FIRE OF THE COVENANT

GERALD N. LUND

FIRE OF THE COVENANT

A NOVEL OF THE WILLIE AND MARTIN HANDCART COMPANIES

DESERET BOOK

SALT LAKE CITY, UTAH

Maps by Tom Child

Visit us at deseretbook.com

First printing in hardbound 1999
First printing in paperbound 2005

Library of Congress Catalog Card Number 99-97186

ISBN 1-57008-685-0 (hardbound)
ISBN 1-59038-411-3 (paperbound)

Printed in the United States of America 8006
Banta, Menasha, WI

10 9 8 7 6 5 4 3 2 1

Let us here observe, that a religion that does not require the sacrifice of all things never has power sufficient to produce the faith necessary unto life and salvation. . . . It was through this sacrifice, and this only, that God has ordained that men should enjoy eternal life; and it is through the medium of the sacrifice of all earthly things that men do actually know that they are doing the things that are well pleasing in the sight of God. When a man has offered in sacrifice all that he has for the truth's sake, not even withholding his life, and believing before God that he has been called to make this sacrifice because he seeks to do his will, he does know, most assuredly, that God does and will accept his sacrifice and offering, and that he has not, nor will not seek his face in vain. Under these circumstances, then, he can obtain the faith necessary for him to lay hold on eternal life.

—Joseph Smith, Lectures on Faith, delivered to the School of the Elders, Kirtland, December 1834

TO ELDERS JAMES G. WILLIE
AND EDWARD MARTIN:

Who bore the weight of responsibility and never faltered in their courage or slackened in their service. How warm a reunion must have awaited them when it was their time to "lay this mortal by"!

TO THE MEN OF THE RESCUE COMPANY:

Who left home and hearth at enormous risk to themselves when they heard the call: "Go and bring in those people."

TO THE MEMBERS OF THE JAMES G. WILLIE AND
EDWARD MARTIN HANDCART COMPANIES:

Who even now, a century and a half later, kindle in us a great desire to let the "fire of the covenant" burn in our hearts like flame unquenchable.

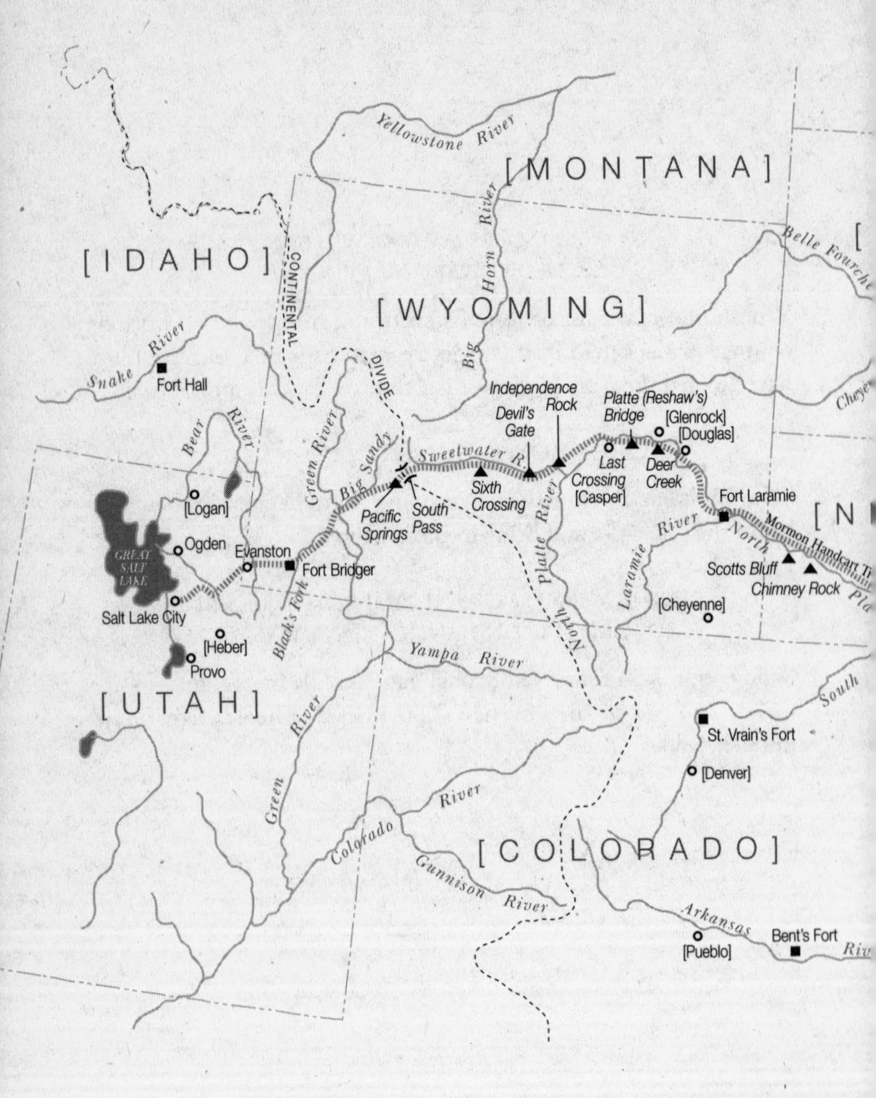
[MONTANA]
[IDAHO]
[WYOMING]
[UTAH]
[COLORADO]
CONTINENTAL
DIVIDE
Yellowstone River
Big Horn River
Belle Fourche
Snake River
Fort Hall
Bear River
Green River
Big Sandy
Sweetwater R.
Independence Rock
Devil's Gate
Platte (Reshaw's) Bridge
[Glenrock]
[Douglas]
Last Crossing
[Casper]
Deer Creek
Sixth Crossing
Pacific Springs
South Pass
Fort Laramie
Mormon Handcart Tr
North
Scotts Bluff
Chimney Rock
Laramie River
[Cheyenne]
North Platte River
[Logan]
Ogden
Evanston
Fort Bridger
GREAT SALT LAKE
Salt Lake City
[Heber]
Provo
Black's Fork
Yampa River
Green River
Colorado River
Gunnison River
St. Vrain's Fort
[Denver]
South
Arkansas River
[Pueblo]
Bent's Fort

Mormon Handcart Trail
Fort
Town
Point of Interest
[Present-day state and town names appear in brackets.]
N
0
25
50
100
200 miles
UTH DAKOTA]
RASKA]
IOWA
[KANSAS]
MISSOURI
Elkhorn River
Middle Loup River
Loup River
Missouri
Iowa River
Mississippi
Des Moines River
Republican River
Blue River
Kansas River
River
Columbus
[North Platte]
Florence
[Omaha]
Council Bluffs
Mormon Handcart Trail
Newton
Fort Des Moines
Iowa City
Rock Island
[Grand Island]
Fort Kearny
Nauvoo
St. Joseph
Independence
[St. Louis]

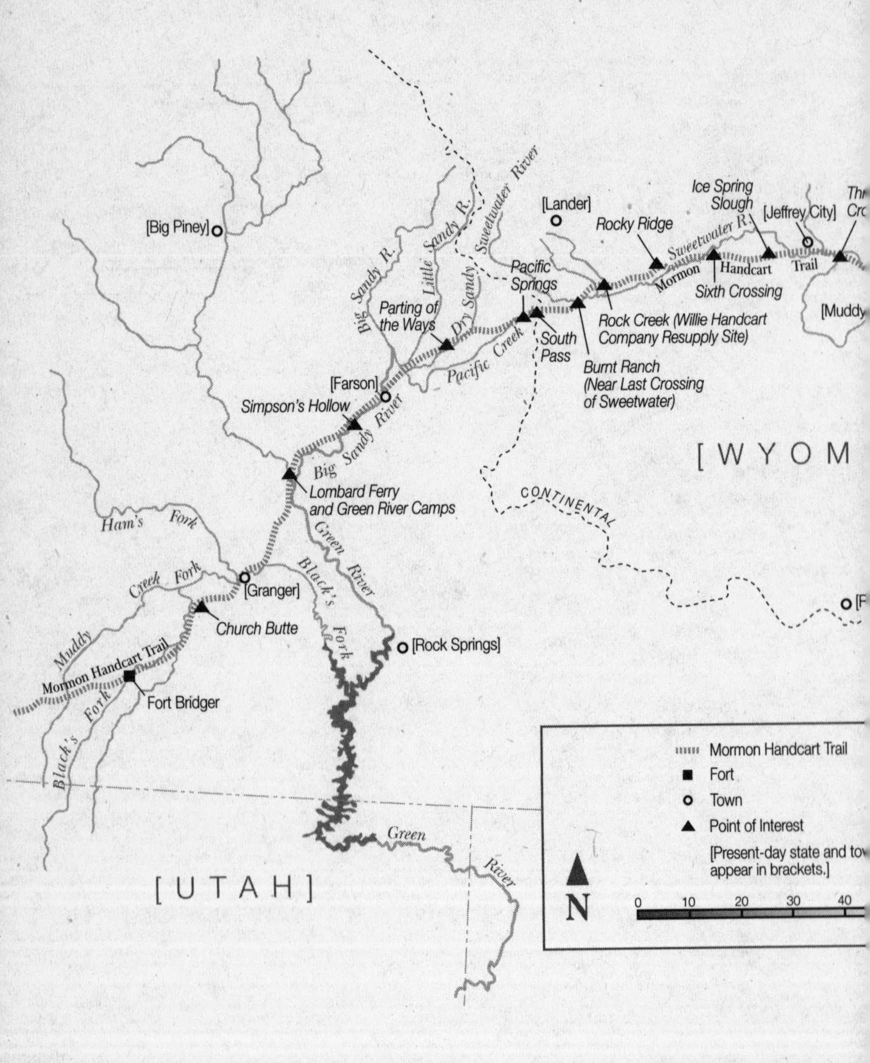

[Big Piney]
[Lander]
Rocky Ridge
Ice Spring Slough
[Jeffrey City]
Sweetwater River
Big Sandy R.
Little Sandy R.
Dry Sandy
Parting of the Ways
Pacific Springs
South Pass
Pacific Creek
Sweetwater R.
Mormon Handcart Trail
Sixth Crossing
[Muddy
Rock Creek (Willie Handcart Company Resupply Site)
Burnt Ranch (Near Last Crossing of Sweetwater)
[Farson]
Simpson's Hollow
Big Sandy River
[WYOM
Lombard Ferry and Green River Camps
CONTINENTAL
Ham's Fork
Green River
Black's Fork
Creek Fork
[Granger]
Muddy
Church Butte
[Rock Springs]
Mormon Handcart Trail
Fort Bridger
Black's Fork
Green River
[UTAH]
Mormon Handcart Trail
Fort
Town
Point of Interest
[Present-day state and to
appear in brackets.]
N
0 10 20 30 40

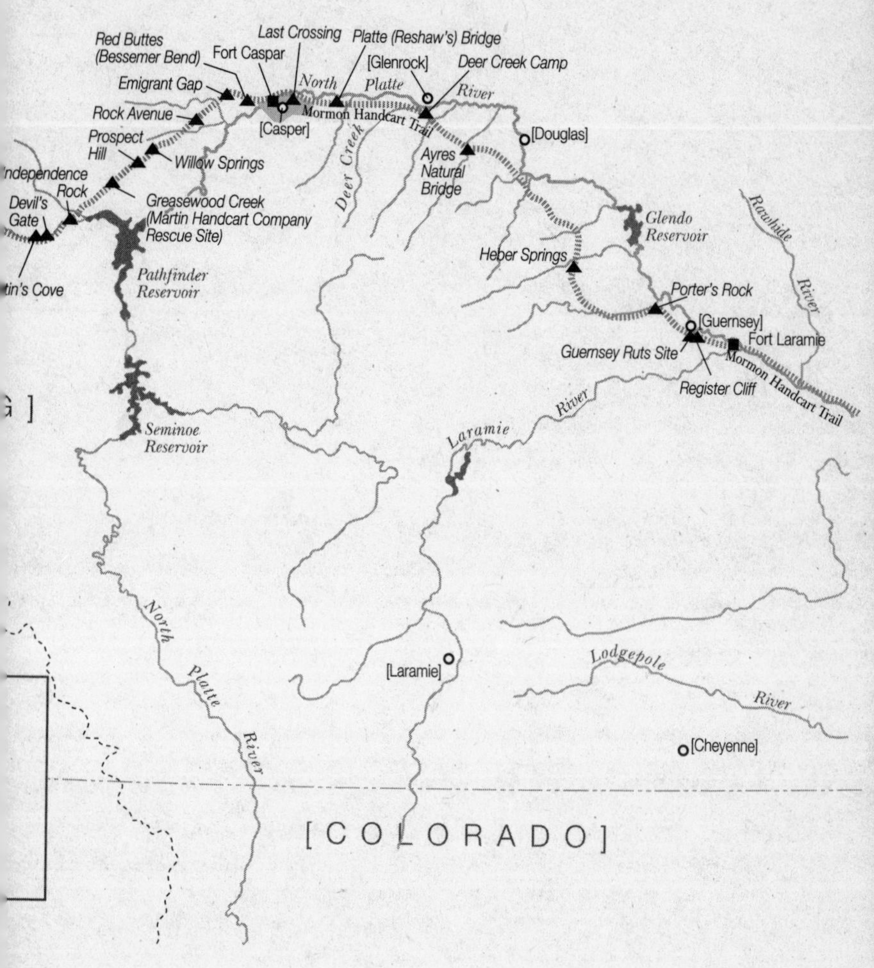

Red Buttes (Bessemer Bend)
Last Crossing
Platte (Reshaw's) Bridge
Fort Caspar
[Glenrock]
Deer Creek Camp
Emigrant Gap
North
Platte
River
Rock Avenue
Mormon Handcart Trail
[Casper]
[Douglas]
Prospect Hill
Willow Springs
Deer Creek
Ayres Natural Bridge
Independence Rock
Devil's Gate
Greasewood Creek (Martin Handcart Company Rescue Site)
Glendo Reservoir
Rawhide
River
Heber Springs
Pathfinder Reservoir
Porter's Rock
[Guernsey]
Fort Laramie
Guernsey Ruts Site
Mormon Handcart Trail
Register Cliff
River
Laramie
Seminoe Reservoir
North
Platte
River
[Laramie]
Lodgepole
River
[Cheyenne]
[COLORADO]

PREFACE

It was the middle of January.

The sun was shining from a cloudless sky of incredible blue. It had been a dry month thus far, and there was only an inch or two of snow amidst the grass and the sagebrush.

I was standing at the top of the great sand hill that sits squarely in the middle of Martin's Cove, not far from Devil's Gate in central Wyoming. All around me in a great half circle loomed the red-brown granite faces of what the locals call the Sweetwater Rocks, a part of the Rattlesnake Range. This is not a mountain range where flatland gives way to foothills and then rises to forested glades and alpine meadows. This is all rock, thrusting out of the flat plain like the sides of a half-buried basketball. Cedar trees dot the hillsides, but most of the range is sheer, naked stone, its stark beauty sufficient to overwhelm the eye.

It was here, in this natural cove formed by the granite ridges, that about five hundred people of the Edward Martin Handcart Company and another four hundred people from two independent wagon companies took shelter in early November 1856. Low on food, desperately cold, they huddled together in misery, waiting out yet another winter storm.

From the top of the sand ridge, I could see down into the cove itself. There was dry, brittle grass, scattered cedar trees, clumps of sage. I could close my eyes and picture the scene as it must have looked back then: round canvas tents, their whiteness almost invisible in the snow; the trails that ran from tent to tent and to the small spring—and to the burial ground. There some fifty-six people had finally escaped the cold and found rest.

On that day I was there, the temperature was hovering somewhere around ten or twelve degrees Fahrenheit. I was grateful. It could have been much worse. On the sixth day of November 1856, the thermometer registered eleven degrees below zero! Ten above in January was pure luxury.

And the wind was blowing. Of course! It is a rare day when the wind is not blowing in this part of Wyoming.

I had come out here fully expecting such treatment from the weather, and I had dressed accordingly. I wore two pairs of jeans and thermal underwear beneath them. Fleece-lined insulated boots with two pairs of heavy woolen socks protected my feet. Beneath a heavy winter parka specifically designed for subzero temperatures I had on a long-sleeved flannel shirt and over that a sweatshirt. My ensemble was completed by heavy snowmobile gloves and a fur-lined hat with earflaps.

I stood there in the wind, shivering violently, stamping my feet up and down, anxiously waiting for the signal to get back into the four-by-fours so we could crank up the heaters full blast.

And I marveled.

The day before, we had stood at Bessemer Bend, about twelve miles south of Casper, Wyoming. Here the North Platte River makes a long, lazy bend and then starts on its long march to join the Platte River somewhere in Nebraska. South of me, in a great arc that covered almost 180 degrees of our view, brilliant red ochre hillsides, studded with the dark green of cedar forests and half-covered in snow, provided a backdrop to the site where the Martin Handcart Company ground to a halt and waited nine days for help. This was what the pioneers called Red Buttes.

A few days before reaching here, in the midst of a howling Wyoming blizzard, women of the Martin Company had hiked up their skirts and plunged into the frigid waters at the last crossing of the Platte. Even though the river is tamed now with a system of dams, where we stood that day it ran swift and deep, fifty yards across. Chunks of ice four and five feet long and half again that wide floated steadily eastward. As I tried to imagine stepping into that current, I was chilled more deeply than I had been by the wind.

And as I stood there, I wondered.

During that January visit to the various handcart company sites along the Sweetwater River, I realized something I had not understood before. That trip was not my first time out across the Mormon Trail in Wyoming, nor would it be my last. It has been my privilege to traverse the trail more than a dozen times and visit the sites that have become so etched in our Latter-day Saint history—Emigrant Gap, Prospect Hill, Independence Rock, Devil's Gate, Ice Springs, the Sixth Crossing, Rocky Ridge, Rock Creek.

I had read the pioneer journals, pored over the accounts written later by the survivors of the handcart disaster. I knew their story well and had been deeply touched by the faith and sacrifice of those handcart pioneers. But on this trip something different happened. I stood there in my fleece-lined boots and snowmobile gloves and Gortex parka and thought of the people who had come through here 140 years before.

And I was astonished.

I knew about the frostbite that took fingers and toes and is some cases feet and legs. I had read about the deaths and the daily burials, sometimes in mass graves. But I had not given that much thought to those who survived. The people of the Willie and Martin Companies had no heavy winter clothing. In the first place, they came from places where the winters are not so terrible and where arctic wear is not required. In the second place, a few days before reaching this bend on the river, they had tossed their heavy clothing and their extra blankets onto their campfires, thinking that if they lightened their loads, perhaps they could meet the wagons from Salt Lake City that much sooner.

As that first October storm ripped down upon them, their clothes were tattered and heavily worn. Shoes and boots were falling apart. Some had no shoes at all and wrapped their feet in burlap. Many had only a single blanket or quilt for bedding. Thin canvas tents provided their only shelter. They were living on four ounces of flour per day—barely enough to make one normal-sized biscuit. And with all of that, they were forced to pull their handcarts through heavy snow—an exhausting task for even the healthy and the strong.

I no longer wondered why so many died. Another question now pressed in heavily upon me. How did anyone survive?

Of the five hundred people who started west from Iowa City with the Willie Handcart Company, sixty-seven would perish before they reached the Valley. Fifteen of those, or about 25 percent of the total deaths, occurred in one day! This was the day after they fought their way in a ground blizzard over a place known as Rocky Ridge. They had no choice. They were out of food, and the wagons from the Valley were waiting for them some sixteen miles to the west.

I have been privileged to pull a handcart over Rocky Ridge. That was on another trip and it was summer then, late in July. It had been hot when we started at the base of the long climb, so I was in Levis, a light summer shirt, and a baseball cap. Then, about two-thirds of the way up, a brief afternoon thunderstorm raced over us. The temperature plummeted fifteen or twenty degrees. It rained for no more than three or four minutes, but enough that we were soaked. The wind was blowing at thirty or thirty-five miles an hour and probably gusting to fifty. In a matter of minutes my teeth were chattering and I was shivering so violently I could hardly walk. I knew that if I stopped I was in danger of suffering a mild case of hypothermia. And that was in July! As I plodded along, feeling like my legs were useless stumps and that someone had poured acid down into my chest, I thought of exhausted, starving emigrants, starting out in the dead of winter, with snow providing treacherous footing in many places.

When we reached the top of Rocky Ridge, our four-by-fours were waiting for us. When the Willie Company reached the top, they had another eleven miles to pull! We took approximately two hours that day. The last of the Willie Company did not straggle in until some twenty-two hours after their departure!

I stood in awe of what they had done.

Standing at Bessemer Bend that day in January, I gazed moodily at the river, watching the ice float steadily past me in the current. My thoughts were on an Englishwoman in the Martin Company. Her husband had died a few nights before, leaving her a widow with three small children. One night she didn't even have a tent to sleep in. That night the ground was so frozen and the few men who were still able to walk were so exhausted that they could not raise their shelter. She sat down on a rock on that bitterly cold night, one child on her lap and one under each arm, as she said, "with nothing but the vault of Heaven for a roof, and stars for companions." And there she spent the night.

As I stood there, chilled and shivering even in my heavy clothing, I began to realize that behind the well-known story of tragedy and commitment and sacrifice, there was another story. A story I had not seen before. A story that needed to be told.

I, along with many others, had wondered why this had happened. These people were faithful. Many of them had sacrificed everything to come to Utah. So why hadn't God tempered the weather? Why was that early storm so vicious and so unrelenting? One experienced guide said he had crossed the trail forty-nine times before and this was the worst he had ever seen. Had God forsaken them because they had foolishly come on so late in the season? That conclusion, which a few writers hinted at, had always troubled me. I did not believe that a loving and merciful Father dealt with His children in that manner.

I went back to the journals again, this time reading with new eyes, this time searching for new insights. Now I saw something else. There were the tragedies, the losses, the daily deaths. The Willie Company lost sixty-seven out of the original five hundred. The Martin Company, with only about seventy more people, lost about twice that number.

But there was something else. There was evidence of the marvelous sustaining power of God. The storms were not turned aside, nor did manna rain down from heaven, but neither were those hapless emigrants forgotten by the Lord. Collectively and individually, they were not forsaken.

Gradually I came to realize that there was an incredible miracle taking place here, a miracle largely unseen and passed over without comment by those who experienced it. It was not only that the marvelous sustaining power of God was there, but that these exhausted, starving, freezing emigrants never lost faith in that power, not even in the hour of their greatest extremity. I realized then that they fully understood the words to one of the popular hymns of Zion, which they sang as they came westward.

> When through the deep waters I call thee to go,
> The rivers of sorrow shall not thee o'erflow,
> For I will be with thee, thy troubles to bless,
> And sanctify to thee thy deepest distress.
> ("How Firm a Foundation," *Hymns*, no. 85)

When I came to that realization, something else happened as well. I decided that this was a story that had to be told.

In the fall of 1846, while the Saints were gathering on the Missouri River, Brigham Young received word that the poorest of the Saints, who had not yet been able to leave Nauvoo, had been driven across the Mississippi River at bayonet point by the mobs. Brother Brigham gathered the brethren around him and reminded them of a covenant they had made in the Nauvoo Temple. Then, calling on them to go and rescue those poorer Saints, he said: "Let the fire of the covenant . . . burn in your hearts like flame unquenchable."

That was what I found as I began to read the journals and accounts with different eyes. I found the fire of faith burning in the hearts of those people so brightly that no amount of cold, no amount of hunger, no amount of suffering could extinguish it. In like manner, it burned in the hearts of those who left their homes and mounted one of the most amazing rescue efforts in American history.

It is my hope that as you read the remarkable story of these two companies, and those who came out to save them, you too will look for evidence of that "fire." If you miss it, you will not fully understand the story these people have to tell.

In writing the story of the handcart pioneers, I ran into several challenges. The first of those was how to tell the actual story of what happened in a way that the modern reader could feel what it must have been like to undergo that experience.

Normally, to say a book is a historical novel means that it is a work of fiction set in a true historical context. How true the author is to that historical setting varies from book to book. *Fire of the Covenant* is neither a work of fiction nor a historical novel in the traditional sense of that term.

This story is true. Most of the characters in the book were real people. This book tells their story as it actually happened to them, relying heavily on their own accounts of their experience. A few fictional characters are created to help convey to the reader the fulness of the experience, but *the story is not fiction*. And therein lies its power to touch our hearts and inspire our minds.

A second challenge lay in the fact that in the minds of some people, the handcart experiment involved only two companies—the Willie and Martin Companies. In actuality, five handcart companies came to Utah in that same year, 1856, three of them arriving without undue incident. Five additional companies came in later years, the last arriving in 1860. They came successfully as well. Only two of the companies ran into tragedy, and this book focuses primarily on that story. But while the others came without disaster, that is not to suggest that they came easily. Each group of handcart emigrants faced the challenge of crossing the plains on foot. Each had to agonize over how to cull out precious possessions in order to reach the required seventeen-pound limit. No handcart could carry sufficient food to sustain full rations across eleven hundred miles of wilderness, so every handcart company faced hunger to one degree or another.

I wanted to help readers glimpse the full handcart experience. Though I focus only on the Willie and Martin groups in this novel, in a few cases I chose to bring in stories from other companies as well. These experiences actually happened but not to people traveling with James G. Willie or Edward Martin. When I do this, the notes at the end of the chapter clearly indicate that that is the case.

Another significant challenge for me as a writer was that we have in the story of the Willie and Martin Handcart Companies two stories in one, and one story in two. These two companies traveled separately, and except for a brief few days' overlap at Iowa City, they did not see each other. Thus, each group has their own story. And yet it is the same story. Both were late in coming to America. Both were plagued with delays, shortages, and setbacks. Though they were separated by more than a hundred miles at that point, both were caught in the same winter storm that struck the high plains on 19 October. And both were saved by the same heroic and courageous men as the Lord moved upon them to become instruments in His hands. So it is one story in two, two stories in one.

To deal with this challenge, I determined that I could not write the book in strict chronological order. Looking at what was happening on any given day to both companies works well in a history book, but it does not work as well when trying to tell the story through the eyes of those who experienced it. Therefore, the chronological sequence overlaps from time to time. We go forward, following the Willie Company to a certain point. Then we go back again, overlapping days already covered, to see what those in the Martin Company were experiencing. Dates are given at the head of each section throughout the novel in hopes that this will help readers keep straight in their minds what is happening.

One other note. Since this is a true story, I decided that instead of simply referencing at the end of the chapter the sources I used, I would include actual excerpts from the writings of those who were there. These journal entries and reminiscences carry great power and emotion, and I wanted the readers to experience that for themselves. Since these original writings now mostly reside in Church archives or library special collections and are not readily available to the average reader, I have chosen to cite them from more recent compilations or reprints. Unfortunately, there is not one source that includes everything, and not all of the sources I have used are still in print. It is hoped that they may still be accessible in libraries or through used-book stores.

As I finish this project, I am once again taken back in my mind to those places that hold so many memories for me. Whether in the stifling heat of July or the frigid days of January, the sites along the Mormon Trail still echo with the voices of those men, women, and children who crossed them so many years before. There is a spirit out there that lifts the heart and renews one's determination to be better, to try harder, to strive to be more faithful. That is the legacy those wonderful Saints have handed to us.

I hope I have told their story in such a way that they would say, "Thank you. We're glad you understand."

GERALD N. LUND

Bountiful, Utah
19 October 1999

Note: It was on October 19, 1856, exactly 143 years ago today, that the first of the great winter storms swept across the high plains of what is now central Wyoming. One hundred and forty-three years ago the Willie and Martin Handcart Companies lifted their heads, steeled their nerve, and called on their faith as they marched forward to meet their destiny.

LIST OF CHARACTERS

Note: Ages shown are at the time the characters are first introduced in the novel.

FICTIONAL FAMILIES

McKensie Family (Edinburgh, Scotland)

MARY—widowed mother; joined the Church with her family three years before; works as a seamstress; husband died two years before; thirty-seven years old.

MARGARET ("MAGGIE")—the oldest of the children; employed at a paper factory in Edinburgh; just nineteen as the book opens.

HANNAH—Maggie's younger sister; very much like her mother; three years younger than Maggie.

ROBERT ("ROBBIE")—Maggie's younger brother; very much in love with life; age twelve.

Pederson Family (Balestrand, Sognefjorden, Norway)

EDVARD—a farmer and fisherman on one of the beautiful Nordic fjords; strong testimony of Mormonism; age forty-two.

KATYA—wife of Edvard; also has a deep conviction of the Church; age forty-one.

ERIC—the oldest son; with his family joined the Church some years before; twenty-two years old as the book opens.

OLAF—Eric's next younger brother; very much admires Eric; will turn sixteen on the ship while crossing the Atlantic.

Kirsten—younger sister to Eric and Olaf; age eight.

Peder—youngest of the Pederson children; six years old.

Granger Family (Great Salt Lake City, Utah Territory)

Jonathan—father and head of the family; joined the Church in Kirtland in 1834; faithful member ever since; farms on the outskirts of Great Salt Lake City; age forty-four.

Eliza—Jonathan's wife; joined the Church with her husband shortly after they were married; forty-two years of age.

David—born in the Church; grew up during age of persecution and exile; helps his father farm; a mail rider and member of the Salt Lake Valley "Minute Men"; turned twenty-one in May of 1856.

Eleanor—David's sister, who is very close to him; turns eighteen in November 1856 and will shortly thereafter marry.

Alma—younger brother to David; fourteen as he is introduced in the novel.

(There are other Granger children, but they are not mentioned by name in the novel.)

OTHER FICTIONAL CHARACTERS OF NOTE

James MacAllister—Maggie's beau; an apprentice machinist; from the Scottish Highlands; one year older than Maggie.

Ingrid Christensen—from Denmark; coming with her uncle and aunt to America; age sixteen in the summer of 1856.

ACTUAL HISTORICAL FAMILIES

Jackson Family (Macclesfield, Cheshire, England)

Aaron—father and head of the family; thirty-one as they prepare to leave England.

ELIZABETH HORROCKS—Aaron's wife; a firm convert to the faith; she has a birthday on the plains and turns thirty.

MARTHA ANN—age seven.

MARY ELIZABETH—four as the book opens, but five when it ends.

AARON, JR.—two years old.

James Family (Worcestershire, England)

WILLIAM—father and head of a large family; joined the Church with his entire family; age forty-seven as he is introduced.

JANE HAINES—wife of William; strong mother and convert; six years younger than her husband.

SARAH—the oldest daughter; of a more serious mind; turns nineteen on the trail.

EMMA—the second daughter; fun-loving and optimistic; turns sixteen years old during the Atlantic crossing.

REUBEN—the Jameses' oldest son; he also has a birthday on the ship as he turns fourteen.

MARY ANN—age eleven.

MARTHA—age nine when they leave England; turns ten on board ship.

GEORGE—the fourth James child to have a birthday on the ship; turns seven then.

JOHN—age three as the book opens.

JANE—nine months as they set sail.

Jaques Family (Leicester, England)

JOHN—converted to the Church over his father's strong objections; became an editor at the *Millennial Star*; articulate writer, poet; twenty-nine years old as he leaves for America.

Zilpah Loader—daughter of James Loader; turns twenty-five while on the ship.

Flora—two years of age in September of 1856.

Alpha—born on 27 August 1856 at Florence, Nebraska.

Loader Family (Oxfordshire, England)

James—a skilled gardener; great love and concern for his family; turns fifty-seven years of age at Iowa City, Iowa.

Amy Britnell—wife of James; fragile health; age fifty-four.

Zilpah—daughter of James and Amy; wife of John Jaques.

Tamar—comes to America with her sister Zilpah and her husband; turns twenty-three years of age somewhere in Nebraska Territory.

Patience—had great concerns about going by handcart; later writes a detailed account of her experience with the Martin Company; turns nineteen about two weeks before Tamar's birthday.

(Other Loader children are not dealt with in the novel.)

Nielson Family (Lolland, Denmark)

Jens—a well-to-do farmer and property owner in Denmark; suffered persecution after joining the Church; tall (six feet two inches) and powerfully built; age thirty-six as the book opens.

Elsie Rasmussen—Jens's wife; a tiny woman, only about four feet eleven; ten years younger than Jens.

Jens, Jr.—the Nielsons' only child; five years old.

Bodil Mortensen—nine years old; comes with the Nielsons to join her sister in Utah (some sources say her father).

OTHER HISTORICAL CHARACTERS

Johan Ahmanson, 29, subcaptain of fifth hundred in Willie Company; later left the Church.

REDDICK N. ALLRED, 34, rescue company; left near South Pass with wagons and supplies.

MILLEN ATWOOD, 51, subcaptain of first hundred in the Willie Company.

MARY BATHGATE, 60's, bitten by rattlesnake; second (McArthur) handcart company.

ROBERT T. BURTON, 35, commander of Salt Lake Cavalry; assistant to Captain Grant in first rescue company; kept journal of rescue company.

JOHN CHISLETT, 24, subcaptain of fourth hundred in Willie Company; wrote detailed and moving history of the Willie Company experience.

HARVEY CLUFF, 20, one of the Minute Men; rescue company; put up signboard at Rock Creek.

ABEL GARR, 22, cattleman, rancher, and scout; member of the rescue company; member of express party sent forward to find the handcart companies.

GEORGE D. GRANT, 40, Church agent at Iowa City; came to SLC with Richards party; captain of first rescue company.

GEORGE W. GRANT, 18, son of George D. Grant; member of the rescue company; one of the young men credited with carrying the Martin Company across the Sweetwater River.

EPHRAIM K. HANKS, 29 or 30, came to the aid of the Martin Company at Cottonwood Creek.

WILLIAM B. HODGETT, 24, led second independent wagon company, which closely followed the Martin Company in 1856.

JOHN A. HUNT, 26, captain of the first independent wagon company, which closely followed the Martin Company in 1856.

CLARK ALLEN HUNTINGTON, 25, a Minute Man in the rescue company;

one of the young men credited with carrying the Martin Company across the Sweetwater River.

DANIEL W. JONES, 26, rescue company; sent forward from Devil's Gate with express party to find Martin Company; left behind to guard goods at Devil's Gate; this is not the same Dan Jones who was in Carthage Jail with Joseph Smith and who was later a missionary to Wales.

DAVID PATTON KIMBALL, 17, son of Heber C. Kimball; one of the Minute Men who joined first rescue company; credited as being one of the young men who carried Martin Company across the Sweetwater River.

HEBER C. KIMBALL, 55, Apostle; pioneer; counselor to Brigham Young in the First Presidency.

HEBER PARLEY KIMBALL, 21, son of Heber C. Kimball; one of the Minute Men who joined first rescue company.

WILLIAM H. KIMBALL, 30, oldest son of Heber C. Kimball; Church agent at Iowa City; came to Salt Lake City with Richards party; assistant to George D. Grant in first rescue company.

EDWARD MARTIN, 38, returning missionary from England; captain of fifth handcart company.

ISABELLA PARK, 60's, companion to Mary Bathgate; second (McArthur) handcart company.

ROBERT AND ANN PARKER, age not known; lost son, then found him again; members of second (McArthur) handcart company.

FRANKLIN D. RICHARDS, 36, Apostle; president of European Mission; organizer of emigration; traveled swiftly across the plains to warn President Young of additional companies.

LEVI SAVAGE, 36, subcaptain of second hundred in Willie Company; at Florence warned Saints not to go on; but when they did, went on with them.

Stephen Taylor, 21, one of the Minute Men; rescue company; member of express party sent forward to find the handcart companies; one of the young men credited with carrying the Martin Company across the Sweetwater River.

Chauncey G. Webb, 44, returning missionary; Church agent at Iowa City; came to Salt Lake City with Richards party; joined rescue company three days later.

Cyrus H. Wheelock, 43, returning missionary; came to Salt Lake City with Richards party; chaplain in the rescue company; member of express party sent forward to find the handcart companies; same man who slipped Joseph Smith the pepperbox pistol in Carthage Jail.

James G. Willie, 42, returning missionary; captain of fourth handcart company.

William Woodward, 23, returning missionary; subcaptain of third hundred of Willie Company.

Brigham Young, 55, prophet; colonizer; second President of the Church.

Brigham Young, Jr., 20, son of Brigham Young; one of the Minute Men; stayed behind and helped tramp the roads over Big and Little Mountain to keep them open for when the handcart companies came in.

Joseph A. Young, 22, son of Brigham Young; returning missionary; came with Franklin D. Richards across the Atlantic and to Salt Lake City; joined rescue company three days later; member of express party sent forward to find handcart companies; also sent forward from Devil's Gate to find the Martin Company.

BOOK 1

THE CALL

JANUARY – MAY 1856

I feel like a father with a great family of children around me, in a winter storm, and I am looking with calmness, confidence and patience, for the clouds to break and the sun to shine, so that I can run out and plant and sow and gather in the corn and wheat and say, Children, come home, winter is approaching again and I have homes and wood and flour and meal and meat and potatoes and squashes and onions and cabbages and all things in abundance, and I am ready to kill the fatted calf and make a joyful feast to all who will come and partake.

—Brigham Young, letter to Jesse C. Little,
written from Winter Quarters, 26 February 1847

CHAPTER 1

EDINBURGH, SCOTLAND

I

Monday, 7 January 1856

"Let's go, Hannah. It's getting lighter now."

Hannah McKensie glanced at her brother, then looked up at the gray, leaden sky. Robbie—it was actually Robert, but not even his mother ever called him that—was twelve. Hannah was sixteen. They didn't look much like brother and sister. Robbie had dark brown hair and round brown eyes. He was stocky and had been shooting up rapidly in the last few months. In a year or two he would definitely pass Hannah up. Hannah was slender of build and was only about five feet three inches tall. She had a fair complexion, and her hair was light brown, almost blond, with just a touch of auburn in it—a gift from her father. Her eyes were green and wide set.

Though they were sister and brother, in some ways the relationship was more like mother and son. In the four years between Hannah's and Robbie's births, Mary McKensie had suffered one miscarriage and given birth to a little girl who had lived only two hours, so there were no other siblings between them. Then two years ago Robert McKensie had taken ill and died. To that point, though they lived a very meager life, the McKensies had determined that the most valuable thing Mary could do for the family was stay home and care for their children. When her husband died, Mary McKensie no longer had a choice. She obtained work in the garment district of Edinburgh as a seamstress. After two years there, she now worked day shift—ten hours Monday through Friday and an eight-hour shift on Saturdays.

Their older sister, Margaret, or Maggie, had obtained work at that same time at the paper mill along the waterfront, but she worked the graveyard shift, ten-thirty P.M. to seven-thirty A.M., six days a week. Her mother was always gone by the time Maggie got home, but if Maggie hurried, she arrived just in time to see Robbie and Hannah off to school. She would then sleep during the day, and finally for a few brief hours in the evening the family would have time together.

Hannah sighed. Recently they had talked about her stopping school and going to work too, but then Robbie would be alone, and Hannah's mother would not hear of that. Sometimes Hannah wanted to just be a young woman, not a mother. Like now. She sighed again and surveyed the clouds above them. "It's still raining, Robbie." It was a typical winter's day in Edinburgh, Scotland. The January wind blew stiffly. The clouds were low and scudding swiftly eastward. The rain, quite heavy earlier, had now lightened to an intermittent drizzle. "Let's wait a few more minutes. Then maybe Maggie will get here."

"Come on, Hannah," he implored. "I don't want to wait any longer."

"Maggie promised she would be here."

"She said she would *try* to come. It's already been ten minutes."

She finally nodded, pulling her scarf up and over her hair. She could see the anxiety in her brother's face and understood it only too well. Every minute she and Robbie waited here at the school increased the potential for problems. She started buttoning her coat, working up her courage. Maybe with the rain, the boys wouldn't show today. Maybe they would just go home.

Robbie took three steps away from the school building. "Come on, Hannah. It's barely enough to wet your face."

With a sigh worthy of a thirty-year-old, Hannah pulled her coat around her more tightly and started after him. "All right," she muttered. "All right."

They moved off briskly, walking almost shoulder-to-shoulder. Robbie kept glancing back nervously. Hannah concentrated on the street in front of them, especially watching doorways that were deep enough to provide a hiding place. When they passed an alley, they moved as one out into the street to give it a wider berth. They didn't speak now. In spite of her attempts to remain calm, Hannah felt her stomach knotting. She saw that Robbie kept licking his lips as well.

By the time they reached King Edward Street and turned south, the rain had become no more than a heavy mist. Four more blocks and they would be home. They had lived there for several years. Most people knew them. There would be safety there. Hannah's hopes rose.

Then suddenly there was a flash of movement out of the corner of her eye. Her head jerked around. "Watch out, Robbie!"

Robbie jumped, but not quickly enough. The apple caught him squarely on the back of his coat, splattering upward and outward.

He gave a cry as his body spun around. Hannah instantly smelled the putrid odor of spoiled fruit and realized that some of the apple had hit her face. She whirled. Across the street there was a small vacant lot protected by a dilapidated wooden slat fence. Through the cracks she could see movement. An arm flashed and a tin can arched skyward. Even before it started downward again, a hail of missiles followed—a whiskey bottle, more tin cans, clods of dirt, sticks, rocks—some of them large enough to be dangerous.

Hannah grabbed Robbie's arm. "Run, Robbie, run!"

A small rock hit her on the cheek, stinging sharply. A half loaf of moldy bread bounced off her arm and slammed into Robbie's shoulder. As they raced away, he began to sob hysterically.

"Get the Mormons!" came the cry from behind them. "Get 'em! Get 'em!"

Hannah glanced back and saw a pack of boys burst out from behind the fence.

"They're getting away!" they shouted, breaking into a hard run. "After them!"

Hannah didn't have to take a second look. It was the same group. There were eight or ten of them. The oldest two were Hannah's age. They were the ringleaders. The rest ranged from twelve to fifteen. A week ago one of the boys, one of the leaders, had somehow learned that the McKensies were Mormons. They cornered Robbie as he tried to leave class, calling him "Mad Mormon," "devil's child," and "crazy boy." When Hannah and Robbie had told their mother she complained to the headmaster. He reprimanded the boys, but only for creating a disturbance in the building. He made little attempt to hide the fact that he held the Mormons in open contempt as well. The boys were too cunning to miss that signal. With others joining in the "fun" every day, they had taken to waiting just off the school yard for Hannah and Robbie. Things quickly escalated from jeers and threats to open bullying, grabbing, and shoving. Last time they had torn Hannah's coat and knocked one of Robbie's books into a puddle before letting them go.

Maggie? Where are you? As they raced along the street, Hannah searched ahead. Gripping Robbie's hand tightly, she angled across the street toward the corner of the next intersection, hoping against hope. Behind her Hannah could hear the boys screaming and yelling, sounding like a pack of dogs in pursuit of a rabbit. *Or two rabbits,* she thought grimly.

"Hang on, Robbie!" She pulled him forward, running all the harder.

As they approached the corner, Hannah glanced back. The two oldest boys were pulling ahead of the rest, and she saw that one of them was Stuart Robison. She felt a chill shoot through her. He was the one who frightened her the most. Foul of temper, a natural bully, and hero of the pack, he had once tried to kiss Hannah on a dare and she had slapped his face. She knew that in addition to her being Mormon and therefore an object that would attract his malice, in his mind there was another score to settle. She could hear him swearing at his comrades, urging them on to greater effort. And then Hannah saw something that really frightened her. Stuart and his friend were both carrying short clubs.

"Run, Robbie! Run!"

Maggie McKensie moved swiftly up the street, only half listening to the squeak of her leather soles on the wet cobblestones. She was berating herself bitterly. She never slept past three in the afternoon. Never! Until today. After all her promises to Robbie and Hannah. She saw again the fear in Robbie's dark eyes. "Please, Maggie, walk us home from school."

This morning Maggie had been exhausted after her shift and had collapsed on the bed when she finally arrived home. But then there had been some children playing in the streets and so she had not been able to sleep well. When they finally tired and went elsewhere, she had slept right through until almost three-thirty. She half closed her eyes. *Wait for me, Hannah. Just wait!*

She broke into a trot, the guilt giving urgency to her feet.

Clutching Robbie's hand even more tightly, Hannah shot around the corner, hair bouncing as she ran. Robbie's feet slipped and he nearly went down, dragging her with him. She yanked up hard. "Don't stop!"

And then down the block she saw the figure of her older sister coming toward them at a run. Hannah gave a cry of relief. "Maggie! Maggie!"

As they raced toward each other, the sound of the pursuit burst upon them. Hannah turned her head. There were five boys in the lead now, with Stuart Robinson at the head. They had closed the distance to thirty or forty yards. The rest of the group was coming hard behind them.

"Help, Maggie! Help!" It was Robbie and it came out in a great sob.

They met in the middle of the block and came to a stop facing each other. "Oh, Maggie!" Hannah blurted. Robbie gave a strangled cry and threw his arms around his older sister.

Up the street the boys pulled up short. Though Maggie was only an inch or two taller than Hannah, they saw immediately that here was an adult. They didn't know that Maggie was only three years older than Hannah, but from where they were, nineteen years old looked like an adult. And that was an unexpected development.

Maggie's face went hard. "Is that them, Hannah? Are those the boys who have been bothering you and Robbie?"

"Yes."

She turned angrily. The group of boys had moved into a tight circle, heads together, talking excitedly, eyes lifting and staring in their direction.

"Get out of here!" Maggie yelled at them.

She heard a younger voice suddenly cry out. "Hey, that's their sister."

"Stay here," Maggie said grimly, stepping forward.

That sent a little ripple through the group, and the boys pulled in more tightly together. But the leader's face went hard. "You looking for trouble, big sister?" Stuart shouted as she closed the distance between them.

Maggie couldn't believe it. This boy, barely starting to shave, swaggered as if he were twice that age. His face was an open sneer. Then

Maggie saw his weapon. She felt a little start of fear, but that disappeared as a great anger washed over her. "No," she cried, stalking forward, "I'm here to give *you* trouble."

That surprised them, and the younger ones shrank a little. Even the two older boys standing beside the leader looked suddenly nervous. Maggie counted swiftly. There were eleven of them, but only these three were of any size or consequence. It struck her suddenly that these were not street urchins, the flotsam of the streets that wandered some parts of Edinburgh and which, in groups, could frighten even the hardiest of adults. They were just schoolboys. But right now, street urchins or not, they were running as a pack and they had been stopped short of their prey. She slowed her step, trying to keep the sudden twinge of anxiety out of her eyes.

"Aren't you the brave warriors?" she hissed as she came to within ten feet of the three leaders and stopped. "Eleven of you to two of them? Why don't you go find some more help? Then maybe you'll feel safer taking on a twelve-year-old."

The leader growled and stepped forward, tapping his stick menacingly against his leg. The other two boys moved with him to provide a solid phalanx. "You watch your tongue, Mormon, or we'll teach you a lesson too."

"Go home," she said in disgust. "The fun's over."

The leader motioned to the group behind him. They moved forward to form a half circle around her. "You want us to teach you a lesson, Mormon?" the leader sneered.

And then behind her, Maggie heard Robbie's soft whimpering as he tried to stop his crying. A great rage welled up inside her. Robbie was of such a tender heart, especially since their father had died. All Maggie had to do was speak sharply to him and he would start to cry. She lunged forward, snatching the stick from the stunned boy's grasp. She turned and flung it away. "How about me teaching *you* a lesson, big man?" Her hands came up to form into fists.

The suddenness of her move broke his will. Disarmed and faced with her fury, he backed up a step. That was all it took. The others moved as one, staying behind him. "Let's get out of here," one of the younger ones cried to his companion. They turned, then broke and ran. The half circle dissolved into nothing.

The two boys who still carried sticks turned in horror; then, realizing they were all alone, they yelled at their buddy and took off as well. It said something for their friend's bravado that he held his ground. His eyes were filled with anger at his being shamed, and for a moment he debated whether he dared go this alone. He was frightened. She leaned forward, thrusting her face next to his. "You think you are such a big man? Then let's see if you're big enough to beat a girl. How about it? Just you and me."

He was startled for a moment, but then he shook his head in disdain. "I don't fight girls."

Maggie straightened. "You know what?" she said. "Neither do I, but in your case I'd make an exception." She straightened to her full height, her eyes smouldering now.

That did it. He muttered something and then bolted. She turned and, without looking back, started for where Hannah and Robbie were watching. When she finally reached them the street behind them was empty. She turned and put an arm around her brother. "I'm sorry, Robbie. I'm sorry I was late."

James MacAllister and Maggie McKensie stood together a few rods down the street from the entrance to the tenement house where Maggie's family lived. Maggie had hoped he would come. She hadn't dared to leave Robbie and Hannah. For all they were putting on a brave face, she could tell they had been deeply shaken, and so she had not gone to the foundry as she usually did to wait for James to finish work. When she had not been there, he had come straight here to see if everything was all right.

And now it was. The rain had stopped, but the temperature had dropped enough that their breath showed in momentary puffs of mist. It was almost seven, and the sky was completely dark. She moved closer to him. In another half an hour her mother would be home and James would leave again. About once a month he would eat with the family, but otherwise he always declined. He still didn't feel comfortable with her mother.

Maggie looked up at James and smiled at him. James MacAllister was twenty, just a year older than Maggie. He was born of Scottish Highland stock and it showed in the ruggedness of his features—the deep-set brown eyes that looked out from beneath thick dark eyebrows, the straight nose, the strong jawline, the mouth that she loved to watch, for it always betrayed his mood. A shock of black hair grew thick and straight, and he was always tossing his head back to take it from his eyes.

They made a striking couple. Everyone said that, though Maggie always felt plain when she was beside him. Her hair was as dark as his and long enough to come below her neck. She had her mother's pleasant countenance, but it was not remarkable in any way. Except for her eyes. She knew they were her best feature—large, almost black, and with long lashes. "Thank you for coming," she murmured.

"Aye," he answered. "Mr. McPhail had me on a job and I was fifteen minutes late finishing my shift. I thought maybe you had come and gone again."

She didn't take her eyes from his face. "I always wait. You know that."

"I wish I had been with you this afternoon. I would have taught them little beggars a lesson or two."

She touched his arm. "I wish you had been too. I don't know what I would have done if that boy had taken my challenge to fight with me."

"You'da popped him one in the nose," he said, smiling at her. He moved closer and put one arm around her. "It was him that was lucky, not you."

She had to laugh. His Gaelic accent was particularly noticeable at times like this. The MacAllisters had been sheep men and farmers in the northern Highlands for generations, unlike her family, who had always lived in Edinburgh. English had been the official language of Scotland since the Act of Union with England and Wales in 1707. But there were some, especially in the north country, who still spoke Gaelic, the language of the Celtic tribes who had invaded the British Isles centuries before.

Then the laugh died. She shuddered slightly, remembering the hardness and hate in the face of the boys.

Feeling her shiver, he pulled her in against him. "You cold?"

She laid her head against his chest. "Mmm. Not now."

"Good." He put his arms all the way around her. Suddenly his voice became hard. "I'll see to it that those slinking mongrels won't be bothering your brother and sister anymore, Maggie."

She looked up, grateful for his strength, grateful that he was angry, grateful that he understood clearly that something had to be done to change things. But then, as so many times before, in looking at him, she was swept away by his deep brown eyes, the dark hair which he left thick and shaggy, the high cheeks, the firm chin with a cleft in it. How had she, Maggie McKensie, ever in the world gotten James MacAllister to take one look at her, let alone become her beau.

"I don't understand it," he said, his eyes still smouldering. "Why would they pick on Robbie and Hannah?"

"Because we're Mormons," she answered in surprise. "I thought you knew that."

"Oh, yeah. Seems like you did say something about that once."

Maggie had lived in fear for a long time, worrying about what James would say or do when he learned that she was a Mormon. But then one day she had mentioned it casually in passing and that had been that. "Why do you suppose they hate us so?"

He shrugged, and she sensed that he had already gone to something else in his thoughts.

For some reason, that irritated her just a little. "They do, you know. They really hate us. I suppose they hear it from their parents."

He pulled back a little and grinned down at her. "Never could understand people getting all excited about this religion or that. Now, take me, for example. I don't have enough religion for anyone to get excited about."

She ignored his attempt at humor. "So that's your answer? Just stop being religious?"

He looked down at her, realizing that he had hit a tender spot. "No. If you want to be a Mormon, it doesn't bother me one way or the other."

"Good." And yet she was somehow not comforted greatly by that response.

"Can I ask you a question, Maggie?"

She stepped back, sensing he was suddenly serious now. "Yes."

"Why *are* you a Mormon?"

Her head came up quickly.

"I know your mother is a strong believer and all that, but it seems like religion doesn't mean that much to you. Why don't you just give it up? Then nobody will hate you."

She stared at him.

"Well, *does* it mean that much to you?"

For a long moment she looked at him; then she turned her head slowly, glancing up at the darkness. "It's getting late, James. Mother will be here shortly."

His face registered surprise and she felt a little stab of shame at turning cold on him. His question had been innocent enough.

"I . . . I think Robbie and Hannah are still upset. I'd better go in."

He gave her a sardonic smile. "If it's none of my business, Maggie, just tell me."

She feigned surprise. "What?"

He just shook his head, then bent and kissed her quickly. "I know a couple of those boys. I'll go around tonight and let them know that if they give Robbie and Hannah more trouble, they're giving me trouble. That should help."

She kissed him back quickly. "Thank you, James."

He was still looking at her, his eyes challenging, but then he grinned. "You're welcome. See you, luv."

She waved and watched him walk swiftly away. But even after he had turned the corner and disappeared she stood there, his words echoing in her mind. *Well,* does *it mean that much to you?*

Her head lifted and she stared at the spot where she had last seen him. "If you have to ask, James," she said softly, "what does that say about me?"

Maggie glanced up at the clock for the third or fourth time in as many minutes. She felt a burst of irritation mingled with growing worry. Her mother finished her shift at seven and was always home no more than half an hour later. Now it was three minutes to nine. Any hope Maggie had of getting some sleep before she had to leave for work was quickly disappearing. She was still feeling the loss of sleep from earlier in the day. It was going to be a very long shift.

She blew out her breath, the concern rising swiftly. The McKensie apartment was on the third floor of a dingy tenement house, one of dozens that filled this part of Edinburgh. It was not a neighborhood with a bad reputation like some of the south side slums, but recently there had been a robbery just four blocks away.

She turned. Hannah and Robbie were at the kitchen table doing their schoolwork, talking in low voices and occasionally laughing softly. Her face softened. The day's confrontation was largely forgotten now, and that was good. That was part of the resilience of youth. It also showed the closeness that had grown between these two. They were more than just brother and sister now. They were friends, confidants, best buddies. In the three years since the family had been baptized into The Church of Jesus Christ of Latter-day Saints, the bond between them had deepened significantly. Being ostracized by most of their friends had left them little choice but to turn to each other.

It left Maggie with a touch of envy. She had never had a close friend such as that. She didn't like to admit it, but she knew that was partly why James meant so much to her now.

Through the door there was the sound of footsteps on the stairs. Maggie swung around. *Finally!* The footsteps grew louder and then stopped outside the door for a moment. Hannah and Robbie turned now as well. Then the door opened and Mary McKensie stepped into the room, holding a folded up umbrella.

"There you are," Maggie said, rising quickly, greatly relieved.

"I'm sorry." Her mother took off her coat and shook it. "I stopped off at Brother Stuart's house," she said. "The missionaries were there."

Maggie noted that she pronounced it "mish-un-AIR-eez" in the American way, and not "MISH-un-reez," as was the common pronunciation in the British Isles. She felt a quick flash of irritation. Maggie genuinely liked the Elders from America, and she found their accent quite amusing, but there was no need to try and imitate it.

Hannah and Robbie were on their feet. As their mother started to hang up her coat on one of the pegs, she suddenly leaned forward. She reached out and touched Robbie's coat. Her fingers ran across the dark stain where the rotten apple had hit him. "Robbie? What happened to your coat?" Then suddenly she understood. She turned and crossed the room swiftly. "Not again!"

Robbie nodded and started to say something, but then his eyes filled with tears and he couldn't speak. Hannah watched him for a moment, then answered for them. "They were hiding behind a fence, Mama. We didn't see them until it was too late."

Mary gathered Robbie into her arms, stroking his hair. "Oh, Robbie, I'm sorry."

"Fortunately," Hannah went on quickly, "Maggie came. She was just in time. Maggie—"

But Maggie shook her head quickly, warning Hannah off with her eyes.

Hannah understood and recovered quickly. "Maggie walked us home."

"I'll talk to the constable again," Mary said to Robbie. "This has gone far enough."

"The constable!" Maggie blurted in disgust. "He's as bad as those boys are. He thinks it's amusing when the Mormons 'get theirs,' as he calls it. But don't worry. James is going to teach them a lesson or two."

A look of alarm crossed her mother's face. "No, Maggie!"

Maggie's jaw set in a stubborn line, but she did not answer.

"I mean it, Maggie. That's no answer, taking things into our own hands. Besides, Jesus taught us to forgive and leave vengeance to Him."

"James and I are not talking vengeance," Maggie shot right back. "We're just going to teach them a lesson."

Her mother's mouth opened and shut again, knowing that this would go nowhere if she pursued it. Maggie turned and looked toward the clock.

"Oh, my!" her mother exclaimed when she followed Maggie's eyes. "It's nine o'clock."

"We were getting worried about you," Maggie pointed out. She hadn't intended it to, but it came out with a touch of snappishness.

There was a quick, apologetic smile. "I'm sorry, Maggie. We got to talking and time just slipped away from us. Go to bed, or you'll not be getting any sleep at all before you have to leave for work. I'm really sorry."

Maggie sighed, feeling instant guilt. Everyone said she was so much like her mother that only their age difference allowed people to tell them apart. They both had dark black hair that was long and straight and which, when washed and brushed out, gleamed like freshly oiled ebony. Their noses—short and upturned slightly at the end—could have been interchanged without anyone's noticing. Just the tiniest hint of what in their childhood had been freckles dusted the high cheekbones. Their eyes were the same deep brown and set beneath thick dark lashes. Maggie's mouth was not quite as full as her mother's, but when they smiled the slight difference between them disappeared.

But the one trait Maggie had not inherited from her mother was her quiet gentleness and seemingly endless patience. At the moment, Maggie was tired, irritable, and badly in need of sleep. But that only made the guilt rise all the higher. She worked an hour less every day than her mother and only half a shift on Saturday. Her mother's Saturdays were celebrated by working two hours less that day. Was it so terrible that she had taken one night to stop and visit with friends for an hour? Did she never get to do anything for herself?

Maggie sighed again. "It's all right, Mama. I slept well this morning. Come on. I think the stew is still warm."

They moved back to the table, but as Maggie turned toward the stove, her mother caught her arm. "Sit down for a moment, Maggie. I have something I want to tell all of you."

"What is it, Mama?" Robbie blurted, suddenly excited.

She just smiled and waved them to their chairs. Then she sat down across from the three of them. She folded her hands, trying to appear sedate, but Maggie could see that there was open excitement in her eyes.

"What, Mama?" Robbie said again. "What is it?"

"I have news," she said with a half smile.

"What news?" Hannah asked, infected with a little of her brother's eagerness. Hannah had inherited her father's green eyes, fair skin, and lighter brown hair, but she was the one who had gotten her mother's temperament. There was little of that patience showing now, however. "Tell us, Mama."

"The missionaries received a letter from President Richards today."

"Who is President Richards?" Robbie asked.

"Elder Franklin D. Richards," Hannah explained. "He's the president of the European Mission. He lives in Liverpool. He's also one of the Twelve Apostles."

Maggie had gone very quiet now, but no one seemed to notice.

"There's good news," her mother said happily. "The Church has found a way to help more people come to America. The missionaries think that we might be able to get on the list this year now."

"Really?" Hannah cried.

"This year?" Maggie burst out. "But how can we? We have hardly anything saved."

"More details will be coming in the near future." Mary reached out and took Robbie's hand and squeezed it happily. "But it looks very hopeful. The missionaries said they are almost certain we won't have to wait another year."

Maggie shot to her feet. "We can't do that."

Robbie had leaped up as well. "Really?" he shouted gleefully. "Really, Mama?"

Mary chose to respond to her son instead of her daughter. "There's a ship leaving from Liverpool in May. They think we can get passage on that one."

"*Mother!*"

Mary McKensie turned to her older daughter. "What, Maggie?" she asked evenly.

"We can't . . . How can we just . . . " She stopped, staggered. Then the anger exploded. "Why do they want us to go to Utah? Why can't we just stay in our own country? We can still be good Latter-day Saints here."

Mary spoke quietly. This was not an unexpected reaction from her oldest child. When they had first joined the Church, Maggie had been excited about the prospects of moving to America someday.

Since James had come into her life, she would not even discuss it anymore.

"Maggie," she said, "it's not that at all. Some people can't go, but our prophet has said that if we can do it, we should gather to Zion."

"But why?" She was near tears now, which only fueled her anger the more.

"So we can be with people who believe as we do. So we can hear our prophet for ourselves. So we can be free to worship as we please." She turned and looked at Robbie. Her eyes became firm and determined. "So Robbie can walk home from school and not be afraid."

Slumping back down into her chair, Maggie just shook her head. "What about your job at the factory? What about *my* job? How will we live?"

"Maggie!" There was a touch of sorrow now along with the effort to be patient. "We've talked about this before. Why are you so surprised? The missionaries say we can find work in Utah. Everyone says that in a few years we'll be better off financially there than we are here."

Robbie, still on his feet, started dancing a little jig. "We're going to America! We're going to America!"

Maggie whirled, her eyes blazing. "Stop it, Robbie! Just stop it."

He froze, the dismay written clearly on his face.

"That's not necessary, Maggie," Mary said slowly. "Just because you're not excited doesn't mean that Robbie can't be."

"Well, I'm *not* excited, Mama! I have friends here. Our life is here. This is our home." Suddenly she was pleading. "You didn't even ask me."

"We've talked about going to America for three years now, Maggie. You know that's been our plan all along."

Maggie shook that off, not wanting to hear it. "If Papa were here," she said suddenly, "he wouldn't make us leave."

There was a quick look of pain in her mother's eyes. Mary took a quick breath, then responded in that same long-suffering tone.

"That's not fair, Maggie. You know that your father wanted to go to Zion as much as anyone. If he hadn't died, we would have gone before now."

For a long moment, Maggie just stared at her, unable to believe the depths of this betrayal. Then her mouth clamped shut. She whirled away, stomping to the door. Snatching her coat off its peg, she yanked the door open. "I have to go to work," she murmured. Without waiting for an answer, she plunged through the door and shut it hard behind her.

Mary McKensie looked at the door for a long time, then slowly shook her head.

"Mama?"

She turned to Robbie, whose face showed his confusion now.

"Why doesn't Maggie want to go to America?"

Hannah sighed. "Because of James."

Her mother nodded and held out her arms toward Robbie. He stepped into them. "She's just upset. She'll be all right in a little while."

"Are we really going to America, Mama?" The excitement was creeping back into his voice now.

She turned to him fully and smiled warmly. "Yes, son. We really are." She half turned, looking at the dark stain on her son's coat behind the door. "We are going to America."

II

Tuesday, 8 January 1856

The heavy clouds that had covered the sky over Edinburgh the day before had finally moved on eastward across the North Sea toward Denmark, leaving the night chilly but crystal clear. The moon would not appear for another hour or more, but a gas lamp half a block down provided enough light for her to see around her. Maggie tipped her head back, looking up at the stars, blowing out her breath so it would cover them momentarily before dissipating again.

There was a noise to her left and she turned her head. A dark figure was approaching the gate of the foundry. She smiled, looking on as he waved to the watchman there, passed through the gate, and came out into the street. She stepped forward. "James?"

He looked up, then changed directions and came toward her. She waited, feeling the familiar stir of excitement at his presence. He was a good three inches taller than she was. His hair was darker than hers and his eyes nearly black. They were large and often danced with humor when he teased her. More than one girl had had her heart broken when James MacAllister had focused his affections on Maggie McKensie.

"Hello," he said, giving her a quick kiss on the cheek.

"Hello, James."

"How are things?"

She tried to smile but didn't quite manage.

He gave her a sharp look. "Is everything all right?"

She nodded quickly.

His eyes narrowed a little and he searched her face, looking openly dubious. She smiled faintly. He knew her too well.

"So what is it?"

She slipped an arm through his. "Let's walk." But she turned him in the opposite direction from the way they would go if he were walking her home. He gave her another searching look but said nothing.

Three blocks from where he worked was a small park, not much more than a vacant lot in which someone had planted grass and a few trees and placed two dilapidated benches. When they reached it Maggie steered him to one of the benches and they sat down. She leaned back, closing her eyes.

He waited for only a few moments and then spoke. "All right, Maggie. What is it?"

She didn't open her eyes. "Mama has decided that we are going to America."

He visibly jerked. "What?"

She nodded glumly. "She came home and told us last night."

"America? But why?"

She didn't answer. She had told him before about the call for all Latter-day Saints to emigrate to America. But she had always said it was just talk. Her mother would never actually do it.

Now he half turned so he was facing her directly. "She can't be serious."

"Oh, I assure you. She is very serious."

"But you can't go, Maggie."

She finally met his gaze. "Do you think I want to?"

"You can't! You just can't."

She turned away. "I thought it was mostly just talk. Ever since we were baptized Mother's talked about it. My father did too, before his death, but . . ." She shook her head.

His mouth tightened. "You told her that you won't be going, didn't you?"

"I . . . I haven't talked to her since last night. I was so angry, I just left."

Something about her answer bothered him. "You're not even thinking about it." He peered more closely at her. "Are you?"

Her shoulders lifted and fell.

He stood up abruptly. "What about us?" he said tightly.

"What about us, James?" she shot right back.

"You know the answer to that. As soon as I finish my apprenticeship we'll be married. Then we'll start our own family."

There was a sharp stab of pain and she had to look away. She and James had been talking marriage for over a month now, but it was always "When I finish my apprenticeship." He was only half through with the four years it took to become a journeyman machinist. She had told him that marriage would actually help him. He wouldn't have to do his own cooking and laundry. Her salary at the mill would help them afford the larger flat they would need.

He had looked at her as though she were daft. He wasn't going to have her living in squalor for two years. Once the apprenticeship was through, he would be able to care for her properly. He wouldn't subject her to anything less than that. Two years wasn't that long.

She barely managed to hide the hurt. Becoming a journeyman machinist would move James MacAllister into the middle class—the working middle class, to be sure, but the middle class nevertheless. Eventually, he liked to say, he might even be able to start his own small machine shop and they could actually become property owners. For someone who had spent most of his life in crushing poverty, such an opportunity could not be jeopardized.

"It's only two years, Maggie."

She turned back. What hurt the most was not that the possibility of her leaving Scotland hadn't changed his mind. What hurt so deeply now was that it hadn't even occurred to him that marriage was the answer to her problem. "You make it sound so simple," she finally said, her voice forlorn.

"Tell her you're not going. That's simple enough."

"Just like that, I say good-bye to my family and never see them again?"

He whirled away, clearly agitated, then swung back. "All right, Maggie, so it's not simple. But it's your mother who is complicating things, not me. I don't understand this whole thing with you Mormons anyway. If you wanted to go to America to make your fortune, I could understand that. I've considered that myself. And maybe we'll do that in a few years. But to go just so you can be with other Mormons? That strikes me as being a bit fanatical, frankly."

That was not the thing to say to Maggie McKensie at that moment. "Fanatical?" she fired back. "My little brother cannot walk home from school without being afraid of being beat up by a group of bullies. My sister was spit upon the other day by a girl who told her she was a child of the devil. And you think it's fanatical to want to get away from that?"

A little taken aback by her sudden vehemence, he just stared at her.

She was breathing hard now. "Before my father died, he lost his job because his fellow workers refused to work alongside a Mormon. Is it fanatical to want to live where we are not treated like a disease?"

"Look, Maggie, I don't want to argue with you. If your mother is such a faithful Mormon, then let her go. You don't have to go to America to worship God. Sure you'll miss them, but when we marry you'll have to be leaving them anyway."

Her chin lifted and she stared at him for several moments.

"What?" he finally said.

In two more years? When it's finally convenient for you, James? The words were like a hollow echo in her mind, but she would not speak them aloud. And then the significance of what he had just said hit her. "You don't think of *me* as a faithful Latter-day Saint, do you, James?"

He reared back a little. "Well, I—"

"You said my mother is a faithful Mormon, but you didn't say anything about me. What about me, James?"

"What about you? I don't care what you believe. You know where I stand. I've not made a secret of that. I haven't got much use for organized religion. All those preachers talking about how we should have faith in a better world in the hereafter. Sounds like a way to keep the poor from being unhappy with their miserable lot in life now, if you ask me."

But Maggie was still marveling at this self-discovery. Why should she blame him? James had no reason to think that her religion meant that much to her at all. "Did you know that our founder, Joseph Smith, was shot dead by a mob while he was being held in jail under false charges?" she asked quietly.

He turned in surprise. "What was that again?"

"Yes, just twelve years ago now."

He looked a little confused. He wasn't sure what had brought that out just now.

"And did you know that our people were driven from three different states at the point of a bayonet by people just like those boys yesterday?"

"Aw, now, Maggie, they're bullies, all right, but they don't mean no lasting harm." He gave her a sharp look. "They didn't give Robbie any more trouble today, did they?"

She shook her head. "No, not in the sense you mean. But in a full day of school among three dozen classmates, not one person spoke to either Robbie or Hannah. They shunned them as effectively as if they were lepers."

He decided to take the conversation back to where it needed to be. "They say Utah is a desert, Maggie. Is that what you want? to live in the desert?"

"No!" she exploded. "You know I don't want to go, James. I don't want to leave Scotland." Her eyes lowered. *And if you don't want me to leave Scotland, why won't you do something about it?*

He came back and sat beside her, facing her. "Then just don't. I'll bet if your mother is really convinced that you're not going, she'll change her mind."

She just shook her head slowly. He hadn't heard any of it—not her words, not her silent cries. "Do you remember what you asked me yesterday, James?"

"Yesterday?"

"Yes."

"I guess not. What?"

"You asked if Mormonism really meant that much to me."

"Oh." He was suddenly wary. "Yes, I remember."

"I didn't answer you. Do you know why?"

He shook his head.

"Because I suddenly realized that if you had to ask, that didn't say a lot about me."

He slipped off the bench and dropped to a crouch in front of her, taking both of her hands. "Look, Maggie . . . "

For a moment, her heart leaped with hope. But his next words quickly dashed it.

"I told you, you can believe what you want."

"I was sixteen when I was baptized, James," she said, her voice wooden now. "It wasn't as if I were a kid who didn't know what she was doing. I didn't just do it because my mother wanted me to. I prayed about it. I really wanted to know if it was true."

He straightened, blowing out his breath. "All right! So you're a good Mormon. That doesn't mean you have to go to America."

She dropped her head, staring at her hands. Then finally she spoke without looking up. "I love my family, James. I love them very much."

"I know that, but–"

Now her head came up. "And believe it or not, I love my church."

She saw his jaw go tight and his eyes narrow. "And what about me? Do you love me?"

She just stared at him for several seconds, unable to believe that she had heard him right. "Do you have to ask?" she whispered.

That seemed to satisfy him. "No, of course not." And that seemed to solve everything, for now his mind jumped to other things. "So then, what we need to do is start looking for a place for you to stay. How soon will your family be leaving?"

She bit her lower lip, her eyes stricken. "Probably in May."

"Well, that's plenty of time to find something." With that settled, he turned and looked around. "Where would you like to go?"

"I'd better go home, James. Mother will be home in a little while."

"Not for an hour," he said in surprise.

She didn't meet his eyes. "I've got to help Hannah with supper."

He stared at her for several seconds, finally sensing that something was wrong. But then his jaw tightened. "All right. Come on, I'll walk you home."

Chapter Notes

Although fictional, the McKensie family and their experiences are based on what is known about some of the Scottish Latter-day Saint families who journeyed to Utah in the 1850s.

Having been called to Church service in the British Isles twice before, Elder Franklin D. Richards, a member of the Quorum of the Twelve, returned to England in 1854 to preside over the Church's affairs in Europe.

CHAPTER 2

EDINBURGH, SCOTLAND

I

Wednesday, 6 February 1856

It was a little past seven-fifteen at night when Mary McKensie opened the door and entered the flat. Maggie turned from the sink where she and Hannah were cutting up the last of the potatoes and carrots for a dinner stew. "Hello, Mama," they both said.

Robbie came out of the bedroom and down the short hallway. "Hello, Mama."

"Hello." She took off her coat and hung it on one of the pegs behind the door.

"How was work today?"

She shrugged. "How is work every day? Long. Tedious. Tiring."

Just as she started to turn back to her work Maggie saw her mother take a newspaper from the pocket of her coat. Curious, she peered more closely, but then Robbie came over and her mother opened her arms to him. "Any trouble at school today?"

He shook his head. Tomorrow it would be one month since the boys from school had attacked Robbie and Hannah. Even Mary now admitted that having James pay a quiet visit to the boys had solved the problem, at least the overt problem. Her children were still treated like pariahs at school, but no one openly bothered them anymore.

"Good." She let him go and moved to the stove, dropping the paper on the table as she passed. From where she stood, Maggie immediately recognized the masthead for the *Latter-day Saints' Millennial Star*, the newspaper published by the Church in England. Maggie stepped closer, squinting a little at the line below the masthead. *No. 4, Vol. XVIII. Saturday, January 26, 1856. Price One Penny.* The headline below the masthead read, "Thirteenth General Epistle."

Maggie's surprise was twofold. That had to be the latest issue, barely more than a week old. Usually it took a couple of weeks before copies started showing up in Scotland. But even more than that, this seemed to be her mother's own copy. The Church kept the price very low so the members could afford it, but the McKensies always had to let the missionaries or others in the branch tell them what the paper contained. Even one penny was badly needed elsewhere.

"That smells good," Mary said, lifting the lid to the kettle and breathing deeply.

"It's almost ready," Hannah said.

Maggie walked back to the sink. Cutting the last potato into small squares, she dumped them into the kettle. Her mother stirred the stew a couple of times with a wooden spoon, then replaced the lid. "You bought a copy of the *Star?*" Maggie asked, keeping her voice casual.

Her mother appeared momentarily startled, but then shook her head. "No. The missionaries were waiting when I finished work. They lent me their copy."

That brought Maggie's head around. The missionaries were actually waiting for her? That had never happened before.

"There's something important they wanted us to be able to read and study carefully."

"What?" Hannah asked. She didn't see the look of dismay on her older sister's face. Maggie didn't know what it was, but she had guessed what it was about.

Mary glanced quickly at Maggie, then away again. "Let's get dinner over with," she smiled, "and then we can talk about it."

"Leave the dishes," Mary said to Robbie. "Let's read what the missionaries brought."

Robbie gave a little whoop of joy. Postponement of doing the dishes for even five minutes was something to celebrate. He and Hannah came over and sat at the table. Their mother retrieved the newspaper, then went to join them. Maggie was wiping off the sink and cupboard beside it. She went on as though she hadn't heard.

"Maggie?"

Still she didn't turn. "I can hear fine, Mama."

"Maggie, I'd like you to sit with us, please."

She wiped at the last spot, then tossed the dishcloth into the sink. She moved over and sat down slowly beside Robbie.

Her mother smoothed the newspaper in front of her. As Robbie tried to read upside down, his face screwed up in puzzlement. "What's an ee-pis-ta-lee?" he said.

"Epistle," Hannah corrected him. "It's a letter, only more important than just a common, everyday letter."

"Yes," their mother said, the first touch of excitement creeping into her voice. "This is the Thirteenth General Epistle sent to all the Church by the First Presidency. It was written at the end of October but was just published in the latest edition of the *Millennial Star.*" She looked at her son. "A general epistle is an important thing. It means the First Presidency has something they want all the Church to know."

"Have you read it, Mama?" Hannah asked, sensing her mother's excitement.

Mary glanced quickly at Maggie, then spoke to Hannah and

Robbie. "President Young has found a solution to the limited amount of funds available for this season's emigration."

"You mean we get to go to America?" Hannah burst out.

Her mother smiled and then nodded. "Yes. It looks like it."

Maggie dropped her hands into her lap and stared down at them. She felt sick.

"President Young is asking all who cannot afford to pay their own way and who are asking for help from the Perpetual Emigrating Fund to cross the plains by handcart."

That brought Maggie up with a jerk. She gaped at her mother. "Handcarts?"

Robbie looked puzzled. "What's that?"

"They are small two-wheeled carts which people push or pull."

"They're asking people to walk across the plains?" Maggie's voice was heavy with shock and disbelief. "I know they've talked about that before, but I didn't think they were serious."

"That's not as bad as it sounds," her mother explained quickly. "Even with wagons, most people walk anyway. The wagons are usually too loaded, and they say that a wagon ride on those rough roads is unbearable."

Maggie was still staring, shaking her head slowly.

"Outfitting a wagon and teams is very expensive, almost a hundred pounds for each outfit," her mother rushed on. "According to the missionaries, that's why the Perpetual Emigrating Fund is in trouble. It is so costly to bring people to America. And last year in Utah there was a drought. The grasshoppers came in and destroyed much of the wheat crop, which is the primary source of funds for the Church. But by forming handcart companies, the First Presidency says they can bring many more people, even with the limited funds."

Maggie looked openly dubious. "This handcart scheme will save them that much money?"

"Yes. If we go by handcart the cost will be only forty-five American dollars. That's less than nine pounds per person."

Hannah's eyes were wide. "Only nine pounds for all the way to America?"

"Yes!" Mary was exultant. "Can you believe it? That counts shipboard passage, the train ticket to Iowa City, and then a handcart and enough supplies to cross the plains."

Maggie finally looked away. "Four people will still cost thirty-six pounds, Mama. That's three times more than we have been able to save."

"I know, I know. But that is what is so wonderful. *If* we are willing to go by handcart, then the PEF will pay for whatever we do not have ourselves. All of us."

Robbie clapped the table in delight. "I'll go by handcart, Mama. I don't mind."

"Me too," Hannah exclaimed, watching Maggie carefully. Hannah was three years younger than Maggie, but they were very close and Hannah well knew that Maggie was greatly troubled by the whole idea of leaving Scotland.

Maggie whirled on them. "You don't know what you're saying. It's not going to be easy or fun."

Hannah gave her a long look; then her shoulders straightened slightly. She and Maggie had talked for a long time about Maggie's determination not to go to America. And Hannah perfectly understood why she felt the way she did. She had no desire to hurt Maggie, but neither was she about to pretend that she was not excited about going, nor would she take Maggie's side against their mother. She took a quick breath. "I don't care. If we get to go to America, I don't care."

Robbie was almost bouncing on his seat now. "Can we go, Mama? Can we go this year?"

There was a long moment of hesitation, and then Mary nodded. "Yes. Several ships are already booked, but with this announcement, they are securing others. The missionaries say that there is one sailing in early May that still has room for us." Now she turned and looked squarely at her daughter, knowing that there was no more time for dodging the issue. "I told the Elders that we would be happy to go by handcart. They will send our names to Liverpool tomorrow."

"*Happy?*" Maggie said in total disbelief. "You told them we'd be happy to go?"

When Mary spoke, her voice was even and filled with patience. "I told them that Robbie, Hannah, and I are going for sure. I told them that you had not yet decided whether you would be going or staying. I didn't want to make that decision for you."

"Well, that's something, at least." She made no effort to suppress her bitterness. "Thank you very much."

Ignoring that, her mother picked up the paper. "It's a pretty long epistle, but let me read you some parts of it."

Maggie stood abruptly. "I've got to get some sleep before I have to go to work."

"It will just take a minute or two."

"I'm sorry, Mother. I'm very tired."

And without waiting, she turned and went down the hall and into her bedroom. She fought back the temptation to slam the door, and shut it firmly instead. Then in three quick steps she reached the bed and sat down heavily upon it. Through the thin door panels she could hear the soft murmur of her mother's voice. She turned to the small table and picked up the box that sat upon it. For a moment she fingered it softly. It was not fancy in any way. There was no design in the wood, and the inside was lined only with a soft cotton cloth and not velvet. But this had been a gift from her father on her twelfth birthday. It was the only tangible thing she had left from him.

Through the door, Maggie heard Robbie laugh. Quickly she turned the box upside down and turned the key. Then she lifted the lid. The tinkling sound of "Loch Lomond," her favorite Scottish folk song, began to sound. Closing her eyes, she laid the box against her cheek. "Oh, Papa," she whispered. "I wish you were here. Oh, I wish you were here."

II

Friday, 8 February 1856

It was two nights later when Maggie came out of the bedroom an hour earlier than usual. Her mother looked up in surprise. She was sitting at the table writing a letter. "Can't sleep?" she asked softly.

Maggie shook her head and walked to the sink, where she dipped herself a glass of water out of the bucket which they filled from the well in the basement each morning.

"You'll be exhausted before morning. Why don't you try again?"

She shook her head. "I'm all right, Mama. I slept hard for about an hour."

Her mother turned and looked at the small clock on the shelf of their dish cupboard. It was barely nine o'clock. That meant that Maggie didn't have to leave for her night shift for more than an hour yet. "Is everything all right?" she asked softly.

Maggie was still drinking from the glass, and so all she did was nod. She and her mother had barely spoken since the reading of the *Millennial Star* announcement two nights previously. Maggie had deliberately gone to bed early that night, and last night she had gone walking with James once supper was over. She didn't want to talk about America. She didn't want her mother asking questions. She had also forbidden Hannah and Robbie to speak of it in her presence.

Mary McKensie gave her daughter a searching look, but said nothing. After a moment, her head dropped again and she continued with the letter.

Still holding the glass, Maggie turned enough that she could study her mother. Once again she was struck with how strong the resemblance was between the two of them. *Except for the aging.* Maggie was a little shocked to see the unmistakable toll that life was taking on her mother. Mary Stuart McKensie had turned thirty-seven the previous November. Yet her hair was already showing gray. There were wrinkles now starting around her eyes and lines around her mouth. Her body was slender, the result of long hours of hard work and a simple diet. Her hands were slender and graceful, but the knuckles seemed more prominent than Maggie remembered. Is that what hour after hour, day after day at the sewing machines was doing? Once her hands had been truly beautiful.

Mary Stuart had married Robert McKensie when she was seventeen years old. Both of them came from poor working-class families. She gave birth to Maggie a little over a year later. Though it was a great challenge to get by, the couple determined that for as long as possible, Mary's work would be the nurture and care of their children. What a bitter disappointment it must have been, Maggie realized now, when time after time after that first birth, Mary would be with child, only to lose it within a few weeks. It had taken three years to get Hannah, and another four before Robert, their "final gift from God," came. Maggie had known about none of that until a year before when she had asked her mother why she had waited so long between children.

A little more than three years ago, Robert McKensie, Sr., had stopped at a street meeting held by two Americans. He learned they were Mormon missionaries and was impressed with their quiet courage and faith in the face of a hostile and jeering crowd. Two nights later he had taken Mary back with him to a meeting in a rented public hall. Though it took them three more months before they were certain that they wanted to be baptized, they knew on that first night that the church the missionaries represented was something that interested them greatly. In the ensuing months, the family met with the Elders often and shared their meager meals with them.

When it became common knowledge that the family had joined with the Mormons, Maggie's father had been called in by the foreman of the plant and fired without explanation. It was shortly after that that he had gotten sick. Three months later he was gone. And the mother who had never worked a day outside the home in eighteen years of marriage had become the breadwinner of the family. Maggie quit school and started work in the paper mill the following month.

Maggie looked away, suddenly filled with pain. Life had not been easy for Mary McKensie, and Maggie couldn't bear to see the growing evidence of that fact in her face. And that made the guilt that filled her now all the more sharp, all the more unbearable. Maggie turned back, realizing that her mother had stopped writing and was watching her steadily now.

"Mother, I . . ."

Mary sat back, her eyes gentle, her face encouraging. "Yes?"

To Maggie's surprise, the response irritated her. She didn't want gentleness right now. She didn't want her mother's patience. It only highlighted Maggie's own turmoil and restlessness. She set the glass down and came to sit down across from her mother. "Mother," she began again, her voice betraying her frustration a little, "is there no way that you would reconsider your decision?"

Mary didn't have to ask what decision Maggie referred to. Her face remained calm, but Maggie saw that her hands trembled slightly as she set the pen aside and pushed the letter back as well. "Maggie, I have thought long and hard about this. I know what it means for our family to leave Scotland. For you especially."

"Do you?" Maggie cried.

"Yes." There was sorrow now in her eyes. "Yes, I do." She began to draw patterns on the tabletop with her finger. "Do you think it's easy for me, Maggie?"

Maggie's head came up in surprise.

"When I think about what it means—leaving our home, sailing to America, having to care for you children . . . I don't have a man to help me, Maggie. Hannah is sixteen, yes. But Robbie is just twelve. He is eager to be the man of the house, but how much can he do? What if I'm not strong enough, Maggie? What if something happens to me along the way? That would leave Hannah on her own." She looked down. "Do you think I've made this decision because it sounds like a lark to me?"

Maggie didn't know what to say. She *had* assumed something very much like that. She also noticed that her mother had said nothing about what help Maggie could provide.

"I have prayed a great deal about it, Maggie. I have begged the Lord to let me know if this is in accordance with His will."

"I've prayed about it too, Mama, and I don't feel like it's right. I don't think God expects us to leave everything that we have here. Can't we serve Him here as well as in America?"

"Of course. There is no question about that."

It came out so simply and in such a matter-of-fact tone, that Maggie was taken aback. "But, why, then . . . ?"

Her mother's head had dropped and she was staring at her hands. There was a long pause. Then, very softly, she said, "Maybe you're not asking the right question."

"What's that supposed to mean?"

"I've learned that it's not enough for us just to pray, Maggie. We have to ask the right questions too." She was watching Maggie closely now. "If you asked God if you can serve Him here in Scotland, then I'm not surprised that your answer was yes."

"And what am I supposed to ask?" she burst out.

"There's only one question that really matters."

Maggie just shook her head, suspecting what was coming and yet not wanting to hear it.

"Does God want Maggie McKensie to go to America at this time or not? That is the critical question at this moment."

"And what if the answer is no?"

"Then Robbie and Hannah and I will bid you farewell. It will break my heart, but we will go knowing that you are doing what God wants you to do."

"But you don't think that will be the answer, do you?"

There was a long moment; then Mary finally shook her head.

"That's not fair, Mama. You know I don't want to be separated from all of you. It tears my heart out too. But . . ." She couldn't finish. She was near tears and it made her angry at herself. She didn't want this to become an emotional outburst. "You really think it is God's will that I go to America?"

Mary's eyes searched Maggie's face before she finally answered. "What I think doesn't matter. You've got to find out what the Lord wants for you, Maggie. I have my answer. But that's for me. Maybe the Lord wants you to stay here and marry James. Sooner or later you'll be leaving our family anyway. Maybe it's not best for you to go."

Maggie's eyes had dropped at the mention of James. Her mother stopped, watching her closely. Then, suddenly understanding, Mary spoke quietly. "Is James not talking about marriage?"

Maggie didn't want to answer, but she had no choice. She knew her mother could see through it clearly. She forced a quick smile. "He's going to help me find a flat where I can stay. When he completes his apprenticeship and becomes a journeyman, then we'll be married."

"I see." It was filled with a deep sadness.

The quiet resignation in her mother's voice irked Maggie, and her Scottish temper flared. "No, Mama," she cried. "You don't see. It's only two more years and then he'll be done. It will make a lot of difference to us if he is a machinist."

"Yes, it will."

Maggie threw out her hands. "Oh, Mother, it's not what you think. I love James and he loves me."

"Do you think I question that?"

"Then what? What are you trying to say?"

She looked at Maggie for a long time, then just finally shook her head. Her voice was weary now, as well as sad. "This is your decision, Maggie. You have to decide. But you have to do it soon. The missionaries need to know whether to book you passage or not."

"Don't change the subject, Mother. What are you trying to say about me and James?"

Again the silence stretched on, but Maggie held her eyes on her mother, challenging her.

"Your father and I never had much when it came to worldly things," Mary finally said. "He always felt bad about that. Especially at the end when he lost his job. But what he gave me instead was the knowledge that I was more important to him than anything else. *Anything else!*" she emphasized softly.

"That's not fair!" Maggie exclaimed. "James just wants the best for me too."

The mention of work and providing for a family brought back to Maggie's mind the series of events that led to James's current situation. After several successive years of crop failure and deepening financial crises in the Highlands, James's father finally sold their land to a neighboring clansman and came to Edinburgh ("Edin-bur-ah," as James pronounced it in his Gaelic accent). James had been fifteen at the time. Now, five years later, his family lived in an even poorer section of town than Maggie's did. His father took day-labor jobs when they were available. His mother worked in a tanning shop, scraping the hair off the hides of goats and cattle. James had gotten a job as a sweeper in an iron foundry. The foreman quickly took a liking to this raw, unlearned boy from the north, and began to ask him to do other things as well. James proved an apt and willing worker, and after three years of his taking on increasing responsibility, the foreman made him an apprentice machinist. In the swelling Industrial Revolution, machinists were considered craftsmen, and a journeyman machinist was a position to be coveted.

James had accepted the opportunity eagerly and never looked back. He moved into a tiny flat just a block from the foundry. He visited his family only every month or so. And in the two years since he had begun his formal training, he had become a skilled and valued worker. He rejoiced in it, exulted in this incredible opportunity to break out of his family's bondage. It was very important to him. More important than— She stopped herself, not liking how she had almost finished that thought.

"Are you against him becoming a journeyman machinist?" her mother asked quietly.

Maggie's face registered dismay. "Of course not."

"If he marries you now, are you going to try and stop him from completing it?"

"Mother, now you're being ridiculous. No, I want to help him."

"Does he know that?"

"Of course." She was finding it hard not to show her exasperation.

"The other men who are apprentices, are they married?"

Maggie winced inwardly. James had finally admitted one day that he was the only single man working on his apprenticeship.

For all her softness and gentle patience, there was a core of steel inside her mother, and now suddenly it showed beneath the surface. Mary mused, as if no longer speaking to her daughter. "If marrying you meant losing what he's after, then maybe I could understand why he wants to wait. I know he's had a rough life. But . . ." She let it hang there in the air.

Maggie pushed her chair back angrily. "You don't understand, Mother."

She looked squarely at Maggie now. "No, I guess I really don't."

Maggie stood, glaring down at her. "I'm not going to America, Mama. It's not because I don't love you. You know that. But I—"

"Will you at least pray about it, Maggie?"

"I *have* prayed about it. I'm just not going. I can't. And that's final."

"And you really feel like that's your answer?"

"Yes, I do," Maggie snapped. "I know that's not what you want to hear, Mama, but yes. I think I have my answer."

"You *think?*"

Maggie blew out her breath in exasperation. "It's not easy, Mama.

Do you think I don't care about you and that's why I'm not going?" Suddenly her eyes were burning. "I can't let myself think about losing you and Robbie and Hannah or I get physically sick," she whispered.

A hand came out and touched Maggie's arm. "I know," her mother said in an equally subdued voice. "I know."

"You don't have to go, Mama," Maggie said with sudden ferocity. "Wait another season. We'll have more money. Maybe . . ." But that was foolishness. James had two more years of apprenticeship. She wouldn't be married in another year. The silence stretched out between them, and finally Maggie started to turn. "I'm going for a walk, Mama."

"Will you do one thing for me, Maggie?" her mother asked softly.

She stopped. "What?"

Mary took a quick breath. "Hear me out first and then you can respond."

Maggie fought back a retort. She didn't need more preaching. "All right."

"I know I have my answer about this, Maggie. I know this is the year for us to go. The news about the handcarts came as an answer to my prayers."

"An answer for you."

Mary gave her a sharp look and Maggie was instantly contrite. "Sorry."

"I know that you have to get your own answer. I know that. And while it will break my heart to say good-bye to you, if the Lord wants you to stay, then I will accept that. But . . ." She took a deep breath. "But I just don't feel like it *is* right for you. I feel so strongly that you should be going with us. Not just because we want you to, but because it's right for you."

"Mama, I–"

"So here's what I would like to ask of you," Mary went on quickly.

"The scriptures teach us that when there is a really challenging problem, we should combine fasting with our prayers."

Maggie's eyes narrowed. "Fasting?"

"Yes. Prayer *and* fasting."

"Mother, I have already asked. Again and again."

"Have you fasted?"

"No, but–"

"That's all I'm asking, Maggie. Will you fast about it?"

"I–"

Once again Mary cut her off quickly. "If you do that and then tell me, 'Mother, I have my answer and it is to stay,' then I'll not say one more word to you about going. I promise."

Maggie looked at her for a long time. She saw the longing and hope in her mother's face. Maybe this *was* the way to settle it. Maybe it would put her mother's mind at rest once and for all.

"It won't make any difference, Mama. I already know."

"Then I'll be content and you'll not hear more about it."

There came a great sigh–of weariness, of frustration, of surrender. "All right, Mama." Not wanting to give her mother a chance to respond to that, she grabbed her coat and quickly went out the door.

James watched Maggie out of the corner of his eye as they walked along slowly. Maggie was aware of it, but did not respond. He had been surprised when she showed up at his door and asked if he wanted to walk with her before she had to go to work. But he quickly learned that what she really meant was *only* walking, not talking. They had been walking now for almost fifteen minutes and she had said hardly anything.

"I've decided not to go," she said abruptly.

He stopped, staring at her.

She continued on and he hurried to catch up with her. "For sure?"

"Yes."

She still did not turn to look at him, and he was wise enough to sense her mood and be a little wary. "Have you told your mother?"

"Yes."

They walked on, him waiting for more, her not offering it. "Well?" he finally asked.

"She said it was my decision."

He guessed that a lot more than that was said, but just nodded. "Good. It *is* your decision."

"Well, it's made. The missionaries will be to our worship services on Sunday. They have to let the people in Liverpool know who's coming for sure. I'll tell them then."

"I know how hard this must be for you."

She brushed that aside. "I talked to Mrs. Campbell at the boardinghouse. She'll give me a room for one pound per week if I'll help her with the cooking at suppertime."

He stopped again, pulling her towards him. "You did?"

Her head bobbed once.

"When did you do that?"

"Tonight. Before I came to see you." She pulled free and started off again, only now she was walking more slowly.

"That's good," he said as he fell in beside her again. "The boardinghouse is not far from your work."

"No."

He was still a little baffled. He knew that the decision to leave her family must be hard, but there was something more going on here. There was no joy in this decision. He shrugged it off, trying to make the best of it. "Well, it will be for only two more years, and then we can—"

"Don't, James."

He turned in surprise. "Don't what?"

"I don't want to talk about marriage."

"But—"

"When it's time, then we'll talk." She stopped, turned quickly to him, and managed a wan smile. "I'm sorry. I'm not very good company tonight."

"It's all right. I know how hard this must be—"

She went up on tiptoe and kissed him lightly on the cheek. "I'd better go."

"But—"

"I'm sorry, James." Leaving him standing there in bewilderment, she turned and walked swiftly away, her head down.

III

Sunday, 16 March 1856

Somewhere far off, the deep sound of the bells of St. Giles Cathedral floated softly on the air. Maggie laid the book down on her lap, listening. It was the call to four o'clock mass. That meant it was three-thirty now.

As the sound died out, she nodded to herself. She would have to leave soon. She had come to the park where she and James often came on their walks. There were rarely people there. It was far too small to attract families. But it was a twenty-minute walk back to the flat where the McKensies lived. Worship services in their tiny branch were held at five P.M. in a member's home on the far side of Edinburgh, and that was a good half an hour walk in the other direction. Her mother always liked to be there early to visit with the other Saints, so they would be leaving by four-fifteen. Maggie had promised she would return in time to join them.

She looked down at the two books—the one in her lap which was opened was the Doctrine and Covenants. The one on the park bench beside her was the Book of Mormon. She had been reading in the latter for most of the day, but in the last hour she had been searching in the Doctrine and Covenants.

With an immense sense of relief she realized that nothing she had found had changed her mind. This fulfilled her commitment to her mother. She had been fasting since yesterday at noon. And nothing had changed. She wanted to tip her head back and shout it out for joy. She had been right. Her mother was wrong. Well, not wrong, but just not getting the right answer as far as Maggie was concerned. Now Maggie could be at peace. She did not have to leave Scotland to be a faithful Latter-day Saint.

She closed the Doctrine and Covenants and set it upon the Book of Mormon. She looked around, grateful that while there was an occasional passerby, no one else had come to the little postage-stamp-sized park to disturb her. She bowed her head and closed her eyes.

"Our Father in Heaven," she began. "I thank Thee for this beautiful spring day. I thank Thee for the privilege of knowing Thee and knowing that I can come unto Thee in prayer." She hesitated for a moment, thinking of how disappointed her mother would be when Maggie told her that she had an answer. "I love my family, Father. Thou knowest that. I do not want to leave them. Help Mother to understand that it is from Thee."

A noise made her open her eyes. What she saw made her jump to her feet. "James!"

"Hello, luv." He came up to her and kissed her quickly on the cheek.

"Hello, James. This is a surprise."

"I went by your place and your mother said you were out alone somewhere. I guessed it might be here."

"I was just getting ready to go. It's church today, James. I've got to go home and be ready."

His face fell. "I was hoping maybe you could skip it today."

She shook her head slowly, strongly tempted for a moment. "I can't. Not today. I promised Mother I would go. And there's something important I have to tell her."

"What?"

She shook her head. "It's just a promise I made to her." She, of course, had said nothing to James about fasting. "You could go with me," she said on impulse, watching his face.

The smile that she so loved broke slowly out, and there was a mischievous look in his eye. "What? And cause your parson to collapse in stunned astonishment?"

"First of all," she replied, smiling back at him, "we don't call them parsons in our church, we call them branch presidents. Second, I think he's up to the shock."

He ignored that. "I've got some things I've got to do. Will you be home by seven?"

She nodded. "Mama likes to talk afterwards, but I'll come right home."

"Good, there's something I want to tell you."

"What?"

He was suddenly mischievous again, teasing. "I thought you had to get home."

Maggie peered up at him, seeing he was excited about something. "What is it?"

"It's just about us," he said nonchalantly. "It can wait."

"James!" She grabbed his arm and tugged on it. There was a sudden leap of hope, which she pushed aside. Surely he wasn't going to . . . "Tell me now," she demanded.

Grinning widely, he took her hand and pulled her back to the bench. As they sat down he took her other hand as well. "Mr. McPhail asked me to help him finish up a job this morning. That's why I didn't get to your house any sooner."

"And?" she asked. Mr. McPhail was the foreman of the foundry and the one who had invited James to become an apprentice machinist.

"We got to talking about the future while we worked."

Maggie felt her pulse start to race. "You did?" she asked, hardly daring to breathe.

"Yes." He leaned back. "Yes, we did."

She socked him on the arm, knowing he was playing with her. "So?"

Now the smile died away and he grew quite serious. "I told him about your family going to America and leaving you behind. He had already heard that. I asked him if he thought being married would make it harder for me to complete my apprenticeship."

Her hands squeezed hard onto his. Her eyes were wide and brimming with hope.

He squeezed back. "He said that marriage wouldn't make any difference to him."

Now it exploded within her. She jerked her hands free and threw her arms around him. "Really, James? He really said that?"

He was laughing now. "Yes, Maggie. That's what he said."

"So we can get married now?"

He reared back, very sober. "I'd have to go home and change my clothes first."

She slugged him. "I'm serious, James. Don't joke about this."

He nodded, pulling her closer to him. "I'm not joking, Maggie. I've been thinking about it all day. What if you take Mrs. Campbell's offer at the boardinghouse for a few months until we can save a little money. Then we can find us a flat and get ourselves married."

"Oh, James!"

Again there was that deep laugh. "Can I take that as a yes, then?"

"Yes! Yes! Yes!" All of sudden she pulled away, staring at him in amazement.

"What?" he asked in surprise.

"This is my answer, James."

"Your answer to what?"

She just shook her head. "It doesn't matter. But this is the answer."

—❦—

Maggie was out of breath by the time she reached the flat and raced up the stairs. In her near delirium of excitement, she and James had talked for another twenty minutes, making plans, talking through what all of this meant and what had to happen next. Then the bells from the cathedral had brought her up short as they tolled the hour of four o'clock. With one last, passionate kiss of gladness, she had left him and raced home.

The moment she opened the door, she knew she had missed them. The apartment was quiet and still. No matter. Singing to herself, she changed clothes quickly, brushed through her hair, dashed water on her face and toweled it off briskly, then ran out again. She was fairly bursting with the news and wanted to catch her mother before the meeting started.

To her great disappointment, for once the branch president had started the meeting on time. She could hear the group singing the opening hymn even before she reached the house. With a rush of keen disappointment, she went inside. The missionaries were still in the main hallway, greeting any latecomers. They pointed to a seat on the very back row of chairs.

As Maggie moved toward it, she saw her mother and brother and sister near the front. There was no place beside them. She took her seat and her mother turned. She gave her a questioning look. Then it hit Maggie that what was exultant joy for her would be bitter disappointment for her mother. She shook her head slightly, not sure how her mother would interpret that.

Normally, Maggie loved worship services. She loved the sermons. She loved partaking of the sacrament. She loved reading the scriptures together. She even loved to sing with this little group, despite the one or two voices that could make one wince in pain. Sister Alice Merriweather, in her mid-seventies, warbled so terribly that her voice always stood out no matter how loud the rest of them sang. But

Maggie loved the hymns of Zion, and—she realized with a sudden pang—she loved these good people in the Edinburgh Branch.

Today, however, her mind could barely focus. During the passing of the sacrament, she tried to concentrate on remembering the Savior, but once she had partaken, her mind was off again, soaring with joy. No more concern about having to leave Scotland. No pulling little carts across a vast desert. She thought of the marriage, wondering if James would mind if one of the missionaries performed the ceremony. She pictured their first apartment. Wondered if their first child would be a boy or a girl. It was like a rush of warm wind blowing the chill from her mind, and she was barely aware of the services around her.

She was surprised when the speaker sat down and the branch president stood back up again. Sheepishly, Maggie realized that she could not remember one thing the speaker had said in over fifteen minutes.

"In light of the fact that some of our number will be going to America shortly," the president said, "I thought it would be appropriate to sing hymn number fifty-one. Sister Tait will give us the pitch and lead us. Then we'll turn the time over to Elder Anderson."

He sat down as the sound of rustling pages could be heard in the room. Maggie turned the pages in her hymnbook as well, trying to remember what hymn fifty-one might be. She knew many of them by number, but that didn't sound familiar.

Then, as she found the page and looked down, her eyes widened. It was not a hymn they sang often, but they had sung it before. Now the opening lines smacked her as sharply as someone's open palm.

Yes, my native land, I love thee.

Sister Tait came forward. She motioned with her hands and everyone stood. Lifting one hand up and holding it there, she smiled, then hummed a pitch. Around the room others matched her pitch softly.

Then her hand dropped and they began. Maggie started with them, staring at the words as she sang them softly.

> Yes, my native land, I love thee,
>   All thy scenes I love them well,
> Friends, connexions, happy country!
>   Can I bid you all farewell?
>   Can I leave thee–
> Far in distant lands to dwell?

Maggie did not make it past the second line before she wanted to shout at Sister Tait to stop. She wanted to bolt outside where she could no longer hear the words, but she couldn't move. Her eyes burned as the words pummeled her.

> Home! thy joys are passing lovely;
>   Joys no stranger-heart can tell!
> Happy home! 'tis sure I love thee!
>   Can I–can I–say *Farewell?*
>   Can I leave thee–
> Far in distant lands to dwell? . . .
>
> Yes! I hasten from you gladly,
>   From the scenes I love so well!
> Far away, ye billows, bear me:
>   Lovely, native land farewell!
>   Pleas'd I leave thee–
> Far in distant lands to dwell.

Maggie looked away, the burning in her eyes now washed with tears. It was not just the words. It was the absolute, unshakable knowledge that they were being spoken directly to her. She let the book drop to her chair and shut her eyes, but she could not stop the words from piercing her heart.

In the deserts let me labor,
　　On the mountains let me tell,
How he died—the blessed Savior—
　　To redeem a world from hell!
　　　　Let me hasten,
Far in distant lands to dwell.

Bear me on, thou restless ocean;
　　Let the winds my canvass swell—
Heaves my heart with warm emotion,
　　While I go far hence to dwell,
　　　　Glad I bid thee—
Native land!—FAREWELL—FAREWELL.

She bowed her head, the tears overflowing now. *Oh, James!* It was an anguished cry deep within her. *I'm sorry! I'm so sorry!*

When the knock sounded at the door, Mary turned to her daughter. "Would you like me to come with you, Maggie?"

Immediately she shook her head. Though dread was like a great black cloud over her, this she had to do alone. She stood slowly.

Mary stood too and went to her. She took her daughter's hand and squeezed it gently, without speaking. She stepped back. Maggie went to the door, opened it, and then, to James's surprise, stepped through it and shut it behind her.

When they reached the street, he gave her a closer look. "I thought we were going to tell your mother about our decision."

"James, I—" She took a quick breath. "Something happened. At church."

"What?"

She took him by the hand. The dread was like a shroud engulfing her. "Let's walk."

He didn't move, even when she pulled on his hand. "Maggie, what's wrong?"

Her shoulders lifted and fell, and then she began. She fumbled at first, looking for a way to ease into it, to somehow prepare him. She told him about her mother's challenge to fast and pray. She told him that's what she had been doing when he found her in the park. He nodded from time to time, made appropriate murmurs to let her know that he was following her, though he had no idea where all of this was going.

"When you came and said you had talked to Mr. McPhail, I thought that was my answer, James. I was ecstatic. I have never been so happy in my life."

He seemed relieved and smiled a little. "Good. I didn't realize I was bringing an answer to a prayer, but I'm glad I could be of service."

"It meant everything to me, James," she whispered, her eyes glistening now.

"Then what's wrong?"

Speaking in a low voice, she described what had happened to her during the worship services. She finished, her voice trailing off lamely.

He had watched her closely throughout, his face showing little expression. When she finished, he waited a moment, obviously expecting more. When it was not forthcoming, he cocked his head. "So? You sang the hymn about leaving your native land and the words hit you really hard. So what exactly did the words say?"

She bit her lower lip. "The words in and of themselves don't matter. I've sung that song before and never thought much about it. But it was *how* it happened, James. The words were suddenly etched into my mind like liquid fire. I knew *that* was my answer. It came with such power, such clarity. I knew it was the Lord speaking directly to me."

He looked openly skeptical. "Through a song?"

"No, James. Through the Spirit bringing those words into my heart with great power."

Suddenly his eyes narrowed and there was a flash of understanding. "What are you saying, Maggie?"

Could she put it into words? She had hoped he would understand. Was she going to have to roll the words up into a fist and club him with them? "I thought I had my answer when you came to see me this afternoon, James. But in church I got the real answer." There was a long pause. "I have to go to America."

"*What!*"

"I know. It sounds impossible. When you said we could get married, that was all I ever wanted. But then the Lord gave me a different answer."

"No! A song gave you a different answer, Maggie. A stupid song! You're not going to listen to that, are you?"

"I have to." It was an agonized whisper.

"You have to? What about us?"

The tears overflowed and she was pleading now. "James, come to America with us. It's a land of opportunity. You can be anything you want to be there."

He just stared at her, his eyes cold and angry.

She wanted to try again, to grab his hands and hold them to her face, to somehow let him feel what she was feeling.

"Do you want to marry me, Maggie?"

"You know I do," she cried. "You know how long I've waited for you to ask."

"Then let's go upstairs right now and tell your mother that you are not going."

At that moment she knew she had lost. It came as no surprise.

She had come down to the street with him without much hope. Her head dropped and she closed her eyes.

He stood there for almost a minute, breathing hard, glaring down at her. She felt his gaze on her like a burning iron but could not bring herself to lift her head. And finally, without a word, he spun on his heel and stalked away.

At last Maggie looked up. James was just rounding the corner, head high, back stiff. She lowered her head again, burying her face in her hands. In a moment, her shoulders began to shake convulsively.

I'm sorry, James. I am so sorry.

IV

Wednesday, 30 April 1856

Maggie watched as Hannah went up on tiptoes, craning her neck to see better. Robbie was searching up the street as well. "He's not coming," Maggie said in a tired voice. "There's no use looking for him."

"But . . . Her sister turned back, the disappointment clearly on her face. "He knows, doesn't he? He knows you're leaving today?"

Maggie shrugged, picked up one of the valises, and carried it to where the rest of the luggage was being collected. The hurt inside her was like a hemorrhaging sore—the pain was always there, weakening her, draining her of all energy and will. She didn't want to talk about it further.

James wouldn't come and it was just as well. In the six weeks since that terrible Sunday evening when she had told him of her decision, she had not heard from him or seen him. There was nothing more to be said now. Her friend Kathryn Moulter had reported that recently James had been seen with another girl on his arm. No surprise. But the pain almost took Maggie's breath away.

Maggie felt her mother come up behind her with the rest of their belongings. She didn't turn. The carriage for Glasgow was due in ten more minutes. She prayed that it would be early this morning. It would take half a day to reach Scotland's main port. Then they would take the train to Liverpool. In four days they would depart for America. Maybe then the pain would start to subside a little.

Her mother laid a hand on her shoulder, but all she said was, "I think that's everything now."

Maggie nodded numbly. "Yes. I think it is."

Chapter Notes

Though Maggie McKensie and her family are fictional characters, the example of their faith and conversion is echoed in the lives of many actual people. For instance, the following excerpt from the life story of a Mary Ann Stucki Hafen, a young girl from Switzerland whose family came to America with the last handcart company in 1860, gives a glimpse of the faith and commitment of these early Saints:

> I was born May 5, 1854, in the valley of Rotenback, about three miles from the city of Bern, Switzerland. I was the second child of my parents, Samuel Stucki and Magdalena Stettler Stucki. . . .
>
> Every Sunday mother would dress us in our Sunday clothes to go to church, as we belonged to the Christian Church. One day my Uncle John Reber, who had married my father's sister, came to see us. He was a young man then, about twenty I guess. I remember watching him as he came through the lot, leaning heavily on two crutches, his hands warped and misshapen with rheumatism, and a great hump on his back.
>
> He told us that he had been to a Mormon meeting and that he believed they taught the true gospel of Christ. . . .
>
> Soon after this the Elders called at our home. They talked to my parents for a while and then asked us to join them in prayer. I still

remember the sweet influence which I felt during this prayer, though I was only a child. . . .

I well remember the day my Uncle John Reber was baptized. He was the first to join the church in that section. It was mid-winter and the ice over the lake was more than a foot thick. He came down on his crutches to where they had picked through the ice. As he was helped into the water he handed his crutches to a friend who stood near. When he came out he walked on without them, while icicles froze on all his clothes before he could get them changed. Never again in all his life did he use crutches. The hump disappeared entirely, and his hands became straight.

Soon after, my parents also joined the Church and made ready to go to Zion. Father tried to sell our property, but was unable to dispose of it, so he was forced to hire an auctioneer. In this way we received very little for our belongings. Mother took with us a large trunk of clothes, some blankets, a feather bed, and a bolt of linen to make up. Father took only his tool chest. This was early in the year 1860. (*Recollections of a Handcart Pioneer*, pp. 13, 15–17)

In the early history of the Church, it became the practice to send out general epistles from the First Presidency to inform the members of developments and exhort them to faithfulness. In the Thirteenth General Epistle, dated 29 October 1855 and signed by Brigham Young, Heber C. Kimball, and Jedediah M. Grant, the call was given for the European Saints to come to Utah by handcart the following season (see Clark, *Messages of the First Presidency* 2:177–86).

The hymn cited in this chapter which changes Maggie's mind can be found in the original 1835 hymnal prepared by Emma Smith.

CHAPTER 3

BALESTRAND, SOGNEFJORDEN, NORWAY
TO
COPENHAGEN, DENMARK

I

Tuesday, 19 February 1856

It was a strange thing, Eric Pederson thought. His boyhood home was no more than a stone's throw from the waters of the North Sea, and yet in his twenty-two years of life, he had never once seen the actual North Sea. Why? Because the tiny fishing and farming village of Balestrand was on the shore of the Sognefjorden, the longest fjord in Norway. From where the wall of mountains opened up on the west coast to let in the North Sea, the fjord snaked its way inland through the towering peaks for almost a hundred and fifty miles. It took the ferryboat, which was now docked at the small wharf in the village, a full day and a half just to make its way up to Balestrand from the mouth of the fjord. And their little village was by no means at the end of the waterway.

He picked up a pebble from the beach and sent it skittering across the water. Each time it hit, it left circular ripples in the smooth surface. In the Sognefjorden, the water was almost always perfectly still. The high mountain walls protected it from all but the most violent storms. In some places the granite cliffs, looking as though they had been sheared off with some giant Viking's ax millennia ago, squeezed the fjord into a space of no more than a few dozen yards. And the fjord was deep. Eric's father said that some people claimed that it was not only one of the longest inlets in the world but one of the deepest as well. In many places its waters were so deep that they were almost black.

He loved it. Except on gray, stormy days, the calm waters mirrored the green mountain walls, the blue sky, and the white puffs of clouds that marched majestically overhead. It was as though the scene were simply too lovely to share only once, and so there were two fjords offered to the view, the actual one and the reflected one.

Eric flipped another pebble across the water, then stood, feeling the stiffness in his legs from crouching for so long. He stretched, loosening the muscles. The Pedersons, like most of the families in Balestrand, were both fishermen and farmers, and Eric's body showed a lifetime of hard work. He was about six feet tall—two inches more than his father—and solidly built. Yet his waist was slim and his stomach firm. A shock of dark brown hair, thick as a horse's winter coat, was getting a little shaggy again. It had been almost a month since his mother had last cut it. His features were what some might call rugged—high cheekbones, a strong jawline with dark whiskers that showed clearly by afternoon, dark eyebrows as thick as his hair, a firm chin with a slight cleft in it. But his eyes belied that ruggedness. They were a clear blue with tiny flecks of brown and were easily filled with laughter. His hands were large and strong. His arms showed the effects of countless days of pulling in nets laden with fish or cutting down weeds in the orchard.

He turned, surveying the long rows of apple, pear, and peach trees which filled the narrow valley. One of the remarkable things about Norway was its climate, and that was directly caused by the warm waters from the Gulf Stream. The Gulf Stream was a vast current that flowed from the eastern part of the Gulf of Mexico northeastward all the way to northern Europe. The waters spawned warm southwesterly winds that tempered the climate of the northerly latitudes. Even in areas above the Arctic Circle, many of Norway's ports were free of ice year round as compared to ports eight hundred miles to the south in the Baltic Sea, which were locked tightly in ice for several months each winter.

That milder climate also meant that along the shores of the Sognefjorden was a great fruit-growing region, and the Pedersons were part of that. They had a small sailboat which they took out into the fjord three or four times a week during the winter months. Then for the greater part of summer they turned their attention to their orchards and vegetable gardens. In the spring, just a few months from now, the narrow valley along the fjord would become a paradise. The spray of color would be almost more than the eye could take in. The air would be thick with the sweet aroma of blossoms and the hum of ten thousand times ten thousand bees.

And it was that thought which left Eric Pederson filled with a deep melancholy. Like most Norwegians, he had a deep, passionate love for his motherland. As with most Norwegians, the land was so much a part of his life that he could hardly fathom what it would be like to live somewhere else. And yet that was exactly what he was going to do. Soon he would get to see the open North Sea for the first time in his life, but with that the Sognefjorden would become only a memory.

"Eric!"

He turned and looked to the east. Their simple home, which stood on the outskirts of Balestrand, was about a half mile from where he stood. Coming toward him was a figure. One hand came up and waved. "Eric!"

He lifted a hand. "I'm here, Olaf." He bent down, selected one last flat rock, and sidearmed it across the water. He counted swiftly, then grunted in satisfaction. It had skipped eight or nine times. His best yet. Then he started walking toward his brother.

Katya Pederson had lost two children between the births of Eric and Olaf—one stillborn and a little girl to pneumonia before she had turned a year old. Thus there were six years between these two brothers. Eric was twenty-two. Olaf would probably celebrate his sixteenth birthday somewhere out on the Atlantic Ocean. But that difference in age mattered little to either of them. They had shared a bedroom together since Olaf had been born. Together they worked the farm, milked the cows, fished the waters of the fjord, hiked the mountain trails, skied the steep slopes in the winter on their homemade skis. They were as close as if they were twins.

Yet, physically, Olaf was very different than his older brother. He was slender of body—almost a stick—beneath his homespun shirt and trousers. His hair was fair and very fine. Even now as they walked back together, wisps of it lifted in the slight breeze. His eyes were also blue, but lighter and more somber than Eric's. He was a good worker on the farm, but his first love was books. Almost every night his parents had to make him close whatever it was he was reading and go to bed. He had devoured the Book of Mormon and had been the first in the family after their father to declare that the gospel was true. Olaf adored and almost worshiped his older brother, but Eric envied Olaf his passion for learning and the depth of his thinking.

They were just a few rods apart now. "Papa wants you to come home."

"Oh?" That surprised Eric a little. He had finished his chores by noon and his father had given him permission to go for a walk. He had come down the beach wanting to be alone.

"The ferry brought some mail," Olaf explained. "There is a letter from Copenhagen. It came on the ferry from Bergen."

"Oh." Bergen was on the coast, forty or fifty miles south of where the Sognefjorden opened onto the North Sea. "Do you know what the letter says?"

Olaf shook his head. "Papa said to get you and then he would read it to us."

"Then let's go."

He started off with long strides and Olaf fell in beside him. "What were you doing, Eric?" he asked as they walked swiftly along together.

"Just thinking."

"About what?"

"About finally getting to see the North Sea."

Olaf gave him a puzzled look. He gestured toward the water which was only a few feet from where they walked. "But this is the North Sea, Eric."

He laughed softly. "Only a very small part of it, Olaf." He increased the pace a little to forestall any more questions.

The silence in the little cottage lay over them as heavy as a wet woolen blanket. Eric sat at the table with his father and mother and Olaf. His sister, Kirsten, who was eight, and his youngest brother, Peder, who was just six, sat on a bench behind them. Their eyes were wide as they watched the older members of the family.

"I don't understand," Eric said after the silence had stretched on for several moments.

His father glanced at him, then turned to his mother. There was a dark hopelessness in his eyes. The letter lay folded on the table between them.

His mother was staring at the table, and Eric could sense that she was very near to tears. Finally, his father turned back to him. "It means that there is not enough money in the Perpetual Emigrating Fund to help all of us go to America. Not this year."

"But . . ."

There was a long sigh. "And with the late frost last spring, we—" He broke off and shrugged. He didn't have to say more. For the past two years they had been saving every *skilling* they could set aside to help pay for their passage to America. It was not enough, but with what Eric's Uncle Gustav was able to send and with the help of the

Perpetual Emigrating Fund, they were going to make it. And then had come the terrible frost. They had been forced to draw from their savings to survive.

Eric looked up. "I thought those who borrowed money from the fund were supposed to pay it back so there would be money for others like us to come."

"That's the principle behind the fund," his father agreed. "But what can they do? The grasshoppers in Utah have eaten their crop. Evidently no one, or at least not everyone, is able to pay the loans back."

"What about selling the farm, Papa?" Olaf asked. "Wouldn't that give us enough money?"

"Yes, of course," his father answered. "But everyone in the village is just as poor as we are. The frost did not choose favorites, Olaf. I have three people who very much want our farm, but they cannot pay me anything now."

"So we can't go this year?" Eric said, feeling bleak. For all he was filled with melancholy at having to leave Norway, there was never any question in his mind about doing it. The call had come to gather to Zion. The Pedersons believed that that call had been given by prophets, seers, and revelators. The decision was easy. They would emigrate as soon as possible.

Katya Pederson managed a wan smile; then she looked at her husband. Edvard cleared his throat, then sighed. It was a sound of resignation, sorrow, frustration. "Your mother and I have discussed another possible solution."

Eric looked up. "What?"

Again the two parents exchanged quick glances. Now his mother's eyes were shining with tears, but she nodded encouragement to her husband.

"I did not read you the last part of the letter. Elder Ahmanson knows of our circumstances and has made a suggestion."

Eric waited. Elder Johan Ahmanson was a leader of the Church in Scandinavia, currently living in Copenhagen. Though born Swedish, he had moved to Denmark and had been one of the early converts there. Called on a mission to Norway, he had come to Christiania, the capital, and it was there that Eric's father had met him and become interested in the Church. Eric's father returned home with a Danish Book of Mormon—no problem for the Norwegians, since at this point in their history the Danes and the Norwegians both read Danish and their spoken languages were very similar as well. They began reading it together as a family, and a few months later, two missionaries trekked over the mountains from Christiania and baptized the whole family. Both Eric and his father were also ordained to the priesthood—Edvard to the Melchizedek Priesthood, Eric to the Aaronic. It was on the night of their baptism that they first heard of the call for all the Saints in Europe to gather to America. From that moment on, the Pedersons began making plans to emigrate to Utah.

Edvard took a deep breath, looking at his two oldest sons. "While there isn't enough to take all six of us this season, there is some money available—especially with what your Uncle Gustav has sent."

"Yes?" Eric was suddenly wary, only just beginning to sense what was coming.

"We still have a little money left in what we were saving."

Now Eric's eyes widened and he reared back a little. "Are you—?" He stopped.

"Elder Ahmanson is going too. He said that if you and Olaf went this spring, he would meet you in Copenhagen and watch over you for the rest of the journey."

"But Papa," Olaf exclaimed in clear dismay. "Do you mean without you and Mama?"

His father rushed on, anxious to have it said. "When you get to Utah, your mother's brother and sister-in-law will take you in and help you find work. Uncle Gustav and Aunt Mary are doing very well in Utah. They will give you a home and help you find work."

"How can we leave you?" Eric cried. "Can't we all just go next year?"

Eric's mother cleared her throat, dabbing at her eyes. "Your father and I talked about that, and yes, we could do that. But what if there still isn't enough money next year? The thought of having you and Olaf leave us is very difficult, but if you get work in Utah, then you boys could send us money as well." The tears welled up again and she had to stop.

Their father picked it up from her. "Next year. Then we'd be sure to have enough money." He sighed. "Mama and I think it is the best way."

Katya was nodding, more enthusiastically now. "Papa and I will work very hard here and try to save even more. This new plan, to go by handcarts, will open the way, but we will still need the money you two can earn in America. It will only be for one year."

"It is the only way," his father said quietly. "The only way."

"Eric?"

"Yes?"

"You weren't asleep, were you?"

"No, Olaf. I am awake."

"Are you thinking about America?"

Eric smiled in the darkness. He could have guessed exactly what was on his younger brother's mind. "Yes."

"Me too."

The two older boys shared one end of the loft that occupied about two-thirds of the upper floor of the family's small hut. Kirsten and Peder shared the opposite end of the loft. Though Eric and Olaf spoke in low voices out of habit, there wasn't much chance of their waking the other two. They had long ago learned to sleep through any noise the older boys made when they came to bed.

Eric listened for a moment to see if his parents were still awake, but no sound came from below. So he turned over on his side and tried to see his brother in the darkness. "And what were you thinking?" he asked.

"Mostly about leaving Mama and Papa."

"Yes," Eric replied in a low voice. That had been much on his mind all day as well. The shock still hadn't completely worn off.

"Are you frightened, Eric?"

"About going to America?"

"Yes, but especially about going alone. Just me and you."

His first reaction was to brush that aside with a laugh. He was, after all, the older brother. It wouldn't do to let Olaf think he wasn't up to the task given him. Yet on the other hand, he sensed that Olaf was in need of reassurance and that bravado wouldn't give him that. "In one way, I guess. Not about the trip itself. We won't be alone. Elder Ahmanson will be there in Copenhagen to help us. And there are other members from Norway going too–some from Bergen, some from Christiania. They may be on the ferry with us to Denmark. And there'll be the ones from Denmark as well."

"The letter said that there will be missionaries from all over Europe returning to America with the emigrants."

"That's right, and they'll be a great help to us. So I don't worry about not knowing where to go or what to do."

"Then what are you afraid of?"

"It's not so much fear as uncertainty, I would say."

"Uncertainty?"

"That's right. We'll be going to a new country where we don't know anyone excepting Uncle Gustav and Aunt Mary. We don't speak the language. That will be hard." Then he grew more thoughtful. "It will be a whole new life, Olaf. New friends, a new language, a new country. Not knowing what it will be like is a little unsettling, don't you think?"

"A lot more than that," came the fervent reply.

"But we'll be fine. We will have family waiting for us."

"Yes. I'm glad for that. Really glad."

The silence stretched on for almost two minutes as both of the brothers retreated into their thoughts. Then Olaf spoke up again. "I don't know if I can leave Mama and Papa. Every time I think about it, it hurts inside."

"Me too, Olaf. That will be the hardest thing of all. And Kirsten and Peder. How we will miss them! But it will only be for a year."

"I am going to work very hard once we get to America. We will earn many *riksdaler* and send them to Mama and Papa."

"In America they are just called *dollars,* Olaf. But yes, we shall send back every *skilling* that we can spare. And that will make the time pass more quickly too."

He felt Olaf touch his arm. "I'm glad I'll be with you, Eric."

Eric laid a hand on his brother's arm. "Yes. It would be really hard if we had to go alone, either one of us."

"I know."

"We'd better go to sleep, Olaf. Papa wants to take the boat out fishing early."

"All right." Olaf rolled over onto his back and wiggled a little as he got comfortable. Again there was a long silence, and Eric wondered if he had gone to sleep so quickly. But then Olaf's voice sounded softly in the darkness. "I'm glad you weren't asleep, Eric."

"Me too, Olaf. I'm glad we could talk."

II

Saturday, 19 April 1856

"Eric!"

"I hear it, Mama," he called toward the stairs. Then he turned back. "Come on, Olaf. The ferry's coming."

In the narrow confines of the Sognefjorden, the steam whistle of the small ferryboat echoed across the still waters and made it sound much closer than it was. It was perhaps still ten or fifteen minutes from docking at the wharf at Balestrand, but once it arrived it would remain there for only five minutes. And there were still farewells to be made.

"I know. I know." Olaf sounded a little frustrated. He was meticulously folding his socks into neat squares, then finding a place in the battered suitcase where they filled in a space and kept everything even.

Eric shook his head. His own valise was neatly packed and showed very little unused space, but nothing like this. But that was Olaf. He liked things in order and in their place. Clutter of any kind bothered him to the point that he either straightened it or had to go somewhere else.

Shutting his valise and buckling the heavy strap, Eric straightened. "It's all right, Olaf. That's fine. Come on. You've still got things you've got to get in there."

"I know. I know," Olaf said again, biting at his lip as he surveyed how much he still had to accommodate. "You go. I'll be down in a minute."

"Boys! The ferry is coming!"

"Yes, Mama. We're almost done." Eric moved across the loft to Olaf's bed. "Here, let me help."

"No, Eric," he said quickly, almost in panic. "I'm almost done. I know where everything needs to go."

Eric held up his hands and stepped back, a little surprised by the intensity of his brother's reaction. Then suddenly he understood. This was more than just Olaf's usual penchant for neatness. When he closed that suitcase, he closed the lid on the first nearly sixteen years of his life, probably never to be opened again. What was the likelihood that they would ever return to this simple farmer's cottage on the shores of the fjord? Not very great.

He watched as Olaf put the last of his things in the case, stepped back to survey it for a moment, then reluctantly moved forward and shut the top. He snapped the two clips slowly, then picked it up. "All right," he said.

Eric laid a hand on his shoulder and squeezed it for a moment; then together they went down the narrow stairs into the main room of their home. At that moment Kirsten, Eric and Olaf's younger sister, burst in from outside. "The ferry is coming around the bend, Papa."

Edvard Pederson nodded. "Thank you, Kirsten."

The "bend" was about a mile away, so they still had nine or ten minutes. The little white ferryboat, with its black smokestack sticking out of its center mass, made steady time, but it was never speedy.

"Can I go see?" Peder cried, getting to his feet.

"In a moment, son," his father answered. "First we would like to have a family prayer for Eric and Olaf."

"And for you and the family, Papa," Eric added.

"Yes, that too." Edvard moved to the simple wooden table and knelt beside it. The others came and joined him. He looked at his wife as though he were going to ask her to offer the prayer, but she shook her head quickly. He turned to Eric.

"You should do it, Papa," his wife said softly.

He paused, then nodded. "Yes."

"O God, our beloved Father," he began. And then, Edvard Pederson found that he was no better at this than his wife would have been. His voice caught. "Please, God, bless our two boys who are about to go before us to America."

He had to stop. Beside him his wife groped for his hand, then held it tightly. Olaf began to cry softly, and Eric buried his face more deeply into his hands to try and stop the burning behind his eyelids.

"Watch over them, dear Father," Edvard finally managed. "They go to Zion in keeping with Thy will. Keep them in the hollow of Thy hand until we can meet again."

Again there was a long silence, but finally he just said, "In Jesus' name, amen."

They hugged, standing together in a tight circle until the shrill whistle sounded again, this time much closer. Eric's father wiped at his eyes with one hand. "It's almost at the dock, Mama. We have to go."

"Just one moment," Katya Pederson said, not even trying to stop her tears. With her eyes glistening, she walked past them and into the small alcove that served as Edvard and Katya's bedroom. It was separated from the rest of the room by a heavy cloth partition. After a moment, she was back, carrying something in both of her arms. She came back to the table and spread the two items out in front of them. They were two thick woolen sweaters, both of matching royal blue wool with a triangular design of reds and oranges in the center of the chest. One was obviously larger than the other. Both represented hours of knitting and an incredible amount of love.

"Oh, Mama," Eric said, stepping forward. He picked the larger one and held it up to himself. "It's beautiful."

"It's for when you get to Utah," she said softly. "Uncle Gustav says the winters are very cold there."

Olaf had his up as well now. He sniffed, blinking rapidly. "Thank you, Mama."

She started to answer that, but then dropped her head. "Goodbye, my sons."

"It will be cool on the boat, Mama," Olaf said, rubbing the thick weave with the palm of his hand. "Can I wear it now?"

"Of course."

Eric went to his mother and took her into his arms. He was a full head taller than she was and it was as if she disappeared into his embrace. They clung together tightly for a long time. Then she tipped her head back and looked up at him. "Watch over your brother, Eric. Keep him safe until we can join you."

"I will, Mama. I promise."

She was not trying to stop the tears now as she moved away from Eric and took her second son in her arms. "You listen to Eric, Olaf. You do whatever he tells you."

"I will, Mama."

"Promise?"

"Yes, Mama."

A soft sound brought Eric around. Kirsten was standing beside her father, tears streaming down her face. "I don't want you and Olaf to go, Eric."

He set the sweater back on the table and went to her. He gave her a fierce hug, picking her up off the floor so that her feet dangled free. "It's only for a year, Kirsten. Olaf and I will have everything ready for when you and Peder come."

He looked down. Peder had gotten off his chair and had come to stand beside them. He was starting to sniffle too now. Eric let Kirsten down and went to one knee, gathering one sibling in each arm. "You promise you won't forget us in a year, Peder?"

His head went back and forth, his eyes filled with the utmost gravity. "I won't ever forget you, Eric. And Olaf too."

"Good. And you can help Papa. Right?"

That won him a smile, and it was filled with pride and determination. "Yes."

"Good." As he stood, the blast of the ferry's whistle shook the windowpanes. It would be at the wharf in another minute or two. He took a deep breath. Olaf was hurriedly putting on his sweater, and Eric decided to do the same. On the water it *would* be considerably cooler, and there certainly was no more room in their suitcases.

"We'd better go," his father said. But he did not move. As Eric finished pulling the sweater down around his body, his eyes caught those of his father. In two steps they reached each other and hugged tightly.

"Godspeed, Eric," Edvard said in a husky voice.

Eric could only nod now, his chest constricted to the point that he could no longer speak.

"Be safe until we are together again."

Olaf came over and stepped into his father's crushing hug while his mother looked on, weeping openly now. And then in a moment they were all together, standing in the center of the room in one tight cluster, everyone trying to hold everyone else all at once. They stood that way for almost a full minute, and then, without anyone giving a signal, they stepped back from each other. Hands came up to brush away the tears. Eric walked to where the two pieces of luggage were and picked them up. He squared his shoulders. Olaf, seeing the movement, followed. And then Eric's father opened the door and they walked out, going down the path to the main road of Balestrand, then turning east toward the wharf where the ferryboat awaited.

Edvard and Katya Pederson stood on the wharf for a long time after the ferry had disappeared. Kirsten and Peder went back to the house once the boat was no longer in sight, but father and mother stood together, not speaking, looking at the spot where they had last seen two small figures waving their arms in final farewell.

"What have we done, Edvard?" Katya said in a bare whisper. "What have we done?"

"We have answered the call of the Lord." His head lifted a little and his jaw set in a firm line. "Our sons go now so that we can follow. It is the only way."

She looked at him for several seconds, then slowly nodded. "Yes," she said simply. "Yes, that is it, isn't it."

III

Wednesday, 23 April 1856

"Eric?"

Eric turned away from the rail. They were near the bow of the large steamer that was moving slowly out of the harbor at Copenhagen. He was looking forward, watching the ship move past the last of Copenhagen's shoreline. As he turned, he saw Olaf looking back toward the receding city, now silhouetted by the setting sun. "Yes, Olaf?"

Olaf didn't look at his older brother, but Eric saw that his face was filled with longing and melancholy. Finally he shook his head. "Never mind."

"What, Olaf?"

"Nothing." He turned away, staring down at the gray water slipping past the hull with a quiet hissing sound.

Eric watched him for another moment, tempted to push harder to find out what was troubling him, but then he decided against it. He knew without asking. Olaf was suffering from a severe case of longing for home. And leaving Copenhagen—"Koobnhaun," as they pronounced it in Danish—meant that they were now leaving Scandinavia.

It had been hard up to this point, but as they sailed down the coast of Norway and then around to Christiania, where a few other Norwegian converts had come on board, it had still felt like home. Elder Ahmanson, true to his word, had come on board this morning and had been careful to see to Eric's and Olaf's needs since. However, Sister Ahmanson had a young child and so her husband had plenty to keep him occupied. Like now. He had planned to be topside when they left the harbor so as to be with the two brothers, but he was down in the hold helping his wife care for their baby boy, who was having a difficult time today.

When Eric and Olaf crossed the channel to Denmark, it was still not a break from all they knew. The Danes were not Norwegians by any means, but they were close cousins. Danish and Norwegian were sister tongues, more of a difference of dialect than language, though some people said that Norwegian was rapidly taking on its own unique character. But they could converse freely with the Danes who joined them at Copenhagen, bringing the number of their Scandinavian contingent up to about a hundred people.

But now as they sailed away from the capital of Denmark, this signaled a final break with their homeland. When they stopped again they would be in England, and they would be foreigners, and the language would not be theirs. That knowledge had only sharpened Olaf's longing for the family and their native village.

Eric reached out and laid a hand on his brother's shoulder. He turned to look at him, then turned away again. "It's only for a year, Olaf," Eric said softly. "And the first three days are already done. We've started."

"I know."

"One year and then we'll all be together again and—"

"*God dag.*"

Eric turned to see who had spoken. There were a few others out on deck, but most were below, getting their things stowed for the six-day journey to Liverpool. Now he saw a man and a woman coming toward him. A young girl was beside the woman, and the man held the hand of a little boy who bore a striking resemblance to his father.

"*God dag,*" Eric responded. Good day. Hello. The man had used the Norwegian pronunciation, and it surprised Eric.

"May we join you?" the man asked pleasantly.

Olaf had turned to watch now too. Both brothers nodded automatically. "Of course," Eric said. "We are just watching the sunset."

"We wanted to do the same," the woman said with a warm smile. She was a tiny thing, no more than five feet, and maybe an inch short of that. If she weighed a hundred pounds, it would have surprised

Eric. But she had a pleasant face and large dark eyes that were filled with friendship and welcome.

The man stuck out his hand. "We are the Nielsons. I am Jens and this is my wife, Elsie."

Eric extended his hand and was pleased with the firmness of the grip. Elsie Nielson might be a tiny thing, but her husband was not. He was solidly built and stood two inches taller than Eric's own six feet. He probably weighed in at two hundred twenty or thirty pounds, more than double what his wife must be. He also looked to be significantly older than his wife. "Eric Pederson, from Balestrand, Norway," Eric said, gripping the hand back. "And this is my younger brother Olaf."

Elsie also took their hands and shook them. She touched the boy beside her husband. "This is our son, little Jens. He is five and very excited that he will have his next birthday in America."

They laughed as she turned to the girl by her side. "And this is Bodil Mortensen. She is nine. She is traveling with our family. She has some family already in America, so Bodil is going this year and the rest of her family will come next season. Her mother asked that we take her with us."

Olaf leaned forward in surprise, looking at the girl, who smiled shyly at them. "We are doing the same thing. Eric and I are going ahead to earn money. Then our family shall come next year."

Bodil smiled and nodded. "It is very hard, isn't it?" she asked softly.

"Yes, very hard," Olaf answered gravely.

"But we have to be brave, don't we?" Bodil said with a smile. "It's what Heavenly Father wants us to do."

Olaf nodded slowly. "Yes," he said, almost as though he had forgotten that important point, "yes, it is."

Eric watched in amazement. It was as though Olaf had just stepped out of a dark room. Bodil was seven years his junior, but she spoke with quiet faith. It seemed to prick Olaf a little. If a nine-year-old could maintain good cheer in the face of leaving her family for a year, then perhaps Olaf ought to try more diligently to do the same.

Brother Nielson let go of his son's hand so he was free to walk around. He seemed a little unsteady, so Bodil went to help. On impulse, Olaf stepped forward and took the boy's other hand. "Come, little Jens," he said. "Let's take a walk around the ship."

As they moved off, the senior Jens turned to Eric. "Where is Balestrand?" he asked.

"In the Sognefjorden, north of Bergen. We live about a hundred and twenty miles inland up the fjord."

"They say that Norway is so beautiful," Elsie said wistfully. "Denmark unfortunately is more like the top of a dinner plate turned upside down."

Eric laughed, watching Olaf and Bodil stopping near the wheelhouse. "Norway *is* very beautiful. Are you from Copenhagen?"

"No," Jens answered, coming over now to lean on the rail beside Eric. Elsie came to stand beside her husband, leaning over to peer forward into the deepening gloom. "I was born on the island of Lolland," he said, "which is to the south, in the Baltic Sea. But most recently we are from the town of Aarhus, which is to the north in Jutland."

"We saw Jutland as we came down," Eric noted.

"Yes," Elsie responded.

"I wish we were in Liverpool right now," Eric said. "I am ready to be started on this journey to America."

"As we are," Jens said with a trace of wistfulness. "Elsie and I had planned to go shortly after we joined the Church. That was on the twenty-ninth of March, just over two years ago now."

Eric thought he understood what Jens was implying. "Our family has been saving to get enough money to emigrate as well, but a heavy frost last season took much of it. That's why my parents decided that Olaf and I should go ahead."

Jens glanced at his wife. "Fortunately, money is not our problem. I have been blessed with a prosperous farm and success in other endeavors as well."

At Eric's look he went on. "No, our delay came for another reason. After we were baptized, I planned to sell the farm and go. But then the president of our conference came to me and told me that I had been warned and that now I had a duty to warn my neighbor. He asked that I serve a mission among my people."

"Oh," Eric said.

"That went contrary to my natural feelings," Jens went on. "We were ready to come to America, but I decided that, as the prophet Samuel taught King Saul, 'obedience is better than sacrifice.' So we delayed our departure until now. I do not regret it for a moment. It was a wonderful experience and I had great success."

"The Church is having great success in Denmark in many places," Elsie said.

"But not without persecution," Eric noted. At least, that was the report they had received in Norway. In Norway, too, the missionaries had been badly treated in some places.

Jens's face momentarily darkened. "Yes, there were those times as well." But he said nothing more, and Eric decided that it would not be polite to ask for more details.

"But now we go to America," Elsie said brightly. "We are so happy."

"We are too," Eric responded immediately. "Except for leaving our family, of course. Olaf is excited at the prospect of pulling a handcart."

"Ah, yes," Jens answered. "Elsie and I won't be doing that."

"Really?" Eric thought everyone was going by handcart.

"No, there will be two or three independent wagon companies. We have sufficient funds to purchase a wagon and team and go with them."

"I didn't know that," Eric said.

"Yes. In fact, I think the plan is to have our wagon companies carry some of the heavier freight for the handcart companies. They say you will only be allowed a small amount of personal things."

"They told us seventeen pounds," Eric agreed.

"Well, I think we'll be carrying furniture and other heavier items for the rest of you."

At that moment Elsie turned away from the rail, then smiled. "Look."

Eric and Jens turned as well. Olaf and Bodil had young Jens between them, helping him walk the edge of a narrow trunk that was near the bow of the ship. "I think your brother will be good for Bodil," she murmured. "We have been afraid that she would be very lonesome."

"This is good for Olaf as well," Eric responded. "He needs to think about something besides our family."

Sister Nielson looked up at him. "We would be very pleased to have you as our friends, Eric. I think it would be very good for our children, and Jens and I would like it too."

"Yes, very much," Jens agreed quickly. "Would that be all right with you?"

Eric was pleased and surprised. "*Vær så snill,*" he said softly. In Norwegian, it was a phrase often used in the sense of "please." But literally it meant, "Be so kind." He added, "We would like that very much as well."

Chapter Notes

The creation of the Pederson family from the Sognefjorden region of Norway is the author's.

Jens (pronounced "Yents") and **Elsie Nielson** were Danish converts who emigrated to America in 1856 and were part of the Willie Company. They had their only child with them and also Bodil Mortensen, whom they were bringing for another family. While on a trip over the Hole-in-the-Rock Trail in southeastern Utah in 1997, the author had a chance to meet with some of the posterity of Jens and Elsie Nielson. From them he learned that Elsie was about four foot eleven inches tall and weighed less than a hundred pounds, while Jens was around six foot two and weighed about two hundred and twenty pounds.

Johan (sometimes reported as Jacob or John) **Ahmanson,** and his wife, **Grethe,** are likewise actual historical people. Born in Sweden, Ahmanson moved to Denmark in 1849, where he joined the Church in 1850. He was a missionary in Norway from 1851 to 1853, and in 1856 served as the leader of the Scandinavian group who journeyed to Liverpool. He was later appointed as a counselor to Elder Willie on board ship and a subcaptain over his group on the journey across the Atlantic and also in the Willie Handcart Company (see Martin, "John Ahmanson vs. Brigham Young," pp. 1–2; Turner, *Emigrating Journals,* p. 2).

The following excerpts are from the life story of Jens Nielson:

> We have no account of [Jens Nielson's] childhood, and much of the little we know of his early manhood is gleaned from a letter he wrote to his son, Uriah, in 1901. In that letter, he says, "I was born April 26, 1821, on the Island of Laaland [Lolland], Denmark, son of Niels Jensen and Dorothe M. Tomson." . . .
>
> How long Jens stayed in Laaland is uncertain, but at sometime he made his way to Aarhus, a coast city on the mainland a hundred miles to the northwest. He belonged to the better middle class. He was thrifty and industrious and fairly successful, and he had many friends, many of them people of some importance. Being a natural farmer, he liked to possess land and livestock.
>
> In this letter, he goes on to say, "I was married to Elsie Rasmussen when I was thirty years old. [Elsie was only twenty at the time, so there was a ten-year difference in their ages.] Soon after that I bought five acres of land that cost six hundred dollars, and I built a house that cost about four hundred dollars. I had very little money to start with, but the Lord blessed me on my right hand and on my left and I was very successful and prospects in temporal concerns were very bright. I was looked upon as a respectable neighbor and many times invited to the higher class of society.
>
> "In the fall of 1852, two Mormon elders came to our neighborhood. I knew nothing of the Mormons except very bad reports. They had the privilege of holding a meeting close to my home. I thought I would go there for curiosity sake. As soon as I saw those men's faces, I knew they were not the men as represented to be, and I told my

friends so before I heard them speak. Before the meeting was out, I knew the testimony they bore was of God. We bought some few of their tracts and studied them for a few weeks and were perfectly satisfied the work was of God.

"On the 29th of March, 1854, I and my wife went into the waters of baptism. From that time on all my former friends turned against me and spoke all kinds of evil against me, and that falsely. All my possessions had no power over me then, my only desire was to sell out and come to Zion. That same year I partly made a bargain with a man for my home but before the bargain was closed, the president of the conference [the equivalent of a priesthood district today] paid me a visit and told me I had not done my duty. He told me I had been warned and it was my duty to warn others.

"That counsel came right in contact with my natural feelings, but the Spirit whispered me I must obey, for 'obedience is better than sacrifice.' Then I was ordained a priest and sent out to preach with another young man holding the same priesthood. We baptized some twelve or fifteen persons but we did not have the power to confer the Holy Ghost. Soon after that I was ordained an Elder and called to preside over the branch where I lived. I was very successful in my mission, after which I received an honorable release to go to Zion. I sold my place, got my money, and paid all my obligations."

As stated in his account, he made positive preparation to come to Utah soon after being baptized, but he accepted the advice to stay and for a year and a half, or more, he was an active missionary to his native land. A full account of this eventful time would be a wonderful story, inspiring us with faith and impelling us to appreciate him even more than we do now.

He referred to some of the impressive events of that time, but so far as we know, he never undertook to write anything like an account. We would like to know whether his missionary work took him back to Laaland and to Copenhagen, the capital, or whether he preached only in the neighborhood of Aarhus. . . .

He did relate in a testimony meeting in Bluff [in southeastern Utah, where the Nielsons later lived], that after he joined the church, he was attacked by an angry mob of his countrymen, that they tore his clothes to rags and left him injured and outraged. When he appealed to the magistrate of the law, presenting his clothes as evidence of what

> he had suffered, he was told there was "no law in Denmark to protect the Mormons."
>
> At another time during his eventful mission in his home country, a mob threw two of the elders into a pond of filthy water declaring they would baptize them. Whenever the elders struggled to the bank and tried to get out, they were struck by some of the jeering crowd on the bank and pushed rudely back into the water. This torment continued till the elders were almost worn out with chill and exhaustion.
>
> In the spring of 1856, he was given honorable release from his call to preach in Denmark. He sold his property at once and went to the mission headquarters at Copenhagen preparatory to starting for Utah. Of this time he says: "When I came to Copenhagen, I paid my first tithing, and I hold the receipt for the sixty dollars to this day." His family at that time consisted of himself and wife, and a little boy, Jens Junior, about six years old. But he was bringing with him a little girl whose father, Lars Mortensen [some sources say that it was a sister], had already come to Utah. (Lyman, "Bishop Jens Nielson," pp. 1–2)

Incidentally, it is difficult to tell how widely the metric system was in use in specific countries in 1856. Though developed in France in the late 1700s, even there it did not become the official sole means of measurement until 1840. Then gradually it came into widespread use throughout Europe, except in Great Britain, where it did not become widely used until the twentieth century. Thus, throughout the novel when the European emigrants refer to any measure of distance or volume, they use standard measurement terms and not the metric system.

BOOK 2

THE GATHERING

MAY – JULY 1856

T[he] subject of the gathering . . . is a principle I esteem to be of the greatest importance to those who are looking for salvation in this generation, or in these, that may be called, "the latter times." All that the prophets . . . have written . . . in speaking of the salvation of Israel in the last days, goes directly to show that it consists in the work of the gathering.

—Joseph Smith, letter to the elders of the Church, September 1835

CHAPTER 4

LIVERPOOL, ENGLAND

I

Thursday, 1 May 1856

As a young girl, Margaret McKensie had decided that Edinburgh, Scotland, must surely be the largest city in the entire world. When her father took her and Hannah for long walks, it had astonished her to learn that the city continued on for blocks and blocks just as it was around their own street. As she got into her teen years, she learned that there were cities, such as London, which were much larger. But she had always had a hard time conceiving how a city could spread out much larger than her Edinburgh.

The memory of those feelings came flooding back into Maggie's mind as she walked slowly along the docks that lined the Mersey River. Liverpool was said to have almost two hundred thousand people in the city alone, and half that many again in the surrounding towns. It was a huge, often squalid, and always smoky city along the River Mersey. The railway station was more than a mile from the docks, and as the McKensies had walked that distance together, Maggie was amazed to see street after street leading off as far as she could see with huge apartment buildings or long, dark factories with tall chimneys. Since reaching the river, they had come another half a mile, and there had been no break in the complex of docks, wharfs, piers, and warehouses. Half a mile and they still couldn't see the end of it! Robbie had started to count the number of ships. When he reached a hundred, he finally tired and gave it up.

"What is the name of the ship again?"

Maggie slowed her step and turned to look back at her sister. Hannah's earlier enthusiasm for this "grand adventure," as she called it, had now been replaced by weariness. They had gone by stage as far as Glasgow the previous night, but had to stay over to catch the morning train to Liverpool. In Glasgow the missionaries had arranged for a dingy dormitory-style boardinghouse. Brother Cunningham, one of the members of their branch, snored so loudly that half the group had lain awake most of the night with their hands over their ears. Maggie and her mother had been able to sleep some on the train down, but Hannah and Robbie had not. For Robbie, young and bursting with enthusiasm, it was not a problem. But Hannah was exhausted.

They were moving slowly up the road, carrying their personal belongings. A lorry had been hired at the railway station to bring their heavier things, and now Maggie wished they had left it all with the driver. It was a warm, muggy day and they were all perspiring heavily now.

"Look," Mary McKensie said suddenly, pointing ahead. Maggie turned her head, then went up on the balls of her feet so she could see better. About fifty paces ahead of them a crowd was gathered, filling most of the dock area. They weren't just milling about, however. They seemed to be in some sort of lines or queues. Just behind them, tied at the dock, was a large ship with three great masts on which the sails were furled. As they looked more closely, they could see people walking up the gangplank and others lining the rails.

"Do you think that is it?" Maggie's mother asked, moving out ahead a few steps to see better.

"I'll go see," Robbie said, lifting his bag and darting away.

Hannah groaned. "How can he do that? I just want to lie down and never move again."

"It's called youth," her mother answered. She reached out and took Hannah's suitcase from her. Hannah started to protest, but her mother hurried on.

Before they had gone another ten steps, Robbie came racing back. "This is it, Mama. It's the *Thornton.* I can see the name on the ship."

"Wonderful," Mary exclaimed. She turned and looked back at Maggie and Hannah. "Come on, girls, we're almost there."

As they approached the crowd, they saw that the people were organized into three rough lines. Each line snaked back from a table where men in suits were seated. The men had sheaves of paper in front of them and seemed to be checking off names. Behind the tables, at the base of the gangplank, there were four other men directing those who finished at the tables. Maggie let her eyes lift to the prow of the massive sailing vessel. She hadn't doubted Robbie, but it did give her great relief to see the name *Thornton* painted there. Behind them, she could hear others in their party calling out in relief and excitement as well.

As the Scottish group began to arrive, the people in the lines turned to look at them and smiled in greeting. Mary, with Robbie at her side now, went directly to the nearest couple. "Excuse me," she said. "Are you Latter-day Saints?"

"Yes." It came out with warm enthusiasm. "And you?"

"Yes. We have come from Scotland."

The man stuck out his hand. "Welcome to Liverpool. We are the Empeys, from Bedford."

Mary set down her case and took his hand. Maggie and Hannah came up and dropped their luggage gratefully to the ground. "We are the McKensies, from Edinburgh."

"Ah," said the man. "Then you'll be wanting to get into the next line." He pointed. "They're checking us in alphabetically. This line is for those with surnames which start with A to F."

Maggie looked where he was indicating and now saw that there were signs over each table. The second line was for G through M, the third for N through Z. Another couple in the adjacent line was watching and listening. "Did you say McKensie?" the woman asked.

"Yes," said Maggie. "We are the McKensies."

Now the woman's husband came forward, hand outstretched. He had a baby in his arms, a little girl. "Then you'll be in our line. We are the James family. I am William James. This is my wife, Jane."

Maggie's mother took his hand. "We are very pleased to meet you. I'm Mary McKensie."

There were several children nearby, and Maggie was surprised to see all of them turn and move closer to the couple as her mother went on. William James motioned them in. "These are our children." He smiled at them. "We have eight."

Maggie was impressed and a little amazed as well. Families with eight children were not that common in the British Isles. It was not that parents didn't give birth to that many, but it was rare for every child to survive. They were clearly not from a well-to-do home, but each child was neatly dressed and well scrubbed.

Brother James was sizing up the McKensies. "I won't introduce you to everyone just now, but I see you have three older children."

"Yes," Mary said. "Let me introduce you. This is Robbie, he's twelve. And this is Hannah, she is sixteen. And—"

"Really?" Jane James broke in with a pleased smile. She motioned to a girl who looked very much like her mother, bringing her forward. "And this is our daughter Emma, who will be sixteen next month."

"Well," Mary McKensie said, "how nice." She turned. "And this is my oldest daughter, Margaret, or Maggie."

"And I would guess you are about eighteen or nineteen, Maggie," Brother James said.

"Nineteen," she said.

Husband and wife looked at each other, smiling. "How nice," Jane said. Then she turned. Behind her a girl who looked to be about

Maggie's age was kneeling beside a young boy, speaking to him softly. Jane said to the girl, "Sarah, this is Maggie."

The girl stood and smiled.

"Sarah will be nineteen in August," Jane James said. "How wonderful. Emma and Sarah have wondered if there would be anyone their age."

"Hello, Maggie," Sarah said pleasantly, reaching out to shake hands. Her grip was firm and assured. She was taller than Maggie and a very lovely young woman. She had long dark brown hair, surprisingly blue eyes, and almost perfect features. As she smiled, Maggie saw a touch of her father in her face.

"I'm pleased to meet you, Sarah," Maggie replied, immediately liking what she saw.

"And I you."

"I hope we can become good friends," Maggie said, surprising herself even as she spoke, first because she had said it, second because she really meant it.

"I am sure we shall," Sarah responded.

"And us too," Hannah said to Emma. "I am sure we shall too."

"Well, well," William James went on, "this is just grand." He looked at Robbie. "And you're twelve?"

Robbie nodded.

William stepped to the oldest boy. "This is Reuben. He's thirteen. He also has a June birthday, when he'll be fourteen, but I'm sure you can be friends as well."

"What a wonderful family," Mary McKensie said warmly.

"Well," Jane James said, "we are very pleased to make your acquaintance. Come, get in line here with us. It shan't be long. The lines are moving along quite nicely."

The two families visited comfortably as the line moved steadily closer to the tables. Emma and Hannah chatted happily away while

Maggie and Sarah helped keep the three youngest James children occupied by playing finger games with them.

Ten minutes later, as they approached the table, Maggie looked back. The line was longer now than when they had first arrived. She shook her head and spoke to Sarah. "Do you think there will be room enough on board ship for all of us?"

Sarah shrugged, but her mother heard the question and turned. "Yes," she said. "There is room for everyone, but there won't be many empty places. I talked to President Richards earlier and he said nearly every berth has been filled."

Mary McKensie turned in surprise. "President Franklin D. Richards? Is he here?"

Jane laughed. "Of course. Don't you know him? That's him at the bottom of the gangplank showing people where to go."

They all turned, Maggie as curious as her mother. The name of Elder Franklin D. Richards was well known to all the Saints in Europe. He was not only the president of the European Mission but also an Apostle, a member of the Quorum of the Twelve. According to what the missionaries had told Maggie's family, it was in large measure his organizational abilities that made all of this possible. He and his staff booked the ships, made the arrangements for train and ferry passage from a dozen different locations, and purchased the huge amounts of supplies required to see seven hundred people through a six- to eight-week voyage across the Atlantic.

And there he was, in person. Maggie was surprised that he was shorter than she had expected. And younger. Then she remembered that someone had told her that he had been ordained an Apostle at age twenty-seven.

"We're the sixth shipload this season," William James said. "Can you imagine how much work that has meant for Brother Richards and the other missionaries?"

"Six?" Maggie exclaimed. She had known there were other emigrant ships, but six?

"Yes," Brother James answered. "And we're not the last, according to Brother Richards. He said they've had so many people apply for passage since the announcement of the handcarts, they had to charter another ship. It will be leaving in two or three more weeks."

"Do you know any of the other brethren there?" Jane asked Maggie's mother. When Mary shook her head Jane started pointing. "The man at President Richard's left, in the long coat, is Elder James G. Willie. He's been a missionary here for the last four years and is going home. He'll be our leader on the voyage. The man at the top of the gangplank, showing people where to go, is Elder Edward Martin. He's also been a missionary here. He'll come with the next ship in about a fortnight."

"And you know Brother John Jaques, don't you?" William asked.

Mary shook her head. "I don't think so."

"That's him at our table, checking us in. You'll get to meet him shortly."

Maggie studied the man at the table in front of them. They were just four or five people back now, and she had a good look at him. He was a handsome man with short hair and piercing dark eyes. He wore both a mustache and a Greek-style beard, though neither was very thick. His hands moved with quick, sure strokes, and he smiled frequently up at the people before him. She turned back to William James. "Is he one of the Church leaders here?"

"In a way. He's one of the editors at the *Millennial Star.*"

Now Maggie's mother snapped her fingers. "Of course," she said. "John Jaques. He writes beautiful poetry."

"Yes, the very one."

"But I thought his name was pronounced 'Jacks.' "

Brother James shook his head. "It's spelled J-A-Q-U-E-S, but he pronounces it 'Jakes,' not 'Jacks.' He's also the one who wrote that letter to his father-in-law in America that was published in the latest issue of the *Star.* Did you perchance read that?"

"I did," Mary McKensie said. "It was very stirring. My, what a call to repentance that was!"

Maggie looked at her mother. "Did I read that?" she said. None of what they were saying sounded familiar.

"Now that you ask, no. The missionaries showed me the latest issue just before we left Edinburgh."

"I'm glad I wasn't the one who wrote the letter to Brother Jaques," Sarah said now.

"Why?" asked Maggie.

Sarah looked at her father. "You understand better who it was and why Brother Jaques responded as he did. Tell Maggie."

"Well," Brother James said, lowering his voice a little so Brother Jaques wouldn't overhear them. "Brother Jaques is married to one of the daughters of James Loader, a good brother in the Church. Brother Loader and most of his family went to America last fall. Brother Jaques and his wife couldn't join them at that time but made plans to go this spring. They'll be going over with Elder Martin's group on the next ship.

"Anyway, once the Loaders got to America, they settled in to wait. Then somehow they got word that instead of going to Utah by wagon, they would be going by handcart. It really upset one of the daughters—her name is Patience Loader. So Patience wrote to Brother Jaques and complained about the decision, saying that she didn't see how their family could do that."

"So it was just the idea of going by handcart?" Maggie asked. "They didn't change their minds about going to Zion?"

Now Sister James came in, eager to help her husband with the story. "That's right. But even so, it must have really upset Brother Jaques. So he wrote a letter back to Brother Loader. I guess he thought Patience was only expressing the feelings of her father. It was quite pointed."

"*Quite* pointed," Maggie's mother echoed. "It was very much a chastisement."

"But also very inspiring," Brother James said quickly. "It's quite the call to remember why it is we are going to America. That's probably why Elder Richards decided to publish both letters in the paper. It's a lesson to all of us about faith and commitment to our covenants."

Maggie turned away, supposedly to look at Brother Jaques again, but actually so her mother wouldn't see her face. Was that why her mother had said nothing about the letters? Because she was afraid that Maggie would think it was a hint for her to develop a better attitude about going?

Thankfully, Hannah changed the subject then with another question. "What about Elder Richards?" she wondered. "Is he going with us?"

"Yes," Brother James said, "but not yet. After he gets the last emigrants off, he and a few of the other missionaries will finish things up here and come on a fast-sailing packet ship. They will go to New Orleans, then up the Mississippi and Missouri Rivers all the way to Florence. It is much more expensive to go around that way but also much quicker. He hopes to catch up with us by the time we get to Florence."

"So are we going to New York?" Reuben James asked his father, who seemed to know everything about what was going on.

"Yes. Then we'll go by train and steamship to Iowa."

Robbie looked up. "Eye-oh-wah?"

William laughed. "Yes. They say it is an Indian name. That is where the railroad ends. That's where we will get the handcarts." Suddenly he had a thought. "Or will you be going with one of the independent wagon companies?"

They all looked at him blankly.

"There are a few in our group, and also some on the next ship, who have sufficient means to buy wagons and teams. Brother Richards says they are going to form independent wagon companies. They call them independent because they will not be directly associated with us handcarters."

Mary McKensie laughed. "Handcarters. That's a new term. I like it."

"So you'll be with us, then," Jane James said to her. "We're certainly in no financial condition to purchase a wagon or team. Not with eight children."

"Nor are we," Mary said. "If it weren't for the handcart plan, we wouldn't be going this year at all."

Maggie reached out and touched Sarah's arm. "I'm glad," she said. "If we're going to have to pull handcarts, then I'm glad it can be with people we know."

"And people we like," Sarah said, squeezing her hand. "It will make things so much nicer."

Nothing in his twenty-two years had prepared Eric Pederson for the experience called Liverpool, England. He and Olaf had spent their lives in a tiny fishing village on a Norwegian fjord. Everyone knew everyone else. Life was simple and moved at its own pace. At night the air was so quiet that sometimes you could hear the animals moving restlessly in the barn.

Liverpool was cacophony, bedlam, riot, chaos. It was an endless sprawl of huge tenement houses going on for blocks in endless dreariness. The streets were so thick with horses and carts that even a cat took a risk to cross them. The air was heavy with smoke and haze and stank with odors that Eric could not identify. Everything seemed to be covered with soot. The streets were filled with garbage, and some ran with raw sewage in the gutters. The people were loud, brazen, brassy, rude, foul, and vulgar. Women flounced by in dresses with impossibly large skirts. Men passed in shirts so dirty you could not tell the original color. Children were as ragged as the mongrel dogs they played with. And here along the docks of the Mersey River, which made Liverpool one of the busiest ports in the world, it all seemed to be compressed into one horrendous and disturbing mass.

Eric didn't like it. He didn't like anything about it. He turned to

Elsie Nielson in astonishment. “Is this what Copenhagen is like?” he asked.

She had a handkerchief to her nose with one hand while she tried to keep Bodil Mortensen in tow with the other. “No. It is nothing like this,” she breathed. “I can’t believe people can bear to live here.”

Her husband grunted. Jens Nielson had his son Jens on his shoulders so as to leave his hands free to carry their bags. “Copenhagen has some places that are not very pleasant too, Elsie.”

“How much farther, Papa?” the boy asked, tugging at his father’s hair.

“Berth seventy-three,” Jens said, peering at the posts that supported the wharf. They were just coming up on one that had the number seventy tacked to it. “We’re almost there.”

The Scandinavians, almost a hundred of them now, increased their pace a little, anxious to find their ship. Coming by both steamer and train, they had arrived in Liverpool two days before. That had been a shock. Would America be like this? Would Utah? If so, Eric wasn’t sure he could bear living in Zion.

“There!” someone cried. “That must be it.”

Up ahead were some tables in front of a gangplank that led up to a large three-masted ship. There was a small crowd of people gathered in front of the tables. They were obviously being checked in for boarding.

A man in a suit and long overcoat saw them coming and broke away, coming swiftly toward them. Brother Johan Ahmanson had been the leader of the group coming from the Nordic countries. He was near the front, and when he saw the man approaching, he moved out ahead of the others. The rest of the group stopped to wait and watch.

The two men shook hands warmly and began to speak. Eric heard a strange language.

"Does Brother Ahmanson speak English?" Jens Nielson asked in surprise.

"He must," Eric replied, as surprised as Brother Nielson.

"Good. I've been worried about how we shall understand what we are to do."

"Brother Ahmanson and his wife, Grethe, are good people," Elsie said. "How did you come to know them?"

"Elder Ahmanson baptized our family while he was a missionary in Norway," Olaf answered.

Eric started to add something but then saw that Brother Ahmanson and the other man were coming toward them now. When they reached the waiting group both men were smiling. "Brothers and sisters," Ahmanson said in Danish, "I am very pleased to introduce you to Elder Franklin D. Richards, president of the European Mission."

That sent a murmur of recognition and pleasure through the crowd. The Apostle's name was well known to everyone. He raised a hand and waved, then turned and spoke to their leader. Elder Ahmanson nodded and translated for the rest.

"Elder Richards says we are all to go to the first table. Don't worry about what letter your last name begins with. I will be there to help you. There we will be checked in and given our assignments on the ship. Bring your personal belongings with you. The heavier baggage will be brought aboard by the sailors."

Elder Richards said something else and Brother Ahmanson nodded, smiling broadly. "He also says, welcome to Liverpool. Things are going very well here and we should set sail first thing in the morning."

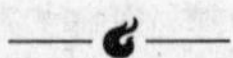

Because they were together in line at the check-in, not only were the Jameses and the McKensies assigned to the same deck—the lower of the two passenger decks—but they ended up in adjoining berths. The bunks, or sleeping berths, were about six feet long and four feet wide, and two adults or three or more children were expected to sleep in one bunk. Maggie McKensie and Sarah James decided to bunk together, as did Hannah and Emma. Maggie's mother and Robbie would share a third bunk. The rest of the James family were distributed between three other berths.

There were two sets of bunks along each bulkhead, one above the other, with the lower being about two feet above the floor. Tables bolted to the deck in the center of the room were equipped with benches, likewise fastened down. These were used for various purposes during the day. For meals they were equipped with attachable leafs with raised edges so the dishes did not slide off as the ship rolled and pitched.

Maggie learned very quickly that they were fortunate to have been assigned to the lower deck. Because it was where the ship's hull was a little wider, each passenger got slightly more room than they did on the deck above. Also, the part of the ship below the waterline stayed cooler. As warmer air always rises, the upper deck was hot and the air stifling. It wasn't as light down below, but it was definitely more roomy and pleasant for those lucky enough to be assigned there.

Robbie set off immediately to explore with Reuben James. Both boys were ecstatic to be on board a real oceangoing sailing ship. After unpacking their personal belongings and getting them "stowed" into small wooden lockers—not much more than boxes built into the bulkheads—Emma and Hannah decided to do the same. Sarah had to help her mother with the three little ones, and so after a few moments Maggie went back up on deck.

It was a hum of activity. Dockworkers were moving back and forth carrying the heavier trunks and baggage of the people down into the belly of the ship. Sailors were checking the rigging or starting to nail boxes and crates to the decks so as to secure them for the rolling motion that would surely come.

Maggie moved quickly over to the rail so as to get out of the way. She had chosen the dockside of the ship and looked down on the three registration tables. The lines for the closest two tables were now down to the last two stragglers. But a large group of people was gathered around the first table. In a moment, as strange sounds floated up to her, she realized that this was the Scandinavian group. Elder Richards and another man, a tall man with a commanding presence, were standing behind the table helping to sign people in. The other man was acting as translator and the process was very slow.

At least I don't have to learn a new language.

It came in a burst of gratitude as she realized what a difference that would make. These people would have to make this challenging journey without being able to understand instructions and commands, participate in worship services, or converse with others besides those in their own little group. What a difference that would make in their experience!

Now other little things jumped out at her from the crowd below that added to the realization that she, Maggie McKensie, was one of the luckier ones. A younger man, probably in his early twenties, was helping his wife toward the gangplank. She moved slowly and laboriously, and Maggie saw that she was heavy with child. *Heavy* with child! The husband's face showed concern. The woman's was filled with exhaustion and pain. Maggie shook her head in wonder. How far had they come in this condition? What if this woman's time had come on a train or on a ferryboat? Was the pull of Zion even more powerful than the concern for a woman's travail? Maggie didn't have to respond to that. The answer was just before her.

Waiting at the table was an old woman with perfectly white hair. She leaned heavily on two canes, waiting for a person who had to be her daughter to help her get checked in. How in the world would she manage in a handcart company? Maggie wondered. There was another blessing she had not really considered before. She was young and strong and healthy.

At the first table, waiting their turn, she noticed two young men who stood close together. Though the similarity was not striking, she guessed they were brothers. For one thing, they both wore beautiful matching hand-knitted sweaters, even though the day was quite warm. Made by a mother or a sister or an aunt, she guessed. The one young man looked slightly older than she was; the other was about Hannah's age. Curious now, she looked around for the rest of their family. There was another couple right behind them—quite a striking couple, actually, for the man was tall, but his wife was tiny and petite, a good foot shorter than he was. They were speaking to the brothers, but after a moment of watching, Maggie decided they were not of the same family. The two boys must be alone.

Again she felt a flash of gratitude. She had left James behind, but she had her family. And now she had found a friend. Why weren't these two brothers with their family? Were they orphaned? Or perhaps they were the only members of their family who were Latter-day Saints. She could only wonder.

As she scanned the crowds, she had differing thoughts and feelings. She saw human beings of every kind—tall and short, rotund and skinny as a reed, the old and the young and everything in between. There were blue eyes, brown eyes, green eyes. There were blonds, brunettes, redheads, grayheads. Directly below her, a woman sat on a box, a baby at her breast. Here and there the wealthy—or at least the well-to-do—stood out from the others by the finery of their dress. One woman with long, elegant gold necklaces and a dark green silk dress directed a manservant, who staggered beneath what Maggie assumed was a trunk of the woman's clothing.

Maggie shook her head as a parable from the New Testament came to her mind. The Savior had said that the kingdom of heaven was like a net, bringing in fish of every kind. Well, here was the living proof of that.

"Maggie! Maggie!"

She turned. Robbie was racing toward her from across the main deck. Reuben James was right behind him. They slid to a halt right in front of her. Robbie's brown eyes, always large and round, now looked enormous. "Guess what, Maggie!"

"What?"

"The first mate—he's the second in command on the ship—anyway, the first mate let Reuben and me go up and see the wheel."

She nodded, holding back a smile. "I didn't think ships had wheels."

He looked disgusted. "Not that kind of wheel, Maggie. The wheel that steers the ship."

She feigned surprise. "Oh, *that* wheel."

"Yes. We even got to turn it, didn't we, Reuben?"

Reuben James nodded gravely.

Robbie rushed on. "This is so wonderful, Maggie! Come on, Reuben, Hannah said we can see down to where there are rocks in the bottom of the ship."

"They call it ballast," Maggie called after them as they darted away.

Robbie said something but it was lost in the noise of the crowd. Maggie smiled, feeling a wisp of envy. Oh, to have that kind of zest!

After a moment, she decided that she would be wise to organize her things while the ship was still docked and steady rather than waiting until they were out to sea. She turned and went below.

II

Friday, 2 May 1856

To get more than seven hundred people all on the main deck at one time required utilizing every inch of available space, but they had done that. Shortly after sunup the call had gone through the ship, asking that all passengers come up topside. To the surprise of many, they found that they were anchored in the main channel of the Mersey River. A tugboat had pulled them away from the Bramberly Moore docks at first light so that another ship could take their place. But they needed to wait one more day for a doctor to come aboard and inspect them so he could certify to the American authorities that there was no smallpox or other contagious diseases being shipped to the New World.

As they gathered on the deck, the ship's captain, whose name was Collins, invited Elder Willie to come up on the fo'c'sle where the people could see and hear him better. Elder Willie was to be their group priesthood leader on the voyage. Spirits were high as they pressed in to hear him better. Though they hadn't sailed yet, in a way their voyage had begun. Most of the emigrants were settled and unpacked. The quarters had been cleaned thoroughly in anticipation of the inspection. There was a great eagerness evident on the faces of all.

Maggie turned as someone came up behind her and touched her arm. It was Sarah James.

"Good morning," Maggie said. For most of their lives Maggie and Hannah had shared a bed, so sleeping with someone was not unusual for Maggie. But the berth that Maggie and Sarah now shared was only two-thirds the width of a bed, and often during the night the two of them bumped each other. Then, just before dawn, Maggie had quietly slipped out of the berth and finally fallen asleep in one of the wooden chairs. To Maggie's astonishment, Sarah wasn't bothered at all. She had slept like one of the stones used for ballast.

"What time did you get up?" Sarah whispered. "I didn't even know you were gone."

Maggie shook her head in wonder. "Where did you learn to sleep like that?"

For a moment Sarah didn't understand; then she laughed softly. "At home Emma and Mary Ann and Martha and me all shared a bed.

I guess I'm used to having somebody next to me." Then she looked horrified. "I didn't snore, did I?"

Now it was Maggie who laughed. "No, not at all. But Old Brother Cunningham did again. For a time there in the night I thought he was sawing a hole in the bulkhead."

"Maggie!"

She turned to see that Robbie, Hannah, and her mother had come up to join them. Emma James was also with them. Maggie's mother was giving her a chastening look.

"Well," Maggie said, a little sheepish, "that's the way it sounded. I just hope that we don't get assigned to the same tent with him, or I'll not sleep a wink until we reach Salt Lake."

"I slept good," Robbie said brightly.

His mother groaned. "Yes, you did. And you slept all over the berth."

Maggie laughed. Robbie was famous for waking up every morning in a different position.

"Did you hear?" Sarah said, nudging Maggie. "There was a baby born on the deck above ours yesterday."

She turned in surprise, remembering the woman and her husband she had seen. "Really? What time?"

"About five o'clock. I guess they had barely made it on board. I don't know them. They said it was a Sister McNeil."

"I think I know exactly which one it was," Maggie said, sobered by how close that sister had come to giving birth in very different circumstances.

"Brothers and sisters."

They all turned. Brother Willie had one arm up, waving to the people to come to attention. Quiet swept across the crowd like a welcome breeze.

"Thank you. As some of you know, my name is Brother James G. Willie. I have been serving as a missionary here in Great Britain for almost four years now. Like many other elders, we are returning home with you. Elder Richards has asked that I serve as the president of this company and escort you to America."

"Hurrah!" someone shouted and Brother Willie grinned.

"Thank you, Brother Baker. Right after the meeting, I will pay you the five quid I promised to give you if you would say that."

That brought a ripple of pleasant laughter across the group. Maggie watched him and smiled too. Willie was about forty and seemed pleasant enough. Several of those from England knew him well and spoke very highly of him. It was good that he had a sense of humor.

He looked down, motioning at some men right below him. Several climbed up to join him. "In this ship's company, we have five hundred and sixty adults, one hundred seventy-two children, and twenty-nine infants. That's a total of seven hundred and sixty-one people. More than enough for one man to govern, I would wager. So, I would like to introduce my counselors for the voyage. Brother Millen Atwood will preside over the main deck of passengers." A man stepped forward and raised his hand. "Brother Moses Cluff will preside over the English portion of the lower deck, and Brother Johan Ahmanson will preside over the Scandinavian Saints on that same deck."

Maggie turned to Sarah. "Brother Ahmanson speaks English. I think he's the one who was translating for the Scandinavians yesterday."

President Willie went on. "The main deck will be divided into four wards with presidents, and the lower into three wards, likewise with presidents."

He motioned to the other men. "Brother John Chislett here has been asked to serve as captain of the guard. You should know that he has been instructed that none of the ship's crew will be allowed to come below on our decks unless they have permission of the ship's captain or his first officer."

Chislett stepped forward, smiled at the crowd, then stepped back.

"Elder Edward Griffith has been appointed steward to have general oversight over all of our provisions." He waited as Griffith stepped forward. "And Brothers John Patterson and Henry Bodenham will serve as our cooks."

As the last two stepped forward, he laid a hand on each of their shoulders. "The rest of us may be your leaders, but these two are the ones you should treat most kindly."

Again that brought an appreciative laugh from the crowd, and a few clapped in response.

President Willie waited a moment as the men rejoined their fellow passengers, then started again. As he did so, Maggie saw that Brother Ahmanson immediately began to translate what was being said to his fellow Saints.

"Brothers and sisters," Willie began, "our voyage on the *Thornton* will take about six weeks. We will be sailing to New York City. We shall then go by railway and steamers across the Great Lakes to a place called Iowa City, Iowa. There is where the railroad ends. That is where the wilderness begins. At Iowa City there are Church agents—likewise missionaries from England—who have gone ahead to prepare things for our arrival.

"While on board ship, we shall conduct ourselves as disciples of the Master. We shall rise at six A.M. and retire at nine P.M. Morning prayers will be at seven, evening prayers half an hour before lights out. We shall have worship services each day at two P.M., weather permitting, and Sabbath day services each week as well. We want to set an example to the captain and the crew. We want to convince them that Mormons are not the horrible creatures some people would make us out to be."

The ship's captain, standing behind Willie, raised a hand. "We already know that. This is the most orderly loading I've ever had."

"Wonderful," Willie said. Then he turned back to the people. "That's what we want. Be cheerful. Keep your quarters clean. Serve one another."

He paused, looking around with affection upon the group. "We realize that these next five or six months will be difficult ones for many of you. We know that you are leaving your homes, and in many cases loved ones."

Maggie's head came up and she looked at her mother sharply. Had she said something to Brother Willie? But her mother seemed as surprised as she was at his words.

"But remember, we are leaving our homes in obedience to the covenants we have made with the Lord. We leave our former lives behind in order to serve the purposes of God. We go forth now to build a heritage and legacy for our children and our grandchildren. Let us go forward with joy, brothers and sisters. We have begun the journey. May we carry on with faith until we bring it to a successful close."

"Hey, you!"

Eric and Olaf Pederson were standing by the rail, watching the activity on the dock. President Willie and the other leaders had taken a boat back to the dock and returned to Liverpool. According to Brother Ahmanson, they would return the next day with President Richards for the final send-off. Eric turned at the shout, though he didn't know what had been said. It was one of the crew about ten feet away. He was working with a large crate near the bow, lashing it down, then nailing boards around the base to secure it in place. He was staring at the two brothers.

"Yes, you!" the man said angrily. "What are you standing around for? Grab a hammer and get to work."

Eric could see that he was talking to him and that he was upset, but had no idea what it was about. Other passengers had stopped to watch curiously. He felt terribly stupid.

"Didn't they tell you anything?" the man snarled. "Get yourself a hammer."

The brothers looked at each other again, clearly dismayed, but not knowing what to do.

The man stood, his face red. "Stupid *Dummkopf!*" he cried.

Maggie McKensie was just coming up the ladder from the hold when she heard the man shouting. It took her only a moment to realize what was happening. These were the two brothers she had noticed yesterday. They were part of the Scandinavian group and therefore likely did not speak English.

She walked swiftly to the sailor, planting herself between him and the two young men. "They don't speak English," Maggie McKensie said. "Or German," she added pointedly. "Can't you see that?"

"I don't care what they speak. Just tell them to get a hammer and get to work."

She felt her temper flare. "How can I do that? I don't speak Danish, or whatever it is they are," she snapped.

"Look, lady," he snarled. "We're crossing the Atlantic Ocean. Anything we don't nail down will go right through that railing and overboard."

"I'm sorry," she said, fighting to keep her voice under control. "But I don't have the gift of tongues any more than you have the gift of good sense."

She threw up her hands and whirled away. What a dolt! As if it were her fault they couldn't understand him.

"May I be of help?"

Maggie turned to see a tall man with graying hair and kind eyes. She recognized him immediately. It was the leader of the Scandinavian group, Brother . . .

She was still groping for his name when he held out his hand. "Johan Ahmanson," he said. His English was slightly accented but very good.

"I am Maggie McKensie." She pointed to the sailor. "He wants these two young men to help, but I don't think they speak English."

He turned to the crewman. "What is the problem?" he asked in Danish.

The man just stared at him. He smiled gently. "I asked you," he repeated in English, "what is the problem?"

"Why don't you speak English, then?" the man growled darkly.

"And why don't you speak to these boys in Norwegian?" he shot right back.

The man saw the point immediately and seemed to soften. There was no animosity or anger in Ahmanson, only quiet patience.

"I need them to help me secure these crates."

"Good. If you will get them hammers and tell me what you want them to do, I'll translate for you."

The crewman nodded, somewhat pacified. "Have them follow me." He looked a little chagrined. "I can show them what to do."

Ahmanson spoke quickly and the two fell into step behind the man. As the older one passed Maggie, he spoke softly. "*Takk. God dag.*"

She looked at Ahmanson.

"That's 'Thank you,' and 'Good day,' " he said with a smile.

"Are they brothers?" Maggie asked as they walked away.

"Yes," Elder Ahmanson said. "They are Eric and Olaf Pederson. They are from Norway."

"I noticed them yesterday. They seem to be alone. Don't they have a family?"

"They are going to Utah by themselves to help earn money. Their family will come next season."

"Oh."

"Well," the leader said graciously, "I'd better go help them. Thank you for intervening."

She blushed a little. "I'm afraid I didn't do it as graciously as you."

He chuckled amiably. "I think you softened the man up so that I could deal with him more reasonably." He waved and walked away.

Just then Hannah came up to stand beside her. "What's the

matter?" she asked, turning to watch the departing group. "It looked like you were fighting with that sailor."

"Nothing's wrong now. Just be thankful that we can speak English. This journey is going to be hard enough without not knowing what is going on around you."

Chapter Notes

The details of the arrival of the Saints at Liverpool and the events surrounding their boarding and preparations for departure are taken from the company journal (see Turner, *Emigrating Journals*, pp. 1–2). For convenience in the novel, everything that was happening in the process of embarking and the events prior to sailing are compressed somewhat.

As noted before, while the Mary McKensie family from Scotland is the author's creation, many others in this book are actual historical characters. Obviously the interactions and conversations of these actual people with the fictional characters are the creation of the author. Also, since in many cases physical descriptions of these people at this point in their lives are unavailable, the descriptions given here are not meant to convey what they may have actually looked like. The actual historical characters in this chapter include:

Franklin D. Richards: He was ordained an Apostle in 1849 at the age of twenty-seven. As the presiding authority over the Church's mission in Europe, he was directly responsible for the massive effort of getting the emigrating Saints outfitted and on their way to America (see *Deseret News 1999–2000 Church Almanac*, p. 58).

Johan A. Ahmanson: This missionary from Scandinavia who became one of the leaders in the Willie Company was introduced in chapter 3.

James Grey Willie: He who would become the captain of the fourth handcart company of 1856 was an Englishman by birth. Born in 1814, he came to America when he was twenty-one and in 1842 joined the Church in Nauvoo. In 1852 he returned to England to serve a mission, and after four years away from his family he was returning home. Elder Richards appointed him president of the group who sailed on the *Thornton* (see Hafen and Hafen, *Handcarts to Zion*, pp. 92–93).

Edward Martin: Also a native Englishman, Martin, born in 1818, was from Preston, England, where the Church's first missionary efforts in the British Isles took place. He was converted to the Church there, and he and his wife came to America thereafter. He was on his way west with the Saints in 1846 when the call for the Mormon Battalion came and he volunteered to go. He too was called back as a missionary to his native land in 1852 and was returning home in 1856 after four years of service. He sailed on the *Horizon* later in May of 1856 and in Iowa City was appointed as captain of one of the two handcart companies formed from that group. At Florence, Nebraska, the two companies were joined and he was kept as the captain. Thus the fifth company of 1856 came to be called the Edward Martin Handcart Company (see Hafen and Hafen, *Handcarts to Zion*, p. 93).

William and Jane James: William was the son of Lee James of Eckington, Worcestershire, England, and was born in 1809. His wife, Jane Haines, also from Worcestershire, was six years younger than her husband. They had eight children, including Sarah, Emma, and Reuben.

John Jaques: Having Brother Jaques as one of the check-in agents for the *Thornton* group is a device of the author to introduce Brother Jaques to the readers. He was not actually there for that sailing, though he did come to America on the *Horizon* with Edward Martin. Brother Jaques had a notable literary gift and was appointed as an editor at the *Millennial Star*. He is the author of the lyrics for the popular hymn "Oh Say, What Is Truth?"

As referred to in this chapter, in the spring of 1856 Patience Loader, Jaques's sister-in-law, wrote him a letter from New York. Upset by what she said, Jaques wrote back to James Loader, her father and his father-in-law. Brother Jaques interpreted Patience's letter as evidence of a lack of faith and evidently assumed that as head of the family, James Loader was responsible for this wavering in the faith. Later, Elder Richards published both letters in the *Millennial Star*. For convenience in the novel, it is suggested the letters had already been published in the *Star* by the time the *Thornton* group gathered at Liverpool. In actuality, they were not published until June, some weeks after the *Thornton's* departure (see *Millennial Star* 18 [14 June 1856]: 369–72; see also Bell, *Life History and Writings of John Jaques*, pp. 72–78, where both letters are printed in their entirety).

Since these letters provide a wonderful insight into the minds and hearts of the Saints of that day, the letter from Patience and excerpts of Jaques's reply to her father are included here:

> Williamsburg, [New York,] April 21, 1856.
>
> Dear Brother Jaques—On the 18th April we received your letter, dated March 29. We had been anxiously expecting to hear from you, and I can say, that when we did hear, we felt somewhat surprised to

find that we have to go by the hand-carts. Father and mother think this cannot be done, and I am sure I think the same, for mother cannot walk day after day, and I do not think that any of us will ever be able to continue walking every day. We think it will be better to remain here or at St. Louis for a time until we are able to help ourselves to a wagon. We are across the water, which is a great part of the way to Zion. Father and mother think you had better come here for a time. We will take lodgings for you if you will let us know. Do you and your wife think it right to go by the hand-carts? If we girls were strong boys then I think it might be done, but father is the only man in our family. I don't feel myself that I can go like this. If, by staying here for a little time, we can get means to go by a wagon, it will be far preferable. Mother, I am sure, can never go that way. She says herself that she cannot do it, and I don't think that any of us can. Why, we understood that the hand-carts were the last resource! Mother says that she must have a revelation before she can see this right. Why, we shall have to sell nearly all our clothes! And what shall we do for things to wear when we get to the Valley? Seventeen pounds weight each is but very little.

We shall be delighted to see you. I wish they in London would come with you. We are doing very comfortable now.

I remain your sister in the Gospel,
P—— —— [Patience Loader]

Liverpool, May 19, 1856.

Dear Brother L—— [Brother James Loader, Jaques's father-in-law].

On May 7, I received with great pleasure the letter written by P——, and dated April 21, because we had been so long expecting one. But my pleasure was changed to great pain and unfeigned sorrow when I read the contents. I have read the letter about half a dozen times. I could scarcely believe that you [Jaques evidently assumed that James Loader was in agreement] could have sent such a one. There is not one atom of the spirit of Zion in it, but the very spirit of apostacy. I felt to exclaim in my heart, "Who has bewitched you, and with whom have you been taking counsel, that you should so soon forget the goodness of the Lord in delivering you from this part of Babylon, and opening up your way to Zion?" . . .

. . . As for me and my house, we will serve the Lord, and when we start we will go right up to Zion, if we go ragged and barefoot. . . .

You have looked upon the journey all in a lump. Recollect that you will only have to perform one day's travel at a time, and the first 200 or 300 miles, from Iowa City to Florence, the hand-carts will travel through a partly settled country, and be lightly loaded, for they will not take their full load for the Plains till they get to Florence. This first part of the journey will just get the Saints used to travelling, without a great deal of toil all at once. You have also thought of performing the journey in your own strength, forgetting that you should put your trust in the Lord, who strengthens even the weak according to their day. . . .

P—— seems very much afraid that she will not have clothes enough when she gets to Zion. Well, if she sets more store upon fine clothes than upon the counsel of the Lord and the blessings of living in Zion, I can say she is different to me. The fact is, she has too many clothes—they are a trouble to her, and she seems willing to hazard her salvation for them. There is such a thing as being ruined by one's riches. . . .

. . . You cannot have much faith in the Lord if you have only enough to take you half way to Zion.

You will say, you never had such a letter before in all your lives. I will say you never before deserved such a letter in all your lives, because you never before turned away from such privileges as you have now within your reach. What! are you going to dash away the cup of temporal salvation from your lips, now it almost touches them? What folly! What madness! It is no little thing to trifle with the Lord, or with His Holy Spirit, or with the counsels of His servants. . . .

You say that you understood that the hand-carts were the last resource. Pray what other resource have you? Those who despise the hand-carts may yet be glad to get to Zion with a pack upon their backs.

What more shall I say? I can but exhort you to repent of your faint-heartedness, repent of your trifling with the salvation of the Lord, and be ready to go with us, with a cheerful heart, trusting in God, and not in your own strength, when we come, and all will be well. . . . Pray unto Him without ceasing. Give your souls no rest till you get the spirit of the gathering burning in your bosoms, like a fire that cannot be quenched. . . .

When your wife has heard this, I think she will fancy she has got revelation enough about the hand-carts.

With love to all, in which my wife and family join, I remain your brother in the Gospel,

John Jaques.

CHAPTER 5

LIVERPOOL, ENGLAND
TO
NEW YORK CITY, NEW YORK

I

Thursday, 8 May 1856

As the sound of the bell came softly through the hatch above her head, Maggie looked up. It was the ship's bell, and it clanged again and then again. Maggie closed her book, a sense of sadness heavy upon her. Here it was again.

The rest of her family and the James family were already topside. She got up and went to the berth where she and Sarah slept. Sarah James was awake, pale as a sheet of parchment, staring up at the bulkhead above her. Maggie noted that it made her look only more lovely. She pulled a face, envious but not resentful. Even when she was seasick, Sarah was lovely.

"Do you want to try and go up on deck?" Maggie asked gently.

Sarah turned. Her eyes closed for a moment, then opened again. "I think so."

"I'll help you." Maggie took her arm and helped her up to a sitting position.

Sarah swayed for a moment and clutched at the side of the berth.

"Don't close your eyes," Maggie suggested. "I found that that only makes things worse."

There was a wan smile, and then Sarah looked at her. "The Americans say that all men are created equal. It's in their Declaration of Independence."

"Yes?" Maggie wasn't sure what had brought that to her mind.

"I don't believe it."

"You don't?"

"No." Now there was just a trace of the spunk that Maggie knew lay inside her new friend. "Otherwise how do you explain why I've been deathly seasick for four straight days now, and yet you were sick for only one day, and Robbie and Reuben didn't even turn pale?"

Maggie put her arm around her and helped her stand up. "I see what you mean. It doesn't seem fair, does it? But then, if we were all created equal, I'd have skin that looks like fine porcelain and eyes as wide and lovely as yours."

"Go on, Maggie," Sarah said, holding on to Maggie's arm to steady herself. "You are very pretty, and you know it."

"And you are beautiful, Sarah James, and you know that."

Sarah looked away, embarrassed by the sincerity in Maggie's voice. "Beauty is as beauty does," she murmured.

And that was Sarah James, Maggie thought with a rush of affection. She was as lovely a girl as Maggie knew, and yet there was not the slightest affectation about it, not the slightest arrogance. *Beauty is as beauty does.* How true. For what made Sarah James truly beautiful was what she was, not simply what she looked like. Maggie once again felt a great burst of gratitude that she had found such a friend so early in their journey.

The sound of the bell came again down through the hatch.

"We'd better hurry," Maggie said, starting toward the ladder.

"Yes." Sarah sighed. "I don't look forward to it. Twice in one day? That's too much."

"I know," Maggie said wearily. "I know."

—❦—

Eric Pederson wanted to avert his head as the four men passed through the crowd. Each held on to one corner of a long board with handles on each end. On the board was a dark shape sewn up into one of the blankets. But then he remembered the words of his father and did not look away. "Death is as much a part of life as birth," his father often said. "While we may not welcome it, neither should we fear to look it in the face, for someday all of us will have to shake hands with it."

But two burials at sea in one day? And when they were barely— He had to stop for a moment and count. They had left the dock and anchored in the river on Friday, but had not actually been towed out into the Irish Sea until Sunday. Today was Thursday. So they had really been at sea for only five days. Five days and they were about to witness their second burial.

Last night, just as the call for evening prayers had gone out, word came that Sister Rachel Curtis, aged seventy-five years, from Norton, in Gloucestershire, England, had passed away from causes incident to old age. Eric and Olaf did not know her personally, but they had seen her as they were checking in at the registration tables. White haired, frail, steadying herself on two canes, she had seemed barely able to hobble. Eric remembered wondering how she could ever manage to cross the plains—in wagon or handcart. But that was no longer a concern for her. Now she had found a different Zion. Now she could rest from those things incident to old age.

The bells had tolled at ten o'clock this morning, and with great solemnity the majority of the passengers gathered on deck for the burial. President Willie had offered up a prayer to the Almighty, and then Rachel Curtis had been consigned to the depths of the sea. It had left a pall over the company, even though all knew that this aged sister was happier now and at peace.

Then the second shock had come. About an hour before, Jens

Nielson came up on deck where several of the Scandinavian Saints were taking the sun and announced that Sister Rasmine Rasmussen, from Jutland, Denmark—a sister that the Nielsons had known well—had just succumbed to an inflammation of the brain. Elsie had been with the sisters who were taking care of the woman and was having a difficult time of it, her husband reported.

Here again, Eric thought, death had not caught them by surprise. On their way down from Norway, when they had docked at Copenhagen, he and Olaf had watched some of the Danish Saints help this sister on board the steamer. She had been suffering from the inflammation for several weeks, but was insistent that she would not be left behind. Now, less than a week into the voyage, she had passed quietly away. This time, because an infection was involved, the ship's captain recommended that there be no delay in the burial. President Willie agreed, and at five o'clock in the afternoon, for the second time that day, the ship's bell began to toll.

Most of the crew were gathered around, faces solemn. They did not like death on their ship, even if it was a common visitor. The ship's captain and President Willie stood side-by-side near the wheel. Almost all of the Saints—except for those who were still suffering from seasickness—were gathered around, heads bare, voices subdued.

This time it was Elder Ahmanson who offered the prayer. He spoke in Danish and Eric was strangely glad. If Sister Rasmussen was allowed to tarry long enough to witness her own burial, she ought to be able to understand the prayer. When the prayer was finished, Captain Collins spoke briefly. Eric didn't know what he said—Elder Ahmanson wasn't there to translate for the ship's captain—but it seemed appropriate. That finished, the four men stepped forward to a place where the railing was open to the sea. There was a moment's hesitation; then the two in the back raised the board up. Eric caught a glimpse of the dark shape sliding downward. There were two or three seconds of silence, then a quiet splash from below.

President Willie stared down for several moments, then replaced his hat. "Thank you, brothers and sisters," he said.

As the crowd returned to their quarters, Eric stood where he was, pensive and reflecting. On Sunday one of President Willie's counselors had married a missionary returning from Bombay and a young Scottish girl from Dundee. On Tuesday a sister had given birth to a baby boy, the second born on board since their arrival. A marriage. Two births. Two deaths. The accounts of mortality. Somehow they had to be kept in balance.

II

Sunday, 11 May 1856

It was evening now and would soon be fully dark. Most of the passengers had gone below immediately following worship services and had not come up again. It had been raining lightly for most of the day, and the wind was stiff and cold, coming directly out of the northwest. But Maggie loved it. She was at the prow of the ship, leaning into the wind, letting it swirl through her hair and make her cheeks tingle. This had proven to be one of the unexpected and yet welcome surprises for Maggie McKensie. She had fallen in love with the sea.

For most of the Latter-day Saints on board the *Thornton*, the crossing of the Atlantic seemed like an interminable string of dreary days and drearier nights. In their eyes it was filled with stupefying monotony—recurring seasickness; drab meals often eaten cold because they could not build fires on deck due to bad weather; unbearable confinement when it stormed and the hatches had to be secured until it passed; constant vigilance required to keep small children from getting into trouble or falling overboard; chilling cold winds or blistering sun.

She half closed her eyes, letting her mind run back over the last ten days. There were the dreary times, there was no disputing that—her brief but violent bout of seasickness when at first she thought she was going to die, and then feared that she might not. Misery took on a whole new depth of meaning to her during that day. There were also the funerals. The one that hit her the hardest was the old woman with the two canes she had watched that first day when they were boarding. Maggie could still close her eyes and picture the snow-white hair and the gnarled hands grasping the handles of her canes.

But there were the lighter moments too. Several of the parents had school for their children. Maggie and Hannah and Emma and Sarah James had volunteered to help with the one that included most of the James children. One day Maggie and Sarah had acted out the fairy tale about Rapunzel. Sarah tied her hair back and became the handsome prince. Maggie borrowed lengths of heavy rope from the crew to become her long "blond" tresses. When she "threw them out of the castle window" so that her prince could "climb up to her," the children shrieked in delight. Maggie and Sarah hammed it up shamelessly.

Maggie now realized that that had been an important day for her. As she and Sarah had collapsed on a bag of wool afterwards, still laughing together, a startling thought hit Maggie. She suddenly realized that while there would always be an empty place in her heart for James MacAllister, Scotland was behind her. She had finally accepted that she was going to America, and was happy with the decision. It had been a significant turning point for her.

"Sister McKensie?"

Maggie turned in surprise. In her reveling in the wind, she hadn't heard anyone come up behind her. She saw that it was the presidency of their company—James G. Willie, Millen Atwood, and the Danish translator, Brother Ahmanson.

"Good evening," she said, turning now fully and brushing at her hair to get it back in its place.

"It's a pleasant evening, isn't it?" Elder Ahmanson said, looking around.

Millen Atwood had his coat pulled tightly about him. "Only someone from Scandinavia would call a night like this pleasant," he grumbled. But it was done with a smile and the others laughed.

"I love it," Maggie said. "I love the wind and smell of the salt water."

"That's not just salt water," President Willie said. He turned and faced into the wind himself. "Captain Collins says that's the smell of icebergs in the air."

That caught them all by surprise. "Truly?" Elder Atwood asked.

"That's what he said. Starting tomorrow, we'll be posting watch because there will be icebergs coming down from Iceland and Greenland."

Maggie was nodding. So that explained the particularly biting nip in the air tonight. She looked at President Willie. "Are you looking for my mother?" she asked. "She's down below."

"No, actually, we were looking for you."

Her eyes widened a little. "Me?"

"Yes, Sister McKensie, we would like a word with you. As your priesthood leaders."

"I . . ." She was completely taken aback. "Of course."

The men moved in around her and found places to sit on the crates and bags lashed to the deck. President Willie pointed to a low trunk and invited her to sit down.

Completely bewildered, she sat down. He sat a few feet away from her, straddling the trunk so he could look directly at her. The others watched but clearly were going to let him take the lead on this.

"May I call you Maggie?" he asked, after a moment.

"Of course."

"Your family is from Scotland? From Edinburgh?"

"Yes."

There was hesitation now. "Your branch president there told me about the difficult time you had in deciding whether to join us or not." As her eyes widened he went on quickly. "I took the liberty to ask your mother for the details."

She rocked back a little, then blushed. Maggie had not spoken to anyone about her struggle, not even Sarah. But to her surprise, she was not upset by the fact that these brethren knew. They were her leaders and they had a right to know about the Saints in their charge. She nodded. The pain was back, almost as piercing as on that Sabbath day. She opened her eyes, but looked away. "I don't know what it was. There were so many reasons why I shouldn't have come. I didn't want to. But . . ." She let her voice trail away to empty silence.

Brother Willie smiled with infinite gentleness. "I think you do know what it was, Maggie."

Her shoulders lifted and fell. "I suppose it was the Spirit." She had told herself that over and over, particularly in those terrible days when James turned away from her and there was nothing but the horrible pain. But to her surprise, he was shaking his head.

One eyebrow lifted.

"Oh, it was the Spirit working on you, of course, but I think it was something more too."

"What?"

"To answer that, let me share something with you, Maggie. This was something that happened in Winter Quarters shortly after we arrived there in the fall of eighteen forty-six. I think it is the explanation for what you experienced."

She was curious now and nodded for him to go on.

"As you probably know, by the fall of eighteen forty-six, most of the Saints had been driven from Nauvoo. But there were about six hundred people who had not been able to come. These were generally widows or those who were too poor to outfit themselves. Then, in September, our enemies decided they would wait no longer. A group of armed militia—really nothing more than an organized mob—laid siege to the city. They started cannonading it and then marched in under arms. The battle was brief but intense. The remaining Saints had no choice but to surrender."

He rubbed at his eyes now, trying to hide the pain. "They were driven out of the city at bayonet point. Some of them—even women and children—were thrown into the river. Others were crowded onto ferries, overloading them to the point where there was risk of them sinking as they crossed. The soldiers stood on the riverbanks, shouting that they hoped the boats would sink."

Maggie's eyes were wide with shock now. He spoke with such intensity that she could almost feel the muddy water beneath her feet. "It must have been terrifying for them."

"I can only imagine." He sighed deeply, then continued. "When word reached Brigham Young in Winter Quarters that the poor Saints had been cast out and were languishing on the west banks of the river, sick, starving, cold, destitute, he called the brethren together."

Now his head came up and there was no more horror in his voice. It was filled with strength and power. "He reminded us of what we called the Nauvoo Covenant. Before leaving we had gathered in the temple, and Brother Brigham put us under covenant that we would not leave anyone behind, even if we had to sacrifice our own goods to bring them along.

"Now, remember, it's not like we had much of the world's goods in Winter Quarters. We too were destitute. We had sent five hundred of our best men off with the Mormon Battalion. We were facing a winter with sparse shelter and limited food. No one was in much condition to go off on some rescue mission."

He leaned forward. "There were so many reasons why we shouldn't have gone, Maggie. So many."

Startled, she stared at him, not sure if he had deliberately chosen to use her exact words or not. She found herself barely breathing, wanting him to finish now.

"Brother Brigham stopped for a moment. I can still picture it as if it happened just this afternoon. He was standing in the back of a wagon. Everything was perfectly still. Every eye was upon him. When he spoke, it was as if he had the voice of a lion. '*Now* is the time for our labor,' he said. 'Let the fire of the covenant, which you made in the house of the Lord, burn in your hearts like flame unquenchable! Rise up, brethren, take your teams and wagons and go straightway to the Mississippi and bring a load of the poor back here where we can help them find shelter for the winter.' "

It was as though James G. Willie had become Brigham Young. His voice rang out, sending chills up and down Maggie's spine. Then gradually he quieted, his shoulders falling again. Now he looked at her squarely. "That's what it was you felt that day, Maggie."

"What?"

"The fire of the covenant."

She pulled back a little, her eyes wide.

"When you were baptized you made a covenant with Jesus Christ. When you sang the words to that song the Spirit brought them into your mind, but what gave them the power to change your heart was the covenant that burned within you."

He stopped, watching her. She was barely aware of him. Was that what it was? Why *had* the words of that hymn hit her so hard? She had reread them several times since and marveled. They were touching lyrics but didn't seem to be anything out of the ordinary. What was it about that final stanza that had swept all of her determination to stay in Scotland aside?

She began to move her head up and down, slowly, almost dazed. "Yes, you are right."

He nodded somberly. "I thought so."

There was a long pause, and then she said, "But knowing that doesn't make it any easier, does it?"

He laughed softly. "No, not in any way. In fact, sometimes the fire is a burden, and you would give almost anything to be rid of it."

"Anything except turning your back on it."

"Exactly." Now he stood, moving away from her to stand closer to his two brethren. "I was touched when your mother told me what had happened. Thank you for letting us talk about it." He took a quick breath. "And that brings us to why we are here, Maggie. We have an assignment for you."

She bobbed her head. That was not unexpected. At worship services earlier that day President Willie had announced that now that the people were getting their "sea legs," it was time to make some work assignments. President Richards had purchased a large quantity of a heavy cotton fabric called "drill" or "drilling" from the cotton mills in Lancashire. It was for making the tents and covers for the wagons and the handcarts they would need in America. Their leader had told them that starting tomorrow, work crews would be assigned—the men cutting up the heavy cloth and the women stitching it together. "I would be happy to help in any way, President Willie. However, I worked at a paper factory. I'm not a good seamstress, but my mother is very good. Perhaps she could teach me and—"

He laughed. "Actually, we weren't thinking of asking you to sew, Sister Maggie. We have something else in mind for you."

Her face registered her surprise. "What?"

"I want you to organize a school."

She rocked back. "A school? Me?"

"Yes. But not for the children. We already have several parents doing that."

"Then what?" She was reeling a little.

Elder Ahmanson stood now too. "An English school," he said quietly.

She stared at him, not sure she had heard correctly.

Elder Atwood jumped in. "The Scandinavians are at a disadvantage. They have Elder Ahmanson and one other brother who can translate for them, but there are over a hundred of them. We cannot possibly teach everyone to speak English now, but if we had even a few who could speak it, it would be a great blessing to the rest of them."

President Willie stepped closer to her. "Once we are on the trail, it will be dangerous if we cannot relay instructions swiftly. We need more translators."

"But I . . . Brother Willie, why would you ask me? I am not a teacher."

"Because we feel impressed that you are the one we need. I will leave it completely in your hands. We will assign five or six people to your class. They will be mostly younger people. We feel like they will be able to learn the language faster than some of the older folks."

Again Elder Ahmanson came in. "I have been trying to teach a few of our people already. For example, remember those two young men who were being yelled at by the sailor and you intervened?"

"Yes."

"I've been teaching them ever since we left Denmark, and they're slowly picking it up. But I don't have the time. It's not been consistent enough to really help them."

Now Maggie understood why President Willie had started by reminding her of the covenant. She felt overwhelmed, terribly intimidated. And yet . . . Since when had God promised that in keeping the covenant one could be completely comfortable?

"I . . ." She took a deep, slow breath. "Yes. I will do as you ask, Brother Willie."

"Good. I knew you would." He reached out and shook her hand. "Thank you. We'll leave it in your hands. Brother Atwood will arrange with the ship's captain a place for you to meet. I'd like you to start tomorrow."

III

Monday, 12 May 1856

"Oh, Sarah, what shall I do?" Maggie wailed.

Sarah James looked up. She and Maggie were the only ones below deck at the moment. The weather had cleared during the night, and the families were taking the opportunity to be up top again. Sarah was seated at the table with baby Jane on her lap. She was bouncing her lightly, making her coo with pleasure. "It will be all right, Maggie," she said. "They're not going to be difficult students."

Maggie started a retort, then bit it off. She remembered the look of pure envy she had seen on Sarah's face when Maggie came back with the news of her new calling. This was something she would love to do too. This morning Maggie had found President Willie again and asked if Sarah could be assigned to help her. "Yes," he had answered, "but only as she has time. The Jameses are a large family, and I can't take her away. Her mother needs her." So Sarah would come to class when she could, but there would be no formal assignment.

Maggie's voice softened. "But these are adults, Sarah. If it were children even, perhaps I could do without textbooks, but I couldn't find a single book that teaches people how to speak English. I've asked everywhere on the ship." She threw up her hands. "How do I teach English without any books?"

Sarah stood up, cuddling the baby against her. "How many are coming again?"

Maggie reached down and snatched up the list President Willie had handed her at the midday meal. "Five. A young married couple, a single girl the same age as Hannah and Emma, and the two Norwegian brothers."

Sarah's head came up. "Eric Pederson?"

Maggie was surprised at that reaction. "Do you know them?"

Her head ducked behind the baby's, but Maggie had already seen the color in her cheeks. "I just know who they are," she murmured. Maggie gave her a sharp look, and her color deepened. "Stop it, Maggie. I just noticed them one day talking with Elder Ahmanson." Then she glanced up from beneath the dark lashes. "But he is very handsome."

Maggie nodded at that. Hannah and Emma had also commented

on Olaf Pederson. The two brothers were both quite good-looking, now that she thought about it. But it surprised her that Sarah—shy, demure Sarah—should have noticed it so quickly.

Then the worry pushed aside any thoughts of shipboard romance. "What am I going to do, Sarah?" she cried. "Class starts in fifteen minutes. I can't even say hello to them. I don't know a word of Danish."

"I thought they were Norwegian."

"The brothers are. The others are from Denmark. But Brother Ahmanson says it is virtually the same language. I don't need to worry about the differences."

Sarah held the baby up high and shook her gently, bringing a delightful little giggle from her. "Why don't you do what we are doing with Jane?" she asked.

Maggie's head came up. "What?"

"Well, think about it. How are we teaching Jane to speak English? We just talk to her. Over and over. We don't worry about having a textbook for her. We just speak English to her all the time."

Maggie frowned, starting to see. "But—" She stopped.

Sarah lowered the baby and picked up a spoon from the table. She held it out for Jane, who grabbed it immediately. "Spoon, Jane. This is a spoon," she said slowly. Then she looked at Maggie and shrugged. "That's how it's done."

Maggie stared at the baby, her mind racing. That was it. It was so simple. She stepped quickly to Sarah and hugged her. "Thank you. Will you come as soon as Jane is asleep?"

"You know I will. Good luck, Maggie."

Laughing, Maggie went to her storage box and began plucking out items and shoving them into a canvas bag. "I don't need luck now," she said, straightening. "Thanks to you."

Maggie's "school" was held up near the bow, away from the major traffic flow of the passengers and crew. Though the *Thornton* seemed huge, eight hundred people, counting passengers and crew, filled up virtually every free space. So Elder Atwood had gotten permission from the first officer to clear a small area near the prow of the ship where they could be largely undisturbed. She looked around, counted five "seats," then folded her arms and settled in to wait. It was a clear evening, promising that the air would be quite cool by morning. She had decided that the time right after the evening meal each day would be the best. They would go for an hour, from six to seven o'clock.

She heard a noise and turned, her heart doing a little flutter. Six people were coming toward her, all in a tight group, laughing and chattering with each other as they approached. One of them was Brother Ahmanson. Good. Trying not to stare, she quickly looked at those with him. There were the two Pederson brothers in their matching sweaters. Beside them was the married couple—the Hansens, according to her list. They had been married shortly before leaving Denmark and so had no children to worry about. They were holding hands as they walked. Coming with the couple was a young girl about Hannah's age. That had to be Ingrid Christensen.

As they approached, Maggie's concerns subsided a little. They didn't look too fierce. In fact, if anyone was intimidated, it seemed to be them. She set the paper back down again, put a block of wood on it so it wouldn't blow away, brushed quickly at her hair with her hands, then stepped to the edge of her "classroom" to greet them.

The group stopped and Brother Ahmanson came forward. He stuck out his hand. "Sister McKensie," he said pleasantly, "I have brought you your class."

"Thank you, Brother Ahmanson."

"Let me introduce you."

Maggie held up her hand quickly. "Thank you, Brother Ahmanson, but no. I have decided that we are going to start right off speaking English, without any translation help. I'll have them introduce themselves in a few minutes."

He gave her a searching look, then nodded approvingly. "A wise decision, I think. Yes, very good." He turned and rattled off something to them, then walked away, much to their consternation. Suddenly Maggie's misgivings shot skyward again.

"Come," she said, motioning with her hand toward their seats. "Come, sit down." She did a little pantomime of sitting. Smiling shyly, they moved past her and took their seats, Ingrid and the Hansens choosing the front crate, the Pederson boys taking two barrels directly behind them.

Maggie waited a moment, then plunged in. "Good evening," she said, fumbling a little at the sight of seven pairs of eyes staring gravely at her. "Welcome to English class. *Anglais classa.*" She frowned. She had no idea if *class* was a word common to other languages. And for that matter, *Anglais* was more French than anything. Did they even know what she was trying to say? No one moved. No one looked away.

She looked at Ingrid, then waved her finger back and forth at her in a gesture of warning. "*Anglais,* Ingrid. No *Danmark. Anglais.* Only English." She frowned. *Danmark* was the name of the country in Danish. She had heard that. But it didn't mean Danish the language.

But the girl smiled and nodded. "No *Danmark. Engelsk.*"

"Yes, that's right. *Engelsk.*" She looked at the other four and again shook her finger. "No Danish. No Norwegian. *Engelsk.* Only English."

"Only English," Olaf Pederson said.

Maggie stopped, remembering that Brother Ahmanson had been teaching these two some. "You are Olaf?" she asked slowly.

"Yah. Olaf Pederson."

"Do you understand what I am saying?"

He nodded, not very sure of himself. "Little."

"Good. That's good." She thought for a moment, then pointed to herself. "My name is Maggie. Maggie McKensie." She kept tapping her chest. "Maggie."

Several nodded, and then Ingrid murmured, "Maggie."

"Good, Ingrid." Maggie reached down and took her by the elbow and brought her up to stand beside her. The girl smiled shyly, blushing almost instantly. Ingrid was adorable. Maggie saw that immediately. Just Hannah's age, she had thick blond hair fastened in a bun at the back of her head. Her skin was fair and her eyes a light blue. She had an upturned nose which seemed to fit her perfectly. When she smiled it was so pleasant and so bright that one couldn't help but instantly want to like her.

Again Maggie pointed to herself. "My name is Maggie." Then she pointed to the girl, speaking slowly and distinctly. "What is your name?"

The girl turned to look at the others, hoping for help. Eric said something to her in Danish.

"No," Maggie said quickly, shaking her finger at him. "*Engelsk.*" She turned the girl back around, touching her chest again. "My name is Maggie." Now she touched Ingrid. "You say it."

Ingrid's face was a bright red, but then she spoke. "Ingrid Christensen," she finally said in a halting manner.

"Good," Maggie exclaimed, nodding up and down enthusiastically. She pointed to her again, still speaking very slowly. "My name is Ingrid. Say it."

"My . . . name is . . . Ingrid."

Maggie clapped her hands. "Excellent. Very good." The others were smiling now too, and Olga Hansen congratulated Ingrid warmly as she sat down again.

Maggie was soaring. She pointed to Eric Pederson and motioned for him to stand up. "Can you tell me your name?" she asked, again speaking slowly and distinctly.

He stood slowly. "My name Eric Pederson."

That pleased her. "Very good. You too speak some English?"

"Yah," he agreed, nodding his head. "But Olaf is better."

She laughed and stepped back. It was going to be okay. Sarah was right. And as soon as she got back down in the hold, she was going to give Sarah one huge hug.

She was pulled back when she saw Eric's hand come up. "Yes, Eric?"

"I wish to say *takk.*" He shook his head in frustration and started again. "Tank you."

Maggie's eyebrows lifted slightly. "Thank you? To me? Why?"

He was struggling, his eyes concentrating fiercely. "For first day."

"For our first day in class?"

"No," Olaf said, standing now too. "For first day on ship. With angry man."

Maggie slowly began to nod. "I see." She began making the motion of hammering. "That man?" she asked.

Both brothers nodded vigorously, smiling now. "Yah, dat man," Eric said. "Very angry at Norwegian *Dummkopf* and brother."

Now she laughed out loud. "He vas da *Dummkopf*, yah?" she said in her best Norwegian accent.

The smiles turned to laughter, but then Eric instantly sobered. "Olaf and Eric tank you, Sister Maggie," he said, laboring with each word. "*Takk.* Very much *takk.*"

IV

Thursday, 29 May 1856

On the morning of their twenty-ninth day after embarkation, Maggie was still in her berth. She had arisen early, as was required, and gone through the usual routine—breakfast, prayers, cleanup of the hold—and then went immediately back to reading the book she had started two days before. One of the ship's officers had lent it to her. It was *The Last of the Mohicans,* by James Fenimore Cooper, and she was thoroughly engrossed. Here was America as she pictured it, with Natty Bummpo—or Leatherstocking, as he was known to his Indian friends—living freely among the natives, in harmony with nature, fighting off danger, fearless in battle. The only drawback was that it left her with a vague sense of anxiety. In a few weeks they would be setting off into the wilderness, and the thoughts of Indians, who were not always friendly to whites, was unsettling. But it was not enough to dissuade her from reading.

"Maggie! Maggie!"

She raised her head in surprise. She heard the clumping of someone coming down the hatch ladder. The door jerked open and Robbie stuck his head in. "Maggie, come quick!"

"What?"

But he was already gone again.

Not sure whether to be alarmed or not, she shut the book, hopped down from the berth, and walked swiftly to the door. As she emerged on deck, she saw a large group of her fellow passengers along the railing near the front of the ship. Robbie was just pushing his way back into the crowd. He saw her and motioned vigorously for her to come.

When she finally made her way to the railing beside him, she had already guessed what it might be. And sure enough, there it was off the port bow. She had heard that they were massive, but nothing she had either heard or read prepared her for the huge mass that lay about a quarter of a mile off the port bow. It looked like an island, except there were no trees, no beach, no life of any kind. The sky was clear, and the sun bouncing off the ice was such a brilliant, dazzling white that she raised her hand to shade her eyes. It was breathtaking and chilling at the same moment.

The previous night, she and Sarah had lain awake much of the night as the ship moved slowly through a thick bank of fog. Above them they could hear the anxious cries of the sailors who were on watch, shouting out every few minutes that all was clear. Maggie kept telling herself that the captain would not sail on blindly and ram one of the floating mountains, but she had not ever been completely successful in convincing herself of that. Now as she thought of the unseen mass below the water—someone said you could see only a tiny portion of the total iceberg—she was grateful that the captain didn't feel a need to take them any closer. It was huge—ten, maybe fifteen times larger than the ship. She felt a little sick as she realized how puny their little wooden raft was when compared to that giant mass.

There were soft murmurs, but the people spoke in awestruck whispers. If the sea ahead was full of these, they were in store for an anxious few days. Then Maggie noticed that Ingrid Christensen was standing at the rail just in front of her. Next to her were Sarah and Reuben James. Smiling, Maggie pushed forward. It had been two and a half weeks now since she had first met Ingrid formally. All of her students were doing well—in fact, remarkably well—but of all of them, Ingrid was the brightest and the quickest. She had a good ear for hearing the correct pronunciation. She also had an impish sense of humor. When she chose she could speak her English words with hardly an accent. Other times she poured them out with such an atrocious Danish accent that Maggie would break out laughing.

Sarah came to class to help Maggie whenever she could. More recently, Emma and Hannah had started coming too. The five girls had quickly become friends, and Ingrid often left her family—she was traveling with her uncle and aunt—to spend time with the Jameses and the McKensies.

"Hello," Maggie said, pushing in between them.

"Ah, Maggie," Ingrid said. "Hello." She pronounced it "Hah-loh."

"Isn't that beautiful?" Sarah said, turning back to the iceberg.

"Incredible," Maggie said in awe. "Absolutely incredible."

"What means *incredible?*" Ingrid asked quickly.

Maggie hesitated. "Wonderful. Marvelous."

Sarah jumped in. "Outstanding. Amazing."

Ingrid still looked blank. Then Maggie thought of a French word.

It wouldn't help Ingrid, but it seemed so appropriate at the moment. "*C'est magnifique,*" she breathed.

Sarah nodded slowly. "Yes," she said. "*C'est magnifique.* It is utterly magnificent."

"Incredible," Ingrid said, trying the word out carefully.

They laughed, enjoying the moment together.

Suddenly there was a shout. Once again it was Robbie. He was at the rail several yards closer to the bow, jumping up and down and pointing at the water. Seeing him, Reuben left them and pushed through the people to join him.

Everyone turned and looked down. There was a stiff wind and the ship was under full sail. It was racing westward at seven or eight knots, as the sailors said. It was fast enough that the water hissed as the sharp edge of the ship's bow cut through it. Then Maggie saw what had caught Robbie's eye.

There was something there, just beneath the surface, in perfect harmony with the ship's progress. No, *two* somethings. "Look!" she cried. "Beneath the water."

Several started pointing. There was a flash as the surface of the water was momentarily broken. For one instant they caught a glimpse of a shining gray-green skin.

"What is it?"

"Sharks," someone cried.

"No!" came the instant response. "There are no fins."

But there was no mistaking it now. There were two shadowy shapes racing through the water, weaving slightly as they kept pace with the ship. A cry went up as one of the shapes momentarily broke the surface again, this time enough that they could see that it was not just a fish. It was five or six feet long. And the wet skin flashed like smooth rubber.

"What could it be?" a woman called out.

"It's the mermaids," came a voice.

In surprise, everyone looked up. Hanging easily from the rigging was one of the sailors. He leaned out so he could look almost straight down at the water. "They love to race the ship," he said, ignoring the skeptical looks from some. "Sure sign there's a storm coming. Always that way. Mermaids bring the storm."

"Are they really mermaids?" Robbie called up in wonder.

"Bet your anchor on that," the man said. "If any of you ladies have got a hand mirror, go get it. If you hold it out far enough, they'll come up to look at their hair."

Maggie studied his face to see if he was feeding them another tall tale from the sea, but he seemed to be as fascinated as the rest of them.

"What are mermaids?" Ingrid asked.

"Sea-maidens," Sarah said. "Girls, like us. But half fish."

"Ah, yah," Ingrid said. She murmured a word which Maggie didn't understand.

They all watched in wonder for several more minutes, and then the flashing shapes dove deep and disappeared. After two full minutes it was clear they weren't going to come back.

"Too bad," the sailor called. "You could have seen them up real close." He swung down and walked away in disgust.

James Willie stood near the back of the crowd. He waited until the man was out of earshot and then he stepped forward. "There are no sea-maidens," he said with a smile. "No mermaids. That's an old sailor's superstition."

"Then what are they?" Reuben James called out.

"Dolphins. For some reason they sometimes like to race the ship."

Maggie had to smile at the look of disappointment on Robbie's face. He knew President Willie was right, but dolphins were not nearly as intriguing as mermaids.

As the crowd began to break up, Maggie turned to her two friends. "Well, that's quite a day," she said. "Mermaids and icebergs all at once. We'd better talk about this in class tonight."

V

Tuesday, 10 June 1856

Maggie rose up on one elbow as Sarah James climbed into the berth beside her. "How is she?"

There was only one lamp lit in the lower deck, and in its faint light she saw Sarah's head move slowly back and forth. "Not good."

"Thrush?"

"Yes, the ship's doctor thinks so." Actually the ship's doctor was the first officer, who had responsibility for dispensing what little medicine they had. "She's got white spots all inside her mouth."

Maggie lay back, the sorrow piercing her like a lance. Jane James had become the delight of the McKensies as well as of her own family. Chubby as a cherub, always quick to smile and respond to whoever paid her attention, she was a child who loved to cuddle. Jane had become the little sister that Maggie had not had since Hannah was a baby. To see her lying in her bed, whimpering softly, barely moving, left Maggie sick at heart.

"What time is it?" she asked, deciding to change the subject and get Sarah's mind on something else.

"It's after three. You've got to sleep, Maggie. I'm sorry I woke you up."

Maggie reached out and put an arm around this girl who now seemed more like her twin than a friend.

"President Willie and Elder Atwood gave her a blessing," Sarah whispered, her voice breaking. "Maybe that will help."

Maggie nodded, not knowing what else to say.

"Will you pray with me, Maggie? for Jane?"

"I've been praying all night, Sarah."

"I know. Let's do it again."

Maggie found Sarah and Emma at the railing near amidships. They were holding each other tightly, the breeze whipping at their shawls and tousling their hair. It was a gray morning, and the seas were heavy. Maggie held onto a rope strung along the passageway to steady herself.

As she approached the two sisters, the ship's bell began to toll slowly. Maggie looked up, hating that sound as intensely as she hated anything she had ever heard.

Somewhere below, William and Jane James were sewing up a tiny blanket around the still form of their daughter. In a few minutes the brethren would bring her up topside, where she would be consigned to the cold gray waters of the North Atlantic.

Maggie stopped and bent over slightly, holding her stomach to stop the pain. "O Lord, why?" she cried. But instantly she pushed it away. Just because there was pain didn't mean there had to be blame. This was life. And for His own purposes God had chosen to take little Jane James to Himself. She remembered what her mother had said when word had come shortly after eight o'clock that the baby had died. Hannah, barely able to speak through her sobbing, had asked why the priesthood blessing had not changed things. " 'Seek not to counsel thy God,' " their mother said, quoting from the prophet Jacob in the Book of Mormon, " 'but seek to take counsel from his hand, for he counseleth in wisdom and justice and mercy.' "

She straightened and quickly walked to where Sarah and Emma stood. They heard her coming and turned. Tears streaked their faces. Maggie opened her arms and Sarah fell into them. "I'm so sorry," Maggie whispered. "I'm so sorry."

VI

Friday, 13 June 1856

Maggie and Hannah McKensie, Sarah and Emma James, and Ingrid Christensen were sitting on crates near the back of the ship.

Supposedly they had come to wash off the breakfast dishes. But the dishes still sat in a pile and the five of them were seated in a circle. As usual, Maggie was drilling Ingrid on her English. She reached down and picked up a cup. "What is it?" she asked.

"Cup," came the immediate reply.

She held up her hand and wiggled her fingers.

"Fingers."

Now Sarah came in, glad for an opportunity to participate and take her mind off of her family's loss three days before. She began to point to herself.

"Nose. Eyes. Ears. Mouth. Hand." Ingrid rattled off the answers as Sarah touched each item.

"Very good," Maggie said, really pleased. She found deep satisfaction in the success of her students. The Hansens—her married couple—had dropped the class. Sister Hansen had learned that she was with child and was having a difficult time with the stomach sickness. They would try to pick up their study again when they got off the ship, but until then it was too much to ask. But the other three were doing very well. Ingrid was making noticeable progress. The Pederson brothers were doing well too. Elder Ahmanson made all three of them speak in English as much as possible. She guessed they were understanding about a third of what they heard now and could communicate about half of that back.

Just then they heard voices behind them. They turned to see Eric and Olaf Pederson with Johan Ahmanson and John Chislett, the captain of the guard. They were examining the lashings on some of the large crates. They did not notice the girls, but Maggie saw Sarah straighten, her eyes fixed on Eric. Without thinking, Sarah reached up and smoothed down her hair. The three younger girls reacted in a similar manner. Though Olaf treated each of them—Ingrid, Hannah, and Emma—with studied equality, each had secret hopes that she might be his favorite.

Maggie decided to have a little fun. "Ingrid?"

She turned.

"In English. Who is that?" Maggie pointed.

"Olaf Pederson," Ingrid said, turning back to watch him.

Hannah giggled. She knew exactly what Maggie was doing. "There are *four* people, Ingrid, not just one."

She blushed. "And Eric. And Brother Ahmanson. I know not . . . I don't know other's name."

"And what is Olaf to Eric?" Maggie prodded. "What is their relationship?"

Ingrid's mouth screwed up for a moment; then she brightened. "Brothers," she said.

"Good." Maggie smiled now, looking at Sarah, whose eyes were still fixed on Eric. Maggie decided to tease her a little. "And how would you describe Eric to Ingrid, Sarah? What word would you use?"

Sarah was startled. She went scarlet, glancing quickly at the figures behind them, who still were not paying any attention to the group of girls, then lowered her eyes. "*C'est magnifique!*" she breathed softly.

The memory of that day when they had seen their first iceberg flashed back into Maggie's mind. She was shocked that Sarah had said it, and with such feeling. She was usually so demure and so private about her feelings. "*Mademoiselle!*" Maggie said in mock horror.

Hannah and Emma hooted aloud. Ingrid, who couldn't follow the French, looked puzzled.

Sarah now was the color of the bright red on the British flag that flew above them. Suddenly feeling a little guilty, Maggie reached out and touched her hand. "I'm sorry," she mouthed.

"I can't believe I said that," Sarah whispered back, laughing softly now.

Then before Maggie could answer, there was a cry from high above them. "There she be!"

Every head turned upwards. In a box-like structure on the top of the mainmast, which the crew called the "crow's nest," one of the sailors was leaning way out, pointing wildly. "There she is. I see it. I see it."

All across the deck, heads lifted, then turned in the direction he was pointing. The girls jumped to their feet. Eric and Olaf and the other brethren forgot about the lashings.

"What?" Johan Ahmanson called. "What is it?"

"Watch!"

And after a moment, there it was. A flash of light, barely above water level.

"That there is the Fire Island lighthouse," the man bawled. "We will be in New York Harbor by tomorrow morning. Welcome to America!"

Chapter Notes

The details of the ocean voyage are drawn from journal entries and histories written later by members of the various handcart companies. The story of the "mermaids" comes from Mary Ann Stucki Hafen (see *Recollections of a Handcart Pioneer*, p. 19).

The statement by Brigham Young about the fire of the covenant was given on September 28, 1846, under the circumstances described here by Brother Willie (see Richard E. Bennett, " 'Dadda, I Wish We Were Out of This Country,' " p. 163).

Jane James, nine months old, died of "thrush of the mouth," a disease caused by a parasitic virus, and was buried at sea on 10 June 1856, just four days before the *Thornton* reached New York Harbor (see Turner, *Emigrating Journals*, p. 7).

The calling of someone to teach English classes is the author's extrapolation and is not based on any specific journal references. It is known from several entries, however, that language barriers were a concern to the leaders of the various companies.

CHAPTER 6

NEW YORK CITY, NEW YORK
TO
IOWA CITY, IOWA

I

Sunday, 15 June 1856

Sarah James leaned over and whispered into Maggie McKensie's ear. "Do you think you can sit through a worship service where the benches are not swaying up and down?"

Maggie laughed softly. "It certainly feels strange, that's for sure."

Hannah McKensie, Ingrid Christensen, and Emma James were sitting directly behind Sarah and Maggie and heard what Sarah had said. Emma James, always the tease and full of life, leaned forward. "To feel normal, in addition to having the room rising and falling we'd have to exchange the chairs and benches for boxes and crates and barrels."

Hannah giggled behind her hand. "And have a sailor in the crow's nest looking down on us while we sing."

They all tittered at that, and Sister Jane James turned and gave them a stern look. They immediately straightened and looked to the front, striving to be a little more prim and proper. But Sarah was right, Maggie thought. It had been only early yesterday morning that their ship had tacked with the wind off Sandy Hook and entered the first of New York Harbor. At eight A.M., a steamboat, appropriately named *Achilles,* the legendary strong man of Greek mythology, came alongside the *Thornton,* threw her a line, and towed her towards the city.

They had been extremely fortunate. A doctor had come on board just off Staten Island and pronounced the passengers fit and healthy with no need of quarantine. That was remarkable. President Willie had warned them that some ships were held up for days while they awaited their health inspection and that some of the doctors would exercise their authority and make anyone who didn't look perfectly fit spend a week or more in quarantine. If there were any signs of real illnesses, such as smallpox or cholera, a whole shipload of passengers might spend a month or more in a quarantine center. Being already very late in the traveling season, that would have been disastrous for the emigrants going to Utah.

A short time later, an equally remarkable event happened. The official from the New York Custom House came on board and, obviously bored, asked a few superficial questions of a few of the passengers. Satisfied, he then passed off all of their luggage without an inspection of any kind. And so by sundown, after forty-two days at sea, they docked at Castle Garden, a large building set aside specifically for incoming emigrants, and stepped on solid ground again.

That was not even twenty-four hours ago, and here they were in New York City joining with the local branch of the Church for worship services. Not even one full day yet. No wonder they missed the perpetual motion of the ship, the rolling with the waves, the swaying from side to side, the sighing of the wind in the rigging, and the crackling of the canvas.

Maggie smiled to herself. *Missed* was probably not the best term. "Noticed its absence" might be a better way to put it. She had never in her life been so glad to be able to walk a few steps as she had been to walk down the gangplank of the *Thornton,* never to see it again.

And if she spent the rest of her life on dry land and never more set foot on a sailing vessel, it wouldn't cause her any noticeable grief.

She pulled out of her thoughts as a stir suddenly swept through the room. Two men had entered the room at the back. Several of the Saints immediately stood to shake their hands. Maggie turned to watch. The first man was President James G. Willie, their group leader. The other she didn't recognize, though he seemed to be attracting the greatest amount of attention among those of the emigrants.

William James leaned over to Maggie's mother. "Do you know who that is?" he asked.

She shook her head. Maggie, Sarah, and the others were shaking their heads as well.

"That's Elder John Taylor," Brother James said.

Maggie started and peered more closely. Here was a name that was well known to the Saints but a face not recognized by many of them. An Englishman himself who had emigrated to Canada back in the late twenties, he had been a missionary to Great Britain, serving considerable time on the Isle of Man, but that had been several years before Maggie's family had joined the Church. He was very distinguished-looking, with a neatly trimmed Greek-style beard and hair that curled in soft waves and was already showing traces of premature gray, though he was not yet fifty years of age.

"Is he an Apostle?" Reuben James asked in a loud whisper. Reuben had just recently turned fourteen.

His father smiled. "Yes, son. He is one of the Twelve. He is also the president of the Eastern States Mission now. So he presides over the Church here."

"He's more than that," Sister James said. "Don't you remember, Reuben? It was Brother Taylor who was in Carthage Jail with the Prophet Joseph. He was shot four times and wounded terribly."

"Really?" Robbie McKensie's eyes grew very large as he stared at the man at the back of the room.

"Yes," Brother James said. "Actually, he was shot five times. But remember? As he was about to fall out of the window, one bullet hit his pocket watch and smashed it, throwing him back into the room. It saved his life."

Sarah was nodding now. Her family had been in the Church longer than the McKensies, and now she remembered Elder Taylor. He had spoken at their Worcestershire Conference when she was younger. "Papa, is it true that he still carries two of those bullets in his body even now?"

"That's right," her father said. "They were never able to remove them."

Robbie's mouth was agape. "Really?" he said again, his voice filled with awe.

"Can you believe it?" Maggie's mother said. "He was actually there that terrible day, and now he's going to speak to us. Think of it, Maggie. Here we are in America, meeting with Latter-day Saints in New York City, and an Apostle of the Lord is about to speak to us. It's a miracle."

II

Tuesday, 17 June 1856

For Eric and Olaf Pederson, much of what was going on around them was a great swirl of confusion. Eric thought they had been making grand progress on their English under the tutelage of Maggie McKensie, but now! People were barking orders, shouting out commands, speaking at what sounded like five hundred words a minute. Here and there a recognizable phrase jumped out at him, but most of it was incomprehensible.

Yesterday he had been greatly encouraged and very much uplifted. On Sunday when the English Saints went into the city to join in the worship services, most of the Scandinavian group had stayed at Castle Garden, the emigrant center where they were temporarily housed. Knowing that the services would be in English, they stayed behind and began sorting through the luggage. Elder Ahmanson had gone into the city with the others, and Eric and Olaf had almost joined him. They changed their minds when Jens and Elsie Nielson had a bad experience with one of the emigrant officials because they couldn't understand what he was asking them to do, and so the two brothers decided they had better stay. Ingrid Christensen also stayed to provide whatever limited translation services she could offer. When Maggie and Hannah, along with Sarah and Emma James, came back and reported that Elder John Taylor had spoken to the group, the three English students were deeply disappointed.

Happily, yesterday President Taylor had come out to Castle Garden to meet the rest of the Saints. He spent a good part of the day giving them instruction and counsel. His style of speaking was careful and measured and much easier for Eric to follow. It had been a wonderful experience. With Elder Taylor came several newspaper editors and journalists, curious to see these emigrants who would be going to Utah by handcart in what the newspapermen termed the "bold experiment." Eric had expected some contempt from such a group, or at least an air of condescension, but for the most part they had manifested friendly feelings for the group and had been quite complimentary on their overall appearance and the general spirit of the company. Curious that he and Olaf could understand some English, one of them had talked with the two Norwegians at some length.

Today had not been so wonderful. More than seven hundred people had come across the Atlantic on the *Thornton.* Getting them aboard ship and sufficiently provisioned for the six-week voyage had seemed an enormous task. But now they had to get that same number—minus a few who had permission to stay in New York for a time—ready for a thousand-mile journey by railway car and steamboat. Railway cars had to be secured, luggage arranged for, tickets purchased, and people assigned. Food enough for the first day or two was brought in, but after that they would have to secure food at the various stops along the way. The Church agents assured them that this would be no problem, but it seemed to Eric that that was easy to say and perhaps not quite so simple to do. He tried not to think about it too much.

At ten o'clock they loaded back onto a harbor boat with all of the luggage and left Castle Garden for the pier that belonged to the New York and Erie Railway line. This was where the railroad picked up the freight that would be carried inland. There things quickly went from pandemonium to total chaos. Each passenger's luggage had to be weighed, for the limit they could take on the train was fifty pounds per adult. That was no problem for Eric and Olaf, who together didn't have enough to make up fifty pounds, but for many it was a difficult and frustrating task. Everything had to be clearly labeled and secured for shipping. Heavier items were sorted out and left behind to be shipped by the Church agents in freight cars, then carried under contract by independent Church wagon companies that were also going to Salt Lake this season.

The weather was hot and muggy, and tempers quickly grew short as the hours dragged on. The Scandinavians had a particularly bad time of it. They were not used to this kind of heat. Then to be jostled and bumped, yelled and shouted at—and frequently sworn at—by frustrated stevedores in a language they didn't understand was not a pleasant experience. It took until seven P.M. before all of that was completed.

Once again they loaded on board the harbor boat and sailed up the Hudson River a few miles to Piermont. Here, a short distance from the dock, was the railroad station. Here, according to their leaders, they would begin their journey across America by rail.

It was eleven P.M. when they finally trooped off the harbor boat and made their way to the railway station—sweaty, grimy, physically exhausted, mentally beaten down, and ready for a chance to lie down and sleep.

"I'm tired, Mama."

Eric turned. The Nielson family was behind him and Olaf. Jens Nielson had Bodil Mortensen, the nine-year-old girl they were bringing to Utah for another family, on his back. Her head lay against him, and she looked like she was asleep. It was young Jens, who was five, that had spoken. He was dragging along, his feet shuffling on the cement walkway, his small valise dragging on the ground behind him. His shoulders were slumped and his eyes heavy.

Elsie turned. She already had both of her hands full with their luggage. "Jens," she said patiently, "we're almost there. Then we can rest on the train."

"Here," Eric said, handing his bag to Olaf. Then he knelt down. "Come on, Jens." He patted his shoulders. "Would you like to ride on my back, like Bodil?"

"Yes!" He ran forward and leaped onto Eric's back. Eric took his small bag in one hand, then hoisted him up with the other. "Hang on, then."

"Thank you, Eric."

"It's a pleasure," he said to Elsie. "All of the children are so tired. It's been a long day."

As they came around the corner of a long brick building, a warehouse of some kind, they saw the train. To Eric's surprise, it was not that long. There was the steam engine and the tender filled with firewood. Next there were two passenger cars with windows. He could see people already filling the benches inside. Then the rest were freight cars—six in all—with a caboose on the end.

Elsie slowed her step, dismay filling her face. "But Jens," she said, "that's not enough cars for our group. And look, they are already full."

Her husband was a little surprised too, but just shook his head.

"Let's be patient, Elsie. President Willie and his counselors know what they're doing."

Eric certainly hoped so, for none of their group had started loading onto the train yet. How could only two passenger cars possibly take them all?

Off to one side they saw President Willie and Elder Millen Atwood, his counselor, standing on a trunk so that they were above the crowd. They were calling to the people and motioning for them to come in close.

As usual, the Scandinavian group was near the end of the line. They had learned that it was easier to let the English speakers go first and then they could watch and get some idea of what they were supposed to do. So when Eric and Olaf and the Nielsons came up to where Brothers Willie and Atwood were waiting, it took only another minute or two before everyone was there.

President Willie raised his hands and the crowd quieted. "Brothers and sisters, this is the New York and Erie Railway station. We have booked passage for all of you from here to Dunkirk, which is at the very western edge of New York State, about four hundred and sixty miles from here."

He paused, letting Elder Ahmanson translate that for his people.

"Dunkirk is a port on Lake Erie. There we have booked passage for our group on a steamship to Toledo, Ohio, which is another two hundred and eighty miles. From Toledo we shall go by rail to Chicago, and from Chicago by way of the Chicago and Rock Island line all the way to Iowa City, Iowa. All together, it is about a thousand miles from here to Iowa City."

There were groans and exclamations of surprise. Eric looked at Jens and Elsie. "A thousand miles?" he mouthed. That was incredible. And that was only to get them to their jumping-off point. Just how big was this North America?

"And how much farther once we get to Iowa?" someone called out.

"Iowa City to the Salt Lake Valley is about fourteen hundred miles. And from there, of course, it will be by handcart all the way."

To a group that was already deeply exhausted, that was devastating information. An appalled silence settled over the crowd.

"I know that sounds terribly discouraging right now, brothers and sisters," President Willie said, forcing a smile, "but remember how fortunate we are. The railroad line to Iowa City was just completed this spring. That saves us an additional week or two over what others have had to do on their own."

When that seemed to settle them a little, he turned and looked toward the train. "As you would probably guess, we do not have the funds to purchase first-class or coach tickets for our group. That would leave nothing for food or for getting you equipped with handcarts. So what we have is what the railroad calls 'emigrant cars.' Those are the last six cars you see on the train."

"But," a woman cried out, "they're just freight cars."

"No," Brother Willie said patiently. "They *were* freight cars. Now they have been outfitted with tiers of benches around all four sides, like seats in a circus tent. Each car will house about eighty passengers."

Every eye was staring at the cars now. *Eighty!* Eric felt his heart drop. Each car looked to be no more than thirty or forty feet long and maybe ten or fifteen feet wide. Could eighty people fit inside? Not "fit." "Live!" Eighty people would have to live inside those cars. They would be their home for the next while. He shook his head, aware that little Jens was almost asleep on his back now.

"I know what you are thinking," President Willie said, speaking more softly now. "But we were fortunate to secure these. In the past some of our people have had to come in cattle cars. And those are not pleasant. Nothing but straw on the floors. Lice everywhere. A terrible smell."

"But where will we sleep?" It sounded like the same woman again.

President Willie audibly sighed. "You will have to sleep as best you can. And the sanitary facilities will not be ideal. But brothers and sisters, it will be only two days and then we will board the steamship. That will be crowded, but you will have a place to stretch out and sleep and will have plenty of fresh air."

He waited. Perhaps it was good that they were all so exhausted, Eric decided. If they had been fresh and rested, there might have been much more protest. As it was, they just stared at the cars, wondering how they would manage.

"Brother Atwood and I have to return to New York to attend to some unsettled business. We are asking Brother Levi Savage to take charge now. We will take an express train to Dunkirk when we are through and meet you at the docks." He looked around. "Are there any questions?"

No one raised a hand.

"All right. Elder Savage has your tickets and your car assignments. Good luck, brothers and sisters. We'll see you in Dunkirk."

III

Friday, 20 June 1856

Maggie found Hannah and Emma James near the front of the *Jersey City* steamship, leaning over the rail staring down into the water of Lake Erie. She pushed her way through the crowds until she reached their side.

"Hi," she said, moving in beside Hannah.

"Hi. Did you finish?"

Maggie nodded. "It's all done." She pulled a face. Scrubbing out their quarters down in steerage had left her a little dizzy. The air was thick and foul and gave her a headache whenever she was down there for very long. Previous passengers were not as concerned about keeping the quarters clean as were the sister Saints. With about seven hundred people in their company, President Willie and his counselors had booked all of the steerage space and put the women and children there. The men had been forced to sleep on the open decks. Immediately the sisters had set to work, much to the pleased surprise of the steamship's crew, to clean out their quarters. They were doing it in shifts, and Maggie and her mother had taken the first turn along with Sister James and Sarah. Hannah and Emma would go down in a few minutes to take advantage of this "opportunity."

Maggie grabbed one of the steel posts that supported the deck of the ship above them. She leaned back, breathing deeply. "That air is wonderful," she said.

"I can't believe they let that compartment get as bad as it is," Hannah said, wrinkling her nose. "I hate it down there."

Emma turned on them. By nature Emma was the optimist, always cheerful, always bright, always trying to see the best side of things. "Well, at least we have a place to lie down when we sleep." She was sixteen now and about six or seven months younger than Hannah.

"Yes," Maggie agreed. Her body still ached from two nights of trying to sleep on the narrow benches of the "emigrant cars," with soot and cinders pouring in through the windows, and the violent rocking. Along one of the stretches, the engineer had opened the throttle and nearly run the train off the track. That had been in the middle of the night and frightened everyone so badly that no one slept until morning. They learned later that the engineer was from Ohio and was a virulent anti-Mormon. When he learned he had a load of Mormon emigrants, he determined that he was going to "drive the Mormons to hell." It had been a very long two days. The steamship was filthy, but Emma was right. The steamer was a welcome change in at least one way.

It was a beautiful day. They had boarded the *Jersey City* at six P.M. the previous evening and sailed shortly thereafter, but dark had quickly settled over the Great Lakes and they had not been able to see much. Now the sky was clear and the morning sun was warm off the water. Moving along at about ten miles per hour, the ship created its own breeze, which made the temperature just about perfect.

"It seems so strange after the ocean," Hannah said. "It's so calm."

"Brother Savage said that in a storm the Great Lakes can get pretty rough too, but it sure doesn't seem that way now," responded Maggie.

Off about two or three miles to their left, the shoreline of Ohio was slipping slowly past them. It was a deep green, broken only occasionally with a house or building. Maggie watched it for a minute or two and then remembered something President Willie had said as they were boarding. "We are going to stop at Cleveland in a little while."

"Yes," Hannah said, "that's what Elder Atwood said too."

"They say that Kirtland is only a few miles from there. Wouldn't you love to go and see the temple?"

Just then Sarah James slipped up behind them and put her arm around Maggie. "What temple?"

"The Kirtland Temple. It's not far from Cleveland, where we'll be stopping for a while."

"Do you think we could go see it?" Emma asked eagerly.

Maggie shook her head. "I heard some others ask, but President Willie said that first, it is too far away. The boat is going to stop for only a short time. Second, the leaders are going to have to work as quickly as possible just to buy more supplies for us. There won't be any time for side trips."

They nodded at that. Purchasing food sufficient for their numbers was an ever-present challenge for their leaders. Coming across New York, it hadn't been quite so difficult. Each place where the train stopped, a whole growing market designed to provide food for the rail travelers was springing up. But coping with seven hundred passengers at once often tested the local resources. In several places the agents bought up all the bread the village had to offer. Twice they had been favored by the "butcher boys," food vendors who worked on the trains themselves. They sold bread, cheeses, and various smoked and dried meats, but most of the emigrants could not afford to purchase much at those prices and had to be content with what the agents procured.

"When do we reach Toledo?" Sarah asked.

"Tomorrow morning about nine," Maggie answered. She had been favored to sit beside President Willie and Elder Atwood for a time this morning and had plied them with these very questions.

"And then back onto the trains?" Hannah said in a despairing voice.

"Yes. We go first to Chicago and then to Rock Island, Illinois. That's where we cross the Mississippi River."

"I'm anxious to see that," Emma said. "They say it makes any river in England look like a trickle of water."

"I'm anxious to see it too," Maggie said, "but not because it's big. Because it means we are almost to Iowa City."

"I can hardly wait," Hannah said dreamily. "It feels like it's been forever since we left Edinburgh."

"Only because it has," Maggie said with a faint smile. "Forever and a couple of days beyond that, actually."

Sarah straightened and looked at Hannah and Emma. "Well, girls, Mama said to tell you it's your turn to go down and clean."

They groaned in perfect unison.

Sarah just smiled. "Maggie and I are going to sit here and enjoy the fresh air while you two do your part to help clean up America."

IV

Tuesday, 24 June 1856

Maggie straightened painfully, bracing herself against the violent, spasmodic jerking from side to side. The noise was constant and loud. She grimaced, doing something she never thought she would ever do again. She actually longed for the quiet of the ship and to have her berth back, crowded as it was with both her and Sarah sleeping in it. Compared to the narrow benches of the railway car, the racket of the engine, the clouds of soot and cinders that blew in through the open windows, the ship had been heaven.

The pain in her neck came because she had fallen asleep, her head at a crazy angle. It was a wonder she had. It was a wonder that anyone could sleep on a train. Yet across from her in the semidarkness she saw Hannah and Emma, heads against each other as they slept. Robbie was across from her, also asleep with Reuben and George James. She turned. Her mother and Jane James were behind her. William James and two more of his children were opposite. They were all asleep.

With a deep sigh she looked around. The car was dark except for the oil lamps at each end, which were turned down low. Just to her left, outside the narrow window, there was a sensation of motion in the darkness, deeper shades of black gliding by. Inside the car, everywhere she looked she could see the dark shapes of sleeping bodies and squarer forms of baggage filling every free space. A heavy weight on her own lap reminded her that John James, who was four, was using her as his pillow.

She reached up behind her head and retrieved the lumpy pillow. Carefully now she lifted John's head, slipped the pillow beneath it, then slid out from under him. He stirred slightly as she laid the pillow down on the bench, but that was all. His breathing deepened again. After a moment she stood, then carefully stepped over Hannah's legs into the narrow aisle.

Seeing two dark figures at the back end of the car, Maggie moved toward them. The one had a cap on. Peering carefully to make sure she didn't trip over anyone, she moved slowly down the aisle. It was a jumble of legs and feet and an occasional head poking out beyond the limits of the benches.

The man straightened as she approached. She saw him flip something away and there was a momentary streak of orange in the darkness. Almost immediately the smell of tobacco mingled with the more pungent smoke from the engine. Then to her surprise, she recognized the silhouette of the other man. It was Eric Pederson. What was he doing way up here? Someone had said the Scandinavian group had taken the last two cars on the train.

At that same moment he recognized her. He too was startled, then smiled. "Hah-loh, Sister Maggie."

She smiled. "Hello, Eric. Did you know when you call me Sister Maggie it makes me feel like my mother?"

He laughed easily. "What I call you?"

"Just Maggie."

"Yes, Sister Maggie," he said. "I can do."

She shook her head, a little taken aback with the realization that he was teasing her. "Can't sleep?" she asked.

He grinned and put his hands over his ears. "Too much quiet," he said.

She laughed. "And too much sitting still." She jerked back and forth in imitation of the train's movements.

"Yah, yah," he said. "Not like ship."

"Not at all." She turned to the other man. She saw now that he was one of the three young railway attendants that had joined them at Chicago. "Good evening."

"Evening, miss," he said, tipping his hat.

She brushed back a strand of hair that had fallen across her eyes, feeling the grittiness, longing for the time when she could wash it again. "Do you know what time it is?"

"Almost eleven o'clock."

"How long before we get to Rock Island?"

"Quarter of an hour. Maybe a little more."

"Rock Island?" Eric broke in. "Is where we go?"

Maggie turned. "Yes. Rock Island, Illinois. It's where we reach the Mississippi River. It's our next stop."

He looked puzzled, but she wasn't sure how to make it any simpler than that. She turned back to the attendant. "Really?" She felt her spirits lift. "We're that close?"

"Yes'm." He was young, she could tell now. No more than a year or two older than she was. His face was pockmarked and the skin looked like sandpaper, but his eyes seemed pleasant enough.

"Wonderful." She started to turn. If he was right, it was time to wake the family and start putting their things together.

"Are you from England?" the attendant asked, bringing her back around.

She managed a smile. Only in America could they mistake the Scottish brogue for an English accent. "From Scotland, actually."

"Oh."

She couldn't tell from his face if he knew the difference or not. She also wondered if he knew they were Mormons. If so, it didn't seem to bother him. In Chicago they had been very badly treated by the railroad conductor, who had insisted on putting them off in the street, baggage and all, then refused to direct them to any shelter, even though a heavy thunderstorm was threatening. Brother Willie finally found the railroad superintendent and prevailed on him to let them take shelter in an empty warehouse for the night. The whole incident had been very depressing for Maggie. Her mother kept saying that they were going to America to escape being persecuted as Mormons. And yet here was the same blind ugliness that had made life for Robbie and Hannah such a nightmare at their school.

"What about him?" The attendant looked at Eric.

"He is from Norway," she answered, forgetting for the moment that Eric and Olaf and Ingrid had been studying English for over a month now and understood much of what was said to them.

"Yah, Norway," Eric confirmed.

"How long have you people been traveling?"

She didn't have to think about it. She had marked every day off with tick marks in her notebook. "Forty-two days at sea. Another nine or ten from New York."

"Wow!" He actually seemed envious. "All by train from New York?"

She shook her head. "No. We took passage on a steamboat across the Great Lakes."

"You'll have to ferry across the Mississippi," the attendant said. "The new bridge collapsed."

"We heard that." She looked at Eric. "They had a new bridge across the river but it collapsed."

He nodded and she wasn't sure if he understood or not.

"But the ferry runs all the time," the attendant went on. "Then you can catch the train again on the other side. It goes all the way into Iowa City. That's where the line ends."

"And how much farther is Iowa City once we cross the river?"

"Fifty, maybe sixty miles is all. You should be there 'fore noon, assuming you get the morning ferry."

She sighed. The original plan had been that they would cross the great river sometime tonight and be to Iowa City by daybreak. She was oh so ready to be off the trains.

"Well," the attendant said, touching the bill of his cap again. "I'd better start waking people up." He moved away and the two of them watched him go.

Maggie suddenly felt awkward. She and Eric Pederson had spent many hours together in class, but this was the first time she had ever been alone with him. "Did you understand that?" she asked. "We'll be stopping soon, Eric."

"Yah. I go and wake Olaf."

"Is he sleeping?" She had pulled a face.

"Oh, yah. He has no ears."

She laughed. This droll humor was a side she had not seen in him before. "My family too. It's disgusting."

"Dis-gust-ing?"

She shook her head, not sure how to explain that. Then she noticed that he had put on his sweater in the night's chill. She reached out on impulse and touched it. "This is beautiful."

"Tank you." He shook his head, instantly correcting himself. "Thank you."

"Where did you get it?"

To her surprise, she saw his face fill with sorrow. "My mother makes special for Olaf and me."

"I see." She made a guess. "As a going-away present?"

He looked at her blankly.

"As a gift? for when you left?"

"Yah," he said. "Is very special to me."

"I understand." Then, to her surprise, she wanted to share something with him. "I have a music box."

"Yah?" he said, seeming to understand but not sure why she said it.

"It was a gift from my father before he died. It is very special to me too."

"Ah," he said softly. "Yes."

She straightened, a little embarrassed now. "Well, I'd better go and wake the family."

"Good-bye, Sister Maggie."

She gave him a stern look. His head tipped back and he laughed easily. Then he turned and started down the line of cars toward the back of the train.

V

Thursday, 26 June 1856

By the time they ferried across the Mississippi—a sight which staggered Eric's mind—and carried their baggage to the train, it had been nine o'clock in the morning. Now it was half past one. The ride to Iowa City had taken four and a half hours.

Eric turned in time to see Sister Elsie Nielson struggling to carry a large suitcase down the steps of the railroad car in one hand. With the other she held little Jens's hand, trying to keep him from pulling away from her and getting lost in the crush of people. The case seemed almost as large as her tiny figure. Eric thrust his own bag at his brother. "Olaf, take this."

He turned and moved swiftly to her, taking the case from her hand.

"*Takk.*" She smiled gratefully at him, then took a firmer hold on her son's hand. "Jens, you stay right here beside Mama."

Eric was struck again with the difference between this woman and her husband who had befriended them as they were leaving Denmark. Elsie Nielson was four foot eleven. She weighed less than a hundred pounds. Jens was a tall and muscular farmer. At six feet two inches, it was always easy to pick him out from the group. Together they were like a towering tree beside a new sapling. When they stood together, people who didn't know them turned to look and then would smile. Eric had learned something, though. They might differ greatly in physical stature, but here was a couple who were one in spirit. Their love for each other was immediately evident, and they were totally united in their love of the gospel as well. Eric felt a deep rush of affection and gratitude for them. Their offer of friendship there on the steamer at Copenhagen had not been an empty one. The Nielsons had taken Eric and Olaf in as though they were their own. It had been wonderful for Olaf. His homesickness had become bearable, and having the two children to help care for had helped keep his mind occupied.

Eric smiled to himself. It wasn't just Olaf who had benefitted from Elsie's mothering and Jens's friendship. It had been good for him as well.

"Thank you, Eric," Jens said as he appeared with another case and Bodil Mortensen.

Eric set the case down and looked around. Beyond the cars of the train he could see rows of buildings on either side of the track. Beyond the buildings was the vastness of the great American prairie. It was a flat, featureless landscape, such a shock to the eyes after the mountains of Sognefjorden. The grass was already starting to turn brown in the June heat. So this was Iowa City. He felt a momentary panic. What if Utah was like this?

And the heat! It was as if they had been dropped into a bathhouse. The air was hot, heavy, almost like a weight pressing against one's body. He could already feel the first prickling of sweat beneath his shirt.

"Let's go, brothers and sisters. The rest are moving."

Eric turned. It was Brother Ahmanson. The Scandinavian group once again had taken the last two cars, so they were at the end of the long line of people who had gotten off the train.

"Brother Willie says the Church agents are waiting for us at the end of Main Street."

Olaf's eyes were wide as the group left the station and started up the main street of Iowa City. The buildings were mostly new. Some were made of logs. Most had tin roofs, but he saw two with grass growing on the top and tugged at Eric's sleeve to show him.

They moved right up the center of the street, a long line of weary emigrants shuffling along in the thick dust. For a moment Olaf wondered why, but then he saw the townspeople. They lined the boardwalks on both sides of the street, leaving nowhere but in the street for the new arrivals. They gaped at the emigrants as they slowly passed. There were men, women, and children. Some of the children pointed, giggling behind cupped hands. "Hey, Mormons!" a young man about Olaf's age shouted. "Go back home where ya come from." But an older man standing next to him cuffed him sharply and he said nothing more.

"This isn't a zoo," Olaf muttered to Eric. "What are they gaping at?"

"Maybe the way we're dressed," Eric responded.

"They're the ones who are dressed funny," Olaf retorted.

"To them, we are the ones who are dressed oddly. We are the ones who are different."

Olaf grunted and lowered his head, not wanting to look at these Americans anymore. In about five minutes they began to leave the buildings behind. As they came to a large field, Eric pointed. Up ahead the crowd was stopping, spreading out like water behind a dam.

"What is it?" Bodil Mortensen asked Elsie.

She shrugged. Jens, who was tall enough to see over most of the crowd, answered for her. "There are some men in a wagon waiting there for us."

Olaf went up on tiptoes. Jens was right. The people were forming into a large circle around four men who stood together in the back of a wagon so that they were above the crowd.

"I think we have arrived," Eric said.

Just then Elder Ahmanson came up. "Eric? Olaf? I know your English is not good yet, but see what you can do to help our people understand what is being said. I will be speaking too, but not all may be able to hear."

Surprised and yet pleased, they both nodded. "Let's go over there," Olaf suggested. "We can be heard better there."

All around, people were sitting on the grass or on their luggage. Women adjusted their bonnets and began fanning themselves with whatever was at hand. Men removed their hats and mopped at their brows. Even that much of a walk in the heat had set them to sweating heavily. Dark spots beneath their arms and on the backs of their shirts were visible on many.

The McKensies and the Jameses found a place near the wagon and gathered in together. Then Hannah saw Ingrid among the last of those coming in and waved. She smiled back and came over to join them. Maggie saw Eric and Olaf move off to one side and remain standing.

At the wagon, President Willie along with Millen Atwood and Moses Cluff, his counselors, were in conference with the four men who had been waiting for the group of Saints. They were far enough away that Maggie could not hear, but she was interested to note that there was clearly agitation among them. Then finally President Willie climbed up beside the other four and raised his hands. "Brothers and sisters, may I have your attention please?"

He didn't have to ask. The crowd had already instantly quieted. Maggie saw that he too looked tired. He was a kind and gentle man in his mid-forties. He had left his family four years before to return to England, his native land, as a missionary. He must be very anxious to return to them. And yet, in the two months of their journey, their leader's first concern had always seemed to be for his people. It was no wonder he was so widely respected.

"After almost two full months," Willie began, "we have finally reached the end—and the beginning—of our journey. We are grateful to the Lord for bringing us safely this far. We pray that His over-watching care may continue."

He half turned. "I would like to introduce you to four men that many of you who are from England already know. These are the Church agents here in Iowa City," he said. "All have been missionaries in the British Isles for the last three or four years. They left England earlier this year at the direction of President Brigham Young. They came here to Iowa City to get things ready for the companies who would be crossing the plains this season. They arrived in March and have been here ever since.

"We are now under their jurisdiction. In charge is Brother Daniel Spencer." One of the men stepped forward, raising a hand in welcome. "With him," President Willie continued, "are Elders George D. Grant, Chauncey Webb, and William H. Kimball, son of President Heber C. Kimball."

As each stepped forward, there were nods and murmurs from those who recognized them. But at the mention of the Kimball name, surprise and admiration rippled through the crowd. Heber C. Kimball was in the First Presidency and was known by name to almost everyone because of his being the first missionary to bring the gospel to Europe.

President Willie stepped back, and the one he had introduced as Brother Spencer moved to the edge of the wagon box, waiting for the group to quiet again.

"Good afternoon, brothers and sisters. Welcome to Iowa City. We are glad to see you here." He smiled broadly. "But I'll wager we're not half as glad as you are to see us."

Suddenly, Sarah was poking Maggie as laughter and applause broke out. "Look, Maggie. Eric and Olaf are helping translate."

Maggie turned and saw that along with Johan Ahmanson the two brothers were helping the people know what Elder Spencer was saying. "Wonderful," she whispered. "There's nothing that will help them more."

Elder Spencer went on. "As Brother Willie has indicated, the four of us were sent here to act as agents for the Perpetual Emigrating Fund. We stand ready to help you in any way possible to further your journey to Zion."

He stopped and the smile on his face slowly died. When he began again the crowd quickly became very, very still.

"Brothers and sisters, I must tell you that we did not expect more emigrants to come this season. Yes, we heard recently from some of our people traveling west that more companies were on their way, but that was only a few days ago. We hoped that perhaps you would stay over in New York until next season. It is very late now. We have already outfitted and sent off three handcart companies in the last six weeks. The last one left just a few days ago. We thought that was it. In fact, we were packing up our things and getting ready to start west ourselves."

Now a buzz swept through the crowd.

Maggie was staring at her mother. *Too late?* She had left James and Scotland and a job that helped her support the family, and now they were being told they were too late? What did the Church agents expect them to do? troop back to the railway station? climb back on the cars and return home? The Scottish in her flared in irritation.

"What will we do, Mama?" Hannah asked.

"It will be all right," Mary soothed. "Let's listen and see what they say."

Daniel Spencer sighed, shaking his head slowly. "To have this many people show up now . . . This will tax our abilities greatly. We have exhausted our lumber supply. We have very little canvas left for the tents. We don't even have a place for you to sleep tonight." There was a long, long silence. Then in a low voice he concluded, "Our resources and funds are nearly gone."

James G. Willie had gone rigid. "But Brother Spencer, President Richards said he had written to tell you of our coming."

Spencer was a middle-aged man of medium build and height. He was clean shaven, and his complexion had been marred some years before by acne or some other infection. His hair and sideburns were very curly and combed back from a high forehead. All of these combined to make him look stern, almost grim. His mood at the moment did little to dispel that impression.

"I suppose he did, Brother Willie, but the mail from Europe—especially out here on the frontier—is very unreliable. Your arrival comes as a great shock to us."

Millen Atwood raised his hand. "We are not the last," he said loudly. "Another ship was supposed to leave about three weeks after us."

Spencer whirled, as did all of his companions. "*What?*"

Willie nodded slowly. "Yes, it's true. It could not be helped. With the announcement of the handcart plan, many more Saints responded than was expected. Brother Edward Martin is bringing another shipload. They were scheduled to leave three weeks after us."

"But it is already way past the time for departure," Brother Grant said. "It is the last of June. By now we should be gone from Florence, and that's three hundred miles farther on from here. And you're saying there are others still three weeks behind you?"

"What were we to do?" Brother Willie answered. "You must realize how things are in England. These people had quit their jobs, or were let go for being Latter-day Saints. They sold everything. When they came to Liverpool expecting passage, they had nowhere to stay, no way to make a living in England. As you know, England's laws are very strict. Many of them would have been thrown into the poorhouse. President Richards did the only thing he could do."

Brother Kimball spoke up now. "How many are there in the next group?"

Willie shook his head. "They were still forming it when we left. President Richards thought perhaps there might be as many as a hundred more than in our company."

"And you're seven hundred?" Grant exploded.

"Yes. Some stayed in New York to come next season, but yes, we are about seven hundred."

The agents huddled and began to talk in great excitement. The crowd erupted in a low roar of sound. Daniel Spencer raised his hand and shouted for order. He had to shout again, and then again a third time before he got their attention.

"Brethren and sisters, obviously this news is distressing to us as it is to you. There is no question but what it is very late in the season." He took a quick breath. "In fact, President Young has counseled us to send no groups west if they cannot leave from Florence by June first."

Maggie felt sick. It was June twenty-sixth and they had just arrived.

The head of the agents in Iowa City shook his head slowly. "This is not good."

Jane James touched her husband's arm. "Surely we haven't come this far only to stop, William?"

"We must not lose faith."

A hand shot up near the front of the crowd. It was one of the English members, Eric saw.

"Yes, brother?" Spencer said.

"Some of us are not going by handcarts. We have sufficient means to go by wagon. What about us?"

Spencer nodded. "We shall be forming one or two independent wagon companies–independent meaning that you can travel on your own without having to go with the handcarts. However, those of you who are in that category will be asked to delay your departure. If the weather does happen to turn cold, the risk to a wagon company is not as great as to the handcarts. You will be able to carry more food and supplies in the wagons than we can in carts. So you will follow after the handcart companies so you can give them aid if they need it."

"Thank you."

Mary was looking at Maggie, seeing the distress in her eyes. "We have to wait and see, Maggie. The Lord didn't bring us here just to forsake us."

Before Maggie could answer, Brother Daniel Spencer cried out again. "Brothers and sisters, please!"

The sound died quickly.

"I'm sorry if we have appeared discouraged. There are hard realities we have to face. *But* . . ." the word hung in the air like a banner. "But it is not upon us that you are relying, it is upon the Lord. That's why you've come. In obedience to His commandment."

Mary shot Maggie a triumphant look. It was nice to have your words validated so quickly.

"We find it hard to believe that the Lord led you this far only to have you stopped. You've come in faith. Let's not let faith die now."

Without conscious thought, Maggie began nodding slowly. Sarah reached out and laid a hand on her arm. "It will be all right, Maggie," she murmured.

Daniel Spencer's face was resolute now, his voice firm. Any feelings of his being harsh or unfeeling were now completely dispelled. "Brothers and sisters, the coming of this many so late may have caught us off guard, but it hasn't caught the Lord by surprise. He who knows all things will watch over our labors. If it is His will that we winter over here at Iowa City or at Florence, then we shall bow to that will. But until He tells us otherwise, we shall go forward with full faith. We shall go to work and secure those supplies that we need. We shall find the lumber. We shall secure the funds. We shall locate the flour we need."

Now all around the assembly, people were nodding as he punched out each sentence. There were smiles too. They were tentative, anxious, but also hopeful. And Maggie's was one of those.

Brother Spencer straightened to his full height. "Brethren and sisters, our outfitting camp is about two miles south of town. As yet we do not have tents enough for all of you. We are pleased to hear that you have sewn some together on your voyage. We shall take those to camp and set them up first thing tomorrow. Perhaps some of the women and children can come with us and stay. In the meantime Brother Webb has contracted with the local superintendent of the railroad to let us have use of one of the large engine sheds for the night."

He glanced toward the west, where far in the distance there was a line of gray clouds. "It looks like we may have rain, so you won't want to be out in the open. Tomorrow the rest of you can come on down and we will go to work."

He stopped and smiled warmly at the faces of these people who were hanging on his every word. "Though we may sound dismayed, make no mistake, brothers and sisters. We are pleased that you have come. You are doing what you have been called upon to do, and we are proud to be associated with you in this great task."

Chapter Notes

The details shared in this chapter about the journey from New York City to Iowa City are drawn from the Willie Company journal (see Turner, *Emigrating Journals*, pp. 1–10). Since the travel by rail and steamboat did not involve the same sacrifice as traveling by wagon and handcart, most of the journal entries that cover the "sail and rail" portions of the journey are not as detailed as those that cover the latter half of the company's journey. However, by modern standards, it is clear that this portion of their travel had its own set of hardships.

One author has written: "Mormons, because they almost always traveled in 'emigrant cars'—that is, the cheap cars rather than the first-class and 'palace' cars—experienced most of the discomforts typical of mid-nineteenth-century railroading. Among the standard problems were crowding (up to eighty-four in each car), uncomfortable cars, poor heating, bad ventilation, dim lighting, marginal sanitary facilities, few if any sleeping arrangements, inadequate eating conveniences, and a lack of drinking water; loud noise, strong smells, jolting, shaking, vibration and fatigue; an abundance of dirt, lice, soot, sparks, smoke, and fire; gamblers, thieves, tramps, drunks, marauding soldiers, impolite railroad personnel, and 'mashers' who tried to 'take advantage' of women; loss of luggage; plenty of snow and ice; and such other inconveniences as sickness, bad breaks, animals on the tracks, derailments, accidents, wrecks, [and] delays" (Stanley B. Kimball, "Sail and Rail Pioneers," pp. 30–31).

The experience with the engineer who declared that he would drive the Mormons to hell is a true one, though it did not happen to the Willie Company as shown here (see Kimball, "Sail and Rail Pioneers," p. 31).

In the Willie Company journal, the entry for 26 June 1856, the day of their arrival at Iowa City, reads: "This morning at 7 a.m., we left and crossed the Mississippi by the steam ferry boat, and at 9 a.m. we left by rail for Iowa City. We arrived there at 1:30 p.m., and camped on the green, but in consequence of a thunderstorm approaching, we obtained possession of a large engine shed and remained there during the night, it raining in torrents all night. Many of the brethren from the camp visited and cordially welcomed us, and on their return, took a large number of the sisters to the camp with them" (in Turner, *Emigrating Journals*, p. 10).

There seem to have been four Church agents operating in Iowa City at this time, and in both the Willie Company and the Martin Company journals frequent mention is made of Daniel Spencer as the presiding agent. All of these brethren, along with most of the leadership of the Willie and Martin

Companies, had gone to England in 1852 or 1854 as missionaries and were returning home after almost four years of service.

There is some confusion as to whether the Church agents in Iowa City had any advanced notice of the late companies. Three handcart companies consisting of about eight hundred Saints had already been outfitted and sent west. The last of these had left Iowa City on 23 June, just three days before the *Thornton* company arrived (see Hafen and Hafen, *Handcarts to Zion*, p. 193). If the agents did know of the coming of the last two shiploads, it couldn't have been very long in advance, and so they were still caught off guard by the numbers and the lateness of the emigrants' arrival (see ibid., pp. 91–92).

The speech given by Daniel Spencer here is not based on any recorded address but seeks to capture some of the concerns these brethren faced with the arrival of two more shiploads of Saints. The reference to President Young's counsel that companies were not to start west from Florence, Nebraska, (Winter Quarters) later than June first is accurate (see Christy, "Weather, Disaster, and Responsibility," pp. 11–12). However, this seems to have been viewed more as a general rule than a specific directive. All of the first three companies of handcarts left Iowa City (three hundred miles east of Florence) after that deadline, and no one seemed too concerned about it.

BOOK 3

THE JOURNEY

JUNE – AUGUST 1856

When I saw Brother [Edmund] Ellsworth come into this city covered with dust and drawing a handcart, I felt that he had gained greater honor than the riches of this world could bestow. . . . The honor any man can obtain by his faithfulness in this cause and kingdom is worth far more than all the honors and riches of the world.

—Wilford Woodruff, address given in the Tabernacle, Salt Lake City, 6 October 1856

CHAPTER 7

IOWA CITY, IOWA

I

Friday, 27 June 1856

President James G. Willie lowered his head and took a deep breath, obviously fighting for patience. Finally he looked up to face the anxious eyes that looked at him from every side. "Brothers and sisters," he said slowly, "sleeping out in the open is just a temporary thing."

That didn't seem to help much. There was a low murmur, much of it grumbling. They were at what the Iowa City residents called "the Mormon campground," two miles south of town. After spending the previous night in town, they had just arrived at the camp and were gathered around President Willie and Brother Daniel Spencer, the chief agent here in Iowa.

Maggie wasn't too surprised at the mood. They had been ten days coming from New York. Those were long, miserable, monotonous days. Nights spent on jolting, swaying railway cars or on the decks of steamers or, in one case, on the cement floor of a warehouse didn't provide significant amounts of sleep, and tempers were growing short.

Brother Spencer had come to give them their instructions, but at the first mention of sleeping outside, a dismayed mutter had erupted and President Willie had jumped in. Now a thought struck him. "How many of you have never slept out beneath the stars before?"

Maggie straightened and looked around as she and her family raised their hands. There was a rustle of astonishment. Fully three-quarters of the people had their hands in the air.

Willie was surprised as well. "Hmm," he said. Then he went on cheerfully. "Well, it is something that every free man and woman ought to do at least once in life. I think you'll find it an invigorating experience."

He stepped back and Brother Spencer came forward. "It shouldn't be for long. As we finish each new tent, we'll assign people to them on the basis of need. Within the week, you should all have shelter."

"How many to a tent?" someone called out.

"Twenty." There were a few groans, but he went on quickly. "We'll organize you into companies of hundreds. There are five tents per company, twenty people per tent. We'll do that by families as much as possible, but there will have to be more than one family to a tent."

Maggie could sense the mood of the crowd beginning to relax. Brother Spencer's easy manner and quick confidence seemed to be what they needed. Actually, she found the idea of sleeping outside intriguing. On the ship the berth above her and Sarah was just six or eight inches above them. Then had come the nightmare rides on the railway cars, which had no beds at all. A ceiling of stars and a "room" full of fresh air sounded wonderful to her.

An elderly man stood up near the front. "I have to get up in the night," he said, his eyes twinkling, "especially if I have a lot to drink. Any advice?"

"Sleep on the far edge of the camp," Spencer shot back without hesitation.

The laughter was spontaneous and sustained. Several clapped their hands at the quickness of the answer. Mary looked at Maggie and smiled. The mood of the group was changing quickly. The man waved amiably and sat down again.

"What about snakes?" another woman, a younger one, asked.

"Aren't any snakes around here," Spencer said. "At least not poisonous ones. Too many people. And besides"—he was warming up to his audience—"all a prairie rattlesnake wants is a warm body to curl up next to during the night. So if you wake up and find something with scales sleeping beside you, just say good morning and roll out of bed the other direction."

There was more laughter, but it was tentative, and several people, especially the women and children, looked at each other nervously. The agent instantly saw his mistake. "I was just joking, folks. There will be places along the trail where we'll have to watch for rattlesnakes, but Iowa City isn't one of them."

Levi Savage was one of the returning missionaries. He had been in Siam for two years and was one of the few in the company who had been across the trail several times before. Now he raised his hand. The agent saw it and nodded. "Brother Levi?"

"You might also mention that snakes have a keen sense of smell. Since the last time any of us had a chance to bathe was in Chicago, I think it's a pretty safe bet no snake with any sense at all is going to come within a hundred yards of our camp."

The people roared. They were all keenly aware of the ripe smell they carried with them.

Spencer smiled and nodded. "Point well taken, Levi. Oh, and one other thing. You parents need to start letting your children go barefoot. It's hard to keep young'uns in shoes on the trail, so most go barefoot. They'll do fine once their feet toughen up."

He waited for a moment, but they had been warned about that back in England and so no one seemed too bothered. Then he became quite serious. "All right, folks. We'll give you the rest of the day to get settled. Find a spot on the prairie and roll out your beds. Tomorrow we'll start you sisters sewing tents while the brethren return to Iowa City and bring the baggage back to camp. The next day is the Sabbath. Worship services will be held at two o'clock. But come Monday morning, we will go to work full speed ahead. There is much to do."

He waited a moment, but now all were quiet. "Iowa City is only a short distance away. If you've got things you want to trade or money enough to buy supplies, there'll be time for that. I hope you got rid of your English money in New York City. The merchants here will probably insist on American dollars. But most of you will be bartering for what you need. This is a good chance for you to divest yourselves of things that you won't be taking with you. We just ask that you wait to go into town until after the work is done each day and that you let your leaders know if you're going."

He looked around. "Are there any questions?"

To Maggie's surprise, Robbie's hand shot up. His mother jerked around too, but before she could make him put it down, President Willie saw it. He leaned over and whispered in Spencer's ear. The agent nodded, then turned to the family. "Yes, young Master McKensie?"

"Brother Spencer?" Robbie stood up. "Do you need someone to stand guard tonight?"

There were soft cries of amusement and admiration. Maggie was astonished. He was twelve years old! But he stood straight and tall with his shoulders squared.

The agent's face softened and there was a pleased smile. "We do, son. Are you volunteering?"

There were a few chuckles, but most of the people were, like Daniel Spencer, suddenly touched by this boy warrior who was about to have his first night sleeping out in the wilderness and who was not in the least bit worried about snakes.

"Yes, sir!" Robbie barked eagerly.

"Great." Spencer's face was completely serious now. "We've already made assignments for the brethren who will be standing duty around the perimeter of the camp, but I'm looking for a man in each family who will be responsible for those he loves. Can you do that, son?"

"Yes, sir!"

"Good. I want you to make sure everyone in your family is together for evening prayers. And when we call lights out, you be sure the campfire is completely out and that all candles and lamps are extinguished. Will you do that for me, Brother McKensie?"

"Yes, Brother Spencer!" Robbie was about to bust right out of his shirt, for the agent was speaking to him as one adult to another. There was no teasing here.

"Thank you." Spencer turned to the audience and there was a sudden catch in his throat. "Oh, my brothers and sisters," he said, "would that we all had such an attitude as that!"

Maggie, her eyes burning, wanted to reach out and hug Robbie, but she saw her mother's eyes—also a little misty—which said, "Don't treat him like a boy. Not right now." And so they just smiled at him and nodded their approval. For Maggie, it was probably the sweetest moment she had enjoyed since leaving Edinburgh.

Suddenly she bowed her head without closing her eyes. *I thank Thee, Father, for speaking to me that day. I have not accepted Thy will graciously. Forgive me. Help me learn to trust more fully in Thy counsel, and to come to understand Thy will.* She paused for a long moment. *And to accept and rejoice in it. Amen.*

II

Monday, 30 June 1856

On Monday morning, immediately after morning prayers, all the adult members of the *Thornton* group began to gather at the large, open area south of camp. The younger children either were sent off to various schools that had been organized or were left with the older girls to be tended. The people were in good spirits this morning. A

Sabbath day's rest and three nights of good sleep out in the open left them rejuvenated and eager.

Precisely at eight o'clock, Daniel Spencer and the other Church agents appeared. They called for the people to gather in close, and Brother Spencer got right to the task at hand. They were divided into work teams. Those with experience in carpentry were sent to help Brother Chauncey Webb build handcarts. Word had already gone through the camp that Chauncey Webb had been the one who made many of the wagons for the pioneers when they went west. Because Eric Pederson had once helped his father build their barn, he went with that group. The rest of the men would go with Brother Grant and begin cutting wood. The younger men and older boys would go with Brother Kimball to purchase more flour.

The women were quickly divided into "cutters" and "sewers" for the tents and went off with Brother Spencer. The younger women who weren't tending children were set to work mending clothes, drying meat, and doing the hundred other minor things that had to happen before the company would be ready to go.

The company was going to be challenged by lack of skilled labor. Most of the emigrants were from England. They were hard workers but they had worked all of their lives in the foundries, the cotton mills, the coal mines, the great pottery factories. Those experiences did not translate easily into trail skills. But they did have one thing in common and that was a determination to go to Zion. They were eager if not immediately capable.

To Maggie's surprise, President Willie sought her out the moment the meeting broke up. The need for translators was more urgent than ever. Ingrid, Eric, and Olaf were being used with the separate work teams, along with Elder Ahmanson. Would she consider starting up the English class again? There had been no opportunity since they left New York, but now she would be excused from any evening assignments. Would she hold class again from six to seven-thirty each night except for the Sabbath?

Maggie agreed instantly, overjoyed that her work would not simply be allowed to die.

—❦—

Chauncey Webb was holding a long piece of board out in front of him, sighting down it with one eye closed. Even from where Jens and Eric stood they could see that it was twisted out of line. The blacksmith lowered it, shaking his head. "Brethren, we have a serious problem, but we have no choice but to make the best of it." He waved the board at them. "Not only are we very short on lumber, but as you can see, much of it is green. That is not good."

Eric thought he caught most of his meaning, but that threw him. He turned to Johan Ahmanson and waited for the translation to make sure he had heard correctly. When Ahmanson finished, Eric stepped to Jens and in a low voice asked, "Does it really matter what color the handcarts are?"

Ahmanson overheard the question and looked startled. Then he understood. "No, Eric. Green in this case is not the color. It means the wood is still new, that it hasn't been properly dried and cured."

"Ah."

They turned back to Chauncey Webb, who was smiling grimly. "When you're out on the trail in this kind of heat, day after day, green wood will start to dry. As it dries it shrinks and warps. It will make for many problems." He straightened, forcing a smile. "Almost all of the lumber we have is still green. But as my father used to say, when you have no choice it greatly simplifies making the decision. And we have no choice."

He moved over to the one existing handcart that was still in camp, motioning for the others to gather around. He picked up a stick and used it as a pointer. "Ideally we use different kinds of wood for the various parts of the handcart—hickory, the hardest of all, for the axletrees"—he tapped the long, thick beam to which the wheels were attached—"red or slippery elms for the hubs, this part here that allows the wheels to turn. We use mostly oak for the bed of the cart and the sides. We try to use white oak for the spokes and the rims of the wheels, and white ash for the shafts." As he said these last words he touched the long, rounded pieces of wood that protruded from the front of the carts and were connected by a crossbar.

The Scandinavian brothers listened as Brother Ahmanson repeated it all in a low voice. Eric began to nod. Yesterday, in worship services, Elder Kimball had spoken to the people about the need to get into good physical shape so that they did not "collapse in the shafts." Now it made sense what he was saying.

"Wherever possible we try to get our wood from timber that has grown on low ground, as that tends to be very tough and easy to bend. The other men will be searching out and sawing that timber for us."

One of the Scottish men raised his hand. "Is it true that the wheels are the most difficult part of the cart to make?"

"Absolutely," Webb said with great fervency. "I guess none of you here are wheelwrights?"

No one moved.

He sighed wearily. "I was afraid of that. Yes, the wheel is a challenge." He walked to the stack of three or four wheels that were behind them and rolled one back to serve as a model. "First of all, we have to soak long strips of oak in water for several days until they can be bent around to make the rim." His fingers stroked the spokes, as though they were the strings of a harp. "Each spoke has to be shaped just right so that it fits tightly in the holes both in the hub and in the rim."

He turned the wheel now so that they weren't looking at it straight on but as though it were rolling toward them. "Do you notice anything unusual about its shape?"

"It curves inward," Brother Ahmanson said.

"Exactly. That is what we call 'dishing' the wheel. We make them slightly concave, like a dish. Why so? Because when the wagon or cart is loaded, the weight pushes directly on the wheel. If it were straight or extended outward, what would happen?"

"The weight is transferred to the spokes and they would pop out," an old Scotsman said. "But in dish shape, the weight actually pushes the spokes more tightly into the hub."

Brother Webb gave him a sharp look. "That's right, brother. Are you sure you've never made a wheel before?"

"No, but our neighbor in Dundee was a blacksmith. He explained all this to me one day."

"Good. I'd like you then to help me with the wheels and see if we can train some others."

He moved and picked up a hub. It was round with a square on the back for the axle and the holes for the spokes already drilled. He held it up high.

"This is the hub, brethren, perhaps the most critical part of the handcart. He turned it so they could see the back. "On the trail we will be in a lot of sand. Sand is death for a handcart. It can grind an axle or the hubs away in a matter of days. We usually try to line the wheel boxes—the place where the axles are connected to the wheels—with tin to prevent that from happening. Unfortunately our supply of tin is also very limited and we have not, as yet, been able to find more. So in some cases we'll have to line the boxes with leather. You'll also need to take something to lubricate the boxes with. Axle grease is best, but—and this will come as no surprise—that too is in very short supply. We may have to use lard, bacon grease, or soap instead. Consider that as you make your plans for what to take."

He stepped back, eyeing the cart. "Well, there you have it. It's not much to look at, but then we're not running a contest here to see who can produce the fanciest equipment. We'll keep the construction simple. The only planing we'll do is to round off the shafts and on the ends of the axle. Oh, also, we round the edges of the rims so that they slough off the sand and dust as they turn. For everything else we can use rough-hewn lumber.

"When done, the cart itself weighs about sixty pounds. But it will easily hold three- or four-hundred-pound loads, which can be pulled by one or two people without a great deal of effort."

He smiled faintly at his "crew." "Well, brethren, I figure if we have five people assigned to each handcart, which is generally what we aim for, between this company and the one that is still coming, we are going to need about two hundred and fifty carts all told."

There were low groans and a soft whistle.

"I couldn't agree more," he said dryly. "So let's get started."

William H. Kimball, Heber C. Kimball's son, and one of the Church agents at Iowa City, had taken his crew in five wagons to a mill in Iowa City. Olaf Pederson was sixteen and in every way considered a man. Also, he could speak some English, so he was assigned to the flour detail. Brother Kimball made a special effort to speak slowly and distinctly so that Olaf could translate for the other Scandinavians. In actuality it didn't prove too difficult, because though it was hard work, it wasn't difficult to understand.

By five o'clock they were loading the last wagon. With a hundred-pound sack on his shoulder, Olaf walked slowly to the back of that wagon, stopped for a moment to line himself up, then heaved the sack of flour up and onto the pile. A small white cloud exploded outward as the wagon creaked beneath the load.

"Four more should about do it," Elder Kimball said, holding up four fingers to Olaf.

Olaf removed his hat and wiped at his brow. It left a white, pasty streak on his shirtsleeve. He grimaced as he looked at it. They all looked like ghosts now, and in the heat the flour stuck to their faces and skin like bookbinder's glue.

The other brethren stopped to rest for a moment as well. An older man from England surveyed the wagons, obviously impressed. "Is this for the next group as well as ours?" he asked Elder Kimball.

"Oh, no," the agent replied with a smile. "This is only for your group. We'll still have to come back and get more."

"It really takes this much?" another man said.

Olaf listened closely, trying to understand as much as possible.

"Figure it out, brethren," Brother Kimball said. "The normal allowance for an adult is sixteen ounces, one pound, of flour per day. Children get about two-thirds that amount. Your company will consist of about five hundred people."

He stopped to let them calculate that in their minds.

"So about five hundred pounds per day," one started.

Kimball nodded. "If you consider the children, a little less than that, but that's close enough. Now figure on just under a month to Florence. We'll resupply there, but just to get us to Florence will take about fifteen thousand pounds, or around eight tons."

Olaf was having trouble following all the figures, but it wasn't hard to read the shock on the men's faces.

"Then think about what it takes from Florence to Salt Lake. That's about seventy days, so for the whole company we need about thirty-five thousand pounds. Seventeen or eighteen tons."

"But how?" one of the brethren blurted. "With only five wagons per company, that's seven thousand pounds per wagon. Surely wagons can't carry that much."

"Well, first of all, we'll be able to purchase some flour as we cross Iowa, so we won't have to carry the full amount to begin with. That's not true once we leave Florence, however. Second, though we're letting you run light from here to Florence—the wagons will carry all the flour until you toughen up some—after that, each handcart will carry a hundred-pound sack. With a hundred and twenty handcarts, that's about six tons of the total. The wagons will take another five tons or so."

"But we'll still be seven or eight tons short," someone cried.

Brother Kimball nodded and went on quickly. "The First Presidency knew from the beginning that handcarts could not carry enough food for the whole distance. That's why they send out resupply wagons from Salt Lake."

"Ah," several said, understanding now.

"We'll meet the supply wagons somewhere between Fort Laramie and the last crossing of the North Platte. They'll load us up again with enough to get us to Fort Bridger, where another group of wagons will be waiting. That's how it's done."

Now the anxiety on the faces of the men disappeared.

Olaf raised his hand. "Do vee haf cows too?"

Kimball nodded. "Yes, each group of a hundred will have a milk cow. That's not much, enough to have a little butter and some milk for the smaller children. We also send with each company about fifty beef cattle that we can butcher along the way for meat."

"What about buffalo?" someone asked.

"We always hope to kill a few buffalo along the way. Also our hunters kill deer and antelope here and there. So we'll be fine." He grinned. "I don't think many of you will grow fat on the trail, but you'll survive."

"What about you?" another man asked. "Do you and the other agents just stay here?"

"No. Once we get everyone off, we'll start out in light wagons and carriages and race ahead to Florence. Elder Franklin D. Richards is coming from England and will meet us there. Then all of us will go on ahead to be sure Salt Lake knows how many are still coming.

"It is a marvelous organization," Kimball concluded. "It gives you a sense for how strongly the First Presidency feels about helping our people gather to Zion. You won't be alone out there, brethren. I can promise you that."

They were nodding now. Olaf had caught only a part of it all, but the last he had understood very well. And it made him proud to think that he and Eric could be part of such an effort.

Brother Kimball straightened and replaced his hat. "Well, brethren, that last wagon isn't going to load itself. And time's a-wasting."

—❦—

By the end of that first Monday after their arrival in Iowa City, the company being led by Elder James G. Willie had made three handcarts and sewn together the first four of an estimated forty or fifty tents that would be needed by the two late-arriving companies. Four tents meant that eighty people would have shelter for the night. The elderly and those with babies were given first priority. The rest would have to wait a little longer. Fortunately, for a third straight day the weather was clear and no rain came. The days were hot, but the nights cooled down to a pleasant temperature.

Elsie and Jens Nielson were not among those assigned to a tent. With young Jens being five and Bodil Mortensen nine, they would have to wait. That was all right with both of them. Though Jens had slept out a few times as a young boy, Elsie never had. She loved the quiet hum of the crickets, the murmur of the creek, the sighing of the wind in the trees. And, of course, there were the stars. For each of the last three nights, Elsie's last waking thoughts had been to wonder at the expanse of the universe above her head. She had always been one to sleep on her side or on her stomach. Now she stayed on her back, hands up beneath her head, for as long as possible.

"Elsie?"

She turned her head.

"Are they asleep?" Jens was whispering.

"I think so."

"Are your fingers still sore?"

"Yes." She rubbed her fingertips together, feeling the tenderness. A full day of pushing the heavy needles through the thick cotton fabric had left the tips of her thumb and forefinger burning and raw. She dreaded another day of it tomorrow.

There was a soft laugh from him. "My blisters now have blisters."

"I saw," she said sadly. Jens thought his hands were tough from his farming, but he had been put on one of the two-man saws for most of the day. Fresh-cut lumber did not provide easy cutting. His hands had blistered, then popped, then blistered again to become ugly sores. Tomorrow he would have to do something else.

"There is something about which I should like to speak with you."

"All right." She turned over on her side so she could look at him directly. The moon wasn't up yet, but it would be in another ten minutes, and when it appeared it would be almost three-quarters full. The eastern sky was already lightened by its promise and gave enough light that she could make out his features. He wasn't looking at her, but his eyes were wide open as he stared upwards.

"We still have more than five hundred *krone,* Elsie. That's about six or seven hundred dollars."

That was totally unexpected. "Yes?"

"That's enough to pay for our wagon and teams and the supplies we need and still have enough left over to buy a farm when we get to Utah."

"I know, Jens. We have been very blessed."

"Very blessed."

She waited, feeling his hesitancy, still puzzled by this particular course in the conversation. They had both talked about how very blessed they were to have the resources they did. Many in their circle were coming only with the help of the Church. Others had enough to pay their own way but didn't know what they would do when they reached Zion, for it would take everything they owned to get there. But even after paying out the required amounts for ship, train, and steamer travel, and 10 percent of the profit on their farm as tithing, Elsie and Jens had spent less than a quarter of their total assets.

"Brother Webb said today that it looks like we can make each handcart for under ten dollars, maybe even five or six," he said.

"Really? That's wonderful. I would have guessed much more than that."

"A wagon costs about fifty or sixty dollars. Oxen are selling for about seventy dollars a yoke."

"And we need two yoke?"

"At least. It would be well to have a spare yoke to trade off the teams."

She nodded, sobered a little. Add in supplies, which the brethren were estimating would be about fifteen dollars per adult and half that for children, and . . . She did some quick calculating and drew in her breath. That was over three hundred dollars, nearly half of all they had left. No wonder he was worrying.

"Elsie, we're young and strong."

Again he had taken her by surprise. "Why do you say that, Jens?"

"What would you think if we went by handcart instead of with the independent wagon companies?"

Perhaps it was just as well that he wasn't looking at her, for she could not contain the shock from flashing across her face. "By handcart, Jens?"

"Yes," he said eagerly. "They say they are not going to load the carts too heavily here in Iowa City. That will give us a chance to get ourselves hardened for when we have to take a full load."

She was still so caught by surprise that she didn't speak.

"Jens and Bodil are in good health. It would be a wonderful adventure for them. Jens has already said he wants to pull a cart."

"But why, Jens?"

She saw his chest rise and fall as he drew in a deep breath. "Elder Spencer came by where we were working this afternoon," he began. "The brethren are worried, Elsie. They have used all of their resources to send off the first three companies. There is not enough money to outfit everybody."

So that was it. She nodded slowly.

"Brother Spencer asked that if any of us had any extra resources, we consider putting it into a common fund, so more people can be taken this season."

She was reeling a little, but now she at least understood. "So if we go by handcart, it will cost us only about fifty dollars instead of three hundred?"

"Yes."

"And would you hold out enough for our farm in Utah?"

He didn't answer for several seconds, and she went up on one elbow. Now she could see that his mouth was drawn into a line and his eyes were wrinkled in consternation. "What, Jens?"

"I would like to hold out enough for us to get a handcart."

She gasped softly.

"And then I would like to give everything else to the fund."

She dropped back to the pillow like a rock. "The farm money too?"

"Everything," he said softly.

She didn't know what to say. He had overwhelmed her.

"We have been blessed, Elsie. We know what the Doctrine and Covenants says. Everything belongs to the Lord anyway. We are only his stewards."

"But, Jens . . ." She didn't know what to say.

"Think about it, Elsie. How would we feel if that were us and there wasn't enough money for us to continue on? Think how we'd feel."

"What will we do when we get to Utah? How shall we make a living?"

He answered without hesitation, and she knew he had thought about this a great deal before he started talking to her. "'Consider the lilies of the field,'" he quoted softly. "'They toil not, neither do they spin, and yet Solomon in all his glory was not arrayed such as one of these.' Are we not more than the lilies of the field, Elsie? Why did we prosper as we did in Denmark?"

"Because the Lord blessed us," she answered at once.

"Yes. If we do His will now, don't you think He will bless us even more?"

"Yes, I do, but–" Then in one instant she saw it as clearly and as simply as he did. "No," she corrected herself.

"No what?"

She heard the disappointment in his voice and scooted over to lie up against him. "No buts, Jens. You are right. We must have faith in the Lord. How can we expect Him to help us if we are not willing to help others?"

"So you agree?" he exclaimed.

"You are a good man, Jens Nielson. The best day of my life was when I married you. Do you think I would try to stop you now from being that kind of man? Yes, Jens, I agree with you completely."

"Then I shall take the money to Brother Spencer first thing in the morning." He bent over and kissed her softly. "Thank you."

"No, Jens. Thank you."

III

Friday, 4 July 1856

By now, one week following their arrival in Iowa City, all but a few of the Willie Company were in tents. To Maggie's great relief, the McKensies and the James family were assigned to the same tent. With the death of baby Jane on the ship, that made nine in the James family and four McKensies. To everyone's delight, Elder Ahmanson asked if Ingrid Christensen could join them. Her aunt and uncle had a full tent without her, and the leader of the Scandinavians wanted Ingrid to get as much exposure to English as possible before their departure. Eventually they would have to have a few more join with them, but for now there were enough people who preferred to sleep outside instead of in the stuffy tents that no one else was with them.

Mary McKensie was especially happy that Ingrid had come over with them. Since the Danish girl had become friends with Maggie and Hannah and the two James sisters, Mary had heard Maggie laugh more in any one given day than she had in the previous three months.

On this morning, which was the Fourth of July, the emigrants who had crossed the Atlantic on the *Thornton* paused with their American leaders and briefly celebrated the birthday of their newly adopted country. Utah was not a state as yet, but Utah Territory was a United States possession and the Saints considered themselves to be U.S. citizens.

Holiday or not, the urgency to prepare for departure did not allow for setting their work aside for even a day. After an hour of celebration, reality set in again. However, instead of normal work assignments, the Church agents had decided that this would be a good day for some special training.

The women of the Willie group followed Brother Grant and Brother Kimball to the west end of the large meadow that served as the Mormon Camp at Iowa City. When they reached the field, there were already two wagons parked and waiting for them. Brothers Grant and Kimball stopped there and waited while the sisters came in close around them.

George D. Grant took the lead while William Kimball watched. "Sisters, in council last night we as your leaders decided that we should better prepare you for your journey. In a week or so—we hope—you will all be out on the trail. It will be a new style of life for most of you. You and the brethren will have experiences you have never had before. And you will be expected to do things that most of you have never done before—simple things like making a fire, cooking a meal over that fire, yoking up a team of oxen, pitching a tent.

"Now, I am happy to say that we have several men who are experienced in these things. Levi Savage, Brother Atwood, and President Willie have been across the trail more than once, but they cannot do everything. Nor should they. You have to learn how to get along out there. You have to know how to take care of yourselves. And that is what we're going to do today."

He raised his arm, pointing at a spot about midway through the group. "Sisters, this half of you over here will stay with Elder Kimball. He is going to teach you how to make a fire and cook over it. Also he will give you a few tips on doing laundry in the middle of the wilderness. The rest of you come with me."

As they started to separate, Grant continued. "Brother Spencer and Brother Webb are going to teach your husbands how to kill, clean, skin, and butcher a beef cow. We send with each company about fifty head of cattle for fresh meat. The men will do the killing, but once the animal is butchered the rest of the task will become yours, sisters. So after fire building you are going to learn how to tan a hide and how to smoke beef so that it will not spoil on the trail."

"Sisters, how many of you recognize what I am holding in my hand here?"

Brother Kimball held up a stone and a flat piece of steel. As he turned it slowly, Mary McKensie shook her head. She looked at Jane James standing beside her. She looked equally blank. The five girls, standing together, also shook their heads.

"All right," Kimball said, lowering the device. "I'm sure that most of you sisters have had to start fires and keep them going in your homes. How many of you used matches to do so?"

Most of the hands came up. The stick match had been invented some twenty or thirty years before and was now to be found virtually everywhere.

"How many of you always kept hot coals in a bucket so you could use those to start your next fire?"

Again many hands came up.

He held up the stone and steel again. "And how many of you have ever used a flint and steel to start a fire without the help of anything else?" This time only three hands came up.

"Well, then," Brother Kimball went on, "since matches get wet and blow out in the wind, we are now going to teach you how to start a fire, even in inclement weather, using flint and steel. This is something they will be teaching the men as well, but there will be many times when it will be up to the women to start a fire."

And so they went to work. For the next hour they learned the art of starting and maintaining a good cooking campfire. They learned how to shave fine slivers off a dry stick or comb the flammable fibers out of linen or wool. The hardest of all was sending the spark exactly into the fibers.

Mary McKensie and Jane James formed one team; Hannah, Ingrid Christensen, and Emma James another; Sarah James and Maggie a third. They worked until their hands were sore. Brother Kimball came over and watched, coaching them as they tried again. When Mary finally sent a spark flying into the wad of fibers and it began to glow, Jane gave a little cry and dropped to her knees. Bending clear over, she blew on it softly. It began to smoke; then after a moment it burst into flames.

You would have thought they struck gold. Mary let out a yell and clapped her friend on the shoulder. The girls gaped, coveting openly what they saw. Quickly the two women added the slivers of wood, then small sticks. In a moment they had a fire big enough to support a frying pan.

At Kimball's insistence, the girls kept trying, and five minutes later Sarah and Maggie had success. In ten more minutes there were fifteen or sixteen crackling campfires burning around the campground.

At that point they moved on to their next lesson. They quickly learned that cooking over an open campfire, especially when the wind was blowing, was significantly different from cooking over a fire in a fireplace or with a stove. Brother Kimball demonstrated some of the basics—how to make a bed of coals and wrap potatoes or other vegetables in leaves until they were steamed through; how to create a spit for roasting meat; how to bring water to a slow boil over a low flame. The ultimate astonishment came when he taught them how to bake bread in what he called a "spider," a heavy black kettle with a thick lid, a handle, and three spindly legs.

At first, when he indicated that that's what they would be doing, the women thought he was teasing them. But when, an hour later, he lifted the spider and dumped out a perfectly browned loaf of white bread, they became believers.

While they waited for the bread to bake, the sisters went over to observe the men in their training. As they arrived, the men had finished butchering a beef and Daniel Spencer was teaching them how to hitch up a yoke of oxen. There would be only five wagons with their company, but everyone would need to help with the animals.

What a sight that proved to be. Maggie's mother wasn't sure whether to feel sorrier for the men or for the animals. Some of the oxen the agents had managed to purchase were unbroken yearlings that had never been yoked before. They fought and bawled and bolted and bucked. The men fought back. They yelled, they bellowed, they jumped out of the way, they tried to hold on to the powerful necks, with no success. One man wasn't quick enough and was sent sprawling. Not a few disparaging remarks were made about both the parentage of the animals and their character.

The sisters hooted as it took seven men to corner one young pair of very frightened and very spooked animals and get the yoke on them. In the end, one of the men actually ended up sitting on the animal's neck before they could subdue it enough to yoke it to its partner.

Through it all the Church agents stood back, just shaking their heads in rueful disbelief. This was proving to be more of a challenge than even they had anticipated.

Chapter Notes

The description of the handcarts and the materials used in their construction comes from two or three sources cited in Hafen and Hafen, *Handcarts to Zion*, pp. 53–55. The shortage of materials and the fact that much of the lumber that could be procured was green and uncured would prove to be a major factor in what happened later. Also, the figures given on the amount of flour needed are accurate. These two things, as much as any other, illustrate the immense challenge it was to outfit a handcart company.

As stated before, Jens and Elsie Nielson were actual people who came with the Willie Handcart Company. It is not stated exactly how much money Jens had realized on the sale of his farm, only that when he reached Copenhagen he paid sixty dollars in tithing, so the assumption is that it was the equivalent of about six hundred dollars. He kept that first tithing receipt throughout his life.

About four hundred of the emigrants who came on the last two ships in the 1855–56 season were well enough off that they planned to cross the plains in wagon companies. These people contracted with many of those going by handcart to carry their heavier goods to Utah for them. The Nielsons had garnered sufficient means from the sale of their farm that they originally planned to go by wagon with one of those independent companies. In a letter written much later to one of his sons, Jens Nielson said only this: "I had enough money to come to Utah, but we were counseled to let all the money go we could spare and cross the plains with handcarts" (quoted in Lyman, "Bishop Jens Nielson," p. 3). That decision would put him and Elsie and the children in the Willie Handcart Company and not with the Hunt or Hodgett Wagon Trains that followed some weeks later.

It seems incredible to modern readers to think that some of the emigrants had so little knowledge and skills about the fundamental kinds of things that are necessary for life on the trail, but it is important to remember that most of them came from the working classes in British industry and were not skilled in living out-of-doors in any way. The following accounts give some clue as to the challenges they faced in preparing to cross some thirteen hundred miles of wilderness:

"The [John Powell] family traveled by train from Boston to the Iowa camp grounds where they helped build their handcarts and joined the company of Captain Edmund Ellsworth [the first handcart company of 1856]. . . . At the Iowa campgrounds they saw the first stove with an oven and they had never seen a washboard until they came to America" (in Carter, comp., *Treasures of Pioneer History* 5:237).

A twelve-year-old daughter in the Powell family later wrote: "We remained in Iowa six weeks. All the men were busy making handcarts. Our bake kettle which Father had ordered had not come. We had to fry our dough in a pan over the campfire. . . .

"Each day I took pains to watch the women bake bread in their bake-kettles. I was taking lessons from them. I knew that I should have to do the baking when our own kettle came and I was anxious to learn the best way to do it" ("Autobiography of Mary Powell Sabin," in Carol Cornwall Madsen, *Journey to Zion*, p. 598). The bake kettle was not delivered before they left Iowa City, but it did catch up to them in Florence, Nebraska, three hundred miles to the west.

Captain Edward Bunker, who led the "Welsh Company" of handcarts, the third company to come west in 1856, wrote of the challenges of leading a company of Saints who did not speak English and who had little experience in dealing with animals: "I had my councilors . . . , neither of whom had had much experience in handling teams. Both were returned missionaries. The Welsh had no experience at all and very few of them could speak English. This made my burden very heavy. I had the mule team to drive and had to instruct the teamsters about yoking the oxen" ("Autobiography of Edward Bunker," as cited in Hafen and Hafen, *Handcarts to Zion*, p. 82).

CHAPTER 8

IOWA CITY, IOWA

I

Tuesday, 8 July 1856

When the *Thornton* reached New York Harbor, Maggie McKensie's English class had been suspended. As they moved across the United States by train and steamer, there simply wasn't time or place for it. Maggie encouraged the two Pederson brothers and Ingrid Christensen to use English as much as possible, but that was all they could do. Then shortly after their arrival in Iowa City, Iowa, Brother Willie asked Maggie if she could start class up again. Once again Maggie felt gratitude for Sarah's wisdom in suggesting that they speak only English in class. The progress of her three students was evident to all. Each of the three of them was now helping Elder Ahmanson translate instructions for the Scandinavian contingent.

Emboldened by Brother Willie's encouragement, Maggie asked if she might have permission to extend the class by half an hour and go two hours. Now that her three students were getting better, she needed more time to allow them to practice their writing and also reading. Without hesitation, both of the brethren approved.

The "desks and benches" made up of crates and barrels on the ship were now replaced by fallen logs and trampled prairie grass. Other than that, and the fact that Maggie had three regular "teacher's helpers" now—Sarah, Emma, and Hannah—everything else was pretty much the same. They came together beneath a grove of trees near the river immediately after the evening meal. There she put them through their paces vigorously for the next two hours until the call came for evening prayer and lights out.

At the moment, Ingrid, Olaf, and Eric were taking turns reading aloud in English from the Book of Mormon. Maggie stood back, watching Sarah, who had moved over beside Eric and watched as his brows furrowed in concentration. If Eric stumbled, Sarah would gently correct him. If he looked up at her, she would look away quickly. When he became absorbed again, she studied his face, her eyes wide and luminous.

Part of Maggie wanted to smile at that; another part of her wanted to cry. With the McKensie and James families sharing the same tent, that put the two sets of sisters—four eligible young ladies—in one tent. With Ingrid assigned to them as well, that made one more. So it wasn't surprising that the young men in camp started "happening by" to stop and talk. Emma, Ingrid, and Hannah brought some attention, but since they were only sixteen, that was more flirtation than any serious courting. Maggie was acknowledged politely, but there was no question what drew them. It was Sarah James. In the minds of the young men in their company—and Maggie agreed completely—Sarah James was the prettiest girl in all of camp. And the fact that she was not promised, even though she was of the age to be married, was like putting wild honey before a pack of bear cubs.

But Sarah had eyes for none of them. She saw only one person in the camp who interested her and that was Eric Pederson. So the young men would come and laugh and chatter and strut a little, but the only time Sarah's eyes would light up and her face start to glow was when Eric was around. And that was where the sadness came in. Sarah James only had eyes for Eric Pederson, but Eric Pederson only had eyes for—Maggie stopped, frowning a little. What? She still wasn't sure. For English? Maybe. He certainly was focused on mastering this new language. But for sure it wasn't for Sarah. Whenever he came to class he was totally absorbed in learning. He treated Sarah in a friendly manner and seemed quite comfortable around her, but if he noticed the way she looked at him, if he saw the way she hung on his every word, if he paid any attention to the longing in her eyes when he was talking to others, he never gave the slightest sign of it. And it was driving Sarah to distraction.

Was he blind? Sarah was so lovely, so captivating, so disarmingly beautiful, and yet Eric seemed unaffected by her. Maggie could not imagine what it would be like to look like that, not even to the smallest degree. There was no resentment in her envy of her friend. Sarah had become far too dear to Maggie for that. But there were times when Maggie just watched her in quiet awe. She was flawless in both inner and outer beauty. How could Eric not see that?

One night, whispering together long after the adults were asleep, the five girls decided that there had been a tragic love in Eric's life or that he had left a fiancée or a special girl behind in Norway. Hannah, never the shy one, immediately took Olaf aside the next day and grilled him on it. There was no one back in Balestrand. So that wasn't it either.

It was a puzzle, and Maggie was trying to work it out. Eric was twenty-two years old, past the age when many young men married. And just as Sarah was drawing the attention of the young men in camp, so Eric was drawing looks from the young women. Even Maggie had to admit that as she had come to know him through class, he was the first person she had found who compared favorably to James MacAllister. In fact—and this admission did not come easily to her—in moments of complete honesty, she knew he was several notches above James. So why couldn't he be like the other young men in the camp? For that matter, why couldn't he be more like his brother?

If Sarah had her eyes on Eric, then both Emma and Hannah had decided that Olaf was the one for them. They flirted with him shamelessly and he reveled in it. He lit up at the sight of them and stayed that way until they parted again. In fact, the two of them had been so encouraged by his response, that they were now beginning to speculate about him as a possible husband. Through all of this, Ingrid said little.

The older sister in Maggie tried to laugh that off, but she finally faced the fact that these two were not girls but young women. Emma had just turned sixteen on board ship, but Ingrid and Hannah would both be seventeen in a few months. Though Olaf might be a year or two away from marriageable age, seventeen was the most common age for young girls in Utah to marry, according to the missionaries.

For a time Maggie worried that having both of them falling for Olaf would create a strain between them, but like Sarah and Maggie, Hannah and Emma were far too close to each other for that. Instead, they simply began to talk about the possibility of Olaf's having two wives. As for who would be first wife, they hit upon a unique solution. They would marry him simultaneously and share first-wife status between them.

Maggie sighed, pulling herself back to what was going on. If she knew how to help Sarah in this matter she would, but she did not. She turned to watch. Eric was still reading. They were in the book of Mosiah.

" 'And it came to pass,' " he read slowly, " 'that there was a man among them whose name was—' " He stopped, leaning over his book more closely. His finger came up to touch the word. "A—," he started, pronouncing it with the same vowel sound as *apple.* "A-bin—"

Maggie wagged a finger at Sarah, warning her not to jump in and help him too quickly. Olaf and Ingrid, reading from Hannah's copy, were likewise peering at the page. Ingrid's lips moved as she experimented too, but she said nothing.

"A-bin-AHD-ee."

"We say it A-BIN-a-dye," Sarah said, smiling at him.

"A-BIN-a-dye?"

"Yes," Maggie and Sarah said together.

His eyes never lifted from the paper. "Say again, please."

"A-BIN-a-dye," Maggie said slowly. "The second syllable is stressed. How do you say it when you read it in Danish?"

He flashed her a sheepish grin. "Ah-bin-AHD-ee. But vee—*we,*" he quickly corrected himself. "We were not sure how to say it." He cocked his head, as though listening to himself. "A-BIN-a-dye."

"Yes, that's it," Maggie said. "Good."

"A-BIN-a-dye," Ingrid and Olaf said together.

"Good." Maggie stepped forward and shut the book. "That's enough reading for now. Before we end class, I would like to teach you a song."

"We learn music?" Olaf said. "That is good."

"This is a song you have not heard before. A man who was here in Iowa City with one of the earlier companies wrote it especially for us handcart people. Brother Spencer came by our tent last night and shared it with Sister James. I think you will like it."

"What is this song?" Eric asked.

"It's called 'The Handcart Song.' "

" 'Handcart Song'?" Ingrid repeated. "This will be good for us, since soon we pull handcarts too, no?"

"Exactly," Maggie said. She reached in the pocket of her apron and pulled out five half sheets of paper. She handed one to each of the students and then one to Hannah and Emma, keeping one for her and Sarah to share. "Here are the words."

After Brother Spencer had left last night, Maggie had carefully printed out the words to the song on five separate pieces of paper. She wanted them to be able to read them for themselves. "Let's read the words together first, and then Sarah and I will sing it for you."

Sarah jerked around. Maggie hadn't thought about doing that until this moment. She just smiled. Sarah had a clear, sweet voice, and the two of them loved to sing the songs of Zion together at worship services. On board ship they had often sung to Sarah's younger brothers and sisters to get them to sleep. Sarah immediately nodded. "All right."

"But let's read it through first. I didn't write down all the stanzas—the verses—but just a few of my favorites. Sarah, will you lead us? Let's all read together. Slowly the first time."

Sarah scooted closer to Maggie and looked at the paper. "All right. Everyone ready."

They read in unison a lot in class now and were getting better at it all the time. As the Scandinavians read with Sarah, Maggie heard them stumble on a word here and there, but they made it through. When they finished she looked at them. "Any questions?"

After a moment Eric pointed at a word. "What is CHORE-us."

"It's pronounced KOR-us," Maggie said. "It's the part that we sing after each verse."

That seemed to be the only question. Maggie waited for a moment, and when they all looked up, she stood up. "All right, Sarah, let's teach them the song." She looked at her students. "The melody is an old Scottish song. Or at least we had it in Scotland. You may recognize it."

They moved together and linked arms. Then Maggie hummed a pitch. "Okay?"

Sarah nodded and they began.

> Ye Saints that dwell on Europe's shores,
> Prepare yourselves with many more
> To leave behind your native land
>   For sure God's Judgments are at hand.
> Prepare to cross the stormy main
> Before you do the valley gain
> And with the faithful make a start
>   To cross the plains with your handcart.

"Okay," Maggie said quickly. "Here's the chorus." She motioned with her hand for Hannah and Emma to join in. They did, smiling and singing in full voice.

> Some must push and some must pull
> As we go marching up the hill,
> As merrily on the way we go
> Until we reach the valley, oh.

"All right," Maggie said. "Have you got it?"

"I like that song," Ingrid said.

"Then let's try it together."

"What means 'the valley, oh'?" Olaf asked.

Emma answered. "It's talking about the Salt Lake Valley. The 'oh' is just a way to emphasize something. It's like saying, '*Oh*, that's wonderful. We will be merry when we reach the valley. *Oh!*' "

"Oh," Olaf said. Then he realized what he'd done and they all laughed together.

Maggie raised her hand again. "All right, second verse. We'll sing it. You try and follow along as best you can. Then we'll all join in on the chorus."

With everyone singing the chorus, it became a little ragged, but they sang it lustily and with enthusiasm. Having the four girls singing along with them helped the students. Maggie was surprised to hear that both Olaf and Eric had clear tenor voices. When they finished the chorus, the four sisters clapped heartily.

"All right, everyone, here's the next verse," Maggie announced. "Sing along if you can, but come in on the chorus for sure."

> But ere before the valley gained
> We will be met upon the plains
> With music sweet and friends so dear
> And fresh supplies our hearts to cheer.

Then with the music and the song,
How cheerfully we'll march along
So thankfully you make a start
  To cross the plains with our handcarts.

Eric and Olaf and Ingrid were following along, humming snatches, heads bobbing.

"All right," Sarah called out. "Everybody now."

Some must push and some must pull
  As we go marching up the hill,
As merrily—

"Sarah. Emma."

They turned in surprise. Jane James was walking swiftly toward them, waving her hand for them to stop.

Sarah stepped away from the others and toward her mother. "What is it, Mama?"

She came up, a little out of breath. "There is good news, Sarah."

"What?"

"The next company has just arrived in Iowa City."

"The next company?" Maggie said.

"Yes! Remember? There was one more ship leaving after ours. They were led by Elder Edward Martin."

"Oh, yes," Sarah said. "And they're here?"

"Yes. And you'll never guess who's with them."

"Who?"

"Elizabeth Jackson!"

Both Emma and Sarah exclaimed as one, "Really?"

Jane turned to Hannah and Maggie. "Elizabeth Jackson is a dear friend of the family. She and her husband, Aaron, and three children were going to go with us on our ship, but there wasn't room. They had to wait for the next one."

"And she's here now?" Sarah said.

"That's what Elder Spencer said. The group is staying in town tonight, just as we did that first night we arrived. I'm going in to Iowa City to try and find them."

"Is Papa going?" Sarah asked.

"No, he'll stay with the children. He says that you and Emma can come in with me if you'd like." She looked at Maggie and Hannah. "And your mother said you can come too."

Maggie nodded, then suddenly remembered her class. She turned to them, but the three Scandinavians had already understood most of what had been said. "It's all right," Eric said. "We shall stay here and practice the song. Then tomorrow we shall sing to you."

"Wonderful," Maggie said, laughing at his enthusiasm. "Thank you."

Fortunately, it was half past eight by the time the five women reached the cavernous roundhouse where the engines were turned around and sent back east across the railway line. Many of the children had already been put to bed, and that made the job of finding the Aaron Jackson family a little easier.

Aaron Jackson and his wife, Elizabeth, were younger than Maggie had expected. She had assumed they were closer in age to Brother and Sister James, who were in the mid-forties. But Sister Jackson was closer to thirty, Maggie guessed, and her husband only a year or two older than that. They had three children—girls seven and almost five, and a boy, named after his father, who was two. Young Aaron was asleep in his father's arms, and the senior Jackson seemed to have no inclination to put him to bed just yet.

Brother Jackson peppered the four girls with questions about Iowa City while his wife and Jane James celebrated their unexpected reunion. Sarah and Emma were drawn into the conversation with the two women, so Brother Jackson made it his task to speak with Maggie and Hannah. He wanted to know when they had come, how long they had been there, why they hadn't left as yet, how many handcarts they had yet to build, when they would be leaving.

As they answered as best they could, Maggie kept letting her eyes sweep across the crowded building. How grateful she was that this wasn't their first night in Iowa City! If all went well they would be leaving within the week. Then she straightened, staring at the back of a man fussing over a little girl with thick dark curls. "Excuse me, Brother Jackson," she broke in, "but isn't that Brother John Jaques?"

He turned, then nodded immediately. "Yes. Do you know Brother Jaques?"

"Not really. We saw him back at Liverpool as we were checking in to board the ship. Brother James told us about him. He was an editor at the *Millennial Star,* right?"

"That's correct. And a very good one too."

Now Hannah remembered. "He's the one who wrote that letter to his father that was published in the *Star.*"

"His father-in-law, actually. James Loader. Yes, that's the same Brother Jaques. In fact, we were berthed close together, our two families. We have become quite dear friends."

His wife turned. "Who is that, dear?"

"The Jaqueses."

Jane James looked surprised. "He's here?"

"Yes," Emma answered. "Right over there."

"Speaking of James Loader," Brother Jackson went on, "you'll never believe what happened tonight."

"Oh, yes," Elizabeth Jackson said. "This is wonderful. You know the story about the letters?"

"Yes," Hannah said. "We just mentioned them, in fact."

"Well," Brother Jackson went on, "while we were getting settled for the night, Patience Loader showed up looking for John and his wife."

"The Loaders are *here?*" Sister James exclaimed.

"Yes. I guess they just got here yesterday on a train from New

York. Brother and Sister Jaques were stunned. As far as they knew, the family was not coming west this year."

"But they are?" Maggie asked. "By handcart?"

"Evidently," Aaron Jackson said. "That's what Patience told them. John's wife went with Patience to join the family. Their baby, little Flora, was so tired that John stayed here with her. But tomorrow they'll all be together again."

"So Brother Jaques's letter made them change their mind?" Maggie asked, interested that someone else who had strong feelings about not coming had experienced a change of heart.

"I suppose," Sister Jackson said. "They're here and preparing to join us in the handcart company."

"Well, well," Jane James said. "So Brother Jaques's letter did some good." Then she shook her head ruefully. "I'll bet there will be some interesting conversations in the Loader tent tomorrow."

Then Maggie had another thought. "Why didn't the Jaqueses look for the Loaders when you came through New York?"

"Because we came through Boston," Aaron replied.

"Oh." Then, thoughtfully, she said one more thing. "I wish I could meet this Brother Loader."

Jane James looked at her in surprise. "Why is that, Maggie?"

"Because when I finally read Brother Jaques's letter, I decided that Brother Loader must not have much faith." Her mouth pulled down. "I judged a man whom I had never met. Now it sounds like I was wrong."

II

Saturday, 12 July 1856

Maggie, Sarah, Emma, Hannah, and Ingrid Christensen were down by the river. They had come to do the laundry, but that had been finished over an hour ago. Generally on Saturday the Church agents left the day free so that the people could catch up on personal items such as laundry, mending, and such. Ingrid, who had now been in the same tent as the McKensie and the James families for almost two weeks, was just as much a part of their families as the other four. Now that the wash was stretched out across the bushes to dry, they lay back on the grassy bank, staring up through the canopy of leaves at the clouds above them. As usual, it only took a few minutes before the conversation turned to love, romance, courtship, and marriage. Maggie didn't mind, really, as she would have in the early weeks on the ship. It drew the five of them closer together and provided a welcome escape from the daily drudgery of sewing tents, drying meat, gathering berries, cooking, doing laundry, or tending children. At the moment the conversation had turned to Olaf Pederson, with Emma and Hannah doing most of the talking.

"It's much too soon," Emma James said coyly. "He's only sixteen. You know, he had his birthday on board ship just like I did."

"But," Hannah came right back, "by next summer, when we're settled in our new homes, we'll all be seventeen then."

Sarah gave Maggie a quick look, her eyes mischievous, then spoke to her sister. "Emma, what if Olaf and Eric are sent off to colonize one of the new settlements while our family stays in Great Salt Lake City?"

Emma turned in surprise, a frown creasing her brow. "Do you think they will be?"

Maggie decided to join Sarah in teasing these two dreamers with stars in their eyes. A little touch of reality might be good for the both of them. "Elder Ahmanson told me that many of the Scandinavians are going down south about a hundred miles in an area they call Sanpete Valley. There are several new settlements there named after scriptural figures–Moroni, Manti, Ephraim."

"But–," Hannah started, then saw through what they were doing. "They're just trying to get a reaction from us, Emma."

But Maggie shook her head. "There is more to it than just teasing you, you know," she said. "President Young wants to colonize the whole Great Basin. The chances of our families ending up in the same place as Olaf is not very high."

The two girls exchanged a look of dismay. "Then we'll just have to marry him before he gets sent away somewhere."

"So it is *we* now for sure?" Sarah teased.

The two of them instantly blushed, looking at each other from beneath lowered brows, but they didn't revise their statement. "We can work it out," Hannah said archly.

Now Sarah got suddenly wistful. "I suppose if it were the right man," she said, "being the second wife wouldn't make that much difference. Especially if you really loved the first wife as your sister in the gospel."

Maggie turned, trying not to look surprised. Did Sarah feel *that* strongly about Eric? There was no question but that it was about Eric that she was thinking. So she knew she didn't stand much chance with him. So she was willing to—

Sarah had seen Maggie's look. She sat up and folded her arms around her knees. "Well, if you believe the principle was given by God through Joseph Smith, then it shouldn't make any difference, should it? I mean, otherwise you'd be saying that the second or the third wife wasn't as important as the first, wouldn't you? And I don't believe that."

Ingrid sat up too, but she was looking at the ground. "I would be willing to be the third wife," she said softly.

"I guess in a way Sarah's right," Emma started to say. Then suddenly she stopped and spun around to stare at Ingrid. Hannah was gaping too. Ingrid's cheeks were deep red and she wouldn't look up.

Maggie began to nod slowly. *I thought so.* Now that she was staying in their tent, Ingrid was almost always around when Emma and Hannah fantasized about Olaf. Maggie had noticed her turn away or look down and not say anything at those times. And why not? She was sixteen too, actually a few months older than Emma. She simply hadn't dared say anything before.

"You like Olaf too?" Hannah said slowly, her eyes wide with wonder.

Ingrid's head bobbed. Her entire face was scarlet now.

Hannah and Emma looked at each other, and for a moment Maggie was afraid they were going to say something that would deeply wound their new friend. But then Hannah sat up and moved over beside Ingrid. She put an arm around her and hugged her tightly. "Maybe they'll let all three of us be number one," she said softly. "If not, I'll be number three."

Maggie had to look away, for suddenly tears sprang to her eyes. Since their baptism, she and Hannah had talked about the possibility that they might be taken in plural marriage some day. Maggie had prayed mightily about the principle of plural marriage as part of her seeking for the truthfulness of the Church. No direct answer came, but she did get a powerful witness that Joseph Smith was God's prophet and seer. It followed, therefore, that since he had taught the principle, it had to be from God. But that still hadn't made it easy to accept. She knew now that in the back recesses of her mind, one of the reasons she had been glad that she would be marrying James MacAllister was that he was not a member of the Church. Since only the most faithful of the brethren were ever allowed to take other wives, it seemed like the perfect solution.

Hannah, in the height of her developing womanhood, had been even more troubled by the question, though outwardly she had avowed that she could accept the principle if ever asked to live it. But more than once she had quietly expressed the hope that her future husband would not be one of the small number of brethren who were asked to live plural marriage. It was only about twenty-five percent of the men who did so; that left a pretty good chance that she wouldn't have to worry about it. So now to have her so openly embrace the possibility because of her love for these two friends touched Maggie so profoundly that she could not stop from wanting to weep. As much as she loved Sarah and as close as they had become, Maggie still wasn't sure she could share a husband with another, even Sarah. Would she ever be able to put aside the fear that she, Maggie, would always be the plain one in her husband's sight? that Sarah would be the more loved because of her beauty and sweetness? She pulled a face. Sweetness was not Maggie's strongest quality. Now, if you were looking for a good streak of stubbornness mingled with a talent for tartness . . . She sighed. Even as she recognized the depth of her feelings for Sarah, she couldn't readily consider sharing a husband with her.

"Maggie?"

They all jumped as though a rifle had just been fired in their midst. Whirling, they saw Eric and Olaf coming through the trees towards them, now just a few yards away. They leaped to their feet, brushing at their skirts. Sarah's hand was at her mouth, her eyes wide. She half turned so that her back was toward them. "Did they hear us?" she mouthed.

Maggie shook her head. "I don't think so," she whispered, but even as she spoke she was desperately trying to remember the last thing that had been said.

"Oh, what if they did?" Emma wailed softly. "I'll never be able to look Olaf in the face again."

Maggie could feel the rush of blood to her cheeks. Emma was right. If they had heard, even the tiniest bit, it was too horrible to contemplate. Then she glanced at her three friends and her sister and laughed out loud. Hannah and Emma and Ingrid were trying to look nonchalant, but their faces looked more as if Eric and Olaf had somehow walked in on them when they were dressed only in their petticoats.

"Hello," Olaf cried. "What are you doing?"

Sarah recovered most quickly. She hadn't said anything for long enough that she felt she was safe. "Laundry," she admitted.

Eric hooted. "Lying down?"

Maggie laughed too. "We have to watch it carefully to make sure it dries well."

The brothers pushed through the bushes and joined them now. Eric became serious again. "There is meeting."

"Oh?"

He nodded. "Your mother and Sister James asked us to find you." He looked at Ingrid. "I told your uncle you would be with them too."

"Brother Willie said all should come," Olaf added.

Maggie looked at the laundry drying on the bushes around them. "How soon?"

Both brothers looked blank. "How soon?" Olaf echoed. "What is meaning that?"

"How soon means when does the meeting start?"

"Ah." Eric understood now. "Very soon. Come now. Is at Elder Spencer's wagon. They will make group lists now."

"Really?" Maggie said in surprise. She felt her heart leap. The Church agents had been talking now for several days about being almost ready for departure. If they were ready to make up the company roster, that was a very good sign. "Is it for everyone?"

"Including the new people?" Sarah asked in surprise.

Now Eric shook his head. "No. Only Elder Willie's people."

That made more sense, Maggie thought. The second group of emigrants under the direction of Brother Edward Martin which had arrived in Iowa City four days before were now all at the Mormon campground. Like their own company, the second group had plunged into the Herculean task of getting a full company of handcarts ready.

"All right," Maggie said. "Tell our mothers we'll be right there as soon as we get the laundry folded."

Eric nodded and both he and Olaf turned and walked away, talking easily with each other.

Hannah sank back down to the earth. "What if Olaf heard us, Maggie? What will we do?"

She laughed, sure now that if the Pedersons had overheard anything she would have seen it in their eyes. "Well, you know," she said lightly, "if you three are going to marry him, someday *he* is going to have to be told too."

Chapter Notes

"The Handcart Song," which Maggie has her class sing in the novel, was written by John Daniel Thompson McAllister. The complete lyrics are found in Hafen and Hafen, *Handcarts to Zion,* pp. 272–73.

The shipload of emigrants that was led by Edward Martin and that sailed on the ship *Horizon* left Liverpool on 25 May 1856, approximately three weeks after the Willie group had left. They arrived in Boston on 28 June and came by rail and steamer to Iowa City, arriving there on 8 July (see Turner, *Emigrating Journals,* pp. 82–87; Bell, *Life History and Writings of John Jacques,* pp. 83–87, 95–101).

The family of **Aaron and Elizabeth Jackson** are actual people. Elizabeth Horrocks was born in Cheshire, England, in 1826. Her father was one of those converted by the early missionaries to England. Elizabeth joined the Church at age fifteen, about a year after her parents were converted. She married Aaron Jackson of Derbyshire, England, in 1848. They had their three children with them as they set out for Zion in 1856: Martha Ann, who was seven; Elizabeth, who would turn five on the trail; and Aaron, who was two (see Kingsford, *Leaves from the Life of Elizabeth Horrocks Jackson Kingsford,* pp. 1–2).

John Jaques, who was introduced in chapter 4, was part of the company who arrived in Iowa City on 8 July. He was traveling with his wife, Zilpah, and their two-year-old daughter, Flora, and with Zilpah's unmarried sister, Tamar Loader. To their utter surprise, the Jaqueses found the Loader family waiting for them when they arrived.

Based on the two letters that were published in the *Millennial Star* (see the notes for chapter 4), one might easily conclude that James Loader's faith was wavering somewhat. From an account written by Patience later, it is evident that perhaps Jaques had misjudged his father-in-law. On arriving in New York the previous winter, James Loader had found work as a gardener in New York City and seems to have been making a good living at it. The Loaders decided they would go by wagon train to Utah once the rest of the family arrived and they had earned enough money to buy a wagon and team. Then they learned about the plan to go by handcart, and that's when Patience wrote to her brother-in-law. She continues the story:

> We were still waiting further orders from Liverpool before we made any move to leave New York.
>
> One day Brother Stenhouse [T.B.H. Stenhouse, who was serving with President John Taylor in New York City] came from President Taylor's office. He said, "Do you know that your name is in the Millennial Star, Brother Loader? You are thought to be apostatizing from the Church. It says that Father Loader, has brought his family out of one part of Babylon and now wants to settle down in another part of Babylon." This hurt my poor father's feelings very much. He said to mother, "I cannot stand to be accused of apostacy. I will show them better. Mother, I am going to Utah. I will pull the handcart if I die on the road." We all knew if our father said he would go that we would all have to go for he would never leave any of us in New York. . . . We all gave notice to quit work and got ready to leave New York on the third of July 1856. (In Bell, *Life History and Writings of John Jaques*, pp. 92–93)

Patience says that she and her family had been in the camp at Iowa City a "few days" when her sisters and brother-in-law arrived. However, if she is correct that they didn't leave New York until 3 July, and knowing that the Martin Company arrived in Iowa City on 8 July, it is more likely that the Loaders had arrived just the day before the Jaqueses, as is shown here.

Though the Church began the practice of plural marriage in Nauvoo while Joseph Smith was still alive, it was not taught publically until 1852. In our day it has become popular in drama and literature to depict the early sister Saints as viewing the principle as abhorrent, something they accepted only under duress. While undoubtedly many found it so, the journals and histories of that time clearly show that many women accepted the principle as having been given by revelation. They willingly (not begrudgingly) accepted the practice. In many cases they saw it as a blessing to them personally as well as to the Church. Some record that the love and the companionship of their sister wives were of sublime and profound importance to them. Thus, while some readers may think it unbelievable that young single women would so easily accept the possibility of plural marriage as Maggie, Sarah, Emma, Hannah, and Ingrid do in this chapter, the records of some of the early sister Saints exhibit that very kind of openness to the principle.

CHAPTER 9

IOWA CITY, IOWA

I

Saturday, 12 July 1856

"Brothers and Sisters." There was a strong breeze blowing and Brother Daniel Spencer had to speak loudly in order to be heard. The people were crowded in tightly around him. "Those of you who came over on the *Thornton* with Brother Willie have been here just over two weeks now. You have worked hard. We now have enough tents and handcarts for your company. More than you need, in fact. The extra ones will be given to Brother Martin's group and will hopefully lessen the time they will have to be here.

"Your company, which will actually be the fourth company of the season, will be leaving very shortly. About five hundred of you have been assigned to that company." He motioned, and Brother Willie stepped forward, climbing up to stand beside him.

"Brother James G. Willie has been asked to serve as captain of the fourth company."

The group nodded. Willie was not only greatly respected but also widely liked by the people.

"As his subcaptains of hundreds, we have asked the following to serve." He looked down at five men waiting beside the wagon. "Brother Millen Atwood, first hundred." Atwood stepped forward and raised an arm. "Brother Levi Savage, second hundred." The missionary who had been sent to Siam and was finally on his way home moved up beside Atwood. "Brother William Woodward, third hundred. That hundred will include most of you who are from Scotland." There was a smattering of applause from the Scottish contingent. Brother Woodward grinned and waved a hand at them. "Brother John Chislett will captain the fourth hundred"—again he let the man step forward—"and John, or Johan, Ahmanson will lead the fifth hundred. The Scandinavians will be in Brother Ahmanson's group, of course."

As the tall Dane translated that quickly for his group, there were murmurs of satisfaction and mild applause. They were pleased to be led by one of their own. Brother Spencer went right on. "We have now made the assignments to the five groups of hundreds. Within each group there will be five people per handcart, which means twenty handcarts per hundred on the average. There will be four handcarts per tent, five tents per hundred. Your handcart group will also be your 'mess group,' or the group you cook and eat with. As much as possible, we have kept families together.

"Now, brothers and sisters," he said, "we have to get ready to leave. As you were told before you ever left Europe, handcarts are limited in how much they can carry. For now you will only have to carry your own personal belongings. The tents, flour, tools, and other foodstuffs will be carried in the five wagons that will accompany you. At Florence, Nebraska, that will change, but for now the lighter loads will give you a chance to toughen up, to get into physical shape before we start out across the wilderness. When you leave Florence you will each have to carry an additional hundred pounds of flour in the cart, or you will not have enough to see you through to the point where we meet the supply wagons from the Valley."

"And where is that?" someone called out.

Spencer turned. "Generally the first wagons meet us at Deer Creek, west of Fort Laramie. That's roughly about five hundred miles from here. Then more meet us at Fort Bridger, and so on." He waited for a moment, but that seemed to satisfy whoever had spoken up, so he went on.

"We have tacked copies of the group lists on both sides of the wagons, and a copy is also pinned on the outside wall of my tent. As soon as we dismiss here, please see which group you are in. We will ask that by tonight you move your things and join together in your new tent groups. The lists also show the tent groups and handcart assignments."

He looked down at the five subcaptains and spoke directly to them. "Brethren, Brother Webb has all of the handcarts down at the cart assembly area. This afternoon take enough men to bring back the handcarts you need for each hundred."

As they nodded, he spoke loudly to the group once more. "Beginning in one hour, Brother Kimball, Brother Grant, and I will come to your tents, where you are now—don't bother trying to move until tonight. We want you waiting outside with all your personal belongings. Each of us will have a set of scales to weigh what you plan to take with you and—"

A great groan went up and he had to stop. He let it roll through the group, then finally raised his hands. "Seventeen pounds, brothers and sisters. That's for each adult. Ten pounds for children. Seven pounds for infants. You were told this before you ever left Europe, so let's hope you have already made many of those hard decisions." He didn't sound very hopeful.

"If you have more than you can take—" He stopped and shook his head. "*When* you see that you have more than you can take, you can go into Iowa City and see if you can trade or sell the surplus to the residents. But don't get your hopes up. They have already seen three previous companies go through, and though I am sad to admit it, they know that once you leave they can come in and, at no cost to them, get those things which you will abandon."

He looked around. "That's it, brothers and sisters. One hour in front of your tents. Seventeen pounds per person. Not one ounce more."

As Eric and Olaf moved to the last wagon to check their list, they saw Jens Nielson pushing his way back out of the crowd. With his height, he was easily seen. He towered over many others in the company. Eric pulled on Olaf's arm and started for him, but Brother Nielson had already spotted them. "Eric! Olaf!" he called. "You are in this group."

As he pushed his way clear of the group, they saw that he had Elsie with him, holding her hand and making a way for her through the people. His wife was so short—barely five feet tall, if that—that she had been lost to them before that. She saw the boys and waved happily. "Wonderful news. Guess what!" she called, smiling broadly.

"Are we still in your tent group?" Eric said, hoping that such was the case but afraid they would be assigned elsewhere.

"Better," she said, as they came up. She reached out and took Eric's hands and squeezed them. "Not only are you and Olaf in our tent group, but you have been assigned to *our* handcart."

"Truly?" Olaf said.

"Yes." Jens clapped him on the shoulder. "I guess since we have two small children they decided we could use some help."

"This is wonderful," Elsie said. "Little Jens and Bodil will be so pleased. And to have someone who can speak English now right with us. It is very good."

"We too are pleased," Eric said earnestly. "This is more than we hoped for."

"Far more," Olaf agreed.

The two brothers started back with the Nielsons. There was no need for them to check the list now. "Then we'd better go and get our things ready for the weight check," Eric said. He grimaced. "That could be more painful than the blisters we got while making the handcarts."

As they made their way, they passed the other groups congregating around the wagons. People called out to each other. There were cries of delight and groans of disappointment as friendships made during the last two months were placed together or split apart. Then Olaf pointed. "Look, there are the McKensies and the Jameses up ahead of us." He raised a hand and shouted. "Sister McKensie! Brother James!"

The two families all turned, waved, and stopped while the brothers came up to join them.

"What group are you in, Olaf?" Hannah asked.

"The five hundred."

"You mean the *fifth* hundred?" she suggested.

"Ah, yah, the fifth hundred. And you?"

"We are in the third hundred," Robbie said. "Brother Woodward's our captain. Most of us from Scotland are in that group."

"And who–," Eric started. He searched for the right words. "Who will be on your tent?"

Sarah smiled. "*In* our tent, Eric. We sleep *on* the ground but *in* a tent."

He nodded sheepishly. They had worked on prepositions in class for several days now, but they were a bewildering whirl in his mind. Or was it *on* his mind?

"The James family and our family get to stay together," Mary McKensie said. "We're still assigned to the same tent. Ingrid too. Isn't that wonderful? She'll get to travel with us."

Brother James was nodding. "Even with both families and Ingrid, we aren't quite enough to fill it, so there will be another family assigned with us when we get ready to leave. We don't know who yet."

Mary smiled. "We wish they would let you and Olaf stay with us as well. Ingrid's English has really improved since she's started staying with us."

Eric shook his head slowly, his eyes grave. "That would not be good."

Surprised, Jane James leaned forward. "Why not?" Then she thought she understood. "Oh, because there would be single young men and single young girls in the same tent?"

"No, much worse."

"Worse? How so?" Mary asked. Now the girls were watching him closely too, puzzled by his somberness.

"In your tent," he said slowly, glancing sidelong at Maggie and Sarah, "there vill be–" He shook his head. Pronouncing the *w* as a *v* was one of the hardest habits to break. "There will be no sleep, yah?"

Mary looked up in surprise. "No sleep? Why not?"

He turned his back on the girls in a conspiratorial manner, then lifted his hands and moved his fingers in a motion that was like a duck's bill opening and closing. "How you say in English? Yakkity yak. Yakkity yak."

William James whooped and slapped his leg in delight. The girls howled. "Eric Pederson!" Maggie cried, hardly believing she had heard him right.

" 'Tis true, no?" Eric said to her mother, still ignoring the girls, who were just coming to realize that he was poking fun at them.

"Oh, yes, Eric," Mary said ruefully. "You're exactly right. These five girls can laugh and giggle all night long."

"Don't tell them I say that," he said soberly. "They will be much angered at me."

"I think it's a little late for that now," Maggie said, trying to look offended but unable to contain her own laughter. His droll manner had once again taken her completely by surprise.

After a moment, when they got more serious again, Olaf looked at Brother James. "Do your family get two handcarts?"

"Yes. Two. Sarah and Emma and Reuben will pull the one, Mother and I will take the other."

Sister James spoke up again. "And since there are five of us who are older, Brother Willie says we can help Mary and her family some days."

"We won't need help," Robbie said calmly. "I'm big enough to pull."

"True, Rob," Brother James said, "but since Brother Spencer asked you to stand guard duty, there may be some days that you'll be out doing other things."

"Oh." That seemed to satisfy him. "In that case, yes. Mother and the girls could use some help."

Maggie and Eric exchanged a look and a smile. "Mother and the girls." Robbie spoke as if he were the one who was nineteen and Maggie was only twelve.

"What about you two?" Sarah asked. "Will you be with that family you came on the ship with?"

"The Nielsons?" Olaf said. "Yes. We are in same tent and we also help them pull the handcart."

"That's good," Mary said. "Don't they just have two children?"

"Yes," Eric answered. "Little Jens, who is five, and Bodil Mortensen, who is only nine. They will need help and we are very happy. They are like our family now."

"Ingrid will help us pull our two carts," Reuben James said. Though he was two years younger than the Danish girl, he and Ingrid had become great friends since she had moved into their tent.

"Very good," Eric said.

"Well," Brother James said to his wife. "We have less than an hour. We'd better get our things together."

"Yah," Olaf responded. "We go to prepare for the weights too." He pulled such a face that everyone laughed.

Sister James sighed. "I think we are all in for a very long afternoon."

—❦—

"Do you think we have too much, Eric?"

Eric looked at the meager pile before him on their bedroll. They were outside the tent where the Nielsons and the others slept. Whenever the weather was clear, Eric and Olaf slept outside. Now they had their things piled up neatly. The sweater his mother had knitted for him was folded on top. After a moment he shook his head. "We don't have much, Olaf, and thank goodness for that."

Olaf slid his hand under his pile and hefted the whole thing, bouncing it up and down to gauge the weight. "It doesn't feel like a lot. I think we'll be all right."

"Remember, you have to count the bedding too."

Olaf pulled a face at that, then set his stack on top of the folded blankets. Then he picked all of it up this time. His confidence was clearly shaken. "Are you going to leave Mama's sweater behind if you have too much?"

Eric instantly shook his head. "No. I'll leave something else. We are going to need Mama's sweaters this winter when we get to Utah." He didn't have to say that this was the only real tie the two of them had to their parents now.

Olaf seemed much relieved. "Good."

There was a shout from behind them and they both stood up. Picking up their things, they walked around to the front of the tent. Brother Ahmanson was there with Brother George D. Grant, one of the Church agents. Grant carried a scale with large weighing pans in one hand and a box of weights in the other. It was time.

In an unplanned but unanimous decision, the Pederson boys were chosen to go first. Olaf placed his stack of belongings on one side of the scales. It clunked to the ground heavily. Then Elder Grant took out the metal weights. On went a ten-pounder. Olaf's pile began to lift, but not high enough. Grant put on a five-pound block, but that was too much. Now the side with the weights dropped lower. He took off the five, added a three. Not quite. He added a one-pounder, and as everyone smiled in surprise, the two sides slowly balanced each other.

"Very good," Brother Grant said. "Fourteen pounds."

Eric was next. He too was under, coming in at a little over fifteen pounds. He breathed a great sigh of relief and looked at the Nielsons. "Now you have an example to follow," he said with a laugh.

"All right, folks," Grant said, looking up at the others who stood around them. "Who's next?"

Jens Nielson stepped forward, raising his hand. He spoke in Danish to Brother Ahmanson. "Can we count all of us together?" he asked.

Ahmanson turned to Brother Grant. "They would like to know if the whole family can be counted together."

Grant nodded immediately. This wasn't the first time he had been asked that. "Seventeen pounds for each adult, ten for each of the two children. That's fifty-four pounds total."

Ahmanson told Jens, and so he gathered everything up into bundles that would fit on the pans. When they were done, again Elder Grant was pleased. They were two pounds under, thanks largely to the fact that little Jens had very little of his own.

"Excellent," Grant grunted, shaking Jens's hand. "Wish everyone would do this well."

Maggie looked up in surprise. Across the tent from her, Ingrid was holding what looked like a brand-new pair of shoes. They were in her lap and she was rubbing the black leather gently with the tips of her fingers.

"Are those new?" Maggie asked.

Ingrid turned in surprise. Then nodded and smiled. Maggie smiled back. How she loved Ingrid's smile! It made her whole face light up. Combined with her blond hair braided in a French braid at the back of her head and the crystal-clear blue eyes, she was the perfect representation of Scandinavia, Maggie decided.

"Yah," Ingrid said, "deese were—" She stopped. "Not deese. How you say it again?"

Emma and Hannah, who slept in the same bedroll, stopped what they were doing to watch now too. "These," Emma supplied.

"Ah, yah. These shoes were given to me by my father as present."

"When you left Denmark?" Maggie asked.

"Yah. He and Mother very sad that I go before them. Father save his money and buy me new shoes."

Now Sarah turned around from what she was doing. "But we've never seen them until now, Ingrid. Have you not worn them before?"

She shook her head, holding them up so they could see them better. Sister James and Maggie's mother also stopped what they were doing to see them. "I decide . . ." It was obvious she was struggling to find the proper words to express herself. "I not want to see President Brigham Young in old shoes."

"Oh," Maggie said slowly.

"If wear them now, they be old by time we get to Salt Lake City, no?"

"Yes," Jane James said, her eyes softening. "They would be old and worn out."

"I want to meet President of the Church in new shoes." She held them against her body. "So I save them now."

Suddenly Reuben James had a thought. "What if you have too much stuff?" he asked. "What if you have to leave something behind? Will you leave your shoes?"

There was not a moment's hesitation. "No. I will leave more important things first. Not my shoes." She put them back in her valise and tucked them firmly into the corner.

"I think that's wonderful," Mary McKensie said quietly. "I wish we could all have new shoes when we enter the Valley."

And that turned Maggie back to her own dilemma. She had

known about the seventeen-pound limit before they ever left Scotland. She thought she had culled out everything that she could bear to leave behind. But now as she eyed the two stacks she had made—one for discard, one for taking—the one looked pitifully small, the other unbelievably large.

Taking a deep breath, she started through the larger stack one more time. Out went her favorite dress. She had bought it a year ago, one of the few times she had spent her wages on herself. It wasn't much in comparison to what she had seen other women wear, even some of those on the ship, but it represented almost half a month of standing at the cutting machine through the long midnight shifts at the factory. It had also been James's favorite. Every time she wore it he would compliment her.

With a sigh she pushed it behind her, where it would not lie there and tempt her. It was old-fashioned now anyway, she told herself. After a moment's hesitation she removed the shoes that went with it. These too were the nicest pair she owned, but they were little more than flimsy slippers with heels. Even if she saved them for that final day of the journey, as Ingrid was doing, they weren't suitable for walking out-of-doors for even half a block. Half closing her eyes, she tossed them over her shoulder onto the dress.

After another five minutes of agonizing, it came down to two things. There was the brass looking glass that James had given her for Christmas last year. She stared at herself, seeing the frustration around her mouth. It was not just that it was a gift from him. She had fully accepted the fact that James was gone from her life now. But she loved the mirror. Embossed in the brass on the back of it was the image of Edinburgh Castle, sitting majestically astride Castle Rock. Beneath it was the word *Dunedin,* the Gaelic name for Edinburgh. She had left the country that she loved. She had left the city that was all she had known for the first nineteen years of her life. Must she part with the only thing she now had left to remind her of her former home?

And yet . . . She laid the mirror down and picked up the plain wooden box. Her fingers moved to the key on the bottom. For a moment she was tempted to wind the key and open the lid, but then she decided against it. As soon as the strains of "Loch Lomond" came from the music box, every eye in the tent would turn to her. The others didn't know about this gift from her father, but her mother did. And Hannah did. And they would feel like they had to say something.

She started a little as she felt a hand on her shoulder. She turned to see Sarah kneeling beside her. "I think I am going to be under weight," she said, half whispering. "I could take one of those."

Maggie reached up and laid a hand on Sarah's, even as she shook her head. "I think I'm close. But thank you." She squeezed her hand, wishing there was some way to say more than that. In one simple sentence Sarah James had once again shown what she was, and Maggie would ever love her for it.

"Hang on to them both for now," Sarah suggested. "Then if you have to give one of them up, I'll take it for you."

"They are both gifts," Maggie said, as if that explained everything.

Sarah nodded. "I'll take whichever one you can't."

———

But in the end, Sarah could take neither.

As the two families lined up in front of their tent, Daniel Spencer and William H. Kimball nodded at the Jameses. "We're ready when you are."

"Can we count ourselves all together?"

Spencer nodded. "You can add your limits together if you wish. You have three adults—" He looked at Emma. "You're how old, Sister James?"

"Sixteen."

"Sorry. Only eighteen and above are adults. You'll have to consider her as a child."

William James nodded in discouragement. "Then we have three adults—that's fifty-one pounds—and seven children. That's seventy more."

With a sharp pang, Maggie suddenly thought of tiny Jane James, who had died on board ship. If she hadn't perished the family could take another seven pounds. How tragic that it came to that, she thought.

"So one hundred twenty-one pounds total," Brother Kimball said. He began setting up the scales. "You can divide it any way you wish, Brother James."

"I have another question. I have brought a shotgun with me to help provide food. I will share that food with others. Do I need to count that as part of my *personal* goods?"

The two agents looked at each other, and then Brother Spencer shook his head. "If you use it to provide food for the company, no. You can exclude that."

There was a sigh of relief. "Thank you."

As everyone watched intently, the first pile of stuff weighed in at twenty-two pounds. Their faces fell. Brother James had put their things in what he hoped would be eighteen- to twenty-pound piles.

The second pile was slightly smaller than the first, but it had some dishes and pictures that looked significantly heavier. When Brother Spencer put on the twenty-pound weight, it barely raised it off the ground. Maggie guessed it would have taken another five to balance it. She was wrong. It took only four.

"Sorry," Brother Kimball said. "That's forty-six pounds so far."

Jane James stared at the scales, her eyes stricken, her hand fumbling nervously at the seam on her dress. As her husband reached for another pile, her hand shot out. "Wait," she cried. She bent down and removed a crystal vase. She held it for a moment, her eyes looking right through it. "This was my grandmother's," she murmured. Then she moved back and set it on top of the pile of their discards. It saved her two pounds.

Even with the two of them removing stuff they had previously deemed to be absolutely essential, they still came in at one hundred thirty pounds—the equivalent of almost another child's full limit. *Almost what baby Jane's limit would have been*, Maggie thought, wondering if that had occurred to them.

Crestfallen, the family gathered together. The others looked away while they whispered together. It seemed obscene to watch while others laid their innermost souls out in the bright sunshine. After a moment they began to go through the stacks again piece by piece.

Out went the family Bible. Out went a small chest filled with something they had previously deemed of great value, though no one now said what it was. John James, who was four, began to weep when his toy wagon filled with carved wooden soldiers was emptied. The soldiers could stay for the ride, the wagon could not. The last to go, and at the dearest cost, was a small portrait of Jane James's grandfather that had been in their family for over fifty years.

Item by item they whittled away at their lives and cast it aside. After fifteen minutes a deeply sobered William Kimball looked up. "That puts you right on, Brother James."

William James nodded and turned to his wife. He put his arm around her and they walked away. Sarah stood slowly, looking down at what would be left behind now, then turned to Maggie. "I'm sorry," she whispered.

Maggie shook her head. "I know. It's all right."

Ingrid was next. Hannah helped her bring her pile of things out and balance them on the scale. Maggie saw that she had discarded her valise and had her things loose now. On the top were the new shoes.

Brother Kimball manipulated the weights with a practiced hand. "A little more than nineteen pounds. Sorry."

Ingrid gave the others a sour look and removed another dress. Up came the scales slightly. But it wasn't enough. She stared at the pile, as if she might reduce something into invisibility. Finally, with a deep sigh, she reached out and took off the shoes. The scales swung upward, the weights now a little lower than her belongings. "I'd say that's about sixteen and a half pounds," Brother Spencer said. "You probably could put the dress back on."

She did and they came into perfect balance. Barely glancing at them, Ingrid took the laces of her new shoes and tied them together. Then, surprising everyone, she slipped them over her head. "You have to weigh those too," Brother Kimball said gently.

"I carry." She looked to Maggie for help.

Maggie stepped closer and they whispered together for several seconds; then Maggie turned to the two agents.

"These were given to her as a birthday present from her father," she said. "She doesn't want to wear them on the trail. She wants to save them for when she first sees President Young. She says she will carry them herself."

Daniel Spencer looked suddenly very tired as he looked up at Ingrid. "You can't take them off later and put them on the cart," he warned.

"No," Ingrid said emphatically. "I carry to Salt Lake."

The two men looked at each other, and then Spencer shrugged. "As long as she understands the conditions, that's her choice."

"I understand," Ingrid said. She was beaming now.

"It's really been something," Brother Kimball said, standing up to stretch his legs for a moment. He was looking at Maggie's mother. "You see just about everything at these weigh-ins. I've seen people hold on to things that won't do them one bit of good, and leave things that could save their lives on the trail. I've seen husbands and wives not speak to each other for days afterwards. Children try to hide things from their parents.

"In the last company, Brother Spencer caught two sisters—literal sisters—trying to beat the limits. Their family was way over the allowance, and these two girls were largely responsible for it. They had a very substantial wardrobe. They excused themselves, supposedly to go off and discard their things, but half an hour later they came back."

Brother Spencer was nodding now. "I did a double take. It looked like the two of them had gained fifteen or twenty pounds in the half hour since they had been gone."

Maggie's hand went to her mouth. "They didn't!" she said.

"Didn't what?" Hannah said, not following yet.

"They did," Brother Spencer chuckled. "They went in their tent and put on two or three sets of clothing beneath what they were wearing."

"So what did you do?" Mary asked.

Now Kimball went on. "We could hardly keep a straight face. Here they were, like two stuffed pork chops, pouring sweat because it was a hot day outside. But we never said a word, just warned them that from time to time after they started, they would be weighed again."

"So they got away with it?" Hannah exclaimed in some dismay.

"Oh, for a little ways, yes. The morning the company left we weighed their things again, so they had no choice but to put all of it back on again. Then Brother Spencer and I rode along with the company for a time to make sure things were all right."

Brother Spencer slapped his leg in pure delight. "Wasn't any problem to follow their trail for about the first five miles," he said. "It was well marked with dresses and petticoats about every five or six hundred yards."

They all had a hearty laugh over that one. Then finally Brother Spencer turned back to Sister McKensie. "Well, I guess your family is next."

Robbie McKensie, who really had nothing other than his clothing and bedding, came in at nine pounds. Hannah was exactly on at ten pounds. Maggie's hopes soared. Then her mother came in six pounds over. An extra cooking pot and one more dress brought the scales down to one pound over. With Robbie, the family was now exactly where they needed to be.

Except for Maggie.

She held her breath as she picked up her stack of things and carefully placed it on the empty pan. Kimball already had put the ten-pound, the five-pound, and the two one-pound weights on the other pan. Gingerly she let the stack settle against the flat surface, then moved her hands away completely, realizing that nothing she could do would alter reality.

The scales reversed directions with a heavy thud. Now the pan with the weights swung slowly back and forth in the air. The other pan rested heavily on the ground.

Brother Spencer gave her a saddened look and reached for more weights. Maggie waved his hand away. She didn't care to know how much she was over. She had already made her decision. She reached for the handle of the looking glass and pulled it out from between her clothing.

For a moment she thought the scales might come in balance. The lower pan lifted for a moment, but then hung silently about an inch above the ground.

She stared at it, her face without expression of any kind. The music box was on the top of the pile and now seemed to loom as large as a chest of drawers. Quickly her eyes scanned the rest of the stack. She knew every single item there.

Maggie McKensie had been born into a family that was part of the working classes of Scotland. She had never known what some might call comfort. Then her father had died and the family faced a crisis. From that time until now Maggie had learned that sometimes decisions had to be made, no matter how unpleasant they might be. As her father had often said, "Postponing it only prolongs the pain."

Her shoulders lifted and fell, but without hesitation she reached out and took off the music box. Slowly the two scales changed position again. They did not come into perfect alignment, but the stack of her belongings was now only slightly lower than the pan with the weights. Brother Kimball nodded. "That's close enough," he said.

Maggie managed a smile and removed her things. She carried them back inside the tent, not looking at the pile of things beside the entrance. Later she would come back and put something over the music box so that the sun wouldn't bleach the wood.

Though Maggie McKensie determined not to brood over her loss as she went about her work for the rest of that day, one thought did keep creeping back again and again into her mind. Though mentally she knew it was foolish, emotionally she couldn't quite push it away.

Perhaps now I have sacrificed enough. My father. Edinburgh. James. My beloved Scotland. The only two things I ever owned that really mattered to me. Maybe finally it is enough.

Before nightfall, she would find out how wrong she was.

Mary McKensie was the first to see them. As the two families finished their evening meal around the cooking fire, she sat facing the river. All she could see from this point was the tops of the trees beyond a sea of tent tops, round and brilliant white in the afternoon sun. It still seemed strange to her that these huge tents, large enough to house twenty people, were circular and not square. She had asked why and been told they were easier to make that way, though no one could tell her how. But all were constructed from the same pattern. With the addition of the Edward Martin group a few days before, there were now more than a thousand people in camp. That meant well more than fifty tents in the camp. It was like a small town, though all the "buildings" were made of white drilling cloth.

The McKensie/James tent was pitched near the western edge of the camp at the end of a central corridor which served as the main thoroughfare through the temporary settlement. From this vantage point they could see all the way to the southeast part of camp, where the wagons were parked. That was where the four Church agents slept, and from there they governed the frantic pace of preparation. And it was from there, coming out from behind the wagons, that three men had appeared. She squinted a little but quickly recognized them. The sun was low in the sky and directly in their faces. It was Daniel Spencer, the leader of the Iowa Mormon Camp; James G. Willie, captain of their handcart company; and Johan Ahmanson, subcaptain of the fifth hundred, the hundred made up primarily of Scandinavians. They were coming swiftly, their heads down in earnest conversation.

Jane James, who sat beside Mary, noticed her watching and also looked up to see. After a moment she said, "They seem in a hurry. It must be something important."

The others turned to look now too. Then Brother James nodded. "We leave in three days. I think those poor brethren have something important weighing on them all the time now."

With Elder Ahmanson accompanying them, Mary half expected them to turn aside to where the fifth hundred was now camped. The Scandinavians were on the south side of camp about midway through. But they strode past those tents and kept coming towards Mary and the others. They were quiet now, and Mary could see that they were quite serious in demeanor.

With sudden intuition, Mary knew the leaders were coming to see them. And in that same instant she was filled with a vague sense of dread. Slowly she set her plate down on the stump and stood up. The others turned in surprise as she did so; then as they realized that the three men had their eyes fixed on them, they too stopped eating and watched.

"Good evening," Brother Spencer called as they approached.

"Good evening," William James replied. He stood and went forward to shake their hands. "Have you had your supper?"

"We have, thank you."

"Sorry to disturb yours," Captain Willie said, looking around and nodding in greeting.

"It's all right," Mary said. "We were just finishing." She noted that Elder Ahmanson smiled in greeting but said nothing.

"We have a problem," Brother Spencer said, as usual not much given to idle talk. In other circumstances it would have made him seem abrupt. With the lateness of the season and over a thousand people to outfit, everyone understood why he might seem a little curt. "We would like to confer with you." He looked around, making it clear he was referring to all of them and not just Brother James.

Maggie was sitting beside Sarah James and Ingrid Christensen. Emma and Hannah were sitting across the fire from them with the younger James children. Eating was forgotten now as every eye was on their camp leader.

Brother Spencer half turned and nodded at Elder Ahmanson. The tall Dane stepped forward. To Ingrid's surprise, his gaze was fixed on her. "As you may know," he began, obviously hesitant, "some of our Danish brothers and sisters will not be going with us but will stay and go with the independent wagon company led by Captain Hodgett."

"Yes," Mary said, "we had heard that."

"In fact, as you may know, my wife and I have a little boy only one year old."

"Yes," Brother James spoke up. "We had heard that."

"With a young babe, we do not see how she can walk or pull a handcart. So I have arranged for her to travel with the wagons."

"Oh?" Sister James said, "But not you?"

He shrugged. He didn't seem very happy.

Captain Willie helped him out. "Brother Ahmanson is captain of the fifth hundred. His people need him."

"Yah," Ahmanson said after a moment. "Grethe will be all right." He didn't sound convinced.

"The wagon companies will leave about the same time as Captain

Martin's group," Brother Spencer said. "So they won't be too far behind us."

Ingrid had stood up now. Her face was grave. "And you would like me to stay with your wife, Brother Ahmanson?"

That brought Emma's head around with a snap. Hannah was staring at her too.

"No, not just that. But—" Ahmanson stopped, his eyes filled with sadness. "I do not want to ask this, for I know how you have become friends with these families."

"Ask what?" Hannah blurted.

"I must go with our people in this company," Ahmanson said. "I am their leader. But we need someone to stay with those who are not going." He reached out as though he would touch Ingrid's arm, but then his hand dropped again. "Someone who can speak English and translate for them."

"Ah," Brother James said with a deep sigh. It wasn't just his daughter who had come to adore this sweet Danish girl who had brought so much laughter to their tent.

"But—," Emma started.

"Especially," Elder Willie cut in, "during this time when they are trying to get ready to go. There are so many instructions they have to understand."

Ingrid turned to Emma and shook her head. "That is why I came to live with your families," she said slowly. She looked at Maggie, her eyes filled with anguish. "This is why you taught me English, Maggie," she said. And then her shoulders straightened as she turned back to the three men. "I shall do as you ask."

Brother Spencer slowly nodded, obviously touched by her simple acceptance. "We have spoken to your aunt and uncle and explained the situation. They have given their permission."

"We talked about having either Eric or Olaf stay," Elder Ahmanson explained, "but they will be helping Jens and Elsie

Nielson with their handcart. Also, as brothers they have only each other for family. We feel like we just can't split them up."

"I understand," Ingrid said, managing a wan smile. "It is best this way. Do you want me to move my things now?"

"No. We are assigning the Roper family to this tent. That will bring it up to full strength, but they won't join the McKensies and the Jameses until we leave on Tuesday. Then you can move into the tent where they are staying."

"I'll go with you, Ingrid."

Mary McKensie spun around. So did everyone else. But Hannah was not looking at her mother. She was not looking at Elder Willie or Elder Spencer. She was staring at Ingrid, and there were tears in her eyes.

"What?" Ingrid exclaimed.

"I'll stay with you."

"Hannah, no!" It was Emma. Already shocked by the thought that after all their plans Ingrid would not be with them after all, she felt that this was too much. Her face was white and she was visibly trembling.

Hannah," her mother began, clearly as stunned as the rest, "you can't just–"

Hannah spun around to Sister James. "Just last night, after Brother and Sister Jackson were here, you said how worried you are about them. They have three young children and you said that Brother Jackson has never had really good health."

"Well, yes, but I didn't mean to say that . . . I wasn't suggesting that we should have someone stay."

Now Hannah ran to her mother and grasped her hands. "It would only be for a little while, Mama. The other company won't be far behind you." She whirled on Brother Willie. "In fact, didn't you say that the next group might catch us by the time we get to Florence?"

"Yes." He was pulling at his lip, watching her closely. "That is our hope. It would be good if the two companies could travel close together once we leave Florence."

Maggie was speechless. Hannah not with them? Like Emma she was still reeling a little from the shock of losing Ingrid, but Hannah? It was one thing to give up her treasured music box, but to lose Hannah? It was as though a sharp stone had pierced her breast. Even as she felt it, she saw the three brethren exchanging looks. Elder Ahmanson was nodding thoughtfully.

Brother Spencer spoke to Elder Willie. "I *was* talking to Aaron Jackson two days ago. I worry a little too. He's so thin. And their oldest child is only . . . what?" He looked at Jane James.

"Martha Ann is seven. Mary Elizabeth will be five in a few days."

"The baby, little Aaron, is only two," William said. "He'll have to ride in the cart. He's just toddling."

Ingrid was still staring at Hannah, her blue eyes registering the same shock as the others. But there was wonder and hope there as well.

"Really, Mother," Hannah rushed on. "Think about it. You said last night you wished there was something we could do to help the Jacksons. Well, now we can."

"Yes, but–"

"I could stay too," Emma said to her father. "Then we could all three be together."

William James slowly shook his head. "We need you, Emma. Especially if Sister McKensie loses Hannah. We'll have to help them."

Brother Spencer was more emphatic. "There's no way we could spare all three of you." He turned to Hannah's mother. "There is something to be said for this, Sister McKensie. What are your feelings?"

Mary started to speak; then words failed her. Her eyes were glistening as she looked at her daughter. Then, slowly, she turned to look at Ingrid. At that moment the Danish girl looked so helpless, and so filled with anxious expectation. Mary turned back. "Are you sure, Hannah?"

Maggie started forward, wanting to cry out, but then stopped. This was not her decision.

"I wasn't," Hannah said slowly. "The idea just popped into my head. But now? Yes, I'm sure, Mama. I feel like it is right. I don't want Ingrid to be alone." She took a quick breath and her shoulders squared. "If I had to leave you for a year, or even months, then I would probably say no. But for just a week or two. Yes, Mama. I'm sure."

Ingrid gave a cry low in her throat and ran to Hannah, throwing her arms around her.

Tears were streaming down Emma's face now. "Please, Papa."

He put an arm around her. "I'm sorry, Emma. We just can't spare you."

Elder Willie, Elder Spencer, and Elder Ahmanson conferred quickly in whispers. Finally they all bobbed their heads in agreement. Daniel Spencer reached out and laid a hand on Mary's arm. "We think there is merit to the idea if you are agreeable."

She took a deep breath and seemed to hold it forever; then it came out slowly and softly. "I am agreeable if Hannah is."

"Then it's settled. Thank you." He stepped forward and stuck out his hand to Hannah McKensie. "Thank you, dear sister. There is nothing sweeter than the pure love between good friends. We'll make the changes in the lists."

As they walked away, the two families stood around in a daze. Still weeping, Emma went to stand by her two friends. They held each other for a time, crying and whispering softly. Then suddenly Hannah straightened and moved back a step. "Do you know what this means, Emma?"

"No, what?"

"You won't be with Ingrid and me, but now you will have Olaf all to yourself." Her voice became husky, and though she tried to smile, it came out sounding quite forlorn. "Maybe you will get to be first wife after all."

Chapter Notes

The following entry for 12 July 1856 is found in the daily journal of the Willie Company: "All are getting their 17 lbs weighed up this morning" (in Turner, *Emigrating Journals*, p. 13).

The accounts below give insights into the "weigh-in" that was required of each handcart emigrant before he or she left Iowa City. Spelling and punctuation are as found in the original sources.

Mary Ann Jones, nineteen, was in the first handcart company of 1856, led by Captain Edmund Ellsworth. She later married Brother Ellsworth when they reached the Valley. "We were allowed 17 lbs. of baggage each, that meant clothes beding cooking utensils etc. When the brethern came to weigh our things some wanted to take more than alowed so put on extra clothes so that some that wore [were] real thin soon became stout so as soon as the weighing was over put the extra clothes in the hand cart again but that did not last long for in a few days we were called upon to have all weighed again & quite a few were found with more than alowed. One old Sister carried a teapot & calendar [colander] on her apron strings all the way to Salt Lake. Another Sister carried a hat box full of things but she died on the way" ("Diary of Mary Ann Jones [age 19] on her trip across the plains," in Carol Cornwall Madsen, *Journey to Zion*, p. 595).

Mary Powell, then twelve, and her family also came west with the Ellsworth Company in 1856. "It became necessary for Mother to dispose of some of our things. She sold a little flat iron that I had taken care to carry with me. How I cried when it was sold. I think this was the only time I cried on the whole long journey. I felt worried and said, 'Whatever will we do for something with which to smooth out our clothes when we get to Salt Lake City'" ("Autobiography of Mary Powell Sabin," in Carol Cornwall Madsen, *Journey to Zion*, p. 598).

Mary Ann Stucki Hafen, from Switzerland, came across the plains in 1860 when she was six. She and her family were in the Oscar Stoddard Company, the last of the ten companies to come to Utah by handcart. "When we came to load up our belongings, we found that we had more than we could take. Mother was forced to leave behind her feather bed, the bolt of linen, two large trunks full of clothes, and some other valuable things which we needed so badly later. Father could take only his most necessary tools" (*Recollections of a Handcart Pioneer*, p. 21).

John Jaques, as noted earlier, came to America and was reunited at Iowa City with his in-laws, the James Loader family. They became part of the Edward

Martin Company. Describing the scene at the Mormon Campground shortly before their departure from Iowa City, he wrote: "As only a very limited amount of baggage could be taken with the handcarts, during the stay in the Iowa camping grounds there was a general lightening of such things as could best be done without. Many things were sold cheaply to residents of that vicinity, and many more things were left on the camping ground for anybody to take or leave at pleasure. It was grievous to see the heaps of books and other articles thus left in the sun and rain and dust, representing a respectable amount of money spent therefore in England, but thenceforth a waste and a dead loss to the owners" (as cited in Bell, *Life History and Writings of John Jaques*, p. 119).

CHAPTER 10

IOWA CITY, IOWA
TO
BRUSHROW CREEK, IOWA

I

Tuesday, 15 July 1856

It was pandemonium. Eric Pederson shook his head. It might be organized pandemonium, but it was pandemonium nevertheless. Dogs barked. Oxen bellowed. People shouted at each other, trying to tell someone else where they should be. They might as well have been talking to the wind on the North Atlantic. Usually they were simply ignored. Occasionally the "someone elses" shouted right back. Children—the only ones finding any enjoyment in any of this—shrieked joyously at each other as they darted back and forth, dodging frustrated adults and ignoring the calls of concerned mothers. Near the front of the line a teamster driving one of the supply wagons was trying to yoke up his newly broken yoke of oxen—or better, Eric thought wryly, judging from what he could see, his *unbroken* yoke of oxen. It was a battle royal and still too early to tell who was going to win. Off to one side a pair of large black mules, already hitched to one of the other wagons, brayed raucously, as though finding the whole scene completely hilarious.

James Willie and the five captains of hundreds strode up and down the line, shouting orders, calling out encouragement, sometimes stopping to help someone with their lashings or to grease a wheel hub. Other times they just passed on, shaking their heads in futility. Willie led a horse behind him. With five hundred people, a hundred and twenty handcarts, five wagons, and about fifty head of beef, the line stretched for about a half a mile along the south side of the Mormon Campground. He had planned to ride back and forth and supervise things, but there were too many things that required his personal attention for him to be able to stay mounted.

The Church agents were likewise engaged. Daniel Spencer, Chauncey Webb, William Kimball, and George D. Grant went up and down the line checking on a thousand details. Today brought to fruition almost three weeks of nonstop effort on their part. The handcarts were constructed. Tents enough for this fourth company of the season were finished and packed in the supply wagons. Each wagon was filled to capacity. The agents carefully checked the inventory of required supplies: tools, rope, black powder, rifles and ammunition, sugar, tea, tent pegs, cooking utensils, bedding, a few bottles and tins of herbs and medicine, a small amount of lumber for repairs on the handcarts—or for coffins, should the need arise.

Eric could hardly take his eyes from the scene. It might be controlled bedlam, but it was also a culmination. Almost a year ago now the First Presidency had made a declaration and sent out a general epistle. Because of crop failures in Utah and tight money, the people would come by handcarts instead of wagon trains. With those few bold strokes of a pen, the Brethren had created the tumble of reality that lay before him.

Olaf was at the back of the cart with Jens Nielson, checking the ropes one last time to make sure the canvas was lashed down tight. Little Jens was right beside his father, his face as sober as that of a mourner at a funeral as he made sure they were doing it right. Unlike some of the handcarts, theirs did not have the rounded cover over the top that made them look like miniature wagons. With the limited amount of canvas, or drill cloth, only those handcarts with small children—defined as under six—were allowed to have covers to shield the children from the sun. Young Jens would not be six until October, but that was only three months away. In the weeks since their arrival at Iowa City, the boy had turned as brown as a piece of shoe leather and, unlike so many of the other Scandinavians who found the heat terribly oppressive, was not bothered by the sun. After almost a month of his running barefoot, the bottoms of his feet were as thick as sole leather and almost as black.

Off to the side from where Eric stood, Elsie Nielson was helping adjust a small shoulder pack for Bodil Mortensen, the nine-year-old girl they were taking to Zion for another family. Eric's eyes softened and a warm rush of affection swept over him. He still missed his family back in Norway, sometimes so keenly that he would lie awake nights thinking about them, but what a blessing it had been to find the Nielsons. They had become family to Olaf and him, and Eric felt a deep gratitude toward them. He saw in Elsie many of the same qualities that his mother had—gentleness, strength, quiet faith, quiet cheer.

Eric smiled. Bodil was only nine, but she was already nearly as tall as Elsie's four foot eleven. This tiny woman, who was such a physical contrast to her husband's height and weight, had enough energy to make up for whatever she lacked in size. She was also a giant when it came to faith. The prophet had said, Come to Zion, and so she was going to Zion. Eric had only just learned about their earlier plan to go to Utah by wagon train and of their decision to change to the handcarts so that they could give their extra money to bless others.

Elsie's skin, which was as fair as a baby's, did not take kindly to the sun. In spite of the bonnets she wore, her cheeks were constantly burned and peeling. Her nose was a bright pink, her lips chapped and bleeding, in spite of small pieces of cloth she stuck on with dabs of butter. Freckles were starting to appear across her cheeks.

One night in English class Maggie had brought a beautiful brass hand mirror as one of the props she always used to help them learn to speak better English. On impulse, Eric had asked if he could borrow it long enough to show Elsie. To his dismay, when he held it up, Elsie burst into tears. Jens had come running over. "What's wrong? What's wrong?" he cried.

Embarrassed, she recovered quickly, but it was clear she was still somewhat shocked.

"What is it, Elsie?" Jens persisted.

"When I get to Salt Lake, none of my friends will recognize me any longer," she whispered. "They won't even know me."

And yet, with all of that, the only thing Eric had ever heard her say that gave even the slightest indication of her feelings was, "Sometimes I so miss the sea air we enjoyed in Denmark."

She turned now and saw that he was watching her and instantly smiled. "Are you ready, Eric?" she asked in Danish.

He grinned. "More than ready. Aren't you?"

She nodded. Jens, finished now, moved up beside his wife and put one arm around her. "At last it comes," he said softly.

"Yes." She smiled up at him. "I'm so glad, Jens."

He turned and looked back toward the camp. There was a small crowd about thirty yards off. It was part of the Edward Martin group. Mingled with them were some of their own number, those who would be coming with the independent wagon trains. They had come out to say farewell.

"Do you think we made the right choice, Elsie?" Jens asked softly.

She looked up in surprise, then instantly frowned. "You know the answer to that," she said firmly.

"I know." His eyes were filled with both love and admiration for her. "Thank you. I still feel that we have made the right decision."

She smiled, then looked at Eric, who was watching the two of them. "Besides, if we were going by wagon company, we would not have these two strong boys added to our family now, would we?"

Eric chuckled. "And handsome too," he teased.

"Yes, very handsome."

Olaf hooted. "That's what Sarah James thinks too."

Eric spun around and glared at his brother. "I was just joking," he said.

Elsie laughed. "Olaf is not the only one who notices how that lovely young girl looks at you, Eric. Why don't you at least smile back at her from time to time?"

Eric started to say something, not realizing that even now he was frowning, but then a noise from off to the left caught his attention and he turned to look, grateful for the distraction. John Chislett, captain of the fourth hundred, was standing with the "footmen," speaking with some animation to two older sisters.

The group that stood off a short distance from the awaiting column did not have handcarts. Each hundred in the company had a small number of people—mostly those without other family members—who were not assigned to a handcart. In some cases it was because they weren't bringing much more than what they wore and didn't need a cart to carry it. Others felt that they were not physically able to pull a cart but could walk. A few were the odd-numbered ones who couldn't be placed easily with any other family group and its cart. They had a tent group and a mess group but not a handcart. The rest of the company had quickly dubbed them the "footmen," or the "walkers."

Curious, and anxious to escape any further taunting about Sarah, Eric spoke to Elsie. "I'm going to see if there's anything I can do to help." Without waiting for her reply, he sauntered over. He had visited with some of the footmen earlier and was impressed with their dogged determination not to be a burden on anyone.

"Sisters," Brother Chislett was saying, fighting for patience, "I find your independence commendable, but I would recommend that you seriously consider Brother Willie's offer."

"We have considered it." The speaker was a heavyset woman. Her hair was nearly white, but her eyes were a dark blue and filled with energy and life. Eric had noticed her before because she reminded him very much of his grandmother on his father's side, who had died two years before.

"And we thank our good captain," she went on, "but Sister Park and I have made up our minds. We shall walk."

In the heat she was fanning herself with a small book–something his grandmother always did–and Eric could see streaks of perspiration coming from beneath her bonnet.

The one called Sister Park nodded vigorously. She was tall, an inch or two more than her companion, and quite slender. At first glance it made her seem more frail, but Eric knew that that was a misleading impression. Her hair was not yet white, but it was graying heavily and was pulled back severely into a bun at the back of her neck. She peered at Brother Chislett. "And we shall not be asking anyone for help."

"But that's just it," Brother Chislett said in exasperation. "You don't have to ask. We are offering to help. They have room for both of you in the wagon company. They'll only be a day or so behind us."

"You think we're too old to walk on our own, don't you?" the first one said snappishly.

Eric smiled. He guessed that both were at least sixty years of age, perhaps as much as sixty-five, but it wouldn't be wise to point that out to them.

Chislett threw up his hands and exploded in frustration. "Sister Bathgate, we are not talking about an easy journey here. We have thirteen hundred miles to go. It is already very late in the season. We may get caught in some snowstorms in the Rocky Mountains before we reach the Valley."

"Then we shall walk through the snow," she retorted. "Sister Park and I will help each other, but we have every intention of walking every step of the way. You don't need to worry about us."

The subcaptain shook his head, starting to turn away. He saw Eric and recognized him. They had worked on the handcarts together. "See if you can talk some sense into these two," he muttered.

Eric smiled. "Hello."

Sister Bathgate squinted her eyes a little, then immediately smiled. "Oh, you're that Danish boy who's been studying English with the Scottish lass."

"Yes. I'm Eric Pederson. Actually, I and my brother are from Norway."

"Hmm," Sister Park said, half to him, half to her companion. "His English is very good. The class must be working."

He laughed. "I have much to learn. But I enjoy." He turned to Captain Chislett. "You are fourth hundred, no?"

"Yes."

"I am in fifth. Elder Ahmanson's group."

"Yes, I know. All the Scandinavians are together."

"Yah. So we will be close together most of the time?"

Chislett nodded. "Yes. Elder Willie plans to rotate the order of march, but we'll stay in the same sequence. So the fourth and fifth hundreds will generally be together."

Eric didn't know what *sequence* meant, but he thought he understood the sense of the man's answer. "Then I shall help," he said, turning to the two women. He held up his hand quickly, as he saw Sister Bathgate start to rear back. "Only when you need help." Then he thought he'd better explain. "You are very much like my grandmother. It would give great pleasure to me to help you. My father and mother would be displeased if they knew I did not help. I will only watch out for you and help when you say."

There was still some hesitation on Sister Bathgate's face, but he could see that she liked what he had said. She looked at the other woman. Sister Park nodded. "There might be times, Mary, when we could use some strong, young hands."

"I think that is a wonderful idea," Chislett said, much relieved. "What do you say, Sister Bathgate?"

She eyed Eric up and down slowly. He couldn't tell what she was thinking, but she didn't seem too pleased. "I look like your grandmother?" she asked. "Is that supposed to make me feel better?"

Then beneath the gruffness, he saw the twinkle in her eye. "Except you seem much younger," he said earnestly.

That did it. She laughed right out loud. "Do you tell such whoppers in Norwegian too, or just in English?" Not waiting for his answer, she turned to Chislett. "If we agree to let this young man help us out from time to time, then will you be satisfied, Captain?"

He chuckled ruefully. "I would feel better about it, yes."

"All right." She stuck out her hand to Eric. "I am Sister Mary Bathgate from England, young man. Eric, is it? And this is Isabella Park, my traveling companion. We thank you for your kindness."

"I am a pleasure to know you," he said gallantly.

She laughed. "And I am a pleasure to know you too. Now, run along. We're about ready to start, and I'm sure you've got things to do."

Captain Willie and the five captains of hundreds had announced that once the company was out on the trail, the groups of hundreds would rotate their position in the train so that one group did not have to be last all the time. But for this first day of the march the companies of hundreds had been asked to line up in order. The first hundred, under the direction of Millen Atwood, was in the front, faces pointed to the west. Next came Levi Savage's hundred. Both Savage and Atwood had been across the trail several times before and were experienced and confident captains. They had their companies well in order and had already sent word to Captain Willie that they were ready whenever he gave the signal.

William Woodward's hundred, made up mostly of the families from Scotland with a few from England, was having a little more trouble. Maggie McKensie watched with some impatience as he helped a family with three teenaged sons who were still trying to pack everything into their cart. Though he was several carts away from where she stood, Maggie could sense Brother Woodward's frustration.

Robbie was watching too. "Why are they taking so long, Mama?"

To Maggie's surprise, her mother's response was quite tart. "I don't know. We all had the same amount of time to get ready."

Maggie's face softened. Maggie had always envied her mother's patience and long-suffering disposition—something Maggie had not inherited—and to see her reacting in this way told Maggie how much she was hurting inside.

Hannah and Ingrid had, of course, come out to see the family off. The Jacksons had come with them as well. Aaron and Elizabeth Jackson stood back with the others of the Martin Company who had come out to say good-bye. Maggie also saw John Jaques and his family with them. She was thankful for that. With the urgency of their own preparations, many of the second company had stayed at their work assignments on this morning. But this was the Jacksons' way of letting the McKensies know that Hannah and Ingrid would be well cared for and loved almost as much as if they were with Hannah's family. And John Jaques had come to Mary McKensie the previous night as well, promising that he too would make a special effort to see that these two young women were properly cared for. It was both touching and comforting, and had meant a great deal to Maggie's mother.

Maggie turned. The William James family with their two handcarts were ahead of Maggie's family. Ingrid and Hannah were with them at the moment, saying their farewells. Emma's eyes were red and swollen. Of the three friends, she was having the hardest time with this farewell.

Maggie couldn't bear to watch, so she turned and let her eyes take in the rest of the scene around them. Their company was at the center of the long column. Behind them was John Chislett's fourth hundred, and then bringing up the rear was the Scandinavian group under Brother Ahmanson. Off to one side, between the fourth and fifth hundreds, she saw the footmen standing together, ready to go. To her surprise, she saw Eric Pederson there with them. He was speaking to two older sisters. Then, even as she wondered why he would be there, he waved his hand in farewell and started back to where his group was waiting.

"Here comes Brother Willie," her mother said.

To Maggie's relief, their captain was mounted now. He was cantering slowly up the line, making one last check on things. Until now he had only been leading the horse. This was an encouraging sign. Elder Willie waved to both families as he passed, then stopped briefly at the cart where Elder Woodward had been helping the family pack their stuff. Captain Woodward was standing back now. The family seemed at last to be finished.

"Everything ready, Brother Woodward?" Captain Willie called as he approached them.

"Yes, sir," Captain Woodward said. "The third hundred is ready to go."

"Good." He dug his heels into his horse and broke into a gallop, heading for the front of the column. That was the signal for Ingrid and Hannah that the time was growing very short. Weeping openly now, they left the Jameses and came back to join Hannah's family.

As they came, Maggie's eyes were drawn to Ingrid. Around her neck she wore the shoes that her father had given her as a present before she left Denmark. They bounced lightly against her blue dress, looking ridiculous against her slender body.

It had surprised all of them when Ingrid appeared with the extra pair of shoes. At the weigh-in she had promised Elder Kimball and Elder Spencer that she would carry them on the trail, but why wear them today? When he saw her, Robbie, with his usual tact, blurted out the question that everyone was wondering. "How come you're wearing those now?" he said.

Ingrid had just smiled, blushing a little. "I need to get used to carrying them," was all she would say.

Ingrid Christensen had one of the sweetest and purest personalities Maggie had ever known. Everyone adored her. Clear blue eyes, a perky, upturned nose, and a broad, ready smile made her a favorite of both children and adults. But Maggie had come to know that within that sweetness and purity there was also a strong will and powerful commitment. How quickly she had learned English was proof of that. Her determination to be properly dressed when she met Brigham Young was another. And so while they might look ridiculous in one way, those shoes were an endearing witness of the true Ingrid Christensen.

As she came up, Maggie reached out and touched the shoes. "We'll watch for you every night," she said, her voice low and strained. "And I'll be looking for someone who's crazy enough to carry a pair of shoes around her neck."

Ingrid's eyes were swimming and she too could barely speak. "I know. That's why I wore them today. I wanted you to know what to look for."

"Oh, Ingrid!" Maggie cried, throwing her arms around her. "We love you so much. I'm so glad Brother Ahmanson put you in our class."

"So am I. Thank you for teaching me how to speak English."

Ingrid stepped back now as Hannah went straight to Robbie, sweeping him up in her arms. A great sob was torn from her as he clung to her. "You take care of Mama, Robbie. You hear me? You take care of her real good."

"I will, Hannah. Hurry so you can catch us."

Mary McKensie wiped at the corners of her eyes with the back of her hand. Her head was high and she was struggling mightily to keep her emotions in check. "It's just a couple of weeks, Robbie. Let's keep telling ourselves that. We'll see Hannah and Ingrid in Florence."

Maggie nodded. They all kept saying that, and yet Daniel Spencer had admitted that it would probably be another two weeks before Edward Martin's company would even be ready to go. Could they make up that much time on them?

Hannah buried her face in her brother's hair, her body shaking convulsively. Then finally she straightened and turned to Maggie. Without a word, they fell into each other's arms, clinging to each other fiercely. "Good-bye, Maggie," Hannah finally said.

"No!" Maggie cried. "Not good-bye. Just we'll see you in a little while."

"Yes." She laughed through her tears. "We'll see you in a little while."

As Hannah finally turned to her mother, Maggie saw that Captain Willie was at the head of the column. He swung his horse around and stood up in the stirrups. For a long moment he let his eyes sweep down the long column, and then he took off his hat and raised it in the air. After a moment his cry came faintly down the line. "Move 'em out."

That broke through the last vestiges of Mary McKensie's control. With a cry of pain, she gathered Hannah against her and began to sob. All up and down the line, the column began to come alive. People called for the children. Teamsters climbed onto their wagons. Drovers began to move around to the back of the herd of cattle. The walkers hoisted their packs and bags. Men and women stepped into the shafts of their handcarts and raised them up to chest level. But beside the three handcarts that belonged to the McKensies and the Jameses, the only sound that could be heard was the soft sound of mother and daughter crying.

II

Sunday, 20 July 1856

For a moment, Maggie thought it was the whistle at the factory, but when she opened her eyes in the semi-darkness of the tent, she groaned. It was one of the few times in her life that she wished she was at the paper factory in Edinburgh. But it wasn't a whistle; it was the camp bugle signaling that it was time to awaken.

She started to roll over onto her side, then winced sharply, gasping in pain. Every muscle screamed out in protest. Her back felt like it had locked into position and that if she moved it, it would snap in two. Her arms ached clear to the bone. Her legs were extensions of the agony that was her body. Her feet and hands were on fire from the massive blisters that filled her palms and covered the balls of each foot.

She rolled back, biting her lip to stop from crying out.

"Can you move?"

Maggie lifted her head and noticed two things simultaneously. Sarah was sitting on her bedroll looking at her. That was the first thing, and it was astonishing. How could she have gotten herself up to a sitting position?

The second thing she noticed was that it was much lighter in the tent than it normally was when the bugle sounded.

Cringing, she pushed herself up beside Sarah. "I didn't think it was possible that one body could experience so much pain," she moaned.

She saw Sarah's head bob. "I think my blisters are having babies," she said.

"And does your whole body feel like it's on fire?"

"Only everywhere that I still have feeling left."

They were still conversing in whispers, for none of the other people in the tent seemed to have stirred as yet. Then suddenly it came to Maggie why it was lighter than normal. "It's Sunday today."

"Yes," Sarah said fervently. "Hallelujah!"

With a groan of sheer pleasure, Maggie fell back onto her bed. So it wasn't four A.M. It was closer to six o'clock. They wouldn't be rolling out this morning. Captain Willie had announced that they would observe the Sabbath by staying in this camp at Brushrow Creek. If he had announced that each person would receive a gift of a thousand pounds or a sack of gold doubloons, it would not have been received any more gratefully than the news that they could rest for a day.

Sarah lay down again too, but scooted over so her head was close to Maggie's. "Aren't we glad that they are letting us begin slowly?" she said, pulling a face.

Maggie hooted softly. "It's a good thing. Otherwise, we'd all be dead."

Sarah was right, of course. Willie and the subcaptains *were* going very slowly. When they had moved out Tuesday afternoon, they had gone only a short distance—a mile, maybe two—from the campground before they stopped. That had come as a great relief to almost everyone. The excitement of being under way quickly wore off as the reality of pulling a loaded handcart across rough ground set in. Less than a mile away from their starting place, they had to ford a creek that supplied water to the camp. It was no more than eight or ten feet across, and the banks were only a couple of feet high on either side, but by the time a dozen carts had crossed, the bottom turned soft and the banks became muddy. It took Maggie, Robbie, their mother, and Emma straining with every ounce of strength they had to make it up the opposite bank. They collapsed thankfully a short distance later when Captain Willie declared that that would be enough for the first day.

The next day they went only three miles before they stopped. The wagons were nowhere in sight, and so the captain took nine or ten men back to find them. It turned out that the young, unbroken oxen and the inexperienced teamsters were a bad combination. But those pulling the handcarts felt nothing but thanks for the chance to rest. Feet and hands were blistered. Lungs burned as though filled with brimstone. People moved gingerly and with constant low groans, even those who thought they were in good physical condition. Seeing their condition, Willie called a halt for all of the third day. That had been

Thursday. But they couldn't make one or even three miles a day for very long. They were already well into July.

On the fourth day, Friday, the bugle blew at four A.M. It took them nearly seven hours to fix breakfast and repack the carts, an amount of time that their leaders said was unacceptable. They moved out about eleven, only to find the road more difficult than what they had previously experienced. The road was rutted and extremely rough in some places. They came to a collapsed bridge and had to ford the small river. The oxen continued to balk and the supply wagons moved forward slowly. By five P.M. the group was totally exhausted. They had come six miles.

Yesterday they had done better but only because the captains had started haranguing them shortly after the bugle call until they were ready to move out at nine A.M. The road was much better, and Captain Willie refused to call a halt, other than to water the cattle once, until seven P.M. the previous evening. He was elated. Twelve miles. They doubled their mileage of the day before. In fact, they had come farther in that one day than in the previous four. He and the subcaptains were the only ones smiling. For the emigrants, they had reached levels of agony never before known to most of the company.

Maggie closed her eyes. They had come about twenty miles. That left them only about thirteen hundred and eighty to go.

When the second of the two Sabbath services broke up that afternoon, many of the people stayed around to talk. The spirit of the group was high, in spite of the aches and pains that everyone was experiencing. Elder Willie had been the main speaker in the morning session. Then Elders Chislett and Savage, two of the captains of hundreds, had spoken this afternoon. The company might be on limited food rations—especially in such luxury items as sugar, rice, and dried apples—but the spiritual nourishment came without measure. It felt good. And they desperately needed the rest from the trail.

Eric and Olaf had been especially gratified, for they had been given their first formal opportunity to serve as translators. Johan Ahmanson divided the Scandinavians into three smaller groups so that the translators could speak in softer voices and not distract the others in the congregation.

"Look," Olaf said, suddenly pointing. "There's Emma." He raised a hand and started to wave. "And there's Maggie and Sarah too. Let's go say hello."

Eric hesitated, then saw that they were waving back. With a nod, he fell into step behind his brother.

Robbie saw them first and gave a whoop. He came on the run and greeted them breathlessly. It was not as if they hadn't seen each other since leaving Iowa City, but with five hundred people in the company and each group of hundred pretty well camping together, they had mostly just waved or called out greetings back and forth.

"Hello, Robbie," Eric said, ruffling his hair. "How are you?"

"Great!"

Eric nodded and smiled. This twelve-year-old's enthusiasm had not dimmed in the slightest. Curious, Eric reached out and took Robbie's hands and turned them up. Sure enough, there were angry red splotches on his palms, just as there were on almost everyone else's in the camp. Eric ruffled his hair again with open affection. It would take more than blisters to dampen this boy's excitement for the trail. Eric held up his own hands to show him and Robbie laughed back at him. "Isn't it great?" he said again. "Mine are getting better every day."

Sarah, Emma, and Maggie came up. Emma greeted Olaf brightly and immediately began to pester him with questions about how they were doing. Sarah watched them for a moment, then smiled shyly at Eric. "Good afternoon."

"Hello, Sister Sarah." He turned a little. "And Sister Maggie."

"How about just Maggie?" Maggie said sternly. She had been trying to get him to call her Maggie since they had first started English class on board ship. He stubbornly refused to do it, and she wasn't sure why.

He nodded, his eyes grave. "Hello, just Maggie."

Sarah laughed lightly as Maggie threw up her hands. "Hello, *Brother* Pederson."

"How are you?" Sarah asked.

Eric shrugged and held up his hands. "Like you. Very good."

Sarah and Maggie both laughed ruefully at that, holding up their own bandaged hands. Emma, hearing that, turned and showed hers as well. "I used Papa's gloves today, but it didn't help much."

"Only because you waited until you had the blisters before you put on gloves," Sarah retorted.

"Well, yes." She seemed puzzled that Sarah would even bring that up.

Maggie watched Sarah for a moment, seeing how alive she had become when Eric appeared. "By the way, were you and Olaf translating today?" she asked. "I saw you standing up and speaking during the meeting."

"Yah." Eric seemed pleased that she had noticed. "We make three groups. Olaf did one. I do one. Elder Ahmanson did one. We did the whole meetings."

"He means we did both meetings," Olaf suggested.

"Yah, we did both meetings."

"That's wonderful," Maggie said.

William James and his children were going back toward the tents, but Mary McKensie and Jane James had seen the boys and come over to join them. "Hello, Olaf. Hello, Eric," Mary said. "And how are you two today?"

"We are fine, thank you," Olaf said. "And you?"

"We are both fine," Jane answered.

"Eric and Olaf served as translators today for both meetings," Maggie said to the two women.

"Yes, I saw," Jane said. "Good for you. Your English is getting very good now."

Eric looked at Maggie, coloring slightly. "We have our teacher to say thank you. Without her, it is not possible."

Maggie was deeply pleased. She nodded slowly. "Thank you, Eric. I wish we had time to continue our classes, but . . ." Without thinking, she looked down at her hands. She had a rag wrapped around each one, which hid the angry red sores. When they left Iowa City she had vowed that they would continue with the English classes, but as yet they hadn't held even one. By the time supper was finished and cleaned up, the only thing anyone wanted to do was to climb stiffly into bed.

"It is all right. The trail is good teacher too, I think."

"Yes. I'll bet you get to use your English a lot."

"Yes. But trail is good teacher for more than English, I think. Some are failing, no?"

Now Mary looked puzzled. "Failing?"

"Sister Baker," he said softly.

"Ah," Mary said, understanding now. Yesterday afternoon, after the twelve-mile push to the campground, a sister from the Southampton Conference in England, a Sister Adelaide Baker, had decided she had endured enough and left the camp. This morning she had come for her luggage and her children and announced she would not be going further with them. When they asked why, she simply shook her head, collected her children and her things, and left, heading for the nearest settlement.

"There were three more who left after worship services this morning," Sarah said sadly.

"More?" Eric said in surprise.

"Yes. Two sisters from the Bedfordshire Conference and a Sister Smith from Bristol. They all turned back."

"It is hard teacher. Worse than Sister Maggie."

Maggie's mother laughed at Maggie's attempt to look offended. "Yes," she said. "The trail is a hard teacher. Much harder than Maggie."

Now Jane came in. "That's what Captain Willie was talking about when he referred to leeks and onions in his talk this morning."

Eric snapped his fingers. "Oh yah, I'm glad you remind me. What is this leeks and onions? Olaf and I did not know how to translate."

"Onions is the vegetable?" Olaf asked.

"Yes." Maggie was carrying her scriptures under one arm. She quickly opened her Bible, thumbing the pages to the back. She let her fingers run down a column of words.

Curious, Eric stepped closer to look. "What is this?" he said, touching the page.

For a moment she wasn't sure what he meant, then saw him examining the page. "Oh, this? It's an abbreviated concordance. It's like a dictionary."

"It tells you what words mean?" he asked, totally focused on the page now.

"No, it tells you where a word is used in the Bible. Here, let me show you."

He moved closer so they were standing shoulder to shoulder.

"Look, here it is. See? It is the word *leeks.* That's what we want to know."

He was nodding thoughtfully. "So what is num one one five?"

"That means the word is used in the book of Numbers, chapter eleven, verse five." She turned quickly until she found it. She pointed with her finger. "See? Here it is. This is what Elder Willie was referring to today. Moses is dealing with the children of Israel, who are rebelling as usual."

Eric got a wry smile. "Like maybe they were unhappy about their blisters."

She laughed at his quickness. It was so easy to think that because he and Olaf could not speak fluent English, they didn't understand things. "Yes, exactly. Even though they are being fed miraculously from heaven with manna, they're still complaining."

Her head bent down. "Listen. This is what it says: 'And the children of Israel also wept again, and said, Who shall give us flesh to eat? We remember the fish, which we did eat in Egypt freely; the cucumbers, and the melons, *and the leeks, and the onions,* and the garlick: but now our soul is dried away: there is nothing at all, beside this manna, before our eyes.' "

She stopped and looked at him. He was watching her closely now, and she flushed a little under the intensity of his gaze. "Do you see what they were saying, Eric?"

"What is cucumber?"

Olaf spoke one word in Norwegian and Eric grunted. "Ah." He bent over, reading the verses again. Finally he looked at her in wonder. "They had bread from heaven but they wanted more."

"Yes. They were murmuring. They wanted to be back in Egypt, where they could have all the fruits and vegetables they wanted."

"Even though Egypt was not good," he said slowly.

"Exactly."

Suddenly Maggie remembered that they were not alone and that they were not in class. She looked around. Emma was quietly trying to explain it to Olaf, who was still looking a little puzzled. Her mother and Sister James were watching Eric, pleased that he had seen it so quickly. But Sarah was looking at Maggie strangely.

A little flustered that she should have gotten so caught away in the teaching moment, she closed the book. "That's what Elder Willie meant when he said that the people who decide to turn back are going after leeks and onions."

If Eric was aware of the others watching them, he seemed not to notice. He was still looking at Maggie steadily. "They wanted that more than the bread from heaven?" he finally asked, shaking his head in amazement.

"Yes, Eric," she said, impressed that he had seen beyond the words to the message they held.

"Just like today," Sister James said. "It's been a difficult few days. We all know that. And it's easy to understand why these people decided to turn back. But . . ." She shrugged. "But if you want to go to Zion, you had better be prepared for blisters."

That sobered every one of them, for their hands and feet bore the marks and their bodies felt the pain of the price that was required of them.

"I wonder how many more will leave," Maggie said quietly. She was thinking about how close she had come to choosing to stay behind in Egypt.

No one answered. No one had to. It was very unlikely that they had seen the last of those who would be turning back.

After a moment Maggie's mother straightened. "Well," she said, putting a cheerful lilt to her voice, "all this talk about fish and cucumbers and leeks and onions has made me hungry." She looked at the two brothers. "Eric? Olaf? How would you two like to join us for supper this evening?"

Maggie turned in surprise, as did Sarah. Emma reacted immediately. "Oh, yes, Olaf, come have supper with us."

"Yes!" Robbie cried. "Do it! Do it!"

Eric was startled by the invitation. "We . . . I don't know. We share supper with the Nielsons each night."

"They won't mind," Olaf said. "Sister Nielson will not have started cooking yet."

"Come on," Emma said, tugging on Olaf's arm. "I'll go with you to tell them."

Eric glanced quickly at Maggie, who clearly was as surprised as he was at this unexpected turn of events. "We'd like that," she said.

To Maggie's surprise, Sarah only nodded. She had thought Sarah would be tugging on Eric's arm by now as well.

Finally he nodded. "All right, I guess. But you go and tell the Nielsons, Olaf."

As Emma and Olaf started away, Robbie grabbed Eric's arm. "Yea!" he shouted. "Come on, Eric. Brother James has been teaching me how to make a whistle out of a willow stick. Come on. I'll show you." He dragged him into a trot.

As they started back toward the tent, Maggie fell in beside her mother and Sister James for a moment, then noticed that Sarah was walking behind them. She dropped back to join her. "Well, that was interesting, wasn't it?"

Sarah gave her a strange look. "It certainly was."

"I thought I was going to have to spell the whole thing out to him. But did you see his eyes? how quickly they understood?"

"Yes," Sarah responded quietly. "I did see his eyes."

Something in the way she said it made Maggie stop. "What?"

Sarah kept walking and Maggie ran quickly and caught up with her again. "What, Sarah? What is it?"

"Nothing."

"Is something wrong?"

"No." It came out too quickly.

"Tell me."

Now Sarah stopped. "You mean you honestly don't know?"

"Don't know what?"

For what seemed a long time, Sarah searched her face. Then finally she shook her head in wonder. "I don't think you do."

"Know what?" Maggie burst out, exasperated now.

Sarah didn't stop, nor did she look at her friend. "Did *you* see his eyes, Maggie?"

"Of course. I told you. You could see how the lights came on and how he saw almost instantly what Elder Willie meant."

"And that's all you saw?"

Maggie threw up her hands. "What else was there?"

Sarah smiled that faint, slightly sad smile again, then put her arm around Maggie's shoulder. "Nothing. I'm just being me today. Forget I said anything."

Chapter Notes

The James G. Willie Handcart Company, the fourth handcart company of 1856, left Iowa City, Iowa, on 15 July. It was seventy-eight days after they had left Liverpool on the *Thornton* and twenty days after their arrival in Iowa. The official count says they had 500 emigrants, 120 handcarts, 5 wagons, 24 oxen, and 45 beef cattle and milk cows (see Hafen and Hafen, *Handcarts to Zion*, p. 93).

One of the difficulties with getting an official count on the handcart companies is that the numbers were constantly changing. Some stayed in New York and Boston to work until they could get enough money to continue. Others decided to winter over at Iowa City. Some, as shown in this chapter (and this was true of both companies), dropped out after they got under way. In a few cases, settlements in Iowa and Nebraska were started by Latter-day Saints who decided they would go no farther. There is an indication that a few in the Willie Company, who evidently were too ill or too weak to continue but who still had a great desire to go to Zion, were picked up later by the Martin Company or the independent wagon companies as they came along.

Several sources provide lists of the emigrants in both the Willie and the Martin Companies, though the lists generally seem to have been drawn from the same basic sources (see, for example, Turner, *Emigrating Journals*, pp. 59–78, 141–64; Hafen and Hafen, *Handcarts to Zion*, pp. 289–302; *Remember*, pp. E-1 to E-23; Susan Arrington Madsen, *The Second Rescue*, pp. 107–37). Those who dropped out are included in some rosters but not in others, and the different lists are not all exactly the same. Because of that, it is difficult to know whether the 500 was the count when the company started or when the numbers finally stabilized.

In his journal Elder Jesse Haven, who captained part of the last company along with Edward Martin, wrote of his approach to those who left the company:

> *30 July 1856*: This morning at prayers, we disfellowshiped Emma Batchelor, who left us yesterday and went out among the gentiles to tarry there. . . . Brother Robert Evans and Sarah White, came to me

> and wished to be excused from going any further because he, Robert Evans, was out of health. I excused them.
>
> *1 August 1856:* This morning, I learned that 3 or 4 left the camp last night; one woman and her child and other children, whose mother died since we started on our journey. . . . Two families talk of leaving and wish to get my counsel. To do so, at the last, I told one of them he might do as he thought proper, and I would not disfellowship him for it. I had established the rule, if any left the camp without counsel, they should be disfellowshiped from the church. Brother Moses left today with his family, also Brother Hunter and his family. (In Turner, *Emigrating Journals,* p. 94)

The reference to Elsie Nielson's shock at looking at herself in a mirror was inspired by a reminiscence of Susanna Stone Lloyd, who was a twenty-five-year-old single woman at the time she traveled with the Willie Handcart Company. "We were near Fort Bridger when they [members of the rescue party] met us, and we rode in the wagons the rest of the way, but we had walked over one thousand miles. When we got near the City, we tried to make ourselves as presentable as we could to meet our friends. I had sold my little looking glass to the Indians for buffalo meat, so I borrowed one and I shall never forget how I looked. Some of my old friends did not know me. We were so weather beaten and tanned" (in Carol Cornwall Madsen, *Journey to Zion,* p. 634).

CHAPTER 11

BRUSHROW CREEK, IOWA
TO
FLORENCE, NEBRASKA TERRITORY

I

Friday, 25 July 1856

Maggie McKensie plodded along, her head down low enough so that her bonnet shaded her face from the western sun. She swallowed and licked her lips, then instantly regretted it as the gritty taste of dust filled her mouth. She had kept a handkerchief over her mouth and nose since early morning, but that didn't stop it from penetrating everywhere. The Woodward hundred, the third hundred of the Willie Handcart Company, was in second position in the column today, and so the dust could have been much worse. Three days before, they had taken the last place in the column, and for nine straight hours they had choked on the great clouds stirred up by the passing of five hundred people and several dozen animals.

Today had been another brutally hot day. Even now, at five o'clock in the afternoon, she guessed it was hovering near one hundred degrees. Every inch of her body was bathed in sweat, and though she kept the neck of her dress and the sleeves around her wrists tied shut, the dust managed to work its way inside her clothing. The wrinkles around her neck and beneath her arms were thick with a gritty paste. The band of her bonnet seemed like sandpaper on her brow. She had long since given up trying to keep the sweat from running in her eyes and simply blinked quickly when the salt began to sting too much.

Ten days. They had left Iowa City just ten days ago. It felt like ten years.

Captain Willie said they had come about seventy-five miles. They were long, hard miles, but at last the emigrants were toughening up. The blisters of the previous week were still red and tender, but the skin was hardening into thick calluses, and new blisters were rare now. Also, the bottoms of their feet were thickening. How wise it had been for the Church agents to have the children go barefoot when they first reached Iowa City! By afternoon the dust of the trail could get hot enough to burn bare flesh, yet the children walked on it without complaint. One boy had even stepped on a prickly pear by accident. They had taken out three long spikes with pliers, but he said he had barely any pain. And no wonder. The soles of his feet were nearly half an inch thick. Maggie wished she had been wise enough to do the same. But like her hands, her feet were tougher now, growing thick skin as tough as dried leather.

The crossbars of each handcart were now polished to a dark sheen. Clothes were stained with sweat and dust. Lips were cracked, cheeks sunburned, eyes wrinkled at the corners from squinting long into the sun. But they were moving steadily westward now. Twelve-mile days were now considered light travel days and came only when they had to stop to make repairs. Just as Chauncey Webb had predicted, the green lumber used to construct the carts was drying and warping in the blistering heat, and time and again they had to stop and put them back together. When there were no delays, sixteen-mile days were common, and they had once gone twenty-one. They were trail tough, and the murmuring had mostly ceased.

But those first few days—a nightmare that she would never forget—had taken their toll. Almost a dozen of their number had turned back or simply stopped where they were. Some promised to wait a season and then come on when they were better prepared. Others made no promises at all. Zion had lost its luster. And two days ago they had suffered their first death. Sister Mary Williams from England, an older woman of about fifty, had died of a severe stomach ailment. They placed her body in one of the wagons and carried her until they found a burying ground in one of the small towns they passed.

The residents had come out to watch, barely speaking to the Mormons but not treating them unkindly either. That was a blessing, Maggie decided. Several nights running now, the locals from surrounding settlements had come out to harass the emigrants. Mostly they just came after dark and stood near the edges of the camp, cursing and calling out obscenities. Often there would be young rowdies waiting at the creek and river crossings. They would whistle and clap vulgarly as the women and girls lifted their skirts enough to ford the water. Tight-lipped, they would ignore them and move on in silence, anxious to be out of Iowa and past the last of the settlements so that there would be no more tormentors.

The cart jolted sharply as the left wheel hit a rock and bounced over it. Maggie straightened. At the moment, her mother and Emma were pulling their cart. Maggie and Robbie were at the back pushing. "Are you ready to switch, Mama?" she called.

"Another few minutes. I think there's a creek up ahead. Doesn't that look like trees?"

Maggie peered forward. There was a dark line along the western horizon.

"It's Muddy Creek," Robbie sang out. "Captain Woodward told me that's where we'll camp tonight."

A creek? To Maggie, that word was like hearing music on the night air. Not just another stagnant slough where they had to strain various particles and small little "wrigglers" out of the water before they could drink it. Not just a creekbed where the men dug down in the sand until water began to seep into the hole, thick with silt and usually a dark brown. In a real creek there would be fresh water for drinking and cooking. In a real creek she could roll up her sleeves and unbutton the collar around her neck and use her handkerchief to remove some of the sandy paste that was driving her nearly insane.

Just then a shout from up ahead brought Maggie's head up. As usual, the footmen were out ahead of the company about a hundred yards. They always left before the main camp so as to avoid the dust and keep ahead of the column. They had stopped and the first of the handcarts were just coming up to them. Then Maggie saw why. Farther away, coming at a steady trot, was a group of horsemen. Captain Willie, at the head of the company, was staring at the oncoming riders. He stood up in the stirrups and called back down the line. "Hold up. Stop the carts."

One by one the handcarts rolled to a stop. The lead company moved up around their captain four and five abreast. The following companies stopped where they were. Those in the back were not even sure at first why they were stopping. As the riders drew closer a tremor of fear swept up and down the line. There were six men and each had a rifle out, muzzles up and pointed at the sky. Mothers beckoned urgently to their children. Fathers stepped in front of their families. The few men who had rifles—primarily the subcaptains and the appointed hunters—stepped closer to the carts or wagons so as to be able to grab their weapons if necessary.

As the column shuddered to a halt, Captain Willie rode his horse slowly forward.

"Is it Indians, Mama?" The question came from Martha James, who was ten. Her father quickly shook his head. "No, it's not Indians. It will be all right."

The group of men had come up to Captain Willie now and the lead rider dismounted. Captain Willie did the same.

"Brother Willie doesn't seem frightened," Mary McKensie noted.

And that was true. Their captain was speaking to the leader of the group. The other men still sat on their horses. The rifles were still out but were held casually. There had been no threatening moves. Maggie saw a flash of white and realized the leader of the group was handing Captain Willie a paper. After a moment, Willie and the man started toward the lead supply wagon, both of them leading their horses. The other five put their rifles in their scabbards, dismounted, and fell into line behind them.

There was an almost audible sigh as the emigrants saw that. There was not going to be trouble. Then, like the hum of an approaching swarm of bees, the word started down the line. "It's a sheriff and some deputies from a nearby town," someone called softly. "They have a warrant to search the wagons."

"What are they looking for?" someone said in a low voice.

"Didn't say. Pass the word back. Captain Willie says everything is all right."

Robbie bolted away, carrying the word back to the next group of emigrants. Every eye was on the wagons now. Elder Willie stood back as the men began opening the canvas covers and looking inside. After a moment, they climbed back down again. Whatever it was they were looking for must be large and easily spotted, for this was not a thorough search.

Then Levi Savage, captain of the second hundred, which was in the lead today, came swiftly down the line. "They're looking for young women," he said. "Someone told the sheriff that we are holding young single women as prisoners."

"What?" several people exclaimed in astonishment.

He laughed. "They think we've got them tied up and are taking them to Utah to be plural wives of the brethren. I think the sheriff realizes now that he's been sold a bill of goods, but he's got to search to make sure. Just cooperate. There won't be any trouble."

Sarah and Maggie looked at each other, and then started to laugh. Sarah held out her hands, wrists together as though they were bound. "At last we shall be free, Maggie. Praise the heavens."

Emma started to giggle and Reuben James hooted. Then Jane James shushed them quickly. "Look," she said.

Captain Willie and the six men were in a circle now. Maggie saw the sheriff wave an arm toward the column. Willie nodded. Immediately the men split up, each heading for a different part of the line, their horses in tow behind them. "Brethren and sisters," Brother Willie shouted. "These men are law officers. They want to search the company. Everything's fine. Please cooperate with them."

The two families stood together now watching as the men approached. The sheriff and Captain Willie angled off for the back of the column. One man started directly toward where the Jameses and McKensies waited. He walked with a swagger, and as he approached, Maggie saw the glint of a silver star pinned to his vest. It was obvious he had seen that there were young women in this group and had chosen them as his target.

"Just stay calm," William James whispered.

As he came up to them, Maggie was surprised to see that he was a young man, no older than her and Sarah. He wore a large hat that had a dark ring around the brim. Like the emigrants, his clothes were dusty. He had narrow green eyes and a thick handlebar mustache that covered most of his mouth. A bandanna was tied around his neck, and he had a pistol strapped to his hip. His face was set as he looked from one to another. But there was no mistaking it. His gaze was fixed on Maggie, Sarah, and Emma.

Suddenly his mouth twisted into a wicked grin that was almost more of grimace than a smile. He swept off this hat. His hair was thick and in need of a cut. There was a ring of red around his forehead where the hatband had been and Maggie saw beads of sweat as well. She took some comfort in knowing that these men too were suffering the effects of a very warm day.

"Ladies," he said, half bowing in mock respect. "My name is Deputy Carl King. I am here as an official officer of the law to ask you some questions."

Emma shrunk back against her father. Suddenly anxious, Mary moved in closer to Maggie and Sarah. "What kind of questions?" she asked.

"Are you married, ma'am?" he replied.

"Widowed. My husband passed away some years ago."

"And you?" he asked Jane James.

"Yes. This is my husband."

The deputy glanced at Brother James and deliberately rested his hand on the butt of his pistol. "Sir, I'll just ask you to stand back and not interfere, please."

There was a sudden chill now. There was not even a trace of friendliness in the man. His voice was cold and his eyes like two pieces of stone. He motioned to Emma. "You there. Come up here beside these other two."

She did so, standing close to Sarah.

"I'm going to ask you three some questions and I don't want no lies, you understand?"

"We don't lie," Maggie said calmly. "Why would you think we would?"

His eyes narrowed as he glared at her, but he let it pass. "How old are you?"

"Nineteen," Maggie responded. "Nineteen," Sarah said. "Sixteen," answered Emma.

"Are any of you married?"

They all shook their heads.

"You're sure you're not one of them there plural wives for some old geezer in the train here?"

Maggie gave him a disgusted look. "We are all single. We are not married to anyone. Nor are we promised to anyone."

He looked at her more closely. "Where you from?" he demanded.

"Scotland."

He swung on Sarah. "And you?" Maggie went cold as she saw that now there was open admiration in his eyes.

Sarah looked away, seeing what Maggie saw as well. "England."

"Jolly good," he said softly, mocking her accent. "And ain't you the pretty one." Then he got serious again. "Are any of you being held against your will?"

Maggie laughed contemptuously. "Does it look like we are in ball and chain?"

"Maggie," Mary warned softly.

The man's lip curled angrily. "Roll up your sleeves," he barked.

"What?"

"Are you deaf?" he snarled. "You heard me. Roll up your sleeves." He jerked his finger at each of them. "All of you. I want to check for rope burns."

Maggie was incredulous. "You surely can't be serious."

"I think you're being taken to Utah as wives for all them poll-iggy-mists there."

Sarah laughed right in his face as she unbuttoned her sleeve and pulled it up. "Another wonderful lie about the Mormons," she said. When her sleeves were up, she thrust her arms toward him.

Maggie and Emma did the same. "Look," Maggie said. "No rope burns. No scars. No whip marks."

"You're kind of a mouthy one, aren't you?" he said, stepping closer.

She didn't flinch or back away but she held her tongue. The hardness on his face told her that she had better keep her Scottish temper in check. But Sarah was angry now as well. Without waiting for his permission she pulled down her sleeves and buttoned them again. "Anything else?" she said coldly.

For the first time he seemed less sure of himself. "You swear that you're going west of your own free will and choice? No one has taken you captive?"

Maggie felt very tired all of a sudden, remembering the confrontation she had faced with another defiant young man on a street in Edinburgh. This man had that same look in his eyes. He hated

Mormons, and he didn't want to hear anything that took away from his reasons for doing so. "We are not captives," she said tightly. "We are not slaves. We are going west with our families because we want to be where people don't tell stupid lies about Mormons and where there aren't other stu–" She caught herself. "And where there aren't other people who believe those lies."

"Maggie," her mother said softly as the deputy stiffened. "That's enough."

Brother James took a step forward but froze as the pistol lifted half out of its holster. "You stay back, mister," the man cried. Then he swung back to Maggie. His jaw was a hard angular line and his eyes were two glittering coals. His lips tightened to a thin line. "Missy, I suggest you just keep your mouth shut. If I want to know anything more from you, I'll ask you. Is that clear?"

Maggie saw her mistake. The deputy had ridden out with grand dreams of rescuing a dozen or so fair young damsels from the clutches of wicked old "geezers," as he called them. Now he looked incredibly foolish and he knew it. And he didn't like that. Not one bit. Though it galled her to do so, she dropped her eyes and stared at the ground. She could feel his glare burning her skin. Finally, he snorted in disgust and turned to Sarah. "Now, you're a looker, that's for sure."

She started to turn away. His hand shot out and grabbed her arm, jerking her back around roughly. "Hey! I'm talking to you."

William James cried out and lunged forward. Almost too quick for the eye to follow, the deputy whipped out his pistol and clubbed downward. There was a solid thud and a low cry, and Brother James went down hard.

"No!" Sarah cried, trying to pull away. Jane gave a soft cry and dropped to her husband's side.

The man spun Sarah around against his body, waving the pistol wildly. "Stay back. Everybody stay back."

When it was clear that everyone was doing exactly that, he

grinned lasciviously. He pulled Sarah closer. "Always wanted to kiss me a Mormon girl. Especially one as pretty as you."

"No, please," Sarah blurted, terrified now.

"Leave her alone," Maggie shouted. "You've got what you're after. Go away."

He whirled so quickly that Maggie gasped and fell back a step. Sarah was freed as the deputy's left hand shot out and grabbed Maggie by the hair. He pulled her head back sharply. Out of the corner of her eye, Maggie saw the pistol waving back and forth. Dimly she was aware of the others around her. Martha James started to cry. Maggie's mother's face was white. Emma looked suddenly sick.

Maggie's mother raised her hands in supplication. "Please," Mary said. "She didn't mean anything. Let her go."

He didn't even glance in Mary's direction. He was breathing hard and Maggie could smell his breath. It smelled of tobacco and, oddly enough, of fried bacon. "I'll tell you when I've got what I'm after," he hissed into her ear, his grip tightening on her hair. Then that terrible grin stole across his face again. "You ain't near the looker that your friend here is, but maybe I'll start with you just to warm up a little."

He yanked her head forward and kissed her hard and full on the mouth.

When he pulled her head back again, he laughed raucously and waved the muzzle of the pistol in her face. "Bet you ain't never been kissed like that before."

Maggie stared at him, the shock and disgust numbing her whole body. She was thoroughly frightened now. In Edinburgh, the boys had carried clubs. Here they carried something much more dangerous. She sensed that he was ready to hurt her, that he would enjoy hurting her.

He jerked her head backwards again, pulling her close to his body. "How did you like it, missy?" he snarled. "Tell me you liked it."

Something deep down in Maggie's Scottish nature flared. She

lifted her chin, clamped her mouth tightly shut, and looked at him defiantly.

It took him by surprise. She saw it in his eyes. But even as the shock registered it turned to fury. He jerked her head back harder, causing her back to bend sharply. "Say it, Mormon! I'm warning you!"

"But she didn't like it."

Everyone whirled as Eric Pederson stepped up beside them. The deputy spun around, letting go of Maggie as he fell back a little, pistol coming up quickly. Maggie dropped to one knee, but quickly recovered and stood again. She saw that others in the company had started to gather around. Captain Woodward was walking swiftly toward them. Then her eyes stopped on Eric. He stood beside her mother. He carried a three-foot length of shovel handle which the men used to lock the wheels when they were doing repairs on the handcarts. He stood casually, his face relaxed and almost smiling, but she saw that he tapped his leg with the handle softly in a slow, easy rhythm.

The pistol came up and pointed at Eric. There was sudden panic in the deputy's eyes. He hadn't been paying attention and now he was nearly surrounded by people. "Who are you?"

"I'm her brother."

King licked his lips, glancing at the others. He waved the pistol at Eric. "Get out of here. This ain't none of your affair."

Eric took a step closer. When he spoke, his voice was almost conversational. "I heard sheriff. He said to learn if anything was wrong. He didn't say you could be—" He turned and looked at Maggie. "How do you say it in English?"

"A dingbat," she said contemptuously.

"Dingbat?" He seemed puzzled.

"Yes, it means empty-headed. Sawdust for brains. A dolt. A fool."

"Why, you—," King cried. He lunged at Maggie, swinging the pistol. She gasped, but the shovel handle flashed in a blur of motion.

There was a sharp crack and the young man screamed. The pistol flew from his hand and hit the ground with a solid thud.

"You broke my arm!" King cried, falling back, clutching at his wrist.

Eric bent over and picked up the pistol. He held it by the trigger guard and let it dangle harmlessly.

"Oh my!" Emma breathed in astonishment.

Maggie gaped at him. Eric had barely moved his body.

"Get on your horse," Eric said easily. "I shall give pistol to the sheriff."

The circle of people parted, opening a path to his mount. Cursing softly, still holding his right arm to his chest, the man backed away. His horse stood waiting a few feet from him. When he reached it he stopped, looking up at the saddle. "I can't get up with my arm," he wailed.

"I will help," Eric suggested, stepping forward.

"No! No! It's all right." He reached up to the horn with his left arm and dragged himself into the saddle, crying out in pain as he did so.

"Go," Eric commanded, motioning with his club toward the head of the column. "Wait up there."

As King rode away, there was a shout from behind them. They turned to see Captain Willie, the sheriff, and the other men on their horses coming toward them on the run. When he saw his deputy riding off, the sheriff spurred his horse. The others did the same. Now the group of emigrants fell back into a line, leaving Eric and Maggie standing in front of them.

The law officer pulled up sharply, staring at Eric, who still had King's pistol dangling from his finger. "What's going on here?" he demanded.

Maggie stepped forward. "Your deputy asked us his questions, Sheriff, and we gave him our answers. Then he got fresh with us." She looked at Sarah, who still looked a little dazed. "He decided he wanted to kiss some Mormon girls."

"He kissed Maggie," Emma blurted. "He forced her to kiss him."

The sheriff scowled, then swore under his breath. He looked at Sarah, his eyes quickly taking in her beauty, knowing he was hearing the truth. He turned to look at the retreating rider and again mumbled something under his breath. He was clearly disgusted.

"Sheriff," Captain Willie said. "You've searched the wagons. You've gone up and down the company. As you can tell, there is nothing wrong here."

The man nodded slowly, staring at Eric. "What did you do to my man?"

"I asked him to leave, that's all." There was a faint smile. "He dropped the pistol." He stepped forward, handing it butt first to the sheriff.

"Fool!" the sheriff said again. He looked at his other men. "I told you to mind your manners."

Maggie's hands had started to tremble now in a delayed reaction, and she pressed them against her body so no one would notice. The relief made her knees feel weak.

The sheriff turned to Captain Willie. "Sir, you have our apology. Clearly the report we were given in town has no basis in fact. We are sorry for troubling you." He looked down at the women and tipped his hat. "And I apologize for this lout of mine who still needs to learn some manners."

Maggie forced a smile. "I think the word we used was *dingbat,*" she murmured.

"Well, he'll not be bothering you anymore." He lifted the reins, and in a moment he and the other deputies were trotting away.

Once they were out of earshot, their captain turned to look at them. "What in the world happened here?" he asked. And then as the group all looked at each other, not sure who should speak, he shook his head. "I'll hear the whole story tonight. For now, we've got to get moving. We'll be stopping at Muddy Creek in about an hour and making camp."

II

Friday, 1 August 1856

Some one hundred and sixty miles and sixteen days out of Iowa City, at a place called Timber Point, Iowa, the James G. Willie Handcart Company was making camp. They had come only fourteen miles that day, but the afternoon heat had been almost unbearable, and several people had fainted, some in the shafts of their handcarts, so Captain Willie had finally called for an early halt.

For the moment, the activity around the camp was in a lull. The large round tents were up now. Supper would come in about an hour, but the camp had basically collapsed in exhaustion. Except for a few young children, who could be heard laughing as they explored the new campsite, the camp looked like a dead zone. Everywhere you looked, people were sprawled out on the ground. Some were dozing; others sat in clusters and spoke quietly.

Near one of the tents, Eric and Olaf Pederson had rolled out their bedrolls. Elsie Nielson had little Jens and Bodil Mortensen seated on a dead log beside her, telling them one of the fairy tales of Hans Christian Andersen, who was almost a national hero in Denmark. The senior Jens had gone off with a couple of the other brethren to look for firewood for in the morning.

Eric stood up. "Sister Nielson?"

Elsie turned.

"Is there anything more you need right now?"

She smiled at him, knowing what he had on his mind. "No, that's fine."

"All right. I won't be long."

The three girls were on their backs in the thick grass. Maggie's bonnet was off and she had spread her thick dark hair out behind her to get it off her neck. On her left, Emma and Sarah looked like corpses laid out for burial. Both of them had their eyes closed, and Maggie wasn't sure but what they were asleep. Maggie's eyes were not closed. She stared up at the leafy canopy above them, listening to the soft gurgle of the creek which was a few feet away. Who would have ever guessed that shade and fresh water would come to be something so luxurious that she would long for it more than the most elegant of dishes? She wanted to savor it, store it up somehow for when they were out on the trail again tomorrow.

Maggie rose up, leaning on one elbow. She looked around. In the dappled light of the wooded grove, the only things she saw standing were the oxen and mules, hobbled and let loose to graze near the supply wagons. Their tails switched lazily back and forth. About twenty yards away, sitting on the grass near one of the wagons, she saw Captain Willie with his five subcaptains. They were talking quietly, not wanting to disturb anyone. She listened but heard nothing from their own tent, which was a few feet away. Like most of the others, the McKensies and the Jameses were taking advantage of the chance to rest.

Then a movement out of the corner of her eye caught Maggie's attention. To her surprise, Eric Pederson was walking at a brisk pace through the trees on the other side of the creek. Surprised, she sat up. What could possibly motivate anyone to be up and moving about right now, and with such purpose? She looked down at the others. Neither Sarah nor Emma had moved. Quietly she picked up her shoes, then stood and stretched. Sarah stirred and opened one eye lazily. "What are you doing?"

"I'm just going to walk about a bit."

"Silly," Sarah mumbled, then closed her eye again.

Maggie laughed softly. "I know."

She slipped away, moving as noiselessly as she could until she was away from them. Then she crossed the creek, loving the feel of the cold water on her bare feet. Eric was now about twenty-five or thirty yards ahead of her and still moving with definite purpose. She sat down and put on her shoes quickly, then jumped up and hurried after him, staying back and keeping trees between her and him so he wouldn't see her. He didn't go far, and when she saw where he stopped, then she understood.

On more than one occasion Maggie had noticed Eric going over to spend time with the footmen of the company. Sometimes it was at night after supper; other times in was in the morning before they departed. Curious, she had asked Olaf about it one day. Olaf had been reluctant at first, but finally admitted that Eric had someone among the footmen that he checked on regularly. When Maggie asked who, he would say no more. It was something Eric did, he explained, and wasn't anxious to have others know about. Olaf's reticence only piqued Maggie's curiosity the more. Was it a young woman? Maybe that was why he treated Sarah's interest in him so casually. Well, now she decided she had a chance to find out for herself.

When he stopped beside one of the tents in the area where the Chislett group was camped, Maggie moved in behind a large hickory tree to watch. To her surprise, he didn't mingle among the group. He called out greetings to several, but he went directly to where two older sisters, one with white hair, one with gray, sat on the ground. When they saw him they rose immediately, their faces wreathed in smiles.

Thoroughly taken aback, Maggie slipped a little closer so she could hear, feeling only a momentary twinge of shame for eavesdropping. Could they be relatives? But then she shook her head. These were English women, as were all of Chislett's group. Eric was Norwegian. She leaned forward to hear better, but the women had their backs to her and their voices were barely a murmur. Twice there was laughter, but she couldn't distinguish what they were saying.

Eric fussed there for several minutes and then stood up. He turned so he was facing them, which put him facing Maggie as well. "Are you sure you're all right?" she heard him ask.

Both nodded but she again couldn't hear their reply.

"You drinking lots of water?" he wanted to know.

They both nodded again.

"All right. I'll come see you in the morning before we leave."

To her further surprise, he gave them both a hug, which was returned with some earnestness, then waved and started toward her. Startled, Maggie realized she was standing directly in his path. For a moment she almost bolted, but then realized it was too late. She stepped out from behind the tree.

Eric stopped, staring at her. "Maggie?"

"What?" she cried, fumbling for a way to deflect his inevitable question. "Not Sister Maggie today?"

"What are you doing here?"

She was tempted to say something about looking for wood or trying to find someone, but she couldn't lie. "Actually," she said, a little embarrassed now, "Olaf told me that you come see the footmen off each day, and I was curious as to who and why."

He laughed and came forward to stand beside her. They turned and started back toward the main camp. "I come to see my granny," he said, smiling.

"That's your grandmother?" she blurted.

He laughed easily. "Sister Bathgate? No, but she is much like my grandmother. I come each day to make sure they're okay."

Maggie stopped, staring at him. He walked on several steps before he stopped too. "What?" he said.

She hadn't realized what she had done and had to recover quickly. "Nothing," she said.

He gave her a strange look, but didn't push further. They walked together slowly, weaving their way through the tents and the people sprawled out around them. She was relieved that it hadn't turned out to be an embarrassment for her. When they reached the creek, she slipped off her shoes again and went across slowly, savoring the cool wetness. He waited until she was across, then jumped it in one leap.

There was a soft sound and Maggie's head came up. Sarah and Emma were sitting up, staring at the two of them in surprise.

"Well, hello," Eric said easily.

They stood quickly. Emma brushed at her hair with her fingers, then picked a piece of leaf from her dress. "Where's Olaf?"

"At the tent. Sleeping probably."

As he spoke to her sister, Sarah shot Maggie a probing look. She shrugged, not wanting to try and explain in front of Eric. Then, surprising them all, Eric sat down and began removing his shoes. When he finished, he moved to the creek and plunged his feet into the water. He closed his eyes and lay back, sheer pleasure on his face.

Not to be outdone, the girls joined him, and soon there were four pairs of feet in the cool water. Maggie could hardly believe it. Eric Pederson? Stopping to take time for a casual visit? She was thoroughly amazed, and yet quietly pleased. Since his intervention with the deputy, she had not had a chance to really thank him. Now perhaps she would.

But Eric took charge of the conversation—another surprise—and kept the conversation away from any mention of the incident with the deputy. They talked about Hannah and Ingrid, wondering if they had left Iowa City by now. Eric reported that Elder Ahmanson said that they should be in Florence in another ten or twelve days and promised that they would stop there for a couple of weeks while they prepared for the jump into the wilderness. Surely that would give the following company time to catch up with them. Thereafter, they hoped, they would be able to travel together.

They spoke of the pitiful state of the handcarts. The lumber was warping to where great cracks were appearing in the boxes of the carts, and in some cases they simply fell apart under the day-long pounding they received. And the sand and dirt were now a serious problem. Without any tin to line the boxes and keep the dirt out of the axle housing, the sand was grinding down the wood at an alarming rate. Also, their axle grease had long since been depleted, and they were down to using bacon grease or lard. They talked about the diminishing food supply. They were on slightly reduced rations now so that they would have enough flour to see them through to Florence.

Maggie kept expecting Eric to bound up at any moment and mumble that he had to go, but he didn't. He was relaxed and seemed to enjoy their company. Then he started recounting his experience in trying to help the teamsters hitch up the mules that morning. For some reason the animals had turned stubborn and balked at every turn. Eric's English was getting quite good now, but when he wanted, he could drop back into a twangy, combination Norwegian-English accent that kept them all laughing. He was a good storyteller and clearly enjoyed entertaining an appreciative audience.

"So," he concluded, "Brother Savage finally had to give that big black mule a whack—" He turned to Maggie. "Is that how you say it?"

"I think Robbie's word is *thwack.*"

"Ah, yah. Anyway we had to give that mule a real thwack. He is stubborn, much like Sister Maggie when we do not say the right verb in English class—"

"What?" Maggie cried.

Feigning innocence, Eric turned to Sarah and Emma. "It is true, no?"

"She is more stubborn than two mules," Sarah agreed. Then she started to mimic. "That is the wrong verb, Olaf. Bad boy."

Maggie's mouth opened wide. "I never said any such thing."

Emma giggled, raising one arm as though she were cracking a whip. "Learn those verbs, Eric. Practice harder, Ingrid."

Maggie looked wounded. "See if I ever teach you one word ever again, Eric Pederson," she vowed.

"Anyway," Eric went on, ignoring Maggie's dark look, "this mule wants to go back to Iowa City. He does not want to pull wagons anymore. So he turned to Captain Willie and said—" Now his voice took on a distinct drawl. "'Cap'n, sir. Don't wanna pull no more wagons, sir. If you don't mind, I think I'll ride in one of the handcarts.'"

Still smarting a little from the teasing, Maggie broke in. "So now you're learning how to speak mule talk as well as English?"

Eric seemed shocked. "Didn't I tell you that?"

Emma grinned, thoroughly enjoying this now. "Say something in mule, Eric. I want to hear you."

He cupped his hands, tipped his head back, and gave such a perfect imitation of the braying of a mule that they all began to laugh. All around, people sat up or stood up to see if one of the animals had gotten loose.

"What do you think, Emma?" Eric said gravely when he finished. "Am I speaking it all right?"

She clapped her hands in delight. "Perfectly."

"Yes," Maggie said, seeing a chance to dig him back a little. "Actually, it's much better than your English."

He never changed expression. "Oh, yah," he said with a deadpan face. "It is very helpful. How do you think I know what that deputy was saying?"

It took one instant to register, and then they all exploded.

He went right on, puckering up his lips and imitating the deputy's voice. "Missy McKensie. I want a kiss. Hee-haw! Hee-haw!"

Maggie couldn't help herself. She doubled over, holding her stomach. Emma was whooping in delight.

He looked at Sarah. "Hey, Mormon girl," he said in the same voice. "You very pretty lady, missy. Come give this handsome donkey one big kiss. Hee-haw!"

Sarah too was clutching at her stomach. “Oh, stop, Eric,” she cried. “Stop. It hurts.”

He did, and gradually a lazy smile stole across his face. He looked at Maggie. “So maybe I don’t study English anymore. Maybe I just go to mule class.”

Wiping at her eyes, she could only nod. Was this Eric Pederson? Was this the man who had seemed so shy and reticent in her English class? the one who had almost fled when her mother invited him to stay for dinner a while ago? She could scarcely believe it.

Then, once again catching everyone off guard, Eric stood up. “Well,” he said, “I’d better go. Sister Nielson will be getting supper.” He said good-bye quickly and walked away.

They waved and called their good-byes, then turned to each other. Sarah was shaking her head. “Was that someone we know?” she wondered.

Maggie was still staring after him. “I’m not sure.” She was having a hard time believing what had just happened. Then a smile slowly stole across her face and filled her eyes. But whatever it was, it had been nice. Very nice.

III

Monday, 11 August 1856

Jens Nielson and Eric Pederson had the handcart turned around backwards. Together they leaned against the crossbar and pushed the two-wheeled cart up the ramp and onto the wooden deck of the ferryboat that would take them across the Missouri River. With the ferryman and Olaf guiding them, they carefully moved it forward, placing the wheels so they overlapped the shafts of the carts that were already there. Satisfied, the ferryman dropped his hands. "That's good, brethren. Let her down right there."

How strange, Eric thought. They had crossed three hundred miles of Iowa, and now as they were about to cross into Nebraska Territory and leave the United States, they had a ferryman who called them "brethren." *How wonderful!* That, more than anything, said what it meant for them to be on the verge of reaching Florence.

They did so and stepped back. Theirs was the tenth handcart on the ferry, and the boat was now almost full. Johan Ahmanson and the other brethren who had put their carts on first stood back, waiting for further instructions. "All right," the heavyset man said, "let's get your families on board." He squinted up at the sun, which was better than halfway down in its track toward the west. "Got one more load to get across before dark. You've got some people waiting for you. Let's move."

Jens Nielson turned to where Elsie, young Jens, and Bodil Mortensen were waiting a few feet away with the rest of the Scandinavian hundred, watching the proceedings with eager faces. He called to them. "Come on. They're ready."

The families moved up the gangplank and joined their husbands and fathers. They were on the eastern bank of the Missouri River. Though the ferryman said the river was low, being late in the season, it was still an impressive sight. Not as much as the Mississippi had been, but it was still wide, deep, and swift nevertheless. Olaf was glad they didn't have to try to ford it.

There was a lurch and the ferry started out into the river. Across, several men guided the yoke of oxen that pulled on the heavy rope that provided the power they needed. Olaf looked at the ferryman, still a little surprised to think that he was a member of the Church, even out here this far in the wilderness. "So that's Florence?"

"Not right there where we land," the ferry captain answered from behind them. "But it's not far. Just up and over the hill. Welcome to Nebraska Territory."

"So we did it," Olaf said to Eric in satisfaction, speaking in Norwegian.

"Did what?"

He looked back over his shoulder. There was no sense of longing in him for what he saw, that was for sure. His face split with a triumphant grin. "Conquered Iowa. She tried her best to beat us, but we punched her in the nose."

"Yes, we did," Eric said. He reached out and clapped his brother on the shoulder. There was still eleven hundred miles to go, but this was a good day. A good day indeed.

Chapter Notes

The details shared here of the Willie Company as they crossed Iowa—including dates of departure, mileage, those who turned back, and the death of Mary Williams—come from the company journal (see Turner, *Emigrating Journals,* pp. 15–18). One entry, that of 25 July 1856, reads as follows: "Traveled as far as Muddy Creek, 13 miles. Stopped twice by the way to rest. The weather being very warm. Just before we camped, we were overtaken by the Sheriff with a warrant to search the wagons, under the idea that the women were detained contrary to their wishes, with ropes. After showing their authority, they had permission to examine any part of the company, and were fully satisfied that the report was without foundation, and they left us."

CHAPTER 12

IOWA CITY, IOWA
TO
INDIAN TOWN, IOWA

I

Monday, 28 July 1856

On the day that the Edward Martin Company marched out of the Mormon Campground at Iowa City, there were no large crowds of people standing by to watch them go as had happened when the Willie Company left. Hannah McKensie clearly remembered that day two weeks before when she and Ingrid had gone out and said good-bye to Hannah's family. She had felt such a burst of longing to be with them instead of standing on the sidelines waving good-bye.

Well, now it was their turn. And who cared if the group come to bid them farewell was pitifully small? There were the five Church agents, with Brother Daniel Spencer at their head, and a few from the independent wagon companies. Ingrid was bothered by that a little, Hannah knew. She had stayed behind specifically to help translate for the Scandinavians who were in the Hodgett Wagon Company. Now only one or two had come out to see her off. It was understandable. They would be leaving soon, probably tomorrow, and final preparations were under way. Time was precious, and even an hour could be costly.

"Where are your thoughts, Hannah?"

She looked around at Elizabeth Jackson. She was holding little Aaron, who was just two, while her husband checked the lashings on their cart one last time. Hannah smiled. "I was thinking about the Scandinavian Saints and if they will come and say good-bye to Ingrid."

"I wondered that too." Sister Jackson half turned. Ingrid was off to one side playing with Sister Jackson's two girls. "Do you think she feels bad that they haven't?"

"She says no, but I think she does a little. She's done a lot for them."

"I know." Sister Jackson's eyes were still on Ingrid. "She has done a lot for us too. As have you, Hannah. We are so thankful that you two were able to stay and help us."

"Yes, we are." Aaron Jackson gave one last yank on the rope, then came around to join them. "We know it was a sacrifice for the both of you."

Hannah was embarrassed now. In the two weeks since saying good-bye to her family, she had drawn very close to the Jacksons. That had helped assuage her loss somewhat, but it had still been hard. "I'm not the only one who's been separated from family. Ingrid is traveling with just her aunt and uncle. Our two friends from Norway left everyone behind. Brother Ahmanson has his wife and child with the wagon company."

Just then they saw Daniel Spencer approaching. He smiled as he reached them. "All set?" he asked.

They all nodded vigorously.

"Good. Again, thanks to you, Hannah, and to Ingrid for staying to help."

"You're welcome," Hannah said. "Do you think we'll be able to catch the others?"

"I hope so. Once we get you out of here, the other agents and I will leave. We have light wagons and carriages and will make much better time than you. We should catch Captain Willie at Florence, if not before, so we'll tell them you're coming."

"Will you tell my family hello when you see them?"

"I will." He looked around. "Well, they're readjusting the load in one of the wagons; then I think Captain Martin is about ready to start."

With that, Elder Spencer tipped his hat and walked away. He stopped for a moment to speak to John Jaques, who, along with James Loader and his family, was just a few carts ahead of them. Jaques was one of the captains of hundreds as well as the historian of the company. When Spencer strode on, he headed for the front of the column where Elder Edward Martin was waiting.

That was the signal the company had been waiting for. Carts were hoisted. Men and women both got inside the shafts and grabbed the crossbars. Teamsters swung up onto the wagon seats.

Edward Martin didn't wait for all of that to finish. Unlike Elder Willie, who had made such a dramatic call for them to move, he simply shook hands with Brother Spencer, swung up onto his horse, and started forward, waving his arm for the others to follow.

As the column began to lurch into motion, Hannah McKensie turned and looked around the campground one last time. To her surprise, she felt a sudden sadness. The campground was littered with piles of materials. There were heaps of books, blankets, clothing, cooking utensils, tools. One only had to look for a moment to realize that there were literally dozens upon dozens of family treasures being left behind here–family pictures taken from walls; furniture that had been in the family for generations; boxes filled with inexpensive jewelry, perfumes, and other toiletry items; small and large chests which held who knew what; full-sized mirrors, vases, china dishes, valued statuary. This was the detritus of the weigh-in held by the Church agents a few days before. If it wasn't within the seventeen-pound limit, it was left behind. Somehow it seemed like the perfect metaphor for this day. Everything they had known, everything they had loved and treasured in their former lives had been discarded. They were already dusty and starting to bleach in the merciless sun.

Hannah straightened her shoulders and raised her head, eager now for that first step. The old was being abandoned, that was true. But the promise of the new was exciting and wondrous. She leaned over, putting her hands against the back of the cart.

Ingrid bent down beside her. They looked at each other for a moment, then grinned happily. "Let's do it, Ingrid," Hannah said. "Let's go."

Ingrid's blue eyes were dancing. "I'm ready, Hannah. I think I could run all the way to Zion."

II

Wednesday, 6 August 1856

Ingrid and Hannah were taking their turn at pulling in the shafts at the moment. The Jacksons had pulled for more than two hours without a break, and the girls were determined to equal that. At Aaron's insistence, his wife was walking alongside now, holding on to little Aaron's hand to steady him atop the cart. Brother Jackson was behind, pushing steadily, keeping the girls moving in order to help them.

The ground was quite level here and the road was good, so the handcart rolled along easily. But Hannah realized that this was the surest sign that they were all, finally, after nine days on the trail, in good physical shape. The blisters were healing, the legs no longer ached, and she could tell that she had significantly greater strength in her arms now.

The two of them—Scottish lass and Danish farm girl—moved along in perfect step, the rhythm of their walking long since synchronized. Their heads were down as they leaned into the crossbar, putting one foot before the other in an endlessly monotonous rhythm.

They nooned atop a large eminence, one of the tallest in the area. The Jacksons sat in the tiny block of shade provided by the handcart, munching on bread and drinking cups of tepid water. Elizabeth Jackson looked around. In every direction the prairie stretched away into nothingness. It was as though they had been dropped back onto the ocean again. Here and there in the hazy distance there were smudges of darker color—a creek or a small grove of trees on some other water source—but otherwise it was perfectly featureless.

"I can't believe it," the Englishwoman said. She was sitting on the ground, her arms folded across her knees and her chin resting on them.

"What?" her husband asked.

"Look. Not a house. Not a building. Not a barn or a shed or even an outhouse. No hedgerows, no village lanes, no churches, no pubs, no farms, no factories. Nothing as far as you can see."

Hannah let her eyes search the emptiness as well. After the lush richness of Edinburgh, this was not something that had drawn her eye.

"Fort Des Moines is only a few miles behind us," Aaron Jackson noted. They had passed through that settlement earlier in the day, but quickly left any other civilization behind.

"Think of Liverpool," she went on, barely hearing him. "Think of London and Manchester. Think how many thousands upon thousands of people there are in England who have scarcely enough room to breathe, who are piled into rows and rows of depressingly dingy tenement houses. There is never enough food to feed them all. And here lies all of this empty land—unowned, fertile, unplowed. Prairie grass and wildflowers. That's all it grows."

Her husband was nodding now.

"Can you imagine us trying to tell people back in England about this? They wouldn't believe it. I can scarcely believe it, and I'm looking at it."

"I'll bet you could fit all of Scotland in what we can see with our eyes from right here," Hannah said.

Sister Jackson nodded, then laid her head down on her arms. "It truly is the land of promise, isn't it?"

At that, Hannah had a sudden thought. "Do you remember what the Book of Mormon says about the land of promise?"

"What?"

"Father Lehi said that none should come unto this land save they should be brought by the hand of the Lord."

There was a soft murmur of assent from all of them. "Well, that is certainly true of us," Aaron Jackson said. "We wouldn't be here if it weren't for the Lord taking a hand in our lives."

"And of me as well," Ingrid said quietly. "I didn't think I would get to come this year."

Hannah once again let her eyes sweep out across the great expanse that lay before them. What if the missionaries had not come to Edinburgh? What if her father had not been impressed enough to listen, then invite them to their home? She believed that was part of the Lord's plan and offered thanks for it in her prayers regularly, but until this moment she had not really considered that her being here, in this very place, in the wide desolation of America's vast prairies, was because of the hand of the Lord in her life. She felt a deep gratitude and promised herself that tonight during evening prayers she would find that passage and read it again. Then she would offer yet another prayer of gratitude to God for his great goodness.

III

Wednesday, 13 August 1856

Captain Edward Martin was standing by a depression in the ground, and the company began to gather around him. "Are we stopping here?" someone called.

It was late in the day, but there was nothing here to indicate a campsite. There was no creek, no river, no springs, no trees, no bushes. There was prairie, and enough of that for a hundred companies like their own. No, Ingrid Christensen thought, there was room for more like a thousand such companies.

"Yes. The next water is still too far to make tonight. We'll have to make do."

"Well," Hannah said beneath her breath. She was standing right beside Ingrid, a few feet away from their captain. "At least we won't have to worry about finding a place to pitch the tents."

Ingrid laughed softly. "But we'll have to hurry before all the spots are taken."

"We'll dig down here," Brother Martin was saying. "This is an old buffalo wallow. When it rains, it collects water, so usually you can dig a hole and eventually water seeps into it."

"Wallow?" Ingrid said. "What is wallow?"

Sister Jackson came up beside them. "It's a low spot, Ingrid. During the spring rains it fills with water and mud, and so the buffalo come and roll in it. It helps keep the bugs away."

"I understand."

Everyone was staring at the low depression. Their last water had been more than six hours ago, and it had been another blistering day. The little children crowded in, pressing against their parents' legs.

"I'm thirsty, Mama," Martha Ann Jackson whispered.

"Me too," her younger brother echoed.

Ingrid didn't doubt that in the least. Her mouth felt like she had just swallowed a cupful of sand. She had sucked on a small rock for some time, trying to keep some moisture in her mouth, but she finally gave up and spit it out. Now, as she looked at the low spot, which was about ten feet across and maybe thirty or forty long, it didn't seem possible that they could get water from this place. As near as she could tell, the surface soil wasn't even wet. But then she was from Denmark. When had anyone in the last thousand years had to worry about water in Denmark?

The captain turned and called. "Brother Jackson. Get a couple of men from your company with shovels and bring them here."

Aaron was already moving before Martin finished. In a few moments he returned with two other men, each carrying a shovel. They stepped down into the depression. Captain Martin touched a spot toward one end with his toe, and the men set to work.

Most of the company had moved in to watch the men dig. No one spoke now. Water was paramount on everyone's mind. With four men working, the hole—about three feet in diameter—quickly deepened. Ingrid watched in fascination as the first shovelfuls were mostly dry. Then the soil darkened. By the time they were down a foot and half, the dirt was clumping together. It was turning muddy. A sigh of relief swept through the crowd. It was working.

At three feet, those close enough could see the water start to trickle into the hole, thick with mud and silt. Another foot and the walls of the hole began to collapse as the water came more quickly. It was black and thick as soup, but it was water.

"All right," Captain Martin called. "That should do it. Let's dig another one at the other end of the wallow. The holes will fill in about an hour, but it will take another hour or two to let the mud settle out of it. Be patient. Just take enough to drink at first. We need to get enough water for the animals too. Then you can get what you need for cooking."

Hannah pulled a face. "We're supposed to drink that?"

Suddenly a young boy of about five broke away from his mother and darted past the diggers. He threw himself down beside the hole and reached in with his hands.

"Tommie Jenkins," his mother yelled, starting toward him. "You get back here."

But the boy had already brought his hands up. They were filled with very wet mud. In wonder he squeezed them together and black liquid squirted between his fingers. He looked up in wonder. "It's cold, Mama," he cried. "And wet."

His mother stopped, her eyes softening. Then to her amazement, Tommie buried his face in his hands. There was a sucking sound as he strained the thick mixture through his teeth.

He stopped and looked up as he realized it had gone totally silent all around him. A ring of black mud covered his mouth, but his eyes were smiling. Then his teeth showed—white lights in a window of black—as he grinned. "It's all right, Mama. It's water. I can get the water." He held up his hands, streaks of black running down his arms. "It tastes good."

That was enough. While the adults grimaced or looked away, several other children darted in and dropped to their stomachs.

Ingrid wrinkled up her nose and started to back away. A moment ago she had felt like she would die for a drink of water. Now she decided that she could wait a little longer.

Captain Martin watched all of this without comment. Then he looked around at the adults. "Well, while you're getting your first lesson in getting water from a 'prairie spring,' you may as well learn about 'prairie firewood' too." He walked away, looking down at the ground. After a moment he bent down and picked up a buffalo chip. He held it up. "You all know what this is."

"How do you say it?" Ingrid asked Sister Jackson. "Buffalo—?"

"Chips. They call them buffalo chips."

"And it is the droppings of the animals?" Ingrid said, wrinkling her nose.

"Yes," Aaron laughed. "It is buffalo dung, but it is all dried out now."

The company moved in close around Elder Martin as he continued. "Well, as you can see, not only do we have no fresh water this afternoon, but for the first time since we left Iowa City more than two weeks ago, we also have no firewood. When you think about it, buffalo chips are really nothing more than dried, digested grass. They burn hot and clean and actually make a very good fuel. While the men start putting up the tents, I suggest the women and children start collecting buffalo chips."

He stopped for a moment, then chuckled softly. "The buffalo may be gone, brothers and sisters, but the essence still remains. Go to it."

As the people began to turn away and head for their carts, Hannah poked Ingrid. As she turned, Hannah pulled a face. "Ooh, let's hurry, Ingrid. I can't wait to eat potatoes which are cooked in muddy water taken from a buffalo wallow over a fire made from dried buffalo dung."

Ingrid's mouth pulled down. "Thanks, Hannah. I think I just lost my appetite."

IV

Thursday, 14 August 1856

On their eighteenth day out of Iowa City, the Edward Martin Handcart Company broke camp and resumed their westward march at eight o'clock in the morning. It was already hot, and now the prairie had given way to rolling hill country covered with scattered groves of trees and brush. It was beautiful after the flat monotony of the prairie, but it also meant pulling the carts up one hill after another. Often the roads changed from hard-packed soil to soft sand.

The wheels sank in three or four inches, and it was like adding two or three hundred pounds to the load. Feet could get no grip, and even as trail toughened as they now were, very quickly the emigrants began to feel the added strain. Calves and thighs began to ache from the lack of good footing. The heat drained moisture from them as if their bodies were wicks in a shallow pan of water. To add further to their misery, many in the company were sick, running high fevers and suffering from dysentery. For them, every mile became pure torture.

There was no question that the trail had become more beautiful now, but it had also suddenly become terribly more brutal.

At eleven o'clock they reached a small, swift-flowing creek which ran through the bottom of a thick stand of woods. Several times now in the last few days they had been forced to dig for water—twice in buffalo wallows, once near a spring which had dried up this late in the season, and once in a sandy creekbed. Captain Martin suspected it was the water that was causing much of their sickness, and knew that fresh water and shade were just too welcome to pass by. He decided they would noon there and ordered a two-hour halt.

When that word reached the Jacksons' handcart, Hannah gave a low cry of joy. Aaron Jackson, who was pulling with her at that point, gestured toward a spot near the creek that was deep in shade. When they reached it, carts were lowered, hats and bonnets removed. All around them, people sank slowly to the ground to give their aching bodies rest. Not Hannah. She walked swiftly to the creek, dropped to her knees, and began scooping up handfuls of the cool water. She drank hungrily, not caring that she was making terrible slurping sounds. Ingrid fell to her stomach beside her and shoved her whole face into the water, gulping loudly. *Wonderful idea,* Hannah thought. She buried her face into the stream as well.

In five minutes they were all sprawled out in various places on the soft, leafy ground. In a few moments more, Brother Jackson began to snore softly.

—❦—

Hannah groaned and sat up. She glanced up at the sky through the canopy of trees. "Has it been two hours yet?" she asked Elizabeth.

Sister Jackson shrugged. She lifted a hand and pointed to where one of the wagons was parked a few feet away. Edward Martin was holding a meeting with the subcaptains beside it. They were talking softly but earnestly. "If it has, they don't seem anxious about getting us up yet."

"Good." Hannah stretched lazily and looked around. She had not fallen asleep, but lying there in the cool air with the soft murmur of the stream beside them had been one of the most restful things she had done since leaving Scotland. It was absolutely wonderful.

"What if we just stayed here for another couple of days?" Ingrid said. She was still lying down with her eyes closed.

"How about a couple of years?" Hannah retorted. Then she looked around. "Where's Brother Jackson?"

"He wanted to get some more flour from the supply wagon."

That gave Hannah a chance to speak about something that was troubling her but which she hadn't dared bring up before. "Is Brother Jackson all right?" she asked his wife.

A shadow fell across Elizabeth Jackson's face. "Yes," she said slowly. "He has had a little touch of the sickness these last few days, but I think he's better."

"Good." It had frightened her to see that their only man on the cart had not been able to pull with the same vigor as on previous days. If it was left to the women, it would be very challenging.

Just then they saw him coming, a sack of flour on his shoulder. As he drew closer, Hannah saw that his face was grim.

"Uh-oh," Sister Jackson murmured, standing up now to await her husband. As he reached them and set the sack in the back of the cart, she spoke. "Aaron, is anything wrong?"

"You haven't seen a young boy wandering around have you? a boy without his parents?"

Hannah, Ingrid, and Elizabeth exchanged looks, then shook their heads. "No."

"His name is Arthur Parker," Brother Jackson said with a worried frown. "His mother came round a bit ago looking for him. They supposed he was with the other children, but it seems he wasn't. Now she's just reported him missing to Brother Martin."

"Sorry." Hannah felt a little sheepish. She had been looking up at leaves, not around the camp. "We weren't really watching for anyone."

"He's probably just off playing with some of his friends," Elizabeth said helpfully.

"Or fell asleep under a bush like us," Ingrid suggested.

Just then they heard a low, far-off rumble. A little surprised, they each swung around to look to the west. There had been a few clouds in the west as they approached the creek almost two hours ago, but Hannah had thought nothing of them. But now through the trees she could see that the western sky was mostly gray.

Then she heard a man speaking. Edward Martin and the remaining captains were on their feet. They too were looking toward the west. Martin's voice came softly to them, muted by the trees. "Stay here," he said to the others. "I want to take a look." He walked away swiftly. The thunder rumbled again, this time more distinctly. Here and there, others in the camp were taking notice now as well.

In a couple of minutes Brother Martin was back. He shook his head. "It's pretty dark. I think we've got a storm brewing." He looked at the others for a moment, then said, "With that and the sickness, perhaps it is best if we make camp here rather than get caught out in the open."

No one disagreed with that welcome news. Their captain nodded. "Let's spread the word."

Hannah almost clapped her hands. "Yes!" she cried. She wouldn't get her wish to stay here forever, but the rest of the day and one full night would be heaven indeed.

"All right, brothers and sisters," their captain called out in a loud voice, turning as he spoke so that all could hear. "We'll camp here for the night. Let's get the tents up quickly and make sure they're staked down good and tight."

All across the wooded glen that meandered along the path of the creek, the sound of voices echoed back and forth. The tents were being pitched. Large enough to hold twenty people and their belongings, putting them up was always a challenge. With the wind rising and starting to gust, it was taking not only the men but the women and older children as well. They were working quickly because now the smell of rain was in the air. This was one of the things that was amazing to Hannah McKensie—the swiftness with which a prairie thunderstorm could approach. It was less than quarter of an hour before when they had first noticed it. Now they would have to hurry to beat it.

As they finished and began to shuttle their things from the carts into the tent, a shrill cry brought them up. "Captain Martin! Captain Martin!"

Across the creek and about thirty feet away, Captain Edward Martin and two other men were securing the covers on the supply wagons. Martin turned, shielding his eyes from the dust and blowing leaves. A couple were making their way quickly toward him. Hannah and Ingrid were by their cart pulling out their bedding. Their tent was up now and they were hurrying to get their things inside. They stopped to watch.

The cry brought Elizabeth Jackson out of the tent. She came to stand beside her two adopted daughters. After a moment she started. "Oh dear."

"What?" Hannah asked.

"That's Ann Parker."

"Who is that?"

"Remember the little boy that was lost today? His name was Parker too."

Now, as the couple reached Elder Martin, Hannah could see that the woman was crying. Her husband, more subdued, looked nevertheless quite grim. "Brother Martin, our son is missing."

"What?" he exclaimed in alarm. "You mean you didn't find him?"

"No, and we've checked everywhere," Brother Parker said. One hand came up and ran through his hair. It said more than words about how distraught he was. "He's not in the camp."

"How long has he been gone?" Brother Martin demanded.

Sister Parker's head dropped and it was her husband who had to answer. He looked pale and drawn. "We're not sure. We thought he was with our other children. When we crossed the creek and stopped to noon, he never came in."

Hannah, Ingrid, and Sister Jackson went over to join them as well.

Brother Martin was firing questions now at Brother Parker. Sister Parker was too ashamed to look at anyone. "As you know, Brother Martin," Brother Parker said, "I've had the fever the last few days and have been riding in one of the wagons."

Ann Parker's hands were twisting and turning. "Our son Maxie, who is twelve, always helps with the cart, and so Martha Alice, who is ten, watches over the younger children. But with Robert too sick to pull, we've had to have Martha Alice help us push. Some of the other children promised to watch Arthur."

"Arthur started in with the fever this morning, too," Brother Parker added. "He was feeling quite poorly."

The woman's eyes lifted briefly, then dropped again. She couldn't bear to meet anyone else's gaze. That was too bad, Hannah thought, for there was no one who was looking at her with condemning eyes. This was one of the universal fears of companies on the trail. Once a large company got under way each day, it was customary for the younger children to gather into their own group and follow along behind or off to one side, away from the heaviest dust. This was not just to free up the parents to push the carts. There was some danger in having the children underfoot. When your eyes were searching the ground ahead for prairie dog holes or the dreaded prickly pear plants, you couldn't watch a child every moment. Each handcart, even as lightly loaded as they were for the Iowa portion of the journey, carried about four hundred pounds. A child run over by one of them could be seriously injured. The wagons and their teams were even more dangerous. Older brothers and sisters too young to pull were given charge of the younger ones and told to keep them away from the line of march. Martha Ann Jackson, who was seven, for example, had the responsibility for Mary Elizabeth, who was only five. It was the only way for families to cope with the double challenge of moving forward at the same time as caring for their children.

Just then the first raindrops splattered on the canvas cover. Elder Martin looked up at the sky, frowning. The air was an ugly black now, and the wind was tearing at their clothes. This was likely going to be another gully-buster. He made a quick decision. "All right, let's get things secure. This looks like a fast-moving storm. Once it clears, we'll make a thorough search of the camp. Then . . ." He let it trail off. Then there was only one thing to do and that was send a party back to search the trail.

The storm lasted about forty minutes, viciously lashing the camp, then passed on to the east. After that it took almost two more hours to confirm that six-year-old Arthur Parker was nowhere in the camp. As Ann Parker wept, Captain Martin called for two men from each company of hundred to form a posse that would accompany Robert Parker back across the trail to look for the boy. They set out immediately, knowing that they would not be able to search the full eleven miles they had come that morning. It was past four-thirty and there was no way they could cover that much ground before dark. If the boy wasn't found, they would resume the search in the morning.

Aaron Jackson was one of those chosen to go, so after the evening meal was completed, Sister Jackson, her three children, and Hannah and Ingrid crossed the creek and walked to the eastern edge of the trees where the company was camped. To no one's surprise, Ann Parker and her four children were already there, watching steadfastly down the road they had crossed earlier in the day.

They quietly found a log and sat down to join in the vigil. One by one the wives and children of the other men who had gone with the posse came out to sit with them.

It was almost full dark when they heard a faint shout. Sister Parker leaped to her feet and shouted back. "Do you have him, Robert?"

Her shoulders sagged and she buried her face in her hands when the faint answer came floating back on the night air. "No! We didn't find him."

V

Saturday, 16 August 1856

Captain Martin kept the company camped at the creek for two additional days while the search posse traced and retraced the trail between there and their last campground. The rainstorm that had been a blessing in letting them rest at camp had proven to be a cursing for the trackers. All traces of their trail had been obliterated. It would seem like an easy thing to backtrack over the path that a company of nearly five hundred people had crossed, but out on the prairie the handcarts moved in and out of the main trail. If the roads were too rutted or had muddy sloughs, they might go off for as far as a mile to find a better place. Also, the column did not stay in a single line. When the ground was good, people would spread out for as much as a quarter of a mile laterally to escape the terrible dust. It was not like following a single track where Arthur Parker would have been. And that was not to consider the fact that a six-year-old, especially if he was lost and frightened, could cover a lot of ground in one day's time.

The second night the search posse came trailing in just at sundown. At least half of the camp, including the Jacksons, were waiting on the eastern edge of the camp to greet them. When her husband shook his head in response to her pleading look, Ann Parker dropped her head and began to sob softly.

Edward Martin visited quietly with different searchers, then came over to stand beside the stricken couple. Sister Parker saw instantly what was coming. Her hand shot out and she clutched at his arm. "One more day, Brother Martin. Please." Her voice was near hysteria and filled with unspeakable grief. "We can't give up."

"Sister Parker," the captain began, "I know how hard it is to—"

"No," she cried. "We can't just walk away. He's alive. I know he's still alive."

"Ann, dear," her husband started, taking her in his arms.

She turned and buried her face against his chest, and her body began to shake violently.

Captain Martin watched her for a moment, his own face torn with pain. Finally, he sighed. "Brother Parker, I—"

"I understand, Brother Martin."

"Our food supply is getting dangerously low. It's almost September and we're not even to Florence yet. We have to keep moving or we face disastrous consequences."

"Yes," Brother Parker said, pulling his wife in tighter against him, trying to stop the shudders. "We'll be ready."

The captain's shoulders lifted and fell, a gesture that more than anything else he could have done showed the burden of leadership. Then slowly he turned and surveyed the faces around him. "Brothers and sisters," he said, his voice heavy. "Even though it is the Sabbath tomorrow, prepare to break camp in the morning. We'll leave immediately after breakfast."

VI

Sunday, 17 August 1856

Hannah and Ingrid were kneeling beside the creek, washing out the breakfast dishes while the others took down the tent and stowed their personal belongings.

"This must be the hardest thing she has ever done," Hannah said softly.

"Who?"

She nodded, indicating a solitary figure off to their left. It was Sister Parker, working halfheartedly at putting her things in the cart.

"Did you hear?" Ingrid said, turning to look at her now.

"Hear what?"

"Brother Parker left early this morning to go back and look for him some more."

"*What?* But I thought that . . . Even after the search party couldn't find him?" And then suddenly Robbie's face flashed into Hannah's mind. If it were her brother who was lost, what would she do? What would her mother be doing this morning? There was no question. If no one else would, then Hannah or Maggie would be going back alone, no matter what anyone else said.

"It was very sad," Ingrid went on softly. "Sister Parker tied a red shawl around her husband's shoulders—I guess he's not completely well yet—and told him if he finds Arthur dead, he should bury him in the shawl. If he is alive, he is to signal to her with it when he returns. She promises to wait at the edge of camp every night and watch for him."

Hannah's eyes suddenly clouded and she looked away. Finally she turned back. "Ingrid? I know we've already had morning prayers, but could we say another one?"

Ingrid nodded almost instantly. "Yes, Hannah. Let's do."

VII

Tuesday, 19 August 1856

The next two days were exhausting ones for the Edward Martin Company. The hill country and sandy roads continued and the sun was merciless. As the afternoon of the second day rolled on, the temperature climbed past ninety, and then ninety-five degrees. People began to lag, and then some of the older folks and young children began to faint from the heat. For a while they placed them in the wagons with those who were still sick and pressed on, but it became painfully evident that they had passed the point of capability. Captain Martin finally called a halt just before sundown. They had come about fourteen miles and it was clear they could go no farther.

Hannah and Sister Jackson were pushing the cart at that point. Brother Jackson and Ingrid were pulling. When the signal came to halt, they stopped where they were, lowered the cart, then sank to the ground. Hannah stretched out flat, one arm up to shield her eyes from the sun, not caring that she was in inch-thick dust.

Sister Jackson sat down cross-legged, pulling off her bonnet and wiping at the sweat that streamed down her face. Though she wouldn't have said anything to her family, she was feeling quite light-headed herself. No wonder some of the older people had fainted. The

Church agents at Iowa City had said they were concerned about the emigrants' being caught in the winter snows before they reached the Valley. At the moment, Elizabeth could not think of anything more welcome than a good, hard snowstorm.

All around them, people were in the same mode. Making camp could wait for a few minutes. For now they were simply too drained to move.

—❦—

An hour and a half later, Hannah and Ingrid sat together with their feet in the creek. It didn't provide much relief. The water was more a trickle than a stream, but it was cooler than the parched earth all around them. They heard footsteps and turned. It was Sister Jackson. She removed her shoes even as she approached; then with a sigh, she sat down beside the two girls.

"Where are the children?" Hannah asked. When they had left to come to the creek, Sister Jackson was reading to her three children.

"Aaron took them over to the cattle. Little Aaron just loves to pet the milk cows."

Ingrid watched her for a moment. "You look tired, Sister Jackson."

Her head came up and there was a faint smile. "That's good, because I sure feel tired." She lay back and closed her eyes. "So what are you two girls talking about?"

Hannah's voice was soft. "About whether our families will still be in Florence."

"Yes," Elizabeth said. "I've been wondering that too. Brother Martin says we should get there in about two more days." She opened her eyes again and looked at Ingrid. "With the wagon company behind us by a few days, you haven't used your English much with them, have you?"

"No, but Brother Spencer knew that might happen. The primary thing was that he wanted me to be a translator at Iowa City while the preparations were being made."

"Well, Aaron and I are certainly glad you stayed. I don't know what we would have done without you. And I'm praying that your families will still be there and that we can travel with them hereafter."

"As am I," Hannah murmured.

They fell silent then, too tired to carry on much idle talk. Hannah brought her knees up and laid her head on them. She closed her eyes. A few minutes later she felt a touch on her arm. She opened her eyes and saw that Elizabeth Jackson was pointing. "Look," she said softly.

Sister Ann Parker, looking drawn and haggard, was walking slowly past them, about twenty yards from where they were. Her head was down and she barely noticed them sitting there. She had her older boy, who was about twelve, with her. As she passed, heads all around the camp turned to follow. Like a fog of chilled air, a great sadness followed her passing. No one spoke as she passed, but every eye followed her. Everyone knew exactly where she was going. Supper was over. Her younger children were settled. It was time to keep her promise. She would go and watch for her husband until it was too dark to see any longer.

They watched as Sister Parker crossed the creek, moved off a few feet, then selected a tall bush and sat down in its shade. Her hand came up to her eyes as she looked to the east, scanning the trail which they had recently covered.

Hannah watched, wondering how this woman could bear it. This was the sixth day now since Arthur had been discovered missing. Six days! How could a boy of five possibly survive that long out alone in a wilderness? How could his mother not lose hope? Every passing day made the chance of Robert Parker's returning with his son more and more remote.

Then to Hannah's surprise, she saw that Ingrid had moved a few feet away from their camp. She was beside a tree, staring at Sister

Parker just as they were. Hannah stood up and went over to stand beside her friend.

"It is so sad," Ingrid said.

"I know." Hannah turned away. "Let's talk about something else."

But even as she said it, she saw Ingrid stiffen. "Oh," she said.

Hannah whirled around.

Across the creek, Ann Parker was still by the bush, but she was on her feet. She was leaning forward, every muscle in her body taut, her hand to her eyes again, shading them as she stared toward the east. Her son was gazing in the same direction. He looked up at his mother and said something, but she neither heard him nor looked at him.

Sister Jackson leaped to her feet. Hannah grabbed Ingrid's hand and they quickly joined her as she crossed the creek. As one, they converged on Sister Parker. Hearing them, she turned. She started to speak but her voice failed her. She gestured toward the east, her eyes pleading.

The three of them stared intently. The sun was almost setting now, and the landscape was filled with a soft orange glow. The trail they had crossed that afternoon was visible for almost a full two miles before it crested a low hill and disappeared. But where it was visible, it was in full sunlight. Hannah gasped. There was movement there.

Sister Parker turned, her eyes huge and filled with hope. "Do you see it?" she exclaimed aloud now, gripping her son's shoulder. "Is it someone?"

"Yes," Sister Jackson exclaimed. "Someone is coming."

And so it was. A small dark speck was visible against the lighter prairie. It was moving slowly towards them, and now they could clearly see that it was a person and not some animal.

"Is it Papa? Is it Papa?" the boy cried.

No one answered him. They were rigid, eyes fixed on the tiny figure that moved towards them. Others had seen what was going on and people were pouring across the creek, coming to see. But no one spoke. It was as if the whole camp were suddenly holding its breath.

And then in a moment that would be frozen in Hannah's mind forever, she saw a glint of red. It moved back and forth above the figure like a flag or a banner. For a moment she didn't understand. Then as a great sob of joy was torn from the lips of Sister Ann Parker, Hannah remembered what Ingrid had reported two mornings before. It was the red shawl. "If you find our son dead," Ann Parker had said to her husband, "use this as his burial shroud. But if you find him alive, wave it as a signal, for I shall watch for you every night until you return." Again the red flashed in the sunlight, like a far-off beacon. Ann Parker sank slowly to the ground, her face in her hands, and she began to sob softly.

Captain Edwin Martin came running up. He stared up the trail for a moment, then dropped to one knee beside Ann Parker. "Sister Parker?" He touched her shoulder. Her head came up slowly. Tears of joy had made streaks through the dust on her cheeks. "Come," he said gently. "We'll send one of the wagons back to get them." He lifted her to her feet. "Let's go get your son."

Chapter Notes

For some reason, the Martin Company did not keep a daily company journal as did the Willie Company. However, several diaries and journals were kept, and some accounts of the journey were written after the arrival in Salt Lake (see Turner, *Emigrating Journals,* p. 81). Together these give a fairly complete picture of the Martin Company's experience. One of the best of these accounts was written by John Jaques, who was appointed to be the company historian. As noted earlier, Jaques was an accomplished writer and poet.

Though not shown in the novel, the company that eventually became the Edward Martin Company—the fifth handcart company of 1856—left Iowa City as two companies, one captained by Edward Martin, one by Jesse Haven. They traveled separately to Florence, Nebraska Territory. There Elder Haven joined the Hodgett Wagon Company. The two companies were then joined and became the Edward Martin Company (see Turner, *Emigrating Journals,* pp. 81, 99, 105).

The material depicted in this chapter was inspired by the following accounts.

C. C. A. Christensen, the famous Mormon artist, came to America from Denmark with his new bride in the 1857 handcart company led by Christian Christiansen. "Our hats, or what might once have been called hats, assumed the most grotesque shapes, seeing that the sun, wind, and rain had the superior force. The ladies' skirts and men's trousers hung in irregular trimmings, and the foot coverings proportional to the rest, with or without bottoms. Our faces were gray from the dust, which sometimes prevented us from seeing the vanguard; our noses with the skin hanging in patches, especially on those who had as much nose as I have; and almost every lower lip covered with a piece of cloth or paper because of its chapped condition, which made it difficult to speak and particularly to smile or laugh" (as quoted in Carol Cornwall Madsen, *Journey to Zion,* p. 592).

Samuel Openshaw, who came west with the Edward Martin Company in 1856, wrote this entry for 7 August: "We started about 7 o'clock this morning and traveled through a beautiful country, where we could stand and gaze upon the prairies as far as the eye could see, even until the prairies themselves seemed to meet the sky on all sides, without being able to see a house. I thought, how many thousands of people are there in England who have scarce room to breathe and not enough to eat. Yet all this good land is lying dormant, except for the prairie grass to grow and decay" (in Turner, *Emigrating Journals,* p. 102).

Mary Powell Sabin was twelve years old when she came in the first handcart company of 1856 captained by Edmund Ellsworth. She later wrote: "Often we would come to a place where the springs had dried down. It might be near midnight. Then little children would form a circle of eager watchers while the men dug down several feet to water. At last when they saw the chunks of wet mud they would lay it on their face and hands. Some of them would suck the water from the mud. When the water burst forth it was usually very thick. The children drank heartily, straining it through their teeth. The next morning it looked quite clear" ("Autobiography of Mary Powell Sabin," in Carol Cornwall Madsen, *Journey to Zion,* p. 603).

Robert and Ann Hartley Parker and their four children came to Utah in 1856 in the second handcart company under the direction of Captain Daniel D. McArthur. Though the Parkers were not with the Willie or Martin Handcart Companies, the story of Arthur's being lost and then found again is included in this novel because it typifies one aspect of the experience of the handcart pioneers. Other than placing the Parkers in the Martin Company, who passed the area where the Parker boy was lost a little more than a month after it actually happened, the novel portrays the details of the story accurately. Here is an account of what happened:

> Robert Parker was stricken with fever that was sweeping the company and Captain McArthur ordered him placed in one of the wagons. Martha Alice had to leave her little brother to the care of the other children while she lent her child-strength to the heavy cart. One day, while going through the timberlands of Nebraska [actually Iowa], Arthur became feverish and ill and unnoticed by the other children sat down to rest beside the trail. He was soon fast asleep. In the afternoon a sudden storm came up and the company hurried to make camp. Finding that Arthur was not with the children, they hurriedly organized a posse and went back to search for him. They returned with grim faces after two days' searching. The Captain ordered the company to move on. Ann pleaded with him, but he set his jaw hard—the food was giving out and not another day could be lost.
>
> Ann Parker pinned a bright shawl about the thin shoulders of her husband and sent him back alone on the trail to search again for their child. If he found him dead he was to wrap him in the shawl; if alive, the shawl would be a flag to signal her. Ann and her children took up their load and struggled on with the company, while Robert retraced the miles of forest trail, calling, and searching and praying for his helpless little son. At last he reached a mail and trading station where he learned that his child had been found and cared for by a woodsman and his wife. He had been ill from exposure and fright. God had heard the prayers of his people.
>
> Out on the trail each night Ann and her children kept watch and, when, on the third night [after she had sent her husband back] the rays of the setting sun caught the glimmer of a bright red shawl, the brave little mother sank in a pitiful heap in the sand. Completely exhausted, Ann slept for the first time in six long days and nights. God indeed was kind and merciful, and in the gladness of their hearts the Saints sang, "All is Well." The good captain speeded a wagon with food and blankets back to meet her husband and son. (In Carter, comp., *Treasures of Pioneer History* 5:240–41)

CHAPTER 13

FLORENCE, NEBRASKA TERRITORY

I

Tuesday, 12 August 1856

The last of the lingering twilight filtered through the thin scattering of trees on the bluffs above the Missouri River. Maggie sat beneath a small oak tree on a knoll just to the east of camp. From here she could look down upon the river and across to the opposite bank. Her eyes lifted slightly. Across the river, on the Iowa side, the first lights in Kanesville, Iowa—what had first been known as Council Bluffs—were starting to show in the gathering darkness. She wrapped her arms around her knees, savoring the light breeze that had sprung up from the west and cooled the air considerably. Above, the evening star hung like a solitary beacon. Soon it would be surrounded with a myriad of others. It was going to be a lovely evening, and she decided that she would talk to Sarah about moving their bedrolls outside tonight.

Maggie smiled to herself. How ironic! For six weeks they had slept in the cramped berths of the ship. For ten days they had tried to sleep in swaying railway cars, on the hard deck of steamboats, or on the concrete floor of empty locomotive barns. And for the last six weeks they had slept in the large round tent that had become their home. And now finally, when there was the opportunity to have an actual roof over their heads, she was considering sleeping outside.

Winter Quarters, or Florence, had once housed thousands of Latter-day Saints. Now they had gone west, leaving little more than a ferry crossing and a way station for the emigrants going to Zion. Hundreds of structures were abandoned. Each new season the Church agents invited the emigrants to take advantage of these shelters as they passed through. The Willie Company had been no different. When the invitation was given, many of their number left their tents packed in the wagons and slept with a roof over their heads for the first time in several weeks.

At the thought of the Church agents, Maggie sighed softly. The men who had worked them so hard in Iowa City had raced across the state in light wagons and carriages and beat the Willie Company to Florence by a day or two. Since it was late afternoon by the time they were all ferried across the Missouri yesterday, the agents had let them have the remainder of that day to rest. But first thing this morning they rounded the emigrants up again and put them to work. If anything, the sense of urgency was even more intense than it had been in Iowa. They had to get carts repaired, clothing mended, and food supplies restocked and be on their way again.

Maggie heard footsteps behind her and turned to see who it was. To her surprise it was Eric Pederson, and she started to scramble to her feet.

"Don't get up!" he said quickly, waving his hand at her. "Please."

She sank back down, feeling her heart race a little. She had been so engrossed in her thoughts, he had startled her.

"May I join you?"

He had not called her Sister Maggie, she noted. That was good. "Of course."

He came over and sat down as well. "It is beautiful night, yes?"

"Very lovely."

He nodded slowly, then turned to look down at the river and across to the east bank. Maggie watched him for a moment out of the corner of her eye, then folded her arms on her knees and rested her chin on them. He did the same, and they sat there for almost a full minute in silence, looking out over the scene before them. Then finally he asked a question. "Were you thinking of Hannah and Ingrid?"

She turned to him in surprise. That was exactly what she had been thinking.

"You are thinking that they will not come before we must go."

She looked away again, nodding. The Martin Company had not left Iowa City until twelve days after Willie had left. Even if they made better time than the Willie Company had, there was no way they could ever get here in time.

"There is some talk of not leaving. Did you know that?"

"Yes. I heard that."

"Some think we must winter over here. Perhaps at the . . ." He stumbled for a moment. "At the Elkhorn River, which is not far."

Maggie had already considered the implications of that. It would certainly solve the problem of Hannah's catching up to them. "Do you think we will?"

He shook his head. "No. I think that is why we have big meeting tomorrow night. Did you hear that some people are here staying no matter what we decide at the meeting?"

"Yes, I heard that too."

"Will your family?" he asked, looking suddenly concerned.

"Not if the rest of the company goes on," Maggie replied. "Mother is adamant about that. Even if it means we don't get to see Hannah until we reach the Valley."

"The Nielsons too," he said. "I for me hope we do not stop. Olaf and I must get to the Valley so we earn money for our family."

Maggie felt a sudden twist of guilt. She had forgotten for the moment that Eric and Olaf had left their entire family and would not see any of them for at least another year. Somehow that made two months without Hannah seem a little insignificant. "Don't you have a sister too?"

"Yah. Her name is Kirsten. She is eight." He smiled softly. "She looks very much like Ingrid—light hair, blue eyes, a smile that . . . She is my little angel. And also my Peder, who wants so much to be a man but is only six."

The longing in his voice made Maggie almost sorry she had asked. "How do the missionaries do it?" she murmured. "They've been gone four years now. Think what that means for their wives and families."

"It is very difficult, I think. But for the gospel . . ." He shrugged and that said it all.

Again they were quiet for a time, lost in their thoughts. Then finally Eric half turned. "Sister Maggie?"

She shook her head, wondering if he could ever not be quite so formal with her. "What?"

"Sister Maggie, I would like to say . . ." His mouth twisted as he felt the frustration of wanting to speak in Norwegian but knowing he had to say it in English. "I wish to thank you for two things."

"For what?"

"For English."

"You and Olaf and Ingrid were a delight to teach. I have enjoyed it a great deal."

"Yes," he said thoughtfully. "That is why you are good teacher. You enjoy and you make us enjoy too."

Touched and surprised at the gravity in his voice, she smiled at him. "Thank you. You said there were two things. What else?"

"For helping stupid *Dummkopf.*"

She just looked at him. "*Dummkopf?* What do you mean?"

"On the ship."

Then she remembered their first day aboard the *Thornton.* One of the sailors had been yelling at Eric and Olaf because they weren't helping. She laughed. "If there was a *Dummkopf* that day, it was the sailor. He was a real donkey. Imagine being angry because someone who can't speak your language doesn't understand what you want."

There was a fleeting smile. "I never say enough thank you for helping me."

"You did thank me. Besides, no thanks are needed. It just made me angry that he was being so stupid."

Now he looked at her directly. In the fading light, his eyes were dark, almost black instead of their usual blue. She could not see the tiny flecks of brown in them that had always fascinated her. She finally had to look away, they were watching her so intensely. "I know," he said. "I thank you for your anger."

She laughed aloud. "My Scottish temper, you mean."

He didn't smile back. "Our Savior was angry when he saw his temple filled with robbers, no? Sometimes it is okay to be angry?"

"Yes," she said in surprise. "That's true. But I think *indignant* might be a better word."

"In-dig-nant?"

"Yes. It means you are angry or upset because things are not right."

"Ah." Now finally he smiled. "Then I thank you for your indignant."

One part of her wanted to laugh at his quaintness, but another part of her was strangely moved. "Thank you, Eric. But really, it was nothing."

"It was important to me . . ." There was a momentary hesitation; then he smiled. "Maggie."

She turned, pleased. "Maggie? Did I hear you say Maggie?" She tried to keep her voice light, teasing.

He nodded soberly. "Yes, Maggie." Then to her surprise, that was it. He stood abruptly. "I must get back." He waved and walked away swiftly, not turning back to see that she was staring after him in complete astonishment.

—❦—

"Maggie?"

"What?"

"I saw Eric go up on the hill tonight."

Maggie came up on one elbow, the lush carpet of stars above them totally forgotten now. She looked directly at Sarah James. "You did?"

"Yes."

Maggie was suddenly flustered. "He wanted to thank me for teaching him English and—" She stopped, realizing that she was sounding guilty. "We also talked about Hannah and Ingrid."

"I thought that's why you went up," her friend said. "I almost came up too, but then decided you wanted to be alone."

"I miss her, Sarah. And Ingrid too."

"I know. I do too. And Emma. She talks about them every day."

"They're not going to get here before we leave, you know." Maggie lay back down. "We're going to leave too soon."

"I'm afraid you are right."

"I wish I had told her how much I love her," Maggie whispered.

"But you did," Sarah said. "I was there, remember?"

"I told her that I loved her," Maggie corrected her, "but I didn't tell her how much."

"Oh."

Both lay back again. They were silent for a long time, and Maggie began to wonder if Sarah had fallen asleep. Then she spoke again. "Maggie? May I ask you a question?"

"Of course."

"Promise me you will answer me honestly."

That brought her head around, and she reached out and touched Sarah's arm. "I'm always honest with you, Sarah. That's one of the things I so admire about you. I can be honest with you and you with me."

"I feel that way too."

"So what is your question?"

There was a long pause; then, "How do you feel about Eric?"

In spite of herself, Maggie jerked around. "What?"

"Shhh!" Sarah whispered. "Don't wake the others."

"What did you say?"

"You know what I said. And remember, you promised to be honest."

"Sarah James, what are you suggesting?"

"I'm not suggesting anything. I just want to know."

"Well, I . . . He's . . . he's very bright. He learns quickly. I think beneath that somber exterior he has a quick sense of humor. He seems to be a good worker. The children love him."

"Yes, they do, don't they?"

"All right," Maggie said sternly. "What is going on here?"

"Let me ask you another question. How do you think Eric feels about me?"

If the first question took her aback, this one floored her. Maggie hesitated. "I . . ." She remembered the hurt she saw in Sarah's eyes whenever Eric was around. He was always polite and friendly, but there was nothing more. "Of course, he likes you. Can't you tell?"

"Don't play games, Maggie. You promised you'd be honest." She was stubborn now, something that Maggie didn't often see in Sarah James. "I'm not talking about just liking me as a friend. Do you think he *really* likes me?"

Maggie didn't know what to say. She thought she knew the answer, but she definitely didn't feel that she should speak for Eric. "Why?" she asked, trying to deflect the question.

"Thank you, Maggie. That's answer enough. Thank you for not lying to me."

"Sarah, I–"

"I already knew that. I'm not blind, you know." Her hand reached out and found Maggie's. "It's all right."

"He does like you as a friend, Sarah. He really does. You know that, don't you?"

"Yes." It was said simply, but that couldn't hide the disappointment.

Maggie lay down again and slid closer until her shoulder touched Sarah, wanting to offer comfort but not sure how.

"If it had to be someone else," Sarah murmured, "I'm glad it was you."

This time Maggie shot up to a sitting position. "*What?*"

Sarah sat up now too. The camp was dark and quiet, but there was a half moon and Maggie's face was bathed in its silver glow. Sarah was staring at her; then suddenly she laughed. "You *don't* know, do you?" Sarah said in soft wonder.

"Don't know what?"

To Maggie's total surprise, Sarah suddenly leaned forward and put her arms around her. "Dear sweet Maggie."

Maggie pulled away. "Don't you 'dear sweet Maggie' me! What are you trying to say?"

Sarah laughed in delight. "This James MacAllister back in Edinburgh. Did he love you?"

"Yes, of course."

"How did you know? I mean, when you first knew that he might like you. How did you know?"

Maggie thought about that for a moment, then answered. "By the way he looked at me."

It was answer enough and Sarah laid her hand on Maggie's arm. "Then I'd say you'd better start paying more attention to Mr. Pederson's eyes, Sister Maggie."

"Sarah, I–"

There was a soft chuckle as she lay back down again. "No, Maggie. That's all I've got to say. Good night." And with that she rolled onto her side away from Maggie and pulled the blanket up and over her head.

Half an hour later, long after Sarah's breathing had deepened, Maggie McKensie still stared up at the stars that filled the night above them. But her thoughts were not on the stars, nor had she thought about Hannah and Ingrid much during that time either.

II

Wednesday, 13 August 1856

Their third day in camp was spent in the same urgent rush of preparations as the previous day. The four Church agents seemed to be everywhere—taking inventory, listing the names of those who had decided to stay for the winter and those who would be going on, seeing to the repairs, sending the wagons to the gristmill built by Brigham Young almost ten years before.

By the time the Willie Company reached Florence, their supplies had dwindled to the point that the daily ration of flour for an adult was cut from sixteen ounces to ten ounces. Rice, sugar, bacon, and other necessities had dwindled to the point that each family was getting almost nothing. Many of those with larger families had begged for food as they crossed Iowa, and surprisingly, the locals had proven to be quite generous. The charity often came with strong encouragement to forget about Salt Lake City and the Mormons and to stay in Iowa—which a few did. But the local settlers still took pity on the long line of emigrants and shared what they had, or sold supplies to them at a very reasonable rate.

Once they reached Florence, the camp was put back on full rations again. Daniel Spencer also ordered some beef killed and the meat distributed throughout the camp. The amount of flour available at the Missouri River was not the problem. The challenge was how to take enough to last the handcart company until they could reach the first place where the supply wagons from Salt Lake would be waiting. Today one sack of flour—ninety-eight pounds—had been given to each handcart. That was sobering. Coming across Iowa, the typical load on the carts was around two hundred to three hundred pounds. They had just increased that load by a third to a half. While there was some grumbling, no one seriously objected. Without food, the trail would prove to be pretty grim.

Eric looked up as Olaf came around the sod hut that was serving as their temporary home. "Ready?" Olaf asked.

Eric glanced up at the sky. The sun was almost gone. Elder Willie had called for all adults in the company to meet together at the public square just at sundown. He reached inside the open door and grabbed his hat. "Yes. Let's go."

The subject for the meeting was known by everyone. It came down to one question. Should the whole company plan to winter over or press on to the Valley. Discussions—and, in some cases, rather heated arguments—had been going on all day long. So it was not surprising that by the time Captain Willie, the Church agents, and the five subcaptains came forward, everyone was already in their place. As John Chislett, captain of the fourth hundred noted, this was going to be a "monster meeting."

As Maggie and her family, along with the James family, passed by the fifth hundred, Eric and Olaf and Brother Ahmanson were dividing the Scandinavians into three smaller groups for translation purposes. Eric saw them and waved. Olaf called out a greeting, singling out Emma as he smiled broadly. Sarah gave Maggie a knowing look, which she blandly ignored.

They found a spot not too far back from the podium, and watched as the leaders came forward. The leaders talked quietly together for a moment, from time to time lifting their heads to look at the people, as if taking their measure, then continued on. To

Maggie's surprise, it was Captain Willie who finally stepped up onto a small platform made with planks laid over two sawhorses. She had expected Daniel Spencer, the leader of the Church agents, to conduct. The moment Brother Willie stood, quiet fell over the assembly. The moment of decision had come.

"Brothers and sisters," he began, speaking loudly so that his voice would carry to the full group. "As you know all too well, our company has reached a crossroads, both literally and figuratively. We are at the last major outfitting center before jumping off into the wilderness." He offered a wan smile. "Now, I know that some of you thought Iowa was wilderness"—he let the laughter ripple across the group—"but I can promise you that in a few days, you will come to think of Iowa as the heart of civilization compared to what you will be seeing.

"We have only Fort Laramie, which is about five hundred miles from here, and Fort Bridger, which is closer to nine hundred or a thousand. Both are small trading posts." His shoulders lifted and fell in sudden discouragement. "Neither is large enough to either resupply our needs or handle a group as large as we are for the winter. What you need to know is that if we decide to leave Florence now, there is no choice but to set our sights on the Valley. There is no other choice . . ." He paused, and the silence hung like a huge weight over their heads. "Unless we choose to winter over somewhere near our present location."

"Can we really do that?" a man spoke up. "I've heard that we don't have enough to care for this large a group here either."

Brother William D. Grant stepped forward to stand beside the platform just below Brother Willie. "That's what makes this decision so difficult," Brother Grant boomed. "Some have already decided to stay, and perhaps the hundred or so who want to wait for spring will be all right. There is some food here and shelter. But we are certainly not equipped to handle five hundred of us. And if you count Brother Martin's group and the independent wagon companies that are still on their way here, that would make well more than a thousand of us.

So the answer is no. We really are not prepared to have a group that large stay for the winter. We could make it, but it would be very difficult."

Now Daniel Spencer called out from where he stood. "And you have to remember something else. An adequate supply of food will be critical no matter where you are, but we will not have wagons coming from Salt Lake all the way out here to resupply us. If you continue, then you can count on that kind of help."

Captain Willie took over again. "I don't have to remind any of you how late in the season we are. We were leaving Liverpool when we should have been leaving Iowa City. We are in Florence when we should be at Fort Laramie or farther. But knowing that doesn't make it go away. It is August thirteenth. The high plains along the trail are known to have frost in every month of the year and snowstorms as early as September. I don't want to sugarcoat this for you. We will almost certainly face some severe weather. But I exhort you to consider moving forward, regardless of whether we may have to endure some suffering, even if some of us may face death. Let us go on to Zion as we have been commanded."

Now he turned and looked at his subcaptains. He was frowning, but he nodded and beckoned with his finger. Levi Savage, captain of the second hundred, came forward. Captain Willie spoke again to the group. "There are only four of us in this company who have crossed the trail before—myself, Brother Woodward, Brother Savage here, and Captain Atwood of the first hundred. Our brethren who are serving as agents know it as well, and we are all inclined to say that we should press forward, in spite of the lateness of the season. However, Brother Savage is of a different mind. We feel that you should have an opportunity to hear his feelings before we take a vote. Brother Savage."

Maggie watched the man closely as he waited for Captain Willie to come down off the platform so that Brother Savage could get up on it. She didn't know him well but had always found him to be a pleasant and practical man. He was in his mid-thirties and, like so many others of those who led the emigrants, had been called as a missionary back in 1852 and was finally returning home. He had gone to the Orient and served as a missionary in Siam and Ceylon.

Brother Savage glanced at the people, then looked down directly at their captain, who stood beside the makeshift platform now. Maggie was close enough that when he spoke his voice carried clearly to her. "Elder Willie, if I speak, I must speak my mind, let it cut where it will."

Brother Willie's jaw tightened a little, but there was a curt nod. "Certainly do so, Brother Savage. Let the people choose for themselves." Then he stepped back so that Brother Savage was alone.

"Brothers and sisters." Levi Savage looked down at his hands, as if he might find something there to help him say what he had to say. Finally, he looked up. When he began, his voice was deep and filled with sadness. "As Elder Willie has said, we face an important time of decision. The consequences of our choices must be considered as carefully as the choices themselves. You need to know that this late in the season we face the possibility of severe hardships. The plains that lie on this side of South Pass are very high, six and seven thousand feet in elevation. It will be October by the time we reach them. We are liable to see snow by then. We may have to wade in snow up to our knees. You will likely have to wrap yourselves in a thin blanket and lie on the frozen ground without a bed.

"It will not be like having a wagon where you can go into it and wrap yourselves in as much covering as you like and stay warm. We have only handcarts and tents. We are destitute of winter clothing and have nowhere to purchase it."

He stopped and let his eyes move from face to face. No one spoke. It seemed to Maggie as if no one breathed. His eyes touched hers and she felt a chill as if the very blasts of winter that he was describing had suddenly swept across the prairie.

"I have great respect for the faith and feelings of my brethren, but I must say my feelings as clearly as I can state them. I am opposed to taking women and children and the weak through the trail this late in the season. We are bound to be caught in the snow before we reach the Valley, and the trials we will be called upon to endure will be severe. I do not condemn the handcart experience. I think it is preferable to unbroken oxen and inexperienced teamsters. My only concern is with the lateness of the season."

Suddenly his voice broke and he had to stop. His head bowed, and for a time that seemed as though it stretched on forever, he stared at the ground. When his head finally lifted again, Maggie was shocked to see tears streaming down his cheeks. "My beloved brothers and sisters," he exclaimed, his voice higher in pitch as he fought to contain his emotions, "let us wait until spring to make this journey. Let us go immediately into winter quarters. In the case of bad weather, some of the strong may get through, but I tell you that the bones of the weak and the old will strew the way if we do not."

For a moment, it looked as though he would say more, but then he changed his mind and stepped down. He didn't return to his seat but waited to see if Brother Willie had anything more he wanted him to say.

Now it was Brother Willie who seemed burdened down. Every eye followed him as he climbed back up on the platform. Maggie leaned forward, still feeling as though she needed to shiver to free herself of the cold feeling that was running up and down her back.

"My beloved brothers and sisters," Elder James G. Willie began slowly, "you have heard Brother Savage on this matter. He is a good brother and a man who has served God faithfully." Now his voice deepened and boomed out with startling intensity. "However, I must say that I cannot agree with his assessment. I know that Brother Savage believes in God, but I have to say that the God I serve is a God who can and will help his children to the utmost. The God I serve has called us to Zion, and I want to answer that call."

Captain Willie turned now to look directly down at his subcaptain. Without waiting for permission, Savage stepped forward a little. "Elder Willie, I have spoken nothing but truth. If you wish to release me from my position as captain of the second hundred, then do so. But you and the others know that what I say is true."

"True or not, Brother Savage, the question is, Shall this company stop here, or somewhere nearby, or shall we press forward in obedience to the commands of our prophet and of our God, even knowing that suffering and death might be our reward?"

Now Willie turned and looked back to the others leaders. "Brethren, have any of you a mind to say more?"

Millen Atwood raised his hand. "I think every family has to pray to God and find out for themselves."

That received a brief nod. William H. Kimball raised his hand and came forward. "It is not as if we have a choice between something that is good and something that is not, between suffering and not suffering. The winter storms blow here in Nebraska as well as on the high plains, let us not forget that. If you go forward, yes, you will likely face storms, but you will reach the Valley by late October, or early November, and then you will have a safe haven. If you stay here you will also face storms, but you will have an additional four months of winter to endure and with no more food coming."

He stepped back. Elder Willie looked to the other subcaptains and the Church agents. "How do you brethren vote?"

"Go," Daniel Spencer said without hesitation.

"Go," said William H. Kimball and George D. Grant. Two of the Church agents who were stationed in Florence that Maggie did not know spoke out clearly. "Go."

Nodding, Willie turned back to face the crowd. "Brothers and sisters, you have heard the feelings of your leaders. Now you must choose. I shall give you a moment to talk about this among yourselves, and then we shall call for a vote. Those of you who have already decided to stay until next season will not be voting. The rest should be prepared to show yea or nay by the uplifted hand."

Maggie turned as the crowd erupted in a buzz of whispering

voices. She looked at her mother, who seemed to be waiting for her to do so. "Is there any question in your mind, Maggie?" she asked.

Before Maggie could respond, Robbie was shaking his head. "Let's go, Mama. We don't want to stop now."

William James looked at his wife. Jane was holding their youngest, little John, who had recently turned four. He hadn't been the youngest when they sailed from Liverpool, but baby Jane had been consigned to the ocean's depths. If death was being talked about, the Jameses knew personally of what they spoke. Sarah didn't wait for her mother. "I'm going," she said. "I believe Brother Willie is right."

"Me too," Emma said. "I don't want to wait out the whole winter here."

"Jane?" William said softly.

"I vote we go."

He nodded and seemed to relax. "Then it's settled for us."

Mary McKensie was still watching her elder daughter. After a moment, though the chill still weighed heavily upon her, Maggie managed a smile. "I don't remember being called to gather to Florence," she said.

Her mother's eyes brimmed with tears. "Thank you," she whispered.

"No," Maggie came right back, "thank *you*, Mother. Someday I hope my faith can grow to be as strong as yours."

Eric looked at Olaf, his eyes questioning. For a moment Olaf seemed startled. Then he shook his head vigorously. "Do you have to ask?" he said.

Eric laughed, a sound filled with pride and affection. "I didn't think so, but I thought I'd better be sure." They were speaking quietly in their own language, as were those around them.

"And you?" Olaf asked.

"Go," Eric said. "There'll be no money earned here for sending back to Mama and Papa."

"I know."

They turned to where Jens and Elsie Nielson were conferring quietly. Jens's back was to Eric and he couldn't see his mouth or hear his words, but suddenly Elsie's head bobbed once emphatically.

"Are you sure?" Jens asked, loudly enough for the boys to hear.

Elsie's head came up proudly. "That's the same question you asked me when you wanted to buy a handcart and give the rest of our money to the brethren. Do you have to ask it again?"

He shook his head, then bent over and kissed her gently on the top of her head. He turned and looked at Eric and Olaf. "Are you going to break up our little handcart family?" he asked.

Eric just laughed. "I'm afraid you must live with us all the way to Salt Lake."

"All right, brothers and sisters."

Like throwing a cloth over a bird's cage, the words brought the noise instantly to a stop.

Elder Willie looked around. "We shall now call for a vote of the congregation. Again, those who are going to stay, please do not raise your hands. This vote is only for those who are considering going forward."

His head swept back and forth, but no one moved or spoke. "All right, then. All in favor of continuing on to the Valley immediately, please show by raising your right hand."

Like almost everyone else in the crowd, Maggie looked around quickly as her hand came up. It was a sea of hands. Here and there were people who didn't have their hands raised, but they were possibly those who had been excluded from the vote. To her surprise she saw Elder Ahmanson. His hand was not up.

"And all of you who would vote with Brother Savage to immediately go into winter quarters and wait until spring to continue on to Utah, please signify."

Again heads craned and people searched across the congregation. Maggie saw a scattering of hands, no more than half a dozen. Puzzled, she noted that Brother Ahmanson didn't raise his hand this time either. As a great rush of noise erupted, she felt her body sag a little with both relief and anxiety. So it was decided. They would go.

I'm sorry, Hannah. We'll see you in Utah.

Instantly the sound was cut off again. Levi Savage had stepped forward again. Elder Willie made a move as though to wave him off, then thought better of it and motioned him forward.

He stood there for a long moment. Then his head came back and he squared his shoulders. "Brothers and sisters, I, like you, have seen the vote of the congregation. I just want to say this much more. What I have said I know to be true. But seeing you are to go forward, I will go with you. I will help all I can. I will work with you. I will rest with you. I will suffer with you, and if necessary . . ." There was a momentary pause. "And if necessary, I will die with you. May God in his mercy bless and preserve us."

III

Friday, 15 August 1856

Mary McKensie looked up in surprise. There was a communal well just two houses away from the empty cabin that her family and the James family had occupied for their brief stay in Florence. She had come out to draw a bucket of water from the well, then stopped for a moment to enjoy the evening air before going back to help start supper. Not far from the well a shed that had been used for making and fixing wagons stood in disrepair. A figure had stepped out from behind the shed and was beckoning to her.

"Eric?" she said as she recognized who it was.

He put a finger to his lips. Then, satisfied that she was alone, he came forward. She saw that he carried something wrapped in a dish towel beneath his arm.

"Good evening, Sister McKensie."

"Good evening, Eric. You startled me a little."

"I'm sorry." He was clearly nervous and kept glancing behind her.

Mary smiled. "Who are you worried about coming out? Sarah, Emma, or Maggie?"

He laughed softly. "I have to get back," was all he said, "and help the Nielsons finish packing."

"Yes. We are busy getting our things together too."

His mouth pulled down. "If we leave tomorrow, you will not see Hannah."

Mary had to look away, for the pain came back as fresh and as sharply as it had earlier today when it was announced that they would leave the following morning. "I know."

"I am most sorry, Sister McKensie. It is not the same for Olaf and me, but we were very much wanting to see Hannah and Ingrid too. They have become most special friends."

She smiled now, blinking back the tears. "I know. Thank you, Eric."

He hesitated for several moments, then took from beneath his arm whatever it was he was carrying in the cloth. "This news makes Maggie very sad too, no?"

Mary's head bobbed once. "Very. She thinks it is partly her fault that Hannah is gone, that she should have been the one to go help the Jacksons."

That didn't seem to surprise him. He held out the bundle toward her. "Perhaps this will help. Will you give it to Maggie?"

She stared at it for a moment, not taking it. "What is it, Eric?"

He shook his head. "She will know. It is my way of saying 'thank you' for teaching us English."

Mary swung around and picked up her bucket. "You stay right here, Eric. I'll send Maggie out."

He jumped as though she had flicked him with a whip. "No, Sister McKensie. You take to her, please."

But she had already started away. She looked over her shoulder. "Don't leave."

Flustered, Eric backed into the shed where he wouldn't be seen by any passersby. Two minutes later he saw the door to the cabin open and Maggie step out. She looked up and down the street, then started for him, walking swiftly. As she neared the well, he walked out where she could see him.

"Eric? What are you doing here?"

"I . . ." He grinned ruefully. "I am here because your mother is stubborn woman."

Maggie laughed lightly. "She is that. That's why I'm here and not back in Edinburgh."

He smiled.

"Say," she said, remembering something, "did you watch Elder Ahmanson at the meeting the other day?"

Eric nodded slowly. He didn't have to ask what she meant.

"He didn't vote."

"I know. I am sad that he is not happy. He complains about how things are. He doesn't want to go on."

"Because his wife and child are with the wagon companies?"

He shook his head. "Perhaps. I worry for him."

That surprised her, but then she decided to get to what she had come out for. She peered at the bundle in his hands. "Mother said you brought me something."

He nodded slowly, his face coloring.

"What is it?"

"It is for making you more happy."

"Me more happy?"

"Yes, because we leave tomorrow and Hannah is not here."

Her chin dropped and the smile was gone. "I know. I had so hoped she would get here by now."

"I and Olaf are most sorry too. I . . ." Then, awkwardly, he held out the bundle toward her.

"What is it, Eric?" She hefted it. "It's heavy. It feels like a box."

He smiled a little, then inclined his head, inviting her to unwrap it.

She did so, slowly, still looking at him with a strange look in her eyes. Then suddenly she gasped. "Oh!" The cloth dropped from her hand as she held the wooden box in both hands, staring at it in total disbelief.

"Where in the world did you—" She stopped, overwhelmed. She lifted the lid and the soft melody of "Loch Lomond" began to sound. Suddenly she was crying as she caressed the wood with her fingers. "But where . . . How did *you* get this?"

His face was red now and he couldn't meet her gaze. "When we weighed our belongings in Iowa City, I was not having enough weight."

She laughed aloud, wiping now at the tears with the back of her hand. "No wonder I couldn't find it. I went back to cover it so the sun wouldn't hurt it and it was gone. I thought someone had stolen it." She shook her head slowly. "So you took this so you could have a full seventeen pounds?"

"Yah, that was it." Now he met her eyes as he fumbled for the right words. "That day, I saw how taking music box away make you very sad. Tomorrow, going away from Hannah make you very sad again. I thought . . . I *hoped* that the music box would give back some happiness to you again."

She looked down at the box, rubbing the lid slowly over and over. "I can't believe it," she said, her voice low. "I thought I had lost it forever."

"Not forever," he said with a crooked grin. "Just until now."

The tears brimmed over and began to trickle down her cheeks. Now she made no effort to wipe them away. She stared at him for several long seconds, her eyes as wide as the wheels of the carts. Suddenly she went up on tiptoes and kissed him on the cheek. "Thank you, Eric Pederson," she whispered. Then she whirled and walked away, her head down as she clutched the music box tightly to her body.

Chapter Notes

On the evening of 13 August, two days after their arrival in Florence, Nebraska Territory, the members of the James G. Willie Handcart Company had what John Chislett described as a "monster meeting." Sources (contemporary journal accounts and later reminiscences) indicate that the issue at hand was whether or not to continue on to Utah. Those sources do include some of the words of Elder Willie and particularly the speech of Levi Savage (see the following for more details: Turner, *Emigrating Journals*, pp. 19–20; John Chislett's narrative in *Remember*, pp. 62–63; Emma James's account in Carol Cornwall Madsen, *Journey to Zion*, p. 625; and Christy, "Weather, Disaster, and Responsibility," pp. 20–21).

Modern students of history may be inclined to critique the decision that was made that day. Two things should be noted. In the first place, James G. Willie and the other leaders were not oblivious to the challenges that could await them if the emigrants continued on. They openly discussed the possible hardships and tribulations and exhorted the Saints "to Go forward regardeless of concequenses" (Savage journal, as cited in Christy, "Weather, Disaster, and Responsibility," p. 20).

In the second place, the fact that the option of continuing on was also very untenable should be taken into account. If the decision to winter over for another season had been made in Liverpool, or even in New York, it might have been possible to wait a season, though even in those two places it would have taxed the Church's resources enormously to do so. But in Florence the resources were already stretched to the limit. Only in Salt Lake City were there the resources and the infrastructure needed to assimilate and care for that many people.

John Chislett, who records the stirring commitment of Levi Savage to stay with the Saints even after they voted against his counsel, adds this significant comment about Savage: "Brother Savage was true to his word; no man worked harder than he to alleviate the suffering which he had foreseen, when he had to endure it" (in *Remember*, p. 63).

Johan Ahmanson, somewhere along the way to Utah, became disenchanted with the Church. He left Utah and the Church the following year after arriving in the Valley. He moved to Omaha and became a prominent citizen there. He sued Brigham Young for not paying him "wages" for his service as subcaptain and also for property he claimed the Church stole from him (see Martin, "John Ahmanson vs. Brigham Young," pp. 1–20). In a later history that he wrote, Ahmanson claimed he was dissatisfied with how things were done on the trek. He does not say whether he voted to stay in Florence or to go, but he was very critical of the decision to go on (see *Secret History*, pp. 29–30).

Having Ahmanson not vote was the author's way of showing that there was a change of attitude happening. It is interesting that, according to the Willie Company journal, on 19 August, just a few days after the company left Florence, a new brother was put in as "interpreter and counsellor to the Danish Saints" (in Turner, *Emigrating Journals*, p. 21). Thereafter, Elder Ahmanson is not mentioned again in the company journal.

CHAPTER 14

FLORENCE, NEBRASKA TERRITORY
TO
SAND HILLS, NEBRASKA TERRITORY

I

Saturday, 16 August 1856 —

This time when the James G. Willie Company lined up for their departure from Florence, Nebraska, it was in sharp contrast to when they had left Iowa City the month before. Expectation had turned to resignation, celebration to hesitation, jubilation to quiet desperation. Where before there had been a sense of festivity, now there was only grim urgency. The only ones to see them off were the hundred or so who would not be going. And there was no cheering here. They watched with long faces, their expressions a mixture of gratitude and nagging shame.

As had become his habit every day while on the march, Eric Pederson ran over to check on the walkers, the footmen of the company. As had become their habit, Mary Bathgate and Isabella Park greeted him brusquely, trying not to show just how much they had come to depend on this morning routine.

"Are you ready?" Eric said cheerfully as he checked Sister Bathgate's pack and made sure it was fastened properly.

"Of course we're ready," she said, trying to sound stern. "Have you ever known a day when we weren't?"

"No," he admitted cheerfully. "Captain Willie says he would like a hundred more like you two. He said it would make being captain much more easy."

"Go on," Isabella said. "You're just funning us, aren't you?"

That was a new one on Eric. "Funning?"

"Teasing," Mary said, squinting at him. "Did he really say that?"

"Yes, he did. Day before yesterday."

"Well, well," Isabella said to her friend, looking quite pleased.

"And he asked me to ask you again if either of you wanted to ride in the wagons."

"And what did you tell him, young man?" Mary said, fixing her gaze on him.

"I said"—he let his voice slide into a low growl—"Captain Willie, sir. These two sisters are going to walk all the way, and don't you forget it!"

Though her eyes were twinkling with delight, Mary harrumphed grumpily. "Good for you. That's what you should have said."

Just then the bugle sounded, calling everyone to their handcarts. Eric turned and looked, then turned back. "I must go. If you need help, send word."

"We won't," Mary Bathgate smiled.

He laughed and trotted away.

"What a fine young man he is!" Sister Park said, watching him go. "I wish he could find some wonderful young girl in this company and set his eye on her."

"He already has," Sister Bathgate said primly.

"He has?"

"Yes. I asked Olaf the other day if there was someone."

"Who is it?"

"His English teacher."

"The Scottish girl?"

"Yes."

Sister Park slowly nodded, obviously approving. "Does she know?"

"Oh, heavens no, Isabella. Our Eric? As shy as he is?"

"Then perhaps, Mary, you and I had better take a hand and give this a little push."

She looked shocked. "Eric would not be happy if he knew."

Isabella clapped her hands. "I know. Isn't it just perfect?"

II

Friday, 22 August 1856

On this, the twenty-sixth day of their march since leaving Iowa City, the fifth handcart company, directed by Captain Edward Martin, rolled out sharply at eight A.M. Two hours later the company crested the top of what had once been known as Council Bluffs. There below them, like a dark brown ribbon stitched against a brilliant green cloth, was the Missouri River. A great collective sigh ran up and down the column. The first leg of the journey was complete.

As the handcart pulled by Aaron and Elizabeth Jackson and pushed by Hannah McKensie and Ingrid Christensen came up beside the others, Hannah ran forward. "Is that it? Is that the Missouri River?" she cried.

Aaron nodded and smiled. "Yes, Hannah. And that's Florence on the far side."

"Oh, Ingrid," she cried, clasping her friend's hands together. "We're finally here. Now we can see if Mama and Maggie and Robbie are still in Florence."

"Yes," Ingrid exclaimed. As on every other day since leaving Iowa City, Ingrid's shoes hung around her neck, the laces tied together. As had become her habit whenever Ingrid stopped, her arm came up and she began to absently wipe the dust from the shoes with the sleeve of her dress. "It's beautiful," she said in awe.

Hannah laughed, feeling a great rush of love for her friend. The young girl from Denmark—blond and blue eyed, with her upturned nose and a smile that started even the hardest of hearts melting—was still there, but she was hidden under sunburnt skin, peeled nose, and cracked lips.

Not that Hannah was any better. She grabbed Ingrid's other shoe and wiped it off for her. Ingrid had been true to her word. Whenever they stopped to rest, she would take the shoes from around her neck and set them carefully on the ground, but she never once put them into the handcart, not even at night when they were camped. That was Ingrid. Quiet, shy, so quick to smile—and stubborn as a piece of knotted oak.

Hannah grabbed her companion by the shoulders and shook her gently. "It's Florence, Ingrid. Florence. My family could be just across the river there."

Elizabeth Jackson watched them, then gave her husband a questioning look. For a moment he wasn't sure what she meant, but then he understood and nodded. Elizabeth looked at the two girls. "It's all downhill to the river," she said. "Aaron and I can manage the cart. Why don't you two run ahead and see what you can find out?"

Hannah's mouth opened in pleased surprise. "Are you sure?"

"Yes, go!"

"Thank you." She grabbed Ingrid's hand and off they raced, the shoes around Ingrid's neck bouncing wildly as they careened down the hill toward the river.

When they reached the river ten minutes later, the ferry was just setting off from the other side, coming toward them. Too excited to sit still, they paced back and forth, their eyes darting to measure its progress every few seconds. When the boat was still twenty or thirty yards away, Hannah could bear it no longer. "Sir?"

There were two men hauling on the rope and one man helping steer with a long pole. They all looked up. The one with the pole answered. "Now, where did you two fine young ladies come from?" Then his eyes lifted to the bluffs where the line of carts and wagons was making its way down the trail. "Ah, you're with the next handcart company."

"Yes, under the direction of Captain Edward Martin, sir. And can you tell me if the company under the direction of Captain Willie is still camped in Florence?"

They were close enough for the man to see the eagerness on their faces. He hesitated, then shook his head. "No, lass. I'm sorry to say that the Willie Company left for points west a week ago tomorrow. They're long gone by now, I'm afraid."

For several seconds Hannah just stared at him, as if he had spoken to her in a foreign tongue. Then she turned away, her eyes burning. "We're too late, Ingrid," she whispered. "I knew it. We are too late."

III

Wednesday, 27 August 1856

"Don't stop! Don't stop!"

Jens Nielson shouted the warning over his shoulder as he threw his full six-foot-two frame against the crossbar of their handcart and lunged forward. Eric and Olaf were together at the back of the cart, arms outstretched, bodies bent, legs digging into the soft sand beneath their feet as they pushed against the tailgate. With all of that, the wheels sunk deeper and the cart came to a shuddering halt.

Eric dropped to his knees, his head down, his chest heaving. As he watched, sweat began to drip off his nose and chin and make tiny dark spots in the sand. Beside him, Olaf turned slowly, then sank down, leaning his back against the one wheel. If the sand—hot enough to burn the skin—bothered him through his trousers, he gave no sign. Like Eric, he seemed totally consumed with trying to get enough air to stop from fainting.

Eric saw the cart move slightly and raised his head. "Jens. Hold up. Let us rest a minute." Then he saw that Jens had only lifted the crossbar enough to slip out from beneath it; then he lowered the cart to the ground.

"Coming through," called a voice.

Turning, Eric watched with envy as a family with five older children came up the hill toward them. The two oldest boys had rope harnesses over their shoulders. These had been tied to the shafts so that they could pull on the cart from out ahead of those in the pulling box. The husband and wife were in what was known as the "pulling box," that area at the front of the cart framed by the two side shafts and the front crossbar. Three other children were pushing at the back of the cart. With that kind of manpower they moved steadily through the heavy sand. They swung out around the Nielson/Pederson cart, calling out encouragement as they passed. "Only about fifty yards more to the top," the man said cheerfully.

"Yeah," Olaf muttered beneath his breath, "and then we get to start on the next hill after that, and the next one after that." Though he and Eric now usually spoke in English when they were alone, they always spoke Danish with the Nielsons.

Eric watched them go by, not even trying to disguise his envy. "Why don't we let them take our hundred pounds of flour if they are finding it so easy?" he muttered.

The sack that they had been given at Florence, and which now sat directly over the wheels, had made a notable difference that they felt every hour of every day when they were pulling. Unfortunately, with Jens Nielson being as tall and strong as he was, and with having the

Pederson brothers—two young "huskies," as Elder Ahmanson noted—they had not yet been allowed to dip into their sack. The sacks of flour from carts pulled by those deemed as weaker cart teams were being used first. When they were emptied, only then would the company start on the others.

Eric blew out his breath, somewhat mollified to see that behind them most of the rest of the company had bogged down and collapsed as well.

"Elsie?"

Elsie Nielson was walking off the trail a little, six-year-old Jens on one side, and Bodil Mortensen, the nine-year-old girl they were bringing to America with them, walking beside her on the other. Seeing them stopped, she was already coming toward them. "Yes, Jens?"

"Where's the bacon? We've got to grease the hubs some more. Pulling through this deep sand is bad enough, but the wheels are binding up again. We need some grease."

Elsie came up beside him, her four-foot-eleven-inch height making her look like a child beside her husband. "I'm sorry, Jens. There is no more bacon."

Eric could have told him that. He had taken the last piece of bacon this morning—fat, lean meat, and all—and greased the hubs as best he could. What little axle grease they had been able to obtain in Florence was gone by the fourth day. Now, when they needed lubricants more desperately than at any time since leaving Iowa City, there was none to be had.

Their captains had warned them that this was one of the most dreaded parts of the trail. They were one hundred thirty-five miles west of Florence and moving up the Loup Fork of the Platte River. The river bottoms were too marshy or choked with underbrush to allow passage, so they had to take to the higher ground where there was hill after rolling hill of sand dunes.

"Then get the soap," Jens said wearily. He removed his hat and wiped at his brow with the sleeve of his shirt. It came away dark with sweat. It was barely noticeable because the front and back of his shirt were likewise wet.

"But, Jens—"

"I know, Elsie," he said, "but we can wash in water alone if we have to. If our wheels freeze on us, we're not going anywhere."

"I'll get it," Olaf said. "I know where it is." He stood and moved to the back of the cart and began to fumble beneath the canvas. In a moment he held up a square bar of soap. It was thick and almost as solid as a rock, the product of animal fat and lye that was strong enough, as Elder Ahmanson put it, to take the freckles off your cheeks.

Jens took the soap from Olaf and moved around to the first wheel. He reached in and began to rub the soap on the axle with short, even strokes. As he did so, he kicked at the base of the tire that was buried six inches deep in the sand. "Would you look at that?" he groused. "Is there no end to how deep it is?"

"Watch this," Olaf said. The sand hills they were traversing were covered with sparse clumps of prairie grass, or what the captains called "prairie wheat." It grew a long stalk that came to a head somewhat resembling mature wheat. Olaf bent down and broke off a stalk, then moved off the road a few feet where no wheels had broken up the sand. The stalk was no thicker than a string and quite fragile. He stuck it thick end first into the sand, then began to push it in deeper and deeper, as though it were a needle and the soil the softest of cloth. They watched in surprise as it went deeper and deeper—four inches, six inches, nine inches. Finally at about ten inches straight down, it would go no farther.

Olaf looked up and shrugged. This wasn't a railroad spike he had driven into the ground. It was nothing but a piece of straw, and it went ten inches down without a strain. It was little wonder that the wheels were buried up to the spokes.

Jens finished and moved around the cart to the other wheel. "Elsie," he said as he began soaping that one, "I'm afraid we're going to have to have your help to get started again." He looked at his foster daughter. "Bodil, you take little Jens and walk alongside until we reach the top of the hill. Then Mama can help you both again."

"Yes, Brother Nielson." She reached out and took the boy's hand and moved off to the side so that she would not be in their path.

"We'll look for lizards, Papa," little Jens said.

That brought Elsie around with a jerk. "Watch closely for snakes, Bodil. Brother Willie said the sand hills were a bad place for rattlesnakes."

Eric shook off a little chill. He hated snakes of any size, shape, or species. He moved up to the front of the cart. "I'll get in the shafts with you, Brother Nielson. Sister Nielson and Olaf can push."

Jens nodded and they lifted the cart together and slipped inside the pulling box.

Olaf stood and put his back against the cart, swishing his feet back and forth until they were buried in the sand deep enough to give him more solid footing. Then he leaned into it, as though he were going to lift the back of the cart off the ground. Elsie moved up beside him.

"Ready when you are," Olaf called.

Jens looked at Eric, who nodded. "All right. One. Two. Three. Heave!"

It was like pulling a heifer out of a mud bog, but as their feet dug down and the veins on their foreheads bulged, the wheels finally began to lift and then started to roll slowly forward. "Don't stop!" Jens Nielson shouted. "Don't stop!"

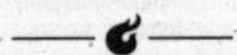

"Why are we stopping?" Olaf, now in the traces with Eric, was peering ahead. One by one the carts ahead of them had come to a stop, and people were sitting down to rest or leaning heavily against their carts.

"Did the bugle blow for nooning?" Elsie Nielson asked.

"No," her husband answered from behind where he had taken his turn at pushing. "It's too early for the noon stop."

Then Eric's head came up as he saw a figure racing back down the line toward them, bonnet in one hand, her dark hair flying. He jerked forward. It was Maggie McKensie!

"Something's wrong," he said. "Wait here." He slipped under the shaft, leaving the cart for Olaf to steady, then broke into a run toward her.

"Eric, come quickly."

"What? What is it?"

"One of the walkers was bitten by a rattlesnake."

He faltered a little. "A walker?"

"Yes. I couldn't see for sure. People were crowding around. But I saw that woman you call your grandmother sitting on the ground."

His heart jumped. "Sister Bathgate?"

"Yes. I thought you'd want to know."

Without thinking, he grabbed her hand. "Come on," he said, breaking into a run.

The cluster of people was out ahead of the lead handcarts. This was no surprise. The walkers always liked to take the lead. That kept them out of the dust and gave them the firmest footing. As Maggie and Eric approached, someone said something to the group. Suddenly Isabella Park was there, waving frantically at them. "Eric! Eric! Come quickly!"

The crowd parted a little to let Eric and Maggie through. Eric felt his stomach plummet. Sister Mary Bathgate was lying on the ground, her face twisted with pain. He dropped to one knee beside her. "Mary?"

She tried to smile, but winced instead. Eric's eyes dropped to where her skirts were pulled up around one ankle. Her leg was turned to the side, so he could see the back of it, just above the ankle bone. He grimaced. There were four puncture marks there, each oozing dark drops of blood. What little flesh he could see was already red and puffy.

"Stupid me," she said between clenched teeth. Her face was white as a sheet. "I was being so careful. Then Isabella and I started talking." She shook her head in disgust. "I didn't hear him rattle until just a second or two before he struck."

Eric took her hand and squeezed it tightly. "*Him?*" he said, chiding her a little. "How do you know it was a male? Maybe it was a girl snake."

She squeezed back and laughed, grateful that he could tease her at this moment. "Because he didn't stay to apologize," she shot back. "Definitely a male."

Eric laughed and put an arm around her back, steadying her. He looked up at the anxious faces surrounding them. "Has someone gone for Elder Willie?"

"Yes," Isabella said. "We sent one of the young girls as soon as it happened."

"Did you kill it?" a boy in his teens asked eagerly.

Sister Bathgate gave him a look that would have melted solid stone. "No, I didn't kill it. Seemed more sensible to sit down and stop the poison from pumping through my body than to get even with that miserable descendant of the serpent who caused Eve to fall."

Maggie dropped into a crouch beside Eric and Sister Bathgate. "Are you feeling faint?"

She nodded. "And sick to my stomach." She bent down and lifted her skirts for a moment. On the upper part of the leg a garter had been tightly tied, biting deep into the flesh. "I stopped it off," she said to Maggie. "My ankle hurts like the devil, but the poison hasn't gotten too far yet, I think."

"Here's Captain Willie," someone shouted. Again the crowd parted as the captain and Elder John Chislett, the captain of the hundred to which the footmen were assigned, came running up. Chislett had a small bottle of olive oil in one hand. Captain Willie had his pocketknife out. He glanced at Sister Bathgate's face, took a quick breath, then went down on his knees beside her foot. Gently he picked it up and pressed against the flesh.

She gasped, and her fingers dug into the flesh of Eric's arm.

"He got you good," Captain Willie said.

Sister Bathgate glared at Eric. "See? I'm not the only one who thinks it was a male."

Maggie just shook her head, amazed that she could joke at a time like this.

Willie laid her foot back down and opened up the blade on the knife. "I'm afraid we're going to have to cut it open, Sister Bathgate, and get that bad blood out."

"Thought you would," she answered. The grim tightness around her mouth belied the forced cheerfulness in her voice. "And I'm glad to see you brought the oil," she said, looking up at Elder Chislett. "There's power in the priesthood and I know it."

"Hold her tight," Willie said to Eric.

Eric looked up, motioning to Maggie with his head. She came around and took Sister Bathgate's other arm. "Close your eyes," Eric said gently. "Won't do no good to watch."

She obeyed. Sister Park came around and knelt down behind her, bracing her back. "I'm here, Mary."

"Be done with it," Sister Bathgate said to Elder Willie. "I'm ready."

Willie wiped the blade of the knife on the sleeve of his shirt, then gripped her ankle firmly with his left hand. He bent over. He made one quick but deep slash between two of the puncture wounds. Under the pressure of the tourniquet, the blood spurted outward. Mary screamed, stiffening against Eric's and Maggie's grip, her body trembling.

"One more." Again there was a quick movement, and another cut was made. Mary moaned, and for a moment Eric thought she would faint. But then her head came up again as she took in air with quick, frantic gulps.

Maggie turned her head away as their leader began to squeeze the leg and blood poured out and dripped onto the sand.

Isabella Park laid her head against her friend's. Mary's eyes were shut and she was jerking spasmodically with every touch. "It's all right, Mary. I'm here. It's all right."

Finally satisfied, Willie stood up. "All right. Let's bandage it up, then give her a blessing."

Two of the women in the company already had thought of bandages and brought out strips of cloth. They undid the garter, then bound the wound tightly, demurely pulling Sister Bathgate's skirts down over the bandage when they finished.

Motioning for Eric to join them, Elder Willie then directed the administration. Elder Chislett anointed her head and then the wound with the consecrated oil. Then Elder Willie blessed her, with Elder Chislett and Eric assisting.

When they finished she reached up and took each one by the hand. "Thank you. I'm feeling better already."

Maggie, still kneeling beside her, nodded. "Your color is better too, Sister Bathgate."

The Englishwoman turned. "Say," she said, her eyes narrowing in concentration. "Aren't you that Scottish lass that was teaching Eric his English lessons?"

"Aye," she said in surprise. She didn't think she was known to this sister.

Mary leaned back and looked up at her friend. "Did you hear that, Isabella?"

There was a smug nod. "I did. When you spoke about doing something about this matter the other day, Mary, I didn't think it would be quite so drastic."

"You hush now, Isabella. If it works, then so much the better."

"If what works?" Eric said, suspicious now. "What are you two doing?"

"Never you mind, Eric Pederson," Isabella said. "This is none of your affair."

Mary gave her an incredulous look.

"Well, not directly, anyway."

"Sister Bathgate?"

She turned and looked up at Captain Willie. "Yes?"

"Now there is no choice. You're going to have to ride in the wagon for a time, whether you like it or not."

She stiffened as violently as if he had cut her again. "No!"

"Oh, yes. Surely you don't think you can walk on that leg?"

"Oh, yes I can." She started to get up, trying to catch Eric's hand for support.

He jerked it away. "Oh, no. Captain Willie is right exactly, yah, and you know it is so."

"Of course he's right," Isabella said sternly. "We'll hear nothing more of this."

Sister Bathgate turned to look at her traveling companion. "And I suppose you'll go right on walking so that you can say that you never had to ride."

"Of course, but I'll walk alongside the wagon so I can be near you."

"Hmmph!" Sister Bathgate said in complete disgust. She turned to Maggie. "I want you to be my witness," she said.

"Witness to what?"

"That I never got into a wagon until I was compelled to by that cursed snake."

Eric and Maggie stood at the back of the wagon, looking at the two elderly sisters lying side by side. "You know, Sister Park," Eric said in a chiding manner, "this was really more than friendship required."

She grimaced. "Couldn't have Mary grousing at me all the way to Utah," she said through clenched teeth.

Sister Bathgate reached over and took her friend's hand and held it tightly, waiting until the pain eased a little. Then she laughed softly. "Can you believe it? I think both of us must be getting old."

Maggie reached in and took Sister Park's other hand. "We're just grateful that it wasn't anything more serious."

Amen to that, Eric thought. Eric and Maggie had followed the stretcher carrying Sister Bathgate back to one of the supply wagons. They had quickly helped the teamster make a bed in the back for the Englishwoman and gotten her settled in comfortably. Throughout, Sister Park hovered nearby, greatly concerned for her companion's welfare. But the tragedy had been averted. Since the time when the wound was cut open and she had received a priesthood blessing, Sister Bathgate's color had returned almost back to normal.

Captain Willie, satisfied that she was situated as well as possible, gave the signal for the column to move out again. They had already been delayed for over an hour. Maggie and Eric were just approaching their handcarts when they heard a terrible scream. They spun around and raced back again. To their horror, Sister Park was just being pulled from beneath the hind wheels of the wagon in which Sister Bathgate was riding.

As it turned out, just as the teamster cracked his whip over the heads of his mules, Sister Park had darted in front of the teams to check on her friend one more time. The teamster didn't even see her. The lead mule knocked her down and she fell beneath the hooves of the teams. How she had avoided being struck in the head was incredible. More incredible was the fact that she had no broken bones.

As those who had witnessed it told the story, Sister Park fell directly in the path of the wagon wheels. The front wheels of the fully loaded wagon went directly over both hips. That was when she had screamed out in agony. Fortunately one of the brethren was standing just a few feet away. When he saw what was happening, he dived for her, grabbed her arms, and dragged her outward. Quick as he was, he wasn't quite quick enough. The rear wheels then passed over both of her ankles. When Eric and Maggie came dashing up, Sister Park was writhing on the ground in agony.

As Eric watched Maggie giving comfort to Sister Park now, he marveled again. The wagon was fully loaded with flour, about four thousand pounds of it. The wheels had struck her squarely and passed directly over her body twice. And there was not a broken bone. Captain Willie and Brother Chislett had carefully checked and found nothing. Though she was in tremendous pain and would surely be heavily bruised, Sister Park had escaped serious injury. Even the thought of that made Eric shudder. Had even one of the ankles been shattered, with nothing but limited medical abilities out here it would probably have meant certain death.

Once again Eric had stood with Captain Willie and administered a priesthood blessing. And once again they had witnessed the power of the Lord. By the time they got a second bed fixed up beside Sister Bathgate and got Sister Park into it, the pain had dropped to bearable levels for the old woman and Sister Bathgate was teasing her companion about wanting to give her company.

Eric shook his head ruefully, looking at these two who had come to mean so much to him. "I have wondered what to do to get you two so that I don't have to worry about you every minute of the day. Well, I think this should do it."

"Pshaw!" Sister Bathgate snorted. "Don't you get used to it, because Isabella and I are getting out of this wagon first chance we get."

Eric just shook his head again. They were hopeless. He hopped up onto the tailgate of the wagon, leaned forward, and kissed them both on the forehead. "Fair enough," he said. "But until then, you just stay here and keep each other company."

IV

Tuesday, 2 September 1856

The Edward Martin Handcart Company left Iowa City, Iowa, thirteen days after James G. Willie's company. They arrived in Florence just five days after the fourth company had continued westward. Elder Franklin D. Richards was waiting for them there, having arrived the day before. He and a small party of British missionaries had come by packet ship from England via New Orleans. There they had caught a Mississippi riverboat to St. Louis, then changed to another, smaller boat and steamed up the Missouri River to Florence. They made the entire trip in twenty-six days. This was astonishing, considering that the group that had come on the *Thornton* was forty-three days just in crossing from Liverpool to New York. The *Horizon* took thirty-five days to cross the Atlantic to Boston. But for the Apostle's group, the winds had been entirely favorable. They sailed directly to New Orleans without a stop, and they had been fortunate to book passage on riverboats without having to wait even a day for their departure.

When the Martin group reached Florence, once again a council was called to discuss the issue of staying in Florence or pressing on in spite of the lateness of the season. Hannah McKensie had been horrified when Elder Richards advised them to consider stopping at Florence for the winter. He noted that Brother Martin's group had many more elderly traveling with them and said that without a doubt some of them and also infants might die by the way. It was deeply sobering. But what wintering over meant for Hannah was that it would be another year before she was reunited with her family.

Fortunately, Cyrus Wheelock, who was traveling with Elder Richards, joined George D. Grant and the other Church agents to put forth that there was not sufficient means to support a group this size for the winter and urged them to go on with all possible speed.

When all were through speaking to the issue, Elder Richards arose again and called for a vote.

It was a solemn moment. Here they sat, these emigrants from a far-off land—bronzed, weathered, and toughened by the trek across Iowa. Hannah was afraid that all the talk of blizzards and high mountains might deter them. She nearly fainted with relief when with uncovered heads and uplifted hands, the company voted almost unanimously to go on.

They spent four more days repairing, refurbishing, and resupplying, and on August twenty-seventh, the fifth and last handcart company of the season rolled out of Florence headed west.

That had been seven days ago—seven hard, long days. Hannah McKensie didn't mind. At noon today they had ferried across the Loup Fork of the Platte River. The ferryman said that the Willie Company had crossed on the twenty-third. That meant they were only about ten days ahead now. In one way, that was discouraging. Ten days was almost two hundred miles. But at one point the two companies had been separated by two full weeks. They were slowly closing the distance.

If Hannah had her way, the company would keep rolling two or three hours longer every day. Each time a cart broke down and they had to stop for repairs made her want to scream. Every delay was maddening. So now, looking at the gathering blackness that spread across the western horizon, she felt anger. *Leave us alone. Take your storm somewhere else. We have to keep moving.*

And yet, even as she said it, she felt a deep dread. She had developed a fear of these prairie thunderstorms. Racing eastward with amazing swiftness, they hit with a ferocity that was never seen back in Edinburgh. In moments the wind could turn from a gentle breeze to a howling gale. Rain came in horizontally like pebbles, feeling like it would strip the flesh from your face. Lightning ripped the sky with blinding intensity. Thunder clapped so loudly that it shook the earth.

It frightened her so badly, she would clamp her eyes shut as tightly as possible, put her hands over her ears, and bury her head in her lap.

She let out her breath, feeling the tension coiling within her. This one was as black as anything they had seen thus far. She looked at Ingrid and shook her head. At Florence some of the agents had talked about the most feared of all American storms, the prairie tornado. They talked of winds that could strip the roof off a house and drop it across town, of pieces of straw being driven like nails into tree trunks. It hadn't done much to cheer the emigrants.

As the wind stiffened, Elizabeth Jackson turned and looked around. The children were off to the side of the main column, walking together as they always did. Holding her bonnet so it wouldn't blow away, she scanned their faces. Young Aaron, her youngest and just two, was nestled in a place they made for him on top of the loaded cart, but her two girls were with the rest of the children. Then she saw her oldest. "Martha Ann! Get Mary Elizabeth. Come quickly. It's going to rain."

Aaron Jackson, pulling in the shafts, came to a stop. Up ahead, Edward Martin was riding toward them, yelling at the people and waving his arms. Aaron didn't have to wait to hear what he was saying. He swung the cart around so that the back of it faced into the teeth of the storm and set it down. "This is going to be a bad one. We'd better get prepared."

They flew into action. Ingrid took off the shoes from around her neck and set them beneath the cart, then ran off to get the girls. Hannah lifted young Aaron from his place and set him down. She gave him a gentle shove. "Under the cart, young man."

Familiar with this routine, he crawled in as far as he could. Being the smallest, he always went in to the front where there was the least amount of room. He snuggled in beside Ingrid's new shoes.

Hannah threw up her hand in front of her face as a gust of wind flung dust and grains of sand into her eyes. She felt the first splash of rain. Aaron Jackson was checking the lashings on the cart. She leaped to help him. "It's coming fast."

There was a brilliant flash and a second or two later a tremendous clap of thunder. Ingrid was just bringing the girls in. They all jumped, and Mary Elizabeth started to cry. "That was close," Ingrid said as she pulled them beneath the shelter of the cart.

All around, people were sprinting for shelter, dragging their children with them. Now the rain began in earnest. The lightning cracked again, and Hannah felt the earth shudder beneath her feet. She closed her eyes and clapped her hands over her ears. "I hate this!" she exclaimed.

The box of a handcart was only about five feet wide—to give it the same width as the wide wagon track—and about five or six feet long. Tipped forward and resting on its shafts, it provided a meager roof for seven people. Huddling in together as tightly as possible, the seven of them crouched beneath the cart as the full fury of the storm descended on the column. Above their heads, the cart shook and shuddered as the wind began to batter at it.

"Grab the wheels!" Aaron yelled at Hannah as he locked his hands on the spoke of the wheel next to him.

Hannah had no choice but to forget trying to shut out the thunder and lightning. She grimaced as she and Ingrid grabbed the other wheel, hanging on fiercely as the cart rocked sharply now. *Boom!* This time the flash and the crash were almost simultaneous. She gritted her teeth and stared at the ground. Praying that it would pass swiftly, she hunkered down to endure it as best she could.

The rain was coming in sheets now, and in moments the ground was covered and water started to run beneath the cart. Brother Jackson tried to dig a furrow with the heel of his boot to divert it, but it was too little too late, and in a few moments Hannah felt the cold wetness through her dress and against her bottom and the back of her legs. Little Aaron began to whimper and Sister Jackson took him in her arms.

Suddenly the roar of the rain changed to a rattling sound. Hannah looked up, instantly understanding. "Look, Mama," Martha Ann shouted. "It's snowing."

"Not snow, dear. That's hail."

The rattling deepened into a drumroll now. The ground all around them came alive with bouncing white pellets. Ingrid reached out and retrieved one, holding it up in wonder. It was as large as the tip of her thumb.

Somewhere off behind them, there was the frantic whinny of a horse. Then an ox bawled. "The stock!" Aaron Jackson cried. "This will drive them mad." He went up to his knees. "Elizabeth. Hold the wheel. I've got to go help."

Setting little Aaron down, Elizabeth grabbed the spokes. Brother Jackson scrambled out, holding his arms above his head. But even as he started to turn, there was a brilliant flash of light and a simultaneous blast. It was as though they were sitting beneath the muzzle of a giant cannon at the moment it fired. There was not just the flash and the deafening roar, but a tremendous concussion as well. Brother Jackson flew forward, landing face first in the mud.

"*Aaron!*" Elizabeth screamed as she came up into a crouch.

Hannah was dazed and it took a moment for it to register that the three children were shrieking hysterically. Then Brother Jackson sat up, shaking his head. His eyes were wide and bewildered. In an instant Elizabeth was at his side, kneeling in the mud, unmindful of the pelting hail. She threw her arms around him. "Are you all right?"

He pushed her back, staring at her. One hand came up to touch his face. "Yes. I—"

"Help. Please, someone! Help me!"

Hannah swung around. Behind them, down the line of carts about fifty feet, barely visible through the pounding hail, she saw a woman on her feet waving frantically. Then she dropped to her knees beside something that had been thrown on the ground. Hannah started. As the hail momentarily lifted, she saw that it was a man, lying on his back in the mud. Strangely, she saw that the front of his shirt was all black.

Aaron stumbled to his feet. "I'm all right, Elizabeth," he said. He squeezed her hands. "Get back under the cart." Then he turned and broke into a stumbling run toward the woman who was calling frantically for anyone to come and help her.

In ten minutes the storm was over. The hail gradually became rain again, the wind lessened, and the horizontal sheets of rain became first a downpour, then a drizzle, and finally a light sprinkle. To the west, they could see the edge of the great cloud that hung over them. Beyond was blue sky. One by one the people began to come out from beneath the wagons and the handcarts. No one seemed to notice that their clothes were soaked and muddy. Every eye was turned to the cluster of people about fifty feet from where Hannah and Ingrid stood. The two older girls had their arms around the two younger Jackson girls, who shivered violently now in their wet clothes. Elizabeth Jackson stood beside them, holding little Aaron against her tightly.

They all straightened as Aaron Jackson suddenly appeared, pushing out from the crowd and starting toward them. His jaw was set and his face grim as he returned to join them.

"Aaron?" Elizabeth said as he came up.

He shook his head. "It's Henry Walker from the Carlisle Conference." He looked away.

"Is he . . . ?" Hannah asked.

He nodded. "The lightning struck him directly. He never had a chance."

Chapter Notes

As in other chapters, actual events from handcart companies other than the Willie and Martin groups have been added to this story so as to give a fuller picture of the handcart experience.

Sisters Mary Bathgate and Isabella Park were actual handcart pioneers. Though depicted here as being part of the Willie Company, in actuality they came with Daniel McArthur's company, the second company of 1856. Their story is included here because it provides one more glimpse into the hearts of the handcart Saints, especially the women. In the novel the rattlesnake incident and the subsequent wagon accident take place on 27 August 1856. They actually occurred eleven days earlier than that and much farther west along the trail than shown here. The details as given here come from Captain McArthur's report of the journey of the second company, including Sister Bathgate's disgust at finally having to ride in the wagon (see Hafen and Hafen, *Handcarts to Zion*, p. 216).

Here is Brother McArthur's description of what happened after Sister Bathgate's injury:

> Sister Bathgate continued to be quite sick, but was full of faith, and after stopping one and a half hours we hitched up our teams. As the word was given for the teams to start, old Sister Isabella Park ran in before the wagon to see how her companion was. The driver, not seeing her, hallooed at his team and they being quick to mind, Sister Park could not get out of the way, and the fore wheel struck her and threw her down and passed over both her hips. Brother Leonard grabbed hold of her to pull her out of the way, before the hind wheel could catch her. He only got her out part way and the hind wheels passed over her ankles. We all thought that she would be all mashed to pieces, but to the joy of us all, there was not a bone broken, although the wagon had something like two tons burden on it, a load for 4 yoke of oxen. We went right to work and applied the same medicine to her that we did to the sister who was bitten by the rattlesnake, and although quite sore for a few days, Sister Park got better, so that she was on the tramp before we got into this Valley, and Sister Bathgate was right by her side, to cheer her up. Both were as smart as could be long before they got here, and this is what I call good luck, for I know that nothing but the power of God saved the two sisters and they traveled together, they rode

together, and suffered together. (In Hafen and Hafen, *Handcarts to Zion,* pp. 216–17)

Henry Walker was a member of the Edmund Ellsworth Company, the first handcart company to come west in 1856. On Saturday 26 July, just west of the Loup Fork ferry, about eighty-five miles west of Florence, a terrible thunderstorm swept over the camp. Archer Walters, a member of the company, kept a daily journal. On that day he records:

> We had [not] got far and it began to lightning and so on the thunders roared and about the middle of the train of hand carts the lightning struck a brother and he fell to rise no more in that body, - by the name of Henry Walker, from Carlisle Conference; aged 58 years. Left a wife and children. One boy burnt a little, named James Studard [Stoddard]; we thought he would die but he recovered and was able to walk and Brother William Studard, father of the boy was knocked to the ground and a sister, Betsy Taylor, was terribly shook but recovered. All wet through. This happened about 2 miles from the Ferry and we then went 2 miles to camp. I put the body, with the help of others, on the hand cart and pulled him to camp and buried him without coffin for there was no boards to be had. (In Carol Cornwall Madsen, *Journey to Zion,* p. 616)

CHAPTER 15

NEAR NORTH BLUFF CREEK, NEBRASKA TERRITORY

I

Thursday, 4 September 1856

It was like a string of pearls, Eric decided. There were occasional jewels of interest or excitement strung together on an endless thread of monotony. Every day was the same as the one before. Rise at dawn. Get breakfast (often cold), strike the tents, pack the carts, roll out at eight or nine o'clock (later, if any of the stock had strayed and couldn't be found), stop or "noon" at midday to rest and eat, roll out again, stop somewhere before sundown and make camp.

And even some of the "pearls" were only notable in contrast to the boredom of the other days. In other circumstances they would probably not even have been worthy of comment. There had been a birth one day and a few days later a death. As on the ship, life went on along the trail as well.

The day that stood out most clearly in Eric's mind was what he thought of as the day of the Indians. After nooning, the company met a large party of Omaha Indians. They were friendly, but carried a letter from an army captain stating that a small wagon train he was escorting had been attacked by a marauding band of Cheyenne. Two soldiers and a small child were killed, and a woman was carried off captive. That sent a shiver through the company, especially among the sisters, but their captains assured them that even warring Indians would not attack a company as large as theirs. That assurance helped, but more than one pair of eyes scanned the horizon anxiously for the next several days. As yet the emigrants weren't knowledgeable enough to understand the differences between the tribes. Children were kept close, the stock was watched with greater care, and those few men with weapons kept them close at hand.

Later that afternoon, as the company moved on, the Indians rode along with the train, fascinated by the carts. One old chief who spoke a few words of English kept pointing and howling with laughter. "Little wagons," he said over and over. "Little wagons."

The day of the Indians ended that evening when subcaptains Millen Atwood and Levi Savage rode to the Indians' camp. There they bartered for a supply of buffalo meat. That night the company had their first taste of the sweet meat about which they had all heard so much.

But even that experience quickly lost its novelty. Seeing buffalo was now almost as common as seeing the ever-present prairie dogs. The great shaggy beasts came close to camp often enough that buffalo meat became a regular supplement to their diet.

"Whoa there, Eric!"

His head came up as the front bar of the cart pulled him to a stop. Olaf, who was standing beside him in the shafts, was looking at him strangely. "Is the heat getting to you?" he drawled. "We're stopping."

Eric grinned, a little sheepish. "Sorry. I was just thinking about how fascinating this journey is. Every day a new and exciting experience."

Elsie Nielson hooted softly. "So where have I been when this was happening?"

Eric only grinned the more broadly. "One thing about monotony," he chuckled, "it doesn't require a lot of attention." Then he looked around. "So why are we stopping?"

Jens Nielson came up. "I think this is where we're stopping for the night," he said wryly, looking at Eric. "Should we join them, or were you thinking of going on by yourself?"

"Oh, you boys," Elsie chided them. "Leave poor Eric alone."

"All right, all right," Eric said. "So my mind was elsewhere." He looked around again. Today their fifth hundred was in the middle of the train. Up ahead the lead carts were already stopped, and people were starting to untie the ropes that held their goods in place. A little farther to the right he could see the wagons of the independent company. For a change, they had been out ahead of the handcarts, and they had already unhitched their teams and turned them out to graze with the beef cattle and the milk cows. That was how it was with a long train like this, Eric thought. It was not a cohesive unit but more like several little pieces which hung loosely together. The first and the last arrivals into camp might be as much as an hour to two hours apart.

He turned and looked. Sure enough, the back half of the train was still coming on, strung out for another quarter of a mile or so.

Elsie was looking around. She pointed. "Let's camp over there."

They turned, then nodded in agreement. The place she had chosen was on an elevated rise, just big enough to hold the tent and give them a place for a fire. If it rained—as it probably would, judging from the gray wall of clouds to the west—the water would not flood their tent.

Jens turned and called back to the others who were part of their tent group. "Over there?" They nodded and also started moving in that direction. Then Eric stopped again.

"Now what?" Olaf exclaimed.

"Listen!"

Eric cocked his head, thinking at first it was the first low rumble from the approaching storm. But then as others stopped and the line quieted, Eric turned. The sound was not coming from the west and it hadn't died away as thunder always did. It was a continuous sound, almost too low to discern but distinct now against the silence.

"What is it?" Elsie said, turning to look in that direction.

Jens raised a hand for silence. Then as they strained to hear more clearly, a shout went up somewhere down the line. "Look!"

About half a mile away one of the gently rolling hills of the great prairie formed the northern horizon. Eric stared. For a moment it looked like someone had spilled a giant kettle of molasses. The ridge was suddenly engulfed with a black flowing mass. Even as they stared, the rumble deepened into a soft but ominous roar.

"What is it, Jens?" Elsie cried again, this time sweeping little Jens up into her arms.

No one answered her. They were transfixed. It took a moment for the image to transfer to the brain and for the mind to process it. Then in one flash of clarity, Eric realized what it was. A huge herd of buffalo was coming towards them at full speed, raising a great cloud of dust behind them. Over the ridge they poured in an endless flow.

"Look at that!" Olaf cried. "There must be thousands of them."

"Tens of thousands," Eric corrected. The mass was still coming with no end in sight.

"Stampede! Stampede!"

They jerked around at the sound of pounding hoofbeats. Captain Willie was racing toward them on his horse, low in the saddle, whipping the reins back and forth. "Push those handcarts together," he screamed. "Get those wagons in a circle. Hurry!"

Eric had been so stunned by what he saw, it hadn't occurred to him that there was danger. Now he realized that the long line of carts and wagons formed a barrier for the oncoming mass. They were coming straight toward them.

"Get those carts out of the way," Elder Willie shouted. "Make an opening!"

"Bodil! Bodil!" Jens spun around, looking frantically for the girl.

"There!" Olaf said, pointing. "I'll get her." He lunged forward, heading for where the group of older children stood rooted to the spot, staring at the scene unfolding before them. Olaf snatched up Bodil Mortensen at a full lope, waving his hand at the other children. "Run!" he screamed. "Get behind the carts."

The children scattered like chickens when a fox enters the chicken coop.

As Eric swung their cart around and started it towards the next cart, he saw Elder Willie, another seventy or eighty yards down the column, yelling and waving at those still in the line. Eric couldn't hear what he was saying, but he immediately saw what he was doing. He was moving those carts back, putting them double and triple. He was doing two things simultaneously—opening up a hole in the line and making a barricade for the people.

Eric whirled and began screaming to those around him at the top of his lungs. "Make an opening! Get the carts up together. Go! Go!"

"What?" Jens Nielson shouted. "Speak in Danish!"

Eric shook his head in disgust. Willie had shouted at them in English, and without thinking he had used the same words. He began again. "Get the carts up in a line together. Make a place for the buffalo to get through. Otherwise they'll go right over the top of us."

Jens Nielson saw it instantly. "Yes. I'll go this way." He leaped forward and grabbed the cart in front of them. The man and his wife were frozen in place, staring at the black mass which was thundering toward them, now less than three hundred yards away. Jens almost knocked the man down as he yanked their cart around and pulled it up beside the next one.

Eric hurtled forward, pulling their cart beside the other two. He dropped it with a crash, leaped out of the shafts, and ran back to the cart that had been behind him. Shouting, yelling, helping where necessary, Jens and Eric began to form a hook in their end of the column, rolling each cart up and behind the others to form a solid wall and open up a great gap. On the other end, Captain Willie and some other men were doing the same, only in the opposite direction.

The earth was trembling now, like the deck of a steamboat under full power. As he looked to the north, Eric no longer saw a shapeless, mindless mass. Now he could make out the individual animals—huge bulls with their shaggy humps and wickedly curving horns, the lighter-colored cows, here and there some yearlings running at full speed to stop from being run over themselves.

"Behind the carts. Stay behind the carts." He raked his eyes up and down the open space now, making sure no one was still there. Suddenly he thought of the McKensies and the Jameses. Where were they? And what about Sister Bathgate and Sister Park, who were still confined to a wagon because of their injuries?

Then he had no more time to worry about others. A hundred yards from him, across the great gap in the line they had created, Elder Willie and some of the other men were jumping up and down and waving shirts, coats, blankets, aprons—whatever they could lay hand on. They were screaming at the top of their lungs at the onrushing animals. Jens grasped what they were doing an instant ahead of Eric. "They're trying to turn them into the gap," he shouted.

Jens ripped off his shirt and began to wave it frantically. Olaf shoved Bodil into Elsie's arms and darted to the cart. In a moment he was at Eric's side with two blankets. They too began jumping up and down.

Now just fifty or sixty yards away, the lead animals closest to the cluster of carts wheeled sharply inward. On the far side the lead animals did the same, squeezing the front of the stampede like water pouring into a funnel. Like sheep, the mass behind followed.

"Get behind the carts!" Jens yelled as the first huge bull bore down on them. He dove and threw his arms around Elsie and the children. Eric and Olaf were right behind him.

For Eric, the only thing that came close to describing what happened next was to compare it to the most severe thunderstorm they had yet experienced. The roar of the hooves was deafening, now added to by the grunts, snorts, and bellowing of the animals and the cries and screams of terrified people. Clods of dirt thrown up by the flashing hooves rained down on them like hail. The dust was thicker than even the strongest wind could create, and they had to throw their arms across their faces to stop from choking.

Behind him, Eric heard a crash and whipped around in time to see a handcart overturned as a large bull tried to leap over it but didn't quite clear it. A woman with a baby screamed and scrambled out of the way. Here and there other animals were breaking through the line and pushing through the wall of carts, but for the most part, Eric saw in relief, Elder Willie's quick thinking had saved the train. The great herd was pouring through the gap in the line, half-hidden in the billowing dust, their hooves churning the soil into powder.

It seemed to Eric as though the dark shapes ran past them for over an hour, but when the last was gone and they slowly stood up, he realized it was probably no more than five or six minutes.

"Oh my!" someone down the line exclaimed.

"Whoo-ee!" cried another.

Elsie looked up at her husband, half-dazed, then finally let go of her son. Little Jens ran to his father. The senior Jens picked him up, still gaping at the disappearing herd.

"Eric! Eric Pederson!"

Eric stood slowly and looked around. He saw Elder Willie's one hand come up and wave. "Eric, can you hear me?"

"Yes, sir."

"Check up and down the line. See if anyone is hurt."

Eric waved back an acknowledgment and turned to Olaf. "Let's go see," he said. "Jens, you stay here with Elsie. We'll let you know if we need help."

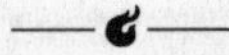

Ten minutes later the first of the handcarts from the back end of the train came up to join the front of the line. Everyone was still talking excitedly, pointing out the great scar in the prairie that marked the path of the buffalo. It was not hard to follow with the eye. If there was a blade of grass that had survived in that path, Eric couldn't see it. Sarah, Emma, and Reuben James had come back with Maggie and Robbie McKensie to see where the stampede had passed. They had been near the front end of the column, preparing to make camp, and the stampede had missed them completely. They were now talking quietly with Eric and Olaf.

At the sound of the carts, Eric turned. James G. Willie was beside them, leading his horse. His eyes scanned the crowd, then stopped on Eric.

Eric didn't wait for him to ask. "Everyone is fine, Elder Willie," he reported.

"What about Elder Woodward's company?"

A man raised his hand. "One girl in our group got a slight cut when a handcart overturned."

John Chislett, captain of the fourth hundred, stepped forward. "A brother in our tent group was hit in the panic to get the carts moved, but other than a bruise, he's all right."

"Thank heavens," Brother Willie said. "Everyone back here is all right too."

"And thank the Lord for that," Johan Ahmanson said in Danish. Those close enough to hear him and understand nodded fervently. "Amen," someone said softly.

"It could have been a lot–"

"Captain Willie!"

Everyone turned. A man was trotting towards them from the direction of the wagons. The captain whirled. "Yes? Is everyone all right in the wagon companies?"

"No one hurt, sir." He frowned. "But . . ." He stopped to catch his breath.

"But what?"

"The cattle stampeded with the buffalo, sir. The whole herd is gone."

II

Saturday, 6 September 1856

It was a grim spirit the emigrants brought to the meeting that morning. No one needed to ask why they had been called to assembly. For the past three days, the fourth handcart company had not moved. For the past three days, parties of men both on foot and on horseback spread out across the prairie searching for their lost cattle. For the third time in as many days, those parties returned at dark without recovering a single head of livestock.

This was a crisis of major proportion. A few of the cattle had not run that far and came back to camp during the first night. The rest were gone. The emigrants were already critically late. To stay in place for three full days was disastrous.

What a dilemma! Maggie thought as she watched the people gather in, looking for all intents and purposes as though they had come to a funeral. The beef cattle were critical to the company's needs. In addition to the thousands of pounds of meat they represented, they also offered the meat in the diet that was so critical in maintaining physical stamina. When you walked fifteen to twenty miles a day pulling three or four hundred pounds in a cart behind you, stamina was enormously important. The loss of the beef cattle was serious.

But even more critical were the draft animals. Most of the oxen that pulled the wagons had been turned out to graze just before the buffalo appeared. A few of them had returned, but not many. The company was now short a significant number of teams. They had little choice but to try and find them.

Yet here was the dilemma. Even as they sought for the meat they needed and the animals required to haul their flour, they were consuming that flour at an alarming rate. The flour ration for the company was sixteen ounces per adult per day, twelve ounces for older children, eight for the young ones. With about four hundred people in the company, they were consuming roughly three hundred pounds of flour per day. This three-day delay had cost them almost a thousand pounds of flour, while they had not moved one single mile closer to their destination! Was it any wonder that a dark gloom had settled over them?

"Brothers and sisters?"

Every eye turned to James Willie, and to no one's surprise he jumped right in without a preamble or introduction. "Here is our situation. We have lost thirty head of cattle. I don't need to tell any of you how critical they are to us. But we are satisfied that further search is useless. Either they have run off to who knows where with the buffalo, or, more likely, they are now fattening the pots of the Omaha Indians we saw the other day. Either way, there is nothing we can do now but press on.

"We no longer have sufficient oxen to pull the wagons. The wagons are full of flour that we need if we are going to get far enough to meet the wagons from Salt Lake. We have no choice but to round up the milk cows and the beef cattle and put them under the yoke."

That was not expected and a low murmur rumbled through the group.

"I know," he muttered. "That's going to be like trying to hold a nest of yellow jackets in your bare hands. They are going to fight like the devil." He blew out his breath. "What is worse, these are not draft animals and so this will almost certainly slow us down. These unbroken teams are not going to be able to pull the same kind of loads as the ox teams did."

Heads came up as some suddenly saw where he was leading them. Their eyes mirrored their dismay.

"We have no choice, brothers and sisters. We're going to have to put another hundred pounds of flour back in each of the handcarts. I'm sorry."

No one moved. No one cried out. He was right. The mathematics were not to be denied.

He looked like he wanted to say more, then changed his mind. He grunted softly, then nodded his head. "All right, brethren, let's round up those cows and get them into the yokes."

—❦—

Once their tent was rolled up and carried to the wagon and their bedding and other personal belongings loaded on the handcart, Maggie took a moment to look around. Over at the wagons the brethren were having a terrible time trying to yoke up the animals. They were at least a quarter of a hour away from being finished, maybe more.

"Mother?"

Mary McKensie was sitting beside Robbie, talking quietly. She turned.

"I'm going over to see how Sister Bathgate and Sister Park are doing. I'll be back before we are ready to go."

"All right. Give them our best."

"I will." Maggie looked to where Sarah James was working with Emma and their father in helping the younger children get their things packed. "Would you like to go, Sarah?"

Sarah shook her head. "We're not quite ready, Maggie. You'd better go. Give them my love as well."

"I will." It had been a little more than a week now since Sister Mary Bathgate had been bitten by a rattlesnake, and then her companion, Sister Isabella Park, was run over by the wagon. The two elderly sisters had so endeared themselves to Maggie, that she had started going over to visit them whenever she could. Sarah had joined her on the second visit and fallen in love with them as well. In addition to visiting, the two girls would help them cook meals, or fetch water for them, or see to whatever needed doing. Since Eric Pederson was also coming almost every day to make sure their recuperation was progressing properly, this provided Maggie a chance to see Eric as well, something she looked forward to more than she openly admitted to herself.

She set off across the campground, moving toward where Elder John Chislett's hundred was camped. Both sisters were still riding in the wagons, but each night they camped with their own tent group.

"Good morning, dear," Sister Bathgate called as Maggie came towards them.

"Good morning, Sister Bathgate. Good morning, Sister Park." When she reached them she took their hands in turn and held them for a moment. She looked down at Sister Bathgate. "And how is the leg doing?"

"Wonderful." She pulled up her dress enough to show Maggie the back of her ankle. The two knife cuts were still angry red welts, but the swelling in the leg was completely gone now and the scabs were off and seemed to be healing nicely. Mary Bathgate reached out and grabbed a stick that someone had whittled down smooth for her. "Watch this." She got to her feet, took the cane, and walked around in a small circle. She still limped heavily, and she was not quite able to hide it when she winced a couple of times.

"Are you sure you should be doing that yet?" Maggie asked, looking concerned.

"Oh, pshaw!" she snapped. "You sound like Captain Willie now."

"And how about you, Sister Park? How are you doing?"

Isabella Park pulled a sour face. "One more week. The soreness is mostly gone now. We've agreed to ride in the accursed wagon a little longer; then we are going to start walking again, whether Captain Willie agrees or not."

"Well," Maggie said, surprised that they had agreed to that much, "we'll see when the time comes."

"Yes, we will," Mary said tartly. "Isabella and I already have our minds made up."

"Where is Sarah?" Isabella asked.

"She was still helping her family pack up. She said to give you her love."

"What a sweet girl she is!" Mary said warmly. "And you tell her we said so."

"I will," Maggie said with a smile. "They don't come much finer than Sarah James."

"No." Mary looked at Isabella. "We have got to find a young man for her."

Maggie swung around in surprise, but the two of them ignored her.

"We have looked over the crop of young men in this company, my dear," Isabella reminded her companion, "and we both agree that we're just going to have to wait until we get to the Valley to find someone worthy of Sarah."

Maggie tried to look suitably shocked, even as she fought back the impulse to laugh. "And does Sarah know that you two are plotting against her like this?"

"Of course not," Isabella said primly. "Do you think we have no sense of decorum?"

Now Maggie did laugh. "And what about me? How come you're only worried about Sarah?"

"Oh," Mary said sagely, "because you are already all taken care of."

"What?" Maggie nearly choked.

"Who is all taken care of?"

They all turned as Eric came around one of the wagons and into view.

Maggie flamed instantly and gave Mary Bathgate a panicked look. She just smiled back at her, then turned to Eric. "Good morning, dear. We were afraid you were going to neglect us this morning."

"Never," he said brightly. He held up a small bag. "I picked you berries from the creek last night. They are tart a little, but very good." He turned. "Good morning, Sister Maggie."

She didn't look up but pretended to be busy with the two small packs that held the belongings of the two women. "Good morning, Eric."

He looked back at Sister Bathgate. "So who is this all taken care of?" he asked again.

"Maggie. She was worried that Isabella and I haven't found her a beau yet."

Maggie's head snapped up. "Sister Bathgate! That's not what I said."

Sister Bathgate ignored Maggie's withering look and smiled brightly. Eric was staring at Maggie, a little dumbfounded.

"Do you know what the word *beau* means, Eric?" asked Sister Bathgate.

He slowly nodded, and now there were spots of color in his cheeks as well. "Yah, I think so." Suddenly his eyes were wary. Maggie shot him a warning look. *Don't ask. Please, Eric, don't ask.*

But the words were already forming on his lips. "Who is this beau?"

Mary Bathgate gave him a look of deep pity, as though he were daft and couldn't do one thing about it. Sister Park just laughed merrily. She looked at Maggie. "You can see why Mary and I have to interfere in the matter."

Maggie stood up, not daring to meet Eric's gaze. "I'd better get back to my family," she stammered. She walked swiftly over to Sister Bathgate and gave her a kiss on the cheek, pretending that nothing out of the ordinary had just happened. "Now, you behave yourself and don't walk on that foot too much."

She went over to Sister Park and bent down and kissed her as well. "I'll come see you this afternoon when we're camped again."

One hand shot out and grabbed Maggie's wrist and held her in place for a moment. "It's all right, dear," she whispered loudly. "We'll see that he comes around."

Her face burning like a hot flatiron, Maggie whirled and walked away, fighting back the temptation to break and run.

Eric watched her in bewilderment, then turned back to the two sisters. "What was all that about?"

"Oh, Eric. Dear, sweet Eric," Isabella said fondly. "Don't you know?"

"Know what?"

"*You* are the beau we have picked out for Maggie."

His mouth opened slightly and then almost instantly he colored deeply.

"Not true," Mary said slowly. "Actually, Eric is the beau that Maggie picked out for herself. You and I just heartily agree with her choice."

He stared at them for several seconds; then he slowly smiled, but it was strained. "You two. You are in the wagon too much now. All you do is dream up things."

"Dream up things?" Mary said indignantly. "Did you say, dream up things?"

"Yes." There was just a touch of exasperation in him now. "Maggie is different than me. She is schoolteacher. She comes from large city. I am a simple farm boy and fisherman. We had no school in our village, only what Mama taught me. All I can do is say, 'Yah, yah,' and . . ." He shook his head. "No. You are wrong. I am not beau."

Mary was looking at Isabella and smiling broadly.

"What?" Eric demanded.

She ignored him. "I think this is going to work out just fine, Isabella, don't you?"

"Indubitably," Isabella said with an equally beatific smile.

Chapter Notes

Ironically, the official journal entry for the Willie Company for 4 September does not mention the buffalo stampede, only that "30 head of cattle strayed away, (most probably a stampede) during the night" (in Turner, *Emigrating Journals*, p. 25). John Chislett, who later wrote an extensive narrative about the Willie Company, said this: "About this time we reached Wood River (a few miles above Grand Island, Nebraska). The whole country was alive with buffaloes, and one night—or, rather, evening—our cattle stampeded. Men went in pursuit and collected what they supposed to be the herd; but, on corralling them for yoking next morning, thirty head were missing" (in Hafen and Hafen, *Handcarts to Zion*, p. 100).

It is from Emma James, a member of the Willie Company, that we get the most graphic details: "One evening as we prepared to stop for the night, a large herd of buffalo came thundering toward us. It sounded like thunder at first, then the big black animals came straight for our carts. We were so scared that we were rooted to the ground. One of the captains, seeing what was going on, ran for the carts which were still coming in, jerked out some of the carts to make a path for the steady stream of animals and let them go through. They went passed us like a train roaring along. I'm sure that but for the quick thinking of these men, many of us would have been trampled to death. The animals acted as if they were crazy the way they ran. We hoped that we wouldn't meet such a large herd soon again. After they had gone somebody called out that the cattle had gone with them. This was our only supply of meat, so the men started right out after them" (in Carol Cornwall Madsen, *Journey to Zion*, pp. 626–27).

Under the date of 7 September 1856, the Willie Company journal states that "President Willie and Captain Atwood and Siler [a captain of the four independent wagons traveling with the Willie Company at this time], with other brethren, yoked up many of the cows, which was an arduous task" (in Turner, *Emigrating Journals*, p. 28).

Writing of the effects of the loss of the cattle, John Chislett said:

> We had only about enough oxen left to put one yoke to each wagon; but as they were each loaded with about three thousand pounds of flour, the teams could not of course move them. We then yoked up our beef cattle, milch cows, and, in fact, everything that could bear a yoke—even two-year-old heifers. The stock was wild and could pull but little, and we were unable, with all our stock, to move our loads. As a last resort, we again loaded a sack of flour on each cart. . . .
>
> It was really hard for the folks to lose the use of their milch cows, have beef rations stopped, and haul one hundred pounds more on

their carts. Every man and woman, however, worked to their utmost to put forward towards the goal of their hopes. (In Hafen and Hafen, *Handcarts to Zion*, p. 100)

CHAPTER 16

LOUP FORK, NEBRASKA TERRITORY
TO
BLUFF CREEK, NEBRASKA TERRITORY

I

Sunday, 7 September 1856

It was Sunday evening and worship services were through. The Saints in the Edward Martin Handcart Company had sung their songs, listened to their leaders, and offered their prayers of thanks. They were back at their campsites preparing to start their suppers, when a cry went up. To the east, perhaps five or six hundred yards away, the trail they had crossed earlier dropped down from one of the many rolling hills and was clearly visible from the camp. There, coming toward them at a brisk pace, a small column had appeared. It was made up of two light wagons and three covered carriages—each drawn by four horses or mules. Immediately they knew it was Elder Franklin D. Richards.

Elder Richards had promised that once he got all the companies off, he and his party—made up of missionaries returning with him from England and the Church agents who had helped them in Iowa City and in Florence—would start by swift conveyance for Salt Lake City. They would not be traveling with the handcart companies. If the truth were known, Elder Richards was deeply worried. The agents in Iowa City had not gotten his letters telling them that two more shiploads were on their way to America. If that was true, what if Salt Lake City did not know either? It was customary to send supply wagons to meet the companies on the plains. It was also customary that as soon as the last company reached the Valley, those supply wagons were called back for the winter. What Elder Richards could not get out of his worry bucket was the nagging fear that President Brigham Young did not know there were two more companies still coming.

At the cry of the people, Hannah McKensie and Ingrid Christensen burst out of their tent to see what was happening. With the rest of the camp they cried out and waved as the small column rolled past them. Then suddenly Hannah grabbed Ingrid's arm. "Do you know what this means?"

Ingrid shook her head.

"In a few days Elder Richards will overtake the Willie Company. He could take a letter to the family for us."

Ingrid looked startled, then pleased. "That is true."

"Come on, Ingrid. I'll write to my family. You write to Emma and hers."

II

Friday, 12 September 1856

The two wagons and three carriages of the Franklin D. Richards party reached North Bluff Creek just before dusk on the night of September twelfth. It had taken the Willie Company twenty-six days to cover the 320 miles from Florence to this spot. The Richards company, their light conveyances pulled in each case by four horses or mules, covered the same distance in eight and half days.

A great hurrah went up in the camp as the emigrants recognized who it was. In addition to Elder Richards and some returning missionaries from England, there were several of the Church agents with whom the emigrants had worked both at Iowa City and at Florence. One of the missionaries, much to the great excitement of the company, was Joseph A. Young, son of Brigham Young. With Brother William H. Kimball being the son of Heber C. Kimball, that meant the emigrants now had an Apostle, the son of the President of the Church, and the son of the First Counselor in the First Presidency all with them in camp.

As soon as supper was completed, the company gathered together beneath a grove of trees near the creek. Elder Willie briefly introduced Elder Richards, and then gave the meeting into his hands to be led by him as the Holy Ghost might dictate.

Elder Richards called on Brother William C. Dunbar, another of the missionaries traveling in his party, to sing one of the songs of Zion, which he did. He had a rich, deep voice, and as he sang, the only other sound to be heard was the soft rushing of the water and the lowing of the cattle some distance away. Eric felt a deep spirit of reverence and gratitude come over him. When it was done, President Richards stood again to address the Saints.

"Brothers and sisters, what a joy it is for us to join you this evening, to be with you in your camp, to have an opportunity to spend the night with you. We are happy to report that everyone we sent to America on those last two ships is now on the trail, with the exception of those who have left us for Babylon or chosen to wait another season to come on. We left Florence the evening of September third. We overtook the rear company of wagons, in the charge of Captain Hunt, during the forenoon of the sixth. He has two hundred forty persons traveling in fifty wagons, not counting four Church wagons which are coming with them.

"On the evening of the seventh, at about five P.M., we overtook Captain Edward Martin's Company about forty miles west of Loup Fork. We are pleased to report that his company was in most excellent spirits, and though he has a greater proportion of feeble emigrants than does your company, the health of his camp was very good. They are averaging about one hundred miles per week without fatiguing his company."

Elder Ahmanson had chosen to translate for his entire group tonight, so Eric and Olaf were sitting near the back listening carefully to what was being said. Olaf leaned over and whispered into Eric's ear. "That's good. Hannah and Ingrid are not far behind us, then."

"Yes. Stopping those three days to look for the cattle helped in that regard at least." Even as Eric spoke, he watched the McKensies, who were across from them. They too were whispering in excitement about that report.

"Refreshed by our short stay with Elder Martin," Elder Richards was continuing, "we drove on another ten miles and there overtook the second independent wagon company led by Brother Hodgett. They have about one hundred fifty people with thirty-three wagons. Though they are generally heavily laden with the goods they are carrying, we were pleased to find that they are in good traveling condition and making excellent progress.

"And now we have come upon you. Altogether, counting your company and Elder Martin's, as well as the two wagon companies, there are about thirteen hundred of you moving west right now. We are greatly satisfied to discover the progress you are making on your journey. We are proving the wisdom of President Young's scheme to come by handcarts. We congratulate you that even though you have lost many of your cattle, under the able direction of Captain Willie's leadership you are pressing forward. If you are willing to be obedient and hearken to the counsel of your leaders to the very letter, this will prove to be your salvation."

He stopped now, letting his gaze sweep across the group. He grew very solemn, but when he spoke his voice rang out like a trumpet. "If you will be strictly obedient to counsel, I feel to promise you in the name of Israel's God, and by the authority of the holy priesthood which I hold, that no obstacle whatever will come in the way of this camp."

Eric felt a little chill shoot up his spine. He looked at Olaf, who was struck with wonder. This was language of great power. Eric turned back, hanging intently on every word.

"I feel to promise you that in your united faith and diligent works, you will be enabled to go through, God being your helper. And, even if something such as the Red Sea should interpose itself upon you, you shall, by the union of heart and hand, walk through it dry-shod, like Israel of old.

"I am not saying there will be no trials between here and there—you may have some trials to endure as proof to God and the brethren that you have the 'true grit' it takes to come through. And yet I say, though it might storm on your right hand and on your left, the Lord will open the way before you and you shall get to Zion in safety."

All around the camp, people were nodding. On the other side of him, Eric saw that Elsie Nielson was weeping quietly but that her face was filled with joy. After all of the fears and anxieties about leaving this late in the season, this was a powerful comfort to them all.

The Apostle fell silent for a time, letting the impact of his words sink into the hearts of his listeners. Then finally he began again. "Now, brothers and sisters, I know there is much anxiety in camp because of the Indian troubles in this vicinity of late."

Again Eric and Olaf exchanged glances. *More than much,* Eric thought. Some days before, a man claiming to be a discharged soldier had ridden into their camp and reported that about seventy miles ahead of them a small train of eastward-bound people had been attacked by the Cheyenne. Two men and a woman were killed after being brutally treated by their attackers. Just today they had come across the site and seen the bloodstained clothing and the burnt-out wagon. That had sent waves of pure terror surging through the camp.

"We feel you are safe, being a large company, but we have recommended to Captain Willie that tomorrow you ford the river and travel on the main part of the Oregon Trail for a time. The military reports that all of the depredations are on the north side of the river, because it is the lesser-traveled route, and we feel crossing to the south to be the safer course of action."

The impact of his words registered on the faces of his audience. The women especially were exhibiting great relief to know that the danger was not being ignored.

"Now, my brothers and sisters, I do not need to remind you that we are very late in the season. I was somewhat disturbed to learn from our brethren who were waiting for you in Iowa City that they were not aware of the fact that more people were coming this season. Evidently the letters I wrote to them did not arrive before you did. So I must tell you that we are concerned that perhaps word of these additional companies has not reached Salt Lake either. If that is so, and the First Presidency think that the first three companies are all that are coming this season, we fear that they may call in the wagons which come out to resupply us."

He might as well have dropped a hive of bees in the center of the congregation. Soft exclamations of alarm and concern erupted, and people began to speak with great agitation to each other. He raised his hands and called for silence.

When they stopped, he took a deep breath. "As you see, my group is equipped with light carriages and wagons and with faster mule and horse teams. We shall leave you tomorrow, hurrying on as rapidly as we can. When we reach Great Salt Lake City, we shall inform President Young of your coming. I can promise you that once President Young learns of your presence, supply wagons filled with flour, food, and warm clothing will be on their way to meet you."

He stopped for the last time, smiling his reassurance. "In the meantime you must go forward in all haste and in faith and obedience. Listen to the counsel of your leaders. Follow that counsel. Press forward with all diligence so that you may claim the promises of the Lord."

The James family and the McKensies stood together speaking softly of what Elder Richards had said. Like many others, once the meeting broke up they seemed reluctant to return to their tents. They wanted to savor the richness of the experience a while longer.

Elder Willie was still in the small group around Elder Richards. They talked for a few moments; then as they broke up, Captain Willie looked around. Seeing the two families together, he started directly for them. "Sister McKensie."

They all turned. He was waving some folded papers. "You'll never guess what I have here. Elder Richards has brought something from the Martin Company."

They were all staring, and then Mary McKensie gave a low cry. "A letter?"

"Two, actually," he smiled broadly as he came up. "One from Hannah for your family and one from Ingrid for the James family."

7th September, West of Loup Fork

Dearest Mother, Maggie, and Robbie,

It is with a joyful heart that I write these lines, knowing that in a short time, Elder Richards and company will deliver this into your hands. How I wish it was me who was handing it to you, but as you well know, such is not to be. How sorrowful Ingrid and I were when we reached the Missouri only to learn that your company had left several days before. Though we were greatly saddened by that knowledge, please know that each night around the campfire when we join together to sing the songs of Zion, Ingrid and I both sing "All Is Well" and mean every word. We miss you terribly and make mention of you in our prayers both morning and night, but we know that we are where we were meant to be and find joy therein.

Since leaving Florence, Ingrid does little translating now. Most of the Scandinavians are traveling with the Hodgett train, but we both know now that it was important that we help the Jacksons. They are such wonderful people and have taken us into their bosoms as though we were their own daughters. Brother Jackson is a wonderful man but not the strongest in body. Having Ingrid and me here to help pull the cart is very important. We are young and strong and can pull as well as anyone now.

I won't give you much news from the camp. I am sure it is very similar to what you have already experienced—long hot days, nights in camp trying to rest, the terrifying occasional thunderstorms. We did lose one of the brethren when he was struck by lightning a few days ago. It was not far from where Ingrid and I were, but neither we nor the Jacksons were hurt.

We are saddened as the rigors of the trail take an increasing toll on our company. As you may know, we have more elderly and weak with us than you do. Generally they do well, but deaths are occurring among the very old or the very young with increasing frequency and this leaves a pall of sorrow over our camp. One man, an old bachelor from England, in the very midst of pulling his cart, fell down dead.

Captain Martin tells us that a common expression among those who cross the Oregon Trail is "seeing the elephant." It means that you come to realize the immensity of the challenge of crossing an entire continent, most of which is through the most desolate of wilderness.

Knowing of the friendship that Brother and Sister James had with John Jaques and his family, they will be saddened to learn that the Jaqueses and the Loaders are seeing the elephant all too much of late. You remember well, I am sure, how Brother James Loader, father-in-law to Brother Jaques, was thought to be in apostasy for wanting to wait another season instead of coming by handcart. And as you know, when he learned that he was being so accused, he came immediately with his family to Iowa City and there met up with the Jaqueses.

Though they joy to be together, things have been difficult for them. Brother Loader has been plagued with dysentery much of the way and has grown very weak. Sister Tamar Loader, who came across the Atlantic with Brother and Sister Jaques, has had mountain fever and also has been too sick to walk. Both father and daughter have had to be carried in the carts on more than one occasion.

As if that is not enough, Sister Jaques gave birth to a son the night we left Florence and camped at Cutler's Park. The next morning, Brother Martin offered to let her and the others that were sick ride in the wagons, but when Patience Loader wanted to ride with them to care for them, Elder Martin had to say no. That seems harsh, I suppose, but there is little choice. This too is part of seeing the elephant. The wagons are filled with the sick and infirm and if each have someone ride with them to watch over them, who shall be left to pull the handcarts? It is a bitter reality, but reality nevertheless. So the Jaques decided to stay behind to let the sick recover somewhat. This created only more difficulties for them because they had to trek long into the following nights to eventually overtake us.

Surprisingly, Sister Loader has done quite well. If you remember the letter Patience wrote to England, she said that her mother could not walk a mile and would need a revelation before she would come by handcart. Now she walks every day and is actually one of the stronger ones in the family. The Lord works in strange ways. But I am happy to report that Tamar is doing better now and Zilpah and the babe, whom they named Alpha, are also well. (Brother Joseph A. Young suggested that the Jaqueses might want to name the boy "Handcart" under the circumstances, but Zilpah said she hoped for something a little more beautiful.)

I'm sorry. As I read over this last part again, I know it will cause Mother worry and I didn't want that, but I knew that Brother and Sister James would want this report on their friends. Know that both Ingrid and I are doing very well. Mercifully, neither of us has been stricken with sickness in any way. Our only malady comes from knowing that it is likely that we shall not see you again until we reach the Valley.

Robbie, by now I am sure you have eaten buffalo meat. We quite like it. What do you think? Elder Martin claims that the early mountain men would take all the fat from the brisket of the animals and melt it over a fire. Then they would drink it straight, a quart at a time. They also thought the tongue was the greatest delicacy. Ugh! But knowing you, I'll bet you would try both just to see what they are like.

Well, soon it is lights out and Elder Richards leaves immediately in the morning, so I shall close. Both Ingrid and I ask that you give everyone a hug, especially Emma. How we miss those nights giggling together in our tent. (I know that Mother and Sister James did not sleep much, but we loved those times together.) Maggie, you and Sarah could even give Olaf a hug for the both of us. (Note that we didn't suggest that Emma do it for us. EMMA: If you read this, we are only joking.) Tell Olaf we miss him too.

Must close. With the blessing of the Lord we shall see you soon.

All my love,
Hannah McKensie

III

Friday, 26 September 1856

When Brother Martin finally gave the signal for evening prayers to end, Hannah got to her feet wearily. It had been another long day. This portion of the trail had gotten quite rough, with long stretches of endless sand or places where the rains had left deep ruts which threatened to jar the carts to pieces. She brushed off the knees of her dress and then helped Martha Ann and Mary Elizabeth Jackson get to their feet.

Brother Jackson smiled gratefully at her, then turned to his wife. "Elizabeth, I fear that we do not have sufficient wood for our fire in the morning. I shall gather some up quickly before it grows any darker."

Ingrid was up now too. She had removed her bonnet for the prayers, though usually the women were not expected to do so, and she replaced it now. "I'll help, Brother Jackson."

Hannah looked over her shoulder toward their tent. "I have the cake cooling in the baking kettle. I shall come help as well as soon as I take it out."

"That would be appreciated." Brother Jackson and Ingrid started away.

"Come, children," Elizabeth Jackson said, scooping her two-year-old up in her arms. "It is time to get ready for bed."

Holding the two older girls' hands, Hannah fell in beside Sister Jackson as they returned to their tent. Hannah went immediately to the heavy black kettle—or "spider," as it was often called because of its black round belly and three spindly legs. Sister Jackson and the girls followed to see the end result. Hannah had filled the spider with the batter before supper and let it cook in the coals for over an hour. Before going to prayers she had taken it from the fire to let it cool. She too was curious how it had turned out. With their limited supplies, she had concocted a batter from corn bread and flour and then sprinkled into the mixture a few wild gooseberries which the children had picked.

"Mm," Martha Ann said. "I can smell it already. Can we have a piece?"

"Not tonight, dear," her mother said firmly. "This is for our breakfast."

Hannah got the tongs and removed the heavy lid. There it was, golden brown and round as a cow's belly. She leaned over and inhaled deeply, then turned to Sister Jackson with a look of longing. "Please, Mama," Hannah said in a little girl's voice. "Can't we have just a little piece tonight?"

Elizabeth laughed. "You're no help."

"Oh, yes, Mama," the girls cried. "Please!"

"All right. Just a little piece."

Getting a towel and wrapping it around the handle, Hannah lifted the kettle so she could tip the cake out on the flat board they used for bread making. She stopped, hefting the kettle up and down. "That's strange."

Elizabeth looked up. "What?"

She was still testing it. "It feels so much lighter than when I put it in."

"It's 'cause it's all baked," Martha Ann said helpfully.

"I guess so," Hannah said. She stepped to the board and tipped the kettle. The cake didn't budge, and Sister Jackson quickly grabbed a large metal spoon and tapped on the bottom sharply. With a soft plop, it fell out upside down.

"Oh!" Hannah set the kettle down with a heavy clunk, her eyes riveted to what lay before her. The outside of the cake, the crust as it were, was perfectly shaped and browned to just the right degree. But now that it was upside down, they could see that the entire inside of the cake was gone.

"What in the world . . . ?" Sister Jackson gasped. "How could it possibly do that?"

Hannah's face had gone dark. "Look. The cake didn't bake this way. Those are finger marks. Someone has been here and helped themselves."

Sister Jackson came closer, bending over. And then she straightened, her mouth pinched and tight. "I can't believe it. Another pilferer."

Hannah just stared, wanting suddenly to cry. Finally she turned to Sister Jackson. "You may as well let them eat it," she said. "There won't be enough for breakfast now." Without waiting for an answer, she turned and started away. "I'll go help Brother Jackson and Ingrid get some fuel for the fire."

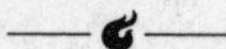

When Hannah, Ingrid, and Brother Jackson returned half an hour later with their arms loaded with dead sticks, three thin pieces of cake were lined up on the tailgate of the handcart.

"We saved you a piece of cake, Papa," Mary Elizabeth told her father proudly as he and the girls dumped their loads off to one side of the fire.

"And you too, Hannah," Elizabeth Jackson said. "It's not much, but it is delicious and—" She stopped, peering at Hannah more closely. Seeing the gravity on her face, she went to Hannah's side, taking her by the shoulders. "It's all right. We'll make another cake tomorrow."

Hannah shook her head.

Aaron stepped to his wife. "It's not the cake, Elizabeth. We stopped by the Loaders' tent."

Her hand came up to her mouth, her eyes suddenly wide. "Is Brother Loader—?"

He shook his head. "No, but he's very weak. When they got into camp tonight, he called his daughters around and apologized to them for not being able to gather firewood. He felt very bad about it."

"He is so conscientious about caring for his family," Elizabeth said. "Perhaps I'd better go help Sister Loader and the girls."

"No, they're all retiring for the night. We left them some wood."

"Then I'll go in the morning."

"That would be nice."

"I don't know if he's going to make it," Hannah whispered. Seeing Brother Loader there on his bed, gray as a rainy sky and barely aware of the conversation around him, had shaken her badly. There had been other deaths in the camp, but no one she knew personally had been among them. This brought it too close to be ignored.

Aaron turned to her. "Perhaps not," he said. In the deepening shadows, he looked suddenly tired and gaunt as well. "But if not, then you know what we sing. 'And should we die before our journey's through, happy day! All is well!' Perhaps he will reach the Valley that much sooner than the rest of us."

Ingrid turned, her face twisting in puzzlement. "I do not understand. We are many miles from the Valley yet."

"We are many miles from the Valley of the Great Salt Lake, that is true. But why do we go to the Valley, Ingrid? Is it not to find peace and a place of safety and refuge?"

"Ah, yah," she said, understanding now. "There is a better Valley, yah?"

"A much better Valley." Now his eyes were filled with a strange light. Hannah was mesmerized as she watched him. Aaron Jackson was not a strong man either, and he too had suffered some rough days since they had left Iowa City. "And you don't have to pull a handcart to get there," he said wistfully.

They stood that way for almost a full minute, the firelight flickering on their faces, their eyes hooded and filled with faraway thoughts. Even the children sensed the somberness of their mood and just stood and watched the adults curiously.

Finally, Aaron Jackson straightened. He looked at Hannah and smiled, then walked over to the handcart. "So this is Hannah's famous cake. I've heard of upside-down cake, but not inside-out cake."

Hannah had to smile in spite of herself. "Or inside-gone cake," she murmured.

"It is delicious, what's left of it," Elizabeth said. "Come on, try it before we go to bed."

Hannah took the proffered piece and began to chew on it slowly. It *was* good, and she wished there were more of it. She closed her eyes, wondering who the thief might be. *How ironic,* she thought. This person, whoever it was, very likely had left everything in his former life—or possibly hers!—in order to come to Zion. Evidently the fact that the very word *Zion* meant to be pure in heart had not yet made a connection in that person's mind.

She took another bite, then licked the crumbs from the tips of her fingers. "I think I'll sleep outside tonight," she said.

"Outside?" Sister Jackson blurted. "But it may rain. And we had frost last night."

"I know," Hannah said wryly, "but if I'm outside I can hear if someone starts moaning in the night with a bellyache."

Brother Jackson chortled, then lifted his last bite of cake as though it were a glass of champagne. "May his belly be filled with cramps until his heart turns back to the Lord."

Hannah joined in the mock toast by raising her own piece high. "Hear, hear!" she said.

IV

Saturday, 27 September 1856

It was a brutal day. The sand hills which lined the north side of the North Platte River were no more than thirty or forty feet higher than the floodplain, but they may as well have been three hundred or four hundred for the toll they took on man and beast.

When the Martin Handcart Company left Iowa City, many of the carts had been given a "harness" to help the emigrants pull. This was really not much more than a braided rope, the one end of which could be tied to the front crossbar or the shafts and the other end formed into a loop that went around a person's chest or waist. It was long enough that the person in the harness would be ahead of those inside the shafts of the cart. All the way across Iowa, Hannah, Ingrid, and the Jacksons had resorted to the use of the harness on only two occasions. By pushing or pulling directly on the cart, they had made their way through without the additional help.

But not on this day.

By ten o'clock, as they reached the first of the rolling hills, the sun was blazing down on them from a perfectly clear sky. Chewed up by four previous companies, the deep sand was soft and provided no solid footing for traction. All up and down the train, the older children were called in. Every hand and every pair of feet would be necessary. Little Aaron Jackson was placed on top of the bedding in the cart and told to hang on tightly. Hannah and Ingrid got in the harnesses, one tied to each shaft. Brother and Sister Jackson got inside the shafts. Martha Ann and Mary Elizabeth, though only five and seven, went to the back to push.

They crossed one hill, then a second. By then their lungs were on fire and their legs were trembling uncontrollably. Even the most callused of hands were getting blisters. Shirts and dresses were stained dark with sweat. The third hill was the longest and steepest. Inch by brutal inch they pulled and pushed and heaved. The wheels were buried several inches in the bottomless sand, and loads of two and three hundred pounds felt like a thousand or more.

Ten yards short of the top, Aaron Jackson went down. His feet were digging deep in the sand and slipped right out from under him. There was a soft cry as he dragged his wife down with him. The rope harnesses snapped back so violently that both Hannah and Ingrid were jerked off their feet and crashed to the ground.

They lay there for several seconds, panting for breath in great heaves, sweat pouring into their eyes, their hands and clothing covered with the fine sand. After a few moments Aaron pushed to his knees. He wiped at his eyes with his sleeve. "Sorry," he mumbled. He stood and helped Elizabeth to her feet. Wearily they lifted the crossbar until the shafts were level again.

Hannah and Ingrid got up slowly, then turned to the front again, adjusting the ropes over their shoulders and around their bodies. Ingrid took the shoes which were ever present around her neck and slid them around so that they fell down her back and didn't interfere with the harness.

"Ready?" Brother Jackson gasped. "Go!"

For a moment nothing happened, except that feet dug into the sand, muscles bulged, veins stood out on their foreheads. And then, ever so slowly, the cart began to inch forward again.

"Keep going!"

Grunting, wheezing, throwing every ounce of strength against the terrible inertia, they moved forward—a yard, two yards, five yards. Suddenly the cart rolled forward as they reached the top and gravity no longer dragged against it. They pulled off the trail and went another twenty yards so as to be out of the way. With a deep groan, Aaron and Elizabeth lowered the cart and stepped out of the shafts. Ingrid and Hannah removed the harnesses and let them drop. They stood there for a few seconds, their chests heaving, and then one by one they slowly sank to the ground. Ingrid reached up and slowly removed the shoes from around her neck. Then she lay out flat in the sand and closed her eyes.

Five minutes later, Edward Martin rode forward on his horse. On the rounded top of the hill there were now about two dozen handcarts. Like the Jacksons, people were sitting in a half stupor. Water jugs were passed around, and the warm, stale liquid was eagerly consumed.

Heads turned as their captain rode up. He reined in and removed his hat. Lines of sweat etched the dust which covered his face. The brim of his hat was dark with the wetness. The horse's flanks were flecked with foam.

"We'll stop here until everyone is up," he announced. "It's

probably going to take us until dark. Some of the oxen have already given out. Any help you could give to the others would be appreciated." He started to rein around, then stopped. "By the way. Keep an eye out for rattlesnakes. This place is known for having quite a few."

People shrunk back and looked around anxiously as he went back down the hill. For a long moment no one moved, and then Aaron Jackson took another long drink from the water jug and got to his feet. Elizabeth started to move but he laid a hand on her shoulder. Her face was bright red and splotchy. "No," he said quickly. "You need to rest for a time. I'll go."

As her husband stepped back, Elizabeth looked up. "Aaron, see if you can find the Loaders and Brother Jaques. They are going to need help."

There was a brief nod as he started off. To that point, Hannah had not moved. Her body was still trembling; her hands were raw. Now, with the greatest of effort, she hauled herself up. She looked down at Ingrid, who had rolled over and was getting up too. "Let's take our harnesses."

What had gotten her to her feet was the image of James Loader. This morning he had been near death. According to John Jaques, he had spoken only one sentence to his wife. "You know I love my children," was all he said. Captain Martin offered to place him in one of the wagons, but the family opted to make a bed for him in one of their handcarts so that they could be at his side at all times. Before they had started up the first sand hill, Elizabeth Jackson had received word that Brother Loader was still alive but evidently had lapsed into a coma.

Yes, Hannah thought. As tired as she was, she would go down and help the Loaders. She called after Brother Jackson. "Hold on. We're coming too."

———

By midafternoon there was no longer any question. Brother James Loader was dying. Through all that morning, through the terrible pull up the sand hills, in the midst of the shouting of men and the bawling of cattle, he had never once opened his eyes or spoken another word. His children spoke to him often, calling to him to see if he would respond. There was nothing.

Now, while the last members of the company clawed their way up the hill, up on top the Loaders placed their father beneath a canvas shelter to spare him from the blistering sun. A group were gathered around him to offer solace to the family in this hour of sorrow. Hannah and Ingrid were there with the Jacksons. After they had been instrumental in helping the family bring their carts up the hill, Sister Loader had asked them to stay.

Hannah watched as two of the subcaptains brought forth the olive oil. After conversing quietly for a moment with Brother Jaques and Sister Loader, one of them put some of the oil on his finger and rubbed it on the parched lips of the dying man. After a moment, Brother Loader's tongue came out and he licked off the oil. There was a momentary smile, but he did not speak.

With Elder Martin acting as lead, they next anointed his head with oil. Several brethren, including Brother James and Brother Jaques, came forward to stand around him. As the blessing began, all bowed their heads, fighting back the tears.

"Brother Loader," Captain Martin said with great solemnity, "in the name of our Savior and Redeemer, even Jesus Christ, we seal you up to the Lord at this time, for He alone is worthy to accept you. You have done your work. You have been a faithful servant in the Church, and we, the servants of God, seal you up unto our Father. And this we do in the name of Jesus Christ, amen."

To everyone's surprise, as the brethren stepped back, Brother Loader spoke in a clear, firm voice. "Amen," he said.

It took most of the day to get everyone over the last sand hill. Finally at six o'clock the last wagon crested the hill. Weary beyond words, Captain Edward Martin gave the signal to move on. They had to find a place with water and wood to camp. At ten o'clock at night the signal finally came back. "We camp here."

Many people simply rolled out their tents flat on the ground, then put their bedrolls on top of the canvas. Though it was going to be another cold night, it was a clear night and there was no threat of rain. Supper was forgotten. Evening prayers were short, though fervent.

As soon as they reached camp Brother and Sister Jackson left to see if they could help the Loaders any further. Hannah and Ingrid got the children some bread and butter and water from the creek, then put them to bed. When the children were finally asleep, the two friends stretched out on their bedroll, too exhausted to stand any longer and yet also too exhausted for sleep to come.

It was half past eleven when they heard the Jacksons making their way toward them and sat up. "We're still awake," Hannah whispered as they reached them. "How is Brother Loader?"

There was a muffled sob from Sister Jackson. Brother Jackson moved over beside the two girls' bedroll and reached out in the darkness until he found their hands. "Brother Loader finally reached the Valley tonight. About fifteen minutes ago." He bowed his head in the darkness. "May he sleep in peace until the trump shall sound and the resurrection shall bring him forth in glory, immortality, and eternal life."

Chapter Notes

Both the Willie Company and Martin Company had some problems with petty theft and pilfering in the camps, something which sometimes brought forth stern calls for repentance from the captains. For example, in the Willie Company journal, part of the entry for 7 September reads: "President Atwood [Elder Millen Atwood, captain of the first hundred] urged the pilferers to come forward and openly confess their faults before their brethren, who would then extend to them the friendly hand of forgiveness" (in Turner, *Emigrating Journals*, p. 27).

In a later recollection, Brother John Jaques noted that the Martin Company also had that problem: "In some of the pinching times there would be a little petty pilfering going on in camp occasionally. The pilferings were usually of bread to eat. The bread was baked in the form of cakes in frying pans, or of biscuits in skillets and bake kettles. In one family there were several grown-up girls, and one of them attended much to the cooking. One evening she had made and baked a very nice cake before going to prayers, and she set it up on edge against the tent while she went to prayer meeting. When she got back to her tent she went for the cake. On picking it up it seemed diminished marvelously in weight. Presently she exclaimed with tears in her eyes, 'Oh! Mother, somebody has been and taken every bit of crumb out of my cake and left the crust.' Some sharper, who either had not been to prayers, or who had loiteringly delayed his going, or had got through them in singularly swift dispatch for his own ulterior purposes, had discovered the girl's cake, taken fancy to it, pulled it in two, eaten the soft, warm inside, put the two crusts together again, and reared them carefully against the tent as they were" (in Bell, *Life History and Writings of John Jaques*, p. 136).

Moving swiftly westward, the company led by Elder Franklin D. Richards overtook the Willie Handcart Company late in the day on 12 September. In the Martin Company journal, those traveling with Elder Richards are listed and thirteen are named (see Turner, *Emigrating Journals*, p. 109).

Elder Richards spoke to the Willie Company the evening after his party arrived and again the next morning. Most of the speech presented here, including his stirring promise given in the name of the Lord, comes from the company journal account (see Turner, *Emigrating Journals*, pp. 30–32) or from a report written by Elder Richards and Daniel Spencer after their arrival in Salt Lake City (see Hafen and Hafen, *Handcarts to Zion*, pp. 218–20).

Though the emigrants were not yet into any kind of severe weather and were still on full rations at this time, the rigors of the trail began taking a toll on the weak and the elderly in both companies. Note the following excerpts from the Willie Company journal:

> *14 Sept 1856, Sunday*: William Haley was buried this morning on our yesterday's campground.
>
> *21 Sept 1856, Sunday*: . . . W. N. Leason . . . died at 11:30 p.m., of canker in the stomach. He was born on 7 Nov 1854.

> *22 Sept 1856, Monday:* W. N. Leason was buried this morning at 7 o'clock. . . . Brother Jesse Empy . . . died from Scrofula [tuberculosis of the lymph glands], aged 31.
>
> *26 Sept 1856, Friday:* . . . Sister Ann Bryant, aged 69 . . . , died this afternoon of general decay of constitution. [Levi Savage's entry for this same day reads: "Sister Ann Briant, 70, found dead in the wagon. She was sitting up, appearing asleep."]
>
> *1 Oct 1856, Wednesday:* . . . Brother David Reeder died, aged 54. . . . William Read died coming into camp in a wagon. He was . . . aged 63.
>
> *3 Oct 1856, Friday:* . . . Peter Larson, aged 43 . . . , died during the day.
>
> *4 Oct 1856, Saturday:* . . . Benjamin Culley, aged 61 . . . , died; also, George Ingra, aged 68 . . . , died; Daniel Gadd, aged 2 . . . , died. (In Turner, *Emigrating Journals,* pp. 33, 36, 37, 38, 39)

Though the Martin Company records are not as complete, during a similar period, at least six deaths are recorded. Hannah's reference to the man who "fell down dead" refers to the death of William Edwards. Josiah Rogerson, Sr., gives this account, which was published in the *Salt Lake Tribune* in 1914. The incident appears to have occurred about 13 September 1856:

> Two bachelors named Luke Carter . . . and William Edwards . . . , each about 50 to 55 years of age, had pulled a covered cart together from Iowa City, Ia., to this point. They slept in the same tent, cooked and bunked together; but for several days previous unpleasant and cross words had passed between them.
>
> Edwards was a tall, loosely built and tender man physically, and Carter more stocky and sturdy. He had favored Edwards by letting the latter pull only what he could in the shafts for some time. This morning he grumbled and complained, still traveling, about being tired, and that he couldn't go any further. Carter retorted: "Come on. Come on. You'll be all right again when we get a bit of dinner at noon." But Edwards kept on begging for him to stop the cart and let him lie down and "dee" (die), Carter replying, "Well, get out and die, then."
>
> The cart was instantly stopped. Carter raised the shafts of the cart. Edwards walked from under and to the south of the road a couple of rods, laid his body down on the level prairie, and in ten minutes he

was a corpse. (*Salt Lake Tribune,* 4 January 1914; also cited in Turner, *Emigrating Journals,* pp. 109–10)

The tribulations of John Jaques and the Loader family are detailed by Patience Loader in a history she wrote some time after their arrival in the Valley (see Bell, *Life History and Writings of John Jaques,* pp. 128–33). As previously mentioned in the notes for chapter 8, in New York City, when Brother James Loader learned that he was being accused of being weak in the faith, he was so upset that he went right home and said to his wife: "I cannot stand to be accused of apostacy. I will show them better. Mother, I am going to Utah. I will pull the handcart if I die on the road" (in Bell, *Life History and Writings of John Jaques,* p. 93).

On 27 September 1856, James Loader offered the ultimate proof of his testimony and his faithfulness. It is typical of the pioneer journals that personal feelings are not often put into writing. One can only wonder what John Jaques must have felt when his father-in-law died, but he gives no indication. In his diary, an entry about emigrant deaths states: "James Loader from Aston Rowant Branch, Warwickshire Conference, September 27 about 11 p.m., west side of sandhill, 13 miles east of Ash Hollow, of diarrhoea. Buried 6 a.m., September 28. Age 57" (in Bell, *Life History and Writings of John Jaques,* p. 140).

However, after reaching the Valley, he who had rebuked his mother-in-law so sharply for her unwillingness to go by handcart paid quiet tribute to her in these words: "His [Brother Loader's] chief solicitude was for his wife, who, he feared, would not be able to endure the journey. But she did endure it. She endured it bravely, although it made her a sorrowing widow. She has lived a life of usefulness to the present time, yet still a widow, for she could never believe there was a man left in the world equal to her husband" (in Bell, *Life History and Writings of John Jaques, p.* 140).

CHAPTER 17

FORT LARAMIE

I

Tuesday, 30 September 1856

It was half past eight o'clock in the morning. Eric Pederson and Maggie McKensie were both at the camp of Mary Bathgate and Isabella Park. Eric was chopping firewood. Maggie was cleaning up after breakfast. Normally they would have been out on the trail by now, but the company was stopped until further word.

After six weeks and more than five hundred miles since leaving Florence, the Willie Handcart Company had reached a major marker on the trail. They were now camped just four miles to the east of the famous Fort Laramie. Last night, as they made camp, everyone assumed that they would be to the fort the next day. But this morning, in council meeting, the captains had decided to let the camp stay put while a delegation was sent to the fort to ascertain if it was possible to purchase additional provisions.

For some reason that Captain Willie did not feel to share with the company, he clearly was nervous about having the company camp for the night right at the fort. Elder Ahmanson thought it was because the fort had a reputation for attracting unsavory characters.

Eric thought it more likely that it was because there would be other emigrants stopped there, and there always seemed to be at least a few who delighted in heckling the Mormons. Or maybe it was because of the Indians. In spite of continual assurance from their leaders, the European emigrants had a natural anxiety around the natives, whether they were reported to be friendly or not.

Whatever the reason, Elder Willie declared that the camp would stay where they were while they waited for the delegation to return. Any stop was welcomed by the company. Instead of the usual cold breakfast, there would be time to cook. The morning would be spent in washing and mending clothes. Out of habit, Eric and Olaf were up early and shared breakfast with the Nielsons. Then Eric set off to check on his two walkers. And they were walkers again now. They had stayed in the wagons for only about two weeks until both of their injuries were healed, and then they were right back on the trail as before. No amount of reasoning or persuasion made a difference.

It came as no great surprise to Eric that Maggie was there ahead of him. She came as regularly as he did, often accompanied by Sarah James. If the two women loved Eric for what he did for them, they absolutely adored the two girls. This morning, though, Sarah was engaged in helping with her own large family, and so Maggie had come alone. The two of them set to work helping Sister Bathgate and Sister Park get a breakfast of their own. That was not a difficult task. With only flour and meat from the cattle, and limited amounts of those, meals were pretty monotonous.

This morning, a fire would be welcomed, Eric thought. It was a brisk morning, the chilliest so far. There had been a heavy frost during the night, and they could still see their breath. For the first time Maggie had her coat on, and also for the first time in quite a while Eric was wearing the sweater his mother had given him the day they left Balestrand.

Finished with getting the fire started and breakfast on, Eric and Maggie went to the two sisters to say farewell. As Eric went to Mary and gave her a hug, she reached out and touched his sweater. "This is beautiful," she said. "I don't think I've seen you wear that before."

"My mother make it for me. One for me and one for Olaf. Before we leave Norway."

"It is lovely."

"Yes."

"The nights are certainly cold enough now," Isabella said. "We had to use another quilt last night."

Maggie bent down and kissed Isabella on the cheek and then went to Mary and did the same. "Well," she said as she did so, "we'll probably see frost most nights from here on in." She could have said much more. It was the last day of September. Over the last week they had watched the leaves in the hills turn to orange and red. Now the aspens, higher up in the mountains off to the west, were showing a brilliant yellow. Autumn was almost gone. Winter was approaching with sobering speed.

Eric and Maggie said good-bye to the two women again and then walked away. Fort Laramie was located near the confluence of the Laramie and North Platte Rivers. Being some distance east of the fort, the company was camped along the North Platte, spread out over a considerable distance so as to get the sites with plentiful firewood and easy access to the water. The sluggish, silty water of the Platte River had been left far behind them now. Here the North Platte was deep, swift, clear, and cold as an icehouse—a joy to the weary travelers. Eric's tent was more than a hundred rods from where Mary and Isabella were camped. Maggie's was another hundred beyond his. They walked slowly, savoring the morning air and the chance for a leisurely moment together.

"Did you know that Fort Laramie is considered the halfway point?" Maggie asked, after they had walked some distance in silence.

"Really?" And then he did some quick figuring in his head. Elder Ahmanson had reported last night that they had come about 550 miles from Florence. If Salt Lake was a little less than eleven hundred miles, then Fort Laramie was almost exactly at the midpoint of their journey.

In the last two weeks they had passed other markers that Eric had long heard and read about—Ash Hollow, a famous stopping place with plentiful wood and water; Chimney Rock, rising majestically some four hundred feet above the plains; Scott's Bluff, which marked the end of the Great Plains and the beginning of the Rocky Mountains. But none of them was as important as Fort Laramie. After almost six hundred miles of emptiness, here was an island of humanity in a wilderness sea.

Eric stopped, his head lifting. High above, an eagle was circling lazily over the river. Maggie glanced up as well, but then lowered her eyes to study Eric's face. She smiled. He hadn't worn his hat this morning, and there was a line across his forehead. Below it, his skin was deeply browned. Above, it was still pale as a piece of parchment. His eyes dropped and caught her watching him.

"What you smile at?" he asked.

Flustered, she looked down. Then she noticed his sweater. "I wish I could knit like that. It really is beautiful."

He reached up with his hand and fingered the wool. "I did not know Mama was doing this," he said, his voice suddenly soft. "She stayed up late nights. She give to me and Olaf the day we leave Balestrand." He looked away, staring out across the river. "It was most special."

Maggie nodded slowly. "You must miss your family terribly."

"Yah, very much."

"I think of how it hurts each time I think of Hannah and I can hardly imagine what it would be like to leave your parents and your brothers and sisters for a whole year."

"It is not easy. But already five months have been done. Seven more only."

Thinking of Hannah only hurt, so she decided to change the subject. "I hope we get a chance to at least stop at the fort for a little while. We still have a little money left. Brother Woodward said we might be able to buy some biscuits or salt, or stuff like that."

"Or trade," he suggested. "Some in our group want to trade their things for food or other things they need."

"Do the Nielsons still have any money?" she asked. "You said they had quite a bit before they gave it to the brethren back in Iowa."

Eric shook his head. "I do not know for sure. I do not think so. Jens did not keep much, I am thinking."

"That is so wonderful. I don't know if I would have that kind of faith."

He gave her a sharp look.

"What?" she said, a little taken aback by the accusation she saw in his eyes.

"You are here, are you not?"

"Well, yes, but—"

He was peering at her now. "Your mother told me about how you are getting your answer about whether to come to America."

Maggie was stunned. "She did? When?"

"Last night."

"Last night? When did you see my mother last night?"

He smiled briefly. "When you and Sarah were with Sister Bathgate and Sister Park."

So that was it. Maggie had wondered why he hadn't been there. But her mother hadn't said one word about Eric's coming to their tent. "And she told you all about Edinburgh?" She was frowning.

"Only because of what I ask her." Now he looked uncomfortable.

"I can't believe—" She stopped, realizing what he had said. "What did you ask her?"

He looked down at his hands, which were twisting nervously. "I ask her if she will allow . . . allow? . . . permit me to court her daughter."

Maggie was so dumbfounded, all she could think of to say was, "Me?"

He laughed. "Hannah is adorable, but I think Olaf would be angry if I court her."

She felt her face burning. "I . . . I didn't mean it that way." She turned now to face him fully. "You really did that?"

"Yah, I did." Now a mischievous grin stole across his face. "I decide that if I do not do it, then Sister Bathgate and Sister Park will do it for me."

Maggie had to laugh and nod at that. "Yes, those two are real conspirators."

He wasn't sure what that word meant, but did not want to be deflected. "In truth, that is not exactly what I ask of your mother."

"Really? What, then?"

For several long seconds he just looked at her; then, without taking his eyes off her, he answered. "I asked for permission to ask her older daughter for permission to court her."

Maggie felt her breath catch. There it was, as direct and unmistakable as she could have hoped for. Her face softened. "And what if the older daughter were to say no?"

He hesitated for only a moment, seeing that she was teasing him now. "Then I shall not go on anymore. I shall wait here for Brother Martin's company and then I shall have to court the younger daughter instead."

That startled her, and then she slugged him on the arm. "Eric Pederson! You leave my sister out of this."

He rubbed his arm, looking rueful. "It would only be if I am desperate."

"How desperate?" she asked softly.

"It depends," he mused. "Does older daughter say no?"

She tried to stay very serious, but she knew there was happiness in her eyes. "If I did say no, you would have to wait here several days. It could get very cold at night without a tent."

He nodded. "Very cold."

"I would hate to think I was responsible for you getting sick."

He never changed his expression. "I would not like either."

She sighed in mock resignation. "Then perhaps the older daughter had better say yes." As his face brightened, she held up her hand. "But there is one condition."

"What?"

"That we don't tell Mary and Isabella about this. I am having far too much fun watching them try to bring us together."

He laughed softly. "How do you say in English? That is deal?"

"Yes. That's a deal."

He stuck out his hand solemnly. "That is deal, Maggie McKensie. Thank you."

She took it and shook it up and down, equally solemn. "Thank *you*, Eric Pederson." Then she poked him with her elbow. "Does this mean no more Sister Maggie?"

He looked offended. "I call you Sister Maggie because from the time I first see you so angry at that sailor man, this foolish Norwegian boy wanted to show how much he is honoring the beautiful Scottish girl, Sister Maggie McKensie."

Suddenly she realized she was still holding his hand. She squeezed it lightly, then let it go. She looked away as she realized her face was burning. "If that is so, this foolish Norwegian boy can call me Sister Maggie anytime he wishes."

At one o'clock that afternoon, word went up and down the camp that they were not going to wait any longer for the men who had been sent to the fort. The camp would move forward in one hour, marching past Fort Laramie to a campsite three miles beyond. That news was met with great disappointment, for there were many in the company who had looked forward to an opportunity to make purchases and just to see the place about which they had heard so much.

Half an hour later another message was circulated. The company would stop near the fort for one hour and a half before moving on to their new camp. Any who wished to trade should avail themselves of that opportunity, for tomorrow the company would continue westward first thing in the morning.

It surprised Eric as he drew closer to the actual fort to see that it was not a stockade made of logs, as he had expected. Rather the walls were made of sunbaked bricks. He had heard that this was in the style of Mexico and was popular in many places here. Shortly after the 1846–48 war with Mexico, the fur-trading post was taken over by the military and became an army fort. Perhaps they were responsible for the sun-dried brick construction. Whatever its source, it was an imposing structure, and certainly the fort itself was the most imposing structure in the complex of barracks and buildings that surrounded it. The bricks had been whitewashed, and they gleamed like marble in the sun from this distance. Near the center of the long and high walls, a tower housed the main gate. Atop the tower was a flagpole from which flew the Stars and Stripes of the United States of America. Defensive towers of lower height could be seen on each corner. Smoke was billowing upward from somewhere inside the fort, perhaps from one of the blacksmith's forges that were said to be there.

Eric was alone at the moment. The company had reached the fort about quarter past three, and Elder Willie called a halt on the fields just to the west of the cluster of buildings. Olaf and Jens Nielson left immediately along with a rush of others. Eric had gone to find Sister Bathgate and Sister Park and see if they needed him to get anything for them. He should have known better. They had already gone in with the others.

The fort was a bustle of activity as he approached. There were several tepees set up near the Laramie River, a few rods from the eastern end of the fort. He could see quite a few Indians there, including numerous children playing some kind of game with half a dozen dogs racing around after them, barking wildly. Closer to the fort, several military-type tents were pitched. On the west, closer to where they had stopped, there were half a dozen wagons and teams, other late emigrants on the Oregon Trail. People were going in or coming out of the fort in a steady stream. Some carried saddlebags, others sacks and boxes, and one man was lugging a heavy bale of skins of some kind.

As Eric reached the huge wooden gate and passed into the fort itself, he stopped in surprise. It was swarming with people, most of them Latter-day Saints. But what completely astounded him was the complex of buildings lining the inside of the massive walls. He turned slowly. Only in the corners were the walls left bare, and here steps led up to the towers. But in every other place he looked, buildings had been constructed in such a way that their back walls were formed by the walls of the stockade. There were stores, workshops, a barber, stables, storage sheds, and even a saloon. Many of the buildings were two stories high, with apartments built over the commercial buildings. He had never imagined such a thing, and for several minutes he just walked around, taking it all in.

He heard someone call his name and turned to see Emma James. She had a wrapped package under one arm as she ran up to him. "Hi, Eric. Are you just getting here?"

"Yah. I went to see Sister Bathgate."

"Oh, she and Sister Park are in the sutler's store."

"Sutler?"

"Yes. It's like a general store but inside a military fort." She indicated a long, low building with her head. Then she turned and pointed in a different direction. Here there was a sign with a word he did not recognize. "There is also the military commissary, but they sell mostly food. The prices are much higher in the sutler's store." She turned back to him. "Do you want me to help you find Sister Bathgate?"

"Thank you, no. I just wondered if they needed help."

She laughed merrily. "I don't think so. When I saw them, they were haggling with one of the clerks over some deerskin moccasins. I think the poor man was getting the worst of it."

Eric chuckled. "I believe that."

"Olaf and Brother Nielson are in the sutler's store too." She started away. "I've got to take this to Mama. It's some cloth for a shirt for Papa. But I'll be back."

He waved to her and moved on. He had nothing to trade and no money, but he decided he wanted to see what a sutler's store was like. Through the windows he could see that it was packed with people. He reached the door and pushed his way inside. It was pure bedlam. The noise was loud and continuous. People held things up, shouting for someone to tell them how much they cost. Others were yelling at clerks in what looked like "to-the-death" arguments. Just to his left, two women—one he recognized, one who was definitely not with their company—were fighting over a small wooden barrel on which was stenciled the word *rice.* A boy was crying loudly, pointing at a jar of hard candy that was marked at three pieces for a penny. His mother was shaking her head.

The store itself was a wonder. Every wall was lined with shelves. Every aisle was crammed with boxes, crates, barrels, and sacks. Wooden and metal tools hung from overhead racks, and the handles had to be dodged as Eric moved along. The place assaulted the nostrils with a dozen or more odors—tobacco, spices, leather, molasses, body odor, pickled something or other, salted pork, slabs of bacon, the sickly smell of something dead as he passed shelves of buffalo, deer, and elk hides.

He saw his two charges, Mary Bathgate and Isabella Park, near the main counter. Evidently the bargaining was over, because the clerk was smiling as he wrapped a small package in plain brown paper. Sister Isabella handed over something small in exchange, perhaps a cosmetic case or a jewel box.

He saw Maggie and Sarah James at another counter and moved closer to see what they were examining with such care. It was sewing materials—some needles and different skeins of yarn. They did not see him and he moved on, not wanting to interrupt.

Convinced that Jens and Olaf were not inside, he finally went out. He let out his breath, grateful to be in the open air again. Half watching for his brother, half just enjoying the wonder of it all, he moved around the compound slowly. He stopped near a table from whence came a pleasant smell. A man in buckskin stood beside an Indian woman who was pounding together a mixture of what looked like dried meat and berries.

The man saw him looking and smiled. "Howdy. You know what pemmican is?"

Eric shook his head.

"Indian food. Best stuff ever made. Keep you going for a hundred miles on a single pouchful."

Eric shrugged. "I have no money."

The man instantly lost interest and turned to a woman who was coming towards them. "You know what pemmican is?" Eric heard the man say as he walked away.

Down near the west end of the large courtyard, things were a little quieter. Here there were several smaller shops, some barely wide enough for a narrow table and an aisle beside it. One had a rope strung across the narrow window. From it hung dried ears of corn tied together in a clump, brightly colored gourds, and bunches of what Eric assumed were spices of some kind. There was no sign. He supposed that with the goods displayed, one was not needed.

Next to that was a similar shop, only this one did have a sign roughly painted in the window: "Metal and Tin Goods." Inside on the long table he saw cups and plates, a coffeepot, a funnel, a colander. He stopped, thinking what some of that tin would mean if it were put inside the axle boxes of their cart.

He looked up as a man came to the door. "Come on in."

Eric shook his head. "I was just looking."

The man looked at him more closely. "A Swede, yah?" His voice took on a perfect Scandinavian accent.

Eric smiled. "No, from Norway."

"Ah, very good. I have seen quite a few from the Old Country here today."

"Are you–"

The man immediately shook his head. "Nope. American true-blue, through and through. But I had a shop up in Wisconsin Territory for a time. Met a lot of Swedes and Danes up there. A few Norwegians too."

"I see."

"Well, come on in and have a look. We have lots of stuff here besides just tin goods. Trinkets. Toys. Jewelry."

On impulse Eric nodded and stepped inside. Perhaps he would find Jens and see if there was any money left for some tin.

The man stepped to the back of the store where there was a larger room behind a half-opened door. "Go ahead and look. Don't cost nothing for looking."

Eric nodded and began walking slowly along, his eyes jumping from one item to the next. It was not the best of quality. Some of the seams on the kettles and pans were roughly made, but the tin was shiny. Spots of rust would have been a concern.

All of sudden he stopped, his eyes pulled to a small box lined with velvet. Inside were a dozen or more slits, and tucked into each slit was a ring. Seeing Eric's interest, the man came forward. He leaned over and picked up the box, holding it out for Eric to take. He did not, but he couldn't pull his eyes away from it. Without realizing it, he was holding his breath, astonished at the thought that had just flashed into his head.

"Are you married?" the man asked.

Eric shook his head.

"Fiancée?"

This time there was a moment's hesitation before he shook his head again. The shopkeeper jumped on that. "A girl you'd like to be your fiancée?" he asked.

When Eric didn't look up, he took out a gold ring. "This is the finest I have. Made it myself from a single nugget I got from an Indian brave. Only ten dollars."

Eric almost gasped.

Immediately sensing his mistake, the man replaced that ring and went to a silver one that was thinner and very plain. "This one is only a dollar."

Eric finally looked up. "I am sorry. I have no money."

"Oh." The man sized him up for a moment, then put the case back down on the table.

"They are very nice, but . . ." He shrugged and started toward the door.

"I understand," the man said, not unkindly. "Wish I could help you."

"Thank you anyway," Eric said, stepping back out into the sunshine.

"Wait a minute." The man grabbed the case and came forward quickly again. When he got to Eric he reached out and touched his sweater, fingering the wool. "This is very nice. Where did you get it?"

"From my mother."

"Oh." Eric could see the wheels churning behind his eyes. "Want to trade it?" the man finally said.

Eric shook his head, but he was staring at the case of rings in the man's hand.

"There won't be another place like this until you get to Salt Lake City. You either get a ring now or not at all."

Two images flashed into Eric's mind at the same time. One was of his mother's tearstained face as she handed him and Olaf the sweaters; the other was the face of Maggie McKensie, her mouth pursed into a small O as she showed him how to pronounce a particularly difficult English word. Finally he looked up at the man. "How much you give?"

He thought for a moment and started to reach for the one-dollar ring. Then he thought better of that. His fingers moved slightly and he chose the one above it. "This one is heavier and has a little design in it." He held it up. "See?"

Eric nodded. It was still quite plain, but there was a pattern in the center of the ring that looked like the waves of the sea.

"This one is one dollar fifty cents. I'll trade you straight across."

For a long time, Eric stared at the ring. Then he took it from the man and looked at it more closely. *This is crazy, Eric Pederson. You have barely started to court her. How can you be thinking about marriage?*

"Wish I could give you more, friend, but I'm not really in the clothing business. I'm not even sure I should do this."

There are times when one's thoughts crystalize and come with such clarity that there is no denying them. This was one of those times. It was not that he decided that Maggie McKensie would marry him. He had serious doubts about that. But in a single instant Eric knew that if he turned and walked away now, he would not be out of the main gate before he turned around and came back. He knew that as surely as he knew that Maggie sent his heart racing every time he thought about her. He could not leave the fort without this ring.

He closed his eyes for a moment. *Mama! Will you ever forgive me?* And then came the second thought, and it came with equal clarity. If his mother were here and she knew it was a choice between the sweater and a wife for her son—especially a wife like Maggie McKensie—she would not hesitate for one second.

He looked up, then slowly began to pull his arms out of the sleeves of the sweater. "All right. It is deal."

As Eric came out of the main gate of the fort and turned toward the line of handcarts, he heard a shout. He stopped and turned, then waved. Olaf was walking across the courtyard with Jens Nielson. Seeing Eric, Olaf said something to Jens, then broke into a trot toward his brother. Eric groaned. Olaf was also wearing his sweater today.

"All done?" he said as he came up.

"It doesn't take long when you have nothing to do," Eric noted dryly. They were speaking in Norwegian.

"Yeah. Same for me. Jens made a good trade for a knife he had. He got two dollars."

Eric winced. Two dollars? He had seen that knife and it was not that wonderful. He wondered if he should have bargained a little more vigorously.

"Did you see Emma?" Olaf asked. "She was in here somewhere."

"Yes. About fifteen minutes ago she was taking something back to her mother."

"I was going—" He stopped, suddenly staring at Eric's chest. "Didn't you have your sweater on earlier?"

For an instant Eric tried to think of ways he could steer around this, but he realized it was of no use. He couldn't lie to Olaf. "Yes," he finally said slowly.

"What did you do, take it off before you came to the fort? It's not that warm today."

"No, I didn't take it off."

Olaf stopped dead, gaping at him. "You traded it?"

Eric nodded and started to turn. Olaf grabbed him and pulled him back around. "You didn't!"

"I did. I made a trade with one of the merchants."

"What did you trade it for?"

"Never mind."

"Eric! Tell me. What was so important that you gave away Mother's sweater?"

"I didn't *give* it away."

"Then what? I want to know."

Eric sighed and pulled him off to the side. People were streaming out of the gate now and turned to look at them as they went by. He took Olaf over to the great wall that loomed above them, glaring at him. "If I tell you, you have to give me your solemn word that you won't tell anyone."

"I promise."

He gripped his arm. "I mean no one, Olaf. Not Jens or Elsie. Not Brother Ahmanson." A look of horror flitted across Eric's face. "And definitely not Emma."

"What about Mama?" Olaf asked, a little defiant now.

Eric sighed. "I'll tell Mama." He tightened his grip and shook his brother a little. "But you can't tell anyone. Swear to me."

"All right, all right."

Eric let him go and stepped back. After a long moment, he thrust his hand into his pocket and withdrew the ring. He held it out.

Olaf glanced at it, then looked back up at Eric. "What's this?"

"This is what I traded my sweater for."

It was like watching a ripple in a pond. Olaf's eyes widened, then widened again. He reached out and took it, bringing it close to see it better. "A wedding ring?"

Eric cuffed him. "You don't have to blurt it out."

"Are you crazy? Who is this for?" The eyes went even wider. "Maggie? Are you—"

"No, we're not. She knows nothing about this, and don't you ever so much as hint to her."

Olaf stepped back, staring at him as though he didn't know who he was. "You are crazy."

Eric took the ring from his brother's hands and slipped it back into his pocket. "I know," he said glumly. He turned and started away. "I know."

The delegation who had ridden ahead to the fort earlier that day did not return to camp until well after dark. They went straight to Captain Willie to report. Captain Willie immediately ordered the horn to sound for assembly. When they were gathered around their leaders, Captain Willie jumped in without introduction.

"Brothers and sisters, it is almost time for lights out, so I will keep this short. Our brethren have been able to purchase a limited number of provisions from the military using the credit of the Church, but our hopes to purchase large quantities of flour were not realized. We know that some of you were able to procure some few things for yourself and that is good. But we certainly have not filled our needs. Today is the last day of September. We are still at least six weeks out of Salt Lake City. We cannot delay even one day now. We will therefore leave first thing in the morning."

There was a collective groan. They knew that was the plan, but after even an hour and a half at the fort, many had hoped they might stay at least one day more.

"Unfortunately, that is not the worst of it. Normally the first place the supply wagons from Salt Lake meet us is at Deer Creek, which is about three or four days farther west from here. We have learned that a group of missionaries from Salt Lake on their way east are camped not far from us. Elder Parley P. Pratt and Brother Thomas Bullock are with them."

That brought a murmur of pleased surprise. Parley P. Pratt was one of the Twelve. He had labored for an extended time in England and was beloved there.

"Hopefully they will be able to join with us and address us tomorrow evening, but . . ." His brow furrowed even more deeply than before. "But they do bring bad news. They passed Deer Creek just three days ago." He stopped, then shook his head wearily. "There are no wagons waiting for us there, and none coming."

Pleased surprise turned to shock and dismay.

He rushed on. "I think it is just as Elder Richards feared. When the third handcart company passed this way a few weeks ago, the supply wagons assumed there were no more coming and turned back. That means . . ." He didn't have to finish.

Now the heavy weight of leadership showed heavily in James Willie's face. "We fear that the soonest we may find wagons from the Valley is at South Pass. That, my brothers and sisters, is another two hundred fifty miles from here."

There was a loud buzz now among the congregation, but he did not try to stop it. He just shouted over it. "That's all I have to say. I suggest that, as always, you make our situation in this matter part of your evening prayers. We are going to need all the help we can get. Please be ready to roll by seven-thirty tomorrow morning."

II

Wednesday, 8 October 1856

The fifth and last handcart company of 1856 reached Fort Laramie late in the afternoon of the forty-third day after leaving Florence, Nebraska. Elder Edward Martin, their captain, chose a campsite about one mile east of the fort. Even before the last carts had stopped rolling, Hannah McKensie and Ingrid Christensen came looking for him.

He had had the same question they did and had sent scouts ahead that morning to learn the answer. Before they could even ask, he was shaking his head. "I'm sorry, Hannah. The Willie Company left here one week ago today."

It was crazy to hope so urgently when you knew there was no hope to be had, but you couldn't help it. Hannah's face crumpled and she turned away before he could see the tears. Ingrid just stared at him for several seconds, then spun around and started after her friend.

"If it is of any consolation," Elder Martin called after them, knowing even as he said it that it would not be, "we are only eight days behind them now. Once we were twelve days behind them. So we are gaining slowly."

Hannah raised an arm in acknowledgment but walked on without stopping.

That night, more out of curiosity than anything, since they had neither money nor trade items, Hannah and Ingrid walked to the fort with Brother Aaron Jackson and Brother John Jaques. While Brother Jaques went into the army commissary to see about purchasing items from the military stores, the girls walked around the main square of the fort. Brother Jackson had some specific things he was looking for and did not stay with them, but they made sure he was always in sight. They received more than a few leers from some of the young men loitering about and one or two invitations from the young rowdies, but if the boys persisted Brother Jackson was right there to send them packing. It was a little frightening, and yet titillating too. For two girls not yet seventeen, there was something exciting in being noticed.

They moved slowly from place to place, barely aware that they were gawking like children. Suddenly, Ingrid grabbed Hannah's arm. She was staring at a storefront. Across the inside of the store window letters were painted: "Metal and Tin Goods." Next to it was a window filled with dried corn, squash, and spices. Hannah looked at Ingrid, then turned to see what she was gaping at. She almost jumped when she saw it. There in the window of the tinsmith was a beautiful blue hand-knitted sweater.

"That's Olaf's sweater," Ingrid gasped. She dragged Hannah forward.

"Are you sure?" But Hannah already knew the answer to that question. She hadn't seen it for several months now, but both Eric and Olaf had worn their sweaters a great deal while they were coming across the Atlantic. "It might be Eric's," she said. "It looks a little big for Olaf."

Ingrid was peering intently through the window. There was a quick intake of breath and she pointed to a small card pinned to the bottom edge of the sweater. It read: "$5.00."

Hannah's mouth dropped open. "*Five dollars?* He got five dollars for that?" Her mind leaped to her own wardrobe, wondering if she had anything that might fetch even half that amount.

"Can I help you ladies?"

They both jumped as the shopkeeper suddenly appeared at the door.

Ingrid mumbled a quick no and backed away, but Hannah's curiosity was too strong. "Did you take that in trade from another handcart company that was here just last week?"

The man looked surprised. "Yes. Why?"

"Was his name Eric?"

He shrugged. "Didn't say. He was a Norwegian, though."

Hannah felt a little sick. Eric had traded the sweater his mother had given him? Were things that desperate for them? She saw the man still watching her.

"Thank you," she murmured, and started to move away. Then she couldn't help it. "And you paid him five dollars for it?"

He straightened, his eyes narrowing. "He drove a hard bargain," he answered in a clipped voice. Then he went back inside, shutting the door behind him.

Chapter Notes

No mention is made of the Willie Company's stopping to trade at Fort Laramie, though the journal does note that they were able to procure some provisions. The author has assumed that, though they did not stay near the fort itself, some of the people did go in to purchase things and make trades.

A week later the Martin Company stayed a full day there, allowing their people to "shop" at the fort. John Jaques recorded his transactions: "Thurs. 9: Many of the brethren went to the fort to buy provisions, etc. I went and sold my watch for thirteen dollars. I bought from the fort commissariat 20 pounds of biscuit at 15 cents, twelve pounds of bacon at 15 cents and 3 pounds of rice at 17 cents and so on" (in Bell, *Life History and Writings of John Jaques,* p. 141).

It is difficult for modern travelers who cross the continent by jet in four or five hours, or even by car at seventy-five miles an hour, to imagine what Fort Laramie must have meant to travelers along the Mormon and Oregon Trails. One small inkling is given in these lines from the Willie Company journal under the date of 1 October 1856: "The first thing this morning, it was discovered that several sisters had left the camp and had taken up their residence at the fort. . . . Lucinda M. Davenport left camp on the previous night with an apostate mormon. It was discovered this morning. She was with Grant and Kimballs wagon on the journey. Christine Brown of the handcart company also stayed at Fort Laramie" (in Turner, *Emigrating Journals,* p. 38).

A party of missionaries from Salt Lake City were traveling the Mormon Trail eastward to begin missions in the United States and Europe. Parley P. Pratt was among them. Though he did not know it then, Elder Pratt would never return to the Valley. He was murdered by an assassin about twelve miles out of Van Buren, Arkansas, on 13 May 1857 (see *Encyclopedia of Mormonism,* s.v. "Pratt, Parley Parker").

BOOK 4

THE STORM

AUGUST – OCTOBER 1856

How could we expect to be joyous and to receive all that "the Father hath" if we do not strive to become like Him? And, in fact, can we, on our scale, be like Him without sharing in the "fellowship of his sufferings"? He shares with us His work; does that not suggest the need for our sharing, too, some of the suffering? . . .

If in all of this there is some understandable trembling, the adrenaline of affliction can help to ensure that our pace will be brisk rather than casual. His grace will cover us like a cloak—enough to provide for survival but too thin to keep out all the cold. The seeming cold is there to keep us from drowsiness, and gospel gladness warms us enough to keep going.

—Neal A. Maxwell, 1982

CHAPTER 18

FORT LARAMIE TO LAST CROSSING

I

Saturday, 4 October 1856

Maggie was not surprised when Eric suddenly appeared. She had taken careful note of where his hundred had camped and calculated the most likely path he would take to get to her tent; then she deliberately went out to intercept him. He had formally asked her permission to come courting just four days before. It had taken only two days for her to realize that having him do so in front of her mother and brother and all of the James family, especially Sarah, was not the most comfortable experience for either him or her.

She smiled. He hadn't seen her yet through the trees, though he was coming directly for her. She could see that his brow was furrowed in concentration as he picked his way over the rough ground. Then she noticed something. The sun was just going down, and while the day had been pleasant, the air was rapidly taking on a chill. Their breath was already starting to show. It would be another night of heavy frost, perhaps dipping into the midtwenties or lower. Eric had on his round-brimmed hat and a long-sleeved flannel shirt, but that was all he wore for the cold. Then it occurred to her that she had not seen him wearing his sweater the last few days.

He slowed as he saw her, then instantly smiled. She smiled back. How she loved that change in his countenance! When he was serious it was as if his face were carved from hickory or one of the other hardwoods. His eyes seemed a darker blue and somewhat withdrawn. But when he smiled, everything changed. The face softened into something wonderful. His eyes became like a . . . what? She couldn't think of an appropriate simile. Well, whatever they were like, she could get lost in them. That was something she had never experienced with James MacAllister.

"Hello," she said as he came up beside her.

"Hello," he answered, clearly a little surprised to see her here.

"I was out walking," she explained, a little lamely, she thought.

He smiled sardonically. "Yah, I understand. We don't get to walk very much anymore."

"All right," she said, laughing through her embarrassment. "I admit it. I thought it would be nice if we had just a few minutes alone before we go into the cage."

"The cage?" He was genuinely puzzled.

"Yes. When we get inside the cage and everyone sits around and stares at us and wonders why we don't feel like talking very much."

Then he understood. He hooted in delight. "Yah. Cage is good. I feel the same."

"So can we take the long way around?" she said, pointing the opposite direction from where her tent was.

"Yes. I like that idea."

She was pleased that as they started walking he moved close enough to her that their shoulders occasionally touched.

"How are Sister Bathgate and Sister Park?" she asked.

He frowned. "Hungry but not willing to admit it."

She nodded. That was no revelation. From the time they left Iowa City, a mild hunger had become a part of their daily regimen. Sixteen ounces of flour per day, supplemented by occasional small portions of meat, was not enough to satisfy the body when it was pulling a handcart fifteen to twenty miles a day. During their brief stay at Florence, there had been more food and the hunger abated. As soon as they departed again, it returned.

Four days ago, that had changed significantly. There had been no flour at Fort Laramie and no oxen to replace those they had lost. There were no supply wagons waiting for them at Deer Creek. Captain Willie had managed to purchase about four hundred pounds of hard biscuits, a small amount of sugar, and a sack of dried apples. The conclusion was inescapable. He and the subcaptains called the Saints together and asked for a reduction by one-fourth in the daily ration. That meant each adult working man dropped to twelve ounces of flour per day; women and children were reduced in a similar manner. The vote had been unanimous in the affirmative. In just four days the effects of that decision were already pressing in upon them. What had been a vague gnawing desire for a little more to put in the belly was now an insistent ache and constant craving.

Maggie started a little as she realized Eric was watching her curiously. As usual, she had gotten lost in her own thoughts. "I'm sure," she said quickly, "that having them walk all day now isn't helping reduce that hunger either."

"That's what I told them too," he said, "but it is good thing they can walk now. We have so many sick that there is no more room in the wagons."

Her eyes dropped and she looked at the ground. "I know. Brother Woodward came by a few minutes ago. He said we've had three more deaths today and that another little boy looks like he will die before the night is over."

"Yah," he said softly. "That is now four in four days. Five if the boy dies."

"I heard that the man who died yesterday was from your group."

"Yes, he was." His eyes were hooded and sorrowful now. "Peter Larson. He was a good friend of Jens and Elsie. He was part of our tent group."

Her hand shot out and she touched his arm. "Oh, Eric. I didn't know that."

"Yes. It has been very hard for Elsie. Sister Larson is a good friend. Now she is left with five children to go alone."

Maggie started, remembering something now. "Sister Larson? Isn't she the one who had a baby just a few weeks ago?"

"Yes. At Iowa City. Now she is widow. It has left great sadness in our tent."

Maggie nodded, greatly sobered by that news. When it started striking within your own tent group, that was like losing family.

"How is your mother and Robbie?"

"Fine." She was glad to change the subject. "She wants to know if you and Olaf would have supper with us."

He laughed shortly. "I ask your mother if I can come courting you, not if she will support me at your table."

"She is the one who insists that I ask you," she protested. "She likes you very much, Eric. This isn't out of a sense of duty."

"I like her very much," he answered solemnly. "I have much admire for your mother."

"Admiration."

"Yah." He shook his head, frustrated with himself. "Yes, admiration."

She smiled up at him. "Your English is getting better all the time."

"If only I can remember to say yes instead of yah."

"I like 'yah,' " she replied. "I think it is—" Suddenly she stopped. "Listen."

He cocked his head a little. From off to their right, not far away, there was the sound of singing. Somewhere in the camp a small group—perhaps just a tent group—had started to sing. They couldn't distinguish the words clearly, but they didn't have to. The words were from a poem written by Eliza R. Snow and then set to music by someone else. It was called, "Think Not, When You Gather to Zion." The words had been published in the *Millennial Star* before they left

England and had quickly become a favorite song among the emigrants.

Think not, when you gather to Zion,
Your troubles and trials are through—
That nothing but comfort and pleasure
Are waiting in Zion for you.

Maggie began to hum along softly. When she realized Eric was watching her, she blushed a little. "I love the songs of Zion. I'm glad that we can still sing them, even though things are not wonderful."

"I too."

"You sing it, then."

He shook his head. "I do not know the words. I still learn 'Some Must Push and Some Must Pull.' "

She laughed. Then, to Eric's surprise, she became suddenly quite somber. "Are we going to make it, Eric?"

He stopped. "Make it?" he asked. "What do you mean?"

"To the Valley. We still have hundreds of miles to go. We don't have enough food. The weather . . ." She didn't finish. One hand began to pluck at the lining of her coat. "I've had this dark feeling lately," she whispered. "I don't know what is wrong. It frightens me."

"Tell me how is dark," he said.

Her shoulders lifted and fell and she exhaled slowly. It was a sound of great weariness. "I don't know. Part of it is being tired and hungry. It wears you down so. And Brother James was sick in the middle of the night. Sarah and I went to the creek and got him some water."

He nodded slowly. He hadn't been up in the night, but he knew exactly what she meant by wearing down. The combination of reduced rations, increasing cold, and continually pressing forward was hitting everyone now. Eric had always worked hard back in Balestrand and had been trim and fit. But two nights before, he had to take his knife and poke two more holes in his belt. It was now overlapping a good two inches more than before.

"And then I've been thinking about Hannah lately." The pain twisted at her mouth. "What if they don't have enough food either? What if—" Tears sprang to her eyes now. "What if I never see her again, Eric? I can't bear the thought of that."

He stepped forward and took her by the shoulders. He turned her so that she squarely faced him. "Is not possible," he said emphatically.

Her eyes came up. "What do you mean it isn't possible?"

"Is not possible that you *never* see her again."

Then she understood. "I know we'll see each other sometime, but I'm talking about this life, Eric. What if she dies?" Her eyes half closed. "What if *I* die?"

To her surprise, he let go of her shoulders and reached out and laid the back of his hand against her cheek. "You will not die," he said very softly.

"Why? How can you be sure?" She felt the first burning of the tears. "It's not just the old people dying anymore, Eric. They said Brother Larson was only forty-three. I don't have any special promises."

For a long time he just looked at her, his eyes that deep, deep blue that pulled her in and held her as tightly as if she were bound. "Tell me, Maggie McKensie. Tell me of that day when the answer came to you."

"Back in Edinburgh do you mean? Mother already told you."

"Not the details. You tell me."

So she did. She told him about James then, the first she had ever spoken to him about it. She told him about fasting and how James had come that day and said they could marry and of the joy she felt. She was so sure that was her answer. Then came the song, with the words burning like fire across her mind. As she said that, she started a little.

"What?" he asked.

"When Brother Willie asked me to teach the English class on board ship, he told me a story about Brigham Young. President Young said that when the fire of the covenant burns in our hearts like flame unquenchable, then we do whatever we are supposed to do, no matter what the consequences. Brother Willie said that was what had happened to me that day. The fire of the covenant was kindled in my heart."

"Ah, yah," Eric said. "Yes. That is true. It is like a fire."

"But . . ." She didn't want to sound discouraged, but this had been lying heavily upon her for the past three days. "These people who died today, they were coming to Zion because of the covenant too. They were doing what the Lord asked of them. So just because I got an answer to come doesn't mean I have a guarantee that I won't die. Or that someone in my family won't die." Her eyes glistened again. "What if Robbie doesn't make it?"

Now he shook her very gently. "Why you think God give you that answer?"

That took her aback. "Why?"

"Yes. Why?"

"Because . . ." She hesitated. "Because I guess he wanted me to come to Zion."

He let her go and stepped back. "You could come to Zion later. Why now?"

"Well, I suppose it had something to do with His wanting me to be with my family."

"Yes, that too." He smiled gently, waiting.

Then her eyes widened and one hand came up as though she were going to reach out to him, but she didn't. The wonder of what he was suggesting struck her hard.

Seeing that she understood, he laughed softly. "Eric Pederson was not coming to Edinburgh. Not ever. Eric Pederson was on the ship *Thornton.* Eric Pederson was the *Dummkopf* who needed some courage-filled young girl to come to his help." He stopped, and now the smile filled his entire countenance. "Eric Pederson needed English teacher."

"I—"

As quickly as the smile had come it left again. Now he was completely serious. "Maggie McKensie better not die," he said slowly. "Not now. Not when she finally say that Eric Pederson can come to court her."

She was so completely taken off guard by his openness that she didn't know what to say. But in that instant, any sense of darkness in her was completely banished. Then her eyes grew mischievous. "And what would you do if I did die?" she teased.

If anything, he became even more grave. "Then," he began, seeming to search for the right words, "then Eric Pederson come to the spirit world and stand behind Maggie all the day long, saying, 'Yah, yah, yah. Yah, yah, yah!' "

The laughter exploded from her and she clapped her hand over her mouth and looked around quickly, afraid someone might have heard her. The singing was still audible, though, and no one seemed to be paying any attention to the two of them. Still laughing, she stepped to Eric and slipped an arm through his. "That would be a fate too horrible to contemplate."

"I think so too," he said.

"Come on," she said happily, laying her head against his shoulder. "Mama will be wondering where we are."

As they started off, she remembered the thought she had had when she first saw him. "By the way, Eric, where is your sweater? I haven't seen you wearing it for a while."

He stopped dead and stepped back away from her. She was surprised to see a touch of panic in his eyes. "It is gone," he finally said.

"Gone? Did you lose it?"

"No. Just gone."

He said it in such a way that it brooked no further questions. As they started off again, Maggie suddenly understood. Tomorrow, when she went to help Sister Bathgate and Sister Park, she would look to see if either of them had acquired a new sweater in the last few days.

II

Wednesday, 8 October 1856

Olaf and Eric Pederson had once again come to have supper with the McKensie and James families. They brought their ration of flour with them so as not to work a hardship on the two families. Tonight, in addition to biscuits and a thin gruel, there would be meat. Elder Willie had ordered another one of the cattle butchered and the meat distributed through the camp. With what was allotted to Eric and Olaf, that gave them about five pounds of food for the fourteen of them. Sarah and Maggie had cut the meat up into small chunks, and then Sister McKensie and Sister James had fried them on a hot griddle, without the aid of grease. Since they had been forced to hitch up the milk cows following the loss of their oxen after the buffalo stampede, the cows were barely producing enough milk to meet the needs of the babies in the camp. That was another loss. The butter and cream had not been much, but they were at least something.

It would be a more substantial meal tonight, Maggie thought, and she thanked the Lord for that. Perhaps tonight the younger children would not have to go to bed holding their stomachs and whimpering about how hungry they still were. Maggie hated that most of all. The little ones weren't old enough to understand covenant and sacrifice and faith and enduring. All they knew was that their tummies hurt.

William James speared a piece of meat with his fork and held it up, eyeing it suspiciously. His wife saw it and frowned at him. "What's wrong, William?"

"Nothing. I was just wondering if this was a piece of meat or a piece of the horn."

They chuckled at the expression on his face. Sarah James stuck a piece in her mouth and began to chew, exaggerating the effort it took to bite into the tough meat. Then she spoke to her father. "It looks like it's meat, but it doesn't have enough flavor to be one of the horns. I'd guess it's one of the hooves."

"All right," Sister James said, trying not to smile. "Complaining about it isn't going to make it any more tender."

"I wasn't complaining," William protested. "I was just wondering."

They were all smiling now. Even the younger James children knew their father was playing. Then the smile died. "It's no wonder we're having problems with dysentery and diarrhea," he said somberly. "It's not just that the meat is tough and tasteless. There's not a trace of fat in it. When this and a watery soup is all you eat every day of your life, no wonder people are getting sick."

The light mood of a few moments before was completely gone now. William James was one of those suffering from the effects of the limited diet. At the moment, he was doing better, but it had taken its toll. His face was gaunt and had lost some of its color. There had been a couple of days when he wasn't able to pull in the shafts and Sarah, Emma, and Sister James had been forced to take over pulling their two carts while he walked behind.

"The cattle are in worse shape than we are," Maggie noted quietly. "I was noticing today that you can count every rib on them."

"Did you hear that one of our best oxen died this morning?" Olaf asked. "They think it ate some kind of poison weed."

They nodded grimly. Yet another setback. They fell silent, contemplating the realities of their current situation. But Emma James didn't like this change in mood. Always cheerful, always teasing, always quick with a smile, now she decided to change the subject. She looked around. "Wasn't it here at Deer Creek that the wagons from Salt Lake were supposed to meet us?"

Eric nodded. He had thought of that very thing when Elder Willie announced that they would stop here for the night. The first three handcart companies—now long since gone on—had found plentiful supplies of flour waiting here. The fourth company—their own—had found nothing but four soldiers from Fort Laramie taking an express to the Platte Bridge outpost.

"It is a beautiful spot," Emma said.

The others looked around. Maggie smiled to herself. *Bless you, Emma,* she thought. This sixteen-year-old would never let them dwell too long on the gloomy side of things. And it *was* a beautiful spot, one of the most pleasant they had seen in the whole journey. Deer Creek was a clear, swift-flowing stream about thirty feet wide and a foot deep. The water was so cold it hurt your teeth. Yesterday they had camped by a stream that was barely a trickle this late in the season and tasted foul. Here tall trees lined the banks on both sides, providing a grove of quiet serenity. The grass was thick and plentiful, something they had not seen for the last few days and something the cattle desperately needed. And in spite of hundreds of people passing through here all season, there was still plenty of firewood to be found.

Emma turned to her father. "Papa? Why don't we build a little log house right here and just stay here forever?"

Setting his plate down, her father stared at her for a moment, not sure if she was serious. Then his face softened. "It is beautiful, Emma, but what would we do for food?"

"Well," she said in surprise, smiling brightly. "We would do what we are doing now. We would simply do without."

III

Friday, 10 October 1856

About one hundred and twenty-five or thirty miles upriver from Fort Laramie, the North Platte River took a sharp turn to the south and entered Jackson Canyon, a narrow gorge too rough and confined for wagons to pass through. Because of that unfortunate accident of topography, after more than six hundred miles of following alongside the Platte and North Platte Rivers, the Oregon Trail left that "highway" for the last time and struck off directly to the west for a sixty-mile run to the Sweetwater River. Thus, this had come to be known simply as "the last crossing."

In the spring runoff, which went well into June and early July, the North Platte swelled tremendously, becoming a treacherous stream that could roll wagons like a wine cork and had exacted more than one human life as its toll for crossing. Even at low water, the main channel was four or five feet deep and the current swift and dangerous. During high water, the river spread across a floodplain a quarter of a mile wide and was eight and ten feet deep in places.

When the Mormons came through in 1847 they learned very quickly that there was no way to ford the river without great risk. Brigham Young ordered a ferry built. When it became immediately obvious that this would be a blessing to those of his people still coming, and that other Oregon Trail emigrants would pay handsomely to take advantage of it, he left eight men behind. Very quickly the "Mormon Ferry" became a mainstay on the upper North Platte, and each season thereafter Brigham would send a crew out to run it through the high-water season.

In 1851, an American-born fur trader of French descent by the name of John Baptiste Richard, which he pronounced "Reshaw" in the French fashion, built a toll bridge across the North Platte River near Deer Creek to provide competition for the Mormon Ferry upriver. Easier, safer, and faster than the ferry—sometimes wagons would end up waiting three or four days for their turn to ferry across—the bridge proved to be quite profitable. When it washed out the following spring, Richard moved upstream to a spot just five or six miles from the ferry site. The bridge he built here was a marvel indeed. It was built on twenty-three cribs made of timbers and then filled with stone. The decking of the bridge, which was ten feet above the high-water mark, was made of sawn planks eighteen feet long and three inches thick. The bridge was wide enough to allow two wagons to pass each other anywhere along its length. But the thing that made the bridge most incredible and a sight that caused jaws to drop and eyes to pop was the fact that it spanned the whole floodplain so that even at its highest stages the river could be crossed without so much as getting one's feet wet. It was 835 feet long from one end to the other!

Though the price for crossing the "Platte Bridge," as most people called it, was exorbitant during the high-water months—five dollars per wagon, four dollars per hundred head of stock—most were willing to pay. Later in the summer Richard might cut those fees in half, but even then it was expensive. Nevertheless, the bridge proved to be so popular that the Mormon Ferry was unable to compete and eventually shut down. To add to his profits, Richard established a small trading post—which was dubbed Fort Bridge—on the south side of the river. Almost all emigrants started out on the trail with overloaded wagons and with goods that were nice but not necessary. By the time they reached the last crossing, they were ready to trade off almost anything for passage across the bridge or for other, more critical items. With tens of thousands of people moving westward across the most significant highway in North America, Richard's success was assured. It was reported that he had made forty thousand dollars the previous season.

It was midmorning on October tenth when the James G. Willie Handcart Company arrived at the Platte Bridge and stopped in a large open field a short distance from Richard's trading post. As the carts pulled up together, everyone stopped to stare at the wonder that lay before them.

"Oh!" Robbie McKensie's mouth was open and his eyes were as wide as the hubs of the carts. "Look, Mama. Look at the bridge."

Reuben James ducked out from beneath the shafts of the second of his family's handcarts and ran to stand beside Robbie. Though he was fourteen, two years older than Robbie, and liked to think of himself as more mature than his friend, he too stopped dead. His mouth opened and there was a sharp gasp. "Jumping grasshoppers," he exclaimed, using a phrase he had picked up from one of the teamsters. "Hurry, Pa. Come look."

They all came over then, as did many others up and down the line. It was a perfect fall day—cool air, bright sunshine, a slight breeze from the west. All along the river the trees were full yellow now. Many had already lost some of their leaves. Against that backdrop Richard's bridge looked endless. Maggie found herself taking a quick breath. Someone had told her how long it was, but knowing the number had not prepared her for the sight. It was huge.

Her eye was caught by a movement. She looked closer. A wagon pulled by three yoke of oxen was making its way across. It was not that far away, but in comparison to the bridge it looked like a tiny white bug inching its way across a very long tree limb.

Robbie turned to Brother James. "Do we get to go across the bridge?" he asked hopefully.

"No, Robbie. Unfortunately we have no money and nothing we can use to trade for the toll. Brother Woodward says we'll ford the river upstream about five miles."

Maggie felt a little shiver. They couldn't see the river from here because of the trees, just an occasional glint of sun on water, but they had camped near it the last two nights. Though it was supposedly in the low season, it was running swift, deep, and very, very cold.

Just then, Brother Woodward, captain of their hundred, came trotting up to where his hundred was talking and pointing at the bridge. "We'll stop here for a little while," he called. "Elder Willie wants to go to the trading post and see what is available."

"Can we go too?" Brother James asked.

Woodward nodded. "Just watch for Elder Willie. When he's through, then you're through. We've got to ford the river later today."

William James turned to his wife. "I'm going to go see what they've got," he said.

"But you don't have anything to trade."

He didn't answer.

There was a soft exclamation of understanding. "No, William. Not your pocket watch. Your father gave that to you. What about your shotgun? That would fetch quite a bit."

William James was shaking his head before his wife finished. "I know I haven't shot much," he said, "but it is a way we can supplement our food supplies. I won't give that up. It's too important for the family."

"But your watch?" Sister James started.

He pulled his hat more firmly onto his head, not meeting her eyes. "If they have food, I'm going to trade, Jane. There'll be other pocket watches."

He turned to Maggie's mother. "Mary?"

She shook her head slowly. "All we have is some pretty threadbare clothing and boots with holes in them. I fancy that won't get us much."

Maggie's head came up sharply at that. She had something more than that. For an agonizing moment she debated about saying something to her mother, but then Brother James was waving and turning away. "I'll be back as soon as I can."

—❦—

Twenty minutes later Emma, Sarah, Maggie, Robbie, and Reuben were lying on the grass, their eyes closed. Any chance to rest, even for five or ten minutes, was always taken now. On the reduced rations, it was the only way to rejuvenate your strength. Where before at such stopping times the children would have been off to play with the rest of their friends, now even the younger James children lay together next to where Jane James and Mary McKensie sat talking quietly. Young John, just four, was curled up on his mother's lap. He had asked for food only once, then closed his eyes and lay against his mother's body.

"Maggie?" her mother called out.

She opened her eyes.

"Eric and Olaf are coming."

Maggie sat up in surprise. Eric was coming to their tent every night now after they stopped to camp, but during the day he usually stayed with his own group. Sarah got up now too. Emma, Reuben, and Robbie rolled over so that they could watch but didn't bother to get up.

As Maggie and Sarah stood, Maggie saw that Olaf carried something folded under his arm. Eric was carrying in his hands the hunting knife he always wore on his belt.

"Are you going over to trade?" she asked, not trying to hide her surprise.

Eric nodded. "Brother Ahmanson just came back. He says there is an Indian and his wife there who have buffalo meat."

Robbie sat up with a jerk. "Buffalo meat?"

"Yes. A hundred pounds or more. We're going to go see."

Now Emma scrambled up beside her sister and Maggie. "Can I go, Mama?" Reuben and Robbie were not a second behind her.

Jane James looked dubious. Mary was shaking her head. Eric smiled. "I'll watch them." Then he asked Maggie, "Would you and Sarah like to come too?"

"Yes." Then she looked at her mother.

After a moment Mary nodded. "All right. But Robbie, you stay right with Maggie."

"By the way," Eric added, "there is some good news. Elder Richards purchased thirty-seven buffalo robes here and left them for us. Brother Willie and Brother Savage are loading them onto the wagon now."

"Thirty-seven!" Sarah exclaimed. "That's wonderful."

"Yes. That's almost two robes per tent. They say they can keep you warm even when the temperature drops below zero."

"They work for the buffalo," Robbie sang out. "And they sleep outside."

Mary looked at her son with great affection. Even now with the hunger and the weariness, he had not lost his enthusiasm for life. "Yes, son, they do work for the buffalo."

"Even if there aren't enough for everyone," Maggie suggested, "it will free up some of the quilts and blankets for others."

"Thanks be to Elder Richards," Jane said warmly. "It's nice to hear some good news for a change."

The trading post was less than a quarter of a mile away, and before they were halfway there they saw William James come out of the low adobe building and start towards them. He was carrying a cloth sack in one hand.

As they met, Emma ran to him. "What did you get, Papa?"

He shook his head, looking quite dejected. "A half pound of sugar, two pounds of beans, and some rice."

"That's all he would give you for your watch?" Sarah exclaimed in dismay.

"It was broken, Sarah. I didn't have the heart to tell your mother that. I broke the crystal about a week ago when I bumped against the cart. It still works, but . . ." He shrugged.

Olaf murmured something in condolence, then said eagerly, "They say there is an Indian with buffalo meat."

Brother James nodded. "Yes. I tried him first, but once I showed him that the watch face was cracked, he wouldn't talk to me. He's driving a hard bargain."

"But it's real meat?" Eric asked.

"Yes." There was a look of pure longing. "It looks fresh and with lots of fat." He sighed softly. "Do you know what that would mean? Maybe we'd all finally have a chance to get well again."

Then as quickly as the dejection had settled in upon him, it left. He lifted the sack and forced a smile. "But at least I got us a little something." He looked at Eric and Olaf, noting what they were carrying. "Good luck," he said.

As he started to go on, Maggie suddenly reached out and grabbed Eric's arm. "Wait, Eric. Wait here. I'll be right back." And without waiting either for an answer or for Brother James, she turned and ran back to their cart.

Puzzled, Eric watched her reach in beneath the canvas, fish around for a minute, then come out with something. She tucked it beneath her apron, then came running back. "All right," she said.

Sarah was staring at her now, eyes questioning. "Maggie? You're not–"

"I'm ready," she said again to Eric firmly. "Let's go."

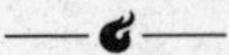

When Olaf unfolded the bundle he had under his arm, all three girls gaped in astonishment. It was Emma, with her characteristic bluntness, who spoke first. "Your sweater, Olaf? You're going to trade your sweater?"

He didn't look around. "I've got a coat," he murmured. "I'll be all right."

"But your mother made that for you special," Sarah said.

"And our father gave Eric that knife." He started to say more, then realized he didn't have to. If a knife, which was a valuable tool, had to go, then a sweater was not a hard decision.

Maggie suddenly remembered the disappearance of Eric's sweater and wondered if this might actually be Eric's. It would be like Eric to give his to Olaf so that Olaf would have something to trade. But as Olaf unfolded it and held it up for the Indian trader to examine, Maggie saw that it was not large enough to be Eric's. It was Olaf's.

The Indian sitting behind the rough-hewn table grunted softly, then took the sweater from Olaf and began to examine it. His wife, sitting beside him, watched as he did so, but her eyes were expressionless. Maggie took the opportunity to study them. According to Levi Savage, these Indians were Sioux, probably Oglala or Mandan. They had been trading peacefully with the whites for some time now. Obviously they traded here with the permission of John Richard, the proprietor of the Platte Bridge and trading post. The table was just a few yards from the door of the adobe building, and inside they could see Mr. Richard waiting on others of their company. Richard probably got a cut of any sales the natives made or some trading concessions with them.

The man looked forty or so, his wife considerably younger than that. His face was dark brown and leathery from a lifetime in the sun. Hers was surprisingly fair, not much darker than Maggie's now after weeks on the trail. As Maggie looked at her, she realized that she was quite pretty, something that Brother Savage had said was typical of many of the Sioux women.

Behind them, a crossbar made from the trunk of a young aspen tree was fixed between two tripods—also made from aspens—which had been driven into the ground. From the crossbar hung a hindquarter of buffalo, or rather what had once been a hindquarter of buffalo. Now it was nearly stripped of all its meat and was mostly bone. A young girl, six or seven, with beetle-bright black eyes, shooed away the flies from the meat with the branch of a cottonwood tree.

On the table, there was one large chunk of meat, perhaps eight pounds or more, and several soup bones with a little fat and shreds of meat left on them. From time to time the woman moved her hand enough to drive off the flies. The bones were not very appealing, but the large piece of meat was marbled with veins of fat and looked very good. Brother James had been right. It looked like excellent-quality meat.

"We should have come first thing," Sarah said softly.

Maggie nodded, wondering how much of that hindquarter had been there when their company first arrived. It had been almost an hour now since then. Behind them, several more families were waiting their turn to bargain with the Indians as well. When they finally marched out again, there wouldn't be much the Indian would have to worry about.

As Maggie watched the Indian turn the sweater over and feel the wool, she held her breath. This meat would be a godsend, especially with the health of their little group failing quickly now. She didn't think they would be able to trade for the whole piece, but even with half, if they were careful they could make it last for several days. Perhaps they could purchase a little salt inside and make it last even longer than that.

"How much?" the Indian asked, finally looking up. Olaf looked at Eric, who stepped forward and put his knife on the table. Now the man's eyes showed definite interest. He took it out and tested the blade with the edge of his thumb. When he put it back in the sheath, Eric took it and placed it on top of the sweater. He motioned to both items, then pointed to the large chunk of meat. "This for that."

The man's head immediately began moving back and forth. "More," he said shortly. "Need more."

Eric held out his hands, showing there was nothing more to be offered. The man leaned across his wife and picked up the largest of the bones. He plopped it down on the table in front of Eric.

"That's all?" Eric cried. "This is very good knife. This"—he touched the sweater—"is very warm."

The Indian shoved the bone a little closer. "Good trade."

Blowing out his breath, Eric turned to the roast. "What if we took only part of it?" He made a sawing motion with his hand, indicating about half.

This time the shake of the head was emphatic and the man's face became stone. "Need more."

Maggie stepped forward, an idea popping into her mind. "Eric. What if we buy the whole piece and share it between our families?"

He turned. "All right," he finally said, but his eyes were asking, *And what do you have that might make the difference?*

Not stopping to think about it, she lifted her apron and brought out the wooden music box. There was an audible gasp from both Eric and Sarah. She ignored them. She held it out for the Indian to see, then turned it upside down and quickly wound the key. Then she set it on the table and lifted the lid. The tinkling melody of "Loch Lomond" began to play softly across the field.

The man's eyes widened. The woman started a little, then leaned forward to stare at it. The little girl rattled off something and darted forward to see.

"Maggie, what are you doing?"

She glanced at Eric, then away. "Olaf can't eat his sweater. I can't fry a music box."

"But–"

She turned, her eyes soft. "I know what you did to save that for me, Eric. And now I know why. It wasn't so I would have music in my tent at night."

She turned back to the Indians, her face determined. The man had it up above his head, peering at it. He shook it gently. His daughter reached out to touch it, but he jerked it away sharply. Maggie gently took it from him and set it on the table and shut the lid. She opened and shut the lid twice more to show him how it worked. Then she placed it on top of Olaf's folded sweater and Eric's knife.

"All of this"—she made a circle with her hands—"for this," and she pointed to the large roast.

The warrior looked at her for several long seconds, his eyes hooded. His eyes moved a little as he looked past her; then he slowly shook his head. There was a brief burst of words aimed at his wife. She picked up the large piece of meat and set it in front of him. Emulating Eric's motions, she pretended to saw off one-third. Then she pointed to what would have been the larger two-thirds.

"No," Maggie shot back at the man, knowing he was the one she had to deal with. "We get it all."

His eyes hardened as he sat back, obviously torn. His wife stared straight ahead, her eyes still as unreadable as before. Then again the man's eyes moved to look past Maggie. Curious, she turned. John Richard was standing at the door of the trading post, watching what was happening. As near as she could determine, he made no sign of any kind, but the Indian turned back to Maggie. Again he "sawed off" one-third and pointed to the larger piece. "Good trade," he barked. "Very good trade."

Maggie swung around to face John Richard. "My father paid three pounds for that music box in Scotland. That's more than ten American dollars."

"Aye, lass," he said. His smile was sympathetic. "And if we were in Scotland, I'd probably offer you four or five pounds for it." He shook his head. "Here, beautiful things come much cheaper."

She wanted to cry or shout at him that it wasn't fair. But she knew it was. He was precisely correct. Out here, priorities got quickly reordered.

"All right," she said, turning back.

"Wait!" Eric was fishing in his pocket.

Olaf leaped forward. "No, Eric."

He pushed him aside, finally finding what he was after. In his fingers he held up a silver ring. He too spoke to Richard. "I'll add this and we take the whole piece."

"What is it?" Emma asked Olaf.

"It's a wedding ring," he answered, his voice stricken.

Maggie whirled. Eric didn't meet her eyes. He just held the ring out as John Richard came over and took it from his hand.

"He traded his sweater for it back at Fort Laramie," Olaf whispered, looking at Maggie, who was thunderstruck. She wasn't the only one. Sarah's eyes were wide. Emma looked a little bewildered.

The black-haired and dark-eyed Richard examined the ring closely, holding it up so it caught the sun. Maggie wanted to leap at him, snatch it from his hands, hold it close so she could at least look at it. But she could only stare at Eric, who finally now turned to her. The pain in his eyes was more than she could bear and she had to look away again.

Richard took a step forward and set the ring down beside the knife, the sweater, and the music box. He gave a quick nod to the Indian, then spun around and went back inside the trading post without another word. The Indian picked up the full chunk of meat and handed it across the table to Eric. When he spoke there was just a hint of satisfaction in his voice. "You make good trade."

Over the vigorous protests of Mary McKensie and William and Jane James, Eric cut the buffalo meat in two slightly unequal pieces, and then took the smaller piece. There were eleven of them, with seven who were adults, if you counted Reuben and Emma, he argued. Even with the Nielsons, there were only four adults and two young children to feed off Eric's and Olaf's portion. When Maggie tried to counter that with the idea that the music box she had contributed was not equal in value to the sweater, knife, and ring that Eric and Olaf had given, it fell on deaf ears.

On the way back from the trading post, Maggie had hung back, hoping Eric would do the same and she would have a chance to question him about the ring. It hadn't happened. If anything, he kept well out in front of them. Now she kept trying to catch his eye, but each time she did he would flush slightly and look away. Finally she just stopped trying.

The children gathered around, eagerly watching, as the meat was cut into two parts. The adults watched with only slightly less interest. Martha, who was ten, looked up at her father with large, pleading eyes. "Can we cook it now, Papa?"

He smiled kindly. "No, dear. We've got to march on and get across the river now. There's no time to build a fire."

"But Papa!" young George said. He was seven. "Can't we have just a piece of it now?"

"It's not cooked, George."

"I don't care. It looks so good, and just looking at it makes my tummy hurt, Papa."

Jane James looked with sorrow on her younger ones. "Children, Sister McKensie and I will cook it tonight so it will not spoil. But even then, we can't eat it all at once. We have to make it last as long as possible."

"We'll cut off a small piece for everyone tonight," Mary McKensie promised. "But now each of you need to thank Maggie and Eric and Olaf for getting this for us. This is a great blessing."

Even Reuben and Emma and the adults turned in compliance to that suggestion. The two brothers tried to put them off and give Maggie the credit, but she said that it was really them who had gotten the whole piece. Through it all, Eric still refused to look at Maggie, and so it came as no surprise that at the first possible moment Eric said they had to go. As he and Olaf walked swiftly away, Maggie's mother turned to her.

"What happened, Maggie?"

She flinched a little. "What do you mean?"

"Something's going on. Eric's twitching like a drop of water on a hot frying pan. What happened over there?"

"I . . . I don't want to talk about it right now, Mama. Perhaps later." And she turned and walked away, moving in the opposite direction from Eric and Olaf.

Sarah almost started after her, then shook her head slightly. This was not the time. Mary saw her and asked, "What is it, Sarah? What happened?"

She blew out her breath. "I think Maggie should be the one to tell you."

Maggie walked down to the river, not far from the great bridge that spanned the North Platte. She passed the structure, barely giving it a second glance, and walked into the trees. She went just far enough so that she wasn't open to view, but close enough to watch for the signal when it was time to move out again. She sat down heavily and closed her eyes, trying to let the tumble of emotions begin to settle a little.

She sat there for fifteen minutes, no more certain of things at the end of that time than she was when she came. Then, as she was considering returning to her family, she saw Olaf. He went to her family, who pointed in her direction. He turned and headed straight towards her.

In a way, she was greatly relieved. She had been afraid that Eric might come and try to stammer his way through an explanation. She didn't know if she was ready to talk with him yet. On the other hand, she was also faintly irritated. Why didn't *he* come? It wasn't Olaf's place to try and straighten this out.

As he entered the trees and saw her, he slowed his step, clearly quite concerned about how she was going to take this. "Maggie?"

She straightened, deciding to just be calm. "Yes, Olaf."

"May I speak with you?"

"Of course." *Where is Eric?* She almost spoke it aloud, but didn't.

"I . . . Eric does not know I am coming to find you."

"Oh?" She relaxed a little. Good. At least he hadn't sent Olaf to work it out for him.

Olaf sighed, sounding more like he was sixty than sixteen. "He is feeling badly most terrible."

Good. I'm feeling pretty confused myself, actually. But she didn't say anything aloud, only watched him steadily. When he began to squirm a little she spoke. "Was that ring for me, Olaf?"

His eyes widened perceptibly. "But of course. What did you think?"

"Why didn't he tell me before?"

Olaf sighed again. "When he trade for ring at Laramie Fort, it was not planned. He saw the ring and said that then he knew."

"Knew what?"

He gave her a pleading look as if to say, *This is hard enough, don't make it more so.*

She softened a little. "So why didn't he just tell me that?" she asked again.

"Eric is . . . He is afraid."

"Afraid? of me?"

He shook his head.

"Then what?"

"That you will not want to marry him. I tell him he is wrong. I tell him you like him very much. But he is afraid. If you say no . . ." He shook his head. "That would be very hard for him."

It was what she had hoped for, and one part of her wanted to shout. But the part of her that was feeling a little frustrated wasn't ready to give up quite yet. She gave him a searching look. "And how long before Eric was going to get up enough courage to tell me all of this?"

Now a slow smile stole across Olaf's face. "Not longer than two years, I think."

"*Two years?*" And then he laughed and she saw that he was teasing her. She laughed with him.

"I keep saying, Eric do it now, but he won't. He says, 'Not yet. Not yet. I am only courting her for one week.' This is why he feel so bad now. Now you know about the ring and there is no chance for him to ask you first how you feel."

She was nodding slowly. "I understand." She decided that there was one thing she had to know for sure, without any misunderstandings. "Is Eric planning to ask me to marry him?"

Again he seemed surprised that she would ask. "Yah, but of course."

"Thank you for telling me."

He searched her face now in return. "And what will Maggie McKensie say if he does?" he asked very quietly.

"Don't you know?" she exclaimed, throwing up her hands in exasperation. "Doesn't *he* know?"

Olaf smiled again, greatly pleased. "Good. This is very good."

Just then there was a shout and they both turned toward the column. Captain Willie was on his horse waving his hat. The people were getting up and moving towards their carts. It was time to move on. Olaf looked suddenly worried. "I must go. If he knows I am talking at you, he will be not happy."

"I won't tell him, Olaf. And promise me you won't tell him either. I want to think about all of this for a while."

He looked greatly relieved. "I say nothing. Thank you, Maggie."

"No, thank *you,* Olaf." She waved as he turned and trotted away, staying along the river before he turned and cut back toward the column. When he was gone Maggie finally stood and started back as well. To her surprise, she was not tired anymore, and for now her hunger was forgotten. *Was that ring for me?* The answer had been instantaneous. *But of course.* She hugged herself as she walked, her step light now. *Is Eric planning to ask me to marry him?* She wanted to tip her head back and shout out the answer. *Yah, but of course!*

Chapter Notes

"A Word to the Saints Who Are Gathering" was a poem written by Eliza R. Snow and set to music by John Tullidge. It came to be known as "Think Not, When You Gather to Zion." It was printed in the *Millennial Star* in March of 1856 (see Hafen and Hafen, *Handcarts to Zion*, p. 271). As the Hafens note, the song served as "a bit of warning for over-enthusiastic converts."

Think not, when you gather to Zion,
Your troubles and trials are through—
That nothing but comfort and pleasure
  Are waiting in Zion for you.
No, no; 'tis design'd as a furnace,
All substance, all textures to try—
To consume all the "wood, hay, and stubble,"
  And the gold from the dross purify.

Think not, when you gather to Zion,
That all will be holy and pure—
That deception and falsehood are banish'd,
  And confidence wholly secure.
No, no; for the Lord our Redeemer
Has said that the tares with the wheat
Must grow, till the great day of burning
  Shall render the harvest complete.

Think not, when you gather to Zion,
The Saints here have nothing to do
But attend to your personal welfare,
  And always be comforting you.
No; the Saints who are faithful are doing
What their hands find to do, with their might;
To accomplish the gath'ring of Israel,
  They are toiling by day and by night.

Think not, when you gather to Zion,
The prize and the victory won—
Think not that the warfare is ended,
  Or the work of salvation is done.

> No, no; for the great Prince of Darkness
> A tenfold exertion will make,
> When he sees you approaching the fountain
> Where Truth you may freely partake.

For all of the handcart companies, hunger was an ever-present factor in their journey across the plains. They simply could not carry sufficient supplies to provide all the food a person wanted. Mary Ann Stucki Hafen, whose family was from Switzerland, came to Utah in 1860 when she was six years old as part of the tenth and last handcart company. She reports that one day they shot two buffalo and distributed the meat to the company.

> When we got that chunk of buffalo meat father put it in the handcart. My brother John [who was nine] remembered that it was the fore part of the week and that father said we would save it for Sunday dinner. John said, "I was so very hungry and the meat smelled so good to me while pushing at the handcart that I could not resist. I had a little pocket knife and with it I cut off a piece or two each half day. Although I expected a severe whipping when father found it out, I cut off little pieces each day. I would chew them so long that they got white and perfectly tasteless. When father came to get the meat he asked me if I had been cutting off some of it. I said, 'Yes, I was so hungry I could not let it alone.' Instead of giving me a scolding or whipping, father turned away and wiped tears from his eyes." (*Recollections of a Handcart Pioneer*, pp. 25–26)

If hunger was a challenge for all of the handcart companies, for the Willie and Martin Companies, who were coming so late in the season, it was particularly critical. By the beginning of the second week after leaving Fort Laramie, the reduced rations and colder conditions were starting to wear heavily on the handcart pioneers. The entry for 8 October made by Levi Savage reads: "Deer Creek. This morning when we arose, we found the best ox on our train dead. In the weak state of our teams, the loss impaired us much. . . . Our old people are nearly all failing fast" (in *Remember*, p. 4).

John Chislett, who was captain of the fourth hundred in the Willie Company, noted the effects of both weather and lack of supplies:

> Our *seventeen pounds of clothing and bedding* was now altogether insufficient for our comfort. Nearly all suffered more or less at night

> from cold. Instead of getting up in the morning strong, refreshed, vigorous, and prepared for the hardships of another day of toil, the poor Saints were to be seen crawling out from their tents looking haggard, benumbed, and showing an utter lack of that vitality so necessary to our success.
>
> Cold weather, scarcity of food, lassitude and fatigue from over-exertion, soon produced their effects. Our old and infirm people began to droop, and they no sooner lost spirit and courage than death's stamp could be traced upon their features. Life went out as smoothly as a lamp ceases to burn when the oil is gone. At first the deaths occurred slowly and irregularly, but in a few days at more frequent intervals, until we soon thought it unusual to leave a camp-ground without burying one or more persons. (In *Remember,* p. 65)

John Jaques, with the Martin Company, wrote: "I believe the company left Fort Laramie the next day [10 October]. . . . Up to this time the daily pound of flour ration had been regularly served out, but it was never enough to stay the stomachs of the emigrants, and the longer they were on the plains and in the mountains the hungrier they grew. It was an appetite that could not be satisfied. At least that was the experience of the handcart people. You felt as if you could almost eat a rusty nail or gnaw a file. You were ten times as hungry as a hunter, yea, as ten hunters, all the long day, and every time you woke up in the night. Eating was the grand passion of the pedestrian on the plains, an insatiable passion, for he never got enough to eat" (in Bell, *Life History and Writings of John Jaques,* p. 142).

Describing conditions as they existed when the winter storms came later that month of October 1856, Jaques wrote: "The cattle had now grown so poor that there was little flesh left on them, and that little was as lean as could be. The problem was how to cook it to advantage. Stewed meat and soups were found to be bad for diarrhoea and dysentery, provocative of and aggravating those diseases, of which there was considerable in the company, and to fry lean meat without an atom of fat in it or out of it was disgusting to every cook in the camp." However, his very next words are of interest: "The outlook was certainly not encouraging, but it need not be supposed that the company was in despair, notwithstanding the situation was rather desperate. Oh! No! A hopeful and cheerful spirit pervaded the camp, and the 'Songs of Zion' were frequently heard at this time, though the company was in the very depths of privation. Though the bodies of the people were worn down, their spirits were buoyant, while at the same time they had become so accustomed to looking death in the face that they seemed to have no fear of it" (in Bell, *Life History and Writings of John Jaques,* pp. 147–48).

The conversation between Emma and her father about staying at Deer Creek actually took place between Mary Powell and her father, John Powell. Mary was almost thirteen and was traveling with the Edmund Ellsworth Company, the first handcart company of that season (see Carol Cornwall Madsen, *Journey to Zion,* pp. 604–5).

The trading post run by John Baptiste Richard (or Reshaw) was sometimes called Fort Bridge because of its being near the famous Platte Bridge. The Platte Bridge is often called Reshaw's Bridge by modern historians. Occasionally in some of the pioneer journals, emigrants refer to Fort Bridge as Fort Bridger. That is an error and shouldn't be confused with the actual Fort Bridger, owned by Jim Bridger, which was near present-day Lyman, Wyoming, another 250 miles from the last crossing of the North Platte.

CHAPTER 19

LAST CROSSING TO DEVIL'S GATE

I

Tuesday, 14 October 1856

"Maggie?"

She opened her eyes. Sarah James was kneeling beside her, pulling the buffalo robe up around her neck.

"How are you feeling?"

It took a moment for Maggie to realize that the inside of their tent was filled with light, which meant it was daytime outside. "Oh!" she cried. She tried to rise. "Is it time to go already?"

Sarah pushed her back down gently. "No, Maggie. We're camped here for the night, but it's not dark yet. You've just fallen asleep again."

She lay back, greatly relieved. "Yes, that's right. I remember now." She did vaguely remember lying on the ground and watching through heavy eyes while the men began to erect the tent. She clutched at the buffalo robe, pulling it more tightly around her body, feeling a sudden chill and reveling in the warmth the heavy covering provided. Suddenly her body convulsed as a deep, racking cough ripped through her. She cried out in pain and hugged herself, feeling the pain down deep in her chest. Sarah watched her with anxious eyes.

"Where are we, Sarah?"

"We are camped between Independence Rock and Devil's Gate."

"Oh, yes. I remember." The other places were a fuzzy blur to her—Emigrant Gap, Willow Springs, Prospect Hill, Saleratus Lake.

Sarah laid a hand on her forehead. To Maggie, it felt cool, wonderful. "Your fever has finally broken," Sarah said. "We're so glad. The priesthood blessing has really helped you."

Priesthood blessing? She didn't remember that at all.

Sarah saw it in her eyes. "Yes. Captain Willie, Brother James, and Eric all administered to you day before yesterday. You had us all very frightened."

"I am feeling a little better." It was a bit of a lie, unless you emphasized "a little," but compared to her few conscious memories of the past few days, this was a definite improvement. "Has it really been two days since we crossed the river?"

There was a tiny smile as Sarah shook her head. "That was four days ago, Maggie."

"Four?" she cried in dismay.

"Yes. You have been a very sick young woman. Your mother has been very worried. Eric has been frantic. You were in and out of delirium—chills, fever."

"Aches," Maggie added weakly. "My body aches everywhere, Sarah."

"I know. I think you got that from crossing the river. A lot of others did as well."

Maggie closed her eyes again. "Ah, yes." That *was* clear in her mind—the stunning shock of stepping into the icy water; the frightening push of the current against the handcart as she and Robbie fought to help their mother keep it moving; the blind panic when her feet had slipped on the rocky bottom and she had gone clear under; the cold wind when they came out on the other side; the violent shivering until she had gotten into dry clothing—which had taken over an hour because they had to get the younger children changed first. Her mother had finally taken her in her arms and held her tightly to get it under control. Oh, yes, she remembered the last crossing very well.

She started to sit up but instantly sensed the depths of her weakness. She gave it up. "Eric? He pulled the cart for a while, didn't he?"

"Yes. When you became too sick to walk, Eric asked Elder Willie if he could help your mother and Robbie pull."

Guilt washed over her. "Why didn't you just put me in one of the wagons?"

"Because every wagon was already full," Eric said.

Maggie turned in surprise. He was at the entry to the tent, holding the flap up. He stepped inside and came over beside them. He looked at Maggie closely for a moment, then turned to Sarah. "How is she?"

"A little better." She stood. "She's remembering more."

"Good."

Sarah smiled down at Maggie. "I'm going to go help Mama with supper, Maggie. If you need something, just call."

"Thank you, Sarah."

As Sarah went out, Eric knelt down beside Maggie. His face was twisted with concern. He reached out and touched her cheek with the back of his hand. "The fever is gone."

She turned her head so as to press her face against his touch. "Yes."

"You have all of us in very big worry, Maggie McKensie."

"I'm sorry."

"Don't be sorry. Just be better now."

"I would like that," she said with a wan smile. "Thank you for helping my family."

He shrugged.

"How are Olaf and the Nielsons? Are they all right?"

"Yah, they are fine. Bodil, the girl who travels with us, was sick too from the wet clothing. But she was better in two days."

"And Sister Bathgate and Isabella?"

"A wonder," he said with a smile. "They are doing well. The crossing did not seem to bother them."

"Good. You said the wagons were full. Are there many who are sick?"

"Yes, very many. The weather has been cold. And like you, many found the crossing of the river very bad. Many others are not sick but just too weak to pull carts any longer." He looked away. "The deaths grow more frequent now. We have lost another in our tent."

"Oh, no."

"And you remember Sister Larson, who's husband died a few days ago."

"Yes. With the five children."

"Yah. The little baby is now very sick. Sister Larson is so worn down she has not enough to nurse him well."

Maggie closed her eyes. More deaths. Young and old, the weak and the helpless. When would it stop?

He exhaled softly. "There were riders going east today. They carried a letter from Elder Richards."

"Really?"

"Yes. Is not good. He says we cannot expect wagons from Salt Lake before Pacific Springs."

She felt her body go cold. "Where is that, Eric?"

"Elder Willie says it is just by South Pass." He paused, debating whether to tell her all of it, then decided she would learn soon enough anyway. "That is yet one hundred more miles."

"A hundred miles?" She felt as if her heart had just fluttered to a stop.

"Yes. At least one week. Maybe eight or nine days."

"How much food do we have left?"

There was a long pause before he went on. "I talked with Brother

Willie before I came here, and he said the captains will meet tonight in council. They have taken accounting of the flour and food. There is not enough. They are thinking that starting tomorrow we will reduce rations even more. They will discuss the matter tonight, but from what Brother Willie says it looks like men will get ten and a half ounces of flour. Women and older children will get nine ounces. Younger children six ounces and infants three."

She felt a deep horror settle in upon her. They were already nearing the limit of their endurance. Didn't the captains know what this would do? But even as the thought came she pushed it away. Of course they knew. What a choice for their leaders to make. Did you give out more flour now so that the company would be strong enough to go forward, knowing you would run out before you reached Pacific Springs? Or did you reduce the rations further now so that the food would last, knowing that it would weaken the people even more so they couldn't make it to Pacific Springs? How terrible to have to make such a choice!

"It is not good, Maggie," Eric went on slowly. "Even the days are cold now. We had a little snow yesterday. Not enough to stay, but it was snow. And the nights are very bitter. We use axes to break the ice on the buckets this morning."

The very mention of ice made her shiver and she cuddled deeper into her bed. "Thank heavens for the buffalo robes. There's that to be thankful for at least."

"Some people throw robes away."

She jerked up, her eyes disbelieving. "No!"

"Yes. They are so heavy and the people are so weak. We pass eight or ten by the trail today." Then as she closed her eyes, deep despair settling in on her face, he was instantly contrite. "I am sorry, Maggie," he said.

She opened her eyes to see his shame.

"Your mother says I am to be making you happy, not sad."

She pulled her arm out from beneath the heavy robe and held

out her hand to him. She wanted to touch him, to let him know it was all right. "I am happy you are here."

"And I am happy you are better. You frighten me very badly."

"Eric? How are we going to get through this?"

"We ask the Lord to strengthen us," he said simply. "We ask Him to bless our food, though it is very little, and He does." Now his head came up. "We ask Him to give us strength in our bodies to go on until the others come. And He does. It is not big miracle, but it is miracle every day."

Now it was she who felt a wash of shame. For a moment there, she had completely forgotten about God. "Yes," she said, lying back. "We must do that."

He was staring out at nothing now. "All the days since my family joined the Church, we say grace on our food. We ask God to strengthen and nourish our bodies." He looked down at her and tightened his grip on her hand. "Now we really mean it. And He hears us. We go on day by day. We are weak but we go on."

"Yes." She reached up and touched his face. How sweet it felt to have him pour out his faith over her! She was so weak and so tired. His quiet assurance that God had not forgotten them was like honey to her soul. Finally, her eyes met and held his. "Eric?"

"Yes."

"Tell me about the ring."

It didn't seem to surprise him. He searched her face, then finally sighed and began to speak slowly. He told her about walking around the compound at Fort Laramie and finding the tin shop and then the ring. He told her about his pain when he thought of giving away his mother's gift, and then how he had known it was all right.

"Why didn't you tell me?" she asked in a whisper.

"I was afraid that you would think I . . ." He looked down at his hands, no longer able to meet her steady gaze. "When I think of asking you to be my wife, I think, 'Why would she say yes?' " His shoulders lifted and fell. "I decide it was better to wait a little while and see how courting goes."

She shook her head, admonishing him with her eyes. "Do you think I would really say no?"

"I had many hopes that you would not, but . . . I was afraid." He looked away. "And now there is no ring."

She was starting to feel tired now, but there was something she had to make clear to him. She pushed back the robe and forced herself up to one elbow. "Eric?"

"Yes?" He was looking at her with great concern now. "I would like it very much if you asked me to be your wife. I want you to know that."

"Really?" His mouth softened. "This is not the fever speaking to me?"

A laugh started to burst out of her, but instantly the cough cut it off. Her body shook as once more the cough racked her again and again. Even as she fought it, she watched the fear in his eyes grow. "I'm sorry," he said over and over.

Finally she got control again. Though spent, she forced a wan smile. "It is not the fever speaking, Eric. But . . ." She clung to him now. "But you can't ask me now."

He looked as if she had struck him. "Why not?"

She took a deep breath, feeling the bleakness come over her, as heavy as the buffalo robe. "Because if I don't make it, I want you to—"

He cut her off sharply. "No, Maggie. Don't you say it."

"Because if I die, I want you to be free to find—"

His hand shot out and he put three fingers over her lips, shutting off the words. Suddenly he bent down. His fingers came away and he kissed her gently.

It so took her aback that all she could do was stare up at him. He reached out and stroked her cheek. "Will you marry me, Maggie McKensie? Will you marry this silly Norwegian who says, 'Yah, yah,' and who does not have a ring, and who is not worthy of you, and whose love for you is stronger than all the hunger and sickness and cold that we have faced and have yet to face?"

"Eric, I . . . I can't. Not now."

He seemed genuinely surprised. "Of course not. It would not be seemly to have you married in your sickbed."

She swung weakly at him, which he dodged easily. "You know what I mean."

"I know what you mean," he said, suddenly fierce, "but I will not let you mean it. Say yes or I shall kiss you again."

A slow smile stole across her face. "No."

He bent down and kissed her once more, this time more firmly and much longer than before. She put her arms up and around his neck. When he pulled back, she was still looking up and smiling into his eyes. "No," she murmured again.

And so he kissed her yet a third time, holding her in his arms now and pulling her tightly to himself. "I will not let you die, Maggie."

"Eric, I–"

He shook his head, cutting her off. "Will you marry me, Maggie McKensie? Please say yes."

There was no hesitation in her anymore. "Yes," she whispered. "Yes, yes."

He closed his eyes and buried his face against her hair. "We will have to wait for a little while. I have not finished my courting of you."

Laughing, she pushed him away. "You'd better get going, then, Brother Pederson."

"I shall. Do you think a week is too soon to be proper?"

"I think a week is much too long, but if you insist . . ." She put her arms around him and clung to him for a long time, growing very quiet now. "In a week, we'll know, Eric. We'll know what's going to happen. Yes, a week is fine."

"I didn't mean that," he started to protest, but she cut him off.

"You must promise me one thing, Eric."

"What?"

He started to pull back, but she wouldn't let him. "Promise me!"

"I promise."

"If I . . ." She couldn't say it. Not now when the happiness inside her was like a glowing ball of light. "If something happens, I expect you to remarry, Eric. I expect—"

"No, Maggie!"

"Just listen to me," she said softly, her heart so filled with love now that she could hardly speak. "I don't care if you remarry. I want you to. But promise me, Eric. Promise me that when you get to Salt Lake you will be sealed to me in the new Endowment House. You can be sealed to more than one woman. Just promise me that I will have you forever."

"You are not—"

"*Promise me, Eric. Please!*"

He clung to her, burying his face against her again. "I promise."

Suddenly she was all matter-of-fact. "Good. Now there is one more thing."

He straightened. "What?"

"I have just discovered the most wonderful medicine for my sickness, Eric."

"What?"

She laughed in soft delight, and tapped her finger to her lips. "I'm not sure what they call it, but it needs to be applied right here at least twice a day."

II

Wednesday, 15 October 1856

When Maggie stepped outside her tent the next morning, Eric was there talking to her mother. She had heard him come, and they were close enough to the tent that she had heard the debate over whether she would have to ride in the wagons or if they could carry her again in the handcart. So she had finished dressing quickly, then stepped outside.

They both turned as she came out. Eric's mouth dropped open at the sight of her. He couldn't believe the transformation. Her head was high and she was smiling radiantly. Her dark hair was pulled back in a French braid—Sarah's doing, Eric guessed—and she walked with a visible bounce in her step. Her skin was still pale, and he could see the shadows around her eyes, but the eyes themselves were literally dancing with life.

"My goodness," Mary McKensie said. "Is that you, Maggie?"

Sarah James came out of the tent right behind her. She was smiling broadly. "No, this is some other young woman who has just joined our company. Let me introduce you."

Maggie laughed merrily and came over and gave her mother a hug.

"You look so much better, Maggie."

"I am so much better." She looked over her mother's shoulder at Eric. "I found some medicine that really made a difference."

Sarah hooted aloud and Eric blushed deeply, suspecting that Maggie had told her friend everything.

"Mother," Maggie said, taking a step back.

"Yes?"

"Eric asked me to marry him yesterday afternoon."

Behind her, Emma James leaped to her feet and squealed aloud. "Really?"

"Ah," Mary said with deep satisfaction. "So that is the medicine."

"Kind of." Maggie reached out her hand and Eric stepped forward and took it.

William James was staring. Sister James had one hand to her mouth, shaking her head with joy, tears springing to her eyes. "Oh, Maggie. How wonderful!"

Robbie was up and bouncing as if he were on a spring. "Really, Eric? Really? You're going to be my brother?"

"Well, I must ask your mother first if it is all right."

"You don't have to ask." Mary was crying now, her face filled with happiness. "You know the answer to that."

"When? When?" Emma was darting around, hurling the question first at Maggie and then at Eric. Reuben James was smiling and pounding Robbie on the back.

Eric turned to Maggie's mother. "I just begin courtship. If this were a normal life, I would ask for maybe one month or two. But out here?" He shrugged. "Would a week be too soon, Sister McKensie?"

She stepped to him and put her arms around him. "A week is fine. If you two decided you wanted to do it today, I would say yes to that too."

"No, Mother," Maggie blurted, a little alarmed. "A week. That will give us time to see if—" As if on perfect cue, she doubled over as another coughing fit struck. Eric stepped to her quickly and held her tightly, his eyes darkening as he heard the deep rasping sound she made. When it passed, she straightened, looking suddenly more vulnerable. "That will give us time to see what is happening," she finished weakly.

Eric shot her a warning glance, which she ignored. She turned as Emma, Sarah, Sister James, and the younger girls swarmed in to throw their arms around her and give their congratulations.

After a moment, Eric called to her. "Maggie?"

"Yes?"

"Before we march this morning, we must tell Sister Bathgate and Sister Park. After all, they think they are responsible."

"Of course." Then she had a thought. "No, you go, Eric. I'm going to write a note to Hannah."

"To Hannah?" Emma blurted. "How will you get a note to Hannah?"

"I'm going to put it on a stick. If someone is going east and sees it they can take it to her. If not, then they are only a week or two behind us. Elder Willie says people do that all the time."

"Oh, yes," Mary McKensie said. "Hannah would never forgive you if you didn't tell her as soon as you knew. You write the letter and I'll go ask Elder Willie where the best place is to leave it for her."

III

Sunday, 19 October 1856

There was no longer any question about stopping to rest for the Sabbath. The race against time and weather had reached the crisis stage. The sky was leaden and lowering. The wind was coming out of the northwest strongly enough to whip the canvas covers on the carts and fill the air with dust and particles of sand. It was their coldest day so far, and the air had that familiar feel that Eric had come to know so well in Norway. They would see their first real snow before the day was out, perhaps even before they stopped to noon. They had seen a few flurries before now but nothing that had even stuck to the ground. And while it was the Sabbath day, the captains had decided that the Lord would not stay the weather simply to give the emigrants a chance to pause for worship.

Eric stamped his feet up and down as he walked along beside Jens Nielson, leaning into the crossbar to keep the handcart moving forward. He wanted to wrap his arms around himself to try and keep warm, and for a moment he felt an intense regret that he had traded away his mother's sweater. If he had that under his coat, then . . . He shook it off. There was nothing to be gained down that path. He felt the cold most in his feet. His right boot had a hole in the sole about an inch in diameter. The left sole was paper-thin in a couple of spots but hadn't broken through yet. Two days before, Maggie had found a small piece of stiff cloth for him, which he slipped inside the right boot. That helped him walk more comfortably but didn't do much for the cold.

He thought back to this morning's meeting around the supply wagons, and shook his head. There was a brief report on those who had died and on the general health of the company. In earlier days, that alone would have been devastating. There had been another death in the night—the sixth since leaving Devil's Gate. The one yesterday had been a Scotsman, one of Maggie's hundred. He was twenty-seven years old! Four of those riding in the wagons were diagnosed as so far gone that they would likely not make it alive to camp tonight. If that was correct, that would mean ten deaths in four days. Now, in addition to morning prayers, each day's ritual included a morning burial.

He shuddered, remembering Maggie's feelings that she was going to die "before our journey's through," as the hymn put it. It had frightened him deeply. Eric lifted his eyes, searching the line ahead. When he finally picked Maggie out, he was relieved to see that she was still in the shafts of her cart, pulling beside her mother. That was good. He knew that she was stubborn enough to try to pull even if she was too weak, but her mother had promised Eric that she wouldn't let that happen. Most encouraging to Eric, Maggie had not mentioned death again since that afternoon in her tent. The deep cough was still of great concern, but she swore that even that was not as painful now as it had been at first.

He felt an overwhelming rush of thanks for the power of prayer and the priesthood. And love. It still astounded him what the promise of marriage had done for her.

Then his countenance fell again. What would this morning's announcement do to her now? The news of the deaths was bad enough, but when they were dividing out the daily rations and the last flour bag was emptied without everyone's getting even their full allotment, it was as though a death knell had sounded.

On the verge of weeping, something the company had never seen him do, Elder Willie announced that there was now nothing left in their stores except for the four hundred pounds of hard biscuits purchased at Fort Laramie—barely one pound per person—a few pounds of sugar, a partial bag of dried apples, and a quarter of a sack of rice. "This is it, brothers and sisters," he said, his voice torn with anguish. "The flour you now have in your hands has to last until the supply wagons reach us."

Eric shook his head. South Pass was still at least three days away. In their weakened condition, more likely four or five. Desperate measures were already being taken. Last night two boys in Eric's hundred had experimented with the hides taken from the two butchered cattle. They held the skins right in the flames to scorch off all the hair. Then they cut off long strips, roasted them until they were crisp, and sprinkled a little sugar on them. They claimed it made an acceptable supper. Even worse, two nights ago, Sarah James had taken her father's knife and cut off the tatters—the ragged pieces—from her shoes and added them to the soup she was making.

Hunger was an endless presence with Eric now, but he wasn't ready to go quite that far yet. He had passed on both the roasted hides and "tatters soup."

"That must be the Ice Springs."

Eric turned to look where Jens was pointing. They were crossing an endless emptiness, where even the artemisia, or sagebrush, was barely three or four inches high and sparsely scattered at that. They hadn't seen trees, other than along the Sweetwater, for two days now. Just ahead of where they were, the handcarts were crossing a low depression in the ground. Meandering through the low spot was a swatch of greener, thicker vegetation, looking almost swampy. Off to the left about a hundred yards, there was a circle of dark green, marking the source of the actual spring.

"Is there any ice left now?" Olaf asked from behind them. He was taking his turn pushing the cart at the moment.

"I don't think so," Jens answered. "Elder Ahmanson said that so many emigrants have dug down to find the ice over the years that it's all gone now."

Bodil Mortensen, the nine-year-old whom the Nielsons were bringing with them for another family, heard that and moved closer. "Was there really ice here, Uncle Jens?"

"That's what they claim. They said that if you dug down through the sod about a foot and a half there by the spring, you would find large slabs of ice. Evidently the water below ground froze in the winter, and then the sod acted like the sawdust in an icehouse and kept it frozen even in the middle of July and August. That's why they called it Ice Springs."

Elsie Nielson was walking alongside the cart, watching little Jens out of the corner of her eye. At the moment he was huddled in a blanket atop the load and seemed almost in a stupor. Elsie had on a thin coat and a shawl over that. Rags wound around her hands served as her mittens. Beneath her summer bonnet, her nose and cheeks were red. "All they need to do," she said, "is leave it open to the air today and they'll have ice here again."

"That's for sure," Olaf said.

Up ahead there was a shout and they saw Elder Willie waving his arms.

"Looks like we're stopping to noon," Jens said. He immediately began to slow. Eric did the same and they let the cart come to a stop. Then they carefully lowered the shafts, not wanting to wake little Jens, and stepped to one side.

Eric looked up as a tiny spot of white fluttered past his face. "Here it comes," he said.

The others looked up as well. Here and there the first snowflakes were slanting in on the cold wind.

"I'm going up with Maggie until it's time to move out again."

Jens and Elsie sank down to the ground beside the cart, grateful to be off their feet. They waved a hand, acknowledging that they had heard.

Eric glanced at Olaf. He was leaning heavily against the cart. "Do you want to come?"

Olaf just shook his head.

As Eric started forward, the snowflakes began to thicken. By the time he had covered the fifty or so yards to where the James and McKensie families were resting beside their carts, it had begun to snow in earnest. As he took off his gloves and dropped down beside Maggie, he turned his back to the wind and took her hand. Even through the layer of her mittens, he could feel how cold her hands were. The flakes were starting to stick to her coat, and he reached up absently and brushed them off her shoulders. "How are you doing?"

She nodded, too weary to answer. Then she turned her face to the northwest, directly into the wind. She half closed her eyes, letting the snow hit against her cheeks. "This is the day we have *not* been waiting for," she murmured. After a moment, she turned again, facing directly west, scanning the endless horizon. Now her eyes were wide and filled with fear. "Oh, Eric. Where are those wagons?"

According to Elder Willie, South Pass and the hoped-for relief were at least three days away, and that was assuming the wagons were there. He didn't have the heart, though, to remind her of that. He just shook his head as he took her hand and held it tightly. After a moment, she hunched over and began to cough, hugging her chest to ease the pain a little. Eric watched her with anxious eyes, rubbing her back softly while she fought to clear her chest again.

Chapter Notes

With the company and its animals failing rapidly now, the news that they could not expect to find the supply wagons before South Pass came as a terrible blow to the Willie Company. Though the letter from Elder Franklin D.

Richards is not mentioned in the company journal, John Chislett says it arrived on 14 October, while they were camped between Independence Rock and Devil's Gate in what is now central Wyoming (see *Remember*, p. 64).

Based on what we know now, they were down to no more than a week's supply of food, and that is taking into consideration the reduced rations and the fact that the increasing frequency of death provided the macabre "blessing" of having fewer mouths to feed. In their weakened state, it would take them at least ten days to reach South Pass. It was that grim arithmetic which, on 14 October as they were camped near Independence Rock, led the company to vote unanimously to reduce their rations even more (see journal entries in *Remember*, pp. 5–6).

Though she does not give a specific date, it would have been about this time that Sarah James came up with an idea that she would later describe thus: "I even decided to cook the tatters of my shoes and make soup of them. It brought a smile to my father's sad face when I made the suggestion, but mother was a bit impatient with me and told me that I'd have to eat the muddy things myself" (in Carol Cornwall Madsen, *Journey to Zion*, p. 628).

George Cunningham, who was a fifteen-year-old boy when he came with his family in the Willie Company, later said this: "Every particle [of the cattle] that could be used was taken, even the hide was rationed and after scorching the hair off, we would roast it a little over the coals and cut it in small pieces and it made what we considered a delicious supper" (in Carol Cornwall Madsen, *Journey to Zion*, p. 638).

Patience Loader, sister-in-law to John Jaques and a member of the Martin Company, wrote about the inadequacy of the food and how they turned to the Lord for help. Speaking of a time when they had obtained a soup bone and used it to make a meager broth, she wrote: "We did not get but very little meat as the bone had been picked the night before and we did not have only the half of asmall biscute as we only was having four oz. of flour aday. This we devided into portians so we could have asmall peice three times aday. This we eat with thankfull hearts and we allways as[k] God to bless to our use and that it would strengthen our bodys day by day so that we could performe our dutys. And I can testefie that our heavenly Father heard and answerd our prayers and we was blessed with health and strength day by day to endure the severe trials we had to pass through on that terrable journey before we got to Salt Lake City. We know that if God had not been with us that our strength would have failed us. . . . I can say we put our trust in God and he heard and answerd our prayers and brought us through to the valleys" (in Godfrey and others, *Women's Voices*, p. 238).

On the eighteenth/nineteenth of October, the Willie Company camped at the Fifth Crossing of the Sweetwater River. The 19 October entry in the company journal records five deaths. In John Chislett's narrative he records that the last of the flour was distributed equally among the camp that morning. Those two sources, as well as Levi Savage's journal, all note that it was bitterly cold and that sometime before noon the first snowstorm of the season descended upon the company. Savage notes that "the poorly clad women and children suffered much" (see *Remember*, pp. 7–8).

CHAPTER 20

DEER CREEK TO LAST CROSSING

I

Friday, 17 October 1856

When the fifth handcart company reached Deer Creek campground, Captain Edward Martin called a halt, even though they had come only five miles that morning. Hannah McKensie assumed they were stopping only to let the teams drink from the stream and to rest for a short time. She and Ingrid, with Sister Jackson pushing from behind, went forward another five or six rods, found a place close to the creek, and set the handcart down.

"What a beautiful spot," Hannah said, looking around even as she sank to the thick carpet of grass beneath her feet. "Let's stay here for a week."

Ingrid took the pair of shoes from around her neck and let them drop to the ground; then she sat down beside Hannah. "How about a month?" she said wearily.

Elizabeth Jackson came forward to lift little Aaron down from the cart. He immediately ran to the water and squatted down so he could put his hands in it. The other Jackson children were with their father far enough back that they hadn't reached the camp yet. Aaron

Jackson was not doing particularly well, and his wife had finally persuaded him—with additional urging from Hannah and Ingrid—to let them pull the cart this day and to simply walk with the children.

Elizabeth turned, searching the faces of those still coming in. "There they are," she said after a moment. "Can you watch little Aaron if I go help Brother Jackson with the girls?"

Hannah started to get up, feeling guilty. "I can go. Why don't you sit down for a while? You look exhausted."

There was a fleeting smile. "Everyone in this company looks exhausted," she said. Then she shook her head. "No. I'll go."

"Tell him we are saving him a place in the shafts tomorrow," Ingrid said.

She smiled. "He would like that, believe it or not. He hates it so badly to think that you girls have to carry his load."

Hannah tried to look stern. "Tell him that we're going to hire a little better-quality help if he keeps hobnobbing with all those sick people."

Elizabeth laughed as she started away. "I'll tell him," she called over her shoulder.

Five minutes later, Brother and Sister Jackson came up with Martha Ann and Mary Elizabeth. Ingrid and Hannah watched Aaron Jackson with some concern. He was walking slowly and looked very tired. "Good news," Elizabeth called out before they even reached them. "Captain Martin has called a halt for the day."

"For the day?"

"Yes. The teams need the rest—not that we don't—and this will also give us a chance to do some washing."

"Wonderful!"

"I'll help the brethren put up the tent," Brother Jackson said.

Elizabeth whirled on him. "You will sit down and rest, Aaron Jackson."

"Elizabeth, I can do that much."

"Do you want to ride in the sick wagons tomorrow?"

That stopped him. He had already done that once, and that was before every wagon was filled chockablock, with the sick jammed in like cordwood or forced to sit up shoulder-to-shoulder.

She glared at him until he finally nodded and found a place to sit down. Little Aaron darted over and climbed onto his father's lap.

"Oh, by the way," Elizabeth said to Hannah and Ingrid, "Elder Martin wants a meeting with all the company this afternoon at two o'clock."

As Hannah watched the people in her company come over to the grassy area beside the wagons and sink slowly to the ground, she found it hard not to give face to her inner apprehensions. She and Ingrid were young and strong, and so far, thank heavens, they had escaped the sickness that was striking down so many now. And yet, with all that, she felt like every step was made with lead boots, that every movement of her body required a conscious act of will. She had never been so totally, thoroughly, utterly tired before in her life. So what must the elderly be feeling now? How did those who were only marginally sick and had to walk keep going?

Two days before, Aaron Jackson had ridden in one of the wagons all day, trying to regain at least some strength. The next morning he had told them that conditions in his wagon were so terrible that he would not go back, no matter what it took for him to continue on.

She looked at the faces around the growing circle. What she saw in many cases was deeply alarming. The deaths were coming frequently now. Almost every morning there was another brief funeral service. Previously, though, it had been the elderly and those who were most seriously ill. Now she saw the shadow of death on the faces of young and old alike. The signs were the same—the gaunt face, the sunken cheeks, the empty look, the utter lassitude.

In two or three more days, according to Elder Martin, they would reach the Platte Bridge. There was a trading post there. Perhaps they could find additional food. Perhaps there would be something to postpone what was quickly becoming the inevitable.

She finally shook it off. She couldn't dwell on this or it would drag her down. She leaned over and nudged Ingrid. "Do you think Eric has worked up his nerve enough to tell Maggie that he likes her?"

Ingrid immediately shook her head. "No. Do you?"

"Probably not. What do you think Emma is doing about now?"

"Flirting with Olaf," Ingrid shot right back.

Hannah laughed. "Oh, yes. I'll bet you're right about that."

Sister Jackson was close enough to have heard. She leaned forward and smiled at her two charges. "The more important question is, what is *Olaf* doing?"

Now it was Hannah who answered without hesitation. "Dreaming of Ingrid and me."

They all laughed, winning questioning looks from some of those sitting around them. Trying not to giggle, Sister Jackson put a finger to her lips. "Shhh! Here comes Elder Martin."

Elder Edward Martin was a strong man and one who seemed to be filled with vigor and energy. As he came forward and climbed up onto the tailgate of the nearest wagon, Hannah saw the price being captain was exacting from him. There were dark circles around his eyes and deep lines around his mouth. He had been a little portly when she had first seen him at Iowa City. Now he was lean as a picket fence, and most of the humor in him had long since disappeared.

Once up, he straightened and took a moment to look around. His five subcaptains were standing nearby. There were a lot of people sitting around waiting for him to begin, but Hannah guessed that at least a quarter, and perhaps as many as a third, of the company had not come. They were simply too exhausted to care. They would hear about any decision eventually.

"Brothers and sisters, as your leaders we have met in council this afternoon to deal with the circumstances we now find ourselves in. This is one of the reasons that we stopped here today. In addition to everyone's needing the rest, we felt that there were critical decisions to be made."

He looked around, searching the faces that were before him. "I don't need to tell you," he finally said, looking at that moment very, very tired, "that our company is wearing down. We have worn ourselves out in getting as far as we have. We are living on reduced rations. Our cattle and oxen are wearing away as well. The weather grows colder all the time. Each day the wagons are filled with more and more who can no longer even walk, let alone pull the handcarts.

"What all of this together means is that in recent days our progress has slowed considerably. We are making fewer miles than we should—than we must!—if we are to survive until help from the Valley reaches us.

"We are still four hundred miles from Salt Lake. We clearly cannot make that on our own. As you know, we recently received a letter from Elder Richards promising that there will be wagons coming, but we likely cannot meet them before South Pass." He stopped for a moment and rubbed at his eyes. "At the rate we are presently going, we will not reach those wagons until at least a week after our supplies have run out. At least a week."

There was no outcry, no exclamations. He was only confirming what they already suspected. The only question was, what could they do differently than they had already done?

"We must increase our speed or we face imminent disaster, brothers and sisters, and yet we are too weak to do more than we are doing. Therefore, as your leaders, we are here to call for a sustaining vote on a proposal."

Now the heads that had been down came up. Those who barely seemed to be listening looked to the front.

"We see no alternative but to lighten the handcarts so we can press forward with greater dispatch." He stopped for just one moment. "I want to say that again so you understand me perfectly. We do not see *any* alternative. Owing to the growing weakness of both our people and our animals, our baggage, including bedding, cooking utensils, and clothing, has to be reduced immediately. We propose that each person eight and older be limited to ten pounds of personal belongings each. Each child under eight is to carry no more than five pounds."

He stopped as if expecting an uproar. It did not come. There were stunned looks here and there, but many more faces were showing relief and gratitude.

"All in favor, please show by raising your right hand."

Hannah looked around. She could not see anyone whose hand was not up.

"If you are opposed to this plan, you may also make that known."

He waited, turning his head back and forth. There was no movement. He nodded curtly. "The voting has been unanimous in the affirmative. All right, brothers and sisters, you'd better go to your tents and go to work."

By the time the sun went down that night, the air temperature had dropped to near freezing. But tonight, at least for a time, the cold would not be a problem. In four different places in the camp there were roaring bonfires. The flames lit up the grove of trees and were reflected off the clear, cold waters of Deer Creek. The choices were painful but relatively easy. Most of the extraneous things—family treasures, personal items of lesser consequence, dressier clothing—had long since been discarded, and the priorities now were simple. Anything that was food stayed. Not that individuals had much of their own any longer, but if they did, that was set aside first. Next came extra clothing. Hannah had only two complete sets of clothing. Inside the tent she removed what she was wearing, and put on her other set, which was cleaner and less worn. She kept a blouse because she could wear it beneath her dress. She also kept one extra petticoat for when they got wet crossing streams. She could put on something dry at least. The rest she folded neatly, then walked to the nearest bonfire and threw it in.

The outerwear was more difficult. They had four hundred miles to go and it was mid-October. So far they had not seen snow. That couldn't last. She picked out her heaviest coat, a pair of mittens her mother had bought before leaving Scotland, and a thick woolen scarf. A sweater, a light jacket, a heavy woolen petticoat, and two extra pairs of stockings went into another pile. She made a second trip to the fire.

When she got back to the tent, Ingrid was just picking up the pile of discards she had made. Off to one corner sat the new pair of shoes that she had carried around her neck since the weigh-in at Iowa City. She saw Hannah look at them and immediately started shaking her head. "Those shoes were never part of my seventeen pounds, Hannah," she said defensively. "They won't be part of my ten pounds now."

Hannah raised her hands in protest. "I wasn't suggesting anything, Ingrid. When I saw them I was just wondering if you were thinking of discarding them."

"I know it's foolish, but I want to have something for when I see President Young. I don't mind carrying them."

Sister Jackson looked up. On the far side of the tent, she was going through her children's clothing, making her separation. She stood, then walked over and laid her cheek against Ingrid's. "Maybe someone needs to do something foolish, just so we don't go insane."

Grateful for her understanding, Ingrid picked up her pile and left the tent. Hannah stood where she was, looking down at the bed where she slept.

"How much are you going to keep?" Sister Jackson asked.

"I'm hoping I am close to my ten pounds now," she answered. "I only have a quilt and one blanket and my pillow."

But Hannah was wrong. When Brother Martin and Brother Jaques came by with the scales, she was still at twelve pounds. Ingrid was the same. As they looked at each other, Brother Jaques spoke quietly. "When the wagons from Salt Lake come, they will bring more blankets. It is better to discard one of them than to give away too many clothes."

"*If* the wagons come from Salt Lake," Hannah responded.

"They will come, Sister McKensie," Elder Martin said firmly. "Our brethren and sisters in the Valley will not forget us."

She nodded. "I know. But will they reach us in time?"

"We cannot lose heart," Brother Jaques said. "If it is our time to find a place of rest and peace, then may His will be done. But if it is not, we must keep our faith up. We must!"

Hannah felt her face grow hot. "I'm sorry, Brother Jaques. You are right. I'm sorry I was discouraged for a moment."

"We all get discouraged," Elder Martin answered. "But Brother John is right. God is still in the heavens and we are still part of His covenant people. He will not forsake us."

Hannah leaned over and removed her woolen blanket from the scales, watching anxiously as the two pans of the scale readjusted themselves. Then slowly they came into balance. "That will do it," Brother Martin said.

Hannah nodded, trying not to think about the last two nights when she had been so cold, even with her clothes on, and that had been with both the blanket and the quilt. Well, tonight she would have to keep her coat and mittens on as well.

Ingrid didn't even wait. She took off her blanket and put it on top of Hannah's. That did it for her as well. As the two brethren turned to weigh the Jacksons' belongings, Elder Martin spied the shoes. He looked at Ingrid, one eyebrow rising.

"I always carry them," she said quickly. "I won't put them on our handcart."

He nodded, something in his eyes showing quiet admiration. "I know you won't, Sister Christensen. I had just wondered if you would keep them."

"Yes, I am keeping them."

Hannah looked at Ingrid, then picked up the two blankets, handing one to Ingrid. "Shall we, my dear?" she said, extending her elbow as if to an escort at a fancy ball.

"Yes," Ingrid said with a smile. "I would be most honored to accompany you."

The flames of the bonfire were now towering ten or fifteen feet in the air. The fire crackled and roared like some wild thing, and the heat radiated outward in shimmering waves. Hannah looked at Ingrid. "Ready?"

She nodded.

"One. Two. Three."

Together they heaved the blankets into the fire, then stepped back. For a moment or two the blankets actually dampened the flames, but the bed of coals—now a good twenty feet in diameter—was glowing white-hot. The blankets began to smoulder, spewing out puffs of dark black smoke. Then there was a sudden *whoosh* and they burst into flames.

Hannah forced herself to smile at her friend. "Did you ever think burning your bedding would be so much fun?"

II

Sunday, 19 October 1856

Hannah McKensie stared into the black water, watching it swirl past her, already feeling the shivers up her back, though she had not so much as put the sole of her foot in yet. All up and down the riverbank, the Edward Martin Company had come to a halt, standing at the water's edge, gazing at this barrier as though it were a stone wall ten feet high and five feet thick.

"Oh, Mother!"

Hannah turned. Aaron Jackson was staring at the swift current in stark horror. He reached out and clutched blindly for his wife's arm. Elizabeth was also gazing at the water, her face like stone. She already knew what this would mean for her husband.

When they had lightened the carts two days before, it seemed to be just what Brother Jackson needed. A wind from the south had also begun to blow, moderating the temperatures somewhat, and that had helped as well. Yesterday he even took his turn pulling the cart and had gone to bed jubilant. It devastated him to think that he could not care for his family and that Ingrid and Hannah had to take over his responsibilities.

Then sometime during the night the wind had shifted around to the northwest. The temperature plunged. When they awoke this morning there was ice along the edge of the creek. The canvas of their tent, still damp from a previous rain, was so stiff they finally had to just roll it up as best they could. By the time they moved out at half past seven, the sky was gray and the wind stiffening steadily. It didn't matter what one had on. It pierced coats, shirts, sweaters, dresses, petticoats, trousers, socks, boots.

It was more than Aaron Jackson could tolerate. Though he insisted on taking first turn in the shafts, he went less than a quarter of a mile before he had to stop. Since then he had plodded along behind them, his head down, helped along by his two young daughters.

"Sit down and rest for a time, Aaron," Elizabeth said. "Brother Martin's not here yet. We have a moment before we have to cross."

He did so, moving around the cart so as to get at least some shelter from the wind. Hannah saw that he averted his face so that he didn't have to look at the river. Neither did he look up at the darkening sky.

In the last hour the clouds had thickened and the wind shifted again until now it was coming nearly straight out of the north. An occasional snowflake whipped by, a dreaded hint of what Hannah was afraid was soon to come.

Beside Hannah, Ingrid sat down on the dry grass and wearily took the shoes from off her neck. Hannah looked around. Evidently it wasn't just the Jacksons who were waiting for Captain Martin to come up and give the signal. No one had ventured into the river as yet. Feeling the weakness in her own legs, she sank down beside her friend and tentmate. She sighed, a sound of deep longing, then lay back and closed her eyes.

"What was that for?" Ingrid said, stretching out now as well.

"I would have paid twice what that trader asked, if I had it," she muttered.

"For the bridge?"

"Yes."

Ingrid nodded and turned her head to look downstream. They couldn't see the Platte Bridge any longer, of course. They had come five miles farther on since they had passed that magnificent structure and the trading post nearby. But she could see it in her mind, etched against the trees and the gray sky, eight hundred feet long and looking as solid as if it were made of steel. The handcart company had stood near its southern end while they waited for Elder Martin and a few other people to finish their meager purchases at Richard's trading post. For almost an hour the bridge had beckoned to them, enticing them like the sound of the Siren in Greek lore. "Come, walk across my spans and escape the black water below. Feel the solid planks beneath your cart wheels. What I cost is only a pittance to the toll the river will exact from you. Come and roll across before the storms descend."

They had not, of course. What little cash reserves they had were used to purchase the few meager provisions still available at the trading post. There was nothing left for paying a toll. And so they had left John Richard's bridge and come another five miles upriver to where the Mormon Ferry had once shuttled wagons and people back and forth. And now they waited for the signal to make that crossing.

Off about a quarter of a mile, Hannah could see the white tops of the Hunt Wagon Company. They would not cross yet. With more ability to carry food, they didn't have quite the same urgency as the handcart company. She turned. Across the river to the north and about a mile west of the crossing, the wagons of the other independent wagon company could be seen. The Hodgett Company had been far enough ahead that they had already crossed and gone into camp. She shook her head. It was hard not to be envious.

The Hunt and Hodgett independent wagon companies had been traveling along somewhat in tandem with their company since they had left Florence. Sometimes they were ahead; often they were behind. Late the day before, the Hodgett Company had passed them and camped out ahead of them a mile or so. Then, as the Martin Company was preparing to roll out this morning, the Hunt Wagon Company had passed them as well. When they reached the last crossing, the Hodgett was already across and the Hunt had gone into camp.

It was discouraging to see them roll past with such ease. Better equipped and provisioned, the wagon companies had not been forced as yet to go on reduced rations or to jettison their belongings. They helped the emigrants in the handcart company when they could, sharing food and offering rides to the sick, but usually they were not traveling together, and so their ability to help was limited. Also, with five hundred people in the Martin Company, more than was in both wagon companies combined, it wasn't possible that the wagoners could relieve even one-tenth of the suffering of their fellow emigrants.

They heard the rattle of a wagon and sat up. Brother Martin was on his horse riding alongside the company's lead supply wagon. The other two wagons were farther behind. The supply wagons had been in the rear of the company, loaded past their capacity with the sick and the exhausted. Even from here, Hannah could see the feet and legs dangling out the back of the first wagon box. Supposedly the wagons were to be used only to carry the company's tents and food. Instead they were now moving infirmaries. Hannah didn't have to look to see who was there. Most would be the elderly or the young children.

Captain Martin dug his heels into the horse's flanks and rode up to the line of people. "All right, folks," he shouted. "We'll take the sick across first." He pointed to a spot where the bank had been cut down by the passage of many wagons. "We'll go in here and then angle upstream to that spot where you can see an opening through the brush. That's the trail."

He waved at the lead teamster, who slapped the reins over the backs of his four mules. "H'yah," he shouted. The animals lunged forward, and in a moment they were into the water.

Now every eye was following. The sick struggled to a sitting position and pulled their feet up as the rear wheels entered the river. Without thinking, Hannah stood up. Ingrid came up beside her. Their gaze was riveted on the wheels. This would give them the measure of the river, only they would be the "mules" and their handcart would be the wagon.

At this point the river was about five rods, or about twenty-five or thirty yards, across. Ten feet out and the hubs of the large back wheels disappeared into the water. In the front, the mules were up to their bellies. The rattle of the metal tires on the cobblestones in the riverbed sounded clearly in the cold air. The second wagon went in behind the first, and Hannah saw some of the walkers, or the footmen, move in behind it, hanging on to the sides of the wagon box so that they had some help in crossing. Another twenty feet and the mules of the lead wagon were chest deep, holding their heads high. One brayed anxiously. A woman in the back of the wagon cried out as the water reached the wagon box and began to seep through the cracks into where she and the others were sitting.

"H'yah, mules!" the teamsters yelled, cracking the whip above their heads. Hannah watched, sick at heart. The water was an inch or two deeper than the wagon box and now all of the sick were clambering to get out of the water. But it didn't get any deeper, and in a few moments the mules were in shallower water again. They broke into a lumbering trot, and in seconds the wagon was across. The second and third followed while those pulling handcarts watched in growing dismay.

Hannah turned to Ingrid. The bottom of a wagon box came about chest high on the two of them. They had hoped that they could keep dry above the waist. Now that they saw how deep the water was, that hope was dashed to pieces.

"All right," Captain Martin shouted. "That's how it's done. You'll have to watch the handcarts. They're a lot lighter and the current will start pushing on them. Just keep angling upstream and head for where the wagon came out."

Up and down the line people got to their feet and moved to their carts. Others walked to the water's edge. Just a short distance upstream from where they were, a man hoisted his wife onto his back. He turned to his two boys, both in their teens. "Wait here. I'll be back and help you with the cart."

Hannah shuddered. That meant he would have to cross the river three times. But he did not hesitate. The moment his wife settled herself onto his back he stepped into the water. There was an audible gasp as the water hit them. Farther on an older brother picked up his sister, a girl of about six, and moved forward. A man and a wife without children followed with their cart, the first to make the attempt.

"Not all at once," Elder Martin shouted. "Don't get tangled up with one another."

Just then a voice from behind them called out. "Brother Aaron, are you all right? Can you make it?"

They turned. John Jaques and his wife, Zilpah, were approaching. John was pulling the cart; his wife was pushing. On top, their little Flora, who was two, sat perched in a place her father had made for her on top of their belongings. She held the baby that had been born the night after the Jaqueses had left Florence about seven weeks before.

"Aaron is going to go over on his own," Elizabeth answered quickly, before her husband could respond. "The girls and I will take the handcart across."

"I can come back," Jaques volunteered.

Aaron Jackson shook his head. He was pale and drawn now. The very sight of the people entering the water and the cries and gasps that were sounding all up and down the line had shaken him deeply. "You have two little ones to care for, Brother John. I'll be all right."

"Thank you for offering," Elizabeth said. "Zilpah, where is the rest of your family?"

Zilpah turned and pointed. "They're coming. Mother has met someone in the Hunt Company they knew in New York. He is going to help her and my sisters."

"Wonderful," Elizabeth said.

There was a sudden cry that spun them around. Another father had a little girl about five or six on his back and had just reached midriver. As the full force of the current caught him, his feet slipped on the rocky bottom. The little girl screamed as he twisted and went down, disappearing into the icy water. In a moment there was a flash of white and another scream. The little girl was flailing wildly as she bobbed to the surface. Then the man's head came up. "Betsy! Betsy!"

Captain Martin shouted something and spurred his horse. The first man to attempt the crossing, the one who had carried his wife over, had just reached the other side. He set his wife down, whirled and saw what was happening, then spurted forward. He ran about ten yards along the bank, then gave a mighty leap out into the water. In a moment Captain Martin reached the floundering father and grabbed him by the hand. He looked around, but the other man had reached the girl and had her in his arms. She was still screaming hysterically. A cry of relief went up as father and daughter were taken safely to the opposite bank.

"Thank heavens," Elizabeth Jackson said, still shaking with the thoughts of that little girl drowning. Then she made up her mind. She reached down, picked up young Aaron, and hoisted him up onto the canvas that covered their belongings in the cart. "Hold on, Aaron. Hold on tight!"

Her husband came forward, nearly stumbling as he tried to grab her arm. "Elizabeth, I'm not going to let you take that over alone."

She took his hands and held them tightly, peering into his eyes. "You know you can't do it, Aaron. We'll be all right. Wait here. If I can't find someone to help you, I'll come back."

"No," he began, but he could barely croak it out. And in that instant he knew that it didn't really matter what the heart wanted to do. If the body was not capable of answering, there was nothing to be done. He let go of his wife and stepped back, lowering his eyes and looking away.

Hannah and Ingrid had come over now. "We'll help, Brother Jackson. It will be all right." Hannah took Mary Elizabeth and swung her up beside her brother. "Hold onto Aaron. Close your eyes if you get frightened."

She started to cry. "I'm scared, Hannah."

Hannah smiled and reached up and squeezed her hand. "My brave little Mary Elizabeth? Frightened? I can't believe that."

The trembling lip steadied and the five-year-old wiped quickly at her eyes. "All right," she said.

"Martha Ann," Sister Jackson said to her older daughter, "you hold on to the back of the cart. If it gets too deep for you to touch bottom, then just float, but don't let go."

"Yes, Mama."

"Elizabeth, I—"

She turned to her husband and hugged him tightly. "It will be all right, Aaron. Just wait here." She kissed him, then hurried to where Hannah and Ingrid were already getting into the pulling box.

"I think you should be at the back, Sister Jackson," Hannah said, "in case Martha Ann needs help."

"Yah, yah," Ingrid said. "Hannah and I will pull."

"All right." Sister Jackson moved around to the back to stand beside her daughter. As she did so, Hannah looked up. What had been an occasional snowflake had suddenly become a swirl, coming in almost horizontally on the gusting wind. To the west, the sky was almost black, promising worse yet to come. It seemed like the wind had become in an instant even more bitterly cold. She grabbed the crossbar, gritting her teeth. "Let's go," she muttered.

Hannah steeled herself, knowing that the water would be an enormous shock to her body, but as she stepped into the river and sank to her knees a cry was torn from her lips. The last four or five creeks had been terribly cold, but this was ten times worse. The cold gripped her with such ferocity that for a moment it felt like her legs had been amputated. She heard Ingrid gasp beside her. "Pull!" she cried. "Pull!"

As the water reached her waist and then her chest, Hannah was breathing in and out so rapidly, trying to cushion the numbing shock that engulfed her, that suddenly she felt light-headed. The current was more powerful than she had expected, and she felt her body start to lift. She drove her legs downward, trying to get some grip on the bottom, but the rocks were like rounded pieces of ice. The skirt of her dress was acting like a sail in the water and dragging her feet along with the current. She was slipping and sliding like a drunken man.

Suddenly the back end of the handcart started to swing around behind them. "Keep going!" Elizabeth screamed. "Don't stop."

Martha Ann was sobbing now and that started Mary Elizabeth. "Mama! Mama!" she wailed.

"Hold on to Aaron!" Elizabeth blurted. "It's all right."

Hannah felt terror now, and it was even more numbing than the water. What if she went down as that man had done? What if she couldn't hold on? She felt the cart swing around so that they were no longer angling across the river but were pointed directly upstream. It was as if it were floating now and no longer under her control. They were not moving forward at all but being carried downstream by the current. Beside her, Ingrid was crying out something frantically. Dimly, Hannah realized she was crying out in Danish.

"Here! Take hold!"

Hannah looked up. One of the men from the wagons had waded out into the river from the far side. He had a lariat curled in one hand. He tossed an end and it hit Hannah in the face. She let go of the crossbar with one hand and clutched at it wildly. Catching it, she yanked it toward her with a sob of relief.

"Wrap it around you!"

Fumbling wildly, she pulled the rope around behind her, then fed it to Ingrid. Ingrid put it around her waist as well, then handed the end back to Hannah. She gripped it with both hands, using only her body now to push against the crossbar. Another man and an older boy splashed out to grab the rope as well. There was a powerful tug as they began pulling it toward them hand over hand.

Hannah cried out with joy. They were moving forward. The cart swung back around now, and through the clouds of snow she could see they were once again headed for the bank where the other carts were coming out. In a moment, the water was only to her waist, then to her knees.

"We made it!" Ingrid said, half sobbing. "We made it."

Once they were on solid ground, Elizabeth came around and she and Ingrid and Hannah fell into each other's arms. Only then did the cold come slamming back at them. Hannah was wet from the neck down, and she could already feel her dress stiffening in the freezing wind. Her body began to shake violently. The snow was coming hard now and she felt the sting of something against her cheeks. Her heart sank as she realized what it was. It was sleet. Mixed with the snow there was a freezing rain.

"We've got to get dry clothes," Ingrid cried.

The problem was, they didn't have a full set of dry clothes now, not after they had lightened their loads by feeding the bonfires day before yesterday. Hannah had an extra petticoat, but that was all.

"Get the blankets," Sister Jackson commanded. "We've got to get warm."

With their teeth chattering and their hands shaking so violently that they could barely grasp the lashing, they pawed at their load. Hannah helped Mary Elizabeth down and then little Aaron. Both were sobbing quietly. Hannah was not the only one who had experienced terror in that crossing.

Holding the blankets up to provide some small amount of privacy, Hannah and Ingrid watched as Elizabeth helped Martha Ann strip down to her underclothing and put on a dry petticoat and then a sweater. They wrung out her dress as best they could and then she put it back on over what she wore. Then Sister Jackson held the blanket for Hannah and Ingrid. Hannah tried to protest that Sister Jackson should change first, but she refused. If she had to go back for Aaron, there was no sense changing yet.

When they finished they wrapped blankets around themselves and now turned to look across the river. In the twenty minutes that had passed since they had arrived on the south bank, the storm had hit with a fury. It was nearly a blizzard now. The wind was tearing at their clothing, making it difficult to stand. The snow and sleet was coming so thick that it often obscured their view for more than a few yards. The ground was already white, showing the footprints and tracks where the people were coming out of the river.

It took a moment for them to spot Brother Jackson. He was standing by a small tree, half hunched over, steadying himself as best he could. Sister Jackson shouted and waved. His head came up, but in the swirling snow he didn't seem to be able to see her. Hannah and Ingrid started waving too. "Brother Jackson! We're over here."

Now he saw them. With an effort he straightened.

"Wait, Aaron, I'm coming to help."

"No!" He waved his hands back and forth. "I'm coming. You stay there."

He stepped to the water's edge, hesitated for only a moment, then walked into the river. They saw him stiffen as the shock of the cold hit him. He came another few feet until he was in the water to his knees, then he slipped on the rocky bottom and went down. Elizabeth lunged forward, crying out. "Keep coming, Aaron! Keep walking."

He looked around, dazed and bewildered, then slowly staggered up again. His head swung back and forth slowly. A short distance away, the water was split by a sandbar about a foot wide and three or four feet long. It was barely out of the water. He turned, stumbling towards it, then collapsed into a heap when he reached it.

"Aaron!" Sister Jackson's cry rent the air. She started forward, hands reaching for him as though she were already to him.

Hannah sprang forward and caught her dress. "No, Sister Jackson. You stay here. I'll get him."

"I'll help you," Ingrid said, running forward with her.

Without hesitation, they leaped into the water again, then pushed forward as swiftly as they could. This time they had two things in their favor. Their bodies were already numbed and half-frozen and the shock was not as great. Also, they were angling downstream now and the current was pushing partially against them. In less than a minute they had crossed to the sandbar and reached Aaron Jackson.

As they got under each arm and lifted him up, Hannah saw Elder Martin crossing the river on his horse. She waved frantically, but he had already seen them and was turning towards them. When he reached them he bent over in the saddle. "Brother Jackson, are you all right?"

Aaron looked up. His lips were blue and his whole body was shaking. "Too weak," he mumbled. "Can't make it."

"Help me get him up on the horse," their captain commanded.

He held out his hand. With him pulling and Ingrid and Hannah pushing, they got Aaron up behind the saddle. Hannah actually had to reach up and put one of Brother Jackson's arms around Captain Martin so he could hold on.

"You two grab hold of the horse's tail," Captain Martin said. "We can at least help pull you across."

In two more minutes it was over. Aaron Jackson sat huddled on the ground as Elizabeth stripped off his shirt and put on a dry one. She had a towel, already quite damp, with which she rubbed him vigorously, trying to restore the circulation.

Captain Martin watched for a moment, the snow swirling around him. Then, seeing that Aaron was going to be all right, he straightened in the saddle and looked to the south. Most of the handcarts were across. The last two or three were now in the river, coming across as best they could. The river was alive with people moving across it, some with children on their backs, some pulling and dragging their carts, some just pushing across alone, no longer aware of where their families were.

"As quickly as you can, start moving," Elder Martin shouted. "We've got to get to camp and get some fires started."

"Thank you, Brother Martin," Sister Jackson said, looking up at him, on the verge of tears.

The captain brushed that aside. "Watch for firewood as you go. There have been so many people pass through here, firewood is going to be scarce."

With a wave he rode away, shouting at those who were standing around in half a stupor to get moving. Sister Jackson wrapped the blanket more tightly around her husband's shoulders, then looked to Hannah and Ingrid. "We're going to have to make a place for him in the cart. He can't walk."

They nodded and went around to the back of the cart, pulling things out and rearranging them as quickly as they could. Both girls were trembling and could barely move their fingers. They had now soaked every piece of clothing they owned. The skirts of their dresses crackled as they moved, already frozen in the howling wind. Their wet shoes slipped on the ground, which was now covered with half an inch of wet, slushy snow.

Finished, they turned around. Sister Jackson already had her husband on his feet. It said something about his condition that he offered not one word of protest as they helped him into the cart. They pulled the canvas around him as best they could.

"Martha Ann," Sister Jackson said, "you get up there with Papa. Hold little Aaron on your lap and stay close together so you can stay warm." She turned. "Mary Elizabeth. You're going to have to walk with Mama. Come, take my hand."

Moving as though their joints had rusted shut, Hannah and Ingrid moved to the front of the cart and prepared to get into the shafts. But as Ingrid bent over to pick up the cart, she cried out. "Oh, no!" Her hands flew up to touch her neck.

Hannah whirled. "What?"

"My shoes!"

Hannah stared, feeling suddenly sick. The new shoes that had hung around Ingrid's neck for almost two full months now, that had become so much a part of her that they were like a coat or a shawl and were barely noticed anymore, were gone. "Where are they?"

Ingrid turned slowly, staring across the river. One hand came up to point. Tears welled up and began to trickle down her cheeks. "They're over there."

Hannah's eyes searched until she recognized the little bush where they had stopped to wait for the crossing. For one quick moment through the storm she thought she could discern a bump in the snow beside the bush. She couldn't be sure. It may have been a large stone.

"Oh, Ingrid!" she cried. She opened her arms and Ingrid fell into them and began to sob. It was the first time Hannah had ever seen her cry openly like this. "Maybe someone in the Hunt Company will see them—" She stopped. They both knew it wasn't true. They were already hidden by the snow. In another hour no one would even notice the bump anymore.

Ingrid pushed away, wiping at her eyes with the backs of her hands. "We have to go," she said. "I'm all right. It will be all right."

Hannah was weeping, feeling as though her heart were breaking. "President Young will understand, Ingrid. He'll understand."

Chapter Notes

Bearing in mind that the Martin Company did not keep a consistent daily journal as did the Willie Company, it is more difficult to put together a detailed and accurate day-to-day picture of what was happening with them. As John Jaques himself wrote: "Thenceforth [after leaving Fort Laramie], until the close of the journey we were so fully occupied in taking care of ourselves that we had little time to spare to note details with exactness, and many notes that were made at that time were lost" (in Bell, *Life History and Writings of John Jaques,* pp. 141–42). But one thing is clear. Their situation only became worse as they approached the crisis brought on by diminishing rations, colder weather, and dying animals. All indications are that the Martin Company, with a higher proportion of the elderly, were having a more difficult time making their way.

No mention is made by those in the Martin Company about the letter from Elder Richards, but it is difficult to believe that he would send information about the supply wagons back to the Willie Company and not do the same for the Martin group. The author therefore has assumed that the same letter continued eastward by the hand of someone and eventually reached the Martin Company too.

It is John Jaques who gives us the detail about the decision to burn badly needed clothing and blankets on 17 October (see Bell, *Life History and Writings of John Jaques,* p. 144). Edward Martin was not a novice on the trail, neither was he foolish enough to think that they could go another four hundred miles in the winter season without suffering from the loss of those goods. That decision says much about how desperate their condition had become at that point. Tragically, it was only two days later that the first snowstorm swept out of the northwest and engulfed the two handcart companies.

As will be seen from later journal entries, this storm was the front end of a massive winter storm coming out of Canada that would cover a huge area of the country and last for several days. It caught the Willie Company at Ice Springs, just west of the fifth crossing of the Sweetwater. It caught the Martin Company at the last crossing of the North Platte, just as they were fording the river.

It is also John Jaques who describes the physical state of the Martin Company emigrants about this time: "In the progress of the journey it was not difficult to tell who was going to die within two or three weeks. The gaunt form, hollow eyes, and sunken countenance, discolored to a weather-beaten sallow, with the gradual weakening of the mental faculties, plainly foreboded the coming and not far distant dissolution" (quoted in Christy, "Weather, Disaster, and Responsibility," p. 36).

Though the Martin Company did not keep consistent records, one event is mentioned in virtually every diary or later account written by members of the company, and that is the last crossing of the North Platte River. The storm alone would have been a crisis of enormous proportions, given the weakened state they were in; but to have it hit when they were soaking wet and already chilled to the bone is almost beyond comprehension. That any survived is a miracle. That most did is almost inconceivable. One tiny glimpse of what they suffered is offered by Josiah Rogerson, Sr., in an account published much later in the *Salt Lake Tribune.* He said that "the results of the wading of this river by the female members of our company was immediately followed by partial and temporary dementia, from which several did not recover till the next spring" (in Turner, *Emigrating Journals,* p. 118).

Aaron Jackson was very sick at this time and stayed behind as Elizabeth took her three children across the river. When he tried to make it on his own, he came only partway before collapsing on a sandbar. In the novel, Hannah and Ingrid go to his aid. In actuality, Elizabeth was traveling with her sister, Mary Horrocks Leavitt, who went back to help Aaron and then later helped Elizabeth pull him in the handcart to the camp. Someone on horseback also came to help and carried him across the river, according to Sister Jackson's later account (see Kingsford, *Leaves from the Life of Elizabeth Horrocks Jackson Kingsford,* pp. 5–6).

Patience Loader, sister-in-law to John Jaques, whose father, James Loader, had died at Ash Hollow, wrote a detailed account of her experience and describes the crossing in some detail. "We traveled on until we came to the last crossing of the Platte River. Here we met the wagon company. They were camped for the night. We of the handcart company had orders from Captain Martin to cross the river that afternoon and evening." In the wagon company was a man they knew who offered to help.

His heart went out in sympathy for mother and us girls when we told him that dear father was dead. He felt sorry to see us having to wade the river and pull the cart through. He took mother on his mule behind him, telling her to hold fast to him and he would return and bring the cart through the river. This we did not know he intended to do so we started to cross the river pulling our own cart. The water was deep and very cold and we were drifted out of the regular crossing and we came near to drowning. The water came up to our arm pits. Poor mother was standing on the bank screaming, as we got near the bank I heard her say, "For God's sake some of you men help my poor girls." Mother said she had been watching us and could see we were drifting down stream. Several of the brethren came down and pulled our cart up the bank for us and we got up the best way we could. Mother Loader showed great wisdom by carrying in her basket dry stockings to put on the family after they had waded streams, and on her body she wore extra underskirts for the same purpose. Mother took off her underskirts and apron and put on us to keep the wet clothing from us. . . .

When we were in the middle of the river I saw a poor man carrying his child on his back. He fell down in the water. I never knew if he was drowned or not. I felt sorry that we could not help him but we had all we could do to save ourselves from drowning.

We had to travel in our wet clothes until we got to camp [on the north side of the river]. Our clothing was nearly frozen on us and when we got to camp we had very little dry clothing to put on. We had to make the best of our poor circumstances and put our trust in God that we take no harm. It was too late to go for wood and water. The wood was too far away. That night the ground was frozen so hard we were unable to drive any tent pins in and the tent was wet. When we had taken it down in the morning it was somewhat frozen so we stretched it open the best we could and got in under it until morning. (In Bell, *Life History and Writings of John Jaques,* pp. 145–46)

BOOK 5

THE RESCUE

OCTOBER 1856

My faith is, when we have done all we can, then the Lord is under obligation, and will not disappoint the faithful. . . .

. . . If there had been no other way, the Lord would have helped them [the handcart companies], if He had had to send His angels to drive up buffaloes day after day, and week after week. I have full confidence that the Lord would have done His part; my only lack of confidence is, that those who profess to be Saints will not do right and perform their duty.

—Brigham Young, discourse given in the Tabernacle, Salt Lake City, 16 November 1856

CHAPTER 21

GREAT SALT LAKE CITY

I

Saturday, 4 October 1856

It was a glorious day. After about a week of rainy, overcast weather, Indian summer had returned in all its splendor. The sky was a deep blue with only a few puffy clouds over the western mountains. There was a slight breeze coming off the Great Salt Lake that kept the air temperature just below seventy, which was perfect for working vigorously.

David Granger stopped, the pitchfork poised for its toss up onto the hay wagon. He let his eyes slowly move across the whole sweep of the mountains that formed the eastern wall of the Great Salt Lake Valley. Just two weeks ago, standing in this same field, he had looked to the mountains, searching for the first signs of color. Then he had seen only a few isolated splashes, as though some painter had accidently flicked his brush on a broad canvas of greens and summer browns. Now the whole mountain was ablaze with orange, reds, and yellows. From the Point of the Mountain down near Draper on the south to the hills around Ensign Peak on the north, it was like some incredible mural spread out by God just for the looking.

"What ya looking at?"

He turned and squinted up at his younger brother. Alma was atop the growing pile of hay, using a smaller fork to spread it around as David fed it up to him. Alma was fourteen, just entering that time of life when he was growing so fast that neither his stomach nor his mother's sewing could keep pace with it. He was skinny as a fence post, freckled from the tip of his head to the ends of his fingers, and impudent as a red squirrel guarding a horde of acorns. A shock of auburn-blond hair exploded on his head, completely untamable by brush or comb.

"Nothing." He tossed the hay up, making Alma jump out of the way rather than get hit with it. As Alma began to spread it around, David took a step forward, sliding the wooden tines beneath the windrows of hay and then moving forward so that it pushed more and more onto his fork. Once it was full, he turned and in one smooth motion, tossed it up to Alma.

Eleanor clucked softly to the team and they moved forward a few feet.

"That's good," David called. He shouldn't have. The horses stopped on their own and immediately lowered their heads and half shut their eyes again.

He looked up at his sister. Eleanor was seventeen, three and a half years younger than David. Another girl born between them had died at birth, so Eleanor was next to David in the family. She was engaged to be married in December to Abner Bennett from the Thirteenth Ward. At fourteen she had been a shorter, female version of Alma, except for the freckles. Now the skinny little girl was gone. The features had softened into something quite lovely. Her hair was long and straight, reminding David of honey being poured out in full sunlight. She had become very pretty, so perhaps there was hope for Alma as well.

David was made from a different mold, more along the lines of his father. He was not quite six feet tall and was solidly built, a trait enhanced by a lifetime of working a farm with his father. His hair was darker, a light brown, and more fine than Eleanor's, which was thick and rich. His eyes were hazel where Eleanor's and Alma's were blue. He had his father's nose and the same high, prominent cheekbones. He realized, without resentment, that those features left him short of the beauty that was his sister's.

He saw that Eleanor was giving him a strange look and realized he had been staring at her. "Wish we could take a ride up through the canyons right now."

She smiled immediately. "Wouldn't that be wonderful! They are so beautiful."

He looked at her slyly. "Bet Abner would go with us."

"I'll go," Alma said eagerly.

Eleanor ignored her younger brother. "He would love it. There's only one problem. We aren't going anywhere unless we get this hay in before the Sabbath tomorrow."

David turned, knowing she was right, but still longing for the mountains anyway. "I'll bet those people in the handcart companies got an eyeful coming up and over Big Mountain."

"Yes," she murmured. "It must be wonderful about now." Her eyes were gazing at the slash in the mountain wall that was Emigration Canyon. They couldn't see much beyond it, but they could picture what lay beyond. The summit of Little Mountain was at the head of the canyon, and beyond that the towering peak that was Big Mountain. It was in 1848, just eight years ago, that the two of them had come with their family over Big Mountain and down Emigration Canyon. They had not left Winter Quarters until late May, so it was late September when they reached the mountains. And those mountains had been on fire with color. To a nine-year-old girl and her thirteen-year-old brother who had grown up on the Great Plains, it was a sight never to be forgotten.

"Heber P. said some of the Minute Men rode up the canyon to meet this last group that came in day before yesterday." He frowned heavily. "Nobody told me about that or I would have been with them, that's for dang sure."

"*David Granger!*"

He pretended surprise. "What?"

"You watch your tongue or Mama is going to make you stop spending so much time with those Minute Men."

"I don't talk no different than Heber P., and his pa is a member of the First Presidency." *That should stop her short,* he thought. He and Heber Parley Kimball, one of Heber C. Kimball's sons—everyone called him Heber P. to distinguish him from his father—were of the same age and best friends. "And I've heard Brigham, Jr., say a 'dang' or two as well."

She decided to avoid that one and tipped her head to one side. "Your wanting to go meet the handcarts wouldn't have anything to do with all those single young ladies in the company, I suppose?" she asked innocently.

He laughed. "Listen, little sister. Just because you're finally getting married, don't be pushing me in that direction."

"*Finally?*" she huffed. "I'll be eighteen in November. Sally Miner was married when she was barely sixteen. So don't you be talking 'finally' with me."

Then she saw that he was baiting her—a favorite pastime of his—and decided to prod him back a little. "Probably none of those girls would want some old man who's already turned twenty-one. You know what President Young says. Your kind is a danger to society."

He laughed, enjoying this little game they had with each other. "Now, sis, you know he said the danger comes only after I'm twenty-four."

"And *you* know he said that a young man—surely that means before twenty-one—should be finding him a wife and getting him some land and building a cottage and settling down."

He looked offended. "But I'm just a boy yet. Me?" he said, stabbing at his chest with his thumb, "I'm going to be a bachelor till I'm thirty or more. Break the hearts of all them maidens who have been begging me to show 'em my favors."

She laughed airily. "All *none* of them?" she said.

Eleanor didn't really mean that. She had four or five friends who would give just about anything if her brother would pay them even the slightest amount of attention, but he showed no interest. That, as her mother kept saying, was directly attributable to his being one of the new Nauvoo Legion's young Minute Men.

Though Brigham Young took the strong stand—based on both wise governmental policy and sound Latter-day Saint theology—that it was better to feed and befriend the Indians than to fight them, it had not worked in all cases. With thousands of Saints pouring into the Great Basin and Brother Brigham colonizing new settlements on a regular basis, clashes with the native Utes, Paiutes, and Goshutes were inevitable. To combat that threat, President Young—who was also Territorial Governor Young—organized local militias in every community. These were armed and trained to respond rapidly to any Indian threats. In Salt Lake City, the "Nauvoo Legion" had been reorganized, and many of the brethren served in its ranks. But the "crack troops," the ones who served as the point of the javelin when trouble broke out, were called the Minute Men. Usually young single men in their late teens and early twenties, they were eager, fearless, and capable.

That wasn't surprising, considering their heritage. For the most part they were the sons and nephews of Saints who had come through the refining days of Ohio, Missouri, and Illinois. Jonathan and Eliza Granger, David's parents, had been at the fall of Far West and in the exodus from Missouri that winter. When persecution broke out again in Nauvoo, they packed up once again and slogged across Iowa. After a very lean year in Winter Quarters they had come across the plains in '48. Nor had the eight years since then been what anyone might call easy ones. And their son had been part of it all. Like the other Minute Men, David Granger had been born in tribulation and nurtured on faith and courage.

By the time David was fourteen, he was doing a man's work on the farm. At fifteen he became a mail rider between Provo and Ogden. The following year he had started riding the "Mormon Corridor," the string of settlements that stretched from Salt Lake to San Diego. The motto of the Minute Man—of which they seemed just a bit too proud, in Eleanor's book—was to keep their powder dry and be ready to ride at a minute's notice. It was common knowledge in the Valley that Brigham Young looked to "the boys" whenever there was a challenge to be met.

As Eleanor watched David, far away from her now as he stared at the looming peaks of the Wasatch, she felt a fierce affection for him and an intense pride. It was David who had made sure a nine-year-old girl got across the plains safely. It was David who had spent the first five dollars he had earned as a mail rider to buy Eleanor the first store-bought dress she had owned since they had left Nauvoo.

"David," she said softly.

Reluctantly, he straightened and turned his head.

"It's getting late. If we don't hurry, we won't get finished before dark."

His shoulders lifted as he took one last, longing look. "Yeah," he sighed. "You're right. Sorry, Alma. I shouldn't be dreaming when there's work to do."

They were almost back to the barn, the wagon creaking beneath the weight of a full load of hay, when David pulled on the reins, bringing the horses to a halt. Out at the gate of their property, which was bordered on the north by Five Hundred South Street, a rider was coming at a hard lope. He slowed only enough to turn in through the gate of the rail fence, then spurred his mount even harder.

"I think that's Heber P.," David said.

Eleanor half stood, looking concerned. "It is. And he's in a mighty big hurry."

It was Heber. He raced into the yard and pulled up in a spray of dust and pebbles. "David! David! Guess what!"

"What?"

"Elder Franklin D. Richards is here."

David just looked at him, trying to think why that would have his friend so agitated.

Heber was aghast at such ignorance. "Elder Richards! From England."

That got through to him. "Oh! *Elder* Richards."

His friend just shook his head, and then he raced on. "He just rode in about an hour ago with a group of missionaries. My brother is with them."

David leaned forward. "William? Really?" Now that *was* exciting news. William H. Kimball, Heber P.'s oldest brother, had gone to England in 1854. A few months ago the Kimball family had received letters from Iowa City saying that William was there helping to outfit the handcart companies and would be coming home once all was finished. And now he was here. "That's great, Heber. I'll bet your father is so–"

"David! There are two more handcart companies out on the plains."

"No, the last one just got in day before yesterday, remember?"

Heber shook that off. "No, two more! Elder Richards and my brother and the others are meeting with President Young and Father right now. They've come all the way across the plains by carriage and light wagons to bring the news. There are another twelve or thirteen hundred people still out there."

"Twelve or thirteen hundred!" Eleanor exclaimed.

"Yes. They left England late. But they're in trouble. Here it is October already."

David had already made that jump in his mind. The days of good weather were numbered now, and that number was not a large one. His face turned grave. "How far?"

"No one is sure. William says that if they're lucky, they'll make it as far as the Green by the time we find them."

"The Green?" David exclaimed. "That's all?"

"Where's the Green, David?" Alma asked. Alma had been only six when they came across the plains and remembered very little of the details of that journey.

"The Green River. That's two days east of Fort Bridger, about a hundred and thirty or forty miles from here."

Heber P. was nodding. "It's likely they'll be farther out than that. William said that when he and his party passed them, the lead company hadn't even reached Fort Laramie yet."

David groaned. "Fort Laramie?"

"Yes. So they might be somewhere along the Sweetwater." He was trying to look grave, but there was excitement dancing in his eyes. "There's going to have to be a rescue party sent out, David." He grinned happily. "And what do the Minute Men always say?" He paused, giving David his cue.

They sang it out together. "*Keep your powder dry and be ready to ride on a minute's notice.*"

David leaned forward, Eleanor and Alma totally forgotten now. "Do you really think they'll call us out?" he asked.

"I don't know," Heber said. "Everyone's meeting right now in President Young's office. But they've got to do something. And when there is something to be done, they almost always call on us. I think we're going, David. I think we are going to go."

II

Sunday, 5 October 1856

"Do you think we'll meet in the Tabernacle or the Bowery?"

David Granger looked at his sister. "I hadn't thought about it."

Eleanor poked him, smiling. "Admit it. You haven't thought about anything except the Minute Men since Heber P. came last night, have you?"

He grinned and touched his cheek along the jawline where he had cut himself. "Nope. Not even shaving."

She laughed and put an arm through his. The Grangers were walking north on West Temple Street and were almost to the "Temple Block," as everyone called it. David and Eleanor had fallen about ten paces behind the rest of the family. Ahead of them, towering above the walls surrounding the block, the triangular roof of the Tabernacle could be seen. The roof of the Bowery, being considerably lower than that of the Tabernacle, was not yet visible.

David's father heard the question and half turned. "With the weather this nice, it will be the North Bowery. It can hold more people."

David nodded. For sure there was going to be a crowd. General conference did not formally begin until Monday, which was the sixth of October, but people had been streaming into the city for two days now. Perhaps it was the weather. More likely it was the news about the late handcart companies. By nightfall the whole city knew of the arrival of Elder Richards's party. The Sunday meeting before conference was always crowded, but it seemed like there were many more people than usual moving toward the temple site this morning.

"Do you think he'll talk about the handcart companies, Pa?"

Jonathan Granger nodded at his oldest son. "I would suspect so. It's a ripe opportunity. With general conference bringing everyone into town, it couldn't be better timing. We'll have Saints from every settlement in the territory here."

Eliza Granger turned. She was out ahead of her husband and Alma a little. She had their two youngest daughters by the hand, hurrying along so they wouldn't be late. "Now, David," she admonished him, "don't you be getting your hopes set too high about this. Going out after those people this late in the year is going to be dangerous."

"So?" he shot right back.

Eleanor laughed. "David survived shaving this morning, Mama. I think he'll be all right."

For a time David was afraid that President Young was not going to bring up the news about the handcarts at all, even though the congregation was humming with speculation about what he would say. He spent almost ten minutes calling the congregation to repentance for being so noisy. And the noise really was terrible.

The Bowery was an open-sided structure made of a roof of leafy boughs and dirt supported by dozens of poles. When the weather was good it could handle more than double the twenty-five hundred that the Tabernacle could house. The problem was, it couldn't possibly accommodate all of the thousands who had come for conference. That left many people outside of its sheltering roof. Many of these wandered about or spoke aloud even after the meeting began. With a crowd this large, every speaker had to shout to make himself heard anyway, but with all the other activity going on it was almost impossible for any but those closest to the speakers to hear.

So with a touch of obvious irritation, their prophet tore into them. He asked for their strictest attention and suggested that if they absolutely had to whisper and carry on conversations they remove themselves far enough away from the Bowery that they wouldn't prevent others from hearing. He rebuked the police who were there to help with the crowd for talking out loud on the periphery of the assembly. He won an appreciative laugh when he suggested that a policeman could much more effectively control the noise by going over and laying his hand on the shoulder of an offending party than by hollering "Silence!" at the top of his lungs.

Next he chided the women with crying babies who refused to take them out, even if they could not silence them. He suggested that it was only a matter of good breeding to be considerate of others in such matters.

"I make these remarks," he said at last, "because I am concerned that you hear the brethren who have just returned to us. We cannot expect them to shout over the whispering and talking, the shuffling of feet, and over crying babies. And I want these brethren to be heard."

David looked at Eleanor in relief. "At last," he whispered.

The chastisement worked. Those outside of the Bowery moved in closer, sheepishly breaking off their conversations. Several women stood up and went out with their wailing children. People stopped shifting around, and the constant squeaking of benches and chairs finally stopped. Everyone focused on their prophet and it quickly became perfectly quiet.

Brigham let the silence become total, then straightened. His face became very grave. "Brothers and sisters, I will now give this people the subject and the text for the Elders who may speak today and during conference, which formally commences tomorrow. As most of you have heard, on this, the fifth day of October, eighteen fifty-six, many of our brethren and sisters are still out on the plains with handcarts. They must be brought here. We must send assistance to them."

David looked across the aisle at Heber P., who was sitting with his mother and other siblings. They grinned at each other. There was going to be a rescue.

Brigham's voice rose sharply. "Here is the subject to which we all shall speak. The text will be—to get them here! I want the brethren who may speak to understand that their text is the people on the plains, and the subject matter for this community is to send for them and bring them in before the winter sets in."

"Hear! Hear!" someone cried out.

President Young clearly heard it, but did not turn. "That is my religion," he said firmly. "That is the dictation of the Holy Ghost that

I possess. *It is to save the people!* We must bring them in from the plains."

He stopped, his head moving back and forth as his eyes locked those of the crowd. His shoulders were squared and his face resolute. "I shall call upon the bishops this day. I shall not wait until tomorrow nor the next day. I want sixty good mule teams and twelve or fifteen wagons. I do not want to send oxen. They are much too slow for this enterprise. I want good horses and mules. They are in this Territory, and we must have them. I want also twelve tons of flour and forty good young men as teamsters."

David nearly leaped up. *Young men!* President Young always called the Minute Men his "boys" or his "young men."

"Next, I want sixty spans of mules, or horses, with harness, whippletrees, neck-yokes, stretchers, load chains, and so forth. I will repeat the division, brothers and sisters. Forty extra teamsters is number one. Sixty spans of mules or horses is part of number two. Twelve tons of flour, and the wagons to take it, is number three."

He shook his finger at the sea of upturned faces. "Let me make myself perfectly clear. I will tell you all that your faith, all your religion, and all your profession of religion will never save one soul of you in the celestial kingdom of our God, not unless you carry out just such principles as I am now teaching you. *Go and bring in those people now on the plains!* Attend strictly to those things which we call temporal duties, otherwise your faith will be in vain. The preaching you have heard will be in vain to you, and you will sink to hell, unless you attend to the things we tell you."

He stopped, his chest rising and falling. There was not a flicker of sound anywhere. Every eye was fastened upon their leader. His voice suddenly dropped in pitch, and though he still had to shout to make himself heard in such a large congregation, it felt like he had suddenly started to whisper. "I feel disposed, brothers and sisters," he went on, "to be as speedy as possible with regard to helping our brethren who are now on the plains. Consequently, I shall call upon the people forthwith for the help that is needed. I want them to give their names this morning, if they are ready to start on their journey tomorrow. Don't say, 'I will go next week, or in ten days, or in a fortnight hence,' for I wish you to start tomorrow morning.

"I want the sisters to have the privilege of fetching blankets, skirts, stockings, shoes, and so forth for the men, women, and children that are in those handcart companies. I want hoods, winter bonnets, stockings, skirts, garments, and almost any description of clothing. I now want brethren to come forward to the stand, for we need forty good teamsters to help the brethren on the plains. You may rise up now and give your names."

David Granger was instantly on his feet and saw that Heber P. Kimball and Brigham Young, Jr., were up as well. He felt a touch on his hand. He looked down at Eleanor, who was smiling up at him through tears. Her eyes were filled with pride. And then to his great joy, he saw that his father was also standing. Jonathan Granger looked down at his wife. "We've got four good horses, Lizzy."

To David's surprise, his mother was weeping too. She reached out and grabbed her husband's hand with both of hers. "Go, Jonathan! You and David go and help find those people."

It was nearing sundown when David Granger left Temple Block and started down West Temple Street towards his home. The Sunday meetings were done. The names were taken, and already donated materials were starting to pour into the tithing store, which had been designated as the collection point.

To no one's surprise, following the meetings Brigham Young formally called up a number of the Minute Men to join the rescue. Not all would go. The community couldn't leave itself vulnerable if any Indian trouble arose, but the Minute Men would be going. And David had been one of those selected. Unfortunately, his father had not been chosen. Brigham noted that the work required in the Valley to supply the rescue effort would be prodigious, and they had great need for help from men like Jonathan Granger.

Afterwards, David and Heber P. and Brigham, Jr., had gathered with their compatriots and talked excitedly about what had to be done. It would be a race to be ready on time, for Brother Brigham was adamant. By Tuesday morning he wanted the first wagons rolling. More would follow as soon as possible, but come Tuesday, the first help had to be on its way. The few voices who expressed doubts about whether that was possible were quickly silenced. Brother Brigham would hear of nothing less. If he had his way, they would be rolling tomorrow morning, but it would take most of Monday just to load the wagons.

David looked up in surprise when he saw Eleanor waiting across the street. When she saw him come out of the gate of Temple Block, she smiled and waved. Waiting for a carriage to roll by, he darted across the street.

"How come you're still here?"

She shook her head, trying to be patient. "What? You think only the Minute Men are working tonight to get things ready?"

"You mean that you are . . ." That thought took him aback a little. "Are you girls doing something?"

"Yes. Some of us who aren't married yet are going to get together in the morning and gather up all the clothing we can find." She blushed a little and looked away. "In fact, we already started."

Puzzled by her sudden embarrassment, he looked at her more closely. She laughed then, stepping away from him, and did a quick pirouette. "Notice anything different?" she said.

It took him a moment; then his eyes widened. Where before her skirts had been full, now they were limp and flat. She looked as though she had shed twenty pounds since he had last seen her. "What happened?"

Still coloring a little, she took his hand and pulled him forward to start walking. "President Young's call for help was so stirring, that while all of you brethren went up to the stand to give your names, we went to the back and made a little circle so we had some privacy. Then we took off our petticoats and stockings and other things we could spare and gave them to the collection."

He was astonished. "Right there in the Bowery?"

She giggled lightly at his expression. "Why not? You jumped to your feet without hesitation. Well, I can't drive a team, and I don't have horses to volunteer. But I was just as moved as you were, David. I wanted to do something."

He had stopped and she had to drag him forward again. He was still staring at her. "What?" she said, blushing even more under the directness of his stare.

"You know what, little sister?" he asked softly.

"What?"

"If I could find someone just like you, maybe I'd consider getting married right away."

"Why, David Granger!" she exclaimed in delight. "That's the nicest thing you have ever said to me."

He didn't smile back. He was completely sober. "I mean it. I'm proud of you, Eleanor."

Now her face softened. "And I'm proud of you, David. Really proud. I wish I were a man and could go with you."

"So do I. I would be proud to ride with you."

Chapter Notes

At about 5:00 P.M. on the afternoon of Saturday, 4 October, Elder Franklin D. Richards and his party of returning missionaries arrived in the Salt Lake Valley, making the eleven-hundred-mile trip from Florence in an astounding thirty-one days (an average of about thirty-five miles per day). They went immediately to the office of President (and Governor) Brigham Young and broke the news that two additional handcart companies and two independent wagon companies were still out on the plains. This must have stunned

President Young. The first two handcart companies had arrived together on 26 September. The third, led by Edward Bunker and composed mainly of emigrants from Wales, had arrived on 2 October, just two days before. Assuming that there were only three companies coming that season, the wagons sent out to resupply the handcarts were already returning to the Valley for the winter (see Bartholomew and Arrington, *Rescue,* pp. 5–6; also see Hafen and Hafen, *Handcarts to Zion,* p. 119).

Based on the minutes of the Saturday evening meeting, it seems that Elder Richards estimated that the Willie Company would be found somewhere around the crossing of the Green River, which is 130 miles east of Salt Lake City (see Bartholomew and Arrington, *Rescue,* p. 10). Perhaps it was the swiftness of their own journey that caused the returning party to so badly overestimate the progress of the last two companies. On 4 October, both companies were still at least five hundred miles from Salt Lake City via the Mormon Trail.

The description of the Minute Men and how they functioned as part of Utah's militia effort at this time is accurate as given here (see Bartholomew and Arrington, *Rescue,* p. 8).

David Granger and his family are the fictional creations of the author, but the others mentioned are not. Heber P. Kimball and Brigham Young, Jr., were members of the Minute Men and did join in the effort to rescue the handcart companies (see Bartholomew and Arrington, *Rescue,* p. 54, n. 31).

The current Tabernacle, with its famous dome-shaped roof, was not started until 1863, and the first conference to be held in it was in October 1867, though it was not formally dedicated until 1875 (see *Encyclopedia of Mormonism,* s.v. "Tabernacle," "Salt Lake City," and "Temple Square"). In 1851–52 the "Old" Tabernacle was built in the southwest corner of the block, where the Assembly Hall now stands. It could seat about 2,500 people. When the weather was good, however, the Bowery was used because it could seat more than twice that amount.

The speech given here by Brigham Young on Sunday morning, 5 October, also incorporates part of what he said in a second speech given after Daniel Spencer and Franklin D. Richards spoke to the congregation. They are combined here for purposes of the novel. However, President Young's words are taken almost verbatim from the report given of the meetings for that day (see *Journal of Discourses* 4:113–14, and Hafen and Hafen, *Handcarts to Zion,* pp. 122–23). It was one woman present that day who later reported: "The sisters stripped off their Peticoats, stockings and everything they could spare, right there in the Tabernacle [actually the Bowery]" (cited in Bartholomew and Arrington, *Rescue,* p. 7).

CHAPTER 22

GREAT SALT LAKE CITY TO SOUTH PASS

I

Tuesday, 7 October 1856

It did not occur to David Granger until it was almost sundown Tuesday afternoon that his wish to see the mountains in their fall colors had been granted. He was standing near the fire beside Heber P. Kimball, heartily putting away a dish of beef and barley stew. Then his eyes lifted to the mountain that towered above them to the northeast. They were camped at the foot of Big Mountain, which now, in the late afternoon light, was awash with color. Tomorrow they would have to go up and over the top—one of the longest steep inclines of the whole eleven hundred miles from Salt Lake to Winter Quarters—before dropping into East Canyon and turning north toward Henefer and the mouth of Echo Canyon. But today, here he was. Was it really only three days before that he and Eleanor paused during hauling hay to wish for the chance to be up in these canyons?

He shook his head. It had been a frantic three days. On Sunday morning President Young had issued the call to action. The rest of that day and all of Monday were spent in urgent preparations—digging out his winter clothing; packing what little personal gear he could carry in his bedroll and saddlebags; checking his saddle and other tacking to make sure they were in excellent condition. Last night he had gone to President Young's office along with the other Minute Men and their leaders to receive a blessing and a final charge from their prophet. Now here they were, on their way.

He had only two regrets, and both of those centered around who was not here with him. He would have been very proud to be in the same company as his father. That had been settled quickly. He and Heber P. were likewise disappointed when Brigham Young, Jr., had also been asked to stay behind and help organize the rescue effort from the Valley side of things. That had been a bitter blow to their friend, but someone had to stay behind and see that the supplies kept coming in. And while he felt guilty about it, David was very glad that it was Brig who had drawn that straw and not him.

"Brethren, can we have you gather round here?"

David turned. It was Brother Robert T. Burton, or rather, *Major* Robert T. Burton. As one of the commanders of the Salt Lake City cavalry, a unit of the Nauvoo Legion, Burton was David's direct line commander in the Minute Men. David gulped the last bite of his stew, followed it down with a long drink of cold creek water, then started moving along with the others to where Major Burton and George D. Grant were standing.

"I think we're about to get our marching instructions," Heber P. said out of the corner of his mouth.

"I hope so. I'm sure ready."

As they gathered into a tight circle, David noticed that a few flakes of snow came floating down in the still air. He looked up and sniffed the air. It shouldn't amount to much, if anything. The overcast didn't seem that thick, and there was not the smell of snow in the air. But it was a silent warning of things to come. *Good,* he thought. It would only lend wings to their feet.

He turned to look at the company and counted swiftly. There were twenty-seven men, counting himself. With the second group camped about ten miles back on the east side of Little Mountain, that made about fifty of them all together. Brigham had called for forty. That was very good. And they were just the first, the ones who had been most eager to answer the call. Hundreds more would be coming over the next while.

But it was not just the numbers that gave him satisfaction; it was also the faces that he recognized. By his own personal knowledge he was aware that at least five or six of these brethren had made the now-famous thousand-mile march to California with the Mormon Battalion. Most had come through the Missouri War and the expulsion from Nauvoo. And, of course, there was no one who hadn't crossed the North American continent to get here.

Here was Charles Decker, who would serve as one of their scouts. Decker was Brigham Young's son-in-law, having married one of the Church leader's daughters back in Winter Quarters in 1847. He and Ephraim Hanks held the contract for carrying mail between Salt Lake City and St. Joseph, Missouri. At last night's meeting, David had heard one of the brethren ask Brother Decker how many times he had been across the trail. He quietly admitted that this would be number fifty for him. That was about as good a qualification for being scout as David could imagine.

Abel Garr stood on the other side of Brother Burton. A young man of twenty-two years, Garr also had served as a scout for the Saints, and currently he and his brothers helped watch over the Church cattle in northern Utah's Cache Valley. For about five or six years prior to that, the Garr family had tended the Church herds out on Antelope Island, a lonely and sometimes dangerous job.

Brother Burton was part of the militia company that became heroes during the "Provo River Battle" of 1850 with the Ute Indians. Three years later he had led the troops in the Indian troubles out west in Tooele County. One time, so the stories went, he and his unit had been caught out there on the desert in the dead of winter without shelter or bedding and still came back victorious. He had proven himself to be not only personally courageous but an inspiring leader as well.

And then there was George D. Grant. David turned and let his eyes stop on Brother Grant, who was speaking quietly with Brother Burton. This was the most remarkable thing of all to David. George D. Grant had been a Church agent in Iowa City and Florence, Nebraska. He had come across the trail with the Franklin D. Richards party, arriving home just three days before. The fact that he would turn around after only three days and hit the trail again was astonishing in and of itself. But what was absolutely astounding was that he was returning from a mission in Europe. So were five others that were with them tonight, including William Kimball, Heber P.'s older brother, and Joseph A. Young, Brig's older brother.

Some of those missionaries had left in 1852, more than four years ago now. Others had gone in 1854. So at the very least they had been away for two years. Others had not seen home for four full years. And when they finally returned after that long absence, they were immediately turning around and leaving again.

Last night, at the meeting with President Young where he had given the rescue group blessings, some had suggested to Brother Grant that no one expected him or the other returnees to leave again. David had been so impressed when Brother Grant shook his head without hesitation. "We encouraged those good people to come on," he said quietly. "How can we turn our backs on them now?"

"All right, brethren," Brother Burton said. "As you know, President Young did not designate an organization for this company but left that in our hands. I would propose that we elect our captain tonight so that we know clearly who leads us."

There were heads nodding all around the circle.

"I would like to propose that the man who is best fit for that job, and who has proven worthy of it by the fact that he stands with us now, is Brother George D. Grant."

Brother Grant ducked his head a little as the group responded to that. "Hear! Hear!" William H. Kimball shouted. "Amen," someone else called out.

Brother Burton nodded. "All in favor?" Every hand came up. "Motion carries." He turned to Brother Grant. "*Captain* Grant, we turn to you for instruction."

"Thank you." He looked around for a moment. "I am greatly pleased to be with you brethren. I couldn't ask for a better outfit and a group better suited to the task at hand. It is an honor to ride with you and to call you brethren."

He paused for just a moment. "The first order of business is to complete our organization. I would therefore like to propose that we select Brothers Robert T. Burton and William H. Kimball as my assistants, Brother Cyrus Wheelock as our chaplain, and Brother Charles Decker as our guide. All in favor?"

Again the vote was not only unanimous but instantaneous.

"All right, brethren. Thank you for your support. As you know, President Young asked all of those who could be ready to leave today to rendezvous somewhere between Big and Little Mountain. As you also know, we have received word that another group of about this same size is camped at the bottom of Little Mountain, about ten miles behind us under the command of Reddick Allred. They will join with us sometime tomorrow and we shall then travel together. Between us we will have twenty-two wagons loaded to capacity with flour, other foodstuffs, clothing, and bedding. More will follow, but we will not wait for them. We all feel a great sense of urgency to go out and find those companies as quickly as possible."

He stopped and looked up at the sky, then reached out and let one of the snowflakes land on his hand. It was still snowing, but very lightly. "Here we are in heavy coats and warm boots and thick gloves, and I still see some of you stamping your feet up and down to keep yourselves warm. If we, who are strong and well fed and rested, find the nights severe, picture if you will the plight of old men, young toddlers, and women who are poorly prepared for such weather. And in addition, they will be short of food as they are forced to pull their handcarts along.

"Our teams—two span per wagon—are strong and fresh. Fortunately, thus far the trail is still dry. The roads are packed hard and easily traveled. Therefore, we shall push on as vigorously as possible. We will not stop and camp at sundown but will go on each day until late in the evening. We will take turns at driving the wagons so that we do not have to stop long to rest. If you get tired, sleep in the back of your wagon, but do not stop."

He looked around the circle, and now his face was lined with worry. "Brethren, we do not know how far we will have to go to find these brothers and sisters. If all goes well, we shall find them in a matter of a few days and return quickly to the Valley. We can all pray for such good fortune."

There was one last pause, and then his jaw set in complete determination. "We promised the Saints we would come. Our prophet has charged us to go out and find them and bring them in, or else our religion is in vain. So find them we will. We shall not rest until they are safely home in the Valley."

II

Monday, 13 October 1856

"Someone's coming!"

The shout passed down the line from wagon to wagon, and with the hearing of it, each teamster pulled his teams up and came to a halt. David Granger and Heber P. Kimball were in the ninth wagon back, taking their turn driving. Heber P. actually had the reins at the moment and pulled them sharply. "Whoa, mules," he called.

David stood up, then stepped up on the driver's seat so he could see better. In a moment Heber P. climbed up beside him. A rider on horseback galloped past them going toward the front of the train. David saw that it was Major Burton, their commanding officer. Grabbing on to the front bow of the wagon, he leaned out so he could see around the wagon in front of them.

"Hey!" he exclaimed in surprise. "It's a wagon train coming."

"Really?" Their own column had come to a complete stop now, so Heber wrapped the reins around the brake handle and hopped down. He went around the back of the wagon and came up on David's side so he could see what David was seeing.

It was late afternoon, and though the overcast of the last several days was still with them, the light was behind them and thus good for seeing to the east. They were moving along the Black's Fork River, about twenty miles north of Fort Bridger. The land here was gently rolling, sagebrush covered hills, one after the other as far as the eye could see in every direction. Half a mile ahead, a line of wagons was coming one by one over the ridge and down the trail towards them. There were already thirty or so wagons visible, with additional ones coming into view every ten or fifteen seconds.

"That must be Abraham Smoot's train," Heber P. said. "It's a big one."

"Abraham Smoot?"

"Yeah. Oh, that's right. You didn't hear that. My brother was telling us that when he was with Elder Richards's party, they were making such excellent time that they passed several companies of Saints along the trail. Brother Smoot's was the largest of those. He's bringing a train of some fifty or so wagons."

"I see. At first I couldn't figure how Brother Smoot had beat us out here."

"He's headed for the Valley."

"I see that now." David was still peering at the oncoming train. Several riders from their own company, including Major Burton, were now going out to meet them.

"Maybe they'll know where the handcart companies are," David suggested.

"I sure hope so. You could tell that Elder Grant was not happy last night when no one at Fort Bridger had heard anything of them."

David nodded. No one had really expected to find the Willie Company as far west as Fort Bridger, but they had serious hopes that there would be at least word of them. Fort Bridger, a Church outpost since Brigham Young had bought it from Jim Bridger, was a major way station for the trains coming and going along the Mormon Trail. It was about a hundred miles east of the Valley. Surely someone there would have knowledge of the whereabouts of the companies. There was none.

Captain Grant's concerns deepened. Cold now gripped the high plains. Fort Bridger was at an elevation of about six thousand feet. It was mid-October, so some cold was to be expected. But when they were waking to ice on the water buckets and finding that the slabs of bacon that hung in the backs of the wagons were frozen through, it didn't bode well for the handcart companies who were out in it. Wanting to press ahead with even more speed than they had been making, Captain Grant ordered some of the flour and other goods cached at the fort so that they could move forward with even greater speed. They would need a supply of food on the way back anyway.

But ten minutes later when Major Burton came riding back down the line, announcing that they would stop here tonight with the Smoot Company, the news was all bad. Brother Smoot knew nothing concerning the whereabouts of the two additional companies. His company had come upon the Willie group in early September, but that had been clear back on the North Platte River. At that point the Willie Company had been stopped looking for cattle lost in a buffalo stampede. Smoot had moved on and had not seen them or heard from them again.

Openly alarmed that nothing was known of their whereabouts, Captain Grant called his other leaders into council. After considerable discussion and numerous suggestions, a decision was made. In the morning an "express" party would leave at first light. They would take a light wagon and the best two span of horses in the company. They would race forward as swiftly as possible to try and find the missing companies. He chose four of his most trusted men–Abel Garr, William H. Kimball, Joseph A. Young, and Stephen Taylor. They wouldn't be able to carry much more than their own gear and food enough for the four of them, plus some bales of hay for the teams, so they couldn't do anything to relieve the plight of the emigrants. What they would carry with them, which probably at this point would be as critical as flour or rice or even warm clothing, was hope. Captain Grant said that if his suspicions were correct, right now hope might be the best possible commodity those struggling Saints could receive.

III

Saturday, 18 October 1856

David Granger was on horseback at the moment, moving at a steady walk off to the side of the trail about midway back in the line of wagons. A movement caught his eye and he turned to see two dozen flashes of tan and white racing across the olive-green landscape. Antelope. At about five hundred yards. Far too distant and far too swift for a possible shot. But in the afternoon sun their bodies were like liquid gold.

"They're beautiful, aren't they?"

He looked at the wagon where Heber P. Kimball was currently at the reins. He was not looking at David but was watching the animals, who were now running at full speed, headed for the top of the ridge, still about a mile away.

"How fast do you think them honeys can run?" David said.

They had been seeing antelope for the past six days now, and it wasn't the first time he had asked that question either to himself or to his friend. There was no answer, of course. They could outrun a horse by double. Some claimed they were faster than the most powerful steam engine. That was hotly disputed because there were no trains out here to match against the fleet-footed animals. But some locomotives were said to be able to reach sixty miles an hour.

As he watched them growing smaller rapidly, David was sure of only one thing. However fast it was, at full speed they were dazzling to watch and he never tired of it. He looked at his friend. "Pacific or Atlantic antelope?" he drawled lazily.

Heber P. looked up in surprise. Then his head bobbed momentarily as he understood what David was suggesting. "I'll say Atlantic."

"And I'll say Pacific," David said, just to be different, even though it looked like they were going straight up and over the top of the ridge.

"All right, let's watch."

The long, low ridge that formed most of the eastern skyline ahead of the wagons was South Pass, the dividing backbone of the North American continent. Currently the antelope were racing for the top of that ridge in full flight. If they went over, they would soon be grazing on sagebrush watered by rain and snow that would eventually flow down to the Gulf of Mexico and the Atlantic Ocean. Behind the column of wagons, still visible, in fact, was Pacific Springs, so named because its waters flowed westward, becoming Pacific Creek, which flowed into the Little Sandy River, which flowed into the Big Sandy and then to the Green and finally to the Colorado, which emptied into the Pacific. So if the antelope didn't turn . . .

Just then the herd wheeled to the left, looking very much like a flock of birds spinning in perfect synchronization. They came almost all the way around, heading back nearly in the same direction they had come, but about a half mile away now. Their headlong flight up and over South Pass now became a sprint for the lowlands behind them.

"Told you," David chortled. "Pacific antelope through and through."

"They really are something," Heber P. whispered as the animals went up and over a low hill and disappeared. "I wish Brig were here. He would love this, wouldn't he?"

"Yeah. You could sure see the disappointment on his face when we left."

David stood up in the stirrups, glad to give his backside a rest for a moment from the hardness of the saddle. He let his eyes sweep the sky and take stock of what he saw. Directly behind them, the sky was blue and the sun was shining. But off to the south it was a different story. The gentle ridge of South Pass rose sharply into a high plateau known as Pacific Butte. Some distance beyond that, the sky was almost black and tendrils of gray hung down like mists, signaling rain or snow—almost certainly snow, as cold as it was. But other than the wind—that incessant, never-ending wind—the temperature here was somewhat bearable.

Heber was watching his friend. "We've been lucky so far, haven't we?"

"Yes, we have." They had seen snow flurries a couple of times, and the days were cold and the nights bitter, but so far they had not had any real storm. The trail had been hard packed and good for traveling and they were making excellent time. "That could end tonight," David suggested.

"I know." Heber clucked at the mules absently, staring out at the top of the ridge, which was now a lot closer. "How far is it after we cross the pass?" he asked.

David dropped back into the saddle again. "Elder Grant said about eight or nine miles before we strike the Sweetwater. You ready to change?"

"After we're over the top," Heber P. replied. "I'm the Pacific teamster, remember? You're the Atlantic."

IV

Sunday, 19 October 1856

"David! David, wake up!"

Coming awake with a jerk, David Granger looked around wildly. The light in their small tent was faint, and he could barely discern the dark figure kneeling over him. "Heber?"

"Yes. Come on, boy. Wake up. Daylight is upon us."

David moaned softly and rolled over on his side. "What time is it?"

"Sun's been up for an hour."

David came up on one elbow and stared at the walls of the tent. The first thing he noted was that the canvas was rippling in and out. Then he heard the sound of the wind. The second thing he saw was that the canvas showed some light through it, but it was hardly bright sun. "What are you talking about?"

There was a soft chuckle. "Okay, maybe it's going to be coming up in an hour."

David swung at him. "Go away. This was not a good night for me."

"You're telling me? It was like trying to sleep in a butter churn. You were rolling all over the place all night long. Bad dreams?"

"Yeah. Wild dreams. Really weird stuff."

"Well, here's something to add to your day." Heber turned and crawled over to the tent flap and raised it up. Now the light flooded in and David had to close his eyes for a minute. When he half opened them and looked outside, he groaned and fell back on his bed. "Snow?"

"Yup. About three or four inches' worth." He let the flap drop again and moved over to sit beside David. "Captain Grant says we're going to stay put for a while this morning. He wants to kill another beef. With fifty of us, we're going through meat like a bear through a beehive."

David reached for his trousers and began to pull them on. "More than fifty, if you count those wagons that came in last night."

"Yeah, that's right. Good thing they got in before the snow started."

David nodded. Three additional wagons with six teamsters from the Valley had come in just after dark last night, very grateful to have finally caught up with the main train. And Captain Grant was grateful to have them. All three wagons were loaded with flour. That meant another six thousand pounds they could count on.

He stood up, pulling on his pants, shivering with the cold. A gust of wind shook the tent, rattling the poles softly. "Is it still snowing?"

"No, but it's blowing hard out of the north now. And colder than cold. I think it's just a matter of time."

David sighed as he hurriedly put on his shirt. "This is the day we've all been dreading. We knew it had to come sooner or later. Too bad it couldn't wait another week."

Now all the humor and teasing in his friend was gone. "Yes, it is," Heber P. answered. "I'm afraid this is going to be a big one."

By ten o'clock, with the beef butchered and quartered, Captain George D. Grant called for a meeting of the camp. The men came in small groups as the word passed from wagon to wagon. They were camped in a scattering of trees and thick willows near what was called the last crossing of the Sweetwater River. For those going east it was actually the first crossing. That gave them some shelter from the wind, but even then the men came bundled up to their fullest. Scarves covered faces; hats were pulled down low to block the blowing snow; gloved hands were thrust deep into coat pockets; feet stomped up and down to keep them warm in spite of heavy boots and two or three pairs of wool stockings.

The wind had picked up force now, and the light snow was already starting to pile up in low drifts. Off to one side, the horses and mules and the beef cattle huddled together, tails to the wind, heads down, a picture of utter misery. The snow was definitely increasing, though at the moment it was hard to tell what was coming down from the sky and what was being whipped up from the ground.

They gathered around the large fire built beside the lead wagon. Someone had thrown the remainder of the firewood on it, and the fire was blazing fiercely. The men gathered around in a horseshoe circle, leaving the south side open for the wind to whip away the smoke and the burning embers.

When the last of them arrived, Brother Grant, Brother Burton, and Brother William Kimball climbed up on the tailgate of their wagon so that everyone could see them clearly. The wind snatched Brother Burton's scarf and tore it away from his face. He had to grab at it to stop it from blowing away. Brother Kimball grabbed his hat and pulled it down more tightly before he lost that too.

"Brethren." Captain Grant's eyes were narrowed to a squint because he was facing into the wind so he could look directly at the men. "Brother Burton and Brother Kimball and I have been discussing our situation. As you see, our weather is deteriorating rapidly and we still have no word of the handcart companies. It has been six days now since we sent four of our brethren off as an express party to try and find the lost sheep. I had fully expected that by now those men would have found our lost Saints and sent word back to us of their whereabouts. The fact that they have not bodes us no good."

David looked at Heber P. and they both shook their heads. The express group had left from Black's Fork. In a light wagon with two span of good horses, they should be covering twenty-five or thirty miles a day. In six days, that was a hundred and fifty miles. Where in the world were they?

"At the time we sent them," Brother Grant went on, "I was sure they would find the handcart companies somewhere along the Sweetwater. It is a real surprise that we have heard nothing. I told the four of them not to go farther than Devil's Gate, but to wait there for us to catch up. I never in the world dreamed that they might actually have to go that far."

"Maybe the companies have decided to winter over somewhere," someone suggested.

Brother Grant immediately started to shake his head. So did Chauncey Webb and William Kimball. "It's possible," Brother Grant admitted, "but not likely."

Chauncey Webb stepped forward. "They don't have either the food or the clothing to get them through a winter out here on the high plains."

"What if they stopped at Fort Laramie?" someone else called out. "That would explain why the express hasn't found them, if they are going only as far as Devil's Gate."

Now it was William Kimball who answered. "Brethren, when we came through Fort Laramie we asked about food. They have very little. We have to face the fact that these people are out here somewhere, and by now they are in desperate need of our help. Their clothes are ragged and worn. Their shoes are in tatters and some are without. Their food will be almost gone by now. It would be nice to think that they are in a safe haven somewhere, but what if we are wrong? Would any of you like to take the responsibility for that?"

No one answered.

"And now the storm has come," Brother Grant came back in. "And it looks like it's going to be a bad one. Therefore, we have decided that we must push on with all possible speed." There was a crooked grin for a moment. "Not that we have been slacking so far."

There was a groan or two to underscore that statement. They had driven hard to this point.

"We can't afford to drive the beef cattle that we got at Fort Bridger. They are slowing us down too much. And yet we need the meat. Some of our teams are starting to fail, and this snow won't help that in any way. Therefore, we have asked Brother Reddick Allred—a courageous and able man, as most of you know—to stay here with the cattle and four of our wagons."

"Well," David said quietly, "that's a surprise." He wasn't speaking about Reddick Allred. Though he didn't know this man as well as some of the others, he knew of his reputation. Here was another Mormon Battalion veteran and a man who had crossed the trail more than once. No, the surprise was the decision to separate their forces.

"Those three wagons that came in last night will also stay here with Reddick. Some of our animals are failing and badly need to rest. We shall leave them here with Brother Allred as well. Once we find our people, we will probably need space in the wagons to carry the sick and the weak, so we are going to off-load here some of the food we have. That way we can travel faster and also have room for those in need of help. Once we find the handcarts, we will send word back to Brother Allred here and have him move forward to meet us. That way we will have food in reserve for when we shall surely need it the most."

He looked around. No one was going to protest this decision. The minute he put it into words, they saw the wisdom of it. "We'll ask Brother Allred to butcher and dress the beef while he is waiting for us." He pretended to shiver. "We're not too worried about it spoiling."

The men hooted. The way things were going, some of those cows risked being frozen solid before they ever killed them.

"Brother Allred?"

"Yes, Brother Grant?"

"Have you selected the men to stay back with you as guards?"

"I have. In addition to the six men who came in last night, I have four others besides myself." He handed a small slip of paper to Captain Grant.

David looked at Heber in dismay. He fully supported Captain Grant in this decision, but he didn't want to be one of those to stay here. To just sit and wait? He held his breath.

Captain Grant perused the list, nodded curtly, then read out the four names. David and Heber breathed a deep sigh of relief. They were not among those called out.

"All right, brethren. Those of you going forward, I want to be moving in the next half an hour. Get those tents down and packed." He looked up. Now there was no question that the snow that filled the air was no longer just blowing up from the ground. The flakes were small, almost pelletized, but they were slanting in thickly on the north wind. He turned back to his men. "The weather is not cooperating. Let's make that fifteen minutes."

As Heber and David turned and headed for their tent, Heber rubbed his gloved hands together. "What must it be like for those poor people who don't have the proper clothing?"

"Unbelievable," David murmured, hardly able to conceive facing this kind of storm when you were not properly prepared for it.

"So where are they, David?" Heber P. muttered. "Where in the world are they?"

"I don't know." He increased his pace a little. "But one thing is for sure. We have got to find them, Heber, and find them fast."

Chapter Notes

The response to Brigham Young's call for help was really quite remarkable. By Tuesday morning, just sixty or so hours after the arrival of Franklin D. Richards in Salt Lake, the first wagons were headed east. Bearing in mind that each wagon could carry close to two thousand pounds of goods, that means about twenty-two tons of supplies were on their way before three full days had passed. About ten thousand pounds of that was flour.

President Young asked those volunteers who could be on their way within twenty-four hours to rendezvous on the trail between Little and Big Mountains. One group led by Reddick Allred stopped at the bottom of Little Mountain (that is, on the east side), while the group led by George D. Grant made it to the base of Big Mountain (see "The Diary of Reddick N. Allred," in Carter, comp., *Treasures of Pioneer History* 5:345; see also Bartholomew and Arrington, *Rescue*, pp. 9–10; "Journal of the First Rescue Party" and "Harvey Cluff's Account of the Rescue," in Hafen and Hafen, *Handcarts to Zion*, pp. 222, 232). The second group caught up with Captain Grant's group on Wednesday and they then became one company (see Allred diary, in Carter, comp., *Treasures of Pioneer History* 5:345).

Though there are slightly different versions of how the rescue company was organized, it seems clear that George D. Grant was captain, with William H. Kimball and Robert T. Burton as his assistants (see Jones, *Forty Years Among the Indians*, p. 63; and Allred diary, in Carter, comp., *Treasures of Pioneer History*, 5:345).

As indicated, six of those in that first rescue party had just arrived in Salt Lake on Saturday afternoon after an absence from their wives and families of from two to four years. On Tuesday morning they were back on the road again. In addition to George D. Grant, the others were William H. Kimball, Chauncey G. Webb—both of whom had also been Church agents in Iowa City—Joseph A. Young, Cyrus Wheelock, and James Ferguson (see Hafen and Hafen, *Handcarts to Zion*, p. 124). Of this sacrifice, John Chislett later wrote: "Among the brethren who came to our succor were elders W. H. Kimball and G. D. Grant. They had remained but a few days in the Valley before starting back to meet us. May God ever bless them for their generous, unselfish kindness and their manly fortitude! They felt that they had, in a great measure, contributed to our sad position; but how nobly, how faithfully, how bravely they worked to bring us safely to the Valley—to the Zion of our hopes!" (in *Remember*, p. 9).

It is interesting that Stephen Taylor, one of the four members of the express party, was another of the Minute Men. A year after this experience he would marry Harriet Seeley Young, one of Brigham Young's daughters. So of the four express riders, one was Brigham Young's son, one was his future son-in-law (though it is not known if he was courting Harriet at this point or not), one was Heber C. Kimball's son, and one was not a member of the Church.

The first rescue party crossed South Pass sometime in the afternoon of 18

October. They were making excellent time. They had covered in twelve days what took a normal wagon train about three weeks to traverse. There were storms around them, but none that directly affected them. The decision to leave wagons and supplies waiting in reserve was made on the nineteenth of October as the storm began to close in. Reddick Allred wrote: "19th–Capt. Grant left me in charge of the supplies of flour, beef cattle, four wagons, the weak animals and eleven men for guard. I killed the beef animals and let the meat lay in quarters where it froze and kept well as it was very cold and storming almost every day. We were reinforced by 3 wagons and 6 men loaded with flour" (in Carter, comp., *Treasures of Pioneer History* 5:345).

CHAPTER 23

ICE SPRINGS TO SIXTH CROSSING

I

Sunday, 19 October 1856

Eric walked as swiftly as his dwindling energy would allow, turning his head away from the wind and the snow, which was coming in hard enough now to sting his flesh. He saw that his coat was wet. There was sleet mixed in the snow. He shook his head. As if the wind weren't bad enough.

As he came to his cart, he saw Jens and Elsie Nielson sitting on the leeward side of the cart, wrapped in a blanket, their backs to the wind, trying to shelter young Jens and Bodil Mortensen as much as possible. Even before he reached them, he could see that Bodil's teeth were chattering. In less than half an hour there was already an inch or two of snow, and it was coming steadily now. The wind was already starting to make small drifts around the little group.

Jens looked up. "Is it time to go?"

"Elder Willie says another five minutes. He knows we need the rest, but with the storm he thinks we'd better start moving again. We've still got eight or ten miles to go." He looked around. "Where's Olaf?"

A figure stepped out from a group who were standing close together a few yards away. "I'm over here." He too was wrapped in a blanket in addition to his coat and gloves and scarf.

"All right." Eric motioned for him to come over. As he did so, Eric dropped into a crouch beside the Nielsons. "Jens?"

"Yes?"

"Do you think you and Olaf can manage the cart for the rest of the way today?"

One eyebrow came up. Olaf gave a quick intake of breath. "Maggie?" Olaf asked.

"No, actually she's doing quite well, except for that terrible cough. But Brother James is not good at all."

"Ah, yes," Jens said. "I saw him this morning. He did not look good."

"He's too weak to pull and there's no room in the wagons. We're going to have to put him into one of their carts. Sarah and Emma and Sister James aren't strong enough to pull both carts alone."

"Yes, you go," Jens said without hesitation. "We will be all right, won't we, Olaf?"

"Yes."

That was a wild exaggeration and they all knew it. "All right" didn't seem to fit anything right now. This morning the last of the flour had been distributed, and even with the reduced rations, they didn't get their full portion at that. The storm was very quickly turning into a full-scale blizzard, and they were at least two days away from South Pass, where supposedly the relief wagons would be waiting for them. "All right" seemed like a profanity under the circumstances.

Eric didn't move. He was looking at this couple who had become his and Olaf's foster parents. Elsie Nielson was a tiny wisp of a woman, being just a shade under five feet tall and weighing no more than a hundred pounds. No, he corrected himself. Elsie *had* once been a hundred pounds when they had first met her on the steamer at Copenhagen. Now she had probably dropped below ninety pounds. Fortunately, Jens towered over her. At six feet two inches, he carried more than double her weight and was powerfully built. His size and strength had been a blessing to them on this journey. More than once Eric had thanked the Lord that Jens and Elsie had decided to give their money to the brethren back in Iowa City and come with the handcarts rather than with the independent wagon companies. But now Eric could see that even Jens was approaching the edge of his limits. And no wonder. He knew for sure that Jens was taking what little rations he was getting for himself and sharing those with Jens, Jr., and Bodil. He was probably living on six to eight ounces of flour per day now. A man could only do that for so long, no matter how strong he was, before the body began to give out.

"Are you sure?" Eric asked anxiously.

"We are sure," Jens said firmly. "Go. Brother James is a proud man. It will take some urging to make him ride."

Brother James was not the only proud man in this company. One of them sat directly before Eric right at that instant. He saw a spot on Jens's cheek, just below his right eye. It was no bigger than the tip of a match, but it looked white and slightly crystalline, as though a snowflake had frozen there. For the first time Eric noticed that Jens did not have a scarf on. Then he saw why. It was wrapped around Bodil's neck.

"Jens?"

"What?"

Eric touched his own cheek. "You'd better warm up that cheek. You're showing the first signs of frostbite."

Jens's hand came up as Elsie gasped. He put it over his cheek and held it there. "I will, Eric. Thank you."

Eric nodded and stood up. "If you need help, just call. I'll be watching back here."

"We will be fine," Jens said again. "Go. We shall see you in camp tonight."

With one last backward glance, Eric turned and moved up the

line of carts again, lifting one arm to shield his face from the wind that felt like it was stripping the flesh off his cheeks.

They had not started moving again when up ahead somewhere Eric thought he heard someone shout. He looked around. Sarah James looked up as well. She and Eric were standing in the shafts of the first of the Jameses' two carts, waiting for the signal to move. Sister James, Emma, and Reuben were handling the second cart, which carried Brother James. "What was that?" Sarah asked.

Eric was peering forward. The snow was blowing in billowing gusts and obscuring the view ahead. He shook his head. "I don't know."

And then Sarah suddenly gasped. "Look, Eric!"

He looked off to the right a little, where she was pointing. For one brief moment the wind lessened and they could see. Ahead of them the trail where they would be going curved slightly to the right. Coming towards them about a quarter of a mile away, its white top almost lost against the snow, was a single wagon, pulled by four horses.

As suddenly as it cleared, the snow swirled in again.

"Was that a wagon?" Eric said in a hoarse croak. His mind was racing. Their own supply wagons were behind the column. And none had passed them since they had left Ice Springs. Then he realized two things at the same instant. The wagon was coming towards them, not going in the same direction. The second thing was even more stunning. As it hit him, he exclaimed aloud, "Those were horses, Sarah. We don't have horses pulling our wagons. It's from the Valley. It's got to be from the Valley."

Elder Willie made the four brethren in the express party wagon wait until the last handcart and last supply wagon had come up and all the people had crowded in around them. That was no small task, because the people were crying and laughing, calling out to the four men in their warm coats and heavy gloves and thick scarves. It was like someone had poured water on a dying plant. New life had surged through the company, and even some of those in the sick wagons or who were riding in the carts had gotten up and hobbled over to see this most wondrous of sights.

When Maggie saw the look in the eyes of the four men as the company pressed in around them, she realized just how shocking their bedraggled appearance must really be.

"All right, brethren," Elder Willie finally said. "We are most anxious to hear what you have to say."

Two of the four men—Cyrus Wheelock and Joseph A. Young—were recognized by the group because they had been with the Franklin D. Richards party when they passed them back in September. The other two were strangers. It was Cyrus Wheelock, clearly the oldest of the four, who stepped forward.

"Brothers and sisters, I can't tell you how relieved we are to have finally found you."

Eric couldn't help himself. He leaned forward, smiling a little. "I think it is safe to say that the feeling is shared by us."

There was actual laughter among the group, a sound they hadn't heard for a time. Maggie moved closer to Eric and took his hand.

"I can only imagine," Brother Wheelock said soberly. He turned to his brethren. "I think most of you remember Brother Young, Brother Joseph A. Young. He and I had a chance to spend a couple of evenings with you a while back. These other brethren are Brother Abel Garr"—one of the two remaining men lifted a hand—"and Brother Stephen Taylor." The second one waved as well. None of the four brethren was smiling, another indication of what the sight of the company was doing to them.

"We are an express party sent out by Captain George D. Grant—whom all of you know—to try to locate your whereabouts. What you need to know is that Captain Grant is in command of a train of about twenty-five wagons, all of which are loaded to the bows with food, bedding, warm clothing, and other things that you need."

He had to stop as cries of joy rang out. "The Lord be praised!" one woman exclaimed. "Hallelujah!" cried another. "God has remembered us," a man said, weeping even as he spoke.

"That's right," Brother Wheelock said forcefully, "God has not forgotten you. Nor have the Saints in the Valley. These twenty-five wagons are only the first of many that are being prepared to come to your rescue."

Maggie felt herself sag against Eric's arm. The pain in her chest was like a fire now, the bitter cold tearing at her throat like a wood rasp. But now they were found. Now there was food on its way towards them. Wagonloads of food. Her cheeks were so cold, when the tears spilled over and started to trickle down her cheeks they felt like scalding water.

"President Richards has reported to President Young your plight, and President Young has called on the Saints to step forward and bring you home."

"How far in back of you are the other wagons?" Captain Willie asked loudly. "We distributed the last of our flour this morning."

"We don't know for sure," Joseph Young said. "A day or two at most, and coming hard. We've only been twelve days out of Salt Lake."

"Wonderful! This is an answer to our prayers."

"Do you know where Captain Martin's company is?" Brother Wheelock asked. "Is there any word of them?"

Brother Willie shook his head slowly. "None, not since Brother Richards passed us. At that point they were about eight days behind us."

That clearly shocked all four of the brethren, but they tried not to show it.

"All right," Brother Wheelock said, straightening now. "We are going to leave you and press on. We must find them as well. When you meet Brother Grant, tell him that we shall go to Devil's Gate as he requested, but no farther. If we haven't found Captain Martin's group we will wait for him there."

Elder Willie nodded. They were only five days' march from Devil's Gate. There was no way that they would find Martin's group by then. But he said nothing.

Brother Wheelock was suddenly all business now. "Captain Willie, we wish desperately that we had some food to leave with you, but we are traveling light so we can make excellent time. We are going to leave you now and go on to find Brother Martin's company. Press on as swiftly as you are able. You have been found and help is on its way."

Ten minutes before, if someone had suggested that the whole company rise up and give a cheer, Maggie would have laughed in the person's face. It would have been an utter impossibility. But as the four men climbed back into the wagon and with a final wave sent the team trotting forward, a great cheer rose up from the ragtag line of emigrants. No one moved until the wagon gradually disappeared into the swirling mists of snow and could no longer be seen.

"All right, brothers and sisters," Elder Willie said, his voice jubilant. "This is the news we have been waiting for. But we are not saved yet. We've still got ten miles to go before we reach the Sixth Crossing, our camping place for the night. But—" He smiled broadly, the first time he had done so in several days. "But knowing that the wagons are coming is a cause for great rejoicing. As we resume our march, do not forget to offer your thanks to a merciful and loving God for answering our prayers."

By five o'clock that afternoon, the rescue company had reached a state of near exhaustion. What had started out as a snowstorm that morning had swiftly escalated into a full-scale high plains blizzard. It was snowing heavily, but due to the shrieking wind, there was no way to tell how much had actually fallen thus far. In some places along the tops of hills or ridges, the trail was down to bare ground. In low spots or where the sagebrush provided a windbreak, the drifts were up to the bellies of the horses. In semi-sheltered areas, the depth was eight to ten inches, probably about the best indicator of how much snow there actually was.

David Granger had ridden a lot of miles in winter weather, especially taking the mails up and down the Mormon Corridor between Utah and California. He was no stranger to cold, but this was like nothing he had ever experienced before. His body was numb, his face—even beneath the woolen scarf—like a raw wound, his fingers so stiff he could barely hold on to the reins.

He and Heber P. Kimball had tied their horses to the back of the wagon and both of them rode on the wagon seat. It wasn't much but the canvas cover did provide some shelter from the battering gusts that shook the wagons like toys.

"Look!" Heber suddenly commanded.

David lifted his eyes, squinting into the flying clouds of snow. One by one the wagons ahead of them were making a sharp right turn. Then they saw Major Robert Burton coming towards them on his horse. He slowed at each wagon, yelling something and pointing.

"We're turning off," David said. He was too tired and cold to feel relief.

In a moment Brother Burton reached them. "Captain Grant says we can't fight this any longer," he shouted.

"Where are we going?" David shouted back.

"This is either Rock Creek or Willow Creek. We'll follow it down to the Sweetwater, see if we can find some willows that will give us some shelter from this hellish wind."

"Yes, sir," Heber P. called. "Glad to hear that, Major."

Burton lifted a hand and rode on. Two minutes later it was their turn, and David pulled sharply on the reins, turning the four mules to the right. For all he was glad for a respite from the storm, he couldn't stop thinking about the handcart companies somewhere out ahead of them. Surely this storm had engulfed them too. And what would they do if their rescuers could not push on?

He leaned forward, concentrating on driving the teams. He couldn't dwell on that. Not when the answer was too terrible to think about and not when there wasn't one thing he could do to change it.

II

Monday, 20 October 1856

Eric Pederson stepped out of his tent and stopped to look around in wonder. He had once seen a pen-and-ink drawing of an Eskimo village in the far northern reaches of Canada. The people were dressed in their furs and stood in front of small round houses made from blocks of ice called igloos. That was what came to his mind now. It was as if he had stumbled into one of those Eskimo villages. The wind had died down considerably now, though there was still a stiff breeze out of the north. It was well below freezing, and his breath came out in explosions of mists which whipped away almost instantly. The snow was eight to ten inches deep and it was still snowing steadily. The roofs of the round tents were completely covered. That and their white sides gave them the appearance of enormous igloos in the early morning light.

They were camped on the east side of the Sweetwater River, which here at the Sixth Crossing ran basically north and south. Some of the tents were out in the open; some were in small clearings in the willows. Having arrived after dark, they had found whatever place was large enough to accommodate their tents and put them up. Though he couldn't see it, he could hear the soft murmur of the river, which was about five or six rods from where he stood. A soft bellow sounded and he turned to see their pitiful little herd of oxen and cattle. They were a short distance away, pawing at the snow to find any kind of forage.

Eric looked down at the ground and saw that he was not the first one up and out this morning. Judging from the tracks in the snow, at least two people had come by his tent in the last few minutes. Then, as he looked around, he saw three men over near where Elder Willie had camped last night. A column of smoke was rising from where they were getting the first fire started.

Good, he thought. He was already feeling the cold through the holes in the bottoms of his boots and felt a wave of depression. Last night he had sat up long after Olaf and the Nielsons and the rest of their "tent family" had gone to sleep, rubbing his feet to get them warm, fearing greatly that they might have been frostbitten after six hours of trudging through the blizzard. The boots were still wet, and the dry stockings he had put on this morning would likely not stay that way very long.

His shoulders straightened as he looked around. Standing here worrying about it certainly wasn't going to warm his feet up. Getting his bearings, he started for one of the tents at the outskirts of the camp. When he reached it, now making his own track through the snow, he paused for a moment. Here no one had been outside yet. Were they awake? And then he heard the murmur of women's voices from inside. He stepped forward and rapped on the tent softly. Snow cascaded down and he had to jump back to avoid being inundated.

"Yes?"

"Sister Bathgate? It's Eric."

"Oh, yes. Good morning, Eric."

"Just seeing how you and Sister Isabella are. Is everything all right?"

"We're just fine, thank you. A little hungry, perhaps, but we'll fix that with a hearty breakfast in a bit."

He laughed. What a joy these two were! Even in the face of near disaster they had not lost their wry sense of humor. "You're sure?" he called softly.

"Yes, really. You go see to Maggie. She's the one we are worried about."

"Yah," he murmured. "Me too." He moved away, heading straight for the river. The James and McKensie tent was set up only a rod or so from the water. A movement out of the corner of his eye brought his head around. It was Olaf, just coming out of their tent. He didn't want to call out, for some might be asleep, so Eric waved at him. Olaf waved back and, guessing where Eric was going, started moving toward the river as well.

"How are the sisters?" Olaf asked as their paths merged.

"They say they're fine."

"And Maggie?"

"That's what I'm going to find out right now."

As the two of them approached the tent, the flap suddenly opened and Robbie McKensie stepped out. He was followed closely by Reuben James. Both were bundled up in their tattered coats and threadbare scarfs. Eric noticed that Robbie's mittens had holes in the palms where he had pushed at the back of the McKensie handcart.

"Good morning," Robbie said when he saw the two brothers.

"Good morning, Robbie. How are you this morning?"

"Hungry," he said without bitterness. Then he grinned. "And you?"

"About the same," Eric said. "We have simply got to start eating better, don't you think?"

"Ha!" Reuben exclaimed. "I would like to do that too. Any suggestions?"

"How's Maggie, Robbie?"

He shook his head. "She was coughing in the night, but she says she's not any worse."

Eric nodded soberly and looked at Reuben. Robbie was twelve

and Reuben was fourteen. Now they both looked like they were in their forties. Their faces were drawn, the flesh stretched tightly over their cheekbones. It was hard to remember that they were still boys. "How's your father, Reuben?"

"Not good, Eric. Mama is really worried. He got really cold riding in the cart yesterday."

"I could tell."

"He won't be able to walk today. And with the snow, I don't know what we're going to do."

Olaf turned and looked across the river where the indentations of the wagon tracks that marked the trail could be faintly discerned. Other than that, the scene was one vast expanse of rolling whiteness, hill after gentle hill of snow-covered desert. "It is not going to be a good day," he said softly.

The four boys fell silent, contemplating what it was going to take to pull handcarts through that country when they were already weak and cold and near exhaustion from yesterday's pull.

"I can help with your other cart again," Eric finally said to Reuben. "Other than that, we will just have to ask the Lord to strengthen us."

"Yah," Olaf responded. "He has done it often enough before. But today we shall especially need it."

Eric turned away from the trail. There was no sense worrying about what lay ahead now. It would be waiting for them soon enough. "Let's get some wood and get a fire started."

"Yes," Robbie said. "That's what Mama and Sister James said too."

As they started for a thick stand of willows, Eric stopped. He was looking in the direction of Elder Willie's tent. Where there had been three men before, now there were five. A sixth man was coming toward them, leading two mules already saddled. Eric watched for a moment, a little surprised. Why were they mounting up this soon? The camp wouldn't be ready to move out for another hour and a half, maybe two.

"Where are they going?" Olaf asked.

"I don't know. Stay here. I'm going to find out."

As he approached the small group of men, Eric immediately saw that it was their subcaptains standing around with Elder Willie—Savage, Atwood, Chislett, Woodward. He noted immediately that Johan Ahmanson was not among them and again felt a pang of grief that his friend and mentor was having difficulty in dealing with the challenges which faced them.

James Willie looked up as they heard his footsteps. "Eric. Oh, good. You can carry the word back to your hundred for us."

"Word about what?" he said, glancing at the mules. The man holding the reins was Brother Joseph Elder.

Brother Willie was pulling on gloves. Once they were on, he blew on them, as though he might warm his hands through the leather. "We're not going to move the camp, Eric."

His eyebrows shot up in surprise.

"There's no way the company can go on," Levi Savage said. "Not in this snow."

"But—"

"The relief wagons are out there somewhere," Brother Willie said grimly. "Brother Elder and I are going to go find them. We're leaving Brother Woodward in charge of the camp."

"You're going alone?" Eric exclaimed.

"There'll be two of us," Brother Elder said.

James Willie hugged himself, turning his back to the fire and moving a little closer. "We fear that they may have stopped in the storm. We've got to find those wagons and tell them how desperate our situation is. Our camp can't go on. We just can't."

Eric had not meant to sound like he was protesting. He was just greatly surprised. In actuality, the news came as a great relief to him. It would mean a world of difference to Maggie and Brother James—to all of the camp, for that matter—if they could rest for the day.

William Woodward was nodding. "Do you want the rest of the provisions distributed this morning, then?"

Their captain hesitated and then nodded. "We don't have any choice. Give out the last of those dried biscuits. There should be about one pound per person left. Thankfully, you have plenty of good water and enough willows to keep the fires going."

"And what about the beef?" Brother Savage asked.

"You may as well kill two more and distribute the meat." Brother Willie sighed. "Not that it will be much good to the people. The meat anymore looks and tastes like chunks of red clay, but yes, kill what you feel you need."

"It's you two that we're worried about," John Chislett said softly. "Do you think you can find the trail in the snow? If that wind picks up again . . ." He just shook his head.

James Willie nodded slowly, his eyes dark and brooding. "We ride with the Lord, firm in the faith that He has not forsaken us. Brethren, Brother Elder and I will not be alone. Nor will you. We ask that you and the camp pray to God with all the energy of your souls that the Lord will hear our cries in this our extremity and bring us deliverance. *We must find those wagons.*"

Then, suddenly determined, he turned to Brother Elder. "Are you ready?"

"Yes, sir. Let's do it."

He handed Captain Willie the reins of his mule and they both swung up. "May God be with you, brethren," Brother Willie said as he wheeled the mule around.

"And with you," Levi Savage said quietly.

When Eric came back to the tent, Sister James and Sister McKensie were outside, bent over the small pile of willows the boys had collected, preparing to start the fires. Mary McKensie straightened. "What's happening, Eric? Where are those men going?"

"To find the wagons." He reached out and touched her arm briefly, then looked at Sister James as well. "Good news. We're going to stay here until Elder Willie gets back."

Jane James stared at him for a moment, then dropped her head into her hands. "Thank heavens."

"Oh, that is wonderful news," Mary cried. "I didn't know how we could do it today."

"We couldn't." Eric paused for a moment. "Is Maggie awake?"

"Yes."

He gave her a questioning look. She finally looked away. "She says she is no worse."

"I asked Brother Woodward to help me give her and Brother James a blessing today."

"That would be wonderful, Eric," Mary said.

"Yes," Jane said. "Thank you, Eric. I am terribly worried about William."

"It's going to be all right," Eric said, trying to sound confident. "If we have—how you say it? lucky day?—then those wagons won't be too far away."

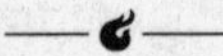

Twenty-five miles to the west, in the thick willows along Rock Creek, near where it emptied into the Sweetwater River, the wind was blowing but at a greatly reduced scale. The snow came down in soft swirls and fell silently among the thickets. But David Granger wasn't fooled by that. He could hear the wind sighing in the upper boughs of the trees along the river, and across the creek about 150 yards away the snow was pouring over a ridge top in billowing clouds and long, misty tendrils, already forming a long drift. That was a clear indicator of what it would be like up in the higher, open country. He shivered a little. It was cold enough down here that the snow squeaked a little beneath his feet. In the wind it would be unbearable. The thought of being out there in the open was not something to comfort the soul.

He turned around, holding out his hands toward the fire. The other men around him were doing the same. They had three fires in the camp and all were crackling and spitting as they consumed the piles of dead willows that had been thrown on them. Someone had nursed the coals during the night, thank heavens, and it had been a simple thing to get them up to full strength again this morning. Around each of the fires, ten or twelve men stood together. They kept glancing over to Captain Grant's tent, wondering what their leaders were deciding.

They didn't have to wait long. George D. Grant, Major Robert Burton, William H. Kimball, and Charles Decker, their lead scout, broke off and turned and walked to the nearest fire. Major Burton waved his arm, calling the others to join them.

David looked at Heber P. and nodded. This was what they had been waiting for. Following the trails through the snow, which down here in the copse of willows was only four or five inches deep, they gathered around their leaders to hear what they had to say.

Brother Grant wasted no time getting to it. "Brethren, under the circumstances, with the storm showing no signs of let up, we think it would be foolish for us to try and go on today."

He stopped to let that settle in. There was worry on the leathered faces and in these eyes that had seen too many summers out in the open or too much sunlight bouncing off snow-covered ranges. Concern for the handcart Saints was evident on the countenances of these men, but there was also relief. A storm of this magnitude and ferocity demanded respect from even the most seasoned outdoorsman. Some of those drifts would be up to the wagon boxes by now, and nothing could take the heart out of a team faster than having to buck their way through that kind of snow. If the men got caught out in the open and ruined their teams, they wouldn't be rescuing a jackrabbit out here, let alone a thousand starving people.

Brother Burton cleared his throat. "If the storm blows through, we'll follow right behind it. Until then, check your gear. Make sure everything's in good repair. And make sure the livestock is secure. We can't afford to lose any teams at this point." He looked around, seeming to be satisfied with what he saw. "Be ready to move out quickly if we decide to go."

Chapter Notes

It was about noon on 19 October, shortly after they left Ice Springs, that the Willie Company met the express party sent forward by Captain George D. Grant. Though the express party could offer no immediate relief from the crisis, the response to their appearance can only be imagined by modern readers. In typical understatement, Levi Savage records: "At twelve o'clock we met Brother Wheelock and company who have come to our relief. . . . This was joyful news to us" (in *Remember*, p. 7). Chislett put it this way: "More welcome messengers never came from the courts of glory than these two young men were to us [there were actually four]. They . . . sped on further east to convey their glad news to Edward Martin and the fifth handcart company. . . . As they went from our view, many a hearty 'God bless you' followed them" (in *Remember*, p. 7).

Once those four intrepid men went on, the grim reality of the situation settled in again on the Willie Company. They were in the midst of a major winter storm. They were still ten miles from their next campsite, and they had issued the last of their flour rations that morning.

As Savage continues with his entry, we get some indication of how serious the situation was: "The wind continued strong and cold. The children, the aged, and infirmed fell back to the wagons until they were so full that all in them were extremely uncomfortable. Brother Knockles, aged 66 years, died during the day in a handcart hitched behind one of the wagons. Sister Smith and Daniel Osborn, age eight years, died in the wagons. They had been ill for some time. The carts arrived at the river at dark. One wagon, it being dark, took another road and did not get into camp until eleven o'clock p.m. They were nearly exhausted and so were myself and teamsters" (in *Remember*, p. 7).

Chislett paints a similar picture: "We pursued our journey with renewed hope and after untold toil and fatigue, doubling teams frequently, going back to fetch up the straggling carts, and encouraging those who had dropped by the way to a little more exertion in view of our soon-to-be improved condition, we finally, late at night, got all to camp—the wind howling frightfully and the snow eddying around us in fitful gusts. But we had found a good camp among the willows, and after warming and partially drying ourselves before good fires, we ate our scanty fare, paid our usual devotions to the Deity and retired to rest with hopes of coming aid" (in *Remember*, p. 7).

By the time they reached the Sixth Crossing of the Sweetwater (located south of U.S. Highway 287 west of Jeffrey City, Wyoming), the Willie Company was near the end of their endurance. In his narrative John Chislett gives some of the grim details:

> The morning before the storm, or rather, the morning of the day on which it came [the 19th], we issued the last ration of flour. On this fatal morning [the 20th], therefore, we had none to issue. We had, however, a barrel or two of hard bread which Captain Willie had procured at Fort Laramie in view of our destitution. This was equally and fairly divided among all the company. Two of our poor broken-down cattle were killed and their carcasses issued for beef. With this we were informed that we would have to subsist until the coming supplies reached us. . . .
>
> Being surrounded by snow a foot deep, out of provisions, many of our people sick, and our cattle dying, it was decided that we should remain in our present camp until the supply train reached us. It was also resolved in council that Captain Willie with one man [Joseph Elder] should go in search of the supply train and apprise its lead of our condition, and hasten him to our help. When this was done we settled down and made our camp as comfortable as we could. As Captain Willie and his companion left for the West, many a heart was lifted in prayer for their success and speedy return. (In *Remember*, pp. 7–8)

Unfortunately, the oncoming rescue party, knowing nothing of all of this, decided that they could not go on in the blizzard. On the evening of the nineteenth, Captain Grant pulled off the main trail at what he said was Willow Creek (but was more likely Rock Creek) to find shelter. The next day, due to the fury of the storm, he determined to stay where he was and wait for the storm to blow itself out.

CHAPTER 24

ROCK CREEK TO SIXTH CROSSING

I

Monday, 20 October 1856

The storm did not blow itself out that day as Brother Grant had hoped it would. The wind howled along the ridges, and the snow kept falling thickly all through the day, a day that to David Granger seemed to go on forever and ever. There were times when it looked as though it might be letting up; then ten minutes later it would be coming down more thickly than ever before. So the men of the rescue party sat in their tents or around the fires talking quietly. Harnessing was repaired; loads were checked and rechecked; snow was cleared so that the horses and mules could find the rich grass below. The one topic of conversation was the whereabouts of the handcart companies, but even that was eventually exhausted. Finally, totally bored, the men lay down on their bedrolls and pulled their hats over their eyes and tried to sleep.

At about half past three, when it was obvious that the storm had not abated and that they would not be moving on that day, the men were rousted out by their leaders. The camp was quickly divided. Some were asked to help Dan Jones start getting their supper ready.

Some, including David and Heber P., were sent to gather more dead willows and brush to keep the fires going through another night. The last group was sent out once again to check on the teams.

Supper was a somber affair. Men sat around the fires or ate in their tents, talking quietly as they consumed another ample meal. Dan Jones, cook for the company, provided excellent meals every day, but guilt was the sauce that flavored their food. Who could eat from such abundance—the wagons around them contained literally tons of food—without thinking of their brothers and sisters out there trying to weather the storm with little or nothing? Yet eat they did, for they knew with equal certainty that once the lost were found, the health and strength of the rescuers would become the salvation of those in need of rescue.

"Brother Grant?"

David's head came up to see who had spoken. It was Harvey Cluff. David knew Harvey, though not really well. Like David and Heber P., he was a Minute Man, but living in Provo, he was part of the Utah County company.

George Grant turned. "Yes."

"I've been thinking," Harvey said, a little tentatively, David thought.

"About what?"

"We're some distance to the south of the trail down here."

"Yes." Grant was watching him curiously. Robert Burton and William Kimball had turned now as well. "Two or three miles probably," Grant acknowledged.

And thank heavens for that, David thought. At least they had shelter down here.

"I was thinking. What if the express party happened to come by tonight? Our tracks have surely long since been covered. They wouldn't know we had turned off the trail."

Major Burton was immediately shaking his head. "No one's going to be out on that trail today. Especially not this late."

"But what if they were?" Cluff said doggedly. "We're too far off the trail for them to see our fire. And with the wind blowing out of the north, they'd never even smell the smoke. They'd go right on by and never see us."

The three leaders looked at each other, considering that possibility. They had been anxiously looking for the express party's return now for several days. What if this *was* the day?

"If we put up a signboard up there where we turned off," Harvey Cluff said, a little less sure of himself now, "then if someone did come along, they'd know we were down here."

"It's a good thought," William Kimball said, "but it's a long way back up to the trail and all uphill in deep snow."

"Yes, sir."

And with that the men went back to what they had been doing before. Nothing more was said about putting up a signboard on the trail.

It was ten minutes later, as David was preparing to go inside his tent for the rest of another long night, when he saw a movement at the back of one of the wagons about three places around the circle from their own. The unseen sun was down now and the light was fading noticeably. In another half an hour it would be full dark. David peered at the figure for a moment until he half turned. David was startled to see that it was Harvey Cluff. He had the wagon cover pulled back and was doing something inside.

As David made sure his own wagon was secure, he kept glancing over at the figure of Harvey Cluff. Whatever it was he was doing, he was certainly staying at it. Finally, done with his own work, David decided he would go over and see if he might help. He made sure the lashings on the cover were secure, then shoved his hands in his pockets and walked over.

"Hi. Need some help?"

Cluff jerked around in surprise, then looked a little sheepish. "No. I'm just done, in fact." Then to David's surprise he straightened and pulled out a three-foot piece of board nailed to a narrow piece of wood taken from one of the crates. Crudely painted on the board were three words and a thick arrow pointing to the left. David moved around so he could see better, then started. The board read, "CAPTAIN GRANT'S COMPANY," and then the arrow was painted below it.

Cluff watched him closely. "I decided I was going to do it," he said quietly. "I talked to Captain Grant and told him I had strong feelings about it. He said it was all right with him."

David nodded. It seemed a little strange, but you had to admire a man for sticking to his guns. "Are you going to take it up tonight?"

"Yes."

David grinned. "Want some company?"

Cluff smiled slowly. "I'd like that."

It took them an hour and a half to go up and back, and it was full dark when David and Harvey Cluff came back to the campsite on the Sweetwater. They were soaked almost to the waist and shivering violently. The men saw them coming and immediately made a place for them by the fire. David's legs trembled as he sat down, and he gave a low sigh of relief to be off his feet. Once they left the shelter of the willows, the snow had doubled in depth and in several places they had to buck their way through drifts that were above their knees. David guessed that the trail was close to three miles away from their campsite. Coming down, following the trail they had already made was easier, but going up there had been a couple of times when he wasn't absolutely certain they would make it.

The men knew where they had been, and it pleased David that there was not one chiding or disparaging remark made. There were some who obviously thought it was a futile gesture, but if Harvey

Cluff was feeling something so strongly, then he had their admiration and respect for following through with it.

"How was it?" Heber P. asked, coming over to sit beside his friend.

"Well, I'll say this much," David answered. "Earlier I questioned Brother Grant's wisdom about laying over here today. I don't question it anymore."

"That bad?"

"This is wonderful," David said fervently. "You don't have to go far up that hill before you know just how protected we are down here."

"Here, let me get you two some hot beef broth," Heber said. He went to the kettle hanging over the fire and dipped out two cups of dark liquid. He handed one to David and the other to Harvey Cluff.

"Ah," David said as the liquid warmed his body. "Thank you."

"Yes," Harvey said. "This is wonderful."

"So where did you put the sign?" Heber asked.

David looked at Harvey, deferring to him, since it was his idea.

"We propped it up in a large sagebrush. We had to put some rocks around it to make sure it didn't blow over."

"But it's easy to see?"

Harvey smiled in satisfaction. "It would be pretty hard to miss, even in the dark."

It was barely five minutes later when a sound brought everyone's head up with a start. "What was that?" Captain Grant said, standing up and peering in the darkness. He was looking to the north, up the path that David and Harvey Cluff had made a few minutes before.

"It sounded like a shout," Robert Burton said. He too was on his feet and staring in that same direction.

"Oh my word!" Grant suddenly gasped.

All of them shot to their feet and were gaping at the same spot.

Against the white snow, barely visible in the darkness, they could see two dark shapes approaching.

"Halloo the camp!"

"It's the express party!" Charles Decker cried out. "They're back!" He and Grant darted forward to the edge of the firelight.

"But they were in a wagon," someone remembered. "These are on mules."

Captain Grant cupped his hands. "Brother Wheelock! Joseph Young! Is that you?"

What came back shocked every man to the core of his being.

"No! It's James G. Willie, captain of the fourth handcart company."

Harvey Cluff jerked around as if he had been hit by an arrow. He was staring at David.

David shook his head in wonder. "They must have gotten to your sign just minutes after we put it up," he said.

Harvey was nodding, his eyes wide. "If we hadn't put it there, they would have gone on past us. And then . . ." Humbled by that thought, he turned back to look at the two oncoming riders. "Who would ever have thought that a signboard could do the work of salvation?" he murmured.

II

Tuesday, 21 October 1856

Maggie opened her eyes as she felt something brush against her cheek. In the dim light of the tent it took her a moment to recognize the dark shape over her and another moment to remember that she was lying in Eric's arms and that he had touched her cheek with the back of his finger a moment before as well. "Hello," she whispered, managing a wan smile.

"Hal-lo, Sester Maggie," Eric said, exaggerating his accent into a broad drawl.

Her smile broadened. "Did I fall asleep again?"

He nodded. "Only for a moment."

"What time is it?"

He shrugged. "About half past five. Almost sundown."

She opened her eyes wider. "You can see the sun?"

"Yes. The storm is finally gone. It is beautiful out there. Very cold, but beautiful."

She started to get up. "Your arm must be tired."

He held her in place gently. "My arm is yoost fine, yah, and tank you vedy much."

She laughed softly, then immediately clutched at her chest as she started to cough.

"I'm sorry," he said instantly. "I shouldn't make you laugh."

The cough passed in a moment, and she looked at him and shook her head. "I need to laugh, Eric. I need to laugh very much." She caught herself. "Vedy much."

Mary McKensie was lying on the bed next to Maggie, with Robbie curled up beside her beneath the blankets. "We all need to laugh," she said.

Maggie turned her head. As their eyes met, her mother smiled. Robbie's eyes were closed and Maggie couldn't tell if he was asleep or not. He had spoken to his mother just a few minutes before. She looked around the tent. The other beds were all full as well. Jane James sat beside her husband, holding his hand. From where she lay, Maggie could see his chest rising and falling in quick, shallow breaths. His face was as white as the canvas of their tent. Sarah and Emma lay together on the other side of their father, also sharing a blanket and each other's body warmth. Reuben and the younger James children were lying close together, Reuben reading to them from the Book of

Mormon, holding the book up so that the light coming through the tent wall illuminated the pages.

"We make a pretty sad group, don't we?" she said, turning back to Eric.

He looked around. "It is good to conserve our strength. How fortunate we are that Brother Willie did not think it wise to push on."

She was instantly sorry for her pessimism. Eric was right. What would it have meant to be out on the trail these last two days? With the last of their food now consumed, it was a great blessing to stay in place. This morning breakfast had been nothing but water with a pinch of sugar in it. The hunger was sapping their strength now at an alarming rate, and they had to conserve their energy and keep warm. And it was working. She could tell that her cough had improved, and Brother James, though still terribly weak, was significantly better than when they had arrived here at the Sixth Crossing. And they were well off compared to others. Eric's tent group had lost four to death now, including a child and a father in one family. Five or six others were still too ill to rise and care for themselves. The reports were that many others were in a similar state.

Eric seemed to sense her thoughts and nodded slowly. "Olaf says there have been four more deaths so far today, including an eleven-year-old Danish girl in our hundred."

Maggie winced. Four today. One yesterday. Four the day before. She closed her eyes, now doubly sorry for her comment. "We are very fortunate, aren't we?"

"Yes," her mother said softly. "And thanks be to the Lord for that."

"I hope Hannah is all right," Robbie said, opening his eyes.

"Hannah will be fine," Mary said, though her eyes filled with sorrow at the mention of her daughter.

"I am so glad she has Ingrid," Maggie said. "I'll bet they have grown so close now."

Sarah sat up now and Emma followed a moment later. "I would so love to see them again," Emma said. "I miss them so much."

"You will see them soon enough," Sister James said. "Once we–"

She stopped. Outside the tent there was a sudden noise. Someone was shouting in a hoarse cry. Then just outside their tent they heard a young girl's voice. "Papa! Papa! Look!"

Sarah leaped to her feet. "Something's wrong," she cried. She darted to the tent flap and, though she had no coat on, slipped outside.

Eric had his head cocked to one side, listening. Now there was a major commotion going on out there. People were shouting and yelling. He laid Maggie back down on her bed and stood up as her mother and Robbie got up quickly too.

"What is it, Mama?" one of the younger children asked Sister James.

"I'll go see," Eric said. He moved to the flap, holding it open as Maggie's mother, Robbie, Reuben, and Emma all went out as well. Maggie rose up on one elbow, listening intently. Then she heard Robbie's voice in a piercing shriek. "Look, Mama! Look!"

Maggie threw back the covers and started to rise, but before she was half up, Eric burst back inside. "What is it, Eric? What's wrong?"

His eyes were registering shock and disbelief. He came to her side and helped her up.

"What, Eric? What is it?"

He just stared at her, his eyes filled with awe.

Jane James was up on her knees now, staring at Eric. "Yes, Eric. Tell us." Beside her, William had awakened and was looking around wildly.

"Come and see," Eric shouted. "You must see this." In that instant he realized that Maggie had no shoes on her feet. With a cry that was half joy, half pain, he swept her up in his arms and moved swiftly to the tent flap. Sister James was there before him, holding it open. Eric leaped through it, then ran awkwardly around to the back of their tent to where the others were all standing.

Maggie threw an arm up across her face. Everything was such a dazzling white that it hurt her eyes. Then as she heard the cries all around her she opened them a crack. Eric had turned so that she was facing to the west. The first thing she saw was a beautiful sunset. The sun was down, but there was a golden glow behind the hill and the clouds were painted with gold.

"What?" she asked, thoroughly perplexed. Surely the people had not gone mad simply because the sun had come out after five or six days.

To her utter astonishment, when Eric looked down at her, his eyes were filled with tears. "Look!" was all he could say. "Look on the ridge."

And then Maggie McKensie saw it too. A movement caught her eye. About a mile to the west of them the flatlands of the river bottom gave way to a sage-covered hillside, perhaps a hundred or so feet higher than where they stood. It was covered with snow and that was why she had missed it at first. But now, silhouetted against the farther hills, she saw a man on horseback–no, muleback. And behind him were– She gave a low cry and her hand flew to her mouth.

Behind him were three wagons, each pulled by four horses. No, four wagons! There came another and then another just behind them.

"What is it?" she exclaimed, not daring to believe.

Eric stared at her, tears streaming down his face now. Then he buried his head against her hair. "It's the wagons, Maggie. Elder Willie has found the wagons."

David Granger started, his head jerking up with a snap. He looked around wildly for one moment, then realized that he had fallen asleep for a second or two. His hands, lying loosely in his lap, still clutched the reins to the four mules. Not that he was making any difference. The mules, heads down and plodding along with their eyes half-closed, were following the wagon in front of them without any help from David.

Surprised that he had dozed off while he was sitting up in a moving wagon—something he had never done before—he turned to see if Heber P. had noticed him. But Heber wasn't noticing anything. His arms were folded and he was leaning back against the sacks of flour that filled the wagon behind them. His hat was pulled down and his eyes were closed.

David half smiled. He wondered how many others up and down the line were struggling to stay awake. He half turned. Behind him, the sun had just gone down, leaving a golden glow all along the horizon and touching the scattered clouds above them with wisps of gold. He guessed it was about half past five or perhaps moving toward six o'clock. He thought about digging out his father's pocket watch to see for sure, then decided it wasn't worth it.

The arrival of James G. Willie and Joseph Elder in camp last night had created a sensation. They had finally found the lost company. But the euphoria quickly faded when the captain told them of the condition his people were in. And they were at the Sixth Crossing, about twenty-five miles farther east. That had settled it for Captain Grant. As soon as Willie and Elder were fed and their mounts seen to, the captain ordered everyone to bed. They were up and gone long before light began to dawn over the east and reveal that the storm had finally blown itself out. They had a quick, cold breakfast and hit the road, barely able to discern the trail in the darkness. That had been about fifteen hours ago. No wonder they were falling asleep.

It had been a very long and tiresome day. They kept the teams moving steadily and took only brief stops to rest. The snow was deep in many spots, and they rotated the lead-wagon position so that one team didn't have to break trail the whole way. The men were exhausted; the animals were nearly at the end of their strength.

Fortunately, twice now in the last twenty minutes they had caught sight of a line of trees in the far distance. Trees out here in this desolation meant only one thing. Once again they were approaching the Sweetwater River. The next time the trail intersected the river was the Sixth Crossing.

They had come down a long, gently sloping hill and entered a low swale before the land rose again. David and Heber's wagon was about midway in the line, and David could see the wagons out ahead of him going up and over the rise, then disappearing again.

Suddenly there was a shout up ahead. As he looked to see what it was, he realized that it was a similar shout a moment ago that had brought him awake. Heber stirred beside him and sat up. He looked around for a moment, trying to get his bearings. "What is it, David?"

"Don't know yet. Someone up ahead is yelling something."

Then as their wagon crested the low hill and started down the other side, David saw what the shouting was about. The low ridge line provided a slight eminence that gave them a commanding view of the landscape below. Stretching across the whole width of his vision was a line of trees marking the serpentine path of the Sweetwater River. Here and there he could see stretches of black where the river itself was visible. But what caught the eye was directly ahead of them, on the opposite bank. There, silhouetted against the darker willows, was a collection of odd mounds, almost like small haystacks buried in the snow. And then David inhaled sharply. There was movement around those mounds—tiny black figures clustered together. Even as he watched, more appeared as if by magic from the mounds themselves.

At the head of their column, Brother Willie had spurred his mule forward. He was standing in the stirrups as the animal loped forward, waving his hat around and around as he shouted at the top of his lungs. The lead wagons were whipping their horses into a lumbering run, following after him.

David felt the breath go out of him in a huge explosion of joy. "It's the camp, Heber! There it is. We've found their camp."

—❦—

David thought that he had prepared himself for what they would find when they finally came upon the emigrants. He had listened intently last night as Captain Willie and Brother Elder described the condition of their people and felt his sense of horror deepen. But nothing anyone could have said or done prepared him for what waited for him as his team splashed across the river and then pulled up to a stop beside the other wagons.

The round tents, buried beneath eight or ten inches of snow, were not placed in any kind of order. They were scattered here and there, some near the river, others among the thickets of willows, a few out in the clearing beyond. Pathways had been trampled in the snow between the tents, giving the area the look of a gigantic prairie dog colony. But it was the people that stunned him. They were pouring out of the tents like ants from a disturbed anthill. Some came out bent over and barely able to move. Others burst forth, leaping up and down, waving their arms.

Everyone was shouting and yelling and laughing and crying. As David and Heber swung down, a woman ran by them with a baby in a tattered, filthy blanket held out in front of her, as though she were beseeching the men to take it from her. "God bless you! God bless you!" she sobbed as she went by. "God bless you."

Directly ahead of David an old man had dropped to his knees and his face was in his hands. His shoulders were shaking convulsively as great sobs racked his body. Suddenly he looked up toward heaven. The dying light from the sunset caught the wetness on his cheeks and turned them to gold as he closed his eyes. David saw his lips begin to move silently.

He turned as a cluster of people caught his eyes. Here were adults and young children as well. One man held a woman in his arms. The younger children were dancing up and down, waving their arms in the air and shouting at the top of their lungs. One little fellow, who looked to be about four, saw David and started forward. His coat was nearly in rags and his battered hat no longer had any color. He wore no shoes but had his feet wrapped in burlap sacks. His blue eyes were wide and filled with wonder. Then he held out his hands and David saw that the tips of his fingers were blackened. He recoiled in horror. Frostbite.

Beside him he heard Heber gasp.

Eyes burning, David ran around to the back of the wagon. He thrust his hand into the nearest sack and grabbed a round, fat onion. He jerked his knife from the sheath on his belt and cut it in two, then darted forward to the little boy, holding out one of the halves to him.

"For me?" the boy cried in a hoarse voice.

David stifled a sob of his own. "Yes. We're here. This is for you."

The boy snatched the onion and bit into it tentatively. The wide eyes closed and there was a murmur of exquisite pleasure as he began to chew slowly.

David turned. A girl was coming toward him now as well. She was perhaps seven or eight. Her hair was dirty and matted and there were smudges of soot on her cheeks. She looked so thin, so frail. Like fragile porcelain. She extended one hand to him, looking almost frightened. David stepped forward, moving slowly so as not to frighten her, and held out the other half of the onion to her. She stared at it for several seconds, then reached out very slowly and took it from him. Then she looked up at him with wide dark eyes. "Are you an angel?" she asked.

David had to turn away as a soft cry was torn from his throat. Suddenly he couldn't see anything but the dark shape of the wagon in front of him. "Get more onions, Heber," he cried in a choked voice.

Together they grabbed the sack and brought it out of the wagon. The little boy and girl had gone back to their family. The boy was holding up the onion for his mother to see; then he turned and offered another sister a bite.

David and Heber lumbered forward, dragging the sack between them. David saw now that it was probably two families. There were two older women but no men who seemed old enough to be their husbands. The younger man who had the woman in his arms had moved forward a little, and David was surprised to see she was barefoot. Then before he could take in more details, a young woman who looked like she might be about the same age as David's sister, Eleanor, broke away from the group and ran toward them. Without a word, she hurled herself at David and he had to drop the sack in order to catch her. She threw her arms around him, clinging to him so tightly that he could hardly breathe for a moment.

"Thank you. Oh, thank you. Thank you."

With each cry of gratitude, she kissed him. On the right cheek. On the left cheek. On his forehead. On the cheek again. And then fully on the mouth.

She fell back, clearly shocked at her own behavior. Blushing deeply, she began to back away. The color only showed all the more dramatically the paleness of her face. "I'm sorry," she blurted. "It's just that—"

"It's all right," David said, swiping at his eyes to clear his vision a little. "It's all right."

"My name is Emma James." She half turned. "This is my family."

Now her mother and an older sister came forward. They were crying openly, unashamedly. "I can't believe it," the woman said. "You've finally come."

"Yes," Heber said. "And we have food." He fumbled in the sack and brought out an onion for the older sister. "Here. There are more."

Sarah James sniffed back the tears. "My father is very ill," she said. "If there are enough, may I have one for him as well?"

Heber just stared. They were on the verge of starvation and she was saying, "May I"? He reached in the sack and brought out another. "Of course. We have other things in the wagons." His eyes dropped to her coat and the dress beneath it. The elbows in her coat were gone. There was a tear in her skirt that had been crudely sewn together. Her shoes were in shambles, and oddly enough, he noticed that some of the tattered places had been cut off as though with a knife.

When he looked back up at her, he saw the shame in her eyes and was himself ashamed that she had seen him looking at her clothing. "We have clothing," he said.

She leaned forward, tears still filling her eyes, and kissed him softly on the cheek. "It's all right. We're all right. Thank you for coming to help us."

David, finally getting a little better hold on his emotions, turned to the young man holding the woman in his arms. Now as he looked at her more closely, he saw that she was no older than the man who held her. "Hello," he said. "My name is David Granger. My companion is Heber P. Kimball. We are so happy that we have finally found you."

"I am Eric Pederson," Eric said. He made no attempt to hide the tears which streaked his face. They were tears of joy and no shame was in them. He looked down tenderly. "And this is my fiancée, Maggie McKensie."

David nodded, surprised and yet somehow deeply pleased to think that young love might be present in a camp such as this.

He felt a tug on his sleeve and turned. A young man who looked to be a little younger than Alma was standing there. Like the others, his clothes were worn and dirty. The knees in his trousers were gone; the fingers of his gloves had been cut away; his scarf looked like one good tug might rip it in half. The face was gaunt, his cheeks sunken, and yet his eyes were as bright as glittering blue buttons. He had his hand out, but not with the palm up. Rather, he was offering his hand in greeting to David.

"How do you do, Brother Granger? My name is Robbie McKensie. I am Maggie's brother. We are very happy to meet you."

David took his hand and held it tightly, feeling the tears come back all over again. "I am very pleased to meet you, Robbie McKensie," he said in a whisper.

Heber stepped forward and laid an arm across Robbie's shoulder. His eyes were red, but he was smiling down at the boy. "Come on, young man. Let's get you some warm clothing and blankets."

In the largest of the clearings near the river, a huge fire was burning, sending a stream of embers into the night air. They had made the fire as large as possible so that all of the emigrants who were able could gather in one place. After the initial ecstatic welcome had spent itself and the first of the food was distributed, Captain Grant sent his men on horseback up and down the river to drag in piles of firewood. There were campfires burning all around the camp, but this one was the largest. Now those Saints who were able to walk about in any way were huddled together around it, their faces lit by the dancing firelight. It was sobering to Maggie to see that only about half of the remaining company was here. Even with the joy, many were too sick to rise from their beds.

With the storm gone, the night had turned very cold, but no one seemed to mind. Maggie looked around. What a miraculous change had come over them in a matter of just a few hours! The despair was gone. Joy infused their faces. Hope swelled their hearts. As for herself, she felt as if the rescuers had brought her a whole new body. Oh, yes, the cough was still there, but she was energized with life and excitement. She had a new coat. Well, it was not new in the sense of being brand new, but it was new to her. Some dear sister in the Valley had given this to the rescuers. It was long and thick and soft. The collar was high enough that she could bring it up and cover her ears. She also had a new pair of mittens and a heavy woolen winter bonnet.

She had protested, saying that others also needed clothing and that she shouldn't get it all. But the two young men who had found them—Brother Granger and Brother Kimball—had watched her double over with her cough, and completely ignored her feeble objections.

Beside her, Eric had a heavy pair of boots. They were scuffed and worn but clearly serviceable. The pair Olaf received was brand new. Perhaps some bootmaker in Salt Lake had been touched by President Young's call for aid and took these directly off his shelf. Sarah and Emma both had coats now, as did Maggie's mother and Sister James. Brother James, significantly improved with the food he had been given, was now comfortable beneath a buffalo robe. Robbie had a thick sweater and new fur-lined gloves. And the list went on.

Food and clothing and bedding and warmth—the change that these had wrought was indeed swift and great. But the greatest change was in their hearts. Maggie closed her eyes. *O Lord, we thank Thee for this day. We thank Thee for these wonderful Saints who have responded to our needs with unbounded love. We thank Thee for Thy goodness and mercy unto us.*

She opened her eyes as she felt a touch on her arm. Turning, she saw Eric smiling at her. "Amen," he whispered softly.

She smiled. *And for Eric, who knows my mind as if it were his own.* "Yes. Amen."

"Brothers and sisters?"

Maggie turned back toward the fire. Across from them, Elder Willie had stood up and come forward. "I—" He stopped, and his head dropped; he was overcome. For almost a full minute he struggled to get control of his voice again. Finally, sniffing back tears, he lifted his head. "The heart cannot express what we are feeling this night." He turned to where George D. Grant, Robert Burton, and William H. Kimball stood behind him. "To you brethren, and the brave men who have come with you, we offer our eternal thanks. May you ever be blessed for what you have done this day."

Brother Grant said something back, but Maggie couldn't discern what it was over the crackling of the fire.

"Brethren," Captain Willie said, "we are in your hands. Instruct us in what you will."

The invitation was not unexpected, for immediately George Grant stepped forward. He looked around the circle, then began to speak in a loud voice. "Brothers and sisters, we have been deeply touched by our experience with you this day. How grateful we are for the Lord's mercies in bringing us to you!"

He stopped and sighed. "Unfortunately, there is still much that must be done. Until we have you safely in the Valley, we cannot rest. The storm has gone on now, but surely more storms will come before we end our journey. We must act swiftly and resolutely now if we are to avert further disaster.

"As you know, there is another company behind you. They too must be in severe straits. We have heard nothing from our express party which we sent forward to find you. Therefore, the whereabouts of Brother Martin's group is still unknown. First thing in the morning I will be taking eight of the wagons on eastward to try and find them."

"Thanks be to God," Maggie whispered softly to her mother.

"Brother Kimball will keep six of the wagons and start back with you immediately."

There were some soft sounds of dismay.

He went on doggedly. "We know how difficult it will be for you in your circumstances to continue forward, but you cannot stay here. We nearly emptied six wagons this evening just to meet your elemental needs. If we are to help the Martin group, we must take the rest of the supplies with us. But there are additional wagons waiting for you. They have flour, beef, clothing, bedding, medicine. And more will be coming from Salt Lake. But they are not coming on, my brothers and sisters. We did not know where you were, and so we left those wagons waiting in place near South Pass. You have to go forward to them."

Maggie shuddered slightly and slipped her arm through Eric's. The thoughts of getting into the shafts again, especially with the ground frozen and snow-covered, left her suddenly fearful. He squeezed her arm, but didn't look at her.

"From here it is about twenty-five miles to Rock Creek Camp." He looked away, turning to the west where the trail waited, hidden now in the darkness. "They are not going to be easy miles. Between here and there lies one of the most difficult stretches of the trail. It is called Rocky Ridge. It shall test your strength and fortitude to the utmost. But you cannot lose faith now. God has not abandoned you, nor shall He. Fortunately, Brother Kimball has six nearly empty wagons to help carry the sick and the weak. You are better clothed now and have at least some food. But I cannot make it seem less difficult than it will be."

He looked around and then finished. "I wish it were not so, my beloved fellow Saints, but such is our lot. Let us press on and not lose hope."

The quiet was broken only by the crackling of the fire. Hundreds of pairs of eyes stared into the fires as the emigrants contemplated the morrow, searching their souls to measure what reserves might still be there. Then after almost a full minute of silence, a single male voice was heard. It sounded out clear and strong and without quavering. Every eye swung around to see where it had come from. Across the fire from where Maggie and her family sat, an older man in his mid-forties had stood up. He was not part of their hundred, and she didn't know his name. His head was tipped back a little and his voice poured out in perfect sweetness.

> Why should we mourn or think our lot is hard?
> 'Tis not so; all is right.
> Why should we think to earn a great reward
> If we now shun the fight?

Maggie straightened, the words piercing her heart like darts of living fire. Her head came up and without conscious thought she joined in.

> Gird up your loins; fresh courage take.
> Our God will never us forsake!

All around, the voices were coming in. Eric's head was up and he sang with full voice, the first time Maggie had ever heard him do so.

> And soon we'll have this tale to tell—
> All is well! All is well!

Now the entire camp joined in. Every head was up; every person, including the young children, was singing without restraint.

> We'll find the place which God for us prepared,
> Far away in the West,
> Where none shall come to hurt or make afraid;
> There the Saints will be blessed.
> We'll make the air with music ring,
> Shout praises to our God and King;
> Above the rest these words we'll tell—
> All is well! All is well!

A sudden thought flashed into Maggie's mind as she anticipated the next words. How many had died to this point? How many graves lay behind them? How many tents had empty places when they rolled out their beds at night? And how many more would there be? In that instant she knew that many others around the circle were having the same thoughts, for there was a moment's hesitation before they took a breath and began to sing the last verse. But when they sang, there were no hushed voices, no flinching from the terrible possibility the words suggested. They looked up at the star-spangled sky above them and sang at full voice.

> And should we die before our journey's through,
> Happy day! All is well!
> We then are free from toil and sorrow, too;
> With the just we shall dwell!

All around them, people were coming to their feet. Maggie leaped up and grabbed Eric's hand, pulling him beside her. Robbie and Sarah and Emma and Maggie's mother were up too. Jane James, who had already lost one child, and who surely was thinking about her husband who was still shivering with chills and fever in their tent, threw her shoulders back and sang into the night.

> But if our lives are spared again
> To see the Saints their rest obtain,
> Oh, how we'll make this chorus swell—
> All is well! All is well!

Chapter Notes

The rescue company journal has this terse entry for 20 October: "Stayed in the same place today [Rock Creek]. Brother Willie came to us near nightfall" (in *Remember,* p. 51).

The story of Harvey Cluff's putting up the signboard is one of the remarkable events of the rescue. Cluff, who was just twenty years of age when he accompanied the first rescue party, later wrote a detailed account of his experience. Referring to that day, he said: "For protection of ourselves and animals, the company moved down the river to where the willows were dense enough to make a good protection against the raging storm from the north. The express team . . . had been dispatched ahead as rapidly as possible to reach and give encouragement to the faltering emigrants, by letting them know that help was near at hand. Quietly resting in the seclusion of the willow copse, three miles from the road I volunteered to take a sign board and place it at a conspicuous place at the main road. This was designed to direct the express party who were expected to return about this time. So they would not miss us. In facing the northern blast up hill I found it quite difficult to keep from freezing. I had only been back to camp a short time when two men road up from Willie's handcart company. The signboard had done the work of salvation. . . . The handcart company was then 25 miles from our camp, and as they [Willie and Elder] had travelled that distance without food for themselves or horses and no bedding, they must have perished. I have always regarded this act of mine as the means of their salvation. And why not? An act of that importance is worthy of record and hence I give a place here" (in *Remember*, p. 51).

By then the conditions in the handcart camp at the Sixth Crossing were critical. John Chislett wrote:

> The scanty allowance of hard bread and poor beef, distributed as described, was mostly consumed the first day by the hungry, ravenous, famished souls.
>
> We killed more cattle and issued the meat; but, eating it without bread, did not satisfy hunger, and to those who were suffering from dysentery it did more harm than good. This terrible disease increased rapidly amongst us during these three days, and several died from exhaustion. Before we renewed our journey the camp became so offensive and filthy that words would fail to describe its condition, and even common decency forbids the attempt. Suffice it to say that all the disgusting scenes which the reader might imagine would certainly not equal the terrible reality. It was enough to make the heavens weep. The recollection of it unmans me even now—those three days! During that time I visited the sick, the widows whose husbands died in serving them, and the aged who could not help themselves, to know for myself where to dispense the few articles that had been placed in my charge for distribution. Such craving hunger I never saw before, and may God in his mercy spare me the sight again. (In *Remember*, p. 8)

As for the day the rescuers arrived, the eyewitness accounts that follow speak for themselves.

John Chislett, of the Willie Company, wrote: "On the evening of the third day [actually it was the second day] after Captain Willie's departure, just as the sun was sinking beautifully behind the distant hills, on an eminence immediately west of our camp several covered wagons, each drawn by four horses, were seen coming towards us. The news ran through the camp like wildfire, and all who were able to leave their beds turned out enmasse to see them. A few minutes brought them sufficiently near to reveal our faithful captain slightly in advance of the train. Shouts of joy rent the air; strong men wept till tears ran freely down their furrowed and sun-burnt cheeks, and little children partook of the joy which some of them hardly understood, and fairly danced around with gladness. Restraint was set aside in the general rejoicing, and as the brethren entered our camp the sisters fell upon them and deluged them with kisses. The brethren were so overcome that they could not for sometime utter a word, but in choking silence repressed all demonstration of those emotions that evidently mastered them. Soon, however, feeling was somewhat abated, and such a shaking of hands, such words of welcome, and such invocation of God's blessing have seldom been witnessed. . . . That evening, for the first time in quite a period, the songs of Zion were to be heard in the camp, and peals of laughter issued from the little knots of people as they chatted around the fires. The change seemed almost miraculous, so sudden was it from grave to gay, from sorrow to gladness, from mourning to rejoicing. With the cravings of hunger satisfied, and with hearts filled with gratitude to God and our good brethren, we all united in prayer, and then retired to rest" (in *Remember*, p. 9).

Harvey Cluff, of the rescue company, recalled: "It was about sun set when we came in sight of the camp; which greatly resembled an Esqumeax Village fully one mile away. The snow being a foot deep and paths having been made from tent to tent gave the camp that appearance. As we reached an eminance overlooking the camp, which was located on a sagebrush plain near the river a mile away. When the people of the camp sighted us approaching, they set up such a shout as to echo through the hills. Arriving within the confines of this emigrant camp a most thrilling and touching scene was enacted, melting to tears the stoutest hearts. Young maidens and feable old ladies, threw off all restraint and freely embraced their deliverers expressing in a flow of kisses, the gratitude which their tongues failed to utter. This was certainly the most timely arrival of a relief party recorded in history" (in Hafen and Hafen, *Handcarts to Zion*, p. 233).

CHAPTER 25

SIXTH CROSSING TO ROCKY RIDGE

I

Wednesday, 22 October 1856

"Brother Granger?"

David was at the back of the wagon, tying the reins of the horse onto the tailgate. He gave a final tug to make sure it was securely tied, then stepped around his horse. To his surprise, it was the young couple he had met yesterday. They stood hand in hand, but it was the woman who had spoken.

He smiled and came forward. "Maggie, if I remember?" he asked.

"Yes, Maggie McKensie."

"And Eric?"

"Yah." He shook that off. "Yes. I am Eric Pederson."

"From Denmark?"

"Norway. Most of the others are from Denmark." Then there was a bit of a mischievous smile. "Was it the 'yah' that gave me away?"

David saw Maggie nudge him a little as though to reprove him. David smiled. "Actually, your English is very good."

"I have very good teacher," Eric replied.

Maggie sobered. "Brother Granger, I–"

"Please, just David. If you've come to thank me, that's not necessary."

"We did not."

He flinched a little, taken aback by her forthrightness. He suddenly realized that beneath the sunburned cheeks and peeled nose and the pallor from having too little food, this was a very pretty young woman. "I'm sorry, I didn't mean to presume."

She shook her head. "It is not possible to thank you. But we pray that you may know for the rest of your life what you have done for us."

"I . . ." He finally just bowed his head. "I will. I will never forget this."

Maggie stepped forward, her eyes suddenly earnest. "I have a favor to ask of you, Bro—" She corrected herself quickly. "David."

"A favor? What?"

"We understand that you are going on with Captain Grant."

"Yes, that's right. My friend Heber—you met him yesterday—he'll be going back with your group. Brother William Kimball and he are brothers."

"I wondered," Eric said. "So he too is President Kimball's son?"

"Yes, but he doesn't like people to make a big thing of it." Then he turned back to Maggie. "What can I do for you?"

"I have a sister traveling with the Martin Company."

That caught him completely off guard. "You do?"

"Yes. She and a good friend, Ingrid Christensen, were asked to stay back and help with that group."

"I see. Is there something you would like me to take to her?"

"Yes." For a moment she hesitated, glancing at Eric. He nodded and she stepped forward and gave David a quick hug. She stepped back, her eyes lowered in embarrassment. "Will you take that to her and tell her that we are all okay?"

He nodded, touched by her concern. "I will. You have my word."

"And will you tell her about Eric and me? She doesn't know we plan to be married. We left a letter for her back on the trail, but with the storm I'm sure she'll never see it."

"I'll do that too."

"I was going to write her a letter for you to take, but there was no time. And we have no paper."

"I'll tell her. And I'll make sure she is all right."

"Would it be too much to ask you to bring her back safely to us?"

Now it was David who hesitated. If the Martin Company was in the same condition as the Willie group, who was to say whether or not she was even alive by now? For that matter, they had no guarantee they would even find them. He began to nod, planning to say, "I'll try." Instead, what came out surprised him. "I will. You have my word on that too."

"Thank you."

A few feet away, in the next wagon, the driver called over to them. "David, I think we're about ready to roll."

Maggie and Eric moved back as he put a foot on the spokes of the front wheel and vaulted up into the wagon seat. He took the reins, got them adjusted in his hands, and then looked down at the two of them again. Before he could say anything more, a shout from up ahead rang out. Brother George Grant, driving the lead wagon, cracked his whip over the head of his four mules. His wagon lurched forward. The second and third fell in line behind him and then it was David's turn. As he snapped the reins and his four animals started forward, he tipped his hat to Maggie. Then suddenly he thought of something. "Hey! What's her name?"

"Hannah," Maggie called. "Hannah McKensie."

"And how old is she? How will I know her?"

"She's sixteen. Almost seventeen. Just ask for her."

He pulled in the animals, keeping them to a walk for a moment. He was grinning as he looked down at her. "Does she look like you?" he asked.

"Much prettier," Maggie said with a laugh.

"Just as pretty," Eric corrected her gallantly.

"Then it will be my pleasure," David called. And with that, he snapped the reins sharply. "Giddap, mules. Let's go."

II

Thursday, 23 October 1856

Not quite twenty-four hours later, Maggie McKensie leaned heavily against her handcart, holding the blanket tightly around her body, one corner of it covering her mouth to keep the cold air from searing her lungs and bringing on the terrible coughing again. She stared at the gray sky, barely seeing the light snowfall whipping past her face in the wind. When she lowered her eyes again, it was to look at the ground and not the rolling hills that loomed over them to the west. She had looked there once already this morning and the sight had nearly disheartened her. Here, they were in a small, narrow valley and the northwest wind was somewhat restrained, though the cold was cutting through her in spite of her new coat and the blanket. Above them, row after row of hills and ridges could be seen. Up there snow boiled in swirling clouds, pouring over the ridges like water sloshing over the top of a kettle. Each ridge wore a long crown of brilliant white, drifts that were six to eight feet deep and a hundred feet or more in length.

She closed her eyes, unable to even bear the sight of the scattered flakes coming down from the sky now. All around her the Willie Handcart Company was preparing to move. Hardly anyone spoke, and then only in short sentences or soft murmurs of assent. Captain Willie and Brother William Kimball and the other rescuers from the Valley moved among the group like grim-faced angels, checking the loads, assessing the condition of each individual. The sickest and the weakest were led off to the wagons. Even with the addition of the six wagons from the Valley, there wasn't going to be enough room to take all of those who needed help.

Yesterday, after Captain Grant took eight of the wagons and continued eastward in search of the Martin Company, William Kimball and his smaller group got the Willie Company ready to move. Maggie remembered with shame the bitter debate that had erupted. Some of the brethren, mostly those with family members who were in terrible shape, had gathered around Captain Willie and Brother Kimball and had begun firing questions at them. Maggie wasn't filled with a critical spirit as a few of them were, but she had listened closely, having the same questions.

Why did they have to move on when they were in such terrible condition? Why couldn't they just wait there at the Sixth Crossing for the rescue wagons to come to them?

Brother Kimball had gone through it carefully. The men under the direction of Reddick Allred who were waiting with rescue wagons at South Pass had no idea that Captain Grant had finally found the first company. They were not coming forward. They were waiting in place until they received word.

All right. So why not just send riders back to South Pass to take word to Reddick Allred and wait until he could come to them?

Again he answered with great patience. South Pass was a good three days away. If they waited for a rider to go back and then for the wagons to come all the way forward, it would be six days. Even with the deaths, the Willie Company roster still stood at about four hundred people. The arrival of the rescue wagons had been a godsend, but in that one burst of need they had nearly exhausted the supply that William Kimball's six wagons carried. They dared not take more from Brother Grant. The Martin Company was larger than their own. And they would have farther to come to reach South Pass. So the hard reality was this: They had food for one more day, maybe two if they stretched it to the limits, but not six. "If we leave you here," Kimball concluded grimly, "there won't be many of you left to save. We have to keep moving west and meet the wagons partway."

Then why not just move forward to the base of Rocky Ridge and wait there? Brother Kimball and Elder Willie had both answered that. They talked about the difficulties of crossing this part of the trail. Actually Rocky Ridge was a misnomer. Rocky *Ridges* was a better description. This was not a single ridge that had to be crossed but a series of rolling hills, steep gullies, and rocky escarpments that stretched on for about five miles. The Sweetwater came out of a narrow canyon about two miles behind where the company was now. The canyon was too difficult for wagons or carts to traverse, so there was no choice. They had to go up and over the top of Rocky Ridge and cut straight across to where the trail met the river again. It was considered the most difficult stretch of trail thus far. More axles were broken, more wheels shattered, more animals ruined on this stretch than anywhere else before the trail reached the mountains around Salt Lake City. Thereafter it was mostly level the rest of the way into Rock Creek.

So why not move forward to the base of Rocky Ridge and then wait? was the next question.

By now, Brother Kimball was getting a little impatient. These people didn't know the trail. They had no idea of the distances or the problems. Maggie could see it in his eyes. Why can't you trust us? Why can't you believe that we have taken all of this into consideration? But he said none of that. He had carefully explained that it was only ten miles from Sixth Crossing to the base of Rocky Ridge. They would take that in one day and then would stop there for the night. But this was not a place to settle in for an extended time. It was two or three miles from the river. There was no wood and no water except for melted snow. And going only ten miles and then stopping wouldn't help enough in solving the problem of meeting the supply wagons farther west.

And so here they were. The ten miles they had come yesterday had been terrible enough. And Brother Kimball's assessment of their campsite had been exactly correct. No wood. No water. The ground had been so hard that many of the emigrants had simply rolled their bedrolls out on the snow last night and huddled in them until morning rather than pitch their tents.

The very sickest and weakest were once again loaded into the wagons. Even with six more wagons added to their own three, it was not sufficient. Jane James had gone to Brother Willie and asked if her husband might be accommodated in one of the wagons. The answer was a reluctant no. If William could walk at all, he would have to do the best he could. The wagons were already so filled that there was fear some might be smothered. Instead, the two captains had another suggestion. The Jameses had two carts. Why not lighten the second cart to the bare essentials? Then Brother James and Reuben could pull that one while the girls and Sister James took the heavier one. So they had divided and redistributed the load. The lead cart, pulled by Sister James, Sarah, and Emma, kept most of their belongings. The second cart, which carried only a few things—probably less than fifty pounds—was then given to Brother James and Reuben to pull together.

It had worked. Though they had fallen behind, father and son made the ten miles on their own. And to Maggie's astonishment, this morning, when a call had been issued for men to help bury the two who had died during the night, William James had gotten a shovel and accompanied Reuben, Eric, and Olaf to go help. He was determined that he would carry his part of the load, no matter how he was feeling at the moment.

But today wouldn't be the same. They had sixteen miles to go today. And the first five miles would be over the dreaded Rocky Ridge.

Maggie stared woodenly at the ground. Did this company have another day in them, especially if that day involved crossing Rocky Ridge? What about William James? How would he do today? Even with the lighter cart, could he and Reuben make it? For that matter, how would *she* do? She knew that similar questions were on everyone's mind this morning.

Maggie hunched over as a spasm of coughing hit her, sending the pain stabbing through her upper body and the fire shooting down into her chest again. When it passed and she straightened again, she saw that her mother was watching her.

"I'm all right," Maggie whispered.

Her mother nodded, but the sorrow in her eyes told Maggie just how terrible she must look right now.

They heard voices and turned. Several men were coming in a group towards them, returning from the burial detail. Maggie's eyes picked out Jens Nielson first. At six feet two inches, he was the tallest man in the group. Then she saw Eric and Olaf beside him. William James and his son Reuben were coming a few feet behind them. Brother James moved with labored and careful steps. As they drew closer, Maggie noted that Captain Willie and Brother Kimball were beside Eric, speaking earnestly as they walked. She saw Eric nod, then nod again.

To Maggie's surprise, Captain Willie came straight to where the McKensies and the Jameses were waiting. He looked as drawn and tired as the rest of them, but nevertheless he walked with a sure step and his shoulders were back. He was their captain, and he would lead them until he dropped if need be.

"Sister James? Sister McKensie?"

Jane and Mary both turned. "Yes?"

"I am assigning Eric to your two families for today."

Maggie snapped around. "You are?"

"Yes. Maggie, I don't want you pulling on the cart today at all. I wish you didn't have to walk, but as you already know, that is not an option."

"I'm all right, Brother Willie. Really, I—"

He shook his finger at her. "You are not all right. I've heard that cough. And if you start straining too hard in this cold wind, you'll get cold air down your lungs and add pleurisy on top of everything else. That won't do your family any good. Do you hear me?"

Eric was nodding, looking at her sternly as well.

She knew they were right, but how could she just stand by and—

"Sister Maggie," Brother Willie said, his eyes pinning her down. "I am speaking both as your company captain and as your priesthood leader. Are you going to be obedient to counsel?"

She looked at him and saw that he was not just trying to tease her into acceptance. He was completely serious. "Yes, sir," she said meekly.

He swung around. William James had just caught up with them. "Brother James, I have the same counsel for you. You are to pull only that second, lighter cart. And let Reuben do that alone whenever you are on level ground. If you reach the point where you feel like you cannot make it, then leave the cart. We have deliberately packed it with things that can be replaced at Rock Creek once we reach the other wagons. So if you have to leave it behind, do it. Do *you* understand me?"

William James lifted his head, the gauntness in his face a little frightening. "Yes, sir." His head dropped again. "I'd like to take my shotgun with me, if that's all right."

Captain Willie hesitated. A shotgun was heavy and virtually useless at this stage. It was not as if there were game roaming around out here right now.

Seeing their leader's expression, Eric stepped forward. William James had brought a fine shotgun with him from England. Along the trail he had shot prairie hens and an occasional rabbit to supplement the family's food supply. "Captain," Eric said in a low voice. "It's because he thinks it will help him care for his family."

Brother Willie finally nodded. "All right." He tipped his hat and he and Brother Kimball moved away, heading for the front of the column.

As soon as they were there, Brother Kimball stepped forward. "Brothers and sisters," he called.

Everyone turned.

"The time has come. We have to begin. I won't lie to you. As we told you yesterday, this is not going to be easy. We are not going to try and keep everyone together. Go at your own pace. As you can see, the wind is going to be a factor. That is typical. Even on the best of summer days, the wind blows very strongly here. Keep yourself wrapped in your blankets and quilts as best you can."

He glanced at Captain Willie. "Brother Willie has asked John Chislett, captain of the fourth hundred, to bring up the rear and watch for any stragglers."

"Brother Chislett is finishing with the burial," Brother Willie said. "He will be along shortly. But brethren and sisters, it is important that you do not stop. In this wind you will freeze to death in a matter of a few minutes. Keep moving. Help one another. Encourage those who falter."

Brother Kimball came back in again. "We shall take my six wagons with the sick and lead out. We will press ahead as rapidly as possible so we can get them to camp."

"Then will you come back for the rest of us?"

Maggie turned. It was the same man who had questioned the two leaders so sharply yesterday morning.

Brother Willie's mouth tightened as he stepped forward to answer. "Brother Foster, this is going to sound very harsh, but the answer is, perhaps. We'll have to see how the teams are at that point The wagons are overloaded now, far more than these teams should carry. The animals are already exhausted from a very hard push from the Valley. I know, I know," he said quickly as the man looked as if he was going to interrupt. "So are you. But we still have two hundred miles to go. If we ruin the teams now, all the efforts of the rescue company will have been for nothing."

To Maggie's surprise, the man nodded somberly. "I understand."

Brother Kimball spoke up again. "We are having your wagons come along at the rear, along with Brother Chislett. If there are those who absolutely cannot make it, then they will pick them up. But I warn you, your ox teams may already be past the point of recovery. Any person who can walk or who can be pulled in the cart is going to have to do it."

He stopped again and his face grew more somber. "Rocky Ridge will be the worst. Once you reach the top, there is a large, flat plain. The road should be easy pulling most of the way after that. Just remember this. Yes, Rock Creek is sixteen miles away—sixteen hard, difficult miles—but when you get there, Brother Reddick Allred will be waiting for us, or at least will be close at hand. He has six wagons filled with food and clothing. His men will be fresh and rested. They will cut firewood for us and help you put up your tents. More wagons will be coming from the Valley every day."

He looked around. Like Elder Willie, he looked exhausted, but now he smiled as warmly as he could manage. "Brothers and sisters, see it through this day and the crisis will be over. It will still be difficult, but we will have averted disaster." His voice rose sharply now. "My beloved Saints, you have suffered so much. But temporal salvation is waiting just sixteen miles from where we stand. May God bless us all with the strength and give us the faith to endure this one last time."

He stepped back. Brother Willie nodded slowly, then looked at his charges. "We will leave in five minutes," he said. "Please be ready."

"What about Olaf?"

Eric looked up from the back of the cart. "He's going to help Jens and Elsie."

"I feel so bad that you—"

His look cut Maggie off. "I am here by assignment from Captain Willie," he reminded her. "You did not ask for this. Neither did Brother James."

She nodded as he came around and lifted the shafts of the cart and stepped into them. Maggie's mother came over and got in beside him. Robbie shuffled around to the back of the cart, adjusting his mittens. Up in front of them, the first of the carts were already moving out, covering the last hundred yards of level ground before the land began to rise. Eric reached out and touched her shoulder. "We're going to make it, Maggie. Just one more day. Don't lose hope."

She nodded, keenly aware of the raspy sound her breath made even as she tried to hold it in as much as possible. Her expression was bleak. "Somehow," she whispered, "the fire of the covenant doesn't seem to be burning very brightly inside me right now."

Eric's eyebrows lowered, but it was Maggie's mother who whirled on her. "What did you say?" she demanded.

"I'm sorry, Mama. It's just that—"

"What do you mean the fire is not burning within you?" Her mother's voice was not angry, but soft and filled with love. "Have you once complained about what we are going through right now? Have you ever once blamed God for our circumstances?"

"Well, no, I don't feel like that. I—"

"And have you ever once said that the answer you got that day to come to America was a mistake?"

Now Maggie turned and looked at Eric, smiling faintly. "No. I know that was the best thing that ever happened to me."

"And do you know, even as you hunch over in pain as the coughing tears at your insides, do you have even the slightest doubt about whether God lives, about whether His Son came to earth and lived and died so that we might live again?"

Maggie straightened slowly, looking her mother directly in the eye. "No," she said. "No, I have not the slightest doubt."

"Then why do you say that the fire of the covenant has gone out in you? Don't you see, Maggie? It is that fire that drives us. It is our faith in the Savior that sustains us. That is what gives us the strength to go on, even now as we start this terrible day."

Her voice dropped suddenly, so low that Maggie had to strain to hear her. "And it is that faith in Jesus Christ and His sacrifice that allows us to say, 'And should we die before we reach Rock Creek this night, then happy day! All is well.' "

Tears welled up in Maggie's eyes and she bowed her head. "Thank you, Mama," she whispered. "I love you."

"And I love you, Maggie."

They turned as the two carts just ahead of them, pulled by the James family, began to move. Maggie reached out and laid a hand on Eric's arm as he leaned into the crossbar. As they began to move, falling into line behind the others, Maggie's eyes lifted. Now, without fear, she scanned the scene before her—ridge after ridge, stretching into the distance. Each was crowned with a long cap of snow, and each was nearly obscured by the howling winds and the boiling snow. It didn't matter. One more day. That was all. Just one more day.

Near the back of the column, Olaf Pederson was on his knees, facing five-year-old Jens Nielson. He fastened the top button on the boy's coat, pulled his scarf more tightly around the lower part of his face, and pulled his hat down more securely around his ears. "Are you sure you don't want to ride on the cart, Jens?"

He shook his head. "It's too cold, Olaf."

Olaf nodded. That was hard to refute. The wind was cutting through whatever clothing they had. The only relief was to jump up and down and move about, stamping your feet, slapping your sides, and doing whatever else it took to stimulate the circulation. Walking would be a blessing on this day, in spite of the challenge it would bring.

"All right, then," Elsie Nielson said to her son. "You stay close beside Bodil. Mama and Papa are going to pull the cart."

"Can Olaf carry me?" Jens asked in a pleading voice.

His father turned and came to him. "Olaf has to help Papa push the cart, son. It is a time to be brave. Can you be brave for Papa?"

Olaf took him by the shoulders. "Your Mama tells me that you will turn six years old next week."

The boy nodded solemnly.

Olaf shook him gently, proudly. "I don't know many six-year-old boys who are as brave as you are, Jens."

"Thank you, Olaf." He turned to look at his father, the brown eyes filled with sudden determination. "I can walk, Papa."

"Good boy."

"Jens?"

Brother Nielson looked up.

Elsie moved to the front of the cart and lifted the shafts. "They're starting to move."

There was one thing about the wind that proved to be a blessing. Anywhere the ground was exposed, every trace of snow was scoured away, leaving the wagon road dry and frozen hard as cement. Across these stretches the handcarts rolled easily and the emigrants moved steadily forward. But other than that, the wind was an inveterate enemy. It fought them every step of the way. Coming directly out of the northwest, it was blowing hard, probably thirty miles an hour or more, Eric guessed. When it gusted it caught the carts and shook them violently. It was enough to knock you off your feet if you weren't constantly bracing against it.

Driven by the wind, the cold became a double-edged sword, cutting every way it turned. It was like a tangible opponent. Eric estimated that the air temperature was hovering somewhere between zero and ten degrees. That kind of cold was a challenge under any circumstances, but when carried by the pummeling wind, it became deadly. The frigid air was like a rasp on exposed skin. It pushed its way into any and every opening in your clothing and seeped through even two and three layers of fabric. It stiffened the hands into frozen claws that could barely keep a grip on the crossbars.

Another way the wind battled them was in the drifting. The very wind which stripped the snow from off the high spots or along the level stretches deposited it into every swale, every depression, every rut. Even the most gentle rise provided a slight windbreak, and drifts would form on the leeward side. You could move along smartly for a hundred yards or more, the wheels rattling loudly on the frozen ground, and then suddenly the road would dip and you would plunge into knee-high drifts, three, four, or five feet across. The lead wagons were breaking trail, thankfully, but almost within seconds after they passed, the tracks began to fill in again. If there was a break of any distance in the column, each drift had to be broached anew by the next group to reach it.

Eric hadn't seen the lead wagons now for more than an hour. In fact, at the moment, there were just the two carts together. The next group out ahead of them was maybe a quarter of a mile away. Behind them, strung out now coming up the long hill, he could see a dozen carts, but the closest was back a good two hundred yards.

At first there had been three carts in their little group. But once they started, Sarah and Emma found that together they could pull the lead cart on their own, so Sister James had dropped back to help her husband and Reuben. Soon, Sarah and Emma were way out ahead of them.

Eric and Mary McKensie were in the lead now, with Robbie pushing and Maggie walking alongside with the rest of the James children. Eric had gone out front deliberately so that Brother and Sister James, along with Reuben pushing from behind, wouldn't have to take the drifts first. It wasn't much help, but the McKensie cart made at least some track through the snow.

Eric glanced back. Even with Mary and him breaking trail, Brother and Sister James and Reuben were falling behind again. Their little group of two carts now was moving more and more slowly as the road grew steeper. They had come perhaps three-quarters of a mile since they had started, and now the incline was taking its toll on Brother James.

Just ahead, the road dropped into a shallow depression. It was no more than five or six feet across, but it was completely drifted in with snow eighteen to twenty inches deep. Without having to say anything aloud, Eric and Mary increased their pace as they approached it. They slammed through, their feet digging gouges in the snowdrift as they strained to keep the cart rolling. In a moment they were through.

Seeing that, as they reached the depression Reuben shouted at his father, "Faster, Papa!" But William James had no more "faster" in him. As their cart wheels plowed into the drift, William's feet slipped out from under him and he went down hard. Reuben yanked back on the cart, barely stopping it from smashing into his father and mother.

"Brother James!" Eric lifted the shafts and ducked beneath them, running back quickly. Maggie heard him shout and turned and raced after him.

As he reached the front of the cart, Eric saw that William James was on his hands and knees. His head was down and he was panting heavily, his breath coming out in tiny spurts of vapor. "I can't do it, Jane," he gasped.

"It's all right. It's all right." She put her arms around him and tried to help him get to his feet. "Rest for a minute."

He shook his head and pushed her away. "You have to go on, Jane. You can't stop."

She was stroking his face, brushing away the snow that was caked on his cheeks. "I can't leave you."

"We'll come on in a minute," he said. "But you can't stop. Take the children."

"I'll help you," Eric said, bending over to look into Brother James's face.

"No!" It came out flat and hard. "You were assigned to help Mary." He stumbled to his feet, leaning heavily on his wife's arm.

"Just help me get the cart off to one side. Reuben and I will rest for a few minutes. Then we'll come on."

Jane James looked at Eric, her face stricken. Maggie saw that look and stepped forward. "Let Eric help them," she said. "I'll help Mother pull."

Brother James jerked free. There was almost panic in his eyes. "No! You heard Elder Willie. You are not to pull."

Jane finally nodded. "He's right, Eric. You have to help Maggie and Mary."

"Just get me off to the side," Brother James said again. "Then we'll come on."

Eric and Maggie and Maggie's mother pulled the cart out of the drift and off to one side of the trail where the ground was bare. As they lowered it again, Brother James sank down beside it. His wife dropped to one knee in front of him, pulling his blanket more tightly around him. "Promise me you'll keep coming, William. Promise."

There was a wan smile. "I will, Jane. Reuben will help me."

Reuben was nodding. His face was determined. "We'll just rest for a few minutes."

Eric turned around and looked back down the hill. Beyond the string of carts he could see the three supply wagons. "Brother Chislett is still back there," he said to Jane, remembering what Brother Kimball had said before they started. "He'll make sure they're all right."

Fighting back her tears, Jane James stood. She reached out and touched her husband's face once more. "We'll see you in camp, then?"

"Yes. I promise."

When John Chislett saw the handcart pulled off to one side of the road, his first thought was that it had been abandoned. Then there was a movement. Looking closer, squinting against the bitter wind, he made out the figure of a man sitting down. No, two men, sitting side by side.

His heart dropped a little. Not already. They hadn't even covered the first full mile yet. There had been a couple of steep slopes, but nothing compared to what still lay ahead. He quickened his pace, motioning for the others to come on.

It had taken him some time back in camp to finish covering the grave, so by the time he finished he figured the company was a good half an hour ahead of him. With that, he had hoped it would be a while before he came across the first stragglers. But within a quarter of a mile he had caught up with the first handcart. And just ahead of it were two of the wagons, the oxen plodding along barely enough to keep the wagon moving. So he had gathered the people up, encouraging them on as best he could, and stayed back with them as Elder Willie had asked him to do. Now there were six handcarts moving along slowly, together with the wagons, helping each other through the drifts or up the steeper parts of the trail.

But this was the first time he had come upon someone who had stopped completely. Concerned, he hurried forward. To his surprise, as he got closer, he recognized William James and his son. Brother James was seated on the ground, his back against the cart, his head down on his chest. He looked like he was asleep, and Brother Chislett felt a sudden start. Was he . . . ?

But at the sound of his footsteps, the boy stood up, waving. Then Brother James's head came up too. Greatly relieved, the subcaptain rushed up to them. "Brother James, are you all right?"

There was a brief nod and a weary smile. "Yes, Brother Chislett. Reuben and I just stopped to rest for a moment."

John Chislett saw the concern in Reuben's eyes. The boy stepped back enough so that his father couldn't see him and held up ten fingers. Chislett shook his head. Ten minutes. That was not good. Without movement, frostbite could start to set in very quickly. He half turned, considering the wagons, but immediately rejected that.

They were already so full that he feared that the animals were not going to keep them moving.

"Come, then," Brother Chislett said cheerfully to Brother James. "You've had your rest now. You can come along with the rest of us laggers."

Reuben bent down and got his father under the arms and helped him to his feet. He stood, but Chislett saw that he was weaving back and forth and had to grab his son's arm to steady himself. Chislett made a decision. He turned to the boy. "Is there anything in the cart you cannot leave behind?"

Reuben considered that for a moment, then shook his head. "It's mostly bedding. Brother Willie says we can get more when we reach the wagons from Salt Lake."

"Good. Then let's leave the cart. You and your father can walk along with us."

"My shotgun," Brother James cried, his head coming up in alarm.

Reuben steadied his father. "It's all right, Papa. We won't leave your shotgun." He looked to Brother Chislett. "He's worried that he won't be able to provide for us."

"Get it for me," Chislett said. "And any other things you may absolutely need." The subcaptain noted that his other charges were going by slowly, barely glancing at the little scene playing out as they passed. He could delay no longer.

Reuben went around to the back of the cart and returned with a finely made double-barreled shotgun. He also had a bag filled with some smaller items. Brother Chislett took the bag from him and quickly tied a knot in the top. He then slipped the bag over the end of the shotgun barrel and placed the gun on William James's shoulder. "There you go. You are good to worry about your family, Brother James. But leave the rest behind. We have to keep moving."

Chislett's eyes were shining as William James gripped the shotgun, straightened, and looked at Brother Chislett. "Thank you."

—❦—

Eric concentrated intently, moving in a dull and monotonous rhythm. One foot up. Swing it forward. Place it down firmly, making sure it doesn't slip on the snow-packed trail. Shift your weight forward. Next foot up. Swing it forward.

His eyes were open as he leaned against the crossbar, but he saw little. There was really nothing to see. The whiteness stretched out in every direction, broken only here and there by small bare patches of ground, or by the jagged edges of the rock escarpment which seemed to beckon to them like the menacing fingers on some unseen hand.

Mary McKensie walked beside him in the shafts. They didn't speak, but without conscious thought they matched their steps in perfect timing as though they were being controlled by the same puppeteer. A short distance ahead of them, Jane James and Maggie were in the middle of the road with the children, plodding steadily forward. Jane had young John, who was four, on her back. Maggie held the hands of Mary Ann and Martha and was almost pulling them along, they were so tired. Robbie brought up the rear, walking with seven-year-old George, too exhausted at the moment to help with the cart. They hadn't seem Emma and Sarah and their cart now for some time.

Eric groaned inwardly. Just ahead of where the family was walking, the trail started to climb sharply again. And here and there he could see the tops of rocks in the middle of the two tracks made by the thousands of wagons which had passed here before them. Beyond that, he could see the tracks going on for some distance, and all uphill. There was no one else in sight now. They were falling behind.

And here was another incline.

The hill would have been challenge enough. They could see dark gashes where previous feet had dug into the snow and reached the dirt beneath. It was not terribly steep but it was sharp enough that they were straining to keep the carts moving. But now the wheels were hitting the rocks in the track. Some of the smaller rocks they bounced over easily, though it rattled the cart and jarred them as they pulled. But some rocks protruded out of the ground three and four and five inches. They tried to steer the cart around them, but they couldn't in every case and the wheels would hang up on them. Then it took superhuman effort to lunge forward and take the wheels up and over.

About two-thirds of the way up the incline, there was a loud crack and the cart jerked Eric and Mary around hard. They grunted, shoving their bodies forward. The cart rocked forward an inch or two, then fell back again.

"Harder," Eric gasped.

They hit it again. Panting and grunting, they threw every ounce of strength they had against the crossbar. The cart lifted slowly. Then suddenly the wheel cleared the obstacle and the cart shot forward. With a startled cry, Eric leaped forward as well. As his feet clawed for leverage, one foot hit a patch of snow and shot out from under him. With a yelp, he went down to one knee, cracking it hard on something sharp. He got up slowly. A red cloud seemed to whirl before his eyes and he shut them quickly to make it go away. Reaching down he started to rub his knee, then winced sharply. He had torn a hole in this trouser leg and he could see the deep abrasion beneath.

"Are you all right?"

"Yes. Just hit my knee a little."

It was burning like fury but he put it aside. Still panting, he looked ahead, tempted to call for help. But Maggie and Sister James were now a good fifty yards ahead of them. If they came back down they would have to ascend the hill a second time.

He looked at Maggie's mother. Her face had splotches of red now and he could see that she was trembling. "Can we do it?"

She lowered her head, taking in deep gulps of air. "I'm all right. Just give me a minute."

—❦—

Eric stopped and licked his lips, looking at Maggie's mother. It was not yet twenty minutes since the last incline. It was not yet fifteen minutes since he had bruised his knee trying to get up one short hill. Now here was another one. He and Mary McKensie were still moving along by themselves. Robbie had come back to help but had lasted for only five minutes before Eric made him quit. His face was white and he looked like he might faint.

Eric pulled a face. His head was light and he felt like he might faint too. Maybe if fortune smiled upon him someone would come along and suggest that he take a break. He smiled grimly. He decided he would get very cold waiting for that to happen.

The next rise was only fifty or sixty feet long before it gentled again, but it was steeper than the last one and the two-track road was once again studded with rocks. He dropped his head and closed his eyes. Not another one. Not now. His lungs burned. His legs were trembling violently. His face was numb and there was a strange tingling sensation in his cheeks. At that moment he knew without the slightest question that his body was no longer capable of what it would take to go up and over that hump. It didn't matter whether or not he had the will. His body would not, could not, respond. He would collapse in the trying.

"I don't know if I can make another one," Sister McKensie whispered beside him.

He turned and saw the same utter hopelessness in her eyes that he was feeling. He nodded, taking in deep breaths to steady himself. Sister James and Maggie and the children were not in sight now. They had gone up and over this rise and on. Eric tipped his head back and shouted. "Sister James!"

A gust of wind snatched the sound away before it was fully out of his mouth. He waited for a moment, but there was no answer.

"I can't, Eric." Mary slumped forward against the crossbar, lowering her head to her hands.

He reached out and laid a hand on her shoulder. He could feel the tremors in her body and knew she was right. He shook her gently, and after a moment she looked up. He forced a smile, which probably looked more like a grimace than anything. "Can I quote you some scripture, Sister McKensie?"

For a moment, she was startled, and then she smiled faintly. "I could use a good one about now."

"It's my father's favorite."

"Which is it?"

"From the book of Ether." He paused a moment, making sure he could remember it correctly. "It goes something like this. 'I give unto men weakness that they may be humble.'" He stopped, shaking his head. "I'm feeling pretty humble about now, how about you?"

"Quite," she said, the smile deepening into something genuine.

Now Eric spoke with greater force. "'My grace is sufficient for all men who humble themselves before me. And if men will humble themselves before me'"—his eyes looked deep into hers—"'and have faith in me, *then will I make weak things become strong unto them.*'"

Mary McKensie slowly began to nod. "I have always loved that scripture."

Eric straightened. "Me too." He looked straight ahead now. "Are you ready, then?"

Her eyes closed for just a moment. "Could we say a little prayer first?"

He nodded, a little chagrined that he hadn't thought of it. Both of them bowed their heads.

"Heavenly Father," Mary said softly. "We cannot do this alone. Wilt Thou help us to get over this next rise, we pray in the name of Thy Son. Amen."

"Amen."

Now she looked up at him, her lips set. "I'm ready."

"Then here we go." In unison they started forward. They broke into a lumbering trot as they approached the bottom of the hill in order to give themselves a little momentum. That carried them up for about twenty feet, but then gravity became more powerful than momentum. Eric dug in, commanding his legs to keep pumping, feeling the pain shoot through his injured knee. To his surprise they kept moving, even though the wheels were bouncing and clattering over the rocks.

"Don't stop," he gasped. "Keep going."

Beside him, Mary cried out as her feet slipped on the packed snow beneath her. She caught herself by hanging onto the shafts of the cart, nearly dragging Eric to the ground with her. But as he staggered forward, she caught her balance again. Suddenly a blast of wind buffeted them, rocking the cart and momentarily blinding them.

And then suddenly, as they fought their way forward, the cart seemed to lighten. Mary McKensie was pulling ahead faster than he was. Scrambling to keep up with her, he was afraid for a moment that the cart was going to hit him in the back.

Then he saw that she was looking at him in astonishment as well. She was pushing, but not that hard.

"Go!" he shouted at Maggie's mother. They spurted upward, in the steepest part of the incline now. But amazingly the cart did not slow.

Eric snapped his head around. It was as if someone had thrown their weight against the back of the cart, as if someone had suddenly come up to help them push. But there was no one there.

"We're going to make it," Mary shouted into his ear.

"Yes!" he exploded. "Yes, we are."

They crested the rise and the trail suddenly leveled again. With a cry of relief they let the cart roll forward another ten or fifteen feet, then brought it to a stop. As they stood there, their chests heaving, their heads down, they looked at each other. Mary's eyes were enormous and filled with wonder.

"What happened?" Eric blurted.

"I don't know."

They both turned. They could see a full half mile back down the trail. No one was in sight. They were totally alone.

"Maybe it was the wind," Sister McKensie suggested.

He started to shake his head and then stopped. He didn't know what it was. He wasn't even sure *if* it was something. Then his head dropped. Hers did the same.

"Thank you, Father," Eric whispered.

"Yes," Mary McKensie added softly.

It was about quarter of an hour later when they heard a shout. Eric looked up. They were coming around the brow of one of the ridges. Ahead they could see where the trail dropped down into a gentle swale, then rose sharply again to a long ridge to the south of them about four or five hundred yards away. As he squinted into the wind, he saw two figures on the far ridge, standing on an outcropping of rock, waving their arms back and forth.

"It's Maggie and Jane," Sister McKensie said, raising an arm and waving. "We're coming," she shouted weakly.

There was a snatch of something they didn't catch.

Eric stopped the cart and cupped his hands. "What?"

A moment later it came in, quite clearly now. "This is the top."

"Glory," Mary breathed in relief.

"All right," Eric shouted hoarsely. "We're coming."

"We're going on. The children are cold." Then there was something else but it was whipped away with the wind.

"What did she say?" he asked.

"Something about Robbie."

Just then a shorter figure appeared beside the others. All three stood there for a moment, and then the adults jumped down and disappeared. Eric nodded. "Robbie's staying to help us with that last pull."

Mary McKensie was already eyeing it. From here it didn't look too terrible, but they had come up this trail enough now to know that when they reached the base, it would look three times steeper than it did from here.

"We can use him," Mary said in a strained whisper.

He knew what she was thinking. If Maggie and Jane knew how close she and Eric were to total collapse, they would stay to help too. But it was too late for that now. "We're almost there," he sighed. "One more pull."

It took them another ten minutes to reach Robbie, who had come down to the bottom of the last incline and was waiting for them. Eric was relieved to see that his color was better and that a bit of his chipper self had been restored.

"Thanks, Robbie," his mother said, as he fell in behind them.

"You're welcome. This one is a bad one." One hand lifted and he pointed ahead. "The rocks at the top are terrible. The worst yet. You can barely get your footing on them."

Eric's heart sank. He could see what Robbie was talking about. Up here on the uppermost ridge top, the wind had whipped much of the snow away. The whole top of the ridge was one long rock escarpment, layer after layer of rock folded in one on top of the other, their protruding edges as jagged as a saw blade. Some jutted up as much as a foot from the ridge itself.

"I'll help," Robbie said.

Eric took a deep breath. The ground was already starting to slope upwards. "All right, here we go."

The first hundred feet or so got them out of the swale and that wasn't so terrible. The ground wasn't rocky yet and was frozen and hard. Even then they were breathing heavily by the time they traversed that stretch. Now the ground rose sharply and they were into the first of the rocks.

"Push, Robbie," he shouted. Eric leaned forward, steeling himself as he felt the weight of the cart start to pull back on them. There was a shout of acknowledgment from Robbie, and Eric felt the cart push forward slightly. *Good. It might just be enough to make the difference.*

"Here we go," he said to Mary through clenched teeth. "Let's keep it moving."

To their surprise, Robbie made a great deal of difference. It took all of their strength, of course, but with him pushing, their progress was steady. The cart clattered and bounced wildly over the escarpment, but they were moving forward with enough momentum to clear every obstacle.

In three minutes it was done. They crested the knife-edge of the ridge, threaded their way through some large boulders, following the other tracks, and came to a stop in a large open area. Eric turned around. "Robbie, thank you. That was—"

But Robbie wasn't there. He looked at Mary in surprise, then dropped the cart and walked around behind it. There was no Robbie. Breaking into a stumbling run, both of them made their way back to the ridge. They stopped dead, gaping in astonishment.

Robbie was trudging slowly up the hill, still two-thirds of the way from the top. They could see that the front of his coat was covered with snow. He looked up when he saw them. "I'm sorry, Mama," he called in discouragement. "I slipped and fell and couldn't catch up with you again."

Chapter Notes

Many years after the handcart companies experiment was over, a Sunday School class in Cedar City, Utah, was discussing the Martin and Willie Handcart Companies. The teacher and some of the class members were sharply criticizing the Church and its leaders for letting the two companies come so late in the season. What happened next provided the inspiration for the experience shared in this chapter by Eric Pederson and Mary McKensie, though the man who stood and spoke, Francis Webster, was part of the Martin Company and what he described did not happen on Rocky Ridge but farther east along the trail. The following recollection was written by William R. Palmer, who was in attendance at the class:

> One old man in the corner [Francis Webster] sat silent and listened as long as he could stand it, then he arose and said things that no person who heard him will ever forget. His face was white with emotion, yet he spoke calmly, deliberately, but with great earnestness and sincerity.
>
> He said in substance, "I ask you to stop this criticism. You are discussing a matter you know nothing about. Cold historic facts mean nothing here, for they give no proper interpretation of the questions involved. Mistake to send the Handcart Company out so late in the season? Yes! But I was in that company and my wife was in it. . . . We suffered beyond anything you can imagine and many died of exposure and starvation. . . . Every one of us came through with the absolute knowledge that God lives for we became acquainted with Him in our extremities!
>
> "I have pulled my handcart when I was so weak and weary from illness and lack of food that I could hardly put one foot ahead of the other. I have looked ahead and seen a patch of sand or a hill slope and I have said, I can go only that far and there I must give up for I cannot pull the load through it. I have gone to that sand and when I reached it, the cart began pushing me! I have looked back many times to see who was pushing my cart, but my eyes saw no one. I knew then that the Angels of God were there.
>
> "Was I sorry that I chose to come by handcart? No! Neither then nor any minute of my life since. The price we paid to become acquainted with God was a privilege to pay and I am thankful that I was privileged to come in the Martin Handcart Company." (In *Remember*, p. 139)

CHAPTER 26

ROCKY RIDGE TO ROCK CREEK

I

Thursday, 23 October 1856

"Hey!"

Eric's head came up and he looked around. The wind was whistling around him, and for a moment he thought it was nothing more than its moaning cry. It was about two o'clock in the afternoon. They had been on the trail now for about seven hours, with no food and only handfuls of snow for water. He was light-headed and for a moment wondered if he was hallucinating. His eyes focused on the carts in front of them. Once they had conquered Rocky Ridge, the ground leveled out in a great plateau. Surprisingly rejuvenated by the miraculous help they had received, they had made better time and just half an hour before had overtaken a group of four other carts. Sister James had hoped that Emma and Sarah would be among them, but they were not. It was amazing. Those two girls were making remarkable time.

"Eric! Stop!"

It was Robbie's voice. Shaking off the lethargy, Eric stopped the cart and looked around. Jane James and her children were just behind the cart, but Robbie wasn't with them.

"Oh, no!" Mary McKensie was looking back too, but to the other side of the trail. Her face was suddenly twisted with horror.

Eric swung around and nearly dropped the crossbar. In back of the cart about fifty feet, Maggie was sitting in the snow. Robbie was standing in front of her, bent over, shaking her shoulders. "Eric!" It was a cry of great distress.

Instantly he was out of the cart and running awkwardly back down the road, with Mary McKensie and Jane James right behind him. Robbie saw them coming and stepped back. Eric slid to a halt in front of Maggie and dropped to his knees. "Maggie! What's the matter?"

Her head came up slowly. Her eyes were glazed and she seemed barely to recognize him. Her lips moved but no words came out. After a moment, her eyes drooped shut and her head flopped heavily down against her chest.

"What's wrong?" Robbie cried.

Eric took Maggie by the shoulders and shook her gently. "Maggie!"

This time her head snapped up. She looked around, a sudden wildness in her eyes.

Mary McKensie was down beside Eric now. She grabbed Maggie's hands and began to rub them vigorously. "Maggie! Wake up! Look at us."

"Tired," she mumbled.

Taking her chin between his fingers, Eric pinched firmly. "Maggie! It's Eric. Look at me."

She pulled away, averting his face. "Go away. Want to sleep."

"It's the cold," Sister James exclaimed. "We've got to get her up and moving."

Eric had decided exactly the same thing. Norway was filled with stories of people who had been out in the cold and let their core body temperature drop to perilous levels. He jumped up, stepped around behind Maggie, and dragged her to her feet. She sagged against him. "Maggie! You're cold. You've got to move around."

"Not cold. Finally warm." She tried to pull away but was so weak she barely moved Eric's hands. "Leave me be."

He shook her again, more roughly now. To his astonishment, she was instantly strong again. She whirled on him, her eyes blazing. "Go away!" She straightened, standing clear of him now. "Leave me alone."

"No. You've got to walk, Maggie. Please. You can't stop."

She backed away, her hands up to ward him off. "Can't go on. Go away." She sank back down to the snow, and curled up in a ball. "So tired."

"Please, Maggie, please!" Robbie was sobbing now.

Eric bent down and grabbed her hands. He jerked her up roughly, making her stand again. She erupted with a terrible fury, swinging wildly at him. "Leave me alone!"

He sidestepped it but didn't move otherwise. She came at him, her fingers like claws, aiming at his face. Instead of backing away, he moved forward and slapped her sharply across the face. Her eyes flew open and she cried out in pain.

Behind him, Eric heard Maggie's mother gasp. Jane James uttered a low cry.

For a moment, Maggie gaped at him. He slapped her again, harder this time. In an instant there was an angry red mark on her cheek showing the outline of his four fingers. Recognition came back to her eyes. "I hate you!" she burst out.

"Do you, Maggie?" he taunted.

She lunged at him. He jumped back, then laughed in her face. "Try it again."

With a scream she ran at him, lumbering awkwardly in the snow. He jumped backward, motioning with his fingers for her to come at him. "Come on, Maggie. You are very slow."

Screaming, she came for him. He danced backwards, staying off the trail, making her plow through the deep snow. After two or three minutes of that, she came to a stop, like a deer run to ground by the cougar. She bent over, hands on her legs, breathing in great gulps of air. He stopped, watching her warily. She was staring at the ground, her eyes wide, her nostrils flaring in and out.

And then gradually her face began to change. The tension around her mouth dissolved. Her eyes became rational again. Finally, she turned and looked at him. There were tears in her eyes now. He took a tentative step forward. "Maggie?"

She nodded, her lower lip trembling.

"I'm sorry."

There was a strangled sob of release and she fell forward into his arms.

She clung to him fiercely as he stroked her hair, kissed her cheeks, touched her face. Finally, he pulled back, looking deeply into her eyes. "You are not going to die on me, Maggie McKensie. Do you hear me? I will not let you."

Olaf and the Nielsons reached the top of Rocky Ridge about noon and collapsed in silent heaps on the snow-swept landscape. Olaf lay back in the snow, not caring that the wind whipped snow across his face like a file on a piece of metal. He wasn't moving any longer and that was all that mattered.

He heard a whimpering sound and looked up. Young Jens Nielson, scarf tied across the lower half of his face, was standing beside him, his arms drooping and his head slumped against his chest. "I'm cold, Olaf."

Olaf sat up immediately and opened his arms. "Come here."

The boy turned and backed into Olaf's lap. Olaf untied the scarf and let it drop, then pulled him close, feeling him shivering through his clothing. On the other side of the cart, Elsie Nielson was talking to Bodil Mortensen, trying to get her to respond. Bodil was staring at nothing, swaying back and forth like a dried reed in the wind.

"Where's Papa?" Jens asked.

Olaf scooted around so that they were facing down the trail. The last fifty or so feet of the trail was filled with jagged spines of rocks, six to eight inches high, which marched away from them in long, parallel lines. Below, just at the base of the last long incline, a solitary figure hobbled slowly towards them.

"Is that Papa?"

"Yes. He's hurt his foot somehow. But he's coming."

They watched together as Jens, Sr., made his way up the final hundred yards of Rocky Ridge. As he reached them and saw Olaf with his son, he nodded. "Thank you for pulling the cart up with Elsie, Olaf. Let me rest and then I shall take my turn again."

"You rest and then we shall see." Olaf's eyes dropped a little. "Is your foot all right?"

There was a slow shake of his head. "It is not good."

"Did you cut it, Papa?" little Jens asked anxiously.

His father came over and dropped to the ground beside them. "No, my son. It is just the cold."

That caused Olaf to start. He had noticed Jens limping heavily about an hour before. He thought the Dane had maybe slipped on the uneven ground and twisted his ankle, or perhaps had bumped against one of the sharp rock edges that were so prevalent along the trail here. Now he saw that Jens's boots were coming apart. The entire toe of the left boot had popped open. The right one had a ragged hole on one side and the sole was flapping loosely. The boots were soaked, and Olaf thought he saw a patch of bright red on one of the stockings.

His eyes widened, but Jens, watching him, shook his head quickly. "I do not want to worry Elsie," he whispered. "I just need to rest."

Olaf felt terrible. He had received a new pair of boots from the rescue wagons. His feet had been terribly cold all day, but the boot soles were thick and protected him from the rough, uneven road. Jens had not gotten any replacement boots because none were large enough to fit him. He had been given a new pair of woolen socks, but that was all.

Jens turned and gazed back the way he had just come. From here they could see a full half mile of the trail. A group of carts was coming around the side of the hill where the trail disappeared again. In a moment two wagons also appeared. It was John Chislett's rear contingent and the company's supply wagons.

Little Jens shivered involuntarily and Olaf pulled the boy in closer to him. He looked at the sky. It was still the color of lead, but thankfully only a few snowflakes were coming down, no different than it had been all morning. If it had been a blizzard . . . Then Olaf laughed mockingly at himself. Maybe there wasn't a lot of snow coming down from the sky, but it *had* been a blizzard all the way up. There had been a dozen or more places where the wind was blowing so hard that visibility had dropped to the point that they could barely see the cart in front of them.

He turned and looked to the south. From here atop Rocky Ridge he could see they had reached an enormous plateau, flat as a board for several miles. That would make the pulling easier. On the other hand, there would be no shelter here from the merciless wind.

Elsie came around, pulling Bodil along beside her. There was some color now again in Bodil's face and she was talking softly to Elsie. Elsie looked down the trail and saw the carts and wagons. "Are we going to wait here for Brother Chislett and the others?" she asked hopefully.

Jens shook his head. "He's still half an hour away, as slow as they're coming. We've got to move on."

"Will you carry me, Papa?" the boy said from Olaf's lap.

Jens turned to his son, and then Olaf saw him recoil in horror. He recovered quickly and held out his arms. "Come here, son."

Young Jens stood up and went over to his father, turning to sit in his lap as he had done with Olaf. Then it was Olaf who gasped. The white spots on the boy's face looked like they had been pasted on.

There was one on his chin, just to the left of center, two high on his cheekbones, and one at the tip of his nose.

"Elsie?" Jens called softly. "You'd better come look."

When they stood up to go ten minutes later, they had been able to bring back a little color to the frostbitten areas. As Elsie looked on, weeping quietly, Jens took his son's face in his hands and held his cheeks in his palms. At first the boy liked it; then as the spots began to thaw he started to cry. It was a sound that wrenched Olaf's heart like nothing he had ever heard before.

Finally the senior Jens took his hands away. He gently wrapped the scarf back around his son's face, then turned to his wife. "Elsie. We have to go."

She nodded. The other carts they had been with had moved out five minutes before. "I know."

"We've still got ten or eleven miles to go. If it gets dark . . ." He looked away.

"I don't want to get back on the cart, Papa," Jens wailed. "It's so cold up there."

Jens bent down and took his boy by the shoulders. "Jens, Papa can't carry you. I wish I could, but Papa's feet are not good."

"I'll carry him."

Jens jerked around. "But–"

Olaf ignored the look. "He'll be warmer on my back." He looked to Elsie. "It would mean you and Jens would have to pull the cart alone."

"Let me try him just for a while," Jens said.

Olaf shook his head. Elsie was shaking hers as well. "You can't, Jens, and you know it. I can pull the cart."

"I could try to carry him for a little while," Bodil said.

Olaf thought his heart would break as he looked into the face of this nine-year-old little woman. "Thank you, Bodil. You are as good to Jens as any sister ever could be. But I am going to do it."

Jens, Sr., stood there, his brow furrowed and his mouth tight. Finally he looked at Elsie. "I can pull if you can push."

She started to shake her head.

"I can pull if you can push," he said again.

Their eyes locked and after several seconds she finally nodded. "All right."

"Come on, Jens," Olaf said, squatting down. "Climb up on my back. Olaf will keep you warm."

Maggie walked along beside the cart, holding onto the shaft next to where Eric stood. She didn't lean on the cart for support, but she found it strangely comforting to keep hold of it, as if she might lose her way otherwise. And it was important to her to be close to Eric. She realized with a deepening sense of awe and gratitude that he had saved her life this afternoon. And now, though the tiredness was more complete, more utterly total than anything she could have imagined, she walked with a determination that was as deep and as absolute as her exhaustion. She *was* going to live. She had to. Wondering what she could do that would ever repay Eric for the gift he had given her, it had come with sudden, perfect clarity. It was so simple. He had saved her life. Now she would give it back to him, for the rest of their time on earth and for all of eternity. She hadn't told him that yet. Perhaps tonight when they finally reached camp.

Then her eyes caught sight of a change in the landscape. They were coming around the bend of a hill and dropping down into a low, narrow valley. It was lined with trees, stripped bare for the winter. "Is that the Sweetwater?" she cried in sudden excitement. "Or Rock Creek?" She had heard Brother Kimball telling some of the emigrants that Rock Creek Camp was near where the stream emptied into the Sweetwater River.

"No, Maggie," Eric said.

Her countenance fell. "Oh."

"I think it's Strawberry Creek. But that means we're only three or four miles from camp now." He glanced up at the sky. The snow had all but stopped, and the gray cloud cover seemed a little higher and thinner. He guessed that it was about four o'clock. If he was right, they should make camp before dark, a prospect that cheered him immensely.

Jane James was in the shafts with Eric at the moment, with Mary McKensie pushing. Robbie plodded alongside with Mary Ann and Martha James. George, who was seven, and little John, who was four, were wrapped up in a quilt atop the cart and seemed to be asleep. Eric looked at Robbie closely. He hadn't spoken at all for over an hour, an alarming sign in light of his usual enthusiasm and optimism. But he seemed to be all right, just completely worn out.

Suddenly Jane James let out a low cry. "Look, Eric! There's a handcart." She was pointing at where the trail intersected the trees. And, sure enough, there was a single handcart waiting there. Two figures were standing beside the cart. Whether it was Jane's cry or the sound of the wheels on the rocky trail that turned them around wasn't clear, but they did turn. As they did so and were silhouetted against the snow, Eric was surprised to see that both wore dresses. Two women alone?

Suddenly one woman began to jump up and down in great excitement. They heard a cry, but the wind whipped it away. Then it came again. "Mama! Mama!"

Jane's hand flew to her mouth and there was a cry of exultation. "It's Sarah and Emma! Thanks be to God. We've found my daughters."

Sarah and Emma had made excellent time. Even though there was only the two of them and they had the more heavily laden cart, they were both still in good health and they were young. But

Strawberry Creek had stopped them. They weren't with anyone else. The wagons had earlier broken through the ice, but it had frozen over again with a thin skin that showed the water flowing beneath it. It was fifteen to eighteen inches deep and looked terribly cold. So they decided it was finally time to stop and wait for their mother.

As mother and daughters talked quietly, Eric walked down to the creek and examined the ford. The stream was twenty or thirty feet across. He walked back to the two families. "How many pairs of dry shoes do we have?"

Sarah and Emma raised their hands, as did their mother, but Jane said that she didn't have a change of shoes for the younger children. Neither did Sister McKensie and Robbie. Eric turned to Maggie. She shook her head slowly, shrinking back at the sight of the water.

He smiled thinly. "I didn't think so." In one smooth motion he swept her up in his arms and started for the creek.

"Eric!" she gasped.

"Hold on." He stepped forward, and felt the ice crack. Though he had clenched his teeth in preparation for the shock, a gasp was still torn from his lips as the water went over the top of his boots. It was as if someone had stabbed him with a dozen knives.

"Eric! Put me down. I can do it."

"Not on your life," he said. He took long strides, breaking the ice open again, setting his feet firmly on the rocky bottom below to make sure he wouldn't slip.

He set her down on the other side, kissed her soundly, then plunged back in again even as she was still protesting. Back with the others, he looked at Sister James. "If I get Martha and Mary Ann, can you and the girls take George and John over on the cart?"

Sister James had already made that decision. The boys were awake and watching what was happening from their perch on the cart. "Yes."

Eric bent down and put Mary Ann, who was eleven, on his back. Then he picked up Martha, who was ten, in his arms.

"Do they get a kiss too?" Emma cried as he started off.

"Yes, but no one older than that," Maggie cried from the other side, laughing now.

In five minutes they were done. Sarah, Emma, and their mother took the cart across and changed into dry stockings and shoes while Eric went back for Robbie one time and Sister McKensie the next. As he set Maggie's mother down, she touched his arm gently. "Thank you, son."

That startled him. She had never used that term with him before. He smiled back at her. "You're welcome."

Then Maggie grabbed at his arm. "Do *you* have another pair of shoes or stockings, Eric?"

He shrugged. "It's only a few miles to Rock Creek," he said lightly. "Come on, let's get going, or my feet are going to get cold."

By late afternoon Olaf Pederson was half stumbling, half walking as he followed the line of tracks in the snow, already half-covered by the blowing snow. He turned, looking back. Elsie and Jens Nielson were now a full quarter of a mile behind him. Even at this distance he could see how badly Jens was hobbling. No wonder they were losing ground on him. Elsie was at the back now, pushing with all her strength, but she couldn't make the cart go faster than Jens could walk. He didn't see Bodil Mortensen and guessed she might be riding in the cart now.

For one brief moment Olaf considered stopping long enough to let them catch up to him. He shook his head. He knew without any doubt that if he stopped now, he would have to sit down. And if he sat down he would not get up again. At least not with little Jens Nielson on his back. And so he lowered his head and plodded on.

His lungs were on fire. His chest hurt with every breath. His back felt as though he carried a barn on it. And his feet. He knew that even the new boots were no longer protecting him. In the last hour, with more and more snow on the trail now that they were on level ground, the boots had gradually become soaked. The progression was interesting to him in a detached sort of way. First there had been the bitter cold and the growing discomfort. Then the wet seeped in and his feet became like two blocks of ice. Then for a blessed time he had felt nothing. Now the first tendrils of pain were starting to shoot through them with each new step. He knew that in another hour or two he would better understand what the senior Jens Nielson was experiencing. He began to sing to himself in English, to take his mind off the pain.

Ye Saints that dwell on Europe's shores,
Prepare yourselves with many more
To leave behind your native land
    For . . .

His eyes were half-closed as he sang and now they snapped open. "For . . ." He shook his head, trying to clear the muddle. But it did no good. Dismayed, he frowned. How would he explain this to Maggie? She had made her students memorize the lyrics. What if she called on him in class tonight?

Frustrated, he jumped ahead to the chorus. That he could remember.

Some must push and some must pull
    As we go marching up the hill,
As merrily on the way we go
    Until we reach the valley, oh.

He grunted softly, pleased with himself. "Hey, Jens," he said in English, turning his head enough to look up at the little person riding on his back. "Are you merrily on the way we go?"

He laughed, pleased with his little joke. Then he realized there was no response. He shook his body a little, switching back to Danish. "Jens. Are you all right up there?"

There was a soft murmur and the weight on his back stirred a little.

"Good." He began humming the next verse, still irritated at himself for not being able to remember the words.

A quarter of a mile back from where Olaf trudged along, Elsie Nielson was also trying to find ways that took her mind off the pain. She hated pushing the cart and would have much preferred to pull. She was so short that even when the cart was level it came to her chest. So to push with any strength, she had to raise her arms to an unnatural level and lean forward. Even after months of taking her turn at pushing, she still wasn't used to it. Her arms and shoulders burned as though someone had rubbed them with a red-hot liniment.

Suddenly the cart jerked violently upward, the tailgate almost smashing her in the face. "Jens! Be careful!"

And then, with a start, she realized what had happened. Her husband had dropped the shafts. The front of the cart had crashed to the ground, jerking the back end up sharply. With a low cry, she darted around. Jens was still in the shafts, but he was on his knees. She stopped as she watched him place both hands in the snow, his arms trembling violently, and try to push himself up. His knees came off the ground for a few seconds, but then he crashed down again. He gave a low sob and buried his face in his hands.

"Jens!" She leaped forward and dropped to his side.

"I can't, Elsie." He turned his face and she was shocked to see wet streaks down his cheeks. That shook her more deeply than anything he could have done. In their six years of marriage and a year of courting before that, she had never seen her husband cry. Now great sobs tore through his body.

With a sob of her own, Elsie threw her arms around him. "Oh,

Jens. It's all right. It's all right." She stroked his face as she pressed against him. "We'll rest for a minute."

For almost a minute, he sat there, his head down, his wife clinging to him. Finally, the shudders lessened and he reached up and wiped at his cheeks. Then he took her by the shoulders and looked deep into her eyes. "I can go no farther, Elsie. You are going to have to go on alone."

"No, Jens!"

He shook her gently. "You have to, Elsie. For the children."

Frantic, all she could do was shake her head. Then suddenly, a great peace came over her. She knew exactly what to do. She stood up and put one hand under his arm. "Jens?"

He looked up.

"Come get in the cart."

Something akin to panic twisted his features. "No, Elsie."

"Yes, Jens."

"My weight will double the load. You're not strong enough."

"I will not leave you." For several long seconds their eyes held and then she said it again. "*I will not.*"

Chapter Notes

The journey from the base of Rocky Ridge to Rock Creek, a distance of sixteen miles, proved to be the greatest ordeal the James G. Willie Handcart Company would face. Though consistent journal keeping had stopped by now, fortunately several participants later wrote of their experiences. These accounts give rich details about what happened, though there are a few minor differences between the accounts, an understandable thing when one considers the trauma of that day. It was twenty hours before the last of the company made it to camp.

Sarah James related the following:

> I can remember the time when one of the men who was pulling a cart just ahead of us laid down in his shafts and started to cry. We all wanted to cry with him. One of the captains, I don't remember just

who, came up to him and just slapped him in the face. It made the man so mad that he jumped right up and started to run with his cart. I remember that it was a mean way to treat the poor fellow but know that it saved his life. . . .

. . . It was a bitter cold morning in October as we broke camp. As usual there were dead to be buried before we could go on. Father and Reuben were with the burial detail. Mother, who was helping to pull the heaviest cart, had stayed behind until they could finish their sad work. After a short service, we, with light cart, went ahead to catch the rest of the company, and mother and Reuben started to follow. Father collapsed and fell in the snow. He tried two or three times to get up with mother's help, then finally he asked her to go on and when he felt rested he would come on with Reuben. Mother knew in her heart that he had given out, but perhaps she said in a few minutes with some rest he could come on. She took the cart and hurried to follow us. (In Carol Cornwall Madsen, *Journey to Zion*, p. 629; see also *Remember*, p. 12)

In his narrative John Chislett recalled:

The day we crossed the Rocky Ridge it was snowing a little—the wind hard from the north-west—and blowing so keenly that it almost pierced us through. We had to wrap ourselves closely in blankets, quilts, or whatever else we could get, to keep from freezing. Captain Willie still attended to the details of the company's travelling, and this day he appointed me to bring up the rear. My duty was to stay behind everything and that nobody was left along the road. I had to bury a man who had died in my hundred, and I finished doing so after the company had started. In about half an hour, I set out on foot alone to do my duty as rear-guard to the camp. The ascent of the ridge commenced soon after leaving camp, and I had not gone far up it before I overtook a cart that the folks could not pull through the snow, here about knee-deep. I helped them along, and we soon overtook another. By all hands getting to one cart we could travel; so we moved one of the carts a few rods, and then went back and brought up the other. After moving in this way for a while, we overtook other carts at different points of the hill, until we had six carts, not one of which could be moved by the parties owning it. I put our collective strength to three carts at a time, took them a short distance, and then brought up the other

> three. Thus by travelling over the hill three times—twice forward and once back—I succeeded after hours of toil in bringing my little company to the summit. The six carts were then trotted on gaily down hill, the intense cold stirring us to action. . . . One old man, named James (a farm-laborer from Gloucestershire), who had a large family, and who had worked very hard all the way, I found sitting by the roadside unable to pull his cart any farther, I could not get him into the wagon, as it was already overcrowded. He had a shotgun which he had brought from England, and which had been a great blessing to him and his family, for he was a good shot, and often had a mess of sage hens or rabbits for his family. I took the gun from the cart, put a small bundle on the end of it, placed it on his shoulder, and started him out with his little boy, twelve years old. His wife and two daughters older than the boy took the cart along finely after reaching the summit.
>
> We travelled along with the ox-team and overtook others, all so laden with the sick and helpless that they moved very slowly. The oxen had almost given out. . . . We struggled along in this weary way until after dark, and by this time our "rear" numbered 3 wagons, 8 handcarts, and nearly 40 persons. With the wagons were Mellen Atwood, Levi Savage, and William Woodward, captains of hundreds, faithful men who had worked hard all the way. (In *Remember*, pp. 10–11)

Levi Savage chronicled the experience thus: "We buried our dead, got up our teams and about nine o'clock a.m. commenced ascending the Rocky Ridge. This was a severe day. The wind blew hard and cold. The ascent was some five miles long and some places steep and covered with deep snow. We became weary, set down to rest, and some became chilled and commenced to freeze. Brothers Atwood, Woodward and myself remained with the teams. They being perfectly loaded down with the sick and children, so thickly stacked I was fearful some would smother" (in *Remember*, p. 10).

Looking back on his experiences, Jens Nielson wrote: "I told you there were five men to the tent, but now the four were dead and I was the only man left so I had to ask some of the largest and strongest women to help me raise the tent. It looked like we should all die. I remember my prayers as distinctly today as I did then, if the Lord would let me live to reach Salt Lake City, that all my days should be spent in usefulness under the direction of his Holy Priesthood. How far I have come short of this promise I do not know, but I have been called to make six homes and as far as this goes, I have fulfilled my promise" (quoted in Lyman, "Bishop Jens Nielson," p. 4). Further describing the ordeal that Jens

Nielson and his wife, Elsie, underwent, the author of Jens's life history states: "In the fury of those storms which raged around them the bishop [Jens later was a bishop in Utah] and his faithful wife toiled through the frozen snow till his feet were shapeless and useless with frost. He could walk no farther. What was to be done? Should he sink in the snow to die of despair? His young wife . . . looked at him, how desolate the world would be without him. 'Ride,' she urged. 'I can't leave you–I can pull the cart'" (Lyman, "Bishop Jens Nielson," p. 4).

The Thomas Moulton family, among whom was eight-year-old James Heber Moulton, were also members of the Willie Company. An account of their experiences includes the following: "Rocky Ridge must have been a real trial, as another terrible wind and snowstorm came upon them. As they struggled up the side of the ridge, they had to wrap themselves in blankets and quilts to keep from freezing to death. Heber took the brunt of the weather. Perhaps there was not sufficient warm clothing to go around for all. A kindly old lady, seeing the freezing lad's dilemma, grasped his hand as he trailed behind the handcart, held by the rope around his waist, and struggling to climb the slopes of the ridge. This kindly act saved his right hand, but his left hand, being exposed to the sub-zero weather, was frozen. The flesh dropped off his poor little fingers to the first joint" (from the autobiography of Charlotte "Lottie" Moulton Carroll, as cited in Turner, *Emigrating Journals*, p. 227).

The reference to the temperature here brings up something that is frequently overlooked. The journal entries and historical accounts about the crossing of Rocky Ridge make frequent reference to the weather, especially the bitterly cold wind, but no specific temperature is mentioned. On November fourth, less than two weeks after the Rocky Ridge crossing, a temperature of minus six degrees was recorded at Martin's Cove. On the sixth, the thermometer showed minus eleven degrees (see Turner, *Emigrating Journals*, p. 201; Hafen and Hafen, *Handcarts to Zion*, p. 224). Those temperatures were recorded near Devil's Gate, which is just under six thousand feet in elevation. The top of Rocky Ridge is 7,300 feet above sea level. So it is possible that temperatures were near zero or below that day.

"Windchill" is a modern device used to calculate the effect of temperature, humidity, and wind on a person. To have a "hard wind" on Rocky Ridge is typical, even in good weather. When storms are brewing the winds can become fierce. Howard A. Christy's study of windchill shows that if the wind was blowing at thirty miles per hour and the temperature was ten degrees Fahrenheit, the windchill factor would be thirty degrees below zero. At zero degrees and forty miles per hour, the windchill factor would drop to fifty-five degrees below zero. At minus ten and forty miles per hour, the windchill effect would be an incredible seventy degrees below zero! (see Christy, "Weather, Disaster, and Responsibility," p. 19).

There is no way to know exactly what conditions were that day on Rocky Ridge, but it is not surprising that severe frostbite became a factor in the emigrants' sufferings.

CHAPTER 27

ROCK CREEK

I

Thursday, 23 October 1856

In the dancing light of the scattered fires, the shapes of the half dozen wagons camped near Rock Creek loomed like ghosts in the darkness. The wagons from South Pass had not been waiting here, as promised, but a rider had come in and said that they would be here in the morning. Six more. Filled with fat quarters of beef, thousands of pounds of flour, more warm clothing, and additional quilts and blankets.

That knowledge warmed Eric as much as the crackling fire. He looked down at Maggie, who was wrapped in a buffalo robe and lying in his arms. "Are you getting warm finally?"

She smiled up at him, her eyes dark and contented in the firelight. "Yes. And full. Can you believe it, Eric? Warm and full. Who would ever have thought that those would be the two most wonderful things in the world?"

"Yes." He held up his feet, which he had been holding near the hot coals. "Even Eric's big feet are getting dry. It is wonderful."

She suddenly remembered something, a sign that she was coming back to normal again. "How are Sister Bathgate and Sister Park?"

"They made it," he said simply. He had gone to see them after supper and was amazed that they seemed to have come through the day without serious setbacks.

He took her hand and held it tightly. "*We* made it too, Maggie," he said quietly.

"I know," she said in wonder.

"We've still got a long way to go, but the worst is over."

She felt a cough stirring down in her chest and willed it to hold for a moment, until she said what she wanted to say. "I was so sure that I was going to die, Eric."

"I told you it would not be."

"I know. Thank you." A teasing smile stole across her face. "Can I tell you something?"

"Of course."

But before she could speak, the coughing started again. He held her tightly until it passed. Then she went on. "Do you remember that day when I told you that if I died before I got to the Valley I wanted you to remarry?"

"Yes?"

She lowered her eyes. "I was just being noble."

He laughed aloud. "I know."

"You knew?" She slapped at him playfully. "Why didn't you tell me that, then?"

He didn't smile back. "I was busy trying to make you believe you would not die."

"Yes," she said. She leaned her head against him, feeling an overwhelming sense of gratitude. It was astonishing the difference that just a few hours could make. She turned and looked across the fire. Over there her mother sat beside Sister James, talking quietly. Sarah sat beside them, listening. Emma was in the tent with the other children, including Robbie, getting them to sleep. Nothing had been heard from any of them for over an hour, and Maggie suspected that Emma had fallen asleep with them. "What time is it, do you think?" she asked.

"Half past ten. Maybe eleven. You should go to bed too, Maggie."

She shook her head. "Not until Olaf and Brother James and Reuben come in."

"And Jens and Elsie," he agreed quietly.

"I'm getting worried. It's so late."

"I know. But Brother Chislett is not here yet either. He was bringing up the last. Maybe they are with him."

"Will you wait up all night for them?" she asked.

"If necessary." And with that he put his arm around her and pulled her in against him. "But you try to sleep."

"Right here?" she murmured.

"Of course," he said, surprised that she had to ask.

They didn't have to wait all night. Fifteen minutes later they heard a hoarse cry and turned to see a figure come stumbling out of the darkness. In an instant people were on their feet and rushing to see who it was. Maggie threw off the robe and grabbed Eric's hand. Her mother and Sister James and Sarah were up too. They walked quickly over to Brother Kimball's fire.

"It's Brother Chislett," Mary McKensie cried as they got close enough to see.

"Thank the Lord," Jane breathed. "But why is he alone?"

As the people crowded in, Brother Willie and Brother Kimball pushed their way through the crowd. Heber P. Kimball was beside his older brother. The crowd instantly quieted as the two leaders reached the subcaptain.

"Brother John," Captain Willie said, gripping his hand. "Thank heavens you've come. Where are your people?"

Chislett stepped closer to the fire, shivering violently. A man nearby stood quickly, took the quilt from his own shoulders, and wrapped it quickly around Chislett's.

"Thank you." He looked at Willie. "We've got forty people at Strawberry Creek."

There was a collective gasp. "Forty!" Brother Kimball blurted.

"Yes. The oxen refuse to cross. And the people are at their limits too. We've got to send someone out to get them."

Brother Willie was nodding. "That's why I couldn't find anyone. I started back to help, but I couldn't make it very far. I had to come back."

William Kimball swung around and began shouting out. "You boys from the Valley. Roust yourselves out of those tents." He turned to his brother. "Get them all up, Heber, and get the teams hitched."

"Yes, sir!" The younger Kimball leaped away.

"There are also some stragglers between here and Strawberry Creek," Chislett said, holding the quilt tightly around himself. "I urged them to come on. You're going to have to tell the men to watch for them along the way."

"We will." William Kimball had heard enough. He said something to Captain Willie, then turned and strode off, headed for the wagons.

Jane James immediately moved forward, with Sarah in tow. Knowing exactly what she was going to do, Eric and Maggie moved in right behind them.

"Brother Chislett?"

He turned. "Ah, Sister James."

"Have you seen my husband and son?"

He sighed, his hand letting go of the quilt to reach out and take hers. "I have, and within the last hour."

Jane's head dropped and there was a choked sob. "Praise heaven!"

Then something in the silence brought her head up again. Brother Chislett was shaking his head. He told them quickly about finding father and son first thing this morning and sending them on without the second cart. But then his voice lowered. "I was chosen by the others at the crossing to come ahead to camp and get help," he said. "I broke through the ice on Strawberry Creek and got my boots filled with water." He looked down and held out one leg for them to see.

The circle of people gasped. Both of his boots were caked with ice.

"I was running, to stop my feet from freezing. Suddenly I saw a figure in the darkness. Then I saw it was two figures, a man and a boy."

"William?" Jane cried.

"Yes. They must have come along all right, because I had not seen them again. But there they were. Your husband was seated by the roadside with your son watching over him."

"Dear, faithful Reuben," Sarah cried, near to tears now.

"Yes. Brother James was very weak. Your son was trying to make him get up and come along, but he couldn't." Now he looked away and his eyes filled with pain. "I tried to help. I got him to his feet and had him lean on me. He did so and we walked a little distance, but then he collapsed again. I half carried him, half dragged him for a ways, your son helping all he could, but my strength failed me."

With eyes that had seen too much in the last fourteen or fifteen hours, John Chislett stared at Jane James. Eyes brimming with tears, she reached out and gripped his hand. "It's all right, Brother Chislett. I thank you for doing what you could."

He barely seemed to hear. He was staring now at something in the fire. "The errand I was on was of a most urgent nature and I could not tarry longer. I took off the quilt I had wrapped around me and rolled your husband into it. I told your son to stay with him but to keep walking back and forth no matter what. If he didn't, I told him he would freeze to death."

Jane turned around, groping blindly. Sarah reached out and took her into her arms, tears streaming down her own cheeks.

Eric stepped forward. "Did you see my brother?"

Chislett turned, grateful for the chance to turn away from his thoughts. "Yes. They are on this side of Strawberry Creek as well, coming on slowly. Your brother is with the Danish couple and their two children."

"Is he all right?"

One hand came up and rubbed at his eyes. "Yes. I think so. He is carrying the little boy." He sighed. "And the tall Dane? What's his name?"

"Jens Nielson."

"Yes, him. His feet are badly frozen. His wife is bringing him on." Again he seemed overwhelmed. He stifled back a sob. "That tiny wisp of a woman has pulled the cart alone, with her husband and the little girl in it, for I don't know how many miles. Hours at least. It's incredible."

Eric bowed his head. *Oh, Elsie! If only I had been with you!* And then he shook it off. If he *had* been with the Nielsons, Maggie would be dead now.

"We offered to have her wait with the rest of us," Chislett was saying. "Maybe she didn't understand what I was saying, but she came on. They crossed the creek on their own—her and your brother—and they're about two miles back."

"The boys will go get them, Eric," Captain Willie said. "The boys from the Valley are still strong and fresh."

Eric turned. "I'll be going with them," he said quietly.

II

Friday, 24 October 1856

The McKensies and the Jameses, along with Eric, had finally reached the Rock Creek Camp just as it was getting dark. Some of the

"Valley boys," as William Kimball called them, immediately rushed out to help. They took their tent and set it up in short order. Food was already in steaming kettles, and though they would not have unlimited quantities until the other wagons arrived, there was enough for a good meal for everyone. Firewood and dry willows had already been cut and piled up near each fire.

That meal along with five or six hours of warmth and rest had done a great deal to rejuvenate Eric's strength, but it would take many days before the terrible weariness in his bones would be gone completely. He could feel that weariness now as he walked alongside one of the wagons moving eastward back towards Strawberry Creek. When they left the camp at Rock Creek shortly before midnight, he had started in the lead wagon along with William H. and Heber P. Kimball. But he soon gave that up and got out to walk. The night was dark and suddenly a solitary figure or a small group pulling a handcart would loom up before them.

At first they tried hailing them to learn who they were. Some responded wearily but coherently; some mumbled indistinguishable words; some just stared at them and stumbled on past as though they were apparitions in the night. Fearing that he might miss Olaf, Eric had climbed down. Soon some of the other rescuers were doing the same, walking along with him, checking each new person or group of people as they came upon them. They would pause long enough to find out who they were and how they were doing. If they were still on their feet, they would encourage them to press forward until the wagons could return for them. If they were on the verge of collapse, they would put them in the wagons and bundle them up as much as possible.

In some cases it was bodies they found, still sitting wrapped in their meager blankets or stretched out in the snow. These would wait until the last wagon returned.

Eric estimated it was now somewhere around two o'clock in the morning. He and Heber P. Kimball walked along with one of the wagons, ignoring their own exhaustion, searching the night with their eyes to make sure that no one was missed.

"Look," Eric said softly. "Up there on the right. Is that someone?" At first he had thought it was a small tree or a bush, but then it seemed to move.

"Yes, I think it is."

They increased their pace, moving out ahead of the wagon. As they drew closer, the dark shape took form. It was a man, and he was waving his arms. "Help!" It was little more than a croak. Eric wasn't sure he had even heard it. "Help me, please."

Heber broke into a trot. That was beyond Eric, but he moved forward as quickly as he could. Only as he reached the person did Eric see another dark shape, this one lying in the snow beside the other. He stopped. "Reuben? Is that you!"

There was a strangled cry of pain and joy.

"It's Eric, Reuben. We're here."

"Papa is sick." He half turned, his hands coming out of his blanket. "The man wrapped him in his quilt. He told me to walk back and forth so I didn't freeze."

Eric and Heber were already on their knees beside the figure in the snow. Eric pulled the blanket back, pulled off his glove, and touched William James's face. To his surprise, it had warmth in it. He bent down, putting an ear to his mouth. He looked up at Heber. "He's alive, but just barely."

Reuben came forward. "Papa?"

Eric stood up and took Reuben James in his arms. In the faint light reflected off the snow, the fourteen-year-old's face looked like that of a tortured old man. "It's all right, Reuben," he said. "We're here to help."

Heber stood up, peering up ahead into the darkness. "Here comes a wagon. Let's get them into it."

Eric nodded and took Reuben's hand. As he started to lead him forward, he saw that Reuben hobbled painfully. He put his arm around his waist. "Your feet?" he asked softly.

There was a silent nod in the darkness. "My hands hurt real bad too, Eric."

"It's going to be all right. Your mother is waiting for you at camp. And Sarah and Emma."

The boy's head came up. "Are they all right?" he whispered.

"Yes. They are all right."

The wagon was already jammed with people, and Eric quickly checked to see if Olaf was one of them. He was not. The emigrants silently rearranged themselves, making room for the two additions. As the wagon moved away, Eric stood silently, wishing that he could get on it too.

"Do you think the old man will make it?" Heber P. asked quietly.

Eric shook his head. "It will be a blessing if he lives long enough to reach camp, so his wife can see him one more time. I do not think he'll make it through the night."

Heber touched Eric's sleeve. "Guess what the father had lying beside him."

Eric could only look at him, too tired to guess.

"A shotgun." He shook his head. "Can you imagine? At a time like this, all you can think about is saving your shotgun?"

Eric stared at him, his eyes suddenly burning. "He wasn't trying to save his shotgun," he whispered. "He was trying to save his family."

Olaf was walking alongside the next returning wagon. At first Eric almost didn't see him as he ran to the back of the wagon and called inside as it moved along. This wagon had two handcarts tied on behind, and they too were filled with people. When he got no response to his calls, Eric turned away, frustrated. Then something about the figure walking on the other side of the wagon brought him around. In the darkness it looked odd and unnatural. He moved forward a few steps before he realized that it was a man carrying a child on his back. With a cry he ran forward. "Olaf!"

The head rose slightly.

Eric leaped forward and grabbed him by the arm. "Olaf!"

Finally, Olaf shook off his grip, not stopping.

Eric jumped forward and stepped directly in front of him. "It's Eric, Olaf."

Olaf shuffled to a stop, his head coming up very slowly. "Eric?" he mumbled.

"Yes! It's me, Olaf. I'm here." Eric peered up at the dark shape on his back. "Is that little Jens?"

"Yes. He is so cold. Didn't want to walk."

"Here let me help you."

Ahead of them, the driver had reined to a stop and was peering around the side of the wagon. He jumped down and ran back to join Eric. "Do you know him?"

"He's my brother."

"I tried to get him to ride in the wagon, but he wouldn't. Said he promised to carry this boy. He's not coherent."

Eric stepped around behind Olaf and reached up. He recoiled as he touched little Jens Nielson's arm. It was cold and stiff. Now the driver was beside Eric. "The boy's dead," he whispered. "We tried to tell your brother that, but he wouldn't listen. He's in pretty bad shape himself."

"Help me," Eric cried softly. Then to Olaf he said, "We're going to get Jens down, Olaf. We'll let him ride in the wagon now."

"Too cold. Have to carry him."

"It's all right," Eric said, fighting to stop his voice from breaking. "We have blankets. Jens will be all right."

Working as gently as possible, Eric and the teamster pried the body of Jens Nielson from off Olaf's back, then carried him to the wagon. Again those inside shuffled around and made room for the still form. Olaf stood where he was, his head down, his arms swinging loose now. Eric went back to him and took him by the elbow.

"There's no more room in there," the driver said. He was young, perhaps even a year or two younger than Eric. His voice was soft and filled with sorrow. "You and him get up in the wagon seat with me."

It took both of them to help Olaf up, and the driver had to hold him steady until Eric clambered up as well and took Olaf in his arms. "All right," Eric said to the teamster.

Maggie and the others had finally gone inside their tent and tried to sleep for a while. But no one did. They had lain there in the darkness for a long time, talking quietly so as not to wake the children. They didn't talk about Brother James or Eric or Olaf. They talked of the Valley and friends that might be waiting for them when they finally arrived, and where they would live, and how they would make a living. Then about an hour after midnight they had heard the rattle of a wagon. They were up instantly and out of their tent. It was a disappointment. The wagon was filled with people but not any of theirs.

The second wagon came in fifteen minutes later. Again they shuffled out as quickly as they could. This time it was to face tragedy. Reuben James was one of the first ones to climb down from the wagon. When he saw his mother he dropped to his knees, buried his face in his hands, and began to sob. The driver and another man then carefully lifted out the body of William James. He had come within half an hour of seeing his beloved family again, but it was not meant to be.

Now Sarah and Emma and Jane James sat by the fire, holding hands, staring numbly at nothing, stricken with grief. The body of William James lay wrapped in a tattered quilt just outside the circle of firelight. Reuben was sleeping now, his hands and feet carefully bandaged. Maggie had nearly fainted when she saw him in the light. The tips of his fingers were as black as if he had been digging in a coal bin. His cheeks had those white crystalized spots they had all come to recognize and dread. And he could barely hobble, even with his mother and sisters holding him up. And in the morning, the four younger children would wake to the news that their father was dead.

Maggie stared eastward into the black night. It was around two or three in the morning now. Eighteen hours ago they had stood at the base of Rocky Ridge and prepared for the day that lay before them. And still it wasn't over. *Oh, Eric! Where are you? Please come back. Please!*

"Mama?"

Maggie turned. It was Emma. She sat beside her mother, who stroked her hair slowly. Sister James finally looked down at her daughter.

Wet streaks on Emma's cheeks gleamed in the firelight. "What are we going to do now, Mama?"

For several moments, Maggie didn't think that Jane was going to answer. Her eyes were lifeless, staring past Emma into the darkness. Her face was like stone. There were no tears here. And then, slowly, her eyes focused. Her mouth softened and she came back to them. Sarah was looking up at her mother now too.

Jane James looked at her two oldest children. On board the *Thornton* she had watched a child be buried in the cold waters of the North Atlantic. In the morning she would attend to another burial. But there were still seven children who were dependent on her alone now. Her head came up a little as she turned to look squarely at Emma. "We shall go on to Zion," she said quietly.

Emma sniffed, wiping at the tears now. Sarah was nodding slowly.

"And there," Jane said with quiet resolve, "there we will live in such a way that when we are privileged to see your father again, he will be very proud of us."

It was just a few minutes later when once again the rattle of wagon wheels on frozen ground sounded across the camp. Maggie whirled. The incoming group was still too far away to see, but she watched steadfastly where the trail dropped down a slight rise into the bottomland of Rock Creek. Her mother had come to her feet to stand beside her, gripping her hand.

And then, as they slowly materialized out of the darkness, she saw the lead mules, followed by the second team and then the wagon. It was pulling behind it two handcarts filled with people. As it came within the full circle of light, Maggie gave a low exclamation. Eric was sitting beside the driver, holding someone in his arms.

Gripping her mother's hand, she started forward. Others were up now and moving towards the wagon as well. There were many who were still on watch for family and friends. The wagon pulled to a stop alongside the ones that had come in earlier. It was quickly surrounded with people. Maggie reached them and pushed her way through, trying to get to the front.

"Eric!" She was calling his name before she even came around to where he was. Then she stopped.

He was still on the wagon seat. Olaf was in his arms, his eyes closed and his face peaceful. Eric was touching his face, tears streaming down his cheeks.

"Oh, Eric. *No!*"

He looked up, his face stricken with such pain that it made her catch her breath. "He's gone, Maggie."

"Oh, Eric." She clambered up and sat beside him. As she touched his arm, Eric's shoulders began to shake.

He dropped his head. His voice was barely a whisper. "I should never have let him trade his sweater for that meat. He wouldn't have gotten so cold."

"Eric, you can't blame yourself."

He was shaking his head back and forth, staring down at Olaf's face. "How am I going to tell Mama?" he whispered. "I promised I would take care of him."

—❦—

Reddick N. Allred, who had been left at South Pass by Brother George D. Grant a few days before, arrived at Rock Creek that morning with six additional wagons filled with provisions. The last of the handcarts of the Willie Company beat them into camp by only a few hours. Captain Willie and William H. Kimball had started the emigrants up Rocky Ridge about nine o'clock the previous morning. The last stragglers had reached Rock Creek sometime around five o'clock this morning, a full twenty hours after they had started.

The arrival was met with general rejoicing, but it was subdued, tempered by the pall of sorrow that lay heavily on the camp. Captain Willie and William Kimball consulted briefly, then determined that in spite of the urgency to move on, with so many dead and dying in the camp they would lay over here for another day. The wind was still blowing hard out of the north and was bitterly cold. With great effort the tents were pulled down and moved downstream into the thickets of willows, which would provide more shelter.

About ten o'clock Brother John Chislett, along with two of the young men from the Valley, began a slow circuit around the camp with an empty handcart. One by one they took the stiff, frozen bodies, many of them nearly covered with the snowdrifts, and carried them to the cart. There were men, women, and children. There were the young and there were the elderly. All were dressed in the clothes they had worn when they started out the morning before.

In a little meadow just east of the creek, another set of men set to work to dig the grave. All who were able came out to help. Eric was among them. They scraped away the snow, then used picks to break through a four-inch layer of rock-hard frozen soil. Once they were through that, the work went more quickly. In less than an hour they had a large hole about seven feet across in both directions, and three or four feet deep. Eric climbed out of the hole, not looking at the rows of bodies now laid out side by side next to the grave. As they finished, a group of women brought another cart heaped to overflowing with willows they had cut from the thickets.

The trumpet sounded through the camp, a low, mournful sound that was snatched away by the wind. Maggie was already there at graveside, holding a blanket tightly around herself, watching sadly as Eric and the other men finished their task. Twice her cough took hold of her and she had to double over before it passed. Both times Eric barely glanced at her, and that frightened her badly. He moved as though he were made of wood or as if in a trance.

One by one, people began to appear. They pulled their coats closer around them, covered their faces and ears with their scarves and hats and bonnets, then came slowly to the grave site. Maggie's mother came out but did not have Robbie with her. Sister James appeared, her head covered with a black scarf. Sarah and Emma followed a moment later with the two younger girls. Reuben, still badly frostbitten, stayed in the tent. His two younger brothers stayed with him.

In the end, not even half the camp turned out for the service. Part of that was understandable. Many were still critically ill. Some, like Reuben or Jens Nielson, were not able to walk and would stay in their beds all day. But some who could have been there, even some who had family members being buried, did not appear.

To Maggie's surprise, Eric suddenly walked away from the group, and for a moment she wondered if he had decided he could not bear to watch further. But in a moment she understood. Elsie Nielson was coming slowly toward the circle of mourners. Her head was up and she seemed to be looking straight ahead. Eric held her arm and spoke softly to her as they came.

Maggie felt her chest constrict, and this time it was not with the cold. Elsie Nielson, this tiny woman with such an enormous spirit, had pulled her husband into camp and saved his life. Unfortunately, that was all she had saved. Jens, Jr., was one of those whose bodies awaited burial. He would have been six in another week. Bodil

Mortensen lay beside him. She had been barely alive when they loaded her into one of the wagons and brought her into camp. By daylight, she too had slipped away. Bodil had become like the daughter Elsie never had and was so close to her that many just assumed Elsie was her mother. And to make it doubly hard, when they reached Utah—if they reached Utah!—Bodil's sister would be there to greet them. What would Elsie say to her then?

Maggie felt the tears come as she watched how tenderly Eric brought this tiny woman, now bowed down even lower with grief, to stand beside him at the edge of the grave.

The services were brief. Elder Willie said a few words. William Kimball also spoke. Brothers Chislett and Atwood offered simple prayers. It was too cold to keep people outside for long, and they desperately needed to rest and recruit their strength. Tomorrow they would have to be on their way again. The worst of the crisis was over, but they were still a long way from the Valley.

Not a sound broke the silence, except for the sighing of the wind above their heads, as the services concluded. Somberly the men walked over to the row of bodies. One by one they picked them up and carried them to the grave and placed them inside it, feet to the center, heads to the outside. When it came time for Olaf, Eric stepped forward. With two others he picked up his brother's body and laid it down with great care. He returned twice more, laying Bodil on one side of Olaf, and young Jens on the other.

Once the bodies were in place, the men laid the willows back and forth in a latticework over the corpses. Then they filled in the hole again, leaving a mound of red-brown dirt in the midst of the snow. As a final gesture of honor and respect, several of the men from the Valley climbed up on the low bluff overlooking the creek and rolled down large rocks. The wolves would come, as sure as the winter winds. This perhaps would thwart their depredations.

As the group broke up and slowly made their way back to their tents, Maggie stood alone—cold, forlorn, stricken with a great sense of loss. She watched as Eric put one arm around Elsie Nielson and started away. For a moment, Maggie was afraid he had completely forgotten her and was going to pass without speaking. But as he came up, he turned his head and motioned for her to come. With a rush of gratitude, she swiftly joined them. He held up his other arm and she ducked beneath it. Together, the three of them walked slowly back towards the camp.

As they approached Elsie's tent, she leaned forward enough to look at Maggie, then looked up at Eric and said something in Danish. He nodded slowly.

"What did she say?" Maggie asked.

"She said that while we are sad that Olaf is gone, Olaf is happy now. Except for one thing."

"What is that?"

Eric bit his lip and looked away. He started to speak, and couldn't. Swallowing hard, he fought back his emotions. Then, in a strained voice, he said, "He will be sad that he did not get to say good-bye to Hannah and Ingrid."

Chapter Notes

Concerning her family's sufferings and her mother's response, Sarah James recalled:

> Toward morning some of the captains who had gone out to gather up the stragglers came into camp bearing the dead body of my father and the badly frozen body of my brother Reuben. His injuries were so bad that he would suffer from them for the rest of his life. . . .
>
> I can see my mother's face as she sat looking at the partly conscious Reuben. Her eyes looked so dead that I was afraid. She didn't sit long, however, for my mother was never one to cry. When it was time to move out, mother had her family ready to go. She put her invalid son in the cart with her baby, and we joined the train. Our

> mother was a strong woman, and she would see us through anything. (In Carol Cornwall Madsen, *Journey to Zion,* p. 630)

Describing events that are related in this chapter, John Chislett wrote:

> We finally came to a stream of water [Strawberry Creek] which was frozen over. . . . We resolved that some one should go on foot to the camp to inform the captain of our situation. I was selected to perform the duty, and I set out with all speed. In crossing the creek I slipped through the ice and got my feet wet, my boots being nearly worn out. I had not gone far when I saw some one sitting by the roadside. I stopped to see who it was, and discovered the old man James and his little boy. The poor old man was quite worn out.
>
> I got him to his feet and had him lean on me, and he walked a little distance, not very far. I partly dragged, partly carried him a short distance farther, but he was quite helpless, and my strength failed me. Being obliged to leave him to go forward on my own errand, I put down a quilt I had wrapped around me, rolled him in it, and told the little boy to walk up and down by his father, and on no account to sit down, or he would be frozen to death. I told him to watch for teams that would come back, and to hail them when they came. This done I again set out for the camp, running nearly all the way and frequently falling down, for there were many obstructions and holes in the road. My boots were frozen stiff, so that I had not the free use of my feet, and it was only by rapid motion that I kept them from being badly frozen. As it was, both were nipped.
>
> . . . I reported to Captains Willie and Kimball the situation of the folks behind. They immediately got up some horses, and the boys from the Valley started back about midnight to help the ox teams in. The night was very severe and many of the emigrants were frozen. It was 5 a.m. before the last team reached the camp. (In *Remember,* pp. 11–12)

The next morning, the cost of Rocky Ridge became evident. Thirteen people had died during the night. Two more would die while helping to bury their comrades. The 24 October entry in the Willie Company journal reads: "Reddin [Reddick] N. Allred & others with 6 wagons came to camp this morning to assist the Handcart Company on our journey to the Valley. It was concluded to stay in camp today & bury the dead as there were 13 persons to inter. William James, from Pershore, Worcestershire, England, aged 46 died; Elizabeth Bailey, from Leigh, Worcestershire, England, aged 52 died; James

Kirkwood from Glasgow, Scotland, aged 11 died; Samuel Gadd, from Orwell, Cambridgeshire, England, aged 10 died; Lars Wendin, from Copenhagen, Denmark, aged 60 died; Anne Olsen, from Seeland, Denmark, aged 46 died; Ella Nilson, from Jutland, Denmark, aged 22 years, died; Jens Nilson [Nielson], from Lolland, Denmark, aged 6 years died; Bodil Mortinsen from Lolland, Denmark, aged 9 years died; Nils Anderson from Seeland, Denmark, aged 41 years died; Ole Madsen from Seeland, Denmark, aged 41 years died. Many of the Saints have their feet & hands frozen from the severity of the weather" (in *Remember*, p. 12).

John Chislett added this: "There were so many dead and dying that it was decided to lie by for the day. In the forenoon I was appointed to go round the camp and collect the dead. I took with me two young men to assist me in the sad task, and we collected together, of all ages and both sexes, thirteen corpses, all stiffly frozen. We had a large square hole dug in which we buried these thirteen people, 3 or 4 abreast and 3 deep. When they did not fit in, we put one or two crosswise at the head or feet of the others. We covered them with willows and then with the earth. When we buried these thirteen people some of their relatives refused to attend the services. They manifested an utter indifference about it. The numbness and cold in their physical natures seem to have reached the soul, and to have crushed out natural feeling and affection. Had I not myself witnessed it, I could not have believed that suffering would have produced such terrible results. But so it was. Two others died during the day, and we buried them in one grave, making fifteen in all buried on that camp ground" (in *Remember*, p. 13).

In his journal Reddick Allred wrote: "The 24th [of October], I took 6 teams and met them [the Willie Company] 15 miles below in such a hard west wind that they could not travel facing the drifting snow even if they had been ready for duty. I found some dead and dying laying over the camp in the drifting snow that was being piled in heaps by the gale and burying their dead. We set in with the rest to make them as comfortable as possible and remained in camp till next day" ("Journal of Reddick Newton Allred," p. 1).

There is another aspect of the story involving Reddick Allred which played an important part in the rescue of the Martin Handcart Company as well as the Willie Company. When Brother William H. Kimball started west with the Willie Company, he asked Brother Allred to remain behind at South Pass once again and wait for Captain Grant and the last of the emigrants. Though no word came, Brother Allred stayed in place for the next two weeks. In his journal he records the following:

John Van Cot and Brother Claudeaus V. Spencer arrived this morning [13 November] but their stay was short as another man was coming down with the smallpox. Brother Spencer tried to induce me to break up camp and return to the city. I declined his proposition and he said he would return. I advised him to stay for the lives of the company depended up[on] us. He then said that he moved that as I was president of the station they center their faith in me, that I should get the word of the Lord to know what we must do, to this I objected as he already said what he would do. They returned the next day. I sent a letter by them to the companies on the road [from Salt Lake City] for them to come on as fast as the condition of their teams would allow, but he failing to present the letter all the companies turned back with them until they got to Bridger where Lewis Robinson prevailed on them to stop until he could send a messenger to President Young, the result of which was to turn them all back again with instructions to go until they met Captain George Grant. Spencers team after reaching the big mountain was turned back and arrived at my camp the same evening that Captain Grant arrived with the last company. . . . President Young told William Kimball that he did not care if he turned some so quick that it would snap their neck. But I saved my neck by sticking to my post. . . .

Captain Grant got into my camp on the 17th of November just 30 days since he left me and saluted me with "hurrah for the bulldog good for hanging on." ("Journal of Reddick Newton Allred," p. 2)

CHAPTER 28

RED BUTTES AND DEVIL'S GATE

I

Saturday, 25 October 1856

On the same day that the James G. Willie Company prepared to roll out from Rock Creek, headed west for the Valley, 140 miles to the east the Edward Martin Handcart Company had ground to a halt. In some ways it was like a team of horses with a magnificent spirit who kept pulling the load even when it became unbearably heavy. But there comes the day when the exertion is too much. Their spirit is broken; their strength is totally spent. Lightening the load no longer fixes things.

As Hannah McKensie stood outside her tent on this bitter cold afternoon, that was the image that came to her mind. She knew this was what had happened to their company. In seven days they had come only ten miles from the last crossing to here at Red Buttes. The heart had gone out of them. The spirit of the company was broken, and they could barely drag themselves forward, no matter how strong their will to do otherwise.

The Martin Company, now traveling with the Hodgett independent wagon company, decided to take a slightly different route after leaving the last crossing. Instead of leaving the river and taking Emigrant Gap road, which cut overland toward the Sweetwater River, they took a southern alternate. Here the trail followed the North Platte for another twelve miles before angling off to the west to rejoin the main trail. This southern option kept them closer to water, and kept them out of the fiercest of the winds. But while the wind did not blow as severely down in the lowlands, it meant the snow was deeper and bare spots on the trail were rare.

Grim reality makes for desperate choices. The emigrants were rapidly approaching a state of collapse. Every day they lingered without meeting the wagons from Salt Lake diminished their dwindling supplies even further. But if they were too exhausted to walk, let alone pull their carts, how could they go forward?

Captain Martin called the subcaptains together. After a brief but intense discussion, the decision was made. The company was simply too weak to go on. The cattle had reached and passed their limit. They would stop here and rest and recruit their strength while they waited for the weather to change. That announcement was met with enormous relief by the emigrants. It also brought a pall over the camp, for the emigrants knew that the longer they stayed in place here, the deeper the crisis would become. As a company they could only add one dimension to this bleak equation. In addition to their evening and morning prayers, Captain Martin suggested that each family spend at least some time each day while they were resting in their tents petitioning the Lord to send help from the Valley as quickly as possible.

Hannah heard a noise and turned. Ingrid Christensen had stepped out of the tent. When she saw Hannah, she came over. "Are you ready?"

"Yes." Hannah bent down and picked up the one small kettle they had kept when they had lightened their loads at Deer Creek. "Let's go."

They moved slowly along one of the paths that linked the camp together, heading for the supply wagons where rations would be distributed again this afternoon. The snow was almost a foot deep and no one wanted to break their own way through it, so the trails were well worn. Wearing every piece of clothing they owned and clutching their only blankets tightly around them, they shuffled along, two dark, despairing figures moving slowly in a world of white.

They joined the line of people waiting in front of one of the supply wagons. John Jaques and another man whose name Hannah couldn't remember were there beside a flour sack with a pair of scales. One by one they asked each person for the total number in his or her tent, then carefully weighed out the daily allotment.

When it was their turn, Brother Jaques looked up and smiled. "Good afternoon."

"Good afternoon, Brother Jaques."

"How is Brother Jackson?"

Hannah shook her head slowly. "Not good. He's still very weak."

"Dysentery?"

"Yes. It's a little better now. We've stopped feeding him meat. That's helped a little."

He nodded grimly. "It's a vicious circle, isn't it? We need the meat from the cattle in our diet, and yet because the cattle are so lean the meat only adds to our misery. It's like eating a piece of boiled cottonwood bark." He sighed, then seemed to shrug it off. "Tell me again how many you have in your tent group?"

"Seven adults, eight children."

The man beside him did some quick calculating. "That would be two pounds twelve ounces," he said to Brother Jaques.

Hannah watched stoically as they measured out the flour and dumped it into her kettle. It did not even fill the bottom third. Not that she had expected it to. Step by step the daily allowance of flour had been cut back. When they found no more flour for sale at Fort Laramie, the daily allotment of sixteen ounces was reduced to twelve ounces per day for an adult. At Deer Creek that dropped to eight ounces. When they reached the Platte Bridge trading post and found nothing there either, Brother Martin had taken stock of what was left. Shortly after they forded the river the announcement had been sent through the camp. Until the supply wagons from Salt Lake were found, the ration for an adult would be four ounces of flour per day. Small children were given half that amount.

"Thank you," Hannah said when they finished.

"Tell Sister Jackson I'll try to come by in the morning and see her husband."

"I will." She and Ingrid turned and started away. Ingrid reached out and took the kettle from Hannah, careful not to let it tip and spill any of the precious little they had.

Hannah shook her head slowly. Four ounces of flour per day. No wonder the company couldn't go forward. If you were careful, you could hold four ounces of flour in one cupped hand. If you used both hands, four ounces wouldn't begin to fill them. So between them right now, Hannah and Ingrid were bringing back a whopping forty-four ounces of flour for their tent group of fifteen people. When they got back to their tent, they would stir in enough water to make a thin gruel, bring it to a near boil over the fire so it would thicken, then either put it on the griddle and fry it into thin cakes or maybe even eat it straight from the kettle.

Somewhere down deep inside her, Hannah wished she could feel anger or frustration or even despair. But the lassitude that engulfed her—and all the others, for that matter—was too complete, the malaise too total, to do anything but walk woodenly back to their group. She wanted to care about what was happening but it took too much effort.

When they reached their tent, Sister Elizabeth Jackson was already waiting for them by the small fire. Her husband sat nearby, a small mass of body hidden in the folds of a quilt, only a tiny circle of his face visible through the folds. The Roper family and the Jackson children were still in the tent. Unless the camp was on the move, most people stayed in their tents now, huddled in their bedding, conserving as much strength as they could.

Sister Jackson had a kettle of water hung over the flames, and when Hannah peered inside, she saw it was already near to boiling. She looked at Sister Jackson, who had a wooden spoon in her hand. She nodded and so Ingrid dumped the flour into the water. As they stepped back, Sister Jackson leaned forward and began to stir the pot with her spoon.

Without waiting to be asked, Hannah got out the plates and spoons and cups from a box in their handcart. As she came back to the fire, Sister Jackson looked up. "I think I'll put the gruel in a cup," she said. "That will be easier for him."

Hannah nodded and set everything down except for one tin cup. Using her apron to hold on to the handle and a rag to grip the bottom, Sister Jackson tipped the kettle and let the steaming batter fill the cup about halfway. Setting the kettle back on the fire, she took the cup, blew on the batter for a moment to cool it, then moved over beside her husband. Pulling the quilt away from his face, she touched his cheek. "Aaron. I have some supper for you."

His eyes were half-closed. They opened slowly and he stared at her for a moment as though he didn't recognize her.

"Here," she said gently. She put the cup to his lips and tipped it up.

Hannah moved a step to the side so she could watch. For a moment she was afraid Aaron Jackson wasn't going to open his mouth, but finally his lips parted, and some of the batter ran inside his mouth. It couldn't have been much, barely a teaspoon, Hannah thought.

His lips closed again, and she could see his cheeks move as he tasted the food in his mouth. But as he went to swallow, he winced sharply, drawing back in pain.

A drop of batter appeared at one corner of his mouth and Sister

Jackson reached up with her apron and wiped it away. "Can you swallow it, Aaron?"

He shook his head.

"Try, Aaron. You've got to swallow it."

His Adam's apple bobbed; then instantly he moaned and one hand came to his throat. His eyes closed in pain. "I can't," he croaked.

"You've got to eat something, Aaron," Sister Jackson said, trying not to let her concern show too much. "Here, try one more."

He turned his head away. "Can't. Hurts too much."

Elizabeth sighed and handed the cup back to Hannah, who poured it back into the kettle.

"Tired," Brother Jackson said after a moment. "Need to rest."

Ingrid and Hannah came forward as Sister Jackson stood up. Working together, they lifted him to his feet and helped him to the tent. As Sister Jackson got him settled in his bed, the girls took the Jackson children and the Ropers outside to have their meager supper.

When Sister Jackson came out a few minutes later, Hannah looked at her. She just shook her head. "He's asleep already," she said wearily. "We've got to get him to eat something. Maybe in the morning."

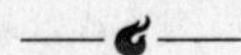

Hannah came awake with a start, looking around wildly. For a moment, she thought she had died. Everything was pitch-black; not even the tiniest glimmer of light shone anywhere.

"Help me."

Hannah rolled over onto her side. "Sister Jackson?"

"Hannah! Help me."

Sister Jackson was in the bedroll next to Hannah's, and so she reached out, groping in the darkness. "What is it? What's the matter?"

Something brushed her arm and she found Sister Jackson's hand. Instantly her hand was seized in a crushing grip. She felt the coldness of the hand on hers. "What is it?" she asked again, rising up on one elbow.

"It's Aaron," came the anguished whisper. "I can't hear him breathing."

And then, before she could answer, Hannah felt her hand being pulled forward. Letting her body follow, she thought for a moment that Sister Jackson was going to take her hands in hers to warm them. Suddenly her hand was placed on something very cold. Her first reaction was to think that Sister Jackson had found a block of ice and wanted her to feel it for some reason.

"No!" Sister Jackson's cry sounded in the darkness. "No! Aaron!"

In that instant Hannah realized with horror that what she was feeling was a face. Here was a nose. Beneath her palm she felt the jawline and the roughness of stubbled whiskers. She jerked her hand away without thinking. A chill more terrible than the cold inside the tent shot through her. And then she got control of herself. As she jerked her hand away, she realized that Elizabeth Jackson's hand was still on her husband's face.

Hannah scrambled to her knees, tossing the blanket back. She moved over beside Sister Jackson.

"Help me!" It was Sister Jackson again, her voice torn with anguish. "Somebody help me!"

Feeling with her hands, Hannah found Aaron Jackson. He was still in his quilt, but one arm was out. When Hannah touched his hand, she recoiled again. It was as cold as the snow outside. With a low sob, she turned and put her arms around the woman beside her. "Oh, Sister Jackson," she cried.

Off to one side, someone stirred. "Sister Jackson, is that you?"

It was Brother Roper, father of the family that shared their tent.

"Yes," Elizabeth Jackson cried, turning toward him. "Can you help me?"

"What's wrong?"

"It's Aaron. My husband."

"Is he . . ."

"He's dead," Hannah said when Elizabeth didn't answer.

"Are you sure?"

"Yes," Sister Jackson finally whispered. "His face is so cold."

There was a long moment of silence; then finally Brother Roper spoke again. "There's nothing we can do now, then. We'll have to wait until first light."

They heard the rustling of blankets and Hannah realized that their tent companion had lain down again. She was on her knees beside Elizabeth Jackson, still holding her. Sister Jackson was rocking back and forth now, and Hannah could feel the trembling in her body. Then she realized that Ingrid was on the other side of Sister Jackson, holding her as well.

"It's all right," Hannah cried, tears trickling down her cheeks. "He's finally at peace now."

"I know." The rocking didn't stop. "I know."

II

Sunday, 26 October 1856

David Granger was tired. He was tired of sitting, tired of the constant hammering of his backside against the wagon seat, tired of staring at the back of the rescue wagon filled with flour sacks in front of him, and tired of the endless miles of snow. He was even tiring of the stunning vista to his left, a long range of mountains made up almost entirely of masses of solid granite that in some places rose from the flat plain as abruptly as a wall. They had been following along this range for two days now.

He sighed and shifted his weight again on the wagon seat, trying to find a more comfortable position. He knew what he was doing. After this long on the road, he always began to get that restless urge to break the monotony. It had been twenty days now since they left Salt

Lake City, and it was their fourth day since the rescue party led by Captain George D. Grant had met the Willie Handcart Company at Sixth Crossing. The rapidity with which they had covered the road from Salt Lake to South Pass was a thing of the past. Here along the river and in the shelter of the great granite upthrust the snow was deeper. One day they had been forced to stop completely as the storm raged around them. Where they had been making twenty-five and occasionally thirty miles a day before, now they weren't even averaging fifteen. And still no sign of the Martin Handcart Company.

Maybe he should have volunteered to go with Heber P. and escort the Willie Company, he thought. At least they had something to do besides sit on a wagon seat and stare forward like a frog frozen in the lamplight. He sighed again and hunched down, stamping his feet up and down to restore the circulation.

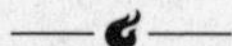

It was about a quarter of a mile later when David lifted his head. The wagons in the lead were pulling to a halt alongside one another. He straightened, his boredom vanishing in an instant. The third wagon in line wheeled out and came up beside the other two. Something was up. David was fifth in line and followed the fourth as he pulled up on the far side of Captain Grant's wagon. In a moment, all eight wagons were parked parallel to each other. David didn't have to ask why they had stopped. The men were already pointing. To the left of the trail and across the river at a distance of about a mile or a mile and a half, the wall of granite mountains curved sharply away to the north. The eastern end tapered off and ended at a point almost straight ahead of them. Here the prairie rose in a gentle incline to make a narrow pass before the next outcropping thrust up and continued on to the east. It was just to the left of that gentle pass that they saw a gigantic cleft in the mountain wall. There it was at last. Devil's Gate. Three hundred and fifty miles later they had reached this important landmark on the trail.

Devil's Gate itself was a narrow gorge through which only the Sweetwater River or a man on foot could pass. When he and his family had come through here in 1848, David had been surprised to learn that the trail did not go through the "gate" but through the gentle pass just to the east of it. He remembered how that night around the fire some of the brethren told the pioneers of the Indian legends about how Devil's Gate had gotten its name. According to the natives, there had once been a great and terrible spirit who haunted the valley of the Sweetwater. In the form of a great tusked beast, it drove off the buffalo and gorged itself on the deer, antelope, and elk. Finally a great holy man called upon all the tribes of the red men to unite together to drive away the evil beast. They surrounded him and filled his body with arrows. Enraged by the attack, the great beast stamped and pawed the ground. Then with one great upward thrust of its tusks, it ripped a huge gash in the mountain wall and fled through it, never to be seen again.

That was the stuff that fired a boy's imagination, and Devil's Gate was a place clearly fixed in David's memory. Now, about three miles off, it lay before him once again, silent, magnificent, awesome.

"Look, there's a column of smoke." One of the men was pointing.

"And there," said another, "behind the building. Isn't that the top of a wagon?"

Captain Grant nodded, looking quite satisfied now. "That's got to be our express party, holed up at the old fort, just like I told them to do." He picked up his reins. "All right, brethren. Let's hope they've got those handcart people with them."

Captain Grant proved to be only half right. Joseph Young, Abel Garr, Stephen Taylor, and Cyrus Wheelock, the four express riders Grant had sent forward from Black's Fork, saw them coming and came out and met them while they were still half a mile out from the fort. All four men were well and reported that their teams were well rested. To the next question there was a slow shake of the head. No, they had found no sign of the Martin Handcart Company or either of the two independent wagon companies reported to be traveling with them.

To a man who had hoped to find his people somewhere around the Green River, almost two hundred miles to the west of where they were now, that was bitter news. As everyone watched their leader, Captain Grant gravely pulled on his lip. Then finally he looked around at his men. "Brethren, we have to find them. They are surely in the most desperate of straits by now." He turned to Brigham Young's son. "Joseph?"

"Yes, sir?"

"Would you be willing to lead another express party and ride as far east as the Platte Bridge?"

"Yes, sir, I would. We're rested and ready to go."

"How far is that?" someone asked.

"Another forty or fifty miles if you have to go all the way," Robert Burton answered, still speaking to Brother Young.

"I want you to leave first thing in the morning," Captain Grant said. He looked around. His eyes settled on Abel Garr, who had ridden with Young as part of the first express party. "Abe, would you be willing to ride with Joseph again?"

"Of course."

He turned once more, and this time his choice surprised a few people. He called upon the camp's cook. "Brother Jones?"

"Yes, Captain? Would you like me to go too?" Daniel W. Jones said.

"I would."

"I would consider it an honor, sir."

"Good. Take the best mounts we have. I want you to take one pack animal loaded with food. It won't be much, but . . ." He shrugged. "I want you on your way at first light."

Then Captain Grant said one last thing that sent a cold shiver through David's back. "If you don't find them by that time, we'll have to assume that either they have decided to go into winter camp somewhere or . . . or else they have perished."

III

Monday, 27 October 1856

While the stronger men gathered the dead from around the camp, including Aaron Jackson, Captain Martin and Captain Hodgett called a meeting with their subcaptains. They hadn't changed their minds about the need to stop for a few days to rest, but they felt there was a better place to do it. About twelve miles upstream from where they had crossed the North Platte—just two or three miles from where they were now—the river made a slow, lazy bend to the south. Here the trail set off across open country to rejoin the main trail near Mineral Springs. But at the bend there was better grass for the animals, more shelter from the wind, and more fuel for the fires. It would provide a better place for an extended stop. And so the signal was given. Strike the tents and pack. Burial service would be at nine o'clock. They would move out immediately thereafter.

They buried the dead as best they could. A hymn was sung and a short dedicatory prayer said over the "grave"—really nothing more than a hole scraped in the snow and then covered with stones and branches and what few rocks could be pried from the grip of the frozen ground. As they marched out half an hour later, no one looked back. Those people had found their rest. Now the living had to find a place to stay for the night.

Captain Martin was right. The camp by the river bend proved to be a better place for an extended stay, and it had not been more than two miles to get there. Even then there were so many delays in getting started and the company moved so slowly, it was almost dark when word came back that this was the place he had in mind. Moving like wooden puppets whose joints were too tight, they set about to cook their meager supper and then to set up camp.

—❦—

Captain W. B. Hodgett, whose wagon company was now traveling together with the Martin Handcart Company, had about 185 people and thirty-three wagons under his command. In the number of people it was less than half of what the handcart group had, but when it came to horses, mules, and oxen, he had far more than Captain Martin did. So, not wanting his greater number of animals to take all the feed, when they reached the bend in the river, Captain Hodgett took his group a little farther on while Captain Martin stopped his company closer to the river.

As the Ropers and the Jacksons, along with Hannah and Ingrid, tried to put up their tent, it quickly became obvious that this was beyond them. Putting up the big round tents usually took four or five men, and that was when they were dry and if there was no wind. With the loss of Aaron Jackson, Hannah's tent group was down to one adult male, Brother Carl Roper, and his fourteen-year-old boy. The rest in the tent were women and children. So there was no choice. Hannah and Ingrid and Sister Roper and Sister Jackson were on tent detail now. By the time supper was done and they turned to the task of erecting the tent, the canvas, wet from almost a full week of snow, was frozen stiff. It was like trying to work with an old dried cowhide. It took all five of them pushing and pulling just to unroll it out into some semblance of flatness. Any thoughts of trying to get it erected were quickly abandoned.

"We'll just have to sleep under the canvas," Ingrid said, stepping back and eyeing the flattened tent as if it were a living enemy.

"I hate that," Hannah said. "I always feel like I'm going to suffocate."

"I won't," Elizabeth Jackson said in a low voice.

Hannah turned in surprise.

"I won't sleep in that. Not like that. Not after Aaron—" She looked away, shuddering.

Brother Roper was staring at her. "What are you going to do, Elizabeth?"

"I shall sit by the fire with my children if need be."

"These fires can't keep you warm," Ingrid said. And she was right. These weren't blazing bonfires. They were sputtering, smokey cooking fires. The willows were either too wet or too green to burn brightly. All of their faces were smudged with soot and streaked from tears caused by the heavy smoke as it stung their eyes.

Sister Jackson's face was set. "I won't sleep under that canvas," she said. "I won't."

IV

Tuesday, 28 October 1856

Twice in the night Hannah woke up and clawed the heavy fabric away from her face. Both times she pulled the flap back enough to peek out. Both times she saw the dark figure of Elizabeth Jackson sitting there in the darkness, just as she had been when Hannah and Ingrid had finally left her and crawled in beneath the canvas.

Sister Jackson found a large rock near the fire, took Little Aaron, who was just two, on her lap, then tucked five-year-old Mary Elizabeth under one arm and Martha Ann, who was seven, under the other. When they were settled, Hannah had taken their one tattered quilt and wrapped it around the four of them. Elizabeth clutched it tightly in one hand and bid her good night.

The second time Hannah had looked out, the fire was down to glowing coals. The dark figure on the rock was so still that for a moment Hannah feared the worst might have happened. But when she started to get up to see, she saw Sister Jackson's head turn. "We're all right," came her voice in the darkness.

"Are you cold?" Hannah whispered back.

"Very!"

"Do you want to come in with us?"

There was not a moment's hesitation. "No!"

Relieved that she was still aware enough to show such resolution, Hannah slipped back beneath the canvas and eventually went back to sleep.

It was just dawning when Hannah awoke for the third time. She lay there for a moment, hating the tent fabric pressing down so heavily upon her; then suddenly she remembered Sister Jackson. Careful not to bump Ingrid or the others, she crawled out from beneath her quilt and through the tent flap. Since they were sleeping now fully clothed, including their boots, there was nothing to do but stand up and stretch.

To her surprise, Sister Jackson was already up. She was kneeling beside the fire, breaking dry willows into smaller pieces and laying them carefully on the hot coals. Thick white smoke billowed upward as she bent down and blew softly, nursing the flames back into life. On the rock her three children huddled together, the quilt pulled tightly around them.

Feeling an immense wave of relief, Hannah started towards her.

Sister Jackson turned. Then with a low cry she ran towards Hannah, throwing herself into Hannah's arms. Completely caught off guard, Hannah held her tightly as Sister Jackson clung to her, rocking back and forth. Finally, she pulled back, and to Hannah's surprise, she saw that tears were streaming down her cheeks, leaving tracks through the soot and dirt.

"What's the matter?" Hannah exclaimed. She jerked around to look at the children, wondering if one of them might be—

Elizabeth Jackson reached up and took Hannah's face and turned it back toward her. "They're all right, Hannah."

"What, then? What's wrong?"

She stepped back, taking both of Hannah's hands in hers and holding them tightly. "You'll never believe what happened just a little while ago."

"What?"

"As you might guess, I didn't sleep much last night."

"You should have come in with us."

"No. Besides the bitter cold, I was so despondent that I couldn't fall asleep. I kept thinking, 'What am I going to do now that Aaron is dead? How will I get on now that I am alone?' I couldn't get those thoughts out of my head."

"We're here to help you," Hannah said, her own eyes starting to mist now. "Ingrid and I were talking about it last night. Now we know why we were supposed to be with you."

Sister Jackson barely seemed to hear her. "Hannah. Aaron came to me."

Hannah gaped at her, not sure she had heard correctly.

Elizabeth shook her hands, squeezing them even more tightly. "Yes, Hannah. It was a dream, I know. But it was so real. Suddenly, Aaron was there, standing beside me." The tears spilled over again. "Oh, he looked so happy. So much at peace."

Hannah felt chills going up and down her body, not from fear but from a sudden thrill of joy. "Oh, Sister Jackson, how wonderful!"

"Yes." She let go of Hannah's hands and gripped her shoulders, pulling her up so their faces were close together. "It meant so much to me to see him like that, to know that he is all right. And then—" She stopped and shook her head a little, trying to get control again. "But here is the most wonderful part, Hannah. After he asked me how I was, he looked me straight in the eye and said, 'Elizabeth, cheer up. Deliverance is at hand.'"

Hannah pulled back, her eyes wide. "Deliverance is at hand?"

"Yes, Hannah! Yes! That's what he said." And with that she threw her arms around Hannah once again. Two minutes later when Ingrid crawled out of the collapsed tent, the two of them were still there holding each other tightly, standing together in front of the smoking fire.

Chapter Notes

On or about 25 October 1856, Aaron Jackson succumbed to the effects of hunger, illness, exhaustion, and the devastating cold of the river crossing. In her written account of those terrible days Elizabeth Horrocks Jackson describes the loss of her husband: "About the 25th of Oct., I think it was—I cannot remember the exact date—we reached camp about sundown. My husband had for several days previous been much worse. He was still sinking, and his condition now became more serious. As soon as possible after reaching camp I prepared a little of such scant articles of food as we then had. He tried to eat but failed. He had not the strength to swallow. I put him to bed as quickly as I could. He seemed to rest easy and fell asleep. About nine o'clock I retired. Bedding had become very scarce, so I did not disrobe. I slept until, as it appeared to me, about midnight. I was extremely cold. The weather was bitter. I listened to hear if my husband breathed—he lay so still. I could not hear him. I became alarmed. I put my hand on his body, when to my horror I discovered that my worst fears were confirmed. My husband was *dead.* He was cold and stiff—rigid in the arms of death. It was a bitter freezing night and the elements had sealed up his mortal frame. I called for help to the other inmates of the tent. They could render me no aid; and there was no alternative but to remain alone by the side of the corpse till morning. The night was enveloped in almost Egyptian darkness. There was nothing with which to produce a light or kindle a fire. Of course I could not sleep. I could only watch, wait, and pray for the dawn. But oh, how those dreary hours drew their tedious length along. When daylight came, some of the male part of the company prepared the body for burial. And oh, such a burial and funeral service. They did not remove his clothing—he had but little. They wrapped him in a blanket and placed him in a pile with thirteen others who had died, and then covered him up in the snow. The ground was frozen so hard that they could not dig a grave. He was left there to sleep in peace until the trump of the Lord shall sound, and the dead in Christ shall awake and come forth in the morning of the first resurrection. We shall then again unite our hearts and lives, and eternity will furnish us with life forever more" (Kingsford, *Leaves from the Life of Elizabeth Horrocks Jackson Kingsford,* pp. 6–7; also in *Remember,* p. 23).

When Captain Grant sent the four men in the express party forward from Black's Fork (which is a few miles northeast of Fort Bridger) on 14 October, he gave them specific instructions that they should go no farther than Devil's Gate. If they had not found the Martin Company by then, they were to wait for further word from Grant himself. When Grant's group reached Devil's Gate on 26 October, the four men reported that they had found nothing of the rear companies. Greatly concerned now because full winter was fast approaching, Captain Grant made one last effort to find them. Three men—Joseph Young, Abel Garr, and Daniel W. Jones—left early on the morning of the twenty-seventh, prepared to ride as swiftly as possible as far as the Platte Bridge (Reshaw's Bridge), which is at present-day Evansville, Wyoming, about six miles east of Casper (see *Remember,* p. 52). Again from the history of Elizabeth Jackson we read:

> A few days after the death of my husband, the male members of the company had become reduced in number by death; and those who remained were so weak and emaciated by sickness, that on reaching the camping place at night, there were not sufficient men with strength enough to raise the poles and pitch the tents. The result was that we camped out with nothing but the vault of Heaven for a roof, and the stars for companions. The snow lay several inches deep upon the ground. The night was bitterly cold. I sat down on a rock with one child in my lap and one on each side of me. In that condition I remained until morning. . . .
>
> It will be readily perceived that under such adverse circumstances I had become despondent. I was six or seven thousand miles from my native land, in a wild, rocky, mountain country, in a destitute condition, the ground covered with snow, the waters covered with ice, and I with three fatherless children with scarcely nothing to protect them from the merciless storms. When I retired to bed that night, being the 27th

of Oct., I had a stunning revelation. In my dream, my husband stood by me and said—"Cheer up, Elizabeth, deliverance is at hand." (Kingsford, *Leaves from the Life of Elizabeth Horrocks Jackson Kingsford,* p. 8; also in *Remember,* p. 23)

CHAPTER 29

RED BUTTES TO GREASEWOOD CREEK

I

Tuesday, 28 October 1856

The Hodgett Wagon Company was separated from the Martin Handcart Company by about a hundred yards of open space, the handcart group being closer to the river, the wagon company a little farther west of them. It was late in the afternoon of the same day that Sister Jackson had her stunning dream. Half an hour before, word had come that some of the brethren had broken a hole in the ice near the riverbank, so Hannah and Ingrid decided to take their bucket down and fill it before the hole froze over again. Thus it was that they were about midway between the two companies when suddenly they heard a woman shouting loudly. Both girls turned around. The sound was coming from where the Hodgett people were camped. Hannah set down the bucket and shaded her eyes. The sky was cloudy and there was no sun, but the light from the west made it difficult to see anything in detail.

"I see them coming! I see them coming!"

Hannah peered more closely, then saw that just to the left of one of the wagons, a woman and two young boys about eight or ten years of age were standing together. The woman was jumping up and down and pointing to the west. She was yelling at the top of her lungs. "Surely they are angels from heaven!"

Ingrid came up beside Hannah now, her hand up to her eyes as well. "What is it?" she cried. "Do you see anything?"

Hannah went up on tiptoe, but beyond the camp there were only the snow-covered hills that rose gently from the river bottoms. "No. I don't see anything." She wondered if one of their company had finally gone mad, but didn't say that to Ingrid.

Now people in both camps were stopping and turning. A man jumped out of a nearby wagon and ran to the woman's side. "What?" he shouted. "What is it?"

"I can see them plainer! Plainer! Plainer!" She was almost hysterical, pointing and waving and hopping up and down.

"Come on," Hannah said. She grabbed Ingrid's hand and started running for the Hodgett camp. As they approached the woman, others were coming toward her too. She ripped off her shawl and began to wave it back and forth. Suddenly the older of the two boys bawled out and started jumping up and down. "Yes, I see them! I see them!"

The man leaned forward now. Then he spun around and grabbed the woman. "Yes!" He picked her up and swung her around and around. "Yes! Hurrah! Hurrah!"

"Where!" Hannah shouted, and then suddenly Ingrid grabbed her arm and pulled her to a halt. "Look, Hannah! On the ridge. Just to the right of the wagons."

Hannah peered more closely, then gasped. She almost dropped the bucket. Just below the crest of the ridge, about two hundred yards away, there were four large dark shapes–horses or mules–moving slowly down the hill toward them. Three of the horses had men on their backs.

"We are saved!" The woman's voice was hoarse now. "It is surely men from the Valley with food for us."

Hannah was utterly astonished. Then she saw that the three men on the horses were waving back. She turned around and stared at Ingrid. Ingrid had one hand up, waving it back and forth. Her eyes were filled with wonder. "It is, Hannah," she said.

Now people from the handcart camp were running towards the Hodgett camp. People were pouring out of their tents. Women were weeping. All over shouts of hurrah rent the air.

"Hannah, what is it?"

Hannah turned around to see Elizabeth Jackson coming toward them, half stumbling in the snow. Her bonnet had fallen back from her head and her hair bounced softly as she ran. Hannah started toward her, the realization coming with such intensity that a great cry of joy was torn from her lips. She fell on Sister Jackson's shoulder. "Your husband was right, Elizabeth," she cried. "What Brother Jackson said was true. Deliverance has come."

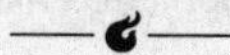

It took almost ten minutes before Captain Martin could press through the celebrating crowd enough to reach the three men. He took one look at the nearest one, and tears sprang to his eyes. "Brother Young?"

Joseph A. Young turned from an older brother who was wringing his hands. When he saw Edward Martin, he came forward and gripped his hand. "Brother Martin. Thanks be to God. We've found you at last."

"And God bless Brigham Young for sending you, young man," a woman cried.

"God bless the Saints in the Valley for not forgetting us," another shouted.

"Hurrah! Hurrah! Hurrah!"

The two men waited, smiling happily as the crowd gave vent to the joy that was in them. Then as it quieted again, Brother Young turned. "You know Abel Garr, I think."

"I do." Brother Martin stuck out his hand. Abel Garr ignored it and threw his arms around him. "We are so happy to see you, Brother Martin," he said as they clasped each other tightly.

Brother Young turned to the third man who had come with them. He had just picked up a young boy, and three other children were clinging to his coat. "And this is Brother Dan Jones."

Captain Martin nodded. "A pleasure, Brother Jones."

"The pleasure is ours, believe me," Brother Jones answered heartily.

Now Captain Martin turned back to Brother Young. "Do you have wagons with you?"

"No, we're an express party sent to find you. But Captain Grant is waiting at Devil's Gate." He turned to look at the people, who were hanging on his every word. "That's a little more than fifty miles from here. He has eight wagons and they are fully loaded with supplies."

"Praise heaven!" "Our prayers are answered." "Thank you. Thank you, brethren." The crowd could not repress their joy at that news.

Joseph Young was just twenty-two years old. He had the clear look of his father about him, and now it was evident he was feeling the same weight of responsibility. "How many dead and how many living?" he asked softly.

That brought a complete hush over the company. When Brother Martin turned back, his eyes were suddenly haunted. "Fifty or more are dead. With those who turned back or decided to stay at Florence, that still leaves us about five hundred in the company. Captain Hodgett has about a hundred and eighty people in his company."

Joseph Young rocked back as though he had been struck. "Fifty dead?"

"Yes. And we're losing five or six a night now."

Abel Garr looked around. "Where's Captain Hunt? We were told he was with you."

Captain Hodgett stepped forward. "They hadn't made the last crossing when we last saw them," he said. "Captain Hunt said he was going to wait for the weather to warm." Without waiting for the question, he gave the answer to what they needed to know. "Captain Hunt has fifty wagons and about two dozen more people than I do."

The three rescuers looked at each other. Though both of the other men were older than Joseph Young, it was clear to everyone that he was in charge, and also that they were happy to have that be the case. Then Brother Young turned back to Brother Martin. "We assume you are on reduced rations?"

"Yes. Four ounces of flour per day for an adult. We figured that is what it would take to make our flour last to South Pass."

Again there was shock, but then Brother Young recovered. The young man's face wrinkled in concentration, and then he nodded. "All right. We have to leave you and go on to the Platte and find Brother Hunt's company. As you see, we have a pack mule loaded with food. It isn't much for so many, but now that you know you don't have to go all the way to South Pass to meet the wagons, I recommend you put everyone back on full rations immediately and—"

He was cut off as again a great shout went up.

He acknowledged it soberly. "Your cheers must be saved for when you reach the Valley, and then you can cheer the Saints who have sent these wagons to you." He turned back to Captains Martin and Hodgett. "You have got to move forward in the morning, even if it is only a few miles at a time. Once we find Brother Hunt's company and get them started, we shall go back to Devil's Gate to alert Captain Grant. But you must go on as rapidly as possible so that he doesn't have to come this far to find you."

"Yes," Brother Martin said. "We understand. We shall leave first thing in the morning."

Joseph Young turned and looked at the surrounding faces. They were gaunt, hollow, smudged. But in the eyes there was something that had not been there just half an hour before. There was hope and rejoicing. "Brothers and sisters," he said in a choked voice. "We have found you at last. God has heard and answered your prayers. *And ours!*

Now, let us set to work and do all we can to bring about your temporal salvation."

II

Thursday, 30 October 1856

Captain Grant was staring moodily into the fire and for once was not participating in the conversation except for an occasional grunt or a brief answer when someone addressed him directly.

David Granger was not surprised by their leader's gloominess. This was the fourth day since Joseph Young, Abel Garr, and Dan Jones had mounted up and ridden east, once again becoming an express party sent out to find the lost handcart pioneers. This was the fourth day that there had been no word of them. This gathering around the fire had become their standard pattern each night. Through the day they would see to their work—checking the gear, making sure the stock had plenty of feed, gathering wood. Then once supper was over and cleaned up, they collected around the fire and talked for a time before evening prayers. David enjoyed these times a great deal. The older men would reminisce about the early days of the Church, or other times when they had crossed the trail, or troubles in the Indian wars in Utah. These conversations made him feel younger than his twenty-one years, but it also brought him a deep sense of gratification to know that he was accepted as a man in these circles. Otherwise he wouldn't be here.

It was dark now and the stars overhead were a brilliant spray of light. Off a short distance to his left, David could just barely make out the deeper black of the granite monoliths that rose like towering walls above the old abandoned fort. Directly in front of him, if he peered more carefully, he could just discern the deep cleft in the rocks that was Devil's Gate.

"This weather is a mixed blessing," Captain Grant suddenly said.

The others stopped and looked at him.

"Having it warmer will bless those poor people, but the roads are going to be a nightmare."

Several murmured their assent at that. Mud was the worst of all for traveling with wagons and teams. Being on foot would only make it all the more miserable.

"Two days won't be enough to thaw it down too deep," Robert Burton suggested, "so maybe it won't be too bad yet."

"True," Grant agreed, "but remember that stretch up and over Prospect Hill and along the top of the plateau? That's the worst mud anywhere on the whole trail. It's like walking through bookbinders' glue. It can gum up a wagon wheel to the point where it won't even turn anymore."

Charles Decker, guide for the company, was laughing softly. "I can remember one time when—"

Captain Grant's head suddenly jerked up. "Hold it!" he said, lifting one hand. He was looking off to his left. It was there that the trail left the old fort and continued northeastward toward Independence Rock. "Riders coming!" He leaped to his feet. The twenty or so men gathered around the fire did the same. Several grabbed for their rifles. They hadn't seen Indians this time out, but they were in Indian country.

In the sudden silence, they all heard it now. Once the sun went down, the temperature dropped below freezing again and they could hear the clatter of horses' hooves on frozen ground.

"It's the express party!" someone said in a low voice.

The sound of the approaching riders grew louder, and then they appeared out of the darkness riding through the gate of the rail fence that had once enclosed the old compound. The men rushed forward. Joseph Young, Abel Garr, and Dan Jones got stiffly down from their mounts. David noticed then that they no longer had the pack animal with them.

"Did you find the handcart company?" Brother Grant blurted even as Brother Young's feet hit the ground.

"We did," Brother Young said wearily. "And both wagon companies as well."

A great shout went up from the men. At last. After more than three weeks of fruitless search, at last they had found the remaining companies.

Brigham Young's son arched his back and yawned mightily, then nodded in satisfaction. "We found Captain Martin's company camped at Red Buttes," he went on. "Captain Hodgett and his group were nearby. We had to ride on another twelve or fifteen miles to find Captain Hunt. They were settled in at the last crossing of the Platte waiting for the weather to break."

"And how are the people doing?" Major Burton asked.

The three men just shook their heads. "The Martin group is in terrible shape," Abel Garr answered for them all. "They're having deaths in the camp every day. They've got a lot of older people."

"They were down to four ounces of flour per day," Dan Jones added.

David Granger started. Four ounces! He wasn't sure exactly how much that was, but he knew it didn't take much of a mixing bowl to hold a full pound.

"Where are they now?" Grant asked.

"Coming on slowly," Brother Young said. He sighed deeply and it was filled with pain. "We camped with them last night at Rock Avenue. This morning we helped them up Prospect Hill." He closed his eyes for a moment. "Ah," he sighed. "What a pitiful sight that was. The wagon companies were both in the rear by then, and we went early this morning to see how they were doing. When we came up on the handcarts again, they were strung out probably three or four miles, all the way from those alkali swamps up past Willow Springs to the top of Prospect Hill.

"It was a scene to wrench the heart. Old men tugging and pulling on their carts, their wives and children riding because they were too sick to walk. You would see women in the shafts, pulling alongside husbands so sick they could barely lift their heads. The children were walking alongside, slipping and sliding in the mud and snow, heads down and mouths pinched with hunger. Their feet were all clotted up with mud and it started to freeze on them as soon as the sun went down. The supply wagons look like funeral carts, stacked so thick with those who are sick that you'd think some would be crushed."

He had to stop. His eyes looked as if he might be sick.

"It was a terrible thing to behold," Abel Garr murmured.

"We used our lariats to help them pull their handcarts up the hill as much as possible," Brother Jones came in. "By the time they reached the top, they were in pretty sad condition."

Brother Young looked up again. "But they haven't lost hope. Our arrival has infused them with determination to come on. When we returned from checking on Brother Hunt's wagon company, all we heard from Captain Martin's group was, 'Let us go to the Valley. Let us go to Zion.'"

"So where are they now?" Brother Charles Decker asked.

"We left them at Prospect Hill about noon today and told them to camp there. We also told them to keep coming on tomorrow morning. We promised that we would bring the wagons out to meet them."

Brother Grant straightened and looked around. "Brethren, get these men some supper. The rest of you see to your gear. I want to be on the road by the time dawn lights the sky."

III

Friday, 31 October 1856

Hannah McKensie had long since stopped looking ahead to see where they were going. First of all there was nothing to see. Since descending from Prospect Hill they had entered a great emptiness unbroken by any landmarks. Second, the glare of the snow, especially now with the afternoon sun directly in front of them, was blinding and it hurt her eyes to look into it. As she and Ingrid moved forward, step after plodding step, they kept their eyes fixed on the ground a few feet in front of them. Now that the trail was on level ground again, Sister Jackson was no longer helping them push. Little Aaron was not feeling well and Sister Jackson was carrying her son on her back. Martha Ann, who was seven, was pushing at the back of the cart, though they could hardly discern any difference, and Mary Elizabeth was riding in the cart for the moment.

It wasn't easy pulling in the mud, but here the mud was not the thick, clutching stuff they had yesterday and earlier today. It was slippery here, but not like some living thing trying to pull them to a stop. And after pulling the cart up the long, seemingly endless incline of Prospect Hill yesterday, this flatland seemed almost like child's play.

A movement caught her eye and she raised her head. Captain Martin was walking toward them, speaking briefly to each family as he passed. He would turn and point as he did so. Squinting against the sun, she saw a dark line directly up ahead of them. Some kind of vegetation, a miracle in this landscape. "It must be a creek or something," she murmured to Ingrid, who was also peering ahead.

Seeing Brother Martin coming, Sister Jackson, who was on the opposite side of the column from him, moved around the back of the cart and came up to walk beside Hannah, moving carefully so as not to wake young Aaron on her back. Hannah looked at the boy. His head was resting on her shoulder, bouncing softly as she walked.

"Is he asleep?" Elizabeth asked.

"Yes."

"Good."

Then Elder Martin came to them. "You see that vegetation up ahead of us? That's Greasewood Creek. We'll stop there for the night."

"Good." Hannah was ready to drop the cart and lie down in the snow, anything to rest her legs and throbbing feet.

Then a smile stole across Elder Martin's face. In his weariness it was almost more like a wince, but there was happiness in his eyes. "There's something else," he said.

"What?" Ingrid asked.

"Look to the left, at about the ten o'clock position."

They turned their heads. All Hannah saw was an unbroken expanse of snow. She shook her head.

"Look more closely. Right at the snow line."

Sister Jackson gave a low cry. "Oh!" One hand came up to her mouth.

"Yes," their captain said in a tired voice. "It's the rescue wagons. At last."

East of Devil's Gate, out past Independence Rock, the land was as flat as a tabletop and just about as empty. The emptiness stretched on for ten to fifteen miles. Then the land began to rise in gentle swells until it topped out on a plateau, of which Prospect Hill was a part. There were a few small and widely scattered upthrusts of rock—the last echoes of the range of granite hills—but other than that, nothing broke this great stretch of nothingness. As David Granger kept his wagon in the tracks of those in front of him, he noticed that even the sagebrush here was stunted, growing in clumps only six to eight inches high and now mostly covered by the snow.

As the rescue party moved eastward and the sun rose higher, the roads began to thaw. At first they were just slushy, but soon the iron tires were digging down into the mud and the horses and mules began to have a harder time of it. This was not yet the stretch of mud that Captain Grant had warned them about, but it was challenge enough.

When they had set out at first light, Captain Grant had left two wagons and four men back at Devil's Gate to prepare for the arrival of the emigrants. To David Granger's pleased surprise, he and Stephen Taylor, another of his companions in the Minute Men group, had been assigned to drive the fourth wagon back in the line. Brother Taylor had ridden with the first express party from Black's Fork and had grown quite impatient waiting at Devil's Gate for Captain Grant's group to finally catch up with them. When Captain Grant suggested that Brother Taylor be one of those that stayed back, he vigorously protested, claiming he had already spent more than his fair share of time at the old fort. Major Burton took pity on him and changed the assignment, putting him with David. Which was fine with David. They had ridden numerous times together and were good friends.

At the moment, Brother Taylor was in the back of the wagon, trying to sleep on the sacks of flour as best he could with all the bumping and jarring the wagon made as it traveled over the rough roads. He had David's full sympathy because David had tried the same thing earlier that afternoon while Stephen drove, and he had barely slept at all.

David lifted his head to gaze out across the great snowfields. Instinctively he pulled down his hat. It was a perfectly clear day, and the sunlight sparkled off the snow in a dazzling glare that even now, as the afternoon wore on, nearly blinded them.

It was about half past four, or maybe even five o'clock, when the company scout, Charles Decker, came riding at a canter back toward the line of wagons. He had been out in front half a mile or more, following the tracks the three express riders had made the night before on their return to Devil's Gate. The sun was dipping low now, and with its less direct rays, the air temperature was dropping again. The roads were still muddy and slushy, but as the temperature dropped, they were starting to firm up again.

The scout stopped for a few minutes and spoke with Captain Grant and Major Burton, then came on again, speaking briefly as he reached each wagon. As Decker came alongside David, he half turned in his saddle, pointing eastward. "See that low slash of black there just off to the left of the wagons, maybe two miles up ahead of us?"

David stood, leaning out to see around the wagon in front of him. "Yes." It wasn't much. More like a black line on top of the snow.

Suddenly Stephen Taylor's head appeared in the slit in the wagon cover. "Where?"

As Brother Taylor climbed out and sat down beside David, Brother Decker pointed again. "That's Greasewood Creek. Captain Grant says we'll stop there and water the teams."

"All right."

As their guide started on again, suddenly there was a shout from up front. Decker wheeled his horse around.

"There they are!" someone yelled.

"Where?" called another.

Decker spurred his horse forward, but David, still standing, had seen what the other man had seen. He didn't need anyone to go and check it out for him. On the right side of the trail, yet some distance off from Greasewood Creek, he had seen movement. At first he thought it was his eyes playing tricks on him. He blinked and looked again. It was not an illusion. There were tiny black specks moving against the endless white background. Handcarts, with people pulling and pushing them. And then behind them he saw teams and wagons, their canvas tops barely discernible against the snow.

He turned to Stephen Taylor with an immense feeling of relief. "They're right," he said. "It's them."

For the second time in ten days, David Granger had the privilege of knowing the joy of being a rescuer. To his surprise, this time it was considerably more subdued than it had been before. At the Sixth Crossing, when the wagons drove in to where the Willie Company was camped, the celebration had been an explosion of joy and exultation. He still remembered the cries of the children, the women throwing off their inhibitions and falling on the men to hug and kiss them. Here, when they drove up to Greasewood Creek, there was joy in the eyes of the emigrants and many cries of welcome, but it was nothing like what they had experienced before.

As he thought about that, he decided part of it was that with the Willie Company their arrival had not been expected. Then, they had come out of the west just at sundown, like angels of mercy descending from heaven. But the Martin Company knew that their rescuers were waiting at Devil's Gate and would come out to meet them. They also knew that this would likely be the day it would happen. It was not that they were less grateful; it was just that they were less surprised.

Yet in another way, while perhaps not as dramatic, this time was even more poignant than the first. David and Stephen Taylor were assigned to distribute the food from their wagon to one of the companies of hundred in Captain Martin's group. It touched David deeply that, as he handed them onions and potatoes and scooped out flour in generous portions, there was no pushing, no fighting for a place in the line, no whining about how hungry they were. They stood patiently, waiting their turn, their eyes large and haunting, the sallow, thin faces enough to make David want to weep. When they finally reached him, they would hold out their hands or their pots without speaking, the very gesture so beseeching and imploring that it became far more eloquent than words. And when he finished giving them their allotment, not once did they forget to express their gratitude. "Thank you, dear brother." "Bless you, son." "The Lord bless you." "Thank you so much for coming to our aid."

Something happened to him this time that hadn't happened in quite the same way with the Willie group. As he looked into the starved faces of these who had been lost, he remembered that they had been living for several days on four ounces of flour per day. And again and again, thoughts of the Savior flooded into his mind. Scriptures he had read since childhood came back to him, this time with such power and intensity he could hardly stop from crying out with the discovery.

The Son of man is come to save that which was lost. What man of you, having a hundred sheep, if he loses one of them, doth not leave the ninety and nine and go into the wilderness to find the one that is lost?

And a woman had ten pieces of silver, and when she lost a piece, she lighted a candle and swept the house clean. And when she found it, she called her friends and neighbors together and said, "Rejoice with me, for I have found that which was lost."

Simon, son of Jonas, lovest thou me? Yea, Lord; thou knowest that I love thee. Then feed my sheep. Feed my lambs.

I am the bread of life. He that cometh to me shall never hunger; and he that believeth on me shall never thirst.

It was as though someone had opened a book that he had never read before. There on every page was the love of the Master he had always known, but now he understood in a way more powerful than he had ever dreamed was possible. No wonder the Lord put His children under covenant to sacrifice whatever was required in order to go out and rescue His children that were lost. No wonder the prophets felt a sense of urgency about sending missionaries out into the world. No wonder Brigham Young chastised the Saints from time to time for turning toward the things of the world. How many of the Lord's fold were lost in the wilderness, perishing for want of bread, slowing dying in the spiritual cold? It was all that David could do not to break down and weep.

"Thank you. You don't know what this means to us."

David pulled out of his thoughts and looked at the young woman in front of him. She was young, maybe a little younger than his sister. Eleanor was almost eighteen now. David had just put a full scoop of flour in her kettle and was handing her an onion. Stephen Taylor had already put three potatoes in her pot. "You're welcome," he said, sorry that he had gotten carried away in his thoughts. "We are so glad that we have found you at last."

She nodded and stepped back to wait. The next person was also a young woman, of about the same age as the first but with light blond hair showing from beneath her winter bonnet. Her eyes were of a startling blue. "Here you go," he said, handing her a large onion, then scooping up another pound of flour.

But she had nothing in which to put it. The first girl stepped forward and held out her kettle. "We are together," the blond girl said in explanation. She pronounced the "we" as "vee."

David nodded and poured the flour in with the first portion. Stephen gave them three additional potatoes. As he did so, David looked at the first girl more closely. These two definitely did not look like sisters. This girl's hair was darker, not black but a light brown. Her eyes were wide set and green. And yet . . .

"Do I know you?" he began, then shook his head, realizing how foolish that sounded. "You look somewhat familiar to me."

Surprised, she shook her head. "I don't think so."

Beside him, he heard Stephen Taylor snigger softly and give him a look of disbelief.

Embarrassed, he stepped back again. "Sorry." But he was still looking at her closely, trying to shake off the feeling that somehow they had met before.

"Thank you again. You are very kind."

He snapped his fingers. The voice did it. "You're from Scotland?"

Her eyes widened. "Yes."

He turned, pointing to the one with blond hair and the

Scandinavian accent. "Then you're Ingrid," he said, almost blurting it out.

Ingrid Christensen was shocked. "Yes, I–"

"And you have to be Hannah."

Both of the girls stared at each other for a moment, and then Hannah turned back to David. "Do we know you?"

He laughed aloud. "That's why you looked familiar. You look like your sister."

"Maggie?" she cried. "You know Maggie?"

David turned to his companion, laughing openly now. "Stephen, can you handle this for a minute?" he said.

His fellow rescuer gave him a strange look, but then nodded. "Sure. We're almost done anyway."

David dropped the scoop in the flour sack and moved over to join the two girls. He took the kettle from Hannah's hands. She barely knew it. She was staring at him in astonishment. "How do you–" Then her eyes flew wide open. "You saw her?"

"Yes. At Sixth Crossing. I was there when we found the Willie Company."

Tears sprang to Hannah's eyes. David had started to walk, but he had to stop again. Hannah was rooted to the spot.

"And she's all right?" she whispered, her voice strained with emotion.

"Yes. She was when I saw her. And your mother and brother too."

A sob was wrenched from somewhere down deep inside her. "Thanks be to God. I've been so worried."

"And they're worried about the two of you."

"Eric and Olaf?" Ingrid said, finally recovering from the shock a little. "Were they all right?"

"Yes. I met them both."

He turned to Hannah. She was struggling to speak through the tears. "Mama? Robbie? You're sure they are all right?"

"Yes." He grinned now. This was an unexpected surprise. He had planned to go around the camp and locate these two after things settled down a little. "Maggie wanted me to bring you two some news."

"What?" They spoke as one.

"She and Eric are engaged to be married."

There was a squeal of delight. Hannah gaped at him for a moment, then swung around to Ingrid. With a shout that turned the heads of others around them, Ingrid cried, "I told you! I told you!"

David watched them, thrilled that it was his privilege to bring something into their lives at this point that could make them shout for joy. Then finally, Hannah remembered that he was still with them. "Thank you. This is the most wonderful thing that could have happened. To know that they are all right and that Maggie and Eric . . ." She couldn't finish and had to look away.

"Maggie also asked me to bring you something, Hannah," he said, less sure of himself now.

Her head came up. "What?"

He hesitated.

"What? What is it?"

Solemnly he set the kettle down in the snow; then, catching her totally by surprise, he took her in his arms and hugged her tightly. When he stepped back, he was blushing and so was Hannah. "I'm sorry," he said, "but she made me promise to do that."

The tears spilled over again. Hannah reached up with the back of her hand and wiped at one cheek. "Thank you," she whispered.

Chapter Notes

The journal entries and histories describing the arrival of the express party from Devil's Gate are too numerous and extensive to include, but the details given here, including the woman who first saw them and her reaction and Joseph Young's response, are drawn from those accounts. Three brief samples will serve to illustrate how those three brethren were received.

John Jaques wrote: "The 28th of October was the red letter day to this handcart expedition. On that memorable day Joseph A. Young, Daniel W. Jones and Abel Garr galloped unexpectedly into camp amid the cheers and tears and smiles and laughter of the emigrants. Those three men being the most advanced relief company from Salt Lake, brought the glad word that assistance, provisions, and clothing were near, that ten [some say it was eight] wagons were waiting at Devil's Gate for the emigrants. . . . All was now animation and bustle in the handcart camp, everybody was busy at once in making preparations for a renewed start in the morning. The revived spirits of the company were still exhilarated by an increased ration of flour that day" (in Bell, *Life History and Writings of John Jaques,* pp. 148–49; also in *Remember,* pp. 23–24).

Patience Loader, Jaques's sister-in-law, added these details:

> [Brother Joseph Young] told Captain Martin if he had flour enough to give us all one pound of flour each and said if there were any cattle to kill, to give us one pound of beef each, saying there were plenty of provisions and clothing coming for us on the road, but tomorrow we must make a move from here. He said we would have to travel twenty-five miles then there would be plenty of provisions and there would be good brethren to help us, that they had come with good teams and covered wagons so the sick could ride. Then he said he would have to leave us. He would like to have traveled with us the next morning, but we must cheer up and God would bless us and give us strength. He said, "We have made a trail for you to follow." . . .
>
> After the brethren had left us, we felt quite encouraged and we got our flour and beef before night came on and we were all busy cooking and we felt to thank God and our kind brethren that had come to help us in our great distress and misery for we were suffering greatly with cold and hunger. When night came we went to bed. We slept pretty comfortably more so than we had done for some time. We felt assured. (In *Remember,* p. 24)

Brother Daniel W. Jones, one of the three express riders, wrote: "This [Martin] company was in almost as bad a condition as the first one [i.e., the Willie Company]. They had nearly given up hope. Their provisions were about exhausted and many of them worn out and sick. When we rode in, there was a general rush to shake hands. I took no part in the ceremony. Many declared we were angels from heaven. I told them I thought we were better than angels for *this* occasion, as we were good strong men come to help them into the valley, and that our company, and wagons loaded with provisions, were not far away" (*Forty Years*, p. 66).

The express party returned to Devil's Gate about seven P.M. on the night of 30 October. The details of Joseph A. Young's report to Captain Grant are drawn from a speech he gave at the Tabernacle in Salt Lake City on 16 November. After the Martin Company was found, Brother Grant sent Joseph Young and Abel Garr to Salt Lake to report to President Young on the rescue efforts (see Hafen and Hafen, *Handcarts to Zion*, pp. 230–31; also *Remember*, p. 53).

There is a stretch along the trail around Prospect Hill that is known for what is called bentonite mud. This is a clay that has the capacity to absorb a great deal of water, and when it does it expands to several times its normal volume. It is used in oil drilling and other industrial applications. After having driven that stretch following a heavy rain, the author had to spend over an hour with a high-pressure sprayer to clean that mud off from beneath his vehicle.

Greasewood Creek (now called Horse Creek) is located about eleven miles northeast of Independence Rock and about sixteen miles from Devil's Gate. It was here, about sundown on the last day of October, that Captain George D. Grant finally met the last company of handcarts. The Hodgett Wagon Company was a short distance behind the handcarts at that time, and the Hunt Company was another day or two back from that, having started later from the last crossing of the North Platte.

As noted, Captain Grant wrote a report on his company's success and sent it by express back to Brigham Young in Salt Lake City. In that report he wrote:

> Not having much feed for our horses they were running down very fast, and not hearing anything from the companies, I did not know but what they had taken up quarters for the winter, consequently we sent on another express to the Platte bridge. When that express returned, to my surprise I learned that the companies [the Martin Handcart Company and the Hunt and Hodgett Wagon Companies] were all on the Platte river, near the upper crossing, and had been encamped there nine days, waiting for the snow to go away, or, as they said, to recruit their cattle.
>
> As quick as we learned this, we moved on to meet them. Met br. Martin's company at Greasewood creek, on the last day of October; br. Hodgett's company was a few miles behind. We dealt out to br. Martin's company the clothing, &c., that we had for them; and next morning, after stowing our wagons full of the sick, the children and the infirm, with a good amount of luggage, started homeward about

noon. The snow began to fall very fast, and continued until late at night. It is now about 8 inches deep here, and the weather is very cold.

. . . You can imagine between five and six hundred men, women and children, worn down by drawing hand carts through snow and mud; fainting by the wayside; falling, chilled by the cold; children crying, their limbs stiffened by cold, their feet bleeding and some of them bare to snow and frost. The sight is almost too much for the stoutest of us; but we go on doing all we can, not doubting nor despairing.

Our company is too small to help much, it is only a drop to a bucket, as it were, in comparison to what is needed. I think that not over one-third of br. Martin's company is able to walk. This you may think is extravagant, but it is nevertheless true. Some of them have good courage and are in good spirits; but a great many are like children and do not help themselves much more, nor realize what is before them. (In Hafen and Hafen, *Handcarts to Zion*, pp. 227–28)

CHAPTER 30

GREASEWOOD CREEK TO DEVIL'S GATE

I

Saturday, 1 November 1856

The James G. Willie Handcart Company left their camp at Rock Creek on October twenty-fifth. They left fifteen people behind them; thirteen of those were buried in a mass grave, and two who had helped dig that grave had to be buried in additional graves of their own. Even with the wagons from the Valley that Reddick Allred had brought from where he was waiting at South Pass, there was barely enough to carry the sick, so once again the emigrants picked up the shafts of their carts and started west.

Being back not only on full rations but having a varied diet—onions, fattened beef, sugar, rice, dried fruit, potatoes—and having far more adequate clothing made a significant difference, but death still exacted its toll as they rolled along. Two died the next day as they crossed South Pass and followed down Pacific Creek. Two more in Eric's hundred died the day they crossed the Big Sandy, thirty-five miles west of South Pass, and two more from England passed away as they reached the Green River, an additional day's journey beyond that.

But it was becoming evident that the full diet and better protection from the elements were having an effect. To Eric's immense relief, day by day Maggie's cough lessened. By the time they reached the Big Sandy, she was back to pulling the cart throughout the full day and would not hear of anyone trying to make her do any less than that. Sarah and Emma James were now able to pull their remaining cart completely alone and leave their mother to care for the younger children. Reuben James, his feet badly frostbitten, was still too crippled to walk and rode in one of the wagons. Jen Nielson, in a similar condition, did the same.

The last day of October proved to be a momentous one. Shortly after leaving their camp on the Green River, they met ten wagons coming east—seven from the Valley and three from Fort Supply south of Fort Bridger. That ended any fears that they might run out of food again and have to go to reduced rations. It also meant there were more wagons in which to put baggage and people. A quick survey was made and several of the most unreliable of the handcarts were abandoned. Even if there wasn't room in the wagons for everyone, walking alongside was a tremendous improvement over having to pull a loaded cart.

The following day another group of wagons from Salt Lake met them on the trail. As important as their presence was, even more significant was the news they brought. They were only the first of literally dozens and dozens of wagons coming east. As they met these welcome messengers, William H. Kimball again stopped the train and ordered more of the handcart loads to be transferred to the wagons.

The Willie Company and their rescuers stopped near the top of a gentle rise in the trail to make the transfer. It was a long ridge that was steep in many places, but here there was a gentle swale through which the trail passed. Maggie and Eric sat in the snow beside their cart, waiting for the decisions to be made on whose carts would be abandoned. Sister McKensie and Robbie sat against the other wheel. Just ahead of them, Sister Jane James and her children waited in like manner.

Brother Kimball and Captain Willie moved slowly along the line. Maggie noted that their captain was limping a little. In all of the concern for those who had died coming up over Rocky Ridge, few had noticed that Captain Willie's feet had been seriously frostbitten too. At Brother Kimball's insistence, he was riding much of the time, so it surprised Maggie to see him on his feet now.

Eric looked up as the two men approached. "Want to buy a cart cheap?" he drawled lazily.

Brother Kimball smiled. Then to their surprise he walked around their cart, looking at it closely as he did so. He even bent down and looked beneath it. Then he rattled each of the wheels. Finally he looked down at Eric. "Sorry, Brother Pederson. I don't think you're going to get much for this one."

Eric sighed. "Well, perhaps in Great Salt Lake City."

"Sorry," Brother Kimball said again, now smiling. "But this one isn't going to Salt Lake."

That brought all of their heads up in surprise.

"Yep. This one is one of the worst. Let's get it unloaded and leave it behind."

Maggie looked up. "We're just going to leave it here?"

"Yes."

"You don't want it for firewood?"

Brother Kimball shook his head. "It's not worth dragging it to our next camp. Leave it for the antelope and the coyotes."

Fifteen minutes later it was done. The cart that Eric and Olaf and Brother James and the other brethren had helped to make back in Iowa City, the cart that had carried their things more than a thousand miles, the cart that had raised blisters and then calluses, that had dragged them back as they went up the hills and pushed them forward when they went down again, was now to be left behind. It was not a prospect that filled them with sorrow.

As they carried the last of their clothing and bedding to the nearest wagon, Brother Kimball nodded. "All right." He looked at Eric. "If you and the McKensies could help Sister James and the girls with their cart until more wagons come along, we'd appreciate it. Pull this one out of the way and let's get rolling again."

Eric nodded, then started for the cart, but Maggie beat him to it. She trotted forward and quickly raised the shafts. As he came to help, she waved him off. "No, Eric. I want to do this."

Surprised, he stopped. She leaned into the crossbars and started forward, the empty cart rolling easily now. "What?" he said, teasing her. "You have so much love for it that you must have one last turn?"

She nodded. Moving faster, she turned off the trail and into the sagebrush. To everyone's surprise, she did not stop but moved upward along the rising ground, following the edge of the ridge.

Her mother began to look concerned. "Maggie, where are you going?" she called.

She waved and called back something that none of them caught. Eric looked at Brother Willie and Brother Kimball. He shrugged, thoroughly perplexed.

The ridge had been swept mostly clear of the snow, so it was not hard pulling for her. Maggie moved steadily along it, looking over the edge of the ridge down below. About a hundred yards out she reached a spot where the ridge dropped off sharply. She was now about fifty or sixty feet above the level ground below. She moved right to the edge of the drop-off, then stepped out of the shafts, still holding firmly to the front crossbar so as to keep the cart level.

"What are you doing?" Robbie shouted.

Eric was suddenly grinning. "Watch," he said.

Steadying the cart now, Maggie gripped the crossbar. With a cry of exultation, she heaved the cart forward. It had enough momentum that it shot over the edge. As the back end of the cart passed her, Maggie aimed a kick at it. She missed, but it still gave her great satisfaction.

Over it went. As the front end dropped, the crossbar and shafts hit the dirt and bounced up again. The cart was careening wildly now as it gathered momentum. The second time the front end came down, the left shaft dug into the soft earth. The back end jerked upward, and then the cart was tumbling end over end, crashing loudly each time it hit. A piece of sideboard went flying. Then the right wheel crumpled. On the third flip, the main body hit a large rock protruding from the ground and the bottom of the cart shattered with a tremendous crack. Splinters of wood went flying everywhere.

In a few seconds it was over. What had once been a serviceable handcart now lay at the bottom of the slope, mangled and twisted almost beyond recognition. Maggie stood there for a moment, looking down at her handiwork; then she brushed off her hands and started back.

To her astonishment, she heard someone start to clap. Then others joined in. As she walked back to where Eric and her family and her two leaders were waiting for her, a great swell of applause went up and down the line of wagons and carts. There were cheers, and one of the newly arrived members of the rescue team even whistled shrilly. She lifted her arms in triumph and waved them back and forth, accepting their cheers for what they were—a deep expression of relief that they had come to this point in their journey.

When she reached the group waiting for her, she looked at William Kimball. Perfectly serious, she nodded. "All right. I think I'm ready now."

Shaking his head and trying not to smile, Brother Kimball gave her an official nod and he and Captain Willie started back for the front of the line.

Robbie was gaping at his sister. She finally let a touch of humor soften her mouth. "I'm sorry, Robbie. If I had been thinking, I would have let you help me."

His mouth was half-open, and then he grinned wickedly. "It was much more fun to watch from here, Maggie," he said.

As Robbie and Maggie's mother moved forward to join the Jameses, Maggie finally turned to Eric. "You didn't know that that was what you were marrying, did you?"

He shook his head in wonder. "No, I didn't."

"Want to change your mind?"

To her surprise, he didn't laugh. "No." He took a deep breath, his eyes pained now. "Since Olaf died, I—" He stopped and took another breath. "I once thought that we should be married before we reached the Valley. When Olaf died, it didn't seem appropriate to talk of happiness anymore."

"I know." She had guessed that that might be the reason he had not mentioned marriage again since that terrible night at Rock Creek.

"But now?" He turned and looked at the shattered cart. "Now I would like to have us be married as soon as we reach the Valley. Would that be all right with you, Maggie?"

She slipped her arm in his. "That would be perfect," she said happily. "Absolutely perfect."

II

Sunday, 2 November 1856

It was about ten o'clock the next morning. According to Brother Kimball and Captain Willie, they were just a few miles away from Fort Bridger, the last major stopping place before they reached the Valley. Maggie and Sarah James were behind the Jameses' handcart, taking their turn pushing at the moment, while Eric and Sister James pulled in the shafts. Emma was getting a rest and was with the children. With both families down to one cart, there were plenty of chances for all to rest more now.

"More wagons coming," Eric called back.

Maggie lifted her head to see over the cart. They were about a third of the way back from the head of the column and had a pretty good view of the trail ahead. But to their surprise, it turned out to be only one wagon. They could see it as it stopped near the front of the line and their captains went over to meet it. But no one ordered the company to stop, and eventually Eric's group came up on the group and passed by it slowly. Captain Willie, Brother Kimball, Kimball's younger brother Heber P., and Levi Savage were all talking to the teamster, who still sat on his wagon seat.

As they went by, Eric saw that the man was slender of build, had long hair that fell down to his shoulders and a full dark beard. He was heavily dressed for the weather, and there was a long-barreled rifle in a holder beside the wagon seat. As he talked with their leaders, the man's eyes would keep shifting to the passing line, and he would lift a hand to wave, or nod in greeting. His eyes were grave and he did not smile.

"That's strange," Eric said.

"What's that?" Jane James asked.

"Only one wagon."

"Hmm." She hadn't considered that. But Eric was right. They had now met more than a dozen wagons, but none of them had been traveling alone. The smallest group had been a group of three. "What do you think it means?"

Eric shrugged. "Maybe he's not from the Valley."

"Maybe he's not even a Mormon," Sarah called up from behind. "He didn't look like one."

Maggie nudged her playfully. "And what is a Mormon supposed to look like?" she asked. "Maybe all the brethren in Utah have long hair and wear full beards."

Sarah pulled a face. "I hope not. I prefer someone like that David Granger that we met."

Hearing that, Eric half turned to look at Maggie and Sarah. "The brethren seemed to know him," he commented.

Five minutes later, as they continued to move slowly along, Heber P. Kimball came sauntering up the line on his horse. Seeing him coming, Eric waved a hand, motioning him in.

"Yes?"

"Was that one of the wagons from the Valley?" Eric asked.

Heber seemed surprised. "Of course. You won't see many other wagons out here now except for ours."

"Isn't it a little unusual to have one wagon traveling alone?"

Heber nodded, understanding the question now. "Normally, yes."

"But this isn't normal?" Maggie asked, curious now as well.

He laughed. "No, this is not normal. This is Ephraim Hanks."

"So you did know him?" Sarah said, seeming a little disappointed.

"Ephraim? Of course. Practically everyone in the Valley knows Ephraim Hanks. He and Charles Decker—" He stopped. "Do you remember Brother Decker? He was our scout. He went on ahead with Brother Grant's group."

"Kind of," Maggie responded.

"Well, anyway, Ephraim and Brother Decker run the mail service between here and St. Jo, Missouri. Ephraim's a real frontiersman, made out of the same mold as the likes of Jim Bridger and the other mountain men."

"So why he is alone?" Eric asked, still surprised to find an isolated wagon out in this desolation.

"Anyone else would be crazy to come out here in this weather on their own. But not Ephraim. He says he's going on to help the rear company." Then Heber got a strange look on his face. "Said he'd gotten a real strong call from the Lord that he ought to come out and help."

"What kind of call?" Sister James asked.

"Wouldn't say. But for all he looks kind of rough, here's a man who's close to the Lord. The Indians call him the man who talks with the Great Spirit."

When it was clear they had no more questions, Heber lifted a hand and rode on. Once he was gone, Maggie turned to Sarah. "I wish I had known that that was what he was doing."

"Why?"

"I would have told him about Hannah and Ingrid and had him make sure they were all right."

III

Monday, 3 November 1856

Rescue did not mean restoration.

David Granger learned that lesson in short order when they found the Martin Company at Greasewood Creek. With the Willie Company, the rescuers had brought in the wagons full of food and clothing, distributed it out to the smiles and tears of the joyous recipients, and then left again immediately. He was not there to see what followed. He came on east with Captain Grant's division while William H. Kimball took the Willie Company west. Somehow in David's mind he still pictured the Willie Company at the Sixth Crossing, enjoying the largesse their rescuers had brought them. Now that he thought about it, he knew that that couldn't be the case, but as they had pressed on eastward he really hadn't thought much about the Willie Company's moving on.

As the rescue company made their camp at Greasewood Creek with the Martin Company on the last day of October, the south wind died; then after a time the wind sprang up again, only this time from out of the northwest. The temperature dropped sharply, and by morning it was clear that another winter storm was coming. From the feel of it, it promised to be another bad one, which shortly proved to be the case. This should have created an air of urgency in the camp, but the emigrants didn't seem to care. Or at least, it was not enough to spur them on to greater speed. And that was when David began to realize that rescue was not the final solution. The mood of the camp that morning had been greatly improved over when they had found them. But one meal on full rations didn't restore strength and energy overnight. One night of hope did not magically regenerate the endurance that had dribbled away over a period of a month or more.

The next morning, as they prepared to break camp and start for Devil's Gate, David began to sense just how far these people had to go before they would be back to any semblance of normality. As he watched them, particularly Hannah McKensie and Ingrid Christensen and the recently widowed Sister Elizabeth Jackson and her children, David decided to ask Captain Grant if Stephen Taylor or someone else might drive the team so that he could help them pull their cart.

He never got a chance to make that request.

As the handcart company prepared to move out, Captain Grant called some of the brethren together. He and Major Burton were going back to find the Hodgett Wagon Company, who were camped just four or five miles behind the Martin group. But the Hunt Wagon Company was still a worry. The last they had been heard from was on the twenty-ninth—three days earlier—when Brother Young and his companions had left them at the last crossing and urged them to come on as quickly as possible. So Captain Grant asked a few brethren under the direction of Cyrus Wheelock to head east and try to find them once again. David was assigned to go with them, and that ended any of his plans about helping with the handcarts—or spending more time with Hannah McKensie.

That had been three days ago, and those three days had turned out to be a little frustrating to David Granger. The Hunt wagons had left the last crossing of the North Platte on the twenty-ninth as they had promised Joseph Young, but their pace could best be described as leisurely. If it was hard to generate a sense of urgency in the handcart emigrants, it was because they had reached the point where all physical, mental, and spiritual reserves were drained. With the Hunt group, the lack of urgency seemed to stem from a blithe unawareness of how critical the situation was becoming. After Joseph Young, Abel Garr, and Dan Jones left them with the command to come on as quickly as possible, the Hunt Company had not moved out until two o'clock that afternoon. They went three miles. The next day they went seven miles and stopped again. Then they stayed in place for another full day while they worked out the purchase of some cattle from the Platte Bridge trading post.

When Brother Wheelock and his small group finally found them, it hadn't been much better. They had finally made it back to Greasewood Creek just today. David blew out his breath. Eighteen miles and it had taken them three days. It was then he decided to go to Brother Wheelock and ask for a favor.

"Brother Wheelock, would you have any objection if I were to ride on ahead to Devil's Gate?"

One eyebrow came up. "Right now?"

"Yes. It's just that . . . well, this company seems to be moving along all right now, and the handcart company seemed in much more need of help. I was just thinking that they are probably getting ready to move on by now. Maybe they already have. They might be able to use some more help." He stopped, realizing that the words had come out in a rush.

For a long moment, Brother Wheelock peered at him. Cyrus Wheelock was a longtime friend of David's father and close to the family. He knew David well and was pleased with how his friend's oldest son was turning out. "This wouldn't have anything to do with those two young ladies I saw you speaking with out here the other day, would it?"

David flinched. How had he noticed that? He had only spoken to Ingrid and Hannah for a few minutes at his wagon. The next morning he had somehow ended up at their tent and helped them take it down, but he had helped others as well.

"I'll take that long silence as a yes," Brother Wheelock said with a sardonic smile.

David grinned sheepishly. "Well, sir, they do seem to be in need of some help."

"Mind if I go with you?" he asked.

David was startled. "Well, no, of course not. But I thought you had to stay with Captain Hunt's group."

Brother Wheelock sighed deeply. "I do. I'll bring them in, but this pace we're setting is enough to drive a teetotaler to drink." He slapped David on the arm. "Saddle your horse and get out of here. Someone needs to tell Captain Grant where we are anyway."

It was almost eight P.M. when David Granger rode into the compound at the old fort at Devil's Gate. He had come seventeen miles in nine hours. Surprised to see a solitary rider, several of those in the rescue company came out to greet him. One of those was Stephen Taylor, his wagon partner when they went out to find the Martin Company. Like David, Stephen was twenty-one and had been in the Minute Men for the last three years.

David climbed down stiffly from the saddle and handed Stephen the reins. "Where's Captain Grant?"

"In that center building there," Stephen answered.

"Good. Will you see to my horse?"

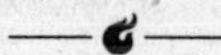

"Look," Ingrid said, poking Hannah on the shoulder. "There he is."

"There who is?" Hannah said, turning to look. She had been talking to Mary Elizabeth Jackson, but looked up to see what Ingrid was looking at.

"You know. *Him!* The one who hugged you."

Hannah's eye caught sight of the figure who had just come out from Captain Grant's cabin. He stopped for a moment to speak to a man standing just outside the door, then started slowly towards the nearest fire. The company had several large fires burning around the compound, and the light illuminated a wide circle in the darkness. Hannah watched him as he moved stiffly and with obvious weariness.

Suddenly Ingrid grabbed her arm. "I'll bet he's hungry. We've still got some stew left."

Hannah turned and gave her an incredulous look.

She went on the defensive. "Wouldn't you be hungry after all day on the trail?"

"*Ingrid!* We barely even know his name."

"So?" A bit of an impish smile played around her mouth. "I thought the scriptures talked about offering help to the stranger."

Hannah was thoroughly shocked. "Have you got designs on that young man?" she said.

Ingrid looked innocent. "What is 'designs'?"

"Don't you play that with me, young lady. You know exactly what I mean. Are you trying to make something happen between you and him?"

Now Ingrid looked shocked. "Not between *me* and him, Hannah."

"*What?*"

"He hugged *you,* you know."

"I . . . that was just from Maggie."

"Did you not see his face? He was red like a beet. It was more than just a hug from Maggie."

"Ingrid Christensen. Is this what a little food and rest does to you? You are losing your mind."

"Come on. Let's ask him." She grabbed Hannah by the arm and dragged her forward.

Hannah was about to pull away when the young man turned and saw them coming. To Hannah's surprise, he immediately smiled and changed direction, coming over to them. "Hello," he said.

"Hello," Ingrid said. "Welcome back."

"Thank you."

"Did you find the Hunt Company?" Hannah asked.

He nodded. "They should be here tomorrow or the next day." He removed his hat, and rubbed ruefully at the stubble on his chin. For a moment Hannah thought he was going to apologize for how he looked, but instead he looked at her. "How are you two doing?"

"Much better," Hannah answered. "Thank you."

"You are hungry?" Ingrid said bluntly.

He turned in surprise. "Yes, very."

"We have stew left over for you if you would like."

His smile was broad and genuine. "Why, thank you. I was just wondering how I might find something when supper is all finished now."

"Sister Jackson," Hannah started, feeling terribly awkward, "the woman we are traveling with, she would be happy to have you share with us. We are very grateful for all you brethren have done."

"It is our privilege," he said earnestly, "believe me."

Ingrid stuck out her hand. "I don't know if you remember, but I am Ingrid Christensen."

He laughed as he took it. "I remember. And I am David Granger."

Hannah colored slightly and put out her hand. "Yes, and I am—"

"Hannah McKensie. I know."

"Yes." She felt herself color more deeply, and so she turned and pointed. "Our tent is over this way."

—❦—

"That was wonderful stew," David said as he finished and set his plate down on the log beside the fire. "Thank you."

Elizabeth Jackson smiled at him. "You lie very well, young man. But I suppose a hearty appetite maketh the best sauce."

David grinned. "Well, then, I had plenty of sauce to add to the mix, that's for sure."

"Having something besides lean beef and flour helps too," Hannah said. "Who would have ever thought that simply adding onions and potatoes to a stew could be so heavenly?"

He sat back and folded his hands across his stomach, obviously not in any hurry to get up and leave. "Well, it was very good. Thank you."

"We are very glad that you found the others and that they are well," Sister Jackson said.

Little Aaron Jackson, who was sitting beside his mother, was watching David with large, grave eyes. Martha Ann, his oldest sister, looked down at him. "Brother Granger drives one of the wagons, Aaron."

He nodded slowly. David smiled at him and patted his lap. "Come here, Aaron. Let me see what a fine boy you are."

To the surprise of them all, little Aaron stood up without hesitation and went to David and allowed himself to be picked up and set in his lap. "Well," Sister Jackson said, "there's a surprise for you."

"And how old are you, Aaron?" David asked.

The boy held up a gloved hand and stuck up his fingers. Then, concentrating mightily, he reached out with his other hand and pushed the thumb and two fingers down again.

"Two?" David said.

He nodded, still very sober.

David pulled the boy back against him and let him snuggle into his arms. "I have a sister that's just about your age." Then he turned to the women. "So did you have much trouble getting here?" he asked of all three of them.

They looked at each other for a moment, and then Sister Jackson spoke up. "The first night was terrible. It was snowing and the night had turned so cold. With so few men . . ." Her voice caught and she looked down at her hands.

Hannah came in smoothly. "With so few men to help, we had a difficult time that night getting the tents up."

He nodded. "So you didn't make it all the way here?"

"No. We stopped at what they called Sweetwater Crossing."

"Ah, yes. There by Independence Rock."

Hannah nodded.

Martha Ann spoke up now. "We didn't have enough shovels. We had to use frying pans and tin plates to scrape away the snow."

"And then," Ingrid added, "it took some of us almost an hour to get the tents up. It was very cold. Even colder than it is tonight."

David glanced upward. There were a few stars showing, and the wind stirred the empty branches of the trees above them. "If it clears off, it's going to turn real cold tonight." Then he turned back to the three women. "Didn't our boys from the Valley help you get your tents up?"

"As much as they could." Hannah smiled. "Is that what they call you? the Valley boys?"

He chuckled softly. "That's kind of what you folks have labeled us. Actually, most of us belong to the Minute Men. That's a group that is part of the militia in the Valley. But I kind of like the title of Valley boys myself. If the name fits, wear it, I always say."

"So you live in Salt Lake Valley?" Ingrid asked.

"Yes. Right in Great Salt Lake City actually. Our family has a farm there."

"Is it wonderful to be there?" Sister Jackson asked softly.

"Yes," came the firm answer. "It is wonderful. You are going to love it there." He hesitated for a moment. "Even though you've lost your husband, Sister Jackson, you and your children will be well cared for."

She looked at him for a long moment, her eyes glistening, then nodded. "Thank you, David."

David turned back to the girls. "So tell me, what has been going on here at Devil's Gate since you arrived? I was afraid you might have gone on again."

"Well, Brother Grant knocked down a house to make us a fire," Ingrid said.

"He did?"

"Yes," Hannah answered. "The first night we arrived. When we got here the men who had been left behind had fires going and supper cooking. We all ran to get close to the fires and get warm. It was so cold. Brother Grant asked us all to be patient and he would get us some wood for our own fires. Well, he walked over to one of these deserted cabins and raised his ax. He gave it one mighty blow and the thing was so decrepit that the whole wall caved in. Then we all got a piece of log to make our own fires."

"By the way," Sister Jackson added, "why are these old buildings here? And doesn't anyone care if they are knocked down and used for firewood?"

David shrugged. "I'm not sure. There was some kind of military post here a while ago, but then it was abandoned. It hasn't been used for some time now."

They fell silent for a moment, and then Hannah spoke again. "They have decided to move us, did you know that?"

"No, Captain Grant and Major Burton didn't mention that." David didn't add that he had been in such a hurry to try and find Hannah and Ingrid that he had stayed only long enough with his leaders to report where Brother Wheelock and the Hunt Company were.

Ingrid spoke up again now. "Yah. They say there is a place not far where we can find more protection from the storm that is coming."

Sister Jackson added further clarification. "Captain Grant says it's too cold and there's too much snow to travel right now. But there is not room enough here for all of us, especially when the Hunt Wagon Company arrives. That will make almost nine hundred people."

Hannah pointed toward the west. "Evidently from what they say, there's a hollow or a cove in these granite mountains just a few miles from here. It's sheltered from the wind and there is water and firewood there. They've decided we should move there until the weather warms again."

"I think that's wise," David said. "That will give you a little more chance to rest before you have to leave again."

"And maybe then more wagons from the Valley will come," Sister Jackson suggested.

David shook his head, reluctant to disagree with her but also knowing that this was a false hope. "I don't think so. Brother Grant told them to stay put at South Pass until they get word from us."

Hannah knew that, but it was something that still puzzled her. "Why do they wait at South Pass? Why don't they come on to find us?"

David's brow furrowed a little. That was a fair question. "You have to remember that when we reached South Pass, we had no idea where you were, or Captain Willie's group either. By then the first snowstorm had hit. Many of our teams were exhausted. Captain Grant was afraid that if he came on with everyone, we might be out here floundering around trying to find you. We couldn't afford to exhaust all the teams that way. Also, there are more wagons coming behind us from the Valley. Captain Grant didn't want them to come on as far as South Pass and not find anyone and turn back."

Now Hannah was embarrassed. "I didn't mean to sound critical," she said. "I was just wondering. We know you are doing everything you can to help us."

"I didn't think you sounded critical," he said.

"Oh," Sister Jackson said, "speaking of sending word, did Captain Grant tell you he sent two men to the Valley with a letter to President

Young asking for more help? They will stop at South Pass and tell the others we are coming and have them start coming forward."

That startled David. Captain Grant had not mentioned that either. "Really? Who were they?"

"Brigham Young's son and the other man who came out to meet us. Abraham . . ." She tried to remember the last name.

"Abel Garr?"

"Yes. Those two."

"My, my," he said. "Those two brethren are going to have leather for backsides before they're done with all this riding." Then he winced and looked at Hannah. "I'm sorry, I didn't mean . . . It's just that–"

Hannah laughed. "We are quite capable of understanding what it means to ride hundreds of miles in the saddle, Brother Granger."

"They are going to empty all wagons," Ingrid said.

"You mean at South Pass?"

"No, here," Hannah said. "They are going to empty out all the Hodgett Company wagons and use them to help carry our baggage and also the sick and the weak."

David could see that he should have taken a little more time with Captain Grant and Major Burton. "You mean they are going to unload all that freight?"

Sister Jackson nodded. "They held a meeting. They will leave all of the goods the wagons were carrying here. From the Hunt Company too, when they arrive. That will give us almost eighty wagons. They plan to leave most of the handcarts behind."

"Whoa!" he said. "Slow down. Are you saying they're just going to leave all that freight here and go on without it?"

"No," Hannah responded. "They're talking about leaving a few of the brethren here to guard it, then sending wagons back in the spring to get it. Brother Jaques says–" Hannah stopped. "Brother Jaques is one of the leaders in our company. He says we will keep only two or three carts per hundred–the very best of them–and put our cooking utensils and kettles and things in them. The food, tents, and everything else will be put into the wagons."

"Everyone who can walk will walk," Ingrid explained. "There are still many sick who will have to ride. But walking will be better than pulling the carts."

"Well, well, I can see they've not been letting things sit idle while they were waiting for us to return." He stood up, lifting young Aaron with him. "I'd better go find out what I'm expected to do in the morning."

He looked down at Sister Jackson, then handed Aaron to her. "Thank you again for supper, ma'am. I am much obliged."

"You are most welcome. And thank you again."

As he started away, Ingrid called after him. "Thank you, Brother Granger, for that hug you brought to Hannah from Maggie."

"*Ingrid!*" Hannah hissed.

David laughed and waved. "It is always a pleasure to do my duty," he called back.

When he was gone, Hannah swung on her friend. "Ingrid! What are you doing?"

"I think he likes you," Ingrid teased. "He talks to all of us, but he looks only at you."

"That's not true," she said, flustered now. She looked to Elizabeth for help.

"Well, it's not completely true," Sister Jackson said with a smile, "but mostly."

"Sister Jackson!"

"Well," Elizabeth said with some warmth in her voice. "He *is* a very nice-looking young man." Then before Hannah could protest again, she stood. "Come, children. It's time for bed."

Chapter Notes

The story of Maggie McKensie and the handcart told in this chapter was inspired by the following story, which has been included in some of the compilations of handcart histories: "Margaret Dalglish, that gaunt image of Scotch fortitude, dragged her pitiful handful of possessions to the very rim of the valley, but when she looked down and saw the end of it, safety, the City of the Saints, she did something extraordinary. She tugged the cart to the edge of the road and gave it a push and watched it roll and crash and tumble and burst apart, scattering down the ravine the last things she owned on earth. Then she went on into Salt Lake to start the new life with nothing but her gaunt bones, her empty hands, her stout heart" (Wallace Stegner, "Ordeal by Handcart," p. 85; also in *Remember*, p. 139).

The story is taken from an account written much later by Margaret Dalglish's granddaughter (see Carter, comp., *Heart Throbs of the West* 1:82), who says her grandmother was in the Martin Company. Some have wondered about the accuracy of this story because Margaret Dalglish is usually listed in the Willie Company and also because some journals say that all the members of both the Willie and Martin Companies were in the rescue wagons by the time they reached the Valley. The author chose to adapt it and make use of it here, not to try to resolve the issues, but rather because whether it happened exactly as described or not, it captures a feeling that many of the emigrants, and especially the women, must have had toward those two-wheeled vehicles that became so much a part of their lives that summer of 1856.

The entry for 2 November in the Willie Company journal reads, in part: "Camp rolled out. Ephraim Hanks passed our camp this morning, bringing news from the valley of many teams being on the road, and that he was going on to the rear companies to meet them" (in Turner, *Emigrating Journals*, p. 51; also in *Remember*, p. 14).

The independent wagon companies traveling in rough tandem with the Martin Handcart Company were obviously not under the same weight limitations that the handcart companies were. Many of them had contracted with emigrants of the Willie and Martin groups to carry heavier items to Utah for them. An entry in the official history of the Church gives some insight as to how the decision was made to cache the freight at Devil's Gate and continue on using the wagons to carry the people: "Soon Bro. Grant arrived and prepared the camp for moving. He said to Joseph A. [Young], 'What would your father do now if he were here?' Joseph answered: 'If my father was here he would take all the books and heavy material and cache them in order to save the lives of the people.' So they agreed to do it. They cached all their articles at Devil's Gate and took up the weak and the feeble and started towards home" (Journal History, 13 November 1856).

The rescue company's journal entry for 3 November reads: "Remained at same place [Devil's Gate]. So cold that the company could not move. Sent an express to G.S.L. City, Joseph A. Young, and Abel Garr, to report our situation and get counsel and help" (in *Remember*, p. 54). This following additional entry gives some indication of the challenge the two men faced riding the 350 miles to the Valley: "Before riding, Young put on three or four pairs of woollen socks, a pair of moccasins, and a pair of buffalo hide over-shoes with the wool on, and then remarked, There, if my feet freeze with those on, they must stay frozen till I get to Salt Lake" (in *Remember*, p. 54).

CHAPTER 31

DEVIL'S GATE TO COTTONWOOD CREEK

I

Tuesday, 4 November 1856

The minute David Granger rolled out of his bed, he knew that they were in for a terrible day. Even inside the tent it was bitterly cold. Once dressed, he stepped outside. One breath of the morning air made him gasp and he quickly pulled his scarf across his face. The snow actually squeaked under his boots, a sure sign that the temperature was below zero.

As he and Stephen Taylor and the other Minute Men set to work, dragging over firewood and nursing the dying coals back into full flame, a few of the people began appearing from out of their tents, but for the most part it was only the men of the rescue company who were up. About half past five, Captain Grant and Robert Burton came out of the old cabin they were using as the camp headquarters. With them were Captain Edward Martin and his five captains of hundreds. Captain Grant called for the rest of his men to come in around them.

"Brethren," Captain Grant said, once they were in a tight circle, "this is not going to be an easy day."

Major Burton broke in. "We just checked the thermometer. Right now it is six degrees below zero."

There was a low whistle from one of the men. David was not surprised. He had been up in the mountains east of Salt Lake cutting firewood enough to know what it felt like when the temperature dropped that low.

George Grant looked up at the sky. Though it was lightening, it was still dark enough for stars to show. The cloud cover was completely gone now, and that partly explained the drop in temperature. Brother Grant turned his face into the wind. It was only a breeze here, coming from the northwest, pouring down gently from the rocky hillsides just behind them. David guessed what his leader was thinking. Once they left the shelter of the rocks and got out in the open, it would be blowing stiffly. As the day wore on, it could become a major factor in dealing with the cold.

Captain Grant turned back, his eyes somber. "The people are rested somewhat, but they are still weak, and as you know, we still have many who are too ill to go on their own. We're going to have to take them in the wagons. We will leave most of the handcarts here. We've instructed the subcaptains to go through their hundreds and select the few carts they feel are still in the best condition. We'll put what tools we have and the cooking utensils—pots, frying pans, skillets, kettles, dishes, cups—into those carts. Food, tents, bedding, and extra clothing will go into the wagons."

"Are we taking all of the wagons from Captain Hodgett's Company too?" someone asked.

"Not today. We've still got to off-load all that freight. We'll take just enough to move the sick and the company's belongings over to that ravine or cove we've found."

"And how far is that?" John Jaques asked. He was one of the subcaptains. He and the other captains of hundreds were standing beside Edward Martin, listening intently.

Brother Grant looked at Brother Burton, then looked back at the men. "If we could go straight there, no more than a mile or a mile and a half. But we're going to have to go west along the trail for a ways to where we can cross the Sweetwater, then we'll cut in from there to the campsite. We estimate it's about three miles all together."

Good, David thought. The cold was going to be a challenge, but three miles was something they could do.

Brother Burton turned to Edward Martin and his captains. "We wish we had enough men that we could pull those carts for you brethren, but we've got to have teamsters for the wagons and we've got to keep some men here to continue the unloading. But we have asked several of our rescue boys to come along with us to help."

Actually he hadn't asked yet, so now he began pointing. "Stephen Taylor. David Kimball. David Granger. Brother Huntington." He hesitated for a moment as he looked at his own son, then went on. "George W. Grant. Dan Jones."

David looked at Stephen Taylor and they nodded in satisfaction. This was what they wanted. They didn't want to stay here unloading freight.

"We'll help you as much as we can," Brother Grant concluded, "but you're going to have to put your strongest people on those carts. The rest who are still able to walk are going to have to do so on their own."

"We understand," Elder Martin said. "When do you want us ready to move?"

Again the two leaders looked at each other; then Brother Grant answered. "Ten o'clock. You'd better roust your people out of those tents."

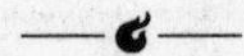

As it turned out, the cart used by Hannah McKensie, Ingrid Christensen, and Elizabeth Jackson and her children was chosen as one of those that were to be taken to the new campsite. As the men stowed the last cooking kettle in its place and pulled the canvas over the top and began to tie it down, Hannah stepped forward. She reached down and tentatively lifted up on one of the shafts. She groaned inwardly. It was significantly heavier than what it had been with only their things in it. She turned and gave Ingrid a look of dismay. How were they going to manage this?

"I am going to help you."

Hannah spun around in surprise, raising one hand to ward off the sun's glare. A man was coming towards them, all but his eyes covered with the scarf he had pulled over his face. As he reached them he pulled away the scarf. To Hannah's pleased surprise it was David Granger.

"Good morning." He turned to Sister Jackson, but looked down at her son, holding out his arms. "How's my young friend Aaron this morning?" The boy was wrapped in his blanket, but he smiled and ran immediately to David, who lifted him up.

"Good morning, Brother Granger," Ingrid said, obviously as pleased as Hannah was.

"David, please. My father is *Brother* Granger." He grinned that wonderful grin of his. "I'm just a boy yet."

Hannah came around to the back of the cart. "I thought you had to drive the wagons."

He turned, squinting, then waved. The man sitting on the wagon seat of the closest wagon waved back. "Brother Taylor's going to drive ours for us."

Ingrid waved as well. "He's the one who helped you give us food."

"Yes. His name is Stephen Taylor."

"And you are friends as well as fellow rescuers?" Hannah asked.

"Yes. All of us in the Minute Men are good friends." David frowned. "We don't have that far to go today, but it is very cold."

Hannah gave him a droll smile. "Really?"

He hooted softly. "You remind me a lot of your sister, did you know that?"

Hannah's smile disappeared instantly. "I hope so. I would consider that a compliment."

Before David could answer back to that, a shout went up to their left. Captain Grant had his hat off and was waving it in the air. "All right," he yelled. "Let's move out."

David was still holding young Aaron, and so he walked around to the back of the heavily laden cart. He reached out with one hand and felt until he found a soft spot, and then he plopped the boy into it. "There you go, young man." He took Aaron's blanket and tucked it around his legs. "You just hang on."

He turned back to the others. "I'll take the first turn at pulling."

Ingrid nodded quickly. "It is Hannah's turn to pull too. I push. Sister Jackson, you can walk with the girls."

Hannah gave Ingrid a sharp look, which she blandly ignored and which caused David to chuckle softly. He went forward and lifted the shafts and slipped under them. He motioned for Hannah to join him. "Shall we?" he asked.

"Oh!" It came out as a soft cry of dismay and brought David's head around to look at her. Hannah looked away, not wanting him to see the fear in her eyes.

David nodded grimly, taking in the scene before them. They were standing on the banks of the Sweetwater River about two miles south of Devil's Gate. The river had been on their right hand all the way from Devil's Gate, meandering in and out in sinuous curves, most of the time between steep banks three or four feet above the water. Here there was a gentle slope down to the riverbank, whether man-made or not, David could not tell. About forty feet farther east, or downstream, there was another cut in the bank on the far side. This was the ford that Captain Grant had talked about.

On the other side of their cart, the Roper family, who shared the tent with the Jacksons and Hannah and Ingrid, stared at the river without speaking. There was a movement behind David and he turned to see Stephen Taylor join them. His wagon was stopped a few rods back from where the handcarts were starting to collect before crossing. David's friend took one look and let out a soft exclamation. "Uh-oh!" he said. "This isn't going to be easy."

David nodded. The sight was daunting, to say the least. Compared to other river crossings, this would not have been worthy of comment under other circumstances. The Green, the North Platte—now, *those* were rivers and usually required ferrying. This was no more than two feet deep and maybe thirty or forty feet across. The current was not terribly swift but enough that you would have to steady yourself against it. The water was clear, and through it he could see that the creek's bottom was sandy, not rocky. That was good in one way. It would not be as slippery as rocks. But it was bad in another. The sand would be soft and the wheels would be more likely to bog down in it.

But none of that was what made him sick to his stomach. It was everything else. The current in the center of the channel was swift enough that it had prevented the water from freezing, but both banks were lined with ice two or three feet out on both sides. Where it met the open water, the ice, two or three inches thick at the banks, tapered off to where the current had formed a knife-sharp edge. Chunks of the ice had broken off and were floating downstream. David made a mental note to watch those and the edges of the ice. Either would be capable of cutting bare flesh, he guessed.

If it had even been straight across, it might not have been so bad. But now as they watched, Captain Grant and Robert Burton were taking the first two carts across. They went down into the water, then turned right and headed downstream. You could see the wheels of the heavily loaded carts sink into the soft sand, roiling the water. They really had to lean into the carts to keep them moving. They moved about forty feet downstream before they turned left again and went out the far side. That downstream turn made the actual crossing more like eighty or ninety feet across and doubled or tripled the time one had to stay in the water.

As she saw the first to cross turn toward the granite mountains, Hannah had to look away. Memories of their experience at the last crossing of the North Platte suddenly overwhelmed her and she shuddered involuntarily. "I can't," she whispered.

David turned to her. To her surprise, he laid a hand on hers. "Yes, Hannah, you can. I'll take the cart."

She shrank back, staring at the water, then closed her eyes. "Oh, dear mercy!"

David turned and Hannah opened her eyes again. Coming up alongside them was John Jaques and his wife, Zilpah. Zilpah carried their baby—the one who had been born at Florence—in her arms. Their daughter, Flora, just two, was perched atop their cart. With them was Brother Jaques's mother-in-law, Amy Loader, and her two daughters, Patience and Tamar. Brother Jaques lowered the cart slowly and took a step forward, peering down at the river. "Heaven have mercy," he whispered. "How are we to cross that?"

From behind him there was a strangled sob. Hannah turned. It was Patience. She was pale as death, and tears were streaming down her face. Then Hannah remembered that last night Sister Jackson had come back to their tent and reported that Patience and Sister Loader were not feeling well. Brother Jaques had inquired if they might ride with the sick today, but the wagons were already loaded.

Patience looked up and saw David and Stephen Taylor looking at her. She turned away in shame, pulling her bonnet down over her face so that they couldn't see her tears. Hannah looked away too, afraid that in a moment she might have to do the same.

Suddenly Stephen Taylor left David's side and went over to stand in front of Patience. He reached out and touched her softly on the shoulder. "Ma'am?"

She looked up slowly, blinking back the tears. "Yes?"

"If you're not averse to riding on my back, I'd be happy to take you across the river."

She stared at him for a moment. He nodded, smiling his encouragement, then turned around and went down to a crouch. Patience turned and looked at her mother, then to her brother-in-law. John Jaques nodded. "Go," he whispered. In a moment, Sister Loader nodded as well. Sniffing and wiping at her eyes, Patience gingerly climbed on the young man's back. Stephen Taylor was not particularly tall, but he had a stout build and like most farm boys was in excellent physical strength. "Hang on," he said, and without hesitation he walked down the bank and into the river. David heard him gasp as he stepped into the water.

"Stay here," David said to Hannah, lowering the cart and stepping out of it. As he walked toward the Jaqueses' cart, he spoke to Ingrid and Sister Jackson. "Wait here. I'll come back."

He went straight to the older woman beside the Jaqueses' cart. "Sister Loader?"

She was staring at her daughter and the young man staggering downstream amidst the floating ice. She turned in surprise.

"I would consider it an honor to take you across as well," David said. He dropped to one knee. She hesitated only a moment, then nodded.

Amy Loader was a thin and frail woman, but David still was shocked by how much she weighed. He tried not to grunt as he stood up, then started for the water.

"Be careful, David!"

He turned and flashed Hannah a smile. "I'll be back."

The wagons had crossed first to break through the ice and make an opening in the ford. As David stepped off into the water, he heard himself cry out, barely aware that it was his voice as the stunning shock of the water hit his legs and feet. It was as if someone had slammed them with a hammer, then slammed them again and again. Then gratefully, as he got to the center of the river and the water reached his knees, they began to numb. Now he was aware that they were sinking into the soft sand. Fighting to keep his balance, he fought his way downstream. Just as he reached the place where he turned right to go up the far bank, Stephen Taylor strode into the water again. He was breathing hard and pounding his gloved hands together. "I'll go get another one," he said between breaths. "Watch out for the ice," he warned. "It's got sharp edges."

David carried Sister Loader up to where her daughter was waiting, then let her slip to the ground. "There you go."

The woman was weeping and reached out and clung to his hands. "Thank you, young man. Thank you."

He squeezed her hands back. "I'll go get your other daughter."

"The other young man already has her," Patience said, pointing.

David turned and saw that Stephen Taylor was coming across with Tamar on his back. And behind him, Allen Huntington was just swinging Sister Jaques and her baby up into his arms. Back in David went, passing the others with a grim nod. He went back across the river, then straight to Hannah, Ingrid, and Sister Jackson and her girls. He pointed to Martha Ann. "You're next," he said with a forced grin. His feet ached terribly and he could feel the water squishing around in his boots. He took the seven-year-old on his back and started away. Seeing a movement out of his eye, he turned. Hannah was following behind him. "No," he said sharply. "You wait."

"I can do it," she said. "You can't keep going back and forth. Your feet will freeze."

"Not if I keep moving," he said, brooking no argument. "Now, you stay here."

He didn't wait for her response. Back into the river he went, grateful for the lighter weight this time.

Now there were several other members of the rescue party shuttling women and children across. David went back and got Mary Elizabeth, who was four. She was light enough that he took little Aaron in his arms and took both across. On the next trip he took

Sister Jackson. Halfway through the downstream portion he felt something strike the back of his legs with a sharp blow. His knees nearly buckled and he had to stumble forward quickly to recover his balance. He caught himself and looked down as a chunk of ice two feet wide and twice that long spun slowly out and around him and continued downstream.

When he came back to the cart, Hannah and Ingrid were bouncing up and down on the balls of their feet trying to keep themselves warm. Then Hannah stepped forward, watching him closely. "You're limping," she said.

He nodded. "A piece of ice struck me in the leg. It's—"

Suddenly Ingrid took a sharp breath, pointing. "It's bleeding."

Surprised, he extended his leg out behind him and looked down. Just below the knee there was a jagged tear in his trouser leg and a three-inch gash in the flesh. It was still streaming blood, which was being diluted as it hit the dripping cloth of his trousers.

"Oh, David," Hannah cried.

He shook his head. "It's all right. The cold water will stop the bleeding. Which one of you is next?"

"Take Ingrid," Hannah said.

Ingrid started to protest, but David turned and knelt down again. "Hurry. We've got to get out of the cold."

As Ingrid climbed on his back and David stood again, he half turned. The stragglers in the column were still approaching the crossing and another handcart was just coming up beside them. It was pulled by two men and there were three women at the back of it helping push.

As David started to turn to the river, he heard one of the men cry out. He turned back again and saw the nearest man looking at the river in horror. "Do we have to go across that?" he cried.

David nodded. It was a fairly obvious answer. Carts were moving through the water, and now a long string of those who had crossed was moving toward the mountain. The men of the rescue company were still shuttling the women and children across on their backs.

"Yes, you do, sir."

David turned. Stephen Taylor had just returned for another person. He was looking at the man who had spoken. "It's terribly cold," Taylor admitted, "but it's not that far across."

To David's surprise, the man dropped his head into his hands and his shoulders began to shake. "I can't go through that," he exclaimed. "I can't." He was sobbing convulsively now.

One of the women came around quickly from the back of the cart. She stepped to the man's side and put an arm around his shoulder. "It's all right, Jimmy," she said soothingly. "Don't cry. I'll pull the cart for you."

The man's head came up and now he was frantic. His eyes fixed on David, who still had Ingrid on his back. Then he jerked to look at Stephen Taylor. "Can you carry me across?"

Taylor turned and looked at David quickly. Then he turned back. "We're trying to get the women and children across first, sir. If you could wait–"

"No! I can't make it." It was obvious that the man was on the verge of hysteria. "Please!"

The woman turned, beseeching Stephen Taylor with her eyes. "I can make it on my own," she said.

"Do it," David said softly to his friend. "I don't think he can make it."

Stephen Taylor nodded and went forward. The man almost leaped upon his back, and Stephen turned and went into the river. David let him go first, then went in behind him. As they reached the center of the current and turned downstream, David slowed. The man was jerking his legs up high, trying to keep them out of the water, and it was throwing Stephen Taylor off balance.

"Please, brother," Stephen cried over his shoulder. "Hold still."

Just at that moment, one of Stephen's boots sunk in the sand and did not pull out as easily as the other. He leaned forward, trying to pull it free. The man on his back yelped in fright and began clawing at Taylor's neck.

Unfortunately the man threw his weight to the left just as Taylor leaned that way to pull his boot free. Down they went with a tremendous splash.

David leaped forward. "Hang on," he said to Ingrid as he reached down and grabbed the man's hand. Spluttering and flailing wildly, the man got to his feet, almost retching as he drew in huge breaths of air in his panic.

"It's all right," David said. "We've got you. The water isn't that deep." Then he helped Stephen Taylor get to his feet.

"Thanks," Stephen said, panting heavily, water dripping from his face. "I've got him."

It was nearly sundown when the men of the rescue company carried the last person over and helped bring the last carts through the Sweetwater River. Hannah and Ingrid and the Jacksons and the Ropers had gone on more than an hour before, following the long, straggling line that moved up the long, gentle slope toward where a deep depression in the granite wall opened before them.

As they watched the last cart roll away from them, David Granger turned to Stephen Taylor. His arms hung down and he felt himself weaving back and forth. Every muscle in his body ached with fatigue. He could no longer feel his feet, and as he looked down at his boots he saw the first little beads of water turning into ice. "Are you ready?" he asked.

"We've got to get to a fire," Stephen Taylor said. He looked around, almost in a stupor.

"One of the others took the wagon over," David said. "Remember?"

"Oh, that's right." That had been a lifetime ago. He reached out and took David's arm. "Let's go, then."

As they started forward, David glanced back at his injured leg. He was not the only one who had been cut by the floating ice today. Fortunately the bleeding had stopped long ago and now the flesh around the gash looked bluish white.

"How's your leg?" Taylor asked.

"What leg?" David responded.

There was a short, mirthless laugh. "Yeah, I know what you mean."

And with that the two of them increased their pace, going from a hobble to a more determined shuffle as they fell in behind the last cart and started toward the cove where they would stay for the night.

II

Sunday, 9 November 1856

For Hannah McKensie the next five days all blurred together. Once settled into what everyone was now calling Martin's Ravine, the Martin Company and the people of the Hodgett Wagon Company mostly stayed in their tents, fully clothed, rolled in their bedding to stay warm. They got up to have meals, to fetch water from the spring. The men who were still strong enough were sent to climb the granite rocks all around them and look for dead cedar trees they could cut down for firewood. Once a day they were called out for another assignment—the burial of the dead.

The weather was still very cold and the snow in the cove was deep. Though they were no longer on severely restricted rations, their food was still limited and meals were simple and never enough to satisfy the hunger. So basically they lay in their tents, talking quietly, occasionally reading when the sun was bright enough to penetrate their tent walls and provide enough light to read by.

Five days of that stultifying sameness. No wonder things seemed like a blur to her.

Hannah looked up in surprise when there was a soft scratching sound on the flap of their tent. She and Ingrid were curled up together beneath a single quilt, speaking with low voices. Sister Jackson had her three children under blankets singing songs softly together. The Ropers were seated together on the opposite side of the tent. They too were wrapped in blankets and quilts and clutched them tightly. Brother Roper was telling his children a fairy tale and actually had them giggling from time to time.

Sister Jackson started to get up, but Brother Roper waved her back. "I'll get it."

He threw off his quilt and crawled over to the center of the tent before standing up. He moved to the flap and opened it.

"Hello."

Hannah came up to a sitting position with a jerk as she heard the voice.

"Good afternoon, Brother Granger," Brother Roper said. "Come in."

Now the others were all getting up too. Ingrid gave Hannah a surprised look, but Hannah was frantically trying to straighten her dress, smooth her hair, and scrub at a smudge of soot on her hand all at the same time.

David poked his head in, but came no farther. He looked around, smiling. "Hello, Sister Jackson."

"Hello, David. What a pleasant surprise!"

"Hello, David." Martha Ann and Mary Elizabeth sang it out in chorus. Little Aaron got to his feet and waved happily.

"Hello, girls. Hi there, young man."

Brother Roper held the tent flap open more widely. "Won't you come in?"

David shook his head. He turned now and looked at Ingrid and Hannah. "Hello to you two. How are you?"

"Fine," Hannah said. "Very good," responded Ingrid.

He looked back at Sister Jackson. "I was wondering if I might have your permission to speak with Hannah for a few minutes."

Elizabeth Jackson smiled warmly. "Of course. Thank you for asking."

Hannah scrambled to her feet and reached for her woollen bonnet. Since she was fully clothed other than that, there was nothing more to get. She moved quickly to the flap, tucking her hair beneath her bonnet, glad for a chance to hide it. As she stepped outside, David moved back to give her room.

She blinked for a moment at the brightness of the light. It was not a sunny day, but with all the snow it was a bit dazzling to her after being in the tent all morning. Then in a moment, knowing that every ear inside that tent would be intently listening to find out what was happening out here, she smiled and pointed to one of the numerous paths through the deep snow. "Shall we walk?"

"If you are feeling up to it," he answered.

"I am more than ready to move," she said. "After five days of lying in bed most of the day, I think I am up to it."

"I'll bet, but that's wise. You're going to need your strength." She looked at him quickly at that, but he went on before she could comment. "How have you been?"

"Hungry. Cold." She smiled faintly. "Normal, like everyone else. How are you?"

"Good. So you've heard that you are leaving in the morning?"

"Yes. Will you—" She stopped. She had been about to ask him if he would be able to help them pull their handcart again, but she decided that that was too forward. "Did you walk out here from Devil's Gate all by yourself?" she asked instead.

He shook his head. "No, I came by horse. And Brothers Grant and Burton needed to talk with Captain Martin. I came with them."

"And how are things at Devil's Gate?"

"Good. All of the Hodgett Company wagons are unloaded and the freight is cached away. They're still working on the ones that came in with Captain Hunt, but there are finally enough wagons to carry most of the baggage and many of the people. That's why Captain Grant thinks it's time to leave."

She let her eyes rise to the steep hillside just to their left. Martin's Ravine—or the cove, as some called it—was formed by a huge U-shaped gouge in the granite mountain wall. All around them the massive sheets and folds of solid rock rose dramatically, studded here and there with cedar trees, now frosted white with snow. But in the center of the huge semi-circle, cutting the cove in half like the prow of a great ship, was a towering sand dune. Over the centuries tons and tons of sand had been blown in here by the wind. The cove provided a leeward shelter, and so like an enormous snowbank, this sand ridge had grown until now it loomed almost a hundred feet above them, the sides of it so steep that it was all a person could do to climb up it. Hannah had done that once since coming here, and walked around the edge of the dune so she could see down into the cove itself. It had been a sight that she would never forget. Dozens of tents covered with snow, the thin trails from tent to tent beaten by the emigrants' feet. Here and there she could see the tracks of individuals who had climbed up the granite mountainsides a short distance in search of firewood. At the north end of the cove, she had looked down at the spot where the snow had been disturbed. Dark soil showed in several spots, marks of the grave diggers' shovels.

"It's time to go," she said, trying to blot that image out of her mind. "Did you know that as of this morning we have had fifty-six deaths since coming here?"

"Yes." David spoke in a hushed voice tinged with horror. "Brother Martin reported that to Captain Grant today."

"That's more than ten a day, David. No wonder they've decided it's time we move on."

"Yes. And not just that. Food is running low again. With almost a thousand people, even eight wagonloads doesn't last long."

She looked up at him, noticing the way his hair poked out from beneath his hat, and the goodness she saw in his eyes. "I guess no more wagons have come from Salt Lake?"

There was a brief shake of his head. "No. Brother Young and Brother Garr will send word for them to come when they find them, but if they are at South Pass it could be several more days before they make it this far."

That was not a surprise. When Elder Martin sent word around the camp this morning that they would start west again tomorrow, he had said that very thing. It would take three or four days for the express riders to reach South Pass and then six or seven more for the wagons to come on this far. They couldn't wait any longer. It would be just a week tomorrow since Joseph Young and Abel Garr had left for Salt Lake.

She shook her head. Only a week? It seemed like a month ago that they had crossed the river and moved up here to Martin's Ravine. She looked down at his feet. "How's your leg?"

He shrugged. "Healing." He didn't tell her that he was still having intense pain in his feet, especially at night when he was no longer up and moving on them. What purpose was there in that? He wasn't the only one of those who had spent that day in the river who was still feeling the effects of the frigid water.

He stopped, reaching out to take her arm and stop her as well. "Hannah?"

She looked up at him, pulling back her scarf so that it left her face free. "Yes?"

"I was going to ask Captain Grant for permission to help you and the Jacksons again."

"You were?" She felt a rush of pleasure.

"Yes. I guess you're going to leave most of the handcarts here, but even with all the wagons available now, they are afraid some are still going to have to walk. I thought—"

"That would be wonderful, David. We already owe you a great debt."

His shoulders lifted and fell. "There was a meeting today at the camp."

"Oh?"

"It's been decided that Brother Dan Jones is going to stay at Devil's Gate until spring. He'll keep a group of men with him to guard all the freight that has been cached now."

She had a sinking feeling as she looked at his face. "And?" she asked quietly.

"And I've been assigned to be one of those who stay."

There was no missing the dejection on his face, and in spite of the instant stab of keen disappointment, it thrilled her to think that that might be because of his having to be away from her. "Did you volunteer?" she asked.

"No. No one did. The assignments were made by the committee." He looked away. "There are some who aren't happy about it." Then he laughed shortly. "Who would be? But someone has to do it."

"I understand."

"Will you be all right?" he asked.

She thought about that, then nodded slowly. "Yes. We are doing better, considering. The rest has been good. Like everyone, we wish there was more food."

"That's why you can't wait any longer. And besides. Those mountain passes around Salt Lake are going to be a challenge to keep open too. They can get twenty to thirty feet of snow in a winter."

"I know."

They stood there together for a moment, neither speaking. Then to her surprise, he reached inside his coat and pulled out a folded sheet of paper. He was suddenly nervous.

As she looked at it more closely, she saw that it was folded on all four sides and then sealed with what looked like candle wax. He held it out to her.

"What's this?"

"Can you take a letter to the Valley for me?"

"Of course. To your mother?"

He laughed, this time with some amusement. "No. To yours."

"What?"

"Promise me you won't read it, that you'll just take it to your mother."

"Of course, but . . ." She was gazing at him quizzically.

"I know. It's strange, but then, my sister Eleanor says I am strange."

"I would like to meet her."

"You will. Once you get to the Valley and get settled a little, will you go see my family and tell them I'm all right?"

"Yes, of course."

"Good."

He fumbled at his coat buttons for a moment. "I hope all is well with your family, Hannah. They should be almost to the Valley now."

"I can't believe that could ever happen."

"I have one other favor to ask."

"What?"

"When you see her, will you give your sister Maggie a hug for me and tell her thank you?"

Now she smiled up at him. "I will." There was a moment's hesitation. "Except for one thing."

"What's that?"

"I don't have a hug from you to give to her."

"Ah," he said with deep satisfaction. And with that he took her gently in his arms and held her tightly for a long time.

III

Monday, 10 November 1856

When the Edward Martin Company, along with the Hodgett Wagon Company, left Martin's Ravine on the morning of the tenth of November, after spending six days there waiting for the weather to soften, Captain Martin told the people that they should come along at their own pace. He was no longer going to try to keep the whole company together in tight order. The original plan had been to put all of the people and their baggage into the Hunt and Hodgett wagons and abandon the rest of the handcarts. As it turned out, they seriously miscalculated. Because they had not arrived at Devil's Gate until later, the Hunt Company had not finished unloading their freight and caching it away, and so there weren't nearly enough wagons after all. Only a few handcarts were needed to come on, but there were still a lot of people who were going to have to walk. Making the decision as to who would walk and who wouldn't, when it was no longer based strictly on physical weakness, became extremely painful. By the time it was made, Captain Martin knew there was no sense in trying to hold them all together, at least not that day.

So they moved out as they were ready, the last not leaving for almost an hour after the first wagons had pulled out. By noon the column of wagons, walkers, and the few remaining handcarts was strung out across a mile and a half of trail, like a long dark piece of yarn being dragged slowly forward through the snow.

By midafternoon the Jacksons and the Ropers had fallen back to somewhere near the end of the column. They barely noticed. Hardly anyone spoke now and few heads came up to take stock of the situation. They plodded doggedly onward, trying not to think about how much longer this never-ending nightmare was going to last.

It had been a solitary three days for Ephraim Hanks. Since he had stopped just this side of South Pass and camped with Reddick Allred, he had not seen another human being. Reddick and his men were still camped with the supply wagons—now supplemented with additional wagons from the Valley—near the Sweetwater, waiting for word from Captain Grant. By then another howling high plains blizzard had struck. Ephraim had crossed South Pass with his single wagon, his horses plowing through snow up to their bellies, and knew he had to let them rest.

Undeterred by the storm, he asked Brother Allred for a good riding horse and a packhorse and left his wagon and teams behind. In spite of the warnings from some of the men that he was crazy to set out in such weather on his own, he turned his face east and rode out that morning. Since then he had not seen another living human being. The first night, Providence had provided him with a nice, fat buffalo bull that had come almost right into his camp, and he spent the night in the snow rolled up warmly in a thick buffalo robe.

Then this morning, as he was crossing Ice Springs Bench, a low flat ridge just west of Ice Springs, to his surprise he came across another buffalo, this time a large, fat cow. Individual buffalo were a bit of a rarity in and of themselves, but by this time of year the buffalo were mostly headed for the lower country where the winds weren't quite so cold and the snow so deep.

Deciding that there might be some Providence in this as well, Ephraim had dropped the animal with one well-placed shot, then spent two hours cleaning her out and cutting the quarters into long strips that quickly froze. When he started on his way again, his packhorse was loaded down with about three hundred pounds of buffalo meat, and he carried another hundred tied to the back of his saddle.

He was glad that along this stretch of the Sweetwater he had the long range of granite mountains off to his left. Any signs of the trail were well buried in the snow, and even as well as he knew that trail, he was glad for the mass of rock hillsides to help him keep his bearings.

It was about an hour away from sundown, and he knew that he was going to have to find a place to camp one more time before he reached Devil's Gate. He let his eyes sweep across the great expanse of white, searching for what he knew should be there. He grunted softly. There it was. About two miles away a small clump of trees showed dark against the snow. He didn't have to guess what they were. He knew they were cottonwoods because he had camped beneath their shelter many times. Also he knew because Cottonwood Creek was the only real water between where he was now and Devil's Gate.

He half turned in the saddle, gauging the height of the lowering sun. He knew from experience that once the sun set behind those hills, it would get dark and cold very quickly.

"Whoa, boy!" he said softly, reining up. He stood up in the saddle, rising as high as possible. He was peering intently directly east. "What in the world . . . ?"

Because Ephraim Hanks was a man who made his living crossing the wilderness, his eyes were trained to pick out anything that didn't belong to nature. At first he thought that what he saw was another line of trees, along a creek or maybe the course of a small spring. But he shook that off immediately. First of all, once you passed Cottonwood Creek, there was nothing except the Sweetwater until you approached Devil's Gate. Second, this wasn't the natural winding of growth along a water course. It was straight as an arrow for almost a mile.

And then there was a sharp intake of breath. "Well, I'll be!" he exclaimed. He lifted a hand, squinting hard now to make sure he had seen it correctly. After a moment he dropped heavily back into the saddle. There was no mistake. That dark line was moving very slowly toward him. And he could see the round tops of many wagons.

He dug his heels into the side of his horse, yanking on the lead rope of the packhorse. "Let's go, boy! I think we've found 'em."

"Mama! Mama! Mama!"

Elizabeth Jackson nearly dropped the pole of the tent she was holding as she whirled around.

Martha Ann came darting around one of the wagons, and nearly went down as she tried to corner in the snow and her feet slipped beneath her.

"Hold it," Brother Roper exclaimed, "don't let go. I've almost got it."

Sister Jackson turned back and pulled the tent pole tight again. On the other side of the tent, Hannah held another pole. Ingrid and Sister Roper were opposite Hannah holding yet another. Brother Roper grabbed a tent peg, pulled the rope taut, then scraped the snow off the ground with the side of his boot. Using the blunt end of a small hatchet, he hammered the stake into the half-frozen earth.

"Mama! Guess what!"

"Just a minute, dear."

Finished, Brother Roper came around and got the rope that would hold up Sister Jackson's tent pole. Martha Ann was jumping up and down, barely able to contain herself. As Sister Jackson felt the pole straighten of its own accord, she let go and stepped back. "All right, Martha Ann, what has got you so excited?"

"There's a man on a horse."

"Okay," she said slowly, a little puzzled. Several of the rescuers rode horses. She wasn't sure why that sight would surprise her daughter.

Martha Ann saw the doubt in her mother's eyes. "No, Mama. From Salt Lake. The man's from Salt Lake. And he's giving away buffalo meat."

Every head turned. Being among the last ones to arrive, they were on the eastern outskirts of the camp. They were staring now towards the western side of their encampment. And now that they had stopped working, they could clearly hear a great commotion coming from that direction.

Martha Ann grabbed her mother's coat, tugging on it frantically. "Hurry, Mama," she wailed. "He's giving it away and we won't get any."

—❦—

Hannah could not take her eyes away from Ephraim Hanks's hands. As he held them out to the fire, they looked huge. His fingers were long and narrow, his knuckles prominent. In the firelight she could see that they were heavily callused and that there was a long white scar on the back of one. She kept glancing up at his weathered face half-hidden beneath a full beard, the long hair that fell loosely around his shoulders, the buckskin jacket with its dancing fringes, but it was those magnificent, expressive hands that drew her eye back again and again.

It was a large fire, perhaps as much as fifteen feet across at the base. The boys from the Valley had dragged in a lot of firewood from the river, and now the central campfire roared and sent embers spinning up and up into the darkness. All around, the people gathered in as closely as they could. Hannah guessed that two or three hundred of the company had come to stare at this man who had so miraculously ridden into their camp and begun delivering chunk after chunk of deep-red buffalo meat, marbled richly with veins of fat. Even now the smell of cooking meat—real meat—seemed to linger in the air. It was intoxicating, even now that they were full.

Captain Grant raised his hands for silence, though at the moment no one was speaking. Everyone was just watching their deliverer in quiet fascination. "Brothers and sisters, Brother Hanks comes as a direct answer to our prayers. As he told me how it is that he happens to be out here all alone with two horses loaded down with buffalo meat, I thought it would be well for you to hear his story. I know that there have been a few who have begun to wonder if God has forsaken us. Well, I think Brother Hanks can answer that for you." He turned. "Brother Ephraim, we would be pleased to have you share with us what you will."

The man stirred slightly, looking a little embarrassed. When she had first seen him, Hannah had thought he was in his late forties or early fifties. Now up close she could see he was closer to thirty, though his face was well weathered by a lifetime in the sun. And the snow, no doubt.

"Brothers and sisters," the bearded man began slowly, "I don't much feel comfortable blowing my own horn, but Captain Grant is right. The hand of the Lord is in this and I've been privileged to be His instrument. And that story is worthy of telling, but the glory is His, not mine."

He leaned back, lifting one knee and locking his hands around it. "I had, of course, heard that there were two handcart companies still out here and that a great rescue effort had been launched by President Young. I couldn't get you folks out of my mind. I kept wondering how you were getting on, especially when the early snows came. Along with everyone else, I was trying to get some things together to see what I might do to help.

"Well, this one night, I think it was about the twenty-fourth of October, I had been down at Utah Lake doing some fishing. I was after a load of fish to sell that time, not just a string for supper. Well, on my way back home, I stopped at the home of a good friend of mine in Draper—that's down in the south part of the Valley. My friend's name is Gurney Brown. Gurney put me up for the night, and being tired, I went right to bed after supper.

"Though the bed was comfortable enough, for some reason I couldn't get to sleep. I tossed and turned like a wild man. Finally, I had just dropped off, when I heard someone calling me. 'Ephraim!' the voice said. Well, that's my name, so I said, 'Yes?' At first I thought it might be Gurney, but it wasn't."

Now his voice took on a low, almost mournful sound. " 'The handcart people are in trouble and you are wanted. Will you go and help them?' I tell you, my heart was like to have pounded right out of my body."

Hannah felt a prickling sensation at the back of her neck. She looked at Ingrid, but she was staring at Brother Hanks in total concentration.

He took a deep breath, looking around at the wide eyes which stared at him. "I turned instinctively in the direction from whence the voice came and beheld an ordinary-sized man in the room. Without any hesitation I answered, 'Yes, I will go if I am called.' I then turned around to go to sleep, but had lain only a few minutes when the voice called a second time, repeating almost the same words as on the first occasion. My answer was the same as before. This was repeated a third time."

Now there was not a sound except the crackling and popping of the fire. Every person was leaning forward to catch his words.

"Well, I tell you, I got right out of bed and told Gurney to get my team hooked up. Sister Brown, she cooked me up some breakfast and I was on my way. I got to Salt Lake from Draper about daybreak, and what should happen but right then I met a messenger from Brother Brigham. He was on his way to come fetch me to go out and help with the handcart people."

He looked up at George D. Grant for a moment, then looked into the fire. He held out those huge hands and rubbed them together, as though they were still cold. "Seems like since I was a boy, the Lord has always been willing to keep in touch with me if I'd keep in touch with Him. Here's the way I got it figured. The Lord isn't going to fool around with any of His gifts just to impress folks. I do know that when a body needs the Lord, needs something the Lord can do for him, so bad that there isn't any other way out, that is the time that the Lord will show His face or His voice."

He stopped, as if lost in memory. "Just after leaving Reddick Allred, had me another interesting experience with a bull buffalo I'll tell you about some other time. But anyway, I got my wagon ready and started east as quickly as possible. When the snow got too deep at South Pass, I traded Brother Allred for these two horses."

Now a smile lit his eyes and he looked around, more jovial now in his countenance. "Yes, the Lord does strange things, but I notice He always counts on human folks to help Him out. Now, I've traveled this road time and again, and at this time of year I wouldn't ever have expected to meet a buffalo there on Ice Springs Bench. But you folks needed meat and that fat old buffalo cow was put right in my way. Now, I'll tell you, if I hadn't been there, or if I couldn't have brought her down . . ." He laughed softly. "Well, anyway, the way I figure it, the Lord wouldn't have bothered to have it there if we couldn't take advantage of it, that's all."

There were appreciative chuckles all around the circle. At that moment Ephraim Hanks could have asked anything from that company and they would gladly have given it to him. And Hannah would have been first in line to do so if asked.

"Now, my brothers and sisters, I know you think that two horses packed to the haunches with rich, fat buffalo meat is about the best news you could have, right?"

Several called out at that. "Yes!" "Amen!" "None better!"

He smiled slowly, his teeth showing like a line of ivory in the darkness of his beard. "Well, I have something better than that to say to you."

Even Captain Grant seemed surprised. "Really, Ephraim? What's that?"

"A couple of nights ago I met Brothers Joseph Young and Abe Garr, riding like the wind for Salt Lake City, bearing a letter for President Young from Brother Grant here."

"Good," Captain Grant said. "Were they making good time?"

"Best as could be expected with all this snow." Now he turned and looked around at the circle of faces. "I told them about Reddick Allred waiting near South Pass with wagons filled with food and clothing and I told them boys to give Brother Allred the word that you folks are in need and to get them wagons rolling, no matter how deep the snow or how cold the wind. Brothers and sisters, I can promise you this. Help now is only a day or two away."

Chapter Notes

The last crossing of the Sweetwater, a mile or two west of Devil's Gate, proved to be the most difficult and daunting of the whole trail experience for the Martin Company. The temperature had plunged to well below zero, and while the ford was neither that wide nor that deep, in the impoverished condition the company was in by then, it proved to be, as John Jaques said, "a severe operation to many of the company" (in Bell, *Life History and Writings of John Jaques,* p. 160; also in *Remember,* p. 28). The details given here—including Patience's hiding her face, "Jimmy's" emotional collapse and then his being accidentally dumped in the water anyway, and the damage from the floating ice—all come from the accounts of those who experienced that terrible day (see *Remember,* pp. 28–29). John Jaques's grandson said that his grandfather carried scars inflicted by the ice for the rest of his life (in Bell, *Life History and Writings of John Jaques,* p. 161).

Some of the accounts credit three young men with the heroic act of carrying the emigrants across the river; others say there were four. Those named are David P. Kimball, seventeen; George W. Grant, eighteen (son of George D. Grant, the rescue company captain); Stephen Taylor, twenty-one; and C. Allen Huntington, twenty-five (see Hafen and Hafen, *Handcarts to Zion,* pp. 132–33; Bell, *Life History and Writings of John Jaques,* p. 160; *Remember,* p. 28). Daniel W. Jones, who was also there that day, makes this comment: "We did all we possibly could to help and cheer the people. Some writers have endeavored to make individual heroes of some of our company. I have no remembrance of any one shirking his duty. Each and everyone did all they possibly could and justice would give to each his due credit" (*Forty Years,* p. 70).

It is said that when President Brigham Young heard the reports of what the young men had done, he wept like a child and said, "That act alone will ensure [these men] an everlasting salvation in the Celestial Kingdom of God, worlds without end" (cited in Hafen and Hafen, *Handcarts to Zion,* p. 133). It has become a popular myth in the Church that these young men all died an early death as a result of their efforts that day. That they suffered the effects long after is true, but David Kimball lived to the age of forty-four and Stephen Taylor to eighty-six (see *Remember,* p. 142).

The various accounts differ in some of the details surrounding the Martin Company's departure from what is now called Martin's Cove near Devil's Gate. Some say the group left on the ninth of November; some say the tenth. Also, some say the Martin Company emigrants were met by Ephraim Hanks the same day they left, while another source says it was the following day. The author here has assumed they left on the tenth and met Brother Hanks just as they were making camp that evening at Cottonwood Creek.

A son of Ephraim Hanks, Sidney Alvarus Hanks, provides a rendition of Ephraim's story as told that November night at the campfire of the Read family. Ephraim himself later gave an autobiographical account to one of the early Church magazines. His speech in this chapter is taken almost word for word from those two accounts (see Sidney Alvarus Hanks, *The Tempered Wind,* pp. 37–39 [also in Bell, *Life History and Writings of John Jaques,* pp. 167–68]; "Ephraim K. Hanks' Narrative," in Jenson, "Church Emigration," pp. 202–5).

Just how remarkable this man was is shown by the following additional details from his history and one additional comment by Ephraim's son Sidney.

> The night after meeting Elders Young and Garr, I camped in the snow in the mountains. As I was preparing to make a bed in the snow with the few articles that my pack animal carried for me, I thought how comfortable a buffalo robe would be on such an occasion, and also how I could relish a little buffalo meat for supper, and before lying down for the night I was instinctively led to ask the Lord to send me a buffalo. Now, I am a firm believer in the efficacy of prayer, for I have on many different occasions asked the Lord for blessings, which He in His mercy has bestowed upon me. But when I, after praying as I did on that lonely night in the South Pass, looked around me and spied a buffalo bull within fifty yards of my camp, my surprise was complete; I had certainly not expected so immediate an answer to my prayer. However, I soon collected myself and was not at a loss to know what to do. Taking deliberate aim at the animal, my first shot brought him down, he made a few jumps only, and then rolled down into the very hollow where I was encamped. . . .
>
> . . . The sight that met my gaze as I entered their [the Martin Company's] camp can never be erased from my memory. The starved forms and haggard countenances of the poor sufferers, as they moved about slowly, shivering with cold, to prepare their scanty evening meal, was enough to touch the stoutest heart. When they saw me coming, they hailed me with joy inexpressible, and when they further beheld the supply of fresh meat I brought into their camp, their gratitude knew no bounds. Flocking around me, one would say, "Oh, please, give me a small piece of meat;" another would exclaim, "My poor children are starving, do give me a little;" and children with tears in their

eyes would call out, "Give me some, give me some." At first I tried to wait on them and handed out the meat as they called for it; but finally I told them to help themselves. Five minutes later both my horses had been released of their extra burden—the meat was all gone, and the next few hours found the people in camp busily engaged cooking and eating it, with thankful hearts. . . .

After dark, on the evening of my arrival in the hand-cart camp, a woman passed the camp fire where I was sitting crying aloud. Wondering what was the matter, my natural impulse led me to follow her. She went straight to Daniel Tyler's wagon, where she told the heartrending story of her husband being at the point of death, and in pleading tones she asked Elder Tyler to come and administer to him. This good brother, tired and weary as he was, after pulling hand-carts all day, had just retired for the night, and was a little reluctant in getting up; but on this earnest solicitation he soon arose, and we both followed the woman to the tent, in which we found the apparently lifeless form of her husband. On seeing him, Elder Tyler remarked, "I can not administer to a dead man." Brother Tyler requested me to stay and lay out the supposed dead brother, while he returned to his wagon to seek that rest which he needed so much. I immediately stepped back to the camp fire where several of the brethren were sitting, and addressing myself to Elders Grant, Kimball and one or two others, I said: "Will you boys do just as I tell you?" The answer was in the affirmative. We then went to work and built a fire near the tent which I and Elder Tyler had just visited; next we warmed some water, and washed the dying man, whose name was Blair, from head to foot. I then anointed him with consecrated oil over his whole body, after which we laid hands on him and commanded him in the name of Jesus Christ to breathe and live. The effect was instantaneous. The man who was dead to all appearances, immediately began to breathe, sat up in his bed and commenced to sing a hymn. His wife, unable to control her feelings of joy and thankfulness, ran through the camp exclaiming: "My husband was dead, but is now alive. Praised be the name of God. The man who brought the buffalo meat has healed him."

This circumstance caused a general excitement in the whole camp, and many of the drooping spirits began to take fresh courage from that very hour. After this the greater portion of my time was devoted to waiting on the sick. "Come to me," "help me," "please administer to my sick wife," or "my dying child," etc., were some of the requests that

> were made of me almost hourly for some time after I had joined the immigrants, and I spent days going from tent to tent administering to the sick. Truly the Lord was with me and others of His servants who labored faithfully together with me in that day of trial and suffering. The result of this our labor of love certainly redounded to the honor and glory of a kind and merciful God. In scores of instances, when we administered to the sick, and rebuked the diseases in the name of the Lord Jesus Christ, the sufferers would rally at once; they were healed almost instantly. I believe I administered to several hundreds in a single day; and I could give names of many whose lives were saved by the power of God. ("Ephraim K. Hanks' Narrative," in Jenson, "Church Emigration," pp. 203, 204; portions of this are also cited in *Remember,* pp. 33–34)

Ephraim's son added this poignant passage: "The next morning everyone in camp was talking about Brother Hanks, about his prayers for the sick, but even more the operations he had performed with his hunting knife. Many of the Saints were carrying frozen limbs which were endangering their lives. Brother Hanks amputated toes and feet and sometimes even legs. . . . First [he] anointed these folks and prayed that the amputation could be done without pain. Then when he took out his great hunting knife, held it in the fire to cleanse it, and took off the dying limb with its keen blade; many with tears in their eyes said they hadn't 'felt a thing'" (Sidney Alvarus Hanks, *The Tempered Wind,* p. 40).

From the journal entries, it is evident that even under the difficult conditions of the journey from Europe to Utah, normal life did not completely stop. There were births and deaths, romance and even marriage. The journals record several marriages on board ship as the emigrants crossed the Atlantic and some between company members once they arrived at the Valley (see Turner, *Emigrating Journals,* pp. 2, 5, 82, 83; Hafen and Hafen, *Handcarts to Zion,* p. 57). However, some readers may think that having romance blossom in the midst of the terrible crisis that struck the handcart companies is unrealistic. Note the following account:

> Another interesting bit of history gives us the story of a beautiful courtship between one of the rescue party, William M. Cowley, and a lovely English girl, who was a member of Martin's Company. This young girl, Emily Wall, . . . had been promised that [she] would reach Salt Lake City. . . . When she reached Devil's Gate where the company of rescuers met the party, one of the boys, William M. Cowley, who

> was a very young printer, came to her aid. In conversation with her he asked if some day she would marry him. Emily said she didn't know and told him he would have to write to England and get permission from her mother. Time went on and the youth was not seen again for three years, as he had been called to San Bernardino to set up a printing press. Upon his return he found the young lady at the home of President Young and asked her if she remembered his proposal. She had, but wanted to know if he had written to her mother. After being informed that a letter had been written to her mother and that an answer had come saying it was all right for them to be married provided he was a good man, Emily consented and the young couple were married. Twelve children were born to them and she remained his only sweetheart. (In Glazier and Clark, comps. and eds., *Journal of the Trail,* pp. 94–95)

And this one:

> James Barnet Cole went with them [the rescue party]. One night he dreamed he would meet his future wife with the stranded Saints. He even was shown what she looked like. She had a fur cap and a green veil tied over her cap to keep the wind off, and she was very beautiful. He told his dream to Brother [William] Kimball and he remarked, "We will see no beautiful girl with a fur cap and a green veil in these frozen Saints."
>
> Reminiscing, James Barnet Cole said that they saw the encampment [at Sixth Crossing] just as the sun was sinking in the west. . . .
>
> When the people caught sight of the train coming, they shouted, they cried, they threw off all restraint and freely embraced their deliverers. Just then, William Kimball caught sight of Lucy Ward in the green veil. He drove up to her and said, "Brother Jim, there is your dream girl." James asked her to get in the wagon and her reply was, "No, I don't know you." She got used to the idea of having him around, because on the way to Salt Lake, on November 2, 1856 [they met at Sixth Crossing on October 21], they were married at Fort Bridger by William Kimball. (In *Remember,* p. 138)

That story is verified by the entry for that day in the Willie Company journal: "James Coll ? of Fort Supply married Lucy Ward of the 4th handcart company at Fort Bridger in the evening" (in Turner, *Emigrating Journals,* p. 51).

BOOK 6

THE VALLEY

NOVEMBER – DECEMBER 1856

And if they die they shall die unto me, and if they live they shall live unto me.

Thou shalt live together in love, insomuch that thou shalt weep for the loss of them that die, and more especially for those that have not hope of a glorious resurrection.

And it shall come to pass that those that die in me shall not taste of death, for it shall be sweet unto them.

– Doctrine and Covenants 42:44–46

CHAPTER 32

GREAT SALT LAKE CITY

I

Sunday, 30 November 1856

"Folks?"

Hannah lifted her head and turned forward. Through the opening in the canvas, beyond the driver, she could see a snow-covered hillside rising steeply on one side of them. It was covered with scrub oak, now totally bare of any leaves. Directly ahead of them the trail was moving through a thick stand of trees, also devoid of any leaves.

Hannah was seated on a pile of empty flour sacks, her back braced against the side of the wagon. Sitting beside her in a similar position, Ingrid Christensen had her head down on her knees. She didn't look up. Neither did the other occupants in the wagon. Elizabeth Jackson was beneath a heavy quilt on the straw mattress that took up the back half of the wagon. She had her three children with her. Hannah could see that Sister Jackson's eyes were open, but the children seemed to be asleep. The other two occupants of the wagon, a man in his sixties and a woman who had lost her husband and two children at Martin's Ravine, also lay with their eyes open, staring up at the canvas above them. The two of them didn't even turn their heads.

"This is something you may want to see," the driver said, speaking softly so as not to wake the children.

Ingrid's head came up. Sister Jackson rolled over on her side and came up on one elbow. "What is it?" she asked.

"See up there through the trees?"

Ingrid leaned forward enough to see around Hannah. Sister Jackson came up to a full sitting position, readjusting the quilt so as to keep the children covered. Hannah was peering forward too. All she could see was blue sky. "I don't see anything," Hannah said, a little puzzled.

"Exactly," the man said with a smile.

For a moment Hannah wasn't sure why he seemed so pleased. He had always seemed a little gruff and distant to her. She didn't mind that. When he had first come up on the struggling emigrants, Hannah had seen the shock and dismay in his eyes. He was not much more than four or five years older than Hannah and Ingrid, and was clearly unprepared for the sight of the emaciated survivors. Hannah had watched his eyes as he took in their ragged, worn-out clothing, their tattered shoes and boots wrapped in burlap sacks, and their gaunt, haggard, frost-nipped faces. She realized that his outer manner was his way of dealing with it. He had been, in fact, very tender and solicitous in seeing to their needs for the last ten days.

So Hannah decided that if there was something important enough for him to disturb them, she would at least give him the courtesy of responding. She got up and crawled forward to the front of the wagon. "What do you mean, exactly?" she started to say, but suddenly she gasped. "Ingrid! Come look!"

Ingrid came forward too, as did Sister Jackson. The driver, smiling broadly at them, pulled back the canvas cover a little more as the three of them knelt behind him.

Ingrid drew in her breath sharply too. "Is that–?" She stopped, gaping.

Hannah reached out and found her hand, gripping it so tightly that Ingrid winced a little. Their eyes were wide, taking in the vast panorama that was opening before them. The hillsides on either side of the wagon were dropping off sharply. Since being rescued by Reddick Allred and the other wagons from the Valley, the Martin Company had abandoned their handcarts and all were riding in the wagons now. Their train had more than a hundred wagons in it and once on the road could snake out for as much as a mile. The wagon that Hannah and Ingrid were in was about halfway back in that column. Ahead of them, wagons were moving slowly down a long and gradual slope. A quarter of a mile ahead of them, the lead wagons were turning to the right, angling northwestward.

The man laughed softly, pleased at their reaction. "Yes," he said in answer to Ingrid's unfinished question, "this is the Valley. Welcome to Salt Lake."

"It's so big!" Sister Jackson said in awe.

Hannah was thinking the same thing. Everything was covered in snow, and in the bright sunlight of a clear, wintry day, the sight was dazzling. A wall of mountains directly in front of them, a good fifteen or twenty miles away, framed the western edge. A little to the left of that, blue as a robin's egg, was a huge body of water, with mountains rising from that as well.

"Is that the Great Salt Lake?" Ingrid cried, pointing now.

"Yes. The big island in the middle of it is Antelope Island. The Church runs its herds there in the summer."

"Then where is Salt Lake City–?" She got that far, and then Hannah stopped. Her eyes had been drawn to a dark cluster about five miles away. She could make out buildings and columns of smoke rising in the still air.

"That's it," the driver said. "Folks, you are almost home."

—❦—

Hannah was amazed at what she saw around her. She and Ingrid were in the wagon seat beside the driver now. Sister Jackson was kneeling on a flour sack behind them, peering out from between their shoulders. Martha Ann Jackson, Elizabeth's seven-year-old, was beside her mother, talking excitedly, pointing out this or that as her eyes fell on it. Mary Elizabeth and little Aaron were still sleeping. Behind Sister Jackson, the old man and the widowed woman still lay on their beds, listening to those who were up front talking, but too weak to get up and see for themselves.

Hannah had heard the missionaries talk so much about how empty and barren the Valley was when they arrived there, she somehow still had that picture in her mind. She expected a tiny cluster of mud huts and outbuildings and, other than that, nothing but sagebrush and coyotes, like what they had seen for most of the last four or five hundred miles. But while the Valley still was largely empty, there were signs of habitation everywhere. Beneath the snow she could see the outlines of plowed fields. Several were filled with the dried cornstalks or stubble from the wheat harvest. Numerous pastures were enclosed with rail fencing, and hundreds of cattle and sheep watched them curiously as they passed by. They passed a large orchard of peach trees as they made the right turn and started angling directly for the city. Peach trees? She had certainly not expected that.

"Where is everyone?" Sister Jackson asked the driver.

As they moved slowly northward, the signs of habitation were increasing markedly. And here again, Hannah was surprised at what they were seeing. There were a few small huts made of adobe bricks, as they called them, but there were solid log cabins and even a few nicely constructed frame homes as well. Barns and other outbuildings were everywhere evident. But so far they had seen only a few people here and there. At the sound of the passing wagons, they came out to watch the new arrivals pass. They waved and called out a welcome, but there were no more than half a dozen.

The driver shook his head. He seemed a little surprised himself. "It's Sunday. On Sunday everyone goes down to Temple Block for worship services." He said it lamely and it sounded like he didn't believe it himself.

"Oh," Hannah said, trying to hide her disappointment. She had hoped that her family would be waiting for them as they came out of Emigration Canyon. Captain Martin had told them it was tradition for the Saints to meet all incoming emigrant trains, usually down at a staging area near the city. But in light of the great effort to rescue them, he fully expected they would have their welcome near the mouth of the canyon.

It wasn't as if the people of the Valley didn't know they were coming. William H. Kimball, one of the leaders of the rescue company who had returned with the Willie group into the Valley, had ridden back out and found the Martin Company near South Pass. With additional wagons meeting them every day now and all of the emigrants finally riding in wagons, Captain Grant decided he could safely leave his charges with Major Robert Burton. Leaving the company near the Big Sandy River, he and Brother Kimball rode on ahead to the Valley to give President Young a report of their progress. And just yesterday, as they crossed over Big Mountain, they found a whole group of men tramping down the snow and keeping the trail open for them. They had been expecting them.

The teamster who was driving their wagon suddenly leaned forward. "Here comes Major Burton," he said.

Hannah leaned forward. There was a rider on horseback coming down the line slowly toward them and she too recognized the man who was leading them home. He was speaking to the occupants of each wagon as he came by. As he reached Hannah's group, their driver tipped his hat back. "Where's our welcoming party?" he called.

Robert Burton slowed his horse. "I think we caught them by

surprise," he said. "If you remember, we thought we'd be camping on the other side of Little Mountain last night. They're not expecting us until tomorrow."

"That's right," the teamster said. He looked at Hannah. "Having those men break trail for us really saved us some time."

"We've sent a rider on ahead," Brother Burton said as he moved on again. "By the time we reach the city, they'll know we're here. They'll be waiting in the streets to meet you."

Hannah's heart soared, the disappointment of a moment before vanished now. It wouldn't be long now and she would see her family again. She had gotten to speak to Brother William Kimball for only a moment there at the Big Sandy before he and Captain Grant left again, but it had been enough. Her family had survived, and she would see them now in just a few more minutes.

She turned to Ingrid. Ingrid's uncle and aunt would be waiting too. As she started to say that, she stopped. From the side, she could see that Ingrid was crying. Hannah reached out, her heart filled with affection for this sweet and wonderful friend the Lord had brought into her life.

"We're almost there," Ingrid cried softly.

To her surprise, when Ingrid looked at her, Hannah saw that these were not tears of joy. She was weeping in sorrow. "Ingrid? What's wrong?"

Her friend shook her head and swiped quickly at her cheeks.

"Tell me!"

Ingrid looked down, then lifted her feet, raising her skirts enough to show the boots she wore. When the supply wagons from South Pass had finally reached the Martin Company, most of the emigrants were given new shoes and boots. Ingrid's feet were so tiny that she had received a worn but serviceable pair of boy's boots. For the next several days, until sufficient wagons came, she and Hannah had been required to walk. The snow was deep, and day after day the boots would become soaked and have to be dried out at night before the fires. They showed that punishment now. The leather was cracked and split in several places. The laces were tied in makeshift knots where they had broken. Any color was long since gone.

And then, as Ingrid let her skirts drop and lowered her feet again, her lip began to tremble.

Now Hannah understood, and tears came to her eyes as well. She reached out and took Ingrid's hand. "It's all right, Ingrid."

"No," she cried in anguish. Then her voice dropped to a whisper. "I'm going to meet the prophet today, and all I have to wear are these ugly old boots."

Maggie McKensie sat beside Eric, feeling the hardness of the bench against her back and legs. Others grumbled about how uncomfortable these hand-hewn seats in the Tabernacle were, but she liked it. There was no slouching down here, no relaxing the body and letting the mind go wandering off. You sat with your back straight and your face turned naturally to the podium that marked the front of the cavernous building with its adobe walls and high triangular roof.

She thought back, trying to remember if she had ever been in a building with twenty-five hundred people. No, she corrected herself, not twenty-five hundred people. Twenty-five hundred Latter-day Saints. And the answer to that was a clear no. It still almost overwhelmed her. Here she sat in the midst of Temple Block. Just a stone's throw to the east of them, the foundations for the great temple were in place. Behind them was the Bowery, a bough-covered shelter used in the summer for larger congregations. Just beyond that was the newly completed Endowment House, where soon she and Eric would kneel before an altar and be married for time and all eternity. Up on the stand were the men whose names she had known and revered before, but now they were more than names. There in person sat their prophet, Brigham Young. On either side of him were his counselors, Heber C. Kimball and Jedediah M. Grant. Behind them were several of the Twelve. And all around her were other Latter-day Saints, hundreds upon hundreds of them.

Suddenly she remembered that day in Edinburgh almost ten months before. It was after her mother had announced they would be going to America, and Maggie, highly upset, had shared that news with James MacAllister. At that point she hadn't known that Eric Pederson even existed, and James MacAllister had been the most important thing in Maggie's life. She remembered now how she had tried to explain to him why the Mormons felt so strongly about going to America. No wonder she hadn't been able to convince him. How little she had known then!

It still filled Maggie with a sense of wonder, being here in the Valley. It was three weeks ago this very day that the Willie Company had come out of Emigration Canyon to the tumultuous welcome that awaited them. In the three short weeks since, her entire perspective had changed. With a rush of gratitude, she reached out and took Eric's hand. He turned and smiled. She smiled back and squeezed his hand.

She had heard the missionaries talk about "the Valley," always seeming to capitalize it with their voices. Now she understood why. It wasn't just a place. It wasn't even just "the right place," as Brother Brigham had said when he first saw it. It was what it meant, what it stood for, what it represented. It was safety and peace from marauding mobs. It was a place of refuge, a haven where one could live without fear. It was finding fellowship with the Saints instead of contempt and mockery and ostracism. It was Robbie walking home from school with newfound friends instead of fleeing from boys pelting him with rotten apples. It was a place where the children could be taught the values and standards and principles that would bring them the greatest joy and then could practice living those values and standards and principles in a setting that supported them. It was sitting in this tabernacle and listening to the words of Brigham Young as they came from his mouth instead of reading his talks months later in the *Millennial Star.* It was walking down the street and hearing people greeting one another as Brother This or Sister That. That was what the Valley was—and how grateful she was that God had not given her the desire of her heart, which was to stay in Edinburgh and marry James MacAllister.

She glanced to her right. On the other side of Eric, Maggie's mother sat with Robbie. And beyond them the James family. She still felt the loss when she saw Sister James sitting without her husband. She felt a touch of the old horror when she looked at Reuben's face and saw the sores that still were not completely healed and pictured the missing tips on several of his toes. But on the other hand, what a change had transpired in those three short weeks! Robbie's face had filled out again, and the smile that had almost disappeared for a time was back in full. His hair was neatly trimmed and combed back and he wore clean, warm clothing. The cracked lips, the snow-burned face, the haunted eyes were gone now.

What a day of celebration that had been when they gathered around the fire in the back of the Granger barn and threw their rags, their tattered shoes, their threadbare blankets and quilts into the flames! Something important had happened to Maggie that day. She would always have the memories of their experience—the days of gnawing hunger, the endless nightmare of Rocky Ridge, the shock at having Eric slap her face, the numbing grief of standing around that mass grave at Rock Creek and seeing the willows laid over the faces of William James, Olaf Pederson, little Jens Nielson, and Bodil Mortensen. But it was as though the worst of the horror of those days was tossed into the fire as well. The memories, though still present, were somehow purged and cleansed by the flames.

With that thought, she turned and looked on the other side of her. Here was the answer to how that healing had come. The Saints of the Valley had taken the haggard emigrants into their homes, fed them at their tables, clothed them from their wardrobes, nursed their frostbitten hands and feet. Truly these Valley Saints had taken the Savior's counsel to heart when He said, "I was a stranger and ye took me in." Now Maggie felt her eyes start to burn as the gratitude she was feeling threatened to completely overwhelm her.

Seated down the bench on the left side of her were the ones who had taken the McKensies in and followed the Savior's counsel. On impulse, Maggie reached out with her other hand and took Eleanor Granger's hand. The girl, just two years younger than Maggie, looked at her, surprised at the sudden gesture. Maggie could only smile at her, squeezing her hand just as she did Eric's. Again the memories flooded over Maggie McKensie.

As the handcart company was nearly swarmed under that day on the ninth of November, Maggie had noticed a young girl going around from wagon to wagon, obviously looking for someone specific. As the girl approached the wagon where the McKensies and the Jameses were, Maggie heard what she was asking. "Does anyone know of the whereabouts of David Granger? He was one of the rescuers."

Maggie called out to her, waving her over. Immediately a man and a woman and several other children came over to join her. The moment Maggie looked at the man, she knew he was David's father.

"We met David," she said. She was motioning for Eric and her mother to come over as well. "He brought us food and clothing at the Sixth Crossing."

"Is he with you now?" his mother asked anxiously.

Maggie's mother had answered. "No. Captain Grant took part of the company on to find Brother Martin's group. David went with them." Then Maggie's mother had begun to weep. "Your son was a godsend to us," she whispered. "Thank you for sending him out to us."

And that had done it. The Grangers opened their home to the McKensies and found a place for the James family on the neighboring farm.

Maggie felt a twinge of sorrow at the thoughts that they would be leaving the Grangers soon. The company that had come so far together, that had suffered and endured so much together, was already scattering. James G. Willie, their faithful captain, and the sub-captains would finally have a chance to be reunited with their families. Assignments to the various settlements were already starting to be made. Jens Nielson and Elsie, now childless, had been assigned to a settlement called Parowan, somewhere to the south. This couple, who could have bypassed so much suffering by keeping their money and coming west with the independent wagon companies, wouldn't leave until spring because Jens's badly frozen feet also needed time to heal. But little Elsie Nielson had saved her husband's life. Now they had a deed for twenty acres of land and would have a chance to start a new life there.

Dear Sister Bathgate and Isabella Park, the two intrepid walkers befriended by Eric who had been so determined to make it on their own, were safe and were going to stay here in the Valley. The James family had already left from the home down the street from the Grangers. They were sharing a farm with another family somewhere along the Jordan River, just a few miles south of the Granger place. Most of the Scandinavians would go to somewhere called Sanpete Valley, also to the south. For a time, Maggie had been afraid that Eric was going to be assigned to go with them, but Brother Granger, she learned later, had quietly reported their coming marriage to Brigham Young, and also the fact that they had family still coming in with the Martin Company. So they were on hold for now, but rumor had it that they too would be staying in the Valley, at least for a time.

And so it went. Names like Provo, Ogden, Bountiful, Nephi, Farmington, Lehi, Alpine, Heber City were being heard now as those in the Willie Company who had survived were given opportunity for a new life. The next to last group of handcart emigrants was finally in safely. There was no profit in lingering overly long on the ordeal they had experienced.

And with that thought, Maggie closed her eyes and silently offered yet again the same prayer she had given so many times before.

Oh, please, dear Lord, bring Hannah and Ingrid safely in. Let them return to us whole and well. And thank you for our safe arrival in the Valley.

It was noon when the meeting ended. Though the sun was shining brightly outside, this last day of November was still a cold one, and the people were not particularly anxious to go back out into it. When the "amen" of the congregation rumbled through the Tabernacle, the people stood up, but most of them stayed where they were, talking with those around them. A few started moving for the doors, but only slowly. Maggie and Eric stood quietly together, waiting for Maggie's mother and Sister James. They had not seen the Jameses for over a week now, and so this was a sweet chance to visit again. Maggie would wait until they moved out into the aisle, and then she wanted to go see Sarah and Emma and learn how their new home was. But just then Eleanor Granger tugged on Maggie's sleeve. When Maggie turned, Eleanor inclined her head toward the pulpit. "Look," she said.

Maggie turned. With everyone standing up, she wasn't sure at first what she was supposed to be seeing. But then as she glanced at the podium, where President Young and his counselors and the other leaders of the Church were gathered in small groups, Maggie saw someone who looked out of place. A man was standing at the side door closest to the podium. He was fully dressed for winter, with coat and hat and gloves still on. In a momentary break in the crowd, Maggie caught a glimpse of riding boots.

As Maggie watched, the man motioned in the direction of the First Presidency. It was Heber C. Kimball who saw him first and went over to see the man. They conferred quietly for several seconds; then Maggie saw President Kimball stiffen. He grabbed the man's arm. The man nodded vigorously. President Kimball spun around and walked swiftly back to President Young.

Now others were noticing what was going on up front and the

buzz of conversation began to die. People nudged each other and pointed. Soon many eyes were watching as Heber Kimball spoke quickly to Brigham Young. Brigham Young jerked around, staring toward the east, even though the building had no windows on either side through which to look out, then whirled back and motioned for the heavily clothed man to come over beside him.

"Brothers and sisters," Heber C. Kimball shouted. "Could we have your attention please."

Now the sound was cut off completely as everyone turned to see what was happening.

President Young stepped forward. "Brothers and sisters." His voice boomed across the large congregation. "As you know, the handcart company is nearing the Valley. We thought they might be arriving tomorrow and planned a warm welcome for them."

Suddenly Maggie was leaning forward on her feet, her breath caught and held. The new arrival had taken off his hat and scarf, and she saw that it was Joseph A. Young.

"Well," President Young said, clapping his hands in delight, "they have surprised us a little. My son has just arrived with some wonderful news."

As he came forward, his father laid a hand across his shoulder. "Tell them, Joseph."

There was a brief nod, and then the son leaned over, looking at the more than two thousand upturned faces. "My fellow Saints," he cried, "it is a great pleasure to announce to you the arrival of the Edward Martin Handcart Company, the fifth and last of this season."

The congregation exploded as surprise and astonishment swept through the crowd.

"How soon will they be here, son?" Brigham called. He already knew the answer, but he wanted the congregation to hear it too.

The noise stopped as cleanly as though chopped through with an ax.

Joseph A. Young smiled broadly. "At this very moment, the first of the nearly one hundred wagons are rolling up East Temple Street, no more than two or three blocks from where we now stand."

East Temple Street, as their driver called it, was surprisingly wide for the main street of a growing city. Once the wagons turned onto it at Five Hundred South Street, they began moving up alongside one another until they were three abreast. That brought the wagon in which Hannah and Ingrid and the Jacksons were riding up to where they were only ten or twelve rows back from the lead wagons.

Hannah and Ingrid were both on their feet now, standing on the wagon seat and trying to see around the wagons in front of them. The streets were not paved and the wagons were chewing the recent snow into a dozen tracks which showed the dirt beneath. But once again Hannah was surprised at what she was seeing. Business establishments lined the street on both sides. There were livery stables, blacksmith shops, millinery shops, dress shops, a dry goods store, an apothecary. After Edinburgh, it looked quite primitive, and perhaps ten months ago she might have sniffed a little at the sight. But after seeing nothing but Fort Laramie and the Platte Trading Post and Fort Bridger in the last three months, it was as if they had been dropped into the most wonderful and glorious place in all of existence.

"Do you see them yet?" Martha Ann Jackson called, tugging on Ingrid's coat.

"Not yet."

"We've still got another two blocks before we reach Temple Block. That's where they'll be meeting." The driver reached inside his coat and drew out a pocket watch from his vest pocket. He opened the lid, then nodded. "It's just a few minutes past noon. They'll be getting out soon." Then he chuckled. "Unless, of course, the Saints haven't been fully doing their duty. Then the brethren might keep them a little longer calling them to repentance."

Then suddenly he stood up as well. He grasped onto the bow of the wagon and leaned way out to the left. Their wagon was on the left side of the street, so he had a clear view all the way up past the other wagons. He straightened again and looked at his charges. A big, slow grin stole across his face. "I think the meeting's out."

"Why? Can you see them?" Hannah blurted.

"I think somebody must have given them the word," he said with forced nonchalance. "There are people pouring out of the gates of Temple Block like bees from a beehive."

The image that came to Maggie's mind was that of turning a stream of water loose into a sluice. If Joseph A. Young had any more to say to the crowd, no one heard it. With his announcement that the wagons were on the street just east of Temple Block, the people gave one roar of joy and headed for the doors. The Tabernacle was in the southwest corner of the block, and there were gates on all four sides. The closest was the one that emptied onto South Temple Street. Seeing most of the people head for that one and pile up as if someone had dropped a board in the sluice, Maggie grabbed Eric's hand and pointed to the east. "Let's go out that one," she cried.

Eric nodded. He had Sister McKensie by the arm, so he pushed forward in front of Maggie, then let go of her. "Stay right behind me," he called over his shoulder. "I'll make us a way."

"Hang on, Robbie," Maggie cried, grabbing at his coat as they rushed forward. The east gate was a good choice, but they still had to slow to what seemed like an agonizing crawl as the crowd packed in to push their way through the narrow portals. Once through the gate, the crowd boiled out into East Temple Street, spreading rapidly.

"There they are!" someone shouted.

Maggie went up on her feet, arching her neck, looking to the south. There was a half sob of joy. The whole of the street to the south of them, which sloped gently away from Temple Block, was filled with wagons. There were dozens of them, and she could see that there were people standing up beside the drivers, jumping up and down and waving their arms. Farther back, people were tumbling out of the wagons like beetles leaving a sinking gourd. "Yes, Mama! I see them. I see them."

After their own experience three weeks ago, Eric knew better than to just search for faces in the crowd. If the Martin Company was no different than the Willie Company, the wagons would be jammed with the sick and the weak as if with cordwood. "You watch the crowd," he shouted into Maggie's ear. "I'll check the wagons."

The street was pandemonium now. Wagons stretched as far down East Temple Street as he could see—a hundred at least, maybe more. Unfortunately the first wagons were like a dam in the river as everyone swarmed around them. As he started toward the nearest one, Eric saw Sister James and Emma and Sarah come in behind Maggie and her mother. Good. They could help. "Sarah, see if they are in these," Eric shouted, motioning at the first row of wagons. "We'll go further on down."

Sarah nodded, and she and her mother turned and started pushing their way in.

"Wait, Maggie," Emma shouted. "I'm coming with you." She darted forward, grabbing for Maggie's hand.

By the time they got to the fifth row of wagons, the crowd was thinning. It hadn't come this far yet. Now Eric leaped forward. "Do you have Hannah McKensie with you?" he called up to the teamster.

The man shook his head. "Not here."

Maggie was already at the back of the wagon on the far side of that one. She stuck her head inside, calling out. Nothing.

They raced on to the next row, calling and shouting and looking into every wagon.

"Hannah McKensie?" Eric called up to a man on a horse. He recognized him as one of the young rescuers Eric had seen at the Sixth Crossing.

"I know who she is. She's with the Danish girl, right?"

Maggie's hand shot out and grabbed at the man's saddle. "Yes! Are they here?"

"Back another couple of rows."

A great cry of relief was torn from Mary McKensie's throat. "Are they all right?"

"Yes, they're fine. They were seated by the driver when I passed them a minute ago."

"Stop!" Hannah grabbed the teamster's shoulder and gripped it hard. "I see them!" Then even as the man began to pull in the reins, she started jumping up and down and waving her arms. "Mama! Mama!"

"There's Maggie!" Ingrid shouted. "And Emma! I see Emma!"

As the wagon came to a stop, the teamster held out his hand to help Hannah down. She didn't even see it. She put one hand on his shoulder and leaped over the side, nearly stumbling as she hit the ground. She was up and running, flinging off her winter bonnet and casting it aside. "Mama! Mama!"

There was a cry as Mary McKensie turned and saw Hannah coming toward her. Maggie also shouted for joy and spurted forward. She could have outrun her mother but at the last moment she held back. With tears streaming down their faces, mother and daughter threw themselves into each other's arms, laughing and crying and kissing each other over and over.

Maggie stood back, her own vision blurred. She should not have been shocked at the sight of her sister. Just three weeks ago she had looked just as terrible, almost frightening herself when she had first seen herself in the looking glass Eleanor Granger had given her. But as she watched her sister clinging to her mother, Maggie's heart wrenched sharply. The light brown hair was dark and matted. There were deep circles around her eyes and they looked almost as if they had been bruised. She wore a shawl over a man's winter coat. The shawl had been pulled on tightly so many times that it hung in loose disarray. Her cheeks were sunken and her mouth pinched.

Maggie felt a tap on her shoulder. She turned, then gasped. Ingrid Christensen was standing before her, her smudged cheeks streaked with tears, her arms half-outstretched.

"Ingrid?" Maggie's cry was one of pain and joy. "Oh, Ingrid!" She threw her arms around her, pulling the frail body in against her, feeling the sobs suddenly begin to shake them both.

Then suddenly she felt other arms around her. Hannah had turned from her mother and come in now too. Maggie felt like she was going to suffocate. Her throat had choked off until she could barely breathe. She let go of Ingrid with one arm and swept her sister into her grasp as well. "Hannah! Hannah! Hannah!" was all she could say.

Ingrid stepped back, letting Sister McKensie and Robbie take her place now. Then suddenly someone picked her up from behind and swung her around. She turned her head. "Eric!"

"Yes!" He set her down. "We are so happy to see you," he said in Danish. "Welcome home."

"Have you seen my uncle and aunt?" she asked.

"Yes." He turned and pointed back up the street. "They were up there. I saw them just a minute ago."

"Thank you." She turned and started away, but she had gone only a few steps when a streaking figure came at them. "Ingrid!"

She turned just in time to have Emma James hurl herself at her. Around and around they danced. "You're here!" Emma shouted exultantly.

Seeing Emma, Hannah let go of her family and rushed in to join her two friends. Now none of them could speak. They just clung to each other, laughing and crying and touching each other's faces. Finally, Ingrid broke free and darted away to find her family.

It was as if there were so much joy that it couldn't be contained.

Hannah took Robbie in her arms one minute, then would let him go and come to Maggie. A moment later she was in her mother's arms again. Then she finally noticed Eric standing back. With a squeal she ran to him. "Is it true?" she cried.

"What?" He laughed, knowing exactly what she meant.

"Are you and Maggie married?"

He shook his head. "Of course not." As she reared back in surprise, he laughed again. "How could we marry without the maid of honor being here?"

Hannah whirled. "You waited for me, Maggie?"

Maggie nodded. "Of course. We knew you'd come soon. We'll be married as soon as you and Ingrid are feeling up to it."

"How about this afternoon?" Hannah exclaimed, giving her sister an enormous hug.

Just then Sarah James came running up and threw herself into the fray. Sister James and the children followed right after her. As they all greeted Hannah, Sister Elizabeth Jackson climbed slowly down from the back of the wagon, then came around with her three children. Jane James saw her and with a low cry ran to meet her old friend.

Suddenly the others went quiet. The joy of reunion was momentarily subdued now as the rest of them watched. "Where's Aaron?" Eric asked Hannah in a low voice.

She shook her head. "He is buried somewhere near Red Buttes. He never recovered from wading across the river at the last crossing of the Platte."

"Oh, no," Maggie said.

Emma stepped up beside Hannah now. "Papa died too, Hannah."

Hannah gave a low cry and rocked back.

"Yes. The night after we came across Rocky Ridge."

Silenced, the family turned to watch Sister James and Sister Jackson, two women who now shared something more than just their friendship.

Suddenly Hannah realized something. She turned to Eric very slowly. “Eric? Where’s Olaf? Why isn’t he here?”

One look told her all she needed to know. There was an anguished cry as one hand came up to her mouth. “Not Olaf!”

Eric nodded slowly, his eyes glistening now in the sunlight.

Hannah buried her face in her hands. “Not Olaf too?”

Eric and Maggie moved forward at the same time and took her in their embrace. “It’s all right,” Eric whispered. He wiped at the corners of his eyes. “He died trying to save little Jens Nielson. I am very proud of him.”

Hannah looked up. Her face crumpled into a mask of sorrow. Now there were no more tears of joy. “There have been so many,” she said softly through her tears. “So very many.”

Now Mary McKensie came forward. She put her hands on Hannah’s shoulders and turned her around to face her. “There have, Hannah. But you survived. You are here with us. And thanks be to God for that.”

And so it was. Joy was tempered by grief. Grief was pushed back by joy.

As they stood together, talking quietly, sharing little pieces of their experiences with each other, another family came forward. As soon as she saw them, Maggie turned to face them. “Did you find him?” she asked.

The woman shook her head. “He’s not here. We found Stephen Taylor. He told us that David was asked to stay at Devil’s Gate and watch the freight that was cached there until spring.”

Hannah, Sarah, and Emma were talking together, but that brought Hannah around. “David Granger?” she asked.

The woman turned. “Yes, that’s our son. Did you meet him?”

Hannah went forward. “He was a great blessing to us.” She stuck out her hand. “It is an honor to meet you, Sister Granger.”

"Thank you. Then he was all right?"

Hannah nodded. Her eyes had become very grave now. "He carried me across the river when it was so cold I knew that if I had to do it on my own, I would very likely die. And I wasn't the only one."

David's father, Jonathan Granger, came forward now to stand beside his wife. With him was a young woman who appeared to be a little older than Hannah. Hannah took one look at her and smiled. "And you must be Eleanor."

"Yes. Did he speak of me?"

"He adores you," Hannah said.

Tears were instantly in Eleanor's eyes. "And I him," she whispered. "You're sure he is all right, then?"

"He was fine," Hannah said, speaking to both of his parents as well as to Eleanor. Then suddenly her mind clicked. She looked at her mother. "He sent you a letter."

"Me a letter?" Mary McKensie said in surprise.

Hannah pulled off her mittens, then unbuttoned her coat and fished inside, trying to find her dress pocket. Then she had it. She brought out the folded paper, still sealed with candle wax. "Yes. He made me promise not to open it."

The disappointment was clearly written on Sister Granger's face. As her own mother began to break open the seal, Hannah turned to David's mother. "He also made me promise to come visit with your family and bring you his greetings."

Now Eliza Granger smiled. "Wonderful. And has Maggie told you that your family is staying with us?"

Hannah just stared. "Really?"

"Yes, really. We will be delighted to have you join us. Then you can tell us all about David."

"I can't believe it. David will be so surprised to hear that."

Before Sister Granger could respond to that, Mary McKensie stepped forward, the letter in her hand. She was looking strangely at her daughter.

"What?" Hannah asked. "What did he say?"

Instead of answering, Mary handed the letter to Eliza Granger. "I think this is for you as well as for me."

Puzzled, Sister Granger took the letter. Her husband stepped up beside her. Eleanor, too curious to be left out, peered over their shoulders. It was Eleanor who reacted first. She clapped her hands in delight. "Well, I'll be." She looked at her mother, who was obviously completely taken aback as well. "I wish he were here so I could give him a big fat kiss," Eleanor said.

"Well," Mary McKensie said, smiling at Eliza Granger. "What do you think of that?"

Eliza glanced at her husband, who was chuckling openly. He was just shaking his head in disbelief.

Sister Granger turned to Hannah's mother. "Just two or three nights ago, I said to Jonathan, 'It's too bad that Eric is such a nice boy or I'd try and get him out of the way and see if we could save Maggie for David.' " She looked now at Hannah, her eyes filled with soft pleasure. "But I think this will be just fine too."

"What?" Hannah cried, exasperated now.

David's mother handed the sheet of paper to her. Hannah took it and looked down. The handwriting was roughly scrawled with a lead pencil, but it was clearly legible.

Dear Sister McKensie:

I know I only met you briefly at the Sixth Crossing and so I have no wish to be presumptuous. However, it has been my great pleasure to make acquaintance with your other daughter, Miss Hannah McKensie. Upon my return, I should like to come to wherever you may be staying at that time and ask for your permission to court your daughter. If Miss Hannah would be willing to accept me as a suitor, under much better circumstances than those which prevailed when we first met, I would be most pleased. I have found her to be someone who impresses me deeply and who has my greatest respect.

Yours respectfully,
David Granger

Hannah lowered the letter slowly, staring first at her mother and then at David's mother. Finally, it was her own mother who spoke. "Well, Hannah?" she asked. "Would you be willing to accept him as a suitor when he returns next spring?"

Hannah turned and looked directly at David's mother. "David Granger was a ray of light in a time of darkness, a candle of courage that relit my faith when I thought it had gone out. If he is still of the same mind when he returns home, you can tell him that I will be waiting for him."

She realized that Maggie had come up beside her. As Hannah turned to look at her, Maggie took Hannah's face in her hands and kissed her softly on the cheek.

"Welcome home, Hannah," she whispered. "Welcome to the Valley."

Chapter Notes

Normally the incoming companies were met outside the city and welcomed warmly by the Saints in the Valley. However, John Jaques indicates that the Martin Company "arrived in Salt Lake City about noon, driving into East Temple Street as the congregation was leaving the old adobie tabernacle in the southwest corner of Temple block" (in Bell, *Life History and Writings of John Jaques*, p. 171; also in *Remember*, p. 35). The assumptions as to why this was the case are the author's.

The Willie Handcart Company arrived in Salt Lake City on 9 November, thirteen days after Captain George D. Grant and his rescue company found them at the Sixth Crossing of the Sweetwater. It is estimated that of the original five hundred emigrants who made up that company, sixty-seven died en route to the Valley.

The Edward Martin Handcart Company, the last to come in 1856, arrived in Salt Lake on 30 November, a full month after being found by Captain Grant at Greasewood Creek east of Devil's Gate. With considerably more of the older and infirm in their company, they suffered more than double the number of deaths that the Willie Company did. Though their records were not as complete, it is estimated that somewhere between 135 and 150 of the original 567 in the company perished somewhere along the trail, a full third or more of those at Martin's Cove alone (see Hafen and Hafen, *Handcarts to Zion*, p. 193).

Though the losses are some of the highest experienced by any emigrant party of that time period (almost triple the number of those who died with the Donner Party), the rescue effort mounted by President Brigham Young and carried out by the courageous and tireless Saints from the Valley averted a major disaster.

Perhaps the most fitting ending to this story was given by Elizabeth Horrocks Jackson, who lost her husband at Red Buttes. As she started her history, she wrote: "I have a desire to leave a record of those scenes and events, thru which I have passed, that my children, down to my latest posterity may read what their ancestors were willing to suffer, and did suffer, patiently for the Gospel's sake. And I wish them to understand, too, that what I now word is the history of hundreds of others, both men, women and children, who have passed thru many like scenes for a similar cause, at the same time we did. I also desire them to know that it was in obedience to the commandments of the true and living God, and with the assurance of an eternal reward—an exaltation to eternal life in His kingdom—that we suffered these things. I hope, too, that it will inspire my posterity with fortitude to stand firm and faithful to the truth, and be willing to suffer, and sacrifice all things they may be required to pass thru for the Kingdom of God's sake" (Kingsford, *Leaves from the Life of Elizabeth Horrocks Jackson Kingsford*, p. 1).

ABOUT THE AUTHOR

Gerald N. Lund received his B.A. and M.S. degrees in sociology from Brigham Young University. He also did extensive graduate work in New Testament studies at Pepperdine University in Los Angeles, California, and studied Hebrew at the University of Judaism in Hollywood, California.

During his thirty-five years in the Church Educational System, the author served as a seminary teacher, an institute teacher and director, a curriculum writer, director of college curriculum, and zone administrator. His Church callings have included those of bishop, stake missionary, and teacher. In April 2002, he was sustained to the Second Quorum of the Seventy. He is currently serving as the first counselor in the Europe West Area Presidency.

Gerald Lund has written many books, including such novels as *The Work and the Glory* series, *The Kingdom and the Crown* trilogy, *The Alliance, The Freedom Factor, Leverage Point,* and *One in Thine Hand.* He has also written several books on gospel studies, including *The Coming of the Lord* and *Jesus Christ, Key to the Plan of Salvation.* He has twice won the Independent Booksellers "Book of the Year" Award and has received many other honors for his works.

He and his wife, Lynn, are the parents of seven children.

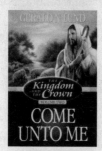

The Work and the Glory Series

by Gerald N. Lund

Unabridged audio read by Larry A. McKeever

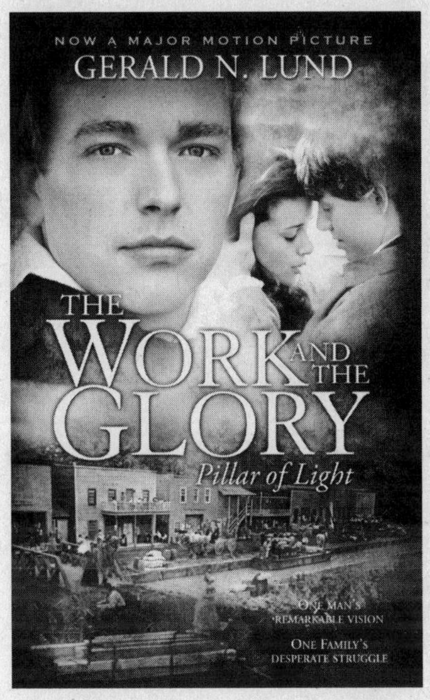

Vol. 1: Pillar of Light

(paperback)
SKU: 4906474
ISBN: 1–59038–363-X

(book on cd)
SKU: 4907251
ISBN: 1–59038–378–8

Available at your local bookstore or on deseretbook.com

The series continues. . .

Vol. 2: Like a Fire Is Burning
(paperback)
SKU: 4037254
ISBN: 1–57345–871–6
(book on tape)
SKU: 3649134
ISBN: 1–57008–471–8

Vol. 3: Truth Will Prevail
(paperback)
SKU: 4037263
ISBN: 1–57345–872–4
(book on tape)
SKU: 3649143
ISBN: 1–57008–472–6

Vol. 4: Thy Gold to Refine
(paperback)
SKU: 4037272
ISBN: 1–57345–873–2
(book on tape)
SKU: 3687483
ISBN: 1–57008–531–5

Vol. 5: A Season of Joy
(paperback)
SKU: 4037281
ISBN: 1–57345–874–0
(book on tape)
SKU: 3687492
ISBN: 1–57008–547–1

Vol. 6: Praise to the Man
(paperback)
SKU: 4037290
ISBN: 1–57345–875–9
(book on tape)
SKU: 3687509
ISBN: 1–57008–548-X

Vol. 7: No Unhallowed Hand
(paperback)
SKU: 4037307
ISBN: 1–57345–876–7
(book on tape)
SKU: 3687518
ISBN: 1–57008–549–8

Vol. 8: So Great a Cause
(paperback)
SKU: 4037316
ISBN: 1–57345–877–5
(book on tape)
SKU: 3687527
ISBN: 1–57008–550–1

Vol. 9: All Is Well
(paperback)
SKU: 4037325
ISBN: 1–57345–878–3
(book on tape)
SKU: 3757346
ISBN: 1–57008–613–3